CORAL BEACH CASEFILES

• HABEAS CORPUS •

Published in Canada by Engen Books, St. John's, NL.

ISBN: 978-1-77478-159-3

Collecting books originally published as:
Black Womb: 978-1-926903-13-2
Transformations in Pain: 978-1-926903-21-7
Smoke and Mirrors: 978-1-926903-24-8

Reprinting material originally presented in: *Call of the Sea, Drawn to the Tides, Return to the Depths,
Fantasy from the Rock* and *Sea Stories from the Rock.*

Distributed by:
Engen Books
www.engenbooks.com
submissions@engenbooks.com

First hardcover printing: April 2017
First Paperback: March 2024

Cover Image: Liz LeDrew
Cover Design: Matthew LeDrew

"The Black Womb lives, thanks to Smoke and Mirrors, Matthew LeDrew's third novel in his saga. Released by Engen Books in 2009, it is a mature and complex tale with many twists and turns that is sure to please fans of action, drama, horror and mystery. If not for a dip in the middle portion, this would easily be the best book – thus far – in the series. As it stands, it may be the most entertaining." - Jay Paulin, author of *Emma Awesome*

CONTENTS

SMOKE & MIRRORS

Introduction
by Matthew LeDrew

A brilliant writer once said, "writing is re-writing." And that's true.
But sometimes, writing is also *not* re-writing.

Over the course of the seventeen-plus years since these books were first printed, I have been tempted to go back and re-write them many times. There's a weird catch-22 that happens when you're a prolific author: everyone wants to read your first book, but by definition, your first book will have been the one you wrote when you had the *least experience*. As such there's a million little things I would change, and I'm always tempted to go back and do so. In those moments of anxiety, it's usually my wife that reminds me that, "these books built our publishing company," flawed as they may be. That people loved them and continue to love them. That there are fans who still write me every other day to remind me that these books helped them *escape* during hard times, and that it's saved lives in doing so.

And that works, for a little while. And I remind myself that, when the book was written I was the age of the characters. That I got criticized by well-meaning-but-silly adults for not understanding the way teens interacted when I was writing the way I saw them act every day. That if I tried to re-write this now as a forty-year-old man, it would lose so much of that authenticity, that understanding of the young world that we all lose as we age.

What would I change? Font choices, a few character arcs, a few lines of dialog. I understand the legal system marginally better now, some of the silliest things happen when approaching that stuff.

But then I remind myself that, just as I grew, these characters grew, too. And that it would be weird to go back and alter who they were just as it would be weird to go back and alter who I was.

So, I hope you enjoy this collection of the first three Coral Beach Case-files novels as much as many others have before, and as much as I did writing them at the time. And I hope you're forgiving of them. And I hope that if you find anything even a little bit interesting in these pages, you strap in, brace yourself, and continue on this journey with me.

Matthew LeDrew
February 25, 2024

BOOK ONE

BLACK WOMB

PROLOGUE: SHE RAN

She turned around fast, too afraid to blink.

She was running so fast that great clumps of her knotted black hair swung into her eyes while she searched the snow covered hillside desperately, brief breaks in the cloud cover providing her with enough visibility to make out movement in the dense forest behind her.

Breath escaped her mouth in great white puffs, swirling around her head like cigarette smoke. Her eyes darted across the waving white horizon of the small clearing she had just sprinted across. Panting loudly, she tried to hear above the sound of her breath and the snow crunching beneath her bare feet, now blue and numb from hours of constant running.

She tried to wiggle her toes but the exertion on her frozen extremities sent bolts of electric pain up her legs and into her spine, finally exploding out the back of her head. She decided not to do it again.

She took one last heave as she leaned against a large oak tree next to her. Her back muscles tensed even more for a moment, then finally loosened for the first time in hours. She closed her eyes only briefly. They stung fiercely from the dry cold and days without sleep. Adjusting the large bulge of blankets she had stuffed under her shirt for warmth, she placed one arm firmly beneath them and huddled them close to her breasts.

A sound in front of her made her eyes snap open once again, her large pupils instantly scanning the landscape relentlessly. There was no wind, and the thick patches of evergreen trees scattered throughout the clearing hung as lifelessly as if they were in a painting. Their heavy branches were weighed down by the snow, making them droop and resemble old sagging faces. They glared at her like gargoyles, each one of them screaming, scowling, laughing and passing judgment on her with their collective brows turned downward in horrible sneers of distaste.

Every movement of the branches, every rustling of a shrub, became a possible danger. Became the idea that something could be there, looking back across the field for any sign of movement, just as she was.

She held her breath until her chest ached even more, her heart rate climbing. Her veins felt like they were on fire, a stark contrast to her skin, which was now turning blue from the intense cold. She knew it had been a bad idea to stop moving, but she had to.

An owl let go of the branch a few feet above her, not making a sound. The snow loosened from the dead branch and fell to the ground, becoming invisible once there. The great bird circled a small area around her before flying silently off to the south and deeper into the woods, where she had been heading.

She chuckled to herself softly, shaking her head at her own paranoia. She had not only doubled, but tripled back upon herself more than once. She had purposely walked in three large circles every mile since she had started running, hours ago. The only thing she had not done was cover her tracks, a near impossibility when wading through three feet of snow.

Keeping a suspicious eye on the open slope before her, she began to examine herself. The black parka she had stolen was still in relatively good condition. It had only been ripped once or twice at the elbows by stray tree limbs. The brown fox fur that lined the neck was still completely intact and had managed to keep her upper body at least a little warm. That kept her heart and lungs warm and kept them pumping warm blood and air through her body, giving them the strength and vitality they would not have had otherwise. Below the waist was only the bottom half of a simple nightdress and a normal paper hospital gown. It provided about as much protection against the cold as 'thinking warm thoughts'.

She grimaced when she noticed a large gash in her right knee, probably from when she had tripped a quarter mile back trying to create a shortcut through a thick patch of shrubs and roots. Bits of twigs and pebbles stuck out of it, along with blood that was now frozen onto the skin. She tried hard not to think about how painful that would be once she got feeling back in the lower half of her body.

She did not even look at her feet, afraid of what she might see. She was afraid that the odd snap she had heard two miles into her run had been one of her toes coming off. She did, however, take note of a viscous green fluid that had splattered all the way up to her pelvis at some point. It seemed to be fading even as she watched it, like suntan lotion as it seeped into your skin. A feeling of relief came over her and she began to think there was at least some hope for her frozen appendages.

Deciding she had wasted enough time, she pushed off from the tree with one arm, her body groaning in rebellion as she forced it into movement again. Looking at the forest ahead of her, she saw no real path in sight. It looked like a black and white etching from a Brothers Grimm story, especially the oaks with their leaves long dead from the fall. Yet as horrible as it seemed, she thought she could see the pale light of civilization past them and she dared to think that she might be close to some form of sanctuary.

She turned and smirked at the tree she had leaned against, looking at the withered knots and crannies that made up its haggard face.

Someone had told her years ago that every tree had a face. She had thought it to be fairy tale bullshit, but if tonight had proven anything it was just the opposite. They had been her only company since she'd entered the tree-line.

"Thanks," she whispered humbly.

Old Man Oak seemed to approve.

2

Then she saw it out of the corner of her eye.

She turned, her hair again catching in her eyes, toward the soft glint she could have sworn she had seen near the edge of the clearing. It was gone now and she squinted and strained her eyes toward the spot where it had been, wishing to the moon for just a little more light.

She got her wish as a pair of headlights turned on from the horizon, illuminating her in bright yellow. Her mouth wide, she thrust up her hands to protect herself from the temporary blindness so instinctively that she almost dropped the blankets she'd been using for warmth.

Immediately after she was doused in light, the source of the glint she had seen was identified. Rifle fire erupted all around her, turning the face of Old Man Oak into sharp splintered sticks. They bounced off her parka as she turned and bolted into the black forest with more gunshots following her, tearing up the virgin snow and sending it sailing in all directions at once.

She pumped her legs harder and faster than she ever had as sweat began to freeze to her scalp. She heard the sound of three... no, four engines revving to life as they started their decent down the clearing after her.

Sharp twigs nipped at her exposed flesh as she fled into the nearest clump of trees too dense for one of their snowmobiles to follow through. She started to make her way toward the light she had seen a moment ago, but had already lost track of.

ʎ^ʎ

The leader of the drivers vaulted off a mogul, landing in an outburst of fresh powder. It sprayed up into his face and parka. The other drivers followed in suit close behind. He leaned over the right edge of his snowmobile and took aim at the woman as her form began to disappear through the trees. He trained his eye on her while struggling to maintain his balance, a circular red lens over his right eye. It looked like a futuristic monocle and displayed information to him, feeding him decreasing statistics on her distance from him, wind resistance, and speed. Smirking to himself from beneath his gray toque, he applied first pressure to the trigger slowly. He fought to keep the barrel in line with the small of her back as she bobbed and weaved through the brush.

His left ski hit a rock hidden by the snow and made his arm jostle to the right, the gun firing at the same time. The shoulder strap on his rifle came loose and he cursed as he was forced to drop it to steady the vehicle. He watched her continue to move away from his team as one of the other drivers stopped at a line of brush to continue on foot, leaving the engine running.

The leader turned toward the front, trying to see if there was a way he could continue with his machine. All at once, it seemed like his snowmobile had stopped moving. The tree that the woman had been standing next to was much closer than he had judged it to be and was moving directly at him.

He barely got the chance to react as the front slammed into the trunk at top speed. He got the chance to think one thought, comprised of exactly one word, before the left side of his face ripped across the jagged, splintered wood of the

3

tree. The momentum carried him forward, slamming his shoulder completely out of socket before launching him into the bushes behind it. The broken red glass from his lens protruded from multiple gouges across the right side of his face. He could already feel his mouth and lungs fill with gummy, coppery liquid and bile through the dual holes in his lungs made by fractured ribs. His spleen had been ruptured. Before he fell into unconsciousness and the certain death that would come soon afterward, he couldn't help but notice his blood. How black it looked against the pure white of the snow, when bathed in the stark moonlight.

ʎ〉ʎ

She saw the light in front of her again now. It flickered on and off, this way and that, like a candle trying to hold its own against a light breeze. She pressed forward with tears streaming down her cheeks and freezing there. Blood poured from the gunshot that had just grazed her hip and now gushed down over her thigh, at least serving to keep her warm.

She could hear him behind her. He was getting closer and closer with every foot they ran, each stride of his powerful legs propelling him at least twice as far as hers were.

The blankets moved and shifted under her breasts, and again she steadied them with her hand.

The light got clearer and clearer and she began to see colours and shapes. Two, then three sources of light and finally a fourth as she cleared a large over-hanging branch. Biting down hard on her lower lip, she clutched her bundle against her chest and ploughed her way through one last thicket. She emerged into a clearing on the other side and stopped dead in her tracks, kicking up powder as she did so.

It erupted out of the ground in front of her as if from nowhere. The lights of civilization were apparent now, a mile or two behind it. Its twin steeples rose high into the mist that she hadn't realized was there a moment ago. The flicker-ing lights behind its massive stained glass windows made the images and char-acters on them dance vibrantly.

It was a convent.

Large wooden doors that looked too big to open were no more than four yards in front of her, their huge brass knockers begging for her to take them in her hand.

She hesitated, staring up this time at actual gargoyles grinning down at her from on high. They protected the central statue on the beautiful architec-tural masterpiece: the mother Mary. She cradled her child Jesus in her arms and stared down at him. She stared not as a woman who gave her son to better the world she lived in, but as a mother, looking upon her one love and greatest achievement.

She unzipped her parka slowly and carefully removed the bundle of dull green blankets held within. Taking off the top layer, she looked down upon her child, curled into a shivering ball to protect itself against the harsh cold. It was devoid of the cuts and scrapes that tattered her body, yet somehow there was blood on its still-pink skin. She realized after a moment that it was her own. The baby's skin was beginning to turn a hue of light blue despite her efforts to keep it warm, and she was relieved when its chest rose and fell before her. Tearing her gaze away from her wonderful child, she turned back toward the convent.

The gargoyles seemed to have turned toward her while she was looking away and now leaned in to stare at the child with renewed interest. Their devilish smiles and curling tongues were lashing out with thirst.

She turned her head when she heard a rustling not far behind her, snapping her out of the momentary trance the sight of the building had placed her in. She bolted forward, grabbing one of the brass knockers and slamming it three times as hard as she could.

There was no response.

Her lower lip quivering and bleeding, she looked down at the child, too cold to even open its eyes. Salt tears streaming down her face, she kissed it once on the forehead then laid it on the stone step.

The gargoyles seemed to dance and bounce with clandestine glee as she turned and ran back the way she came.

The sound of her footfalls continued for a moment or two before a shot rang out onto the chilled air, followed only by silence.

Several long moments passed. The biting winter wind began to pick up again, making the few hairs on the baby's head stand on end as it shivered and shook.

A light went on upstairs in the convent, then another, not far from the doors.

Crouched at the tree line, a dark-skinned man wearing another gray toque and parka uniform peeked through the clearing at what was taking place. He knelt down low and aimed his rifle, set the crosshairs to intersect at the child's head, and placed his finger on the trigger.

The massive front door of the building creaked open, sending a beam of light down onto the infant. It winced, raising its chubby arms to block the new brightness as it washed over him, suddenly replaced by a shadow.

Sister Ruth Main looked down at the helpless child, still squinting from the brightness. Her old sagging features went from shocked to a kind smile as she pushed either side of her habit behind her shoulders and knelt down, picking up the baby and holding it close to her warm body. The infant opened its eyes and looked at her, the light from inside streaming around her head as she smiled at it, cooing softly. She looked like an angel.

The man in the brush shifted his gun sight, making sure it still intersected with the child's head.

Ruth let her hand rest on the child's head, pushing back its soft hair until it stood on end. The golden crucifix that dangled around her neck caught the child's eye and it followed it intently, its small mouth opening in toothless awe.

He paused, slowly taking pressure away from the trigger before finally letting go of it altogether. The barrel dropped away as he watched Ruth cradle the child and look all around the grounds, before taking the babe back inside. He frowned, a determined look coming over him, then turned around and began the walk back toward his snowmobile.

January 28. Subject female, early twenties, caucasian, roughly 150 pounds. Reference number 08276. Was exposed to the darkness during first trimester of pregnancy. Subject is now twenty one days pregnant. This one appears hopeful.

February 12. Subject showing rejection to vitamins and other birth enhancing chemicals. There are an unusual number of white blood cells in the patient's blood stream. Further studies into possibilities of diabetes and other diseases' are pending. Considering Philidamide.

March 1. Subject has gone into early labor. Child appears to be perfectly healthy, with no sources of the darkness within his genetic structure. The project has been terminated, marked FAILURE.

March 7. Female subject has fled with her child. One soldier killed during said escape. Female subject was captured approximately five miles from town. As per procedure she was made insulin-deficient prior to testing. Prolonged time away from treatment center caused kidney failure and other complications resulting in her death. However, the child was too young to be altered in any such way...

HE WILL SURVIVE . . .

CHAPTER ONE: SMALL TOWN

15 YEARS LATER

"So, you going to Julian Grendel's party on Friday?" she asked him, paying little attention to his response or even if he gave one. It was one thing he almost admired about Sara Johnson; she had a way of controlling you without even letting you know you were being controlled. Maybe it was her lips, or how she subconsciously played with her curly blonde hair all the time, but she always did it. She was good at it, and she knew it.

"Uh, I'm not sure. I was thinking about hitting the Factory with Mike," Alexander Drew replied, half concentrating on her and half watching out for Grendel himself. For whatever reason, Grendel didn't like people not coming to his parties. He brushed a hand through his dark brown hair. His eyes darted about skittishly, meeting those of every person who walked past the two of them, then immediately dropped to the floor. Finally, they found her. Her perfect body, not too thin, those lush pink lips, short blonde hair and the way her blue eyes looked right through you, slicing at you.

"Oh, come on, Xander," she whined. She said his name like it was some kind of a joke.

He didn't remember the orphanage, but he remembered how he got stuck with the name Xander. Every child had been named after a saint. There were three children who had been given the name Alexander by separate caretakers. For identification purposes, one was Alexander, another was Alex, and he was just plain Xander.

He hated the name; it was just another thing to make him stand out that tiny bit when all he wanted was not to be noticed... and the one person he did want to notice him said his name as if it were a joke.

"Alright, I'll come. But you have to promise me you'll make sure Mike and Cathy don't ditch me like the last time," he reasoned, heaving a massive sigh as he gave in.

"They didn't ditch you."

He gave her a droll, tired look.

"They didn't!" she laughed, slapping his arm playfully.

He frowned, then rolled his eyes and nodded.

"Oh, come on. Don't sulk. You know I'm right. They love you."

"They do," he agreed finally. "They really do. They love me and they're there for me and they are the best of friends - except in public. In public, it's like we never met."

"Drama queen."

"Oh, I'm not saying they *try* it or anything... it's just the way things are. I get it." He forced a smile, making eye contact with her. "I don't even think they realize they do it."

She gave him a little smile, the right corner of her lip curling just enough to make her irresistible as she fixed her black tube top, even though it hadn't really needed it. In all honesty, it was not so much a tube top as it was a strip of black tape going across her chest. That was the other thing about Sara. Besides having the looks of a goddess and the voice of an angel... she dressed like the devil. Skimpy tank tops and hip-hugger jeans. Fishnet stockings wrapped around her hands and covering her forearms. Large hoop earrings, at least two rings on each finger (silver on the left and gold on the right) and all that was just one outfit.

"I promise," she said, after she had spent enough time fiddling with her attire to make him twitch. "They'll be good little boys and girls, as long as you are."

He snorted, rolled his eyes, and closed his locker door with a clang. He pulled his book bag onto his back as the two of them started walking toward the front exit of Coral Beach High, the flat-out boring high school in the mediocre town of Coral Beach, getting ready to walk home together just like they did every day.

"So, what's new today?" he asked, shooting her a smile. "Anything scandalous going on?"

Now it was his turn to know the answer before she gave it. He asked something like that of her every day, because to her there was always something scandalous happening. Everywhere. Always. But to be fair, scandalous things seemed to happen around her anyway.

"Well," she started, smirking to herself proudly. "I heard from Julie Peterson today that the reason Derek has been so on edge lately is because Theresa had to take the test."

"Yeah," Xander nodded. "That Family Living test was bad news. I think I must have only gotten an eighty-five or something..."

She turned and gave him a little slap on the arm. "Not that test, you halfwit. A pregnancy test."

Xander's eyes went wide for a moment as he held open the front door for her, which she barely acknowledged. "Oh."

"Yeah."

"Why would Derek be messed up over that?" he asked naively.

She shot him a look.

"Ah. Forget I asked."

"Done."

"Wasn't she supposed to be with Jamie?"

"They broke up."

"Why? I mean, besides the 'she may be pregnant from another man' thing?"

"That's just a rumor. The real reason was because he cheated on her," she smirked to herself coyly.

"With who?" he moaned, feeling a relationship headache coming on.

"Me," she said proudly, and he realized that this would become a migraine before it was over.

Xander finished walking home with Sara, like always. They lived next door to one another, and had since either of them could remember. Since they were children. Every day he'd remember little things like where he'd fallen out of the tree trying to sneak up to her room when they were six, when she had been sick and wanted to play. Or on his lush, green lawn where she had found out how he felt when they were twelve.

He had had a huge crush on her that summer and had been sitting on the sidewalk between their houses, burning their initials into a piece of wood. She had started toward him on roller blades and he had dropped the wood and ran into his house. She'd picked it up and looked at it, then thrown it into the trees on her way down the road, never actually speaking of it. He could still remember the scent of the wood as it burned every time he thought of it. It was the way love smelled.

At that age, most children were confident of their own immortality. That they could do anything, and go anywhere. But it was then that he realized how different he was from his friend. She was a princess in their school. Other kids wondered why she lowered herself to talking to him. He was... abnormal. Subnormal. Less than human. Those who actually took notice of him could barely stand him. But when he was around her, none of it mattered. On that ten minute walk from home to school and back again, the world could fall down around his ears and crush him every day, and he wouldn't care. He would ask for more.

"So, about the party..." Sara stared, looking up at him, her eyes sparkling.

"Yeah?" he said, his voice rising with the smallest speckle of hope.

"Jamie's going to be coming with me, so you better not get all weird with him... okay? I like him."

"Yeah, sure," he said softly, his eyes fading back downward.

She walked up her driveway and through the off-white door into her house.

He watched it for a second after she was gone as if she were still there, then walked into his own house.

He went straight up his stairs and into his room, passing by his father quickly to avoid the usual barrage of questions.

He logged onto his computer and suddenly he wasn't a loser anymore. He wasn't anybody's doormat. He was the king of everything. He was everything. The ultimate hacker.

A sly smile spread over his face as he turned on the screen, illuminating his face in bright blue in the dark room, his eyes alive with vindictive excitement as he opened up all of his programs.

ʎ◇ʎ

The Factory.

A local arcade/club/dance hall where all the teens went when there was nothing else to do. Located in the scenic downtown of Coral Beach, which was roughly a five minute walk from 'up' town, the Factory jutted up from the otherwise calm landscape, always loud and exciting and neon.

Jamie Dawkins leaned over one of the many pool tables that adorned the club, raising an eyebrow as he tried to figure out his shot. His leather sports jacket crumpled and scrunched noisily every time he moved, impeding his ability to shoot. Many times he had pushed up the sleeves in an effort to alleviate the inconvenience, but they always fell back down almost immediately. But he dared not take it off. His brother had worn that jacket when he was captain of the Coral Beach Cougars, and his father before that. Now that he was finally captain, it barely ever left his back. Some even said he showered with it on.

As good as he was at football (almost undisputed as the best in the entire region), his abilities did not translate into every sport. Pool, as it turned out, was not one of them. His face began to turn red as he huffed in frustration. Standing back up and grabbing the chalk, he fumbled it over the top of his stick and smeared a little onto his hands as he had once seen some pool champ on ESPN do. Nervous and more than a little agitated, the bulky teen rubbed a hand over his close-cut hair, accidently leaving some of the blue powder there as well.

Across the table his opponent, Mike Harris, snickered a little at the sight. Mike nearly had all of the high balls sunk, but Jamie was still on his third low. It was probably a good thing that this wasn't one of the high profile tournaments that were held here once or twice a month, or Jamie would've been the laughing stock of the school for at least a week.

9

Mike glanced into the large, circular mirror that was mounted in the top corner of the room, watching a cute black-haired girl without her even realizing it. She had an adorable round face with rose-red lips and wore a tight top over her slim figure to match them. Her eyes were almost almond shaped, a trait accentuated by how she wore her eyeliner. She wore loose, relaxed jeans with frills going down the sides, and held her Coke near her breasts, playing with the straw a little with her tongue.

Smiling, he turned back to the game.

On the other side of the room, Cathy Kennessy sipped on her soda subconsciously. She wasn't really paying attention to the game. She was watching Mike. Very intently. The way he moved with his large, square shoulders and tall frame. The way shocks of his blonde hair fell over his brow, touching his sky blue eyes in places. The way his freckles dotted his cheeks. And his arms, she couldn't forget his arms. Those large, muscular arms that he used to pick her up and spin her around and hold her when she was cold.

From across the room, Grendel watched Cathy from the bar, smirking to himself. He was wearing a ratty button-down shirt as a coat over his tee shirt, the sleeves of which extended well over his hands, absorbing moisture from the bar into their tattered fibers.

He took one last swig of cola from his glass, feeling it sizzle as tiny flickers of it connected with his cheeks. He took notice of the waitress as she wiped a ring of condensation from his glass away even as he picked it up, throwing her a wink. She rolled her eyes at him.

Wiping the pop from his face, he started across the room.

He popped up next to Cathy, producing a smile so large it made his ears wiggle.

"Great music, huh?" he said cheerfully, looking her up and down.

She turned to him, glancing at his large, innocent eyes for a moment. His bald head and his attempt to grow scruff along the sides of his face and chin made him look just a little silly, enough to make her laugh whenever she saw him.

She stopped for a second to acknowledge the very music he was talking about. She had been so engrossed in watching her boyfriend that she had barely even noticed it. They were a local band called Ragnarok, playing their own rendition of *Superman's Dead* by Our Lady Peace. It was good, but not as good as the original and definitely not as good as the band's own music.

She gave Grendel a little nod.

This was how it always was. She had her outside image, she attended the games, listened to the music, put on the face. But all she really cared about was her boyfriend and her friends. Friends like Sara and Xander.

Poor Xander.

She called him that so much that some of the juniors had actually started to believe it was his name. She'd always thought he and Sara were perfect for one another, but Sara had, like, serial boyfriends. She went through them like popcorn. Cathy always warned her that she would eventually hit a kernel and get a bad one, or she'd pass over a really good one.

"So, what's going on?" Grendel asked, leaning against the counter next to her. He followed her gaze until he was watching the game as well.

"Not much," she said, an evil smirk spreading across her lips. "Mike's kicking Jamie's ass."

Grendel laughed. "What else is new? Jamie's about as good at pool as he is at football."

"That why he's captain and you didn't make the team?" she poised playfully, raising an eyebrow in his direction. She turned away from Mike for the first time since the conversation began.

"Hey, I just couldn't take the politics of the game, is all."

"How is a bunch of testosterone crazed idiots running around and slamming into each other wearing glorified coconut shells and pouring Gatorade over each other political?"

"I see no differences between what you just said and what goes on in government." He paused. "Except football players usually have more going on for them upstairs than your average president."

Across the room, Jamie finally parted with his jacket, laying it on a hanger near him. He leaned in for his shot as Mike, Cathy and now Grendel all watched. He tried to get the seven ball in the side pocket with an easy straight shot, but the table was old and the cloth was lumpy and torn in spots. The cue missed the seven completely and ended up bouncing harmlessly off the side.

Smiling, Mike leaned in quickly (almost before the cue had stopped rolling) and finished the game with a bank shot that sunk the eight ball into the side pocket.

Jamie looked enraged, but he suppressed the anger and calmly put down the pool cue.

"Good game," he mumbled under his breath.

"Yes, it was." Mike laughed, shaking his opponent's hand curtly. "Now pay up."

Jamie sighed, then reached into his pocket and pulled out a five, grumbling as though he had expected Mike to forget.

"Wanna play again?"

"Ha," Jamie smiled. "Not likely. I think I'm just gonna head home and call Sara."

"Cool," Mike shrugged, putting his stick away and walking over to where Cathy and Grendel stood. He placed the five down on the counter and waited for Roxanne to come around so that he could buy Cathy a snack before they left.

"You won!" she chirped happily, spreading out her arms as though she were cheering him on from the sidelines of the Superbowl.

"I did," he laughed, placing a hand on her hip. "Wait, was that in doubt? Did you have doubt-face?"

"Never once," she assured him, glancing from the five dollar bill to rack of snacks and goodies behind the bar. She knew what it meant. She'd seen it

11

before.

He gave her a quick kiss, then extended it into a longer one.

Jamie shrugged, justifying his loss with the fact that the money would be put to good use buying Cathy and Mike dinner, but more importantly, some much needed alone time. Life was busy, even if their parents would argue that they were lazy.

He grabbed his leather Cougars jacket and waved a goodbye to Mike and Cathy, although they hardly noticed. He smirked to himself as he opened the door and walked out.

Grendel looked away from Mike and Cathy as they went deeper and deeper into their kiss. As he glanced back at them, a disgusted look coming over his face. His eyes slowly fell down her backside until he found himself looking at things he knew that he shouldn't. He turned toward the door and smiled a little. "I think I'll head out, too. You two seem like you wanna be alone."

They didn't answer, each of them too deep in the other.

He got up and walked for the door, slamming it behind him.

Neither of them noticed or cared.

Jamie started to walk down the street. It was getting dark, and he lit up a cigarette and took a long draw. Then he looked down at it and got suddenly revolted with himself. He'd smoked for years. He knew what it was doing to him, why he was having trouble running the whole distance of the field now. He finished the smoke on the corner and threw the smouldering butt down onto the sidewalk, swearing to himself that he'd never touch another one of them.

He thought he heard something behind him, then started walking again, zipping his jacket to protect himself against the harsh cold of night. He could see his own breath as it swirled up around his head like a wreath.

A dark figure stepped out of the shadows behind him and stepped in time with him, squishing the discarded cigarette beneath his heavy feet.

Jamie heard it now, he was sure of it. The footsteps were getting closer and closer to him. He started to pick up his pace, and so did the second set of footsteps. He broke into an all out run, hearing the second set do the same, close behind him. He got to the end of the block and made a sharp turn, beads of sweat already forming on his forehead. He got to the end of the next block and bent over from the pain in his side. He shouldn't have gotten such a painful stitch already. He ran three times this far on the football field every day. Yet his lungs heaved, each breath brought agony, and he made a small grunt from the pain. He looked up, turning around to face his attacker for the first time.

There was nobody there. He searched the streets and doorways around him with his eyes, seeing nothing.

Suddenly, he started to laugh.

He stomped his foot down onto the black pavement, listening to the echo of the sound returning to him. He'd been running from noises, shadows. He laughed once more at his own stupidity.

"You're losing it," he whispered to himself softly.

12

He turned the corner and immediately bumped into a large, dark figure. The person was covered by a coat that seemed to be made out of shadows, with eyes burning bright with hatred as it moved toward him menacingly.

Jamie screamed loudly and took off in the other direction, but his stitch got the better of him again, this time right away. The shadow-figure grabbed him, and pulled him into the darkness. A dagger appeared from his coat and jabbed into Jamie's right side.

Blood gushed from the treads etched into the sides of the blade, splattering onto the street with a sickening splashing sound.

As Jamie's vision became hazy and he realized it was over, he stopped struggling against his killer's iron grip. He fell to the ground, and the last thoughts to run through his head were that maybe if he had given up smoking just a little earlier, he might have been able to run just that little bit further...

ʎ〈〉ʎ

Xander woke up at his computer, his hair a tattered mess.

He fell asleep on the keyboard like that often, staying online to the point past exhaustion. He wiped a bit of drool from his chin. His skin felt sticky and wet, like he had just gotten out of a bath of honey. He touched himself, and found that his flesh was clammy and warm. Glancing up at his screen, he noticed he had mail. Babygurl@firsttimebreak.com. That was Sara's e-mail.

He opened it and scrolled down through the prattle that headed most of her e-mails, more gossip about Theresa and Derek, along with a few other tidbits about who Julie and Tommy were dating now... Then he noticed a little sentence at the end.

Do you know where Jamie is? He was supposed to call me...

At the mention of Jamie Dawkins, Xander's nostrils flared. He closed and deleted the e-mail, then logged back onto his usual chat page, rubbing his tired eyes. He felt as though he hadn't gotten any sleep at all.

He hated all of Sara's (what was it Cathy had called them?) serial boyfriends. Sometimes he really just wished that all the Jamie Dawkins of the world would just drop dead.

Suddenly, he heard the familiar chime as someone online contacted him.

Hello Pinkerton, came the instant message. Xander looked at it and smirked. He hadn't been called that in real life in years, but it had always made for an entertaining screen name.

Oh. Hi soul. How's life? he replied, typing quickly.

Alright. I've been looking at something weird online. I discovered some kind of bizarre... thing. I don't have a password decoder as sophisticated as you do, I thought you might wanna take a look at it.

Sure. What's the site?

Something called engen.com. Oops. Gtg!

'got to go'?, Why?

But he was gone, just as quickly as he had come online. Xander frowned. Soul had always specialized in finding weird stuff online. Weird government conspiracy videos, proof that the Moon landing was faked, the Paris Hilton vid-

13

eo... This was probably nothing, but still, it was worth checking out.

But it would have to wait until morning.

He let out a long yawn, then got up and walked the two feet to his bed, fell onto his mattress, and slept.

Officer Tom Lensherr of the Coral Beach police precinct wasn't used to weird stuff.

That's partly why he joined the force of this town. He had always said that nothing ever happened in Coral Beach. And by nothing he didn't mean nothing bad. Literally *nothing* ever occurred here. It was as if this town's purpose was solely to exist.

Lensherr never much cared for gore either. He hadn't seen a real dead body since his first day on the job a few months ago, and that had only been a heart attack victim.

So what he saw as he shone his flashlight into the darkened alley made his stomach turn. The image was permanently burned into his mind, enough so that he would spend the remainder of his days curling into his wife for comfort every night as he cried himself to sleep.

Jamie Dawkins was sprawled out on the ground in a dark alley, thrown down like a piece of trash. There was blood all around him, smeared onto the brick walls that must have been the last thing he saw. His torso had been cut open revealing the inner body cavity and places where organs should have been, but weren't. His skull had been bashed in, and looked like it had been done over and over again.

There was a yellow, gloppy substance all around him, something that Lensherr recognized as intestines from a report he'd seen on the Discovery Channel a few weeks ago. The distinct aroma of dung and blood assaulted his senses, making him gasp for air that only brought more of the foul odor. Flecks of marrow and bone checkered the ground around them, and the boy's empty eye sockets glared at him, screaming at him, his broken nose and shattered teeth turning his face into one bloody maw.

Lensherr nearly vomited before picking up his radio and calling for reinforcements from the morgue. Then he shone his flashlight onto the blood blurred walls and saw what the blood spelled: **Black Womb**.

CHAPTER TWO: CADAVER

"Did you hear about what happened to Jamie Dawkins?"

The news spread through the school like wildfire. Within moments of opening its doors, it seemed as if everyone in school knew. It was the hushed topic on everyone's lips, in every gaze, in every movement. It was like a thick fog had descended into the halls, one so blinding that nobody could see anything but it.

Sara and Cathy were both still crying to Dr. Phillips, the guidance counsellor, while a shocked Mike gave statements to the police about what time Jamie had left last night.

Xander just watched, feeling terrible and guilty, thinking (if only in the back of his mind) that his wish had somehow caused this tragedy. He stared through the guidance counsellor's window at Sara as she bent over and buried her face in her hands, tears streaming down, and her eyes red and puffy. Her usually perfect blonde hair was a tangled mess from the number of times that she had run her fingers through it. Her blouse was wetted with the salt water pouring out of her eyes.

Cathy was crying too, but was still more composed than Sara. She managed to keep Dr. Phillips' gaze, nodding to his questions and comments at the appropriate times, only now and again bringing up a hand to wipe her runny nose. She let the tears fall, making no attempt to catch them. They just fell to the floor, softly pitting against the carpet.

Xander's gaze fell from them. He pictured Jamie's face, the way he had looked last year when the Cougars had won the semi-finals, his face filled with a transcendent joy. Or the way he looked the first time he and Greer Donaldson had danced at last year's spring formal. Or the way he'd sounded the last time they'd spoken, outside in the parking lot, when he had offered to walk home with him and Sara.

Sighing, he walked over to the nearest chair and collapsed into it. Leaning back, eyes closed shut, he banged his head off of a metal filing cabinet behind him.

"Ow," he said flatly, barely acknowledging it.

He opened his eyes and stared up at the ceiling. There were papers leaning over the side of the cabinet with police stickers on them.

Sticking out of a pale yellow folder amongst the files were pictures of Jamie.

Raising an eyebrow, he quickly glanced over at the police officer who was now talking with Tommy Irons. Biting his lip while he fought the urge to do it, he grabbed the file and stuffed it into his jacket, rising up from his chair and out of the counsellor's office.

Trying to remain as unseen as possible, something that he had become adept at over the years, he snuck through the halls and into the library. Hurrying to the back row of seats behind a bookshelf, he opened up the file and peered inside.

What he saw was horrific. The pictures depicted the last few moments of Jamie's life clearly. The rumors Xander had heard about the body had been true, and worse. His clothes were in shreds, especially the Cougars leather jacket he had cherished so much. The cloth that normally would have been silky was now rough and hard with dried blood. You couldn't really tell from the pictures, but he was sure he saw claw marks on him. His organs were all missing. Heart. Kidneys. Liver... everything except the lungs.

"What's that?" Mike said from somewhere in front of him.

Xander closed the folder quickly, but without arousing caution.

"Um... Lit Assignment."

"Ugh. Keep that crap away from me. I don't need anything like that right now," Mike droned as he sank down into a chair next to his friend. His face was flush white, his eyes distant and sad.

Good, thought Xander. "So how are you and Cathy getting along?" he chimed, understanding his friend's need to not talk about what was going on right now.

"Oh. Great. But this thing with... well, it doesn't help matters."

"Why? What's wrong?"

"It's Grendel. I know how she feels about him..."

"Yeah," Xander said calmly, getting up from his seat. "And she feels better about you. You know how lucky you are to have a girl like that love you?"

"Yeah, but..."

"But nothing. It's not worth the crap it'll cause for you two."

Mike frowned, then smirked a little. "I hate it when you're right, you know that?"

"Then you're just going to have to stop being so damn stupid all the time," Xander replied, slapping him on the back heartily.

"You wanna get a bite at Tiffany's?"

"Sure." They headed off, and Xander took one last look back at the pictures in the folder. "I don't think I'm gonna eat though. I haven't really got that much of an appetite today."

⋀⟨⟩⋀

As much as we'd like to forget it sometimes, everyone remembers a death. Not only friends and loved ones, but also acquaintances. Even people we have never met will mourn our passing thanks to media, the internet, and word of mouth. Whether we like it or not, death is always a recorded event in our society.

Especially by the body experiencing it.

Be it for explanations natural or external, an examination of any cadaver will tell you how it came to be in that state. Every body has a story to tell, it just cannot form the words all on its own.

If the victim or victims were shot, there will be an entry wound of a certain size and depth depending on the weapon fired. It will tell us the positioning of the weapon, the victim, and the shooter. In some cases there is an exit wound and gunpowder residue as well, all of which can be used to reconstruct the events leading to the person's demise.

If the victim was strangled, veins in the eyes will appear bloodshot and pronounced.

If the victim was stabbed, taking a mold of the puncture wound can reveal the size, shape, and sometimes even the origin of the weapon used.

Hairs, slivers of glass, fibers, bug cocoons, defensive wounds and other foreign substances all contribute to figuring out how and under what circumstances death finally occurred.

"Coral Beach Precinct Morgue, Tuesday the twentieth. My name is Harry Ford. I'll be your mortician for this evening."

"Come on, Harry. Quit fooling around and start the tape. This guy's creepy," Lance Berkshire said to his partner. He scratched the few strands of remaining hair around his right ear, his stocky frame jittering a little as he did so. He always found it cold here, and just a little moist.

He stared down at what remained of Jamie Dawkins, struggling to sum up enough saliva to allow him to speak again. After a moment, he clicked on the tape recorder. The plastic gears spun the film around them for almost a full minute before he had gathered up enough courage to start. "Subject name: Dawkins R. Jamie. Male. Caucasian, five-five, two-hundred fifty-five pounds. Cause of death: undetermined. Hey Harry, pass me the scalpel."

Harry's hand convulsed as he picked up the thin titanium knife and handed it to his partner. The flippancy known as Gallow's Humor he had clung to wavered for a moment, as he found himself unable to tear his eyes away from the vacant stare of their patient.

Lance began poking at the cold body, making one clean slice to fully expose the thorax. He wouldn't have to do much cutting though since the entire chest cavity had been pretty much removed. There were rips and tears around the edges of the hole the killer had made, each of them with four distinct claw marks, that had made the first officer on the scene think it had been an attack by a wolf or a bear.

His final cuts made at the neck and pelvis, Lance braced a hand on either side of the chest cavity and pushed. It opened like a hinge in dire need of oiling, and the sound it made was a wet suck followed by a snap. He looked at the rib cage he had just forced open, which was now just broken shards of bone, except for one which was smooth.

"Harry, look at this."

"What? It's a rib. So?" Harry said, raising an eyebrow and leaning his lanky frame inward, peering down at what Lance was indicating, a bit of his blonde hair falling down into his eyes.

"So? Look at it. It's been perfectly sawed off, like it was done with a tool. And look here," Lance said, making a broad sweeping motion across the corpse's torso. "All the body cavity organs have been taken, except the lungs. They haven't even been touched. They even worked *around* them to get to other organs. I don't know any animals that picky."

Harry maneuvered the light hanging from the ceiling to get a better look. "You mean a human did this? Something with a soul? Geez."

"That's what I think," he heaved, his frown seeming as though it were trying to escape the sides of his mouth. He checked a box and scribbled something down on his chart, his eyes darting back and forth to Jamie's open chest.

"What?" Harry asked, trying to follow Lance's gaze. "What is it?"

"The lungs are a bit dark."

"Probably a smoker."

"He's just a kid."

"Most smokers are."

Lance shot him a wry look, then laid down his clipboard and picked up his scalpel again. "Why weren't the lungs taken, anyway?" he asked rhetorically, fortifying one hand against the body's shoulder as he stuck his scalpel into one of the lungs. It resisted at first, the rubbery flesh bending inward against the pressure, then eventually opened with a slight hiss of air. He slid the knife down several inches, then put his blade aside and stuck in a gloved hand, stretching the organ until that part was inside out. Seeing the inside of the boy's lung revealed the blackness inside. It looked as though tar had been marinated into the meat. "Guess you were right. Looks like our Mr. Dawkins was actually a pretty heavy smoker. Our killer didn't want any damaged organs. Only the best."

Harry looked up, shivering a little as he felt the cold, sterile environment of the morgue get just a little bit colder.

ʌϒʌ

The bathroom at the Factory was one of the filthiest in town, coming in second only to the bar on Spring Street.

The floors were a dark green tile and grew mold so fast that you could almost watch it, first starting in the gray hued cement that held one to the other around their edges, then slowly working its way in until the original colour was just an odd dot in the centre.

There was a space heater against the far wall that never worked, and would occasionally shoot radiant blue sparks at people walking by if there was enough water on the floor. It was a sickly nicotine yellow and always smelled like burning hair. If you looked inside the grate near its top, you could see bits of paper and beer stoppers that had been shoved inside by idle hands. Some were charred beyond recognition, others with simply singed along their edges. Once someone had found a hockey card lodged in there, wrapped in a plastic sleeve and in mint condition.

While there were no separate bathrooms for different genders, this had clearly been the boy's bathroom. There was a urinal not far from the heater that always stank of warm piss. It was stained a dark orange around the sides and near the bottom where it met the pipe. There were still little blue cakes placed in it every day (likely tossed in from a safe distance of several feet), but it had gone largely unused for almost two years. Very few men had wanted to put their manhood anywhere near its corroded porcelain surface.

The girl's room had been commandeered by the staff several years back, when they'd decided they no longer wanted to share a bathroom with their customers.

Sara let out a long, mournful wail as she stared at herself it the filthy mirror, trying to force herself to stop for the third time. More tears welled up and blocked her vision until she couldn't even recognize herself, her soft features coming out like a picture taken while someone had spread Vaseline on the lens.

She let out another long, baleful moan that turned into an "oh" sound, glancing back at the bathroom door nervously to make sure it was locked.

There were white, milky stains around the edges of the mirror. Her gaze found them again and again, no matter how hard she tried to look away.

She dabbed at her eyes with the stocking wrapped around her hand, clearing her vision again. She sniffed back, trying to stop her face as it insisted on leaking from every available crevice. She wiped her nose, so hard that her rings scraped against its tip and made it red.

"Fuck," she cursed, reaching down and retrieving her purse from her side and laying it on the edge of the sink. With trembling hands she worked the clasp, her vision becoming muddy and blurred again.

"Stop it!" she snapped at herself, finding her foundation and slamming it down on the sink.

She turned on the tap cautiously, only touching it with the tips of her fingers. It was just as dirty as everything else here was. There was a brown sticky substance on one end that had been there for months. The janitors avoided it as much as the patrons did.

The water that spouted from the tap was yellow at first, then slowly faded to a more normal shade. It never completely lost that hue, and gained something that again looked like diluted milk, but was serviceable.

She cupped her hands beneath and waited until they were full, then splashed it onto her face. It left a sour smell on her skin, but the cold was refreshing and brought her back to reality, at least for a moment.

When she looked at herself again the sparkling treads her tears had left were gone, but her nose was still red. The skin under her eyes was red too, and had become puffy and pronounced.

She huffed, unscrewing the top of her makeup and beginning to apply it methodically. In some odd way it soothed her, the way any familiar task soothed the weary. She'd been applying foundation in these same motions since she was eleven, and returning to it somehow brought her to a calm place. Not necessarily a place of peace, but a place where she could get lost in the routine of the mundane until the storm finally passed.

By the time she finished, she wasn't even sniffling anymore.

She looked back down into her purse.

There was an orange prescription bottle there that until a few hours ago had resided in her mother's medicine cabinet. It was filled with small blue pills with a diagonal indentation on the back. She watched it for a moment, as if expecting it to do something, then picked it up and popped the top off with her thumb.

She poured a handful of the little blue circles her mother called happy pills and her father called Valium into her hand, forming a neat little mountain in her palm. She looked at it again, wriggling her fingers and feeling the way they moved and shifted with her every motion, then poured them back into the bottle until there were only two left. Those two stared back at her like two pale eyes.

She turned on the tap again and was about to cup her other hand underneath to get enough water so she wouldn't have to dry swallow them, then stopped. She sighed and placed one back in the bottle. She held the other between her thumb and forefinger, hovering it over the bottle as if threatening to throw it back with the others.

Turning back to the door again, she sniffed back hard.

"Fuck it," she said, then pushed the pill between her pursed lips. She bent down and stuck her mouth into the stream of milky liquid coming out of the faucet, sucking back more than enough to make the pill go down easily. Her hair got wet as she did this.

She turned off the tap and placed the cap back on the bottle, then gave herself one last look in the mirror. She adjusted her bra strap so it wasn't quite so visible, then nodded approvingly and stepped toward the door.

When her hand touched the knob, her vision became hazy again. She paused, bit her lip, and forced herself not to start crying again.

To her surprise, it worked this time. She glanced at her reflection in the cruddy mirror one last time, forced a smile onto her face, then walked out of the bathroom and back out into the Factory.

She and Xander had decided to join Mike and Cathy that evening. They had agreed beforehand to walk home together, and nobody had blamed them. On their way there they had seen people affixing new locks to their windows, shops closing down early... and people only seemed to get more and more paranoid as they got closer to the club. Many older people gave them hard stares, following them with their eyes as they walked by.

Xander and Mike were caught deep in battle on an arcade game, which Mike appeared to be winning judging by the curses spewing from Xander's lips and the way he was rattling his joystick.

Cathy sat in the driving simulator, not actually playing it. She pried her eyes from Mike long enough to acknowledge Sara's return, but did not question her absence.

"What do you think of Grendel?" Sara asked, looking over at the buff hockey player.

"Ugh. I'm afraid to say. Mike's all upset over me and Gren. He won't accept that we're just friends," she tisked, pulling her hair back into a ponytail and tying an elastic in it.

"I meant for me."

Cathy rolled her eyes. "Don't you think it's a little soon? Kinda pushing it."

"Oh, yeah. The mourning has begun," she laughed. The smile she had practiced in the mirror was more natural now, and she herself did not know whether she was faking it or not.

Cathy laughed too, but only to be polite. She didn't see anything funny about it at all.

"Kick 'em! No! How'd you... argh!" Xander finally admitted defeat and stepped back from the joystick. "Dammit! How'd you do that last bit?"

"Well, it's all about a delicate balance of concentration, discipline, and not being a spaz. You wouldn't understand," Mike grinned as he straightened his collar.

"You're not a very good winner. Has anyone ever told you that?"

"Hmm," Mike responded, pretending to look thoughtful. "I don't know.

You'd think I would be a better winner, what with all the practice I have."

Xander sighed, fumbling around his pockets for a quarter. Finding one, he held it up toward Mike at eye level, an evil grin spreading across his face. "Play again?"

"No way man. I gotta save some money to buy Cathy dinner."

Xander made a little sound like a whip under his breath.

"What was that?"

"I didn't say anything."

Mike eyed his friend for a moment. "One more game."

🦇

Detective Carl Dent had seen his fair share of weird stuff. Sick stuff. The stuff that they leave out of even the worst horror flick, he lived every day of his life. Things that wake you up at night in cold sweats. Children massacred in hoards and piled up in men's sheds. People half eaten by some postal worker turned cannibal. Even a guy skewered on a lamppost. But when his commissioner passed him that folder, his gut turned over inside him. All he could think of was the sick, revolting, abhorrent nature of man.

He brushed a hand through his fast fading hair, briefly disrupting his comb-over before subconsciously putting it back into place. Flipping through the files on Jamie Dawkins, he felt himself unable to take his eyes away from the photographs or miss a single syllable written on the pages. He placed a hand over his mouth as he got to the part with close up photos of his organs, or where they should have been.

They had been extracted meticulously, with the preciseness and care of a practiced surgeon. The organs would be usable afterward if stored properly, if that was, in fact, the killer's intent. But the area *around* where the organs had been lifted was the exact opposite, slashed and mutilated and mauled. Like once the operation had been completed the person had purposely caused as much damage as possible to whatever remained, for no other reason than the pure, undiminished joy of it.

Worst of all, autopsy tests revealed that the victim may have been alive when the operation was happening. Or at least when it had begun.

Detective Tim White walked by Dent's desk, taking a peek over his shoulder at his friend as he did so. He frowned, his exaggerated lips and dark African-American complexion only bringing out the emotion more. "Jeez, Carl. What're you doing?"

Dent did nothing for a moment, so engrossed was he in the information in front of him. He seemed to be fixated on one photo, taken of the boy's lungs in the state they were in at the crime scene. Suddenly, his head snapped up to look at Tim, as if his reaction to his coworker's comment had been a delayed one. "Sorry. What?"

"Hard case?"

Dent emitted a low growl in the back of his throat. "They're all hard. Especially when there's kids involved."

21

Tim nodded, prying his own eyes from the open folder. "I hear that. How old was he, anyway?"

"Eighteen."

"Ugh."

"What kind of monster could do something like this? And for what reason? There's just no logical sense behind it. This guy had no enemies, no grudges, he wasn't in a gang, there was nothing. He was clean."

"Maybe one of those idiot kids from the Cove?" Tim suggested, hating himself for saying it. "I mean, he was a star player. Maybe it's some kinda team rivalry."

"Yeah," Dent snorted. "And maybe they ate his organs to absorb his talent."

There was a look between them then as they both mentally examined the insanity and yet plausible validity of the comment, then brushed it aside.

"I'm glad you've got this one and not me," Tim admitted, tapping the top of Dent's cubicle wall once. "I don't think I'd be able to handle it."

Dent sighed, glancing back at the file. "Look at this: 'It is in the CS unit's professional opinion that the victim was attacked with a large, two-edged blade with a hilt, driven directly through the victim's right side.' I mean, that's a sword. That's a sword, right?"

"Or a machete."

"Who even does that? Really?"

"Dunno," Tim admitted reluctantly. "But I guess now it's your job to find out."

He gave his friend a curt wave then threw his jacket over his shoulder and started toward the exit.

Carl watched him go, then picked up the file again, immediately re-absorbed in the disturbing photographs.

ᚠᚥᚠ

Sara stepped out in front of them, her shoes tapping along the sidewalk and her arms held just above her head as she turned the streetlight into a spotlight. Her jacket bobbed to the beat her feet created, flapping under her arms like the garments of some Broadway jazz dancer.

"What is she doing?" Mike laughed, walking slowly alongside Cathy and Xander. He'd been slapped on the arm by the former a few times already for walking too fast, his long legs making his strides command many more inches than theirs.

Cathy watched her for a moment, tilting her head to one side. "Hop scotch?"

"There's no squares."

"*Invisible* hop scotch then?"

"No, there's a beat to it. Watch."

Sara tapped and scuffed her feet as though she couldn't hear their critique, mouthing along to the song in her head as she did.

22

Xander smiled.

"It has a long body to it," Cathy said.

Mike nodded.

Sara continued to skip, the way her shoes worked along the pavement making different sounds, like morse code. Short short short short short short short, long long!

"Do do do do do do do, dah dah," Mike repeated, in time with her as she started again. "What is that?"

"It's Spirit in the Sky," Xander said finally, unable to keep his mouth shut any longer.

Sara stopped, spun around, and glared at him. "Tattler."

"They wouldn't have got it."

"Hey!" Mike spat, turning and pushing Xander with one finger. "It was on the tip of my tongue."

"Sure."

"It was!"

"Uh-huh."

Cathy laughed, entwining her fingers into Mike's as the three of them caught up to Sara and they began to walk in unison.

Xander paid particular attention to their legs for a moment. It seemed as though Mike, Cathy and Sara were unintentionally stepping in unison, like soldiers on the march. He tried for a moment to force himself to be in synch with them but could not and eventually gave up. Still, it nagged at him.

They walked like this often, most of the time with no particular destination in mind. On nice summer nights they'd walk from one end of town to the other, just enjoying one another's company and making fun of anything they saw that had amused them that day and complaining about how none of them had a car.

They turned down Xander and Sara's street, a long stretch of road that connected Norman's Lane to Laird Street. Their houses loomed in the distance, the lights in Xander's house all dark. From where they were, it looked abandoned.

All the lights were on in Sara's house, blaring out into the night like it was on fire. Her mother's silhouette could be seen in the window, staring out into the street like a fisherman's wife looking out to sea.

Sara rolled her eyes. "I told her not to wait up."

"It's not even ten," Mike drawled. "I'd lay wages she was up anyway."

"You know what I mean."

"She's just worried," Cathy said, her voice smooth as silk. "Everyone is. Everyone should be."

"She's always like this. Ever since the crash," Sara continued, as though Cathy hadn't spoken. "This just gives her a good reason. Now I can't talk her out of it again."

"Pity," Xander smirked at her. "You might actually have to start being respectable."

She punched him in the arm even as she started laughing, and continued to laugh as she did it more and more. He raised his hands to try and defend himself, but kept lowering them to clutch his sides as rolls of laughter came out of him as well.

Cathy smiled, watching the two of them play. After a moment she leaned in and kissed Mike on the neck, the highest point she could reach without stopping in mid-stride and standing on her tip toes.

He smiled as her hair tickled his collarbone, squeezing her hand lovingly.

When they reached the walkway to Sara's house her mother opened the door, bathing the cobblestone in harsh bright light.

"Sara!" she snapped, her foot stomping a little when she did. It was a Johnson family trait, Xander had noticed, to talk with your feet. "You had me worried sick!"

"It's not even ten," Sara huffed as she walked toward her house, turning back to Mike as if to quote him. "Don't be such a drama queen."

"Don't take that tone with me, not after the other night. I have every right to be worried, and you know it."

She turned back to the rest of the group and smiled glumly, shrugged her shoulders, then entered her house without another word.

"This isn't a good time to be out and about like this," her mother continued, even as she closed the door. "I don't know how you can be so aloof when --"

The door closed, blotting out the light and muffling the sound of her scolding until they couldn't hear it at all.

Cathy sighed, then started walking again, towing Mike along with one hand.

Xander continued to watch the spot where Sara had disappeared for a moment, then stepped quickly to join them.

"Why do people say it like that?" he asked to no one in particular as they walked across the threshold into his yard. "I mean, we all know what happened. It'll probably even make the national news tonight. So why is everybody acting like it's some kind of a secret?"

"Because," Cathy explained, her silky voice singing through the cold night. "People don't like to know things like that. So they pretend they don't. Nobody likes to walk down the street, wondering what's behind them. But we do. Because if we don't... well..."

"Well, look what happened to Jamie," Mike finished, his eyes cast downward.

Xander paused, his head looming downward as he pondered that for a moment, then reluctantly accepted it as fact. He gave a curt wave goodbye to Cathy and Mike when they reached his door, then walked into his house and up the stairs toward his room, not saying a word to wake his parents.

When he got to the top, he got a sharp pain in his right side and nearly fell, but caught himself on the rail. The pain went away as quickly as it had come over him, but even after it was gone there was a steady ache as he entered his room. It reminded him of when people lost their limbs in wars yet said they could still feel them, even though they were gone. Pausing for a second while he leaned on his desk to make sure that it had passed, he shrugged it off, thinking nothing of it beyond the moment. He wasn't terribly athletic and he had been walking for a while. Usually he'd get online after getting home, but tonight he felt tired. He could barely keep his eyes open, and Cathy had caught him yawning more than once on the walk home. He got to his room and was about to lie down when he thought he heard something off in the corner of his room, and suddenly he got very scared.

It's just the house settling, he told himself, but still he turned on the light and looked around. He checked under his bed and around the room. He found nothing, but then he heard the sound again behind him. He turned sharply.

The light bulb on his ceiling went out with a sudden flash and he was left in the dark, his eyes seeing spots everywhere.

His heart skipped a beat. He tried to swallow but it got stuck in his throat as sweat began to bead on his brow.

The sound, now that he actually listened, was like a long shuffle. Like someone trying to find something while scuttling about in the dark. There was the slight flicker of paper.

He stopped breathing to listen hard. He couldn't hear anything now, not even the usual sounds that the house made. He turned on the computer screen to give himself a little light, bathing the room in an eerie green glow. He stopped again to listen hard and heard it a second time, in the corner. He went over, pulled away a box and revealed... an old computer magazine flapping against his air conditioner.

He laughed at himself, breathing a sigh of relief. He walked over to his door and locked it, then got in his bed and slipped into a long, deep sleep.

As Xander Drew slept, Cathy and Mike walked down the street toward her house. They hadn't said much since leaving Xander's place. They both knew what was on each other's mind.

Jamie.

He had been Mike's friend, not Cathy's. So it was okay for Cathy to talk about it, but not okay for Mike to hear about it. What resulted was a weird sort of silence that made them both uncomfortable, and yet left them no way to escape from it.

There was a thick mist of fog rolling onto the streets.

Cathy stopped him on the corner by touching his arm and forcing him to face her, then leaned in slowly and kissed him. He kissed her back, only for a moment, and then they resumed walking across the road.

"So can we talk about it now?" she asked, the words coming with a sigh of relief that they had finally found their way free.

He took her hand in his own. "Not yet. It's still... too early."

"When then?"

He sighed, thinking ahead a little more than he usually liked to. "Um, how about at Grendel's party Saturday?"

"Three days?" she whined, pouting her lower lip. She didn't like holding things in. She was the type of person who said whatever was on her mind whenever she wanted. Not that she was a flake. Actually, she was the exact opposite. Those who knew her knew that she took responsibility for everything. She probably even blamed herself for Jamie's death in some way.

She leaned in to kiss him again, but they were interrupted by a sound behind them. Cathy jumped into Mike's arms and he laughed at her.

"What?" he asked, holding her lightly by the shoulders.

"I- I thought I heard a sound," she stammered.

He laughed at her again. "You could not be more cliché if you tried. You really think there's some crazed killer on the..."

Shink.

This time he heard it too. The sound of metal scraping on metal. They both stood perfectly still, neither making a sound.

Shink.

Again. Closer this time. It was coming from across the street, around the corner that they had just come from.

"Come on," he said, taking her by the arm and they broke into a fast walk down the street toward her house. They rounded the next corner and stopped for a moment to listen. They could hear it.

Shink. Shink. Shink.

Metal scraping across the pavement, getting closer and closer to them. They broke into an all out run as they passed under a street lamp next to a gas station. Cathy stopped for a minute and banged on the windows as she went. "Help us!" she screamed to arouse the curiosity of anyone who might be inside, but there was no response.

Mike stopped a few feet past her, turning around when he heard the noise she was making, the expression on his face turning from unadulterated fear to pity for just a moment.

She stared into the tinted windows of the station, only the night lights on to let her see that everyone had left, every business had closed early. Everyone in this town had been spooked by Jamie Dawkins' death. So the two were alone. Her lower lip shook as her eyes searched frantically amongst the dimly lit potato chip and cigarette displays for any sign of movement, desperation beginning to pump through her fragile body as fast as adrenaline.

Shink.

Mike jogged back toward her, taking her firmly but gently around her upper arm. "Come on. We don't have time," he said, his voice the only part of him showing his exhaustion.

She looked around the gas bar again, her hair whipping around her head, when the sound came again.

Shink.

It was so close she thought she had felt the blade graze the goosebumps on the back of her neck. She started to run with Mike again without even looking where he was leading her, taking off away from the abandoned station and back onto the street toward her home.

Mike turned around momentarily, looking into the gaping darkness through the thick fog. He heard the sound again, followed by a sight. The gleam of a long, curved piece of metal shining in his eyes. He turned back toward the front, the voice of his junior high gym coach ringing in his ears, telling him to keep his eyes facing forward. You run faster when you're facing forward.

Cathy didn't get far before she buckled over in pain. They'd been walking for hours, and now all this running had produced a spasmodic ache in the muscles of her stomach, sending shots of agony down her legs and upwards into her chest. She tried to get up, but her body automatically cried out in rebellion sending her back down to her knees. Mike looked back again.

Nothing.

He helped her to her feet and listened for a moment. Then, from the darkness, something slashed at her.

"Ah!" she cried, as she felt the heat of pain rip up and down her thigh. Something had tried to cut through her hamstring. She quickly propped herself onto Mike's shoulder and then began to run, but Mike knew it was hopeless. She was hopping around on one foot, and he wouldn't be able to take her added weight for too much longer.

When he looked over his shoulder again, he saw it. A tall, dark figure steadily making its way toward them. It wasn't running, and yet it was making progress on them. With a single thought of horrible brilliance, a light went on in Mike's head and he realized that they both wouldn't make it. He stopped when they passed the next corner, a shocked look on his pasty white face.

The guy was close; they both knew it. Cathy's house was only about a block away, but they wouldn't make it. They both knew it.

"Why are you stopping?" she asked, wide eyed with astonishment and pain, tears already streaming down her face.

Holding her arms with both hands, he pulled her in and kissed her, then pushed her in the direction of her house. "Go."

She started to cry fresh tears, but turned and ran toward her home.

Mike turned around to face their attacker. Suddenly, he felt a sharp pain in his right side as a long, double-edged sword plunged into him. He screamed as the attacker twisted the blade slightly before ripping it out again. Mike felt his blood flow freely from the wound. He turned. He wanted to know. *Had* to know who this mysterious figure was before he died.

But there was no one there. He was alone.

He turned and ran for Cathy's home. The pumping of his legs increased the blood flow, and as her house came into sight, he started to feel light headed. He stopped for a moment on a bench to catch his breath. He put his hand on his side and pressed, shooting pain all through his torso. He looked down at his hand, soaked in blood, looking black in the darkness of the night street. Closing his eyes, he let his head rest a minute. Then he remembered what they tried to tell you on those medical shows that he and Xander loved so much. When you got a wound like this, you don't close your eyes. There's a good chance that you'll never wake up again.

So he clenched his teeth and got up.

He fell immediately to the sidewalk, skidding his knees against the concrete. He vomited onto the gray stone, but then realized that it was blood, its coppery taste filling his mouth and throat. Mike had always hated the taste of his own blood, and now he was drowning in it. He wrapped his hands around his sides, trying desperately to stop the stream of red fluid coming from them.

CHAPTER THREE: INJECTED

"Mike? Dear God, Mike?" came a voice from ahead. The sound was muffled by the throbbing pain in his skull. It sounded like someone talking while under-water.

Mike looked up. Even his vision had begun to get hazy, but he could plainly see Cathy's dad coming toward him. He was a hard man to mistake for anyone else. David Kennessy was portly and kind of shaped like a pear, with saggy jowls that shook whenever he spoke. His eyes always looked kind and often concerned, as they did right now as he looked down at the open wound on Mike's side.

Mike only grunted in response.

"Oh, fuck," he said as he picked Mike up and put his arm around his shoulder. "Let's get you into the warm, son."

The walk back to the house was both slow and rushed at the same time. With every agonizing step they took, David could feel the boy in his arms tremble. He could see the blood as it continued to soak through his shirt at an alarming rate, faster than he would have thought possible.

He'd never seen that much blood before, not in real life.

There was a sound behind them and David pressed forward, glaring back between them with eyes filled with fear. Mike kept up the new pace for only a moment, then let out a long grunt and slowed down. David obliged. It was like trying to run a three-legged race when the prize is your life and your partner was a toddler.

"M'sorry," Mike hummed painfully.

"It's okay," David said, patting him on the chest.

It wasn't.

They made their way to the house without incident, David opening the door with a firm kick. The latch had never been good, and opened with even the slightest force.

Cathy and her mother, Karen, were still on the couch crying. There were first-aid bandages in place on Cathy's calf, and Karen had just hung up the phone with the hospital. When she heard the door open, she got up and yelled: "David? Dear god, did you find him?"

Then she saw him. She gasped at the sight of the boy she loved like her own son with his clothes and hands drenched in blood. She hurried Cathy upstairs despite her screams and cries of protest.

They laid Mike onto the couch, placing pillows under his neck and head to prop them up. David wrapped some makeshift bandages tightly around his torso to stop the bleeding, and placed blankets on him to keep him warm. They could hear the ambulance's siren in the distance.

Cathy gave up fighting her mother and went into her room, slamming the door behind her so hard it rattled pictures all over the house. There was only a second's worth of silent pause before they heard her scream.

All eyes in the room went wider than ever, a difficult feat considering the situation.

David looked from his wife to Mike and then back again before he rushed up the stairs, leaving Mike momentarily to see what was wrong. Karen followed.

He reached his daughter's room and opened the door. He found his daughter curled into a ball on the floor next to her double bed, crying and holding her legs tightly against her body. She peered over her knees with panic stricken eyes, unable to pry her gaze off the foreign object in her room.

There was a long, double-edged sword sticking out of her floor. It had golden lining and a rubber handle in the middle, and was perfectly clean. No blood was on it.

David ran to the window and looked out. There was nothing there except the ambulance pulling up, its flashing red lights making eerie shadows on the street. He turned to his wife and daughter. "Did he hurt you?"

"There was nobody h-here. Just the... the thing," Cathy stammered hysterically.

David turned and looked at the blade, put in so little time ago that it was still wobbling like a tuning fork.

"How could someone have sunk that in without anyone hearing?" he breathed to himself.

He ran back downstairs, leaving his wife and child in the room. He thanked God that his younger daughter was staying at a friend's house.

He greeted the paramedics quickly and led them into the living room, where Mike was drifting in and out of consciousness. One of the younger medics lifted up the blanket and looked at the wound as they hefted him onto the stretcher.

"Fuck," he mumbled so that only he could hear. "Gutted like a friggin' fish."

They rushed him into the ambulance and began work right away, giving him morphine for the pain as they tried urgently to staunch the blood flow. Cathy got into the van with him. She had wounds to treat as well. She started to bawl as she saw the blank look in her boyfriend's eyes, which were faded and rolled back into his skull. The doctors began to stitch up the wound before they even arrived at the hospital. They rushed him into emergency as Cathy went into a smaller doctor's office. It was the first time she wondered if she would ever see him again. And for a while, the only sound she could hear was her own heart breaking.

29

Xander woke up the next morning and stretched, scratching his sides. He heard the familiar crack of his bones and the creak of his bed as he got up, his skin still sticky and clammy from the warm night's sleep. He went over to his computer, whose alarm clock program was beeping the "time to wake up" song it played every day at seven. He jiggled the mouse to get rid of the saver, then clicked the off button on the beeping clock.

He hauled on a new shirt and jeans and opened his door. He stopped dead in his tracks, staring at the door, his lower lip quivering just a little.

His door had been locked last night. Now it wasn't.

He looked around his room quickly for anything out of the ordinary and saw nothing. Just stacks of Popular Science magazines and clothes scattered all over the floor, along with a pile of CDs he'd been meaning to give back to Sara for some time. Taking a long, slow pan of the room to make sure, he decided that it had to be nothing. Maybe the lock had slipped, as it had sometimes in the past. No big deal.

He walked down the stairs and into the kitchen. He turned sharply to see his mother crying and his father sitting at the table.

Xander's father was old and scrawny, wearing a flannel shirt and suspenders he refused to admit were out of style. His shoulders were slumped forward and his face sagged more than usual as he clenched his wife's hand tightly around her fingers.

She was a little younger and usually hid her years much better. Today her hair wasn't curled and Xander noticed she was only wearing one earring. The makeup on her round face was smeared by tears and tissues, and when she looked at Xander he could see her eyes were bloodshot.

Xander's eyes widened in shock. "What's going on?" He almost didn't need to ask. It was as if he knew before the words even escaped his mother's lips. The image of what he knew had happened came to his brain. He could practically hear her saying the words in her head.

"Xander, son, you should sit down," his mother coaxed, motioning toward an empty chair at the table.

"No. No way. Just fucking tell me," he said slowly but defiantly, hating it when people started bad news with sit down. It just made it worse by drawing it out.

"Sit," his father said in a stern voice, frowning in disapproval of his son's choice in language.

Xander took a step toward the chair without even realizing it, almost as a reflex, his father glaring at him as he did.

"Alex, sweetie, were you with Mike and Cathy last night?" his mother asked, her voice unwavering even through her tears.

"I... what?" Xander asked, getting confused as his head spun a mile a minute.

"Son, Michael and Cathy were attacked last night," his father said bluntly, placing an open palm on the table as if he were laying out the facts.

Xander could feel the words cut through him like a dagger. He ran into the porch and hauled on his shoes, unlocked the front door and ran out.

His mother started to get up and go after him, but his father touched her on the arm quickly, shaking his head.

He hopped across the threshold they had passed over only last night. He ran to Sara's doorway and started banging on her door.

She opened it, still wearing her nightgown, her eyes red and puffy.

Without a word, he took her into his arms and cried.

ϺϺ

Carl Dent slammed a fist down on the folder in front of him, this one marked Harris/Kennessy. "Fuck!" he yelled, getting the attention of the entire wing. Nobody dared to say anything to him, as the entirety of his balding head turned red with livid anger.

He ran a hand through his remaining hair, clenching his teeth as he opened both this and the Dawkins file.

"What am I missing?" he mumbled to himself, waiting for something to jump out at him. A tattoo, a locale, anything besides the manner in which the people were attacked.

Suddenly, his phone rang.

He glared at it, willing it to stop on its own.

Which of course, it did not.

Cursing again, he picked it up and put it to his ear. "Dent," he grumbled, scraping his teeth together.

"Yes, this is Don Smith. I'm a reporter with Beach News Daily..." said the polite yet exhausted voice on the other end of the line.

Dent rolled his eyes, throwing his free hand up in the air. He hated reporters, always had. More than anything, he hated the way they introduced themselves, putting emphasis of their job title, the newspaper, and even their name. It was as if they were trying to make themselves sound so much more important than they really were. "Yes?" he sighed reluctantly.

"... I was wondering if you had any information regarding the attack?"

"All information associated with Jamie Dawkins that we are willing to disclose at this time has been released in a press release to all media outlets. I would suggest you get off the phone with me and check your fax machine. Besides, I only deal with Tom Drake. He's the only decent reporter at that rag."

There was an audible silence on the line as Don took a deep sigh, composing himself before speaking again. "I wasn't talking about that attack. I meant the attack last night. On Mike Harris and Cathy Kennessy?"

Dent raised an eyebrow. "And how do you know shit about that?"

"My son told me. He goes to their school. They all seem to know..."

Dent narrowed his eyes. "Then why don't you go ask them?" he hissed, slamming the phone down onto its receiver as hard as he could.

He immediately grabbed the file on Mike and Cathy and threw on his jacket,

31

cursing as he walked toward the door.

"Bout time I stopped sitting on the sidelines anyway..." he mumbled, slamming the door behind him.

Xander and Sara both took that Wednesday off school to go visit Mike and Cathy in the hospital. Cathy was as good as new. The blade had only breached the skin.

Mike was a different story. The killer's blade had punctured the right side of his abdomen and gone in several inches. The flesh there had required fifty-two stitches and ten staples to stay closed. The blade had missed the major organs, although the attending physician still was not sure how. It had ruptured one organ however, nearly slicing it half and resulting in its immediate removal from Mike's body.

"Your appendix?" Sara repeated, fighting to control her laughter. "Some people have to pay to get that useless ball of flesh removed, and you're all whiny cause some creep did it for free?"

Mike laughed weakly at that, feeling his stitches stretch. He knew she was joking. "Ha. Yeah, guess it is kinda funny when you look at it like that. If you're a twisted freak like you are."

Cathy did one of her famous fake laughs, then gave Mike a kiss on the cheek.

"The doctors even say if I rest up, I'll be out of here in time for Grendel's party," Mike added happily, squeezing his girlfriend's hand tightly and giving her a happy smile.

"Great. Perfect," Xander joked cheerfully. "But I think Cathy's going to be disappointed. She was looking forward to some alone time with ol' Gren."

Both Sara and Cathy laughed at that. Mike did not.

Xander coughed awkwardly. "Well, if you feel up to it later, I think I spotted an arcade down near the waiting room. Maybe they've got --"

"Nope," Mike cut him off. "Sorry buddy, our game isn't there."

"Dammit," he whined, stomping his foot dramatically.

"They've got Marble Mutant Super Heroes though."

"Cool enough, I guess," he shrugged, scuffing his feet along the tile floor in disappointment.

There was a knock at the door and a tall, important looking man stepped into the room. He wore a cheap black suit and a leather tie. He had a dulled toothpick between teeth that looked jaundice, which he took out when he entered the room and flicked into the medical waste bin on the wall. His eyes were small and beady. They glared down Xander before even meeting with anyone else. He had a bad comb-over and cheeks that were just a little chubby, but not overly so. He reached into his suit and produced a badge, let it gleam brightly in the light from the window, then shoved it back.

"I'm Detective Carl Dent. Is this..." he looked at his papers, quickly finding the name he was looking for, "Mike Harris' room?"

"Yeah, that's me." Mike paused after speaking, breath catching as his side ached at him.

"He's the one in the bed," Sara smirked. "I think that should have been obvious."

"That's Sara, and this is my girlfriend Cathy. Can we... help you?" Mike continued, as though Sara hadn't spoken.

"Yes. I need to ask you a few questions regarding your attacker. Do you mind, or would you like me to come back later?" he smiled politely, again shooting a look at Xander.

Xander raised his eyebrows in response, not knowing what he had done to upset the man.

"No, now's fine," Mike smiled, then added quickly, "Oh! As long as you don't mind my friends being here."

Dent looked down on Xander again, this time making long eye contact.

"Not at all," he smiled. "Now I've worked on cases like this before, and I know you may have trouble spelling out the details over and over... so, all I want for the moment is a description on your attacker."

"I wouldn't be able to tell you. We never really saw him," Cathy replied solemnly.

"And you, sir?" He pointed with his pen to Mike.

"Same story."

"So, you're telling me you saw nothing, even though my report says you were stabbed under a street light?"

"Yes, sir," Mike said through barred teeth.

"And then the killer had to go past your girlfriend's oncoming father and get into her room, plant the sword in her floor (which would have been loud), all without making a sound and then get out again?"

"If that's what he said happened," Sara interrupted, "then that's what happened."

"I didn't ask you," he snapped curtly.

"Hey!" Xander jumped from his seat and glared into the detective's eyes. "What do *you* think happened?"

Dent took a deep breath and closed his folder. "I think that these last two attacks were gang related. The same stupid town pride crap that's been happening between here and Coral Cove for years. And that you made up these stories, maybe even stabbed each other, to protect a friend in the gang that you know did it."

Mike tried not to laugh. And failed.

Xander got up in Dent's face again and gave him a little shove. Not enough to get him in any kind a trouble, just a rude nudge, finding a backbone that he never even knew he had as the hairs on the back of his neck stood on end.

"Get out," he said simply, cocking his head toward the door.

"Okay," Dent said as he raised his hands up in defeat calmly. "But I think I've got my gang banger right here." He motioned toward Xander and walked away.

There was a long silence even after he left the room.

"What a jerk," Cathy said after what felt like forever. She sat down on the bed next to Mike and kissed him.

Still the others were quiet.

"Come on!" she said in a more cheerful voice, getting out a wheelchair for Mike. "Let's go down to that game room like Xander said."

At Coral Beach High School, everyone was scared out of their minds. People were going crazy. There were wild rumors spreading all over the hallways now, with each student putting their own spin on what had happened and who had done it. Everyone had been blamed -- every student, every teacher, everyone that was known to be blamed had been blamed. There had even been recurrences of an old urban legend involving a man with hooks for hands that preyed on kids that went behind the Factory to make out at the kissing stone. In any case, students and parents alike were freaked. Every shadow was a killer, every movement a danger. Every sound was someone waiting to slice them open. And the teachers' suggestions to get a walk home buddy didn't help either.

Grendel roamed the hallways after his fourth period English class had gotten too boring. He had a slight smirk on his face, the satisfaction he always got after he'd done something he knew he shouldn't have. The halls were empty, and eerily quiet. Only the squeak of his footsteps on the wet floor could be heard. After a while the squeak wore off, and he had renewed hope that the principal would not catch him.

He heard the sound of scuffed, smooth shoes and recognized them immediately as Principal Shnieder's. He was a fat little troll of an administrator with ears that wriggled when he talked about geography and *only* when he talked about geography.

And he *loved* giving out detention slips.

Grendel ducked into the boy's bathroom just as Shnieder was coming around the corner, feeling his heart jump up into his chest when he did.

Tommy and 'Sud' were in the bathroom, where they spent most of their classes.

"What's up, Gren?" Tommy said in the halfway-mocking tone he almost always used. He was tall for his age at almost six foot five, and spiked his hair to add even a little more height. His grin seemed to stretch beyond the borders of his face as he greeted Grendel, opening his jean shirt to reveal a 'Hello Nasty' tee underneath. Sud sat next to him on the sink counter, scratching the stubble that composed his hair. He was a larger boy wearing a sweater even though he was clearly warm and his arms seemed a little too long for the rest of his body. He did not greet Grendel, but that was normal. Sud almost never spoke, except to back up Tommy.

"Nothin' much, man," Grendel replied, still listening for Shnieder to pass as he slapped hands with Tommy. "You guys still coming to my party this Saturday? It's gonna be a wild one."

"Yeah. Yeah, we'll be there," Tommy smiled, then dropped his voice, even though there was nobody else around. "Have you, ah, made your move with Cathy yet?"

Grendel lowered his voice too. "Not yet. I'm gonna do it at the party. I figure after all this Jamie business, and with Mike in the hospital, she'll need a shoulder to cry on."

"Yeah, and then a person to lie on."

They all laughed.

"Hopefully," he smirked, licking his tongue against his teeth. They stopped talking as they heard Shnieder pass the bathroom and continue around the corner. "Well, I gotta go. It's only so long before he checks in here. Talk to you later, guys."

Grendel stepped out into the quiet hallway once again. His shoes made no sound now.

Then suddenly, they did.

He stopped, but the squeaking continued for a moment or two. He put his back to the corner and poked his head out to check for Shnieder.

The halls were clear.

He looked back from where he came to see if it was Tommy or Sud coming out of the washroom, but that hall was clear as well. He began to walk again, and again the squeaking started, out of synch with his own footsteps. Then he heard it.

Schenk.

The sound of cold metal on the stone walls of the school. His body broke out in gooseflesh as he began to run up the halls toward his classroom. The sound and the squeaks sped up as well. He rounded the second-to-last corner to his class, and slipped on the floor, ploughing into the wet floor sign and then slamming into the lockers. Hard.

He picked himself up as he heard the squeaks, still coming now even though he had stopped. He heard the sound again, and suddenly remembered the rumors of the man with hooks for hands. He broke into a run, turning the next corner and running right into Carl Dent.

"What the hell are you doin', boy?" Dent bellowed.

"N-nothing," Grendel stammered as he looked down at Dent's metal coat strap, clinking against the wall, and sighed at his own silliness.

"I should report you to your --" Dent stopped for a moment, looked in his folder, then back up at Grendel. "Is your name Julian Grendel?"

"Uh, yeah. That's me. It's just Grendel though."

"Son, do you know an Alex Drew?"

"You mean Xander?"

"Come with me, boy."

"Son," Dent said as he glared at the boy from across the guidance counsellor's table. "How well do you know this... Xander, is it?"

"Yeah. He's all right. I invited him to a party coming up Saturday."

"So, you'd say that you were friends?"

"More like a friend of a friend," Grendel said, mulling the term 'friend' around in his head for a second.

"You mean Michael Harris?" he pushed, checking his file just to be sure of the name.

"Mmm. More like Cathy Kennessy," he corrected quickly, a sly grin prying over his lips.

"I see. Alright, how would you describe Xander Drew?"

"He's cool enough. He knows what goes on. A little bit of a loner though."

"What do you mean?" Dent picked up his pen and paper and began to write.

"Well, he mainly only hangs around with these three people..."

Dent again looked at his notes. "Mike Harris, Cathy Kennessy and Sara Johnson."

"Yes." Grendel was starting to get a little freaked about how much Dent knew about the life of an average kid. "And when he's not shooting pool with them, he's usually inside on his computer. Guy fancies himself a bit of a hacker."

"So he keeps to himself a bit."

"Um, yeah. A little, I guess. Acts like he doesn't have the time of day for anyone else then wonders why they ain't got it for him. Truth is, if Sara didn't like him so much, he wouldn't be coming near my place this Saturday. Dunno what she sees in the guy."

Dent gathered up his papers, smiling from ear to ear. "Thank you for your help, son."

Grendel furrowed his brow, getting up the same time that Dent did, more than a little confused. "Wait, I thought you were going to ask me what I knew about the murderer?"

"I just did," he said under his breath, heading toward the door.

Grendel's mouth went slack, then turned up into a grin.

"Well, this is just... neat," he cackled, turning toward the door himself.

"Son of a bitch!" Xander screamed as Mike's character laid another triple punch combo into his. "Even in a damn wheelchair he manages to beat me!"

Xander had chosen the Granite Gladiator, a gray behemoth wearing armor that made him look like Russell Crowe, thinking his brute strength would more than make up for his own inexperience with the game. He was wrong, as per usual. Against the strength and speed of Mike's character, the Stone Spider, the Gladiator was all but helpless. Mike did a half swivel with the joystick and pressed 'punch' three times in succession to initiate the 'Ultimate Spider' move, where the Spider just zipped around the screen, hitting the Gladiator about a hundred times as he went. The Granite Gladiator went down for the second time and the gold letters "Stone Spider Wins" appeared on the screen. The digital spider creature made the remark that the loser would 'Make a good sidekick.' With Xander's defeat the game went into one player mode and Mike fought the computer's character, randomly chosen as Obsidian. The scrawny little black statue came to life and leaped into the playing field, sprouting four sparkling claws at the end of each wrist as he did so.

"Dammit. I can't beat this guy," Mike muttered as Obsidian started off with something called a 'Hazard-O' attack, swirling his claws all around the screen in great gaping circles.

Xander wandered over to where the girls had been sitting, cursing all the way.

"Hi guy," Cathy said to him, "Get bored of the game?"

"Naw. Just bored of losing the game. But I think it cheered Mike up."

"Good." She leaned over and gave her friend a little kiss on the cheek. "Thank you."

"Whatever. If you need me, I'll be playing pinball," he said, motioning to where that game stood. "It's easier to take losing against a small metal ball. Mike's victory dance is even more demeaning when he's in that damn chair."

She giggled, knowing exactly what he was talking about.

"Kay," she said cheerfully, watching him as he made his way over to the pinball machine, digging change out of his pocket along the way.

With Xander gone, the girls could resume their talk. Cathy turned back to Sara, a concerned look upon her face.

"What do you think that investigator guy meant when he accused Xander of being in a gang?" Sara asked out of the blue, as she was known to do every now and again.

"I don't know. Maybe he thinks it's him because you and him were the only two people who knew that Mike and I were on that road."

A look of panic flashed across Sara's face, and her voice had a little more edge in it. "Hey, what makes you so special? Why would he think that you were actually targeted, instead of just a random victim like Jamie?"

"I don't know," Cathy said, just taking a sip of her soda. "But you damn well better hope someone figures it out. I don't know how Mike got away from that guy, but he was absolutely brutal."

"Argh!" Mike said, slamming his hands against the machine. Even Cathy noticed. The computer-controlled Obsidian had just finished him off with a move called 'Insanity Rage', and Stone Spider went spinning into the air before landing on his back with a thump. Mike wheeled himself over to where Xander stood searching his pockets for change after losing another quarter to the pinball game.

"That one's impossible, man," he said to his friend, motioning toward the air hockey tables. "Let's try our hand at a real sport."

Xander grabbed the handles on the wheelchair and put him in place at one end.

"Two paddles?" Xander asked, picking them both up and displaying them to his friend.

"Of course. But I'll use one. I figure with the wheelchair, and the one paddle, that'll mean I won't *totally* kick your ass."

"Hardy har," he said, throwing Mike his second paddle and putting a dollar into the side of the machine. It slowly buzzed to life.

"So, you are still going over to Grendel's... right?" Sara asked, almost out of boredom. "I mean, it is the social event of the season." She did a mock British accent when she said that, but it sounded more like Australian.

Cathy laughed at the horrifically bad impression, then brushed a strand of her long black hair back behind her ear. "I want to," she said, but there was that implied 'but' at the end of it, one that was left hanging there open-ended for Sara to pick up and follow on.

"So, why won't you? And don't give me any of that 'Mike thinks Gren wants me' crap either."

"I dunno," Cathy mulled, fiddling her straw up and down in her drink. "Don't you think it's possible? I mean, he does come off a little..."

"He doesn't," Sara assured her, placing one hand on her friend's knee to emphasize the sentiment. "Take it from someone who dated him. If he liked you, you'd know it."

"Really?" Cathy frowned, still visibly unsure.

"Absolutely," Sara laughed. "And even if he does, Gren's cool. He'd never act on it. Gren's good at keeping secrets. His own, and other peoples."

⋀⋋⋏

"I'm telling you guys. Xander Drew is the *killer*!" Grendel shouted. A small legion consisting of Sud, Tommy, Derek and a few others had gathered around him as he stood on one of the picnic tables outside school. "That guy from the cops practically *said* it!"

"No way," Tommy muttered under his breath, his eyes widening as he thought of all the times he and Xander had talked in the halls, or passed him in the stalls, or let him copy his history notes.... The thought made him shudder. "There's just *no way*." He smoothed a hand through his spiked hair, frazzling it as he played with the settings on the camera that hung relaxed around his neck.

"Yeah," echoed Sud, moving to fiddle with his own hair as Tommy had, only to remember that his head was, in fact, shaved. He quickly brought his hand down, hoping that nobody had noticed. "No way."

"Anyway," Grendel continued, giving Sud a look that completely disregarded his last comment. "The evidence is all there! He hated Jamie because Sara liked him. Everyone sees the way he chases her around, been doing it since he was six goddamn years old. He tried to kill Cathy and Mike because he's angry at them for ditching him all the time. He sees what they've got and he knows he's never going to have that with Sara. Plus, he's the only one who knew where they would be that doesn't have an alibi. I mean, think about it. I couldn't accept it at first either but... no, just *think* about it and you'll see it."

"Yeah," Derek piped up. He shrugged, his black plastic jacket making ruffling sounds as he did. "And while we're at it, we'll all think about how the hell that whiny little weakling could even punch somebody enough to hurt them, let alone do any damage." He shrugged his shoulders again and walked away from Grendel.

"Yeah," Tommy said, ignoring Grendel's protests as he followed Derek's lead and walked back toward the bathrooms.

"Yeah," Sud said, mimicking Tommy's exact movements.

Grendel just got down off of the table as the rest of the crowd dispersed. He sat back, a look of hatred and darkness in his eyes.

You'll all pay for this, he thought. *Nobody ignores Julian Grendel.*

ʎ⟨ʎ

"Hey Dent," Tim said as he slipped on his suede jacket. "Find anything connecting those kids yet?" He smiled at Dent. The man was dedicated, that was for certain. He'd never let go of a case like this, not until he brought in the killer.

"No. Not yet," Dent admitted, not even looking up from the photos comparing Mike and Jamie's wounds.

"You should go home. Get some rest," he remarked, a faint sound of concern in his voice. "Fresh eyes would do that case better then tired ones."

"Tim, there have been two teen attacks in the last two nights. Tonight could mean another one for this killer. This kid may not be as lucky as the last two."

"Yeah, and it's an hour before sunset," Tim sighed, motioning toward the open window with his head.

Dent looked down at his watch in genuine astonishment. He had completely lost track of time. "Man oh man oh... wait."

Tim's eyes went up. "What?"

"I'd probably need another victim to prove this theory, but both Harris and Dawkins were adopted."

"Come on, Carl," Tim said, sighing as he shook his head at his friend. "So are thousands of kids all over America. You're grasping at shadows. What about the Kennessy girl?"

"She could have been just an innocent, in the way of the killer's attack."

"I think I liked your gang theory a little better. Besides..." his voice trailed off for a minute as he looked out the window at the sun. "It is now fifty-five minutes to sunset. I don't think you have time to run birth records on every kid in this town before then."

Dent cursed under his breath, running his hand over his mouth as he watched the sun slowly set. He glared at the bright orange orb as if it had betrayed him horribly.

"It's going to happen again, you know," he said finally, in a defeated, barely audible tone.

"Yeah," Tim reciprocated, pulling up a chair next to him. "I know."

"Dammit!" Xander yelled as Mike won his third straight game of air hockey. Xander had won the first game, but once Mike had gotten a handle on playing in the wheelchair, there was no hope. Goal after goal -- Mike had just hammered them in without remorse.

"I guess that means I win... doesn't it?" Mike gloated, getting as much enjoyment out of the moment as he possibly could.

"Get up out of that chair. You've gotta be milking it or something."

They all laughed. Cathy came over and gave Mike a short kiss, and there was an awkward pause between Xander and Sara.

"Ugh," Xander let out a little grunt.

"What is it?" Cathy asked, coming to his side.

"Um..." he paused for a second, putting pressure on his right side. "It's nothing. Really, it happened last night too. It's just a lot of pain in my right side."

Mike's eyes widened momentarily. *Could it actually be some kind of... sixth sense humans had to danger?* he thought, his mind going a mile a minute. *Was it possible that the killer was close by, in the building even.... no. God no, of course it wasn't.* He laughed at himself as he took Cathy in his arms again. Coral Beach was a big enough place that whoever this sicko was he didn't need to come looking for his targets.

"Come on," Sara chimed. "We have to call our parents if we're gonna be home in time for dinner."

Xander got home at around quarter to six. It was only just beginning to get dark. He ran up the stairs two steps at a time, knowing that his dinner would be waiting for him in his quiet room at the top. He opened the door and the smell of fried chicken made his mouth water. He sat down next to it and turned on the computer, taking a copy of the Beach News Daily that his mother had left on the keyboard and tossing it to one side.

Taking a sip of his coke from the large cup, he started browsing through his files looking for something to do.

He decided to check out that website that Soul had been talking about.

What was it called?

He took a big bite of gravy-covered chicken breast and licked his fingers, then checked his computer's chat history, pulling up the conversation he'd had with Soul earlier.

"hello Pinkerton.

Oh. Hi soul. How's life?

Alright. I've been looking at something weird online. I discovered some kind of bizarre... thing. I don't have a password decoder as sophisticated as you do, I thought you might wanna take a look at it.

Sure. What's the site?

Something called engen.com. Oops. Gtg!

40

'got to go'?, why?"

"There," he said to himself, reading aloud off of the screen. "Engen.com."

He punched the address into his computer's web browser. Automatically, odd midi music started to play. A badly done gif animation of what he could only assume was the Engen logo came up onto the screen. It was a blue circle with a spike running through it from side to side, containing the word 'Engen'. When that was done, the main home page loaded up. It was filled with a bunch of different links going down the side, stuff like music, comic books, novels, the names of a few people he didn't recognize... all the trademarks of a well-designed and never visited personal web site.

"Welcome to Engen.com," a muffled voice recording said loudly, forcing Xander to turn down the volume on his control panel. "Your one-stop location for all MP3's and other music files, comic book updates, and everything else you could have read on the side bar, you illiterate fool." Then the voice went away and was replaced by a looping midi rendition of *Highway to Hell* by AC/DC.

Xander wasn't all too impressed. He was expecting some kind of freaky government place.

"But why would Soul need a decoder for this place?" He frowned, his eyes darting over the information presented. He scrolled down further. The site seemed to go on forever, with links to every torrent and hack he'd ever heard of.

Music by title, music by artist, music by style, music by date, music by era... the list seemed endless. Then he saw a little symbol on the bottom right-hand corner of the screen, set apart from the menu. Someone would have to scroll down a long time after the menu had ended to have even noticed it.

"What the hell?" he breathed, straining his eyes to see the minuscule font, which was obviously not meant to be seen. It was three little letters.

GTG

"Soul wasn't saying 'got to go'..." he realized suddenly. "He was telling me what to look for."

He hesitated momentarily, something inside him telling him not to proceed, then clicked on the small acronym. His monitor immediately turned black, and Xander wondered for a second if he had struck the off button. Then he saw it at the top of the screen. The link had opened up a kind of dos prompt within the site, and in very small letters read: PASSWORD PLEASE.

Xander grinned, resizing his browser window so that he could see his desktop, and clicking on a folder labeled *family photos*. When the folder opened there were no photos inside, just dozens of program icons. Some of them were of keys or padlocks while others had odd smiley faces or letters. One named *Devil's Advocate* had a cartoon image of the devil on it, and he right-clicked on it and clicked open. A new program window opened, the devil face in the upper left hand corner. He went back into his browser and copied the link for the password prompt he had gotten, then pasted it into the address bar of Devil's Advocate and pressed enter.

The hourglass spun for a moment, then three words popped up underneath it and the devil's face turned to a frown: **NO PASSWORD FOUND.**

Growling under his breath, he closed out that program and opened up another, repeating the action. This time it was a smiley face that turned into a frown as the same words appeared on the screen.

He opened up a program with a key for an icon that he had created himself. The hourglass animation was replaced by one of a key turning in a lock, then after a moment the key broke. **PASSWORD NOT FOUND.**

One by one he tried with all his programs to figure out the password, but could not. He gave up, sliding a floppy disk into the drive and copying the site location onto it. Then he took the disk out of the computer and shut his bedroom door. He pulled back his dresser, revealing an old ventilation duct that wasn't used anymore. It was where he kept all the things he didn't want anyone else to find. He put the disk in there and pushed the shelf back into place.

He thought he heard a sound behind him, like the metallic clicking sound an old-fashioned clock made. He turned around fast. Pain again erupted from his right side when he was in mid-turn, sending him to the floor.

The pain was unbearable. He ground his teeth together against it, digging his fingernails deep into his carpet.

What the hell is this crap? he thought as he fought back tears. *It's like my side is on fire!*

Something inside him twitched and there was another burst of agony, stopping all coherent thought.

Struggling, his every move stiff and forced, Xander pulled himself into his bed. His muscles aching as if he'd just run a marathon, he rested for a moment and then quickly fell into a profoundly deep and dreamless sleep.

Carl Dent slipped silently past Mike's hospital bed, snagging some of his charts. He glanced up at the sleeping child, making sure he was in fact fast asleep, then turned and opened the file.

He looked them over quickly, jotting notes on what medication he was on and when he was getting out. His eyes widened a bit. They were letting the kid out next week.

"Gawd dammit," he cursed, biting his lip when he realized how loud he had said it, throwing another look at Mike to make sure he hadn't awoken the child. That didn't grant him much time.

Mike stirred.

Dent looked up momentarily, then quietly put the chart back in its rightful position. He looked at his pad with glee. It was Mike's social security number, birth date, and all other information. With it, he could find out exactly where Mike had been adopted from.

As he left the room, he saw a small security camera aimed directly at him. He realized quickly that he had no warrant to have invaded this boy's privacy. He reached up and unplugged the camera with one swift tug. No one could know. Frowning at his own actions he continued on, trying his best not to look back.

As Dent walked past the nurses' station, a tall nurse with a pronounced upper lip and a nametag that read 'Riley' gave him a hard look as he hurried onto the elevator. As he got on, a man dressed all in black bumped into him while getting off.

"Watch it!" Dent stammered, his papers scattering.

The black man just walked by, barely noticing Dent was even there.

Dent hurried his papers together, then got on the elevator, muttering a long string of curses under his breath as he did.

The black man walked past the nurses' station and over to the room where Mike was staying. A room whose security camera happened to be offline. He took a piece of paper out from under his arm. It was the same one that Dent had been copying notes onto, his jot notes scrawled onto it in his almost illegible shorthand. He compared the number on Mike's door to the number on the paper and walked in. Smiling and as silent as the dead, he took an I.V. bag from inside his jacket and switched it with Mike's. He moved with such swiftness, as if every move he made was calculated, no movement made for no reason. The new liquid dripped down into the tube, then pumped itself into Mike's very veins, as the man slipped back out as quickly as he had come.

⋀⟨⋏⟩

Dent walked down the street in a hurry. He wanted to get this information back to the station so that he could process it. Sweat began to bead on his forehead. It was unusually hot for this time of night. His bones began to ache as he walked faster and faster, accidentally dropping the stack of papers again.

"Fuck," he uttered, bending down to pick them up. A small pain was developing in his right side, but he ignored it. He had to catch the creep that was murdering these kids. As the pain only seemed to get worse the more he tried to ignore it, he mentally swore off Dunkin Donuts for the third time this week.

He heard a sound up ahead of him. He looked up, but saw nobody. The streets were deserted, an eerie quiet surrounding them. The type of quiet that was almost louder than sound itself could ever be.

The sound happened again, louder this time. Metal on metal.

Dent drew his weapon from its holster. *Maybe I won't need to track down the dirtbag,* he thought to himself, smirking a little. He put his back to the brick wall and slid on it to the corner, bringing his gun up to eye level. He swallowed hard and listened.

Several long moments passed, with no sound at all.

Then suddenly, a loud crash.

Dent spun around the corner and yelled "Police! Stop right there!"

The alley was dark and for a minute he thought the killer was hiding in the shadows, until he saw a small kitten crawl out of an old, dented garbage can. Dent sighed with relief, putting the gun back in its place. He turned to walk back toward the precinct.

He slammed face first into a large black figure. The person raised his long

43

blade and drove it into Dent's side, jigging it up even further once it was in.

Dent shoved past the killer and broke into a run down the street toward the station. Each breath caused his body to ache, every step making him want to bend over and throw up. He listened hard, hearing the click of the killer's boots as they stepped past the rocky path. They echoed loudly, the sound reverberating off all the buildings then back again, making it seem as though it was coming from all directions at once. He felt the blood run openly from his wound as he tried desperately to tap just a little more speed into his legs. Dent sped around a corner at top speed, finally ducking behind a doorway. He pulled out his weapon again, then looked through the door of the house he was standing in front of. It was deserted. There would be no aid there. He once again brought the gun up to eye level, peeking his head around the corner. Nothing. The street and all those connecting to it were completely void of all life. Dent once again breathed a sigh of relief as he lowered the weapon.

Smash. A great black gloved hand broke through the window of the house, grabbing Dent. He felt the broken glass rip at his flesh as he was pulled into the home.

He looked around and saw the corpses of an elderly couple sprawled onto the floor. Dent could tell that they had been dead a long time by the way the flesh was beginning to rot away, their icy cold gazes begging him for aid he could not give. Then Dent realized... *If they've been dead that long, this guy must've planned all this.*

Dent's eyes went wide as the killer stabbed once. Twice. Three times, then threw his now limp body to the floor. The killer put the weapon away, replacing it with a small scalpel. He bent over, stepping into the pool of fresh blood, letting the small, sharp knife cut through Dent's tender stomach flesh, making a long line all the way down...

CHAPTER FOUR: SPIDER WEB

Sara Johnson was home alone that night. Her parents were over at Jamie Dawkins' house, helping his parents through this 'hard time'.

Why do people do that? she wondered silently. *They go over to comfort people they've barely spoken to before after a tragedy happens, to 'make things better', but they usually end up just making things worse. They remind these families of their loss, when these people should be getting into a routine to distract themselves from it. Some people think it best to face things like this. Sheyeah. Right.*

Sitting at her desk with her laptop in front of her, she ran a hand through her blonde hair, messing it into a tangled knot on one side. Taking a bite out of her Kit-Kat bar, she signed out of her e-mail account after deleting all the old messages from Jamie. The chocolate goodness gave her a slight lift that she had been in desperate need of and she couldn't help but smile as she took another nibble, brushing wafer crumbs off the breast of her shirt.

-BEEP- -BEEP- -BEEP- Sara's instant messenger called out to her from her computer. She jiggled the mouse a bit to turn off sleep mode, then brought it down to the little yellow man in the corner of her screen.

"Spider?" she asked out loud, reading the name that popped up as the message's author. "Who the hell is Spider?"

She double clicked on the name to receive the instant message, and began to read it aloud. Her eyes went wide with fright and she backed away from the computer. She raced over to her door and locked it, then froze in mid-step and listened. From downstairs came the slow creak of footsteps.

"No way. It's just some moron screwing with me," she whispered to herself, then looked back at the screen.

I'm outside house.

She looked around the room carefully, her eyes darting every which way, searching for any sign of movement or life.

-BEEP-!

She jumped with fright, quickly putting her hand on her chest. With tears forming in her eyes, she went around to the computer and pressed enter.

Go to the window, came the new message, as cryptic and disturbing as the one before.

As salt water found its way down Sara's cheek, she made her way over to the window. The blinds were closed. She grabbed the swinging rope that would open them, closed her eyes, and took a deep breath. Biting her lip, she mustered up the strength to pull down on it, causing the venetian blinds to rise.

Stepping over to the window and looking down at the ground below, she saw nothing. Leaning out, she turned her head to look out to the side of the driveway. Still, there was nothing.

She let out a long sigh, realizing she'd been holding her breath the entire time she was at the window.

"Sara!" the voice came suddenly as a head with scruffy dark brown hair popped out from the side of the window.

"Ah!" Sara let out a short yelp and held her chest as she realized who it was. "Xander! What are you doing here?"

"Good day to you too," he said cheerily, climbing in through the window as he wiped the sweat from his forehead.

"You jerk!" she yelled, slapping him playfully on the arm. "What are you doing here?"

"My parents went over to Jamie's too. I thought we could hang out a bit." He looked her over once, chuckling. "Have a small heart attack, why don't you?"

"Shut up! You would too if you got messages like that!"

"Messages?" Xander raised his eyebrows. "What messages?"

"Shut up!" Sara said. "You're always trying to scare me!"

"Usually yeah, but not this time, no."

They both stepped over to the computer and looked at the messages. "Are you telling me that isn't you?"

"Come on, you know my tag is Captain America. Besides, how could I have

45

messaged this and gotten to your house in that amount of time? This is probably just some freak trying to scare you. It's just a cool coincidence that I came at the same time."

She nodded, acknowledging the impossibility of him sending those messages. She glanced down at the plastic bag in his hand, then looked up at him with a grin, her eyes both expectant and more than a little flirtatious. She did know him so well. "Movies?"

"Yup. One chick-flick, one for me, and a comedy for both."

"Should last us all night. What do you plan on doing in that amount of time?"

He smiled, blushing despite all his attempts not to. "I got *Sweet November* for you, *Apocalypse Now* for me, and *Big Daddy* for the required comedy."

"Let's pop 'em in," she laughed, as the two headed downstairs.

Nurse Riley was on duty early Thursday morning. It was only six o'clock and still quite dark out as she checked through all of the rooms to make sure everything was all right with the patients. She reached room 205 and looked down her charts. Harris, Mike. She glanced up at the unplugged security camera, sighed, then plugged it back in.

"Kids," she muttered.

She walked into the room and checked his vital signs.

"Well, you're doing better," she said. She looked at the charts from last night and compared them with the new signs. Her eyes went wide with shock.

"Oh! Way better!" She stepped out of the room for a moment. "Dr. Marx! Come take a look at this!"

A few hours later, Nurse Riley stripped the bandages off Mike as Cathy and both their parents stood and watched.

"...I can honestly say I've never seen anything like this," Dr. Marx attempted to explain, stuttering once. "He's almost made a complete recovery. I'm recommending him off the wheelchair and onto crutches immediately."

Marx was a stocky little man that looked like a cartoon mole, his lab coat hanging lopsided over a growing hunch on his back. Large rimmed glasses perched precariously on the edge of his nose and he adjusted them nervously as he spoke.

"That's great," Mike's father said, smiling at his son. He placed a hand on Mike's shoulder, as if to take his son's strength as a compliment to his own. "But how did this happen?"

"We're... uncertain, but we think that... actually, we have no idea what to think... but something, very strange, is going on here... ... yes," he said, looking over the reports as if to give validity to his response.

Cathy raised an eyebrow toward the older man. "Are all those technical terms why they pay you the big bucks?" she asked sarcastically, cuddling up close to Mike for the first time in days without fear of harming him.

"Yes... well..." Dr. Marx stammered again, attempting to explain again and then deciding it best not to even attempt to do so.

"Besides, who cares?" Cathy said, leaning over and kissing her boyfriend. "He's back with us, isn't that what matters?"

Mike smiled at her, touching her hair and pushing it back behind her ear.

She did have a way of putting things into perspective.

When Sara got up that morning, she threw the covers off herself playfully. She hopped out of bed with her nighty on (which was actually an oversized tee-shirt that had once belonged to Xander, featuring the Transformers symbol) then stepped into her walk-in closet to change into some clothes she didn't mind the world seeing.

She came out wearing a sleeveless shirt that read *0% Angel* across the chest and some slightly worn jeans that rode low in the front. She brushed a hand through her hair and made a small, disgusted grunt at how tangled it had become, then walked over to her dresser to get some socks, stopping to smile at the panda bear Xander had won for her at a fair. She gave it a little kiss, then walked over to the window to let the sun in.

Squish.

She looked down.

"Fuck," she said to herself, rising up her foot.

On the floor was a large muddy footprint. *Xander must have left it there when he came over last night. I'd better clean it up, or mom and dad might think I had a boy over.*

She laughed at her own little joke, then walked into the bathroom and grabbed a handful of paper towels. Getting down on her hands and knees, she began cleaning up the glob of foot-shaped mud. She brushed her hair back as she looked out the window over at Xander's bedroom.

She saw a little light go on, meaning his computer's alarm clock had just gone off. She smiled as she imagined him getting up and going through a similar ritual as she just had, wondering just how alike it actually was.

She finished cleaning the last of the mud and went to put the towels into the toilet for easy disposal. She dropped them in and was about to flush when she caught something out of the corner of her eye. She looked at the towels floating there for the first time since she had started cleaning. They were... red. She inhaled through her nose, and was immediately filled with the undeniable scent of copper.

The footprint had been made in blood.

She let out a little yelp as she realized what that implied.

"Sara?" her mother called out from downstairs. "Are you alright?"

"I'm fine, Mom!" she lied, running her hands over her head again and again, unsure of what to do.

"Come down for breakfast soon."

"Uh-huh!"

She stared at the red liquid on the paper towel for a moment. The blood was already seeping off of the paper into swirly rings around the top of the water, spinning around and making the entire bowl look dark red.

She quickly flushed the paper towel down the toilet, then walked silently back into her room. She looked out her window again and saw Xander at the computer. Suddenly, there was a loud -BEEP- behind her. She went over to check her instant message.

~CapTainaMeriCa~.

That was Xander. She couldn't talk to him right now. She clicked ignore, and began to think of *other* ways that Xander could have gotten blood on his shoe as she walked down the stairs to get breakfast.

The list was short.

"Ignore?" Xander read to himself as the little caption appeared on his screen. "Why would she ignore my message?"

He took a monster bite of the sausage that he was having for breakfast, then dipped the remaining morsel into a bit of mustard and popped it into his mouth, giving the screen a frustrated glare before closing it out.

He brought the mouse up to the left-hand corner of the screen and clicked on his bookmarks, scrolling down until he found engen.com.

He clicked on the little icon that represented engen.com and once again the animated symbol went through its cycle, only this time it ended with 'Stiff Upper Lip' by AC/DC. He quickly scrolled down the page and found the gtg icon and clicked on it. The dos password prompt overtook his screen again, the tiny cursor blinking next to the words PASSWORD PLEASE.

Wracking his brain and rubbing his eyes, which had veins like crow's feet from watching TV all night with Sara, he typed in Soul.

Password rejected.

Sighing, he typed in: Engen, and then Engen User.

Again, password rejected.

Groaning, he looked over on his desk and saw a newspaper. In it were the photographs of the alley where Jamie's body had been found, along with a story by Tom Drake and a one-column sidebar written by Don Smith. On the wall of the alley were those words again: 'Black Womb'. He glanced back at the computer, furrowing his forehead. It had the right number of characters.

The password please option came up on his screen again, and he typed in the letters: b - l - a - c - k - w - o - m - b and hit enter.

Immediately his screen became filled with image after image, windows popping up and then shutting themselves down before he could really see them. The screen began to flicker and he thought he was going to have a seizure. He strained his eyes against the brightness, trying to see at least *some* of the information before him. There was a headshot I.D. photo of a man with spiked hair and a devilish grin. Another showed an Asian woman with clear skin and tiny lips.

A third showed what he thought was the street outside the Factory.

The more he watched the flickering images, the more pain began to build in his abdomen and at the base of his skull. Growling under his breath, he re-opened the family photos folder and double clicked an image of a safe.

The images stopped flashing by, staying on the screen as the computer locked itself up. Not even the mouse would move.

"It worked," he said in astonishment, glancing over the page. "This shit looks... government."

He looked over the frozen window, seeing files on Jamie, Mike, even Cathy. Then he saw one that was marked classified. To him, that was an open invitation. He began to read down through this new information.

black womb, the. A project started through joint commission of governments to try to expand on the possibilities of genetic memory in stem-cell research. The end result would take decades, but would have eventually given way to a new age in foreign policy and sending men overseas. It would have been a super soldier. Although all tests failed to some degree, there was substantial increase in the field. The government project is currently owned by Owen McMasters, the lead research developer of the project, despite

The computer made a little noise. A caption came up that said 'location being tracked'.

"Fuck," Xander cursed, trying to regain control of the mouse and close out the program. The pointer stayed there no matter how much he jiggled it, as if it were paralyzed. Grunting angrily through gritted teeth, he held down the 'control' and 'alt' buttons on the keyboard then tapped 'delete' frantically.

At first nothing happened, the icon in the bottom right still spinning around and telling him he was being tracked.

Finally, the task manager popped up in the centre of the screen. He let out a sigh of relief as he ended all the programs one by one.

'Location being tracked' still dominated the bottom right of the screen.

Cursing again, he deleted the engen.com bookmark off of his desktop then pushed in on the computer's power button and held it until it was off.

He stared at the black screen for a long moment, resting his head against his hand as he leaned on his desk. He scooped up the last taste of mustard onto his finger and put it into his mouth.

"What the hell was that?" he asked himself, not surprised when he got no response.

꒰꒪ꆛ꒪꒱

Grendel flicked his pencil up at the ceiling, causing it to stick into the tile.

He wasn't interested in this biology lecture, not that he ever was. He was thinking about his party. With any luck, Mike wouldn't be able to make it. And even if he could, Sud, Tommy and Derek would take care of him. Either way, he'd finally get his crack at Cathy tomorrow night.

Tomorrow night.

It seemed so immediate and so far away all at the same time.

After Mike, the only problem would be that freak, Xander, and Sara. But they were easy enough to deal with. This weekend, he and Cathy would have his parents' house all to themselves...

"Julian!" Professor Miles slapped his hand down on Grendel's desk. His Boston accent was muddled by years in rural Maine but still very condescending and better-than-thou. A hail of pencils slipped from their places on the ceiling, crashing down onto Grendel's head. "Julian, you have not paid attention all class, your feet are on the desk... By god, you don't even have the right book!"

"But that's the book I've been using since the beginning of the year," Grendel objected, motioning toward it with both open palms.

The tired old teacher rubbed the bridge of his nose with his thumb and forefinger. "That... that actually doesn't shock me. I must be getting used to this." He took off his glasses and wiped them in his shirt, chuckling softly. "Dear lord, that is a scary thought, isn't it?"

"Can I use the bathroom?" Grendel asked.

Miles looked up, eyes wide in astonishment. "What?"

"Well, as Mr. Calendar once said 'better I am in the halls than in here bothering the students who want to learn.'"

"You are excused, Mr. Grendel."

Grendel hopped out from his desk and out the door as fast as he could, before Miles had a chance to change his mind.

He strutted up and down the halls of Coral Beach High as he'd often done before. The pale green lockers and tan walls were all very familiar to him, some even sparking fond memories. There was a spot between a row of lockers and the girl's rest room where he'd carved the anarchy symbol with a protractor late last year. It had been the only constructive use he had gotten out of the tool that semester. One of the lockers on his right still had a dent in it from where he had punched it after Greer had broken up with him.

He stopped at one classroom and looked into it.

There she was.

Cathy Kennessy, in all her grace and style. Her long hair shimmering in the morning light, her lips so juicy he could practically taste them... and he was convinced he could smell her specific aroma from where he stood.

She intoxicated him.

She spotted him outside, and smiled at him.

"Come out!" he mouthed silently, motioning toward himself with both hands.

She shook her head no, giggling.

"Come on!" he pretended to plead, bending down as if he were about to get onto his knees.

She relented, raising her hand.

"Yes, Miss Kennessy?" Mr. Calender said, pointing to Cathy.

"May I be excused? I kinda need to go to the little girls' room."

Calender smiled, motioning toward the door. "Go right ahead."

Cathy smiled, scooping up her book bag and heading for the door as the class resumed its discussion. She joined Grendel and the two of them began walking down the hall away from the classroom together.

"So, how's Mike?" Grendel asked Cathy in mock concern. Although he was looking at her, he was not even attempting to make eye contact with her as he asked.

"Fine. In fact, he'll be out this evening, so we'll both be at your party," she smiled, relishing in the news.

"Cool," he said, trying to sound overly enthusiastic about Mike's presence. *Looks like I'll be going with Plan 'B' then*, he thought to himself. "So what about Xander, is he..."

"Yup. In fact, I've been thinking about trying to fix him and Sara up," she said in a hushed tone, as if there were someone around to hear it.

"That'd be great. We should talk about that at the party."

"Sure," she said before she gave him a little hug and walked back to class. He watched her walk away intently, paying close attention to the slight swivel of her hips.

Tomorrow.

3:15.

Xander Drew got home from school and walked into his room. He went over to his computer, as usual, and jiggled the mouse.

Nothing.

"Oh yeah," he remembered, slapping himself in the forehead. "I had to turn it off."

He pressed the on button.

Still, nothing.

"What the hell?" he almost shouted.

He grabbed a screwdriver and opened up the tower, looking inside. The CPU was completely fried, melted to the rest of the machinery so bad that he wouldn't even be able to pry it off. It would take him weeks to replace, and that was if money was good.

"Damn," he sighed, tossing the screwdriver down and taking a chip out of the floor.

4:30.

"Frig!" Mike screamed at the little computerized character named Quartz on the screen as he let out a full force eye beam on his character, Ragna-Rock. Ragna went down easily, but then Diamond, the tag-team partner in this match, came out and started to lay it into Quartz. Diamond was the only female character in the game, and sparkled just like her namesake on the screen. She did a kiss attack, using her powers to sap Quartz's energy. It always reminded him of the effect that Cathy's kisses had on him, making him smile just that little bit more. Then, just as Mike was about to finish off Quartz 'HERE COMES A NEW

CHALLENGER!' flashed across the screen in bright gold letters. He turned to see who had placed the money into the game, and smiled when he did. "Jerk. Why'd you do that?"

"Ah, you would've lost anyway," Xander replied, with Cathy and Sara behind him. "After the kiss attack, Diamond is really vulnerable to Quartz's punches and kicks."

Mike sighed. "How true. But I can still beat you."

"Right," Xander replied sarcastically, then took the opposing control stick and selected Granite and Obsidian to battle Mike's Diamond and Ragna-Rock. "I thought these guys didn't have any decent fighting games?"

"Came in yesterday," Mike answered absentmindedly, his tongue sticking out as he concentrated on the game.

Cathy and Sara took that as their cue that there would be no more attention paid to them for at least five minutes, both of them walking across the room.

"Boys will be boys," Cathy muttered to herself, sitting down on the racecar ride. The comedic cartoon announcer was taunting them from within the screen, telling them to 'race against ten other competitors for the world cup'. It was already beginning to get annoying.

"Yeah, but did you hear?"

"Hear what?"

"That secret service guy got killed last night, along with some old couple."

"No way," Cathy said, her eyes widening.

"Do you think the guy was right?" she whispered.

"What?" Cathy responded, astonished.

"About Xander doing it."

"No way! It's *Xander* we're talking about."

"Yeah, but if you did it, wouldn't you kill only the guy who thought you did it?"

Cathy acknowledged this. "Still. Sorry, Sara, it's just not in him."

Sara sighed. "You're right," she admitted, sounding less then sure.

"Autopsy report, Coral Beach Morgue. Thursday, the 22nd. Second report of this nature in three days. First of three victims, beginning autopsy now."

Harry Ford had lost his patented sense of humor. Some would call the jokes he made while dissecting the victims of horrendous acts of man disgusting. The truth was he had to joke just to keep from vomiting.

Lance Berkshire had a much stronger stomach, but a much softer heart. He handed the scalpel over to Harry, then realized it really wasn't necessary in the case of Carl Dent. His torso had a square hole cut into the centre of it, revealing cracked bones and a barrage of vital organs. "This time the killer took lungs, heart, intestinal tracks.... geez."

"Yeah, I know, Lance. I've been afraid to let my kids outside the house at all, let alone at night." He took a small pause before returning to business. "Serial killer?"

"That'd be my best guess. I hear the police are exercising the possibility of gang and cult killings."

"God, what is wrong with this world," he murmured, but it wasn't a question so much as a general statement towards the plight of their town.

"It was definitely the same guy though. He took the lungs he didn't get the first time. Also the heart, small and large intestines..."

"Anything our creep hasn't got yet?"

"Well, muscle tissue, brain matter... he got kidneys and livers from the old couple..."

"Why? Wouldn't he want a younger one?"

"It appears our Mr. Dent had a bit of a drinking problem. But there's something even stranger."

"I'm almost afraid to ask."

"In every case, even that poor kid who wasn't killed... the appendixes were completely removed. But in the first case it was smooth, cut edges. Like one of us did it. This time... it's like it was done in anger."

6:00.

Dusk.

Tim parted two sections of his venetian blind and peered out into the street, making striped shadows across his face. The body count was now four, with a possibility of it rising within the next eight hours. He let the blinds fall back into place and paced back to his desk. On it were Carl Dent's files, both those he kept at the precinct and those found scattered near the murder scene. The only lead or suspect that actually made any sense at all was the Xander Drew file. A dark loner of a kid who hung around with the same people all of the time. It fit, but it wasn't enough to put anything on the kid. There were probably a hundred kids like that in this city. But then Dent went to that Grendel kid and that pushed the focus of this case in Dent's favor. *And now Dent's dead, but that may help the case, god forgive me for thinking it.* All they needed now was something solid. Some actual evidence...

"Sir?" the skinny blonde secretary called out, popping in her head from outside the door.

"Yes, Felicia. What is it?"

"There's a young girl here. I believe Carl Dent questioned her briefly in the hospital. She says she has some information which may be helpful. I think her name is Johnson."

"Send her in."

Darkness covered Coral Beach that night. And when it came, the city closed its doors. Roadblocks were set up. Police were even borrowed from nearby towns to patrol the streets, which were like vacant lots, giving the entire town a ghostly tranquility. Everything was silent and still.

The only place still open was, naturally, the Factory.

The musicians had gone home and many of its workers wouldn't have stayed there for a million dollars, but the four owners and three of the customers still remained. Sud, Tommy and Derek.

Sud sat on the pool table opposite the one that Tommy and Derek were playing at. Derek leaned over the table and easily sank the eight ball into the corner pocket.

"Damn man. How'd you learn to play like that?" Tommy chided, shaking his head as he looked at the massive amount of balls he still had on the table.

"I just learned. That's all," Derek shrugged.

"You going to Gren's party tomorrow night?"

"Who isn't? Something tells me it's gonna be a wild time."

"Yeah," Sud grunted in agreement.

"Alright boys," Roxanne, one of the ladies that owned the Factory, called out from behind a desk. "We're closin' down. Pack it up and get out."

The three of them grabbed their coats from the rack and started out the door. They all lived in opposite directions. Derek was right across the street from the Factory, so they walked him to his door.

"You guys could come in a while if you wanted," Derek offered. "Call your 'rents, ask them to come and pick you up."

"Naw, man," Tommy shrugged. "We'll be fine."

Sud nodded in agreement.

"You sure?" Derek pushed, taking a quick glance around the street. "It's not safe out there, man."

Tommy just chuckled a little at that. "I don't think there's anybody stupid enough to try to take on us... not even lil' Xander Drew."

Sud laughed, but it seemed forced.

Derek smiled. "Yeah, I guess you're right. Take it easy, boys."

"You too," Tommy said, as the duo started walking home.

The street was cold. It wasn't winter yet by any means, but Tommy had noticed that ever since school started the temperature around town had become a fickle thing - warm one moment and then freezing cold the next.

The cold left an odd crispness on the street they walked on, like stepping into one of those walk-in freezers in the back of a restaurant. It sent sparks of life up through his calves and created swirls of dancing white mist that could only been seen in the direct light of the street lamps.

The rest of the street was covered in a sort of soft stillness. It felt like he imagined the inside of a snow globe would feel between shakes.

All of the storefronts were closed and the street was deserted, so much so that neither of them had ever seen the like before. Typically, Tommy found that every time he found himself noticing that the town was vacant, some car would pull out from behind a corner or some classmate would reveal himself from a doorway to prove him wrong. Tonight it was just the street... although the street itself seemed alive.

There was an energy to the street that came from the cold and the moon, that sort of electric vibrance that animated everything. The buildings seemed to loom high above the street lights until they were impossibly high and looking down on them. The houses they passed had dim lights in their windows and looked like jack-o-lanterns, their malformed and disfigured scowls glaring out at them.

Tommy pulled his shirt closer around him.

After a moment of silent walking he realized that it was up to him to initiate a conversation, because his near-mute partner never would. "Lookin' forward to the party?"

Sud nodded.

"Yea," he smirked. "I can't wait. It's gonna be a hell of a time. Julie told me she's gonna show, and Greer and Liz should too. Those girls..." He paused, throwing a smile at his compatriot. "Know how to party, if you catch my drift."

Again Sud nodded, this time adding a sly smile.

Then Tommy stopped.

Sud stopped too, more so to copy Tommy then for any other reason.

"You hear something?" Tommy said, swallowing hard.

"No. Why, did you?" Sud asked, his eyes starting to wander from side to side.

"Shh. Listen."

They did. And for a moment, there was nothing. Then it came.

-click-

Metal. The unmistakable sound of metal on metal sliced through the foggy air. They waited still.

-click-

Again, louder now, followed by a quick scuff like a boot or sneaker against the gravel. Sud and Tommy glanced at each other briefly, then broke into a run.

They crossed the street at the next intersection, ignoring the 'Don't walk' sign, then turned and ran up the next avenue toward Tommy's house. They could hear the metal scrape getting louder behind them. Louder and faster. Whoever was following them was also picking up speed. Then Sud tripped, falling onto the sidewalk and scraping his knee.

"Fuck!" he yelped.

"Clumsy bastard!" Tommy yelled, stopping to help him up.

They looked back and he was there. A large, dark man looming over them, raising a long, curved blade. They both closed their eyes and prayed to god, waiting for the inevitable to happen... but it didn't. They opened their eyes and there was nobody there.

"Boys? You okay?" came a voice from behind them.

They both turned simultaneously to see Tim White standing by his patrol car about ten feet behind them.

They ran to him despite how their legs begging for them to stop, so fast that they slammed into the side of the car.

Tommy laid his head against the metal roof, sweat dripping from his nose and chin as he tried desperately to catch his breath in worn, wet gasps.

Sud fumbled with the door handle of the cruiser.

"Hey!" Tim protested.

"You gotta help us man, you gotta get us out of here!" Tommy cried, near literal tears.

Sud got in the car and just laid his head back on the cushion, trying hard to catch his breath. Tommy shoved him to one side and followed him in.

"Easy boys. It's okay now. You're safe," Tim said, trying to calm the boys. He turned around and looked at them, shaking his head.

Almost lost another two.

He turned the keys to start the engine. It started for a moment, then revved and went dead.

The boys looked at each other in the backseat. White looked up and down the street to make sure nobody was coming, then turned back to the boys with fire in his eyes.

"Get out," he told them flatly.

They looked at him oddly, then got out.

"Run. To the Factory. It shouldn't take us too long."

They obeyed and broke into a slow jog, trying to conserve their energy. But as they turned the first corner, Sud and Tommy both buckled over in pain.

"What?" Tim exclaimed, stopping to help them up. "What's wrong?"

"My... side," Tommy replied, clutching his right side and clenching his teeth.

"The appendix," Tim whispered, realizing something else all of the victims had in common. Even as the thought crossed his mind, he nearly fell over in pain himself, Sud catching him.

Tim glanced around nervously. "We've got to keep moving."

They began moving slowly through the streets on their way to the Factory. They crossed the next corner and it was in their sights, but the pain grew with each and every step. Sud had to ward off vomiting each time the heel of his shoe scratched against the cold pavement. Then, from behind them, came the sound that they had all knew was coming yet dreaded the arrival of.

-clink-

Metal, dragging against stone walkways. Then again: -clink-. Much sharper this time than the last. When the sound happened again, Tim noticed that the gap was narrower then the first. *Whoever he is, he's running.*

They were on the home stretch now, running up the Factory's long driveway. They reached the door and began to thump on it loudly, trying to draw the attention of those inside.

"It's no use," Tommy sighed, motioning toward the driveway. "There's no cars. They've left."

"Damn," Tim muttered to himself. For a moment, all was quiet.

-clink-

They all glanced up in the direction that the sound had been coming from. Sud started banging on the door once more, followed by the others, this time in an effort to break it down. After a few moments, Tim motioned for the boys to stand back and gave the door a hard kick, knocking it off its hinges.

They entered. The lights were out, but the multiple arcade game screens created an eerie glow as their shadows flickered and danced on the wall. Tim made an effort to make the door look like it had been untouched, so that the killer might not suspect they had entered. Then, from behind them, they heard a loud thump. They all jumped around, staring into the gaping darkness.

"Roxanne?" Tommy called into the darkness. There was no response except for a sudden, sharp -clink-.

Tim pulled his gun out of its holster, stepping toward the entrance to the back room. He looked at the boys, then at the front door. "On three," he whispered.

They nodded.

"Three!"

The three of them bolted for the door and across to Derek's house. They looked behind them, seeing nothing. Derek's driveway was only a few feet away.

Tommy tripped on the sidewalk and fell to the ground, hitting the side of his face and drawing blood. White helped him up, looking around again. Nothing to be seen but cold, damp streets. They walked up to the front door and burst in. Derek's father came rushing in from the dining room, and Tim just held up his badge and tried to catch his breath.

ᚹᚷᚹ

Friday.

That was the first thought on Xander Drew's mind when he woke up the next morning. Every Friday was like a thousand years for him, with the boring drudgery of schoolwork to contend with. Each minute dragged on as if it were an hour and it was nearly impossible to get any work done because he couldn't stop thinking about the weekend if he had wanted to. More specifically, tonight. This was the night of Grendel's big party. It was to be (how did Sara put it?) the social event of the season.

The next thought to cross his mind was: *school.*

He brought his watch up to his face and pressed a button on its side, illuminating it in indigo light. The black numbers on the little screen read 8:50. The homeroom bell rang in five minutes. He jumped out of bed and pulled on a pair of tattered jeans, running down the stairs. His hair and skin were sticky, wet and more than a little warm. He made a mental note to take some of the covers off of his bed before he went to sleep tonight.

Halfway down he saw Sara, who was completely out of breath.

"School," she managed to stammer. Apparently she had slept in too.

"Yeah, I... Why didn't my computer's alarm clock wake me?" he thought out loud.

Sara stood up straight. "Yeah, mine didn't either."

They both pondered it for a moment, until Xander flicked on the hall light. Nothing happened. "Power's out."

Sara flicked the light off and on. "You're right. It's probably off at my place too."

Moreover, my CPU's fried, Xander remembered. *But I can't tell you that.*

They both thought about that a minute more, before they realized that they were already late for school. Xander grabbed his book bag and opened the door for Sara, then followed her out and started to run.

When she didn't run he stopped, figuring that she was tired from running to his house. She didn't say anything, merely nodding at him for waiting.

He motioned to put his arm around her, but she jerked away quickly.

He looked at her awkwardly for a minute, then started walking next to her. As they walked down the same road that they often had before, she noticed a growing pain in her side and bit her lip to steel herself against it.

She remembered that day, all those years ago. It was her sixth birthday. When most little girls turn six they have a party with all their wild friends and eat cake until they puke, but not Cathy Kennessy. She spent her sixth grade birthday in an old, musty car with her parents driving to Coral Beach. It didn't matter to her where she was going at the time. All she knew was that all of her friends were back home in Pittsburgh and she was in the car. Because they were moving to a new place where her Daddy could get a job and make lots and lots of money.

They arrived at her new home at eight o'clock in the night and it was almost her bedtime. But she didn't have a bed yet, so she would have to sleep on a mattress on the cold floor.

From across the street came a little boy. He was about her height, his face covered in freckles. They looked at each other for a minute, almost wondering exactly what to think of one another.

The boy broke the silence. "Wanna play?"

She looked at him for a minute, then replied, "Okay. What's your name?"

"Michael David Harris. What's yours?"

"Cathy Elizabeth Kennessy. Do you know how to jump rope?"

"That's for girls..."

Cathy smiled at Mike from across the classroom. He winked at her briefly, then went back to finishing his question sheet. *Not exactly love at first sight,* she thought calmly as she went back to her own sheet. *But it'll do for a story our kids'll hear until they want to strangle us with it.*

Fourteen years old. That's when Sara Johnson thought it was all over. She was riding in the back seat of her boyfriend Justin's new car. He had just gotten his license and they were celebrating. In the car with her was Grendel in the back, and Cathy up front. She hadn't been dating Mike for very long then. They had just come from one of Derek's parties and Justin was about to bring them home, but he'd had a few too many drinks at the party. The car hit a bump in the road and started to swerve. The next thing she knew, she was being thrown from the car and onto the sidewalk. She didn't know how long she was out, but when she woke up there were red and blue lights flashing.

Police.

God, Mom is gonna kill me, she remembered thinking. That was when it struck her that she had almost died. She opened her eyes and there was a blurry image of a man looking down on her.

"Justin?" she murmured. Her eyes cleared and she saw the face she'd never forget. Xander Drew, her next door neighbour. She hadn't seen him much these last couple years; they'd drifted apart. But now, she jumped into his arms and cried on his shoulder.

Then she looked around. "Justin?"

That was when she saw it -- the limp body of her boyfriend being lifted onto a stretcher. There were cuts and bruises on his body everywhere and the chest of his shirt was soaked in blood. His eyes were open in an eerie gaze that sent chills down her spine. His hand fell limply over the side of his stretcher as they checked his pulse. The paramedic looked at his watch as his fingers pressed on the boy's neck. He shook his head and the two doctors put the white blanket over Justin's head.

She buried her head into Xander's shoulder and cried. He just held her. He didn't say a word, either from being in shock himself over seeing the body or just because he couldn't think of anything to say. Whatever the reason, he just held her for hours and hours. Long after the police, the paramedics and everyone else had left, he stayed there just holding her.

How could someone as sweet- Sara's thoughts were interrupted by Mr. Calendar raising his voice slightly in the middle of his sentence. Not out of anger, but more so to get the attention of the entire class. She looked up, slightly startled. *It just isn't possible.*

The voice of Principal Shnieder came over the intercom, which squealed a bit as it was turned on. "This is Principal Shnieder speaking. Due to the recent incidents in town, there will not be school until further notice. Also, a seven o'clock curfew has been placed on the town. Anyone caught out past seven will be brought home by a police escort immediately."

The announcement of school closing was followed by a barrage of hoots and hollers from students as they flooded out the doors. All except Cathy and Mike, who both realized what this meant: the killer had struck during the night.

CHAPTER FIVE: GOOD TIME

6:00

The party was just starting. Grendel didn't really want to start this early, but the curfew forced him to. It also ensured that once everyone got in, they had to stay until morning. Which was just fine for him, and one other person.

"School's out for summer!" Cathy and Xander chanted along with the music blaring over the speakers. "School's out forever!"

Grendel's front yard was packed with kids and it was hard for Mike, Cathy and Xander just to stay close to one another. Sara was over by Grendel, chatting away to him, although he didn't really notice. He was watching Cathy. Intently.

"This is a great party, Gren!" Tommy shouted over the speakers.

"What?" Grendel replied, putting a hand to his ear.

Tommy motioned for Grendel to speak in private. They walked away from the yard and into the kitchen.

"When are we doin' it?" he asked.

"Shh." Grendel put a finger up to his mouth and took a quick glance around. "You want everyone to hear? Alright, around seven o'clock, you, Sud and Derek ask Mike to help you lift something. You do whatever it takes to keep him out there. That's when I'll take Cathy upstairs to talk to her. If Xander starts being a problem, just dump him. Got it?"

"Yeah. What about Sara?"

"That fucking airhead slut? She won't be a big problem."

About forty minutes later, music still blared over the stereo. Everyone in the yard was bouncing and singing. Grendel's backyard was a large open space contained by high wooden fences stained a rich rusty colour that kept out prying eyes. There was a large brick barbeque a few feet from the north wall that was currently covered with speakers, and a metal fire pit near the centre that was clogged with cigarette butts.

The yard was filled with people attending the party.

From one end of the fence to the other, it was packed so tightly that it was hard to move, let alone dance, although people still managed. Drinks were passed from the cooler from person to person until they found their desired party. People jumped and swayed and pushed, turning the backyard into a giant mosh pit.

Jeffery Dunam made out with a girl a few years younger than him against the back wall of Grendel's house. He had a beer in one hand that was half empty, and was so drunk that every time he took a drink great splashes of it dribbled down over his chin.

Beverly Mass was throwing up into the barbeque, the roar of the speakers making her stomach do a back flip every time it urged.

Sara smiled, raising both her hands up into the air and bobbing along to the beat, bending her knees and thrusting her arms. "Whoo-hooo!"

Xander followed at her, watching the way every part of her danced. Her hair, her jacket... every part of her moved to the heavy bass beat. He smiled.

She turned and looked at him, both hands clenching his drink to his chest and his feet planted firmly to the grass.

Frowning and rolling her eyes, she slapped the drink out of his hands.

"H-hey!" he stammered.

"If it's not alcohol, it's not abuse," she stated in a factual tone. She reached over and grabbed both his hands.

His heart began to beat faster.

She raised their hands above their heads and pumped them, her fingers laced around his until he got the rhythm and started to do it on his own.

He smiled.

"You looked like one of the lawn gnomes," she said, pointing to a small cluster of little ceramic men that had been arranged in the corner so as not to get hurt. One of them was even holding a drink, in much the same way Xander had been. "It *had* to be corrected."

"Thanks," he beamed, continuing to pump his arms to the beat that Sara had started them on, even when the beat of the music changed. After a moment he started to bend his knees as well, trying his best to mimic her.

She laughed. "You're dancing like a girl."

He stopped, his already pink face becoming red.

"Here." She reached over and took his hips in her hands and started to show him how to move.

He could feel sweat trickle its way down his forehead. His throat became dry and his tongue refused to move.

"Move with it, first with one then the other," she said, biting her lip a little as she looked down at the way their hips pressed together, hers moving along with his. "Don't be afraid to lean into me. And don't over think it. Just... do it."

She looked up at him, meeting his gaze for a long moment.

She cleared her throat, then stepped away from him.

He continued to move, taking a breath for the first time in what felt like minutes.

"Yeah," she said, grabbing a cube of ice from the cooler and popping it between her lips. "That's better."

Around her the others continued to bump and grind.

ᚹ

Cathy sat near the fire pit and watched Sara as she tried to teach Xander to dance, a wry smile finding its way onto her lips even as people pushed and shoved each other all around her. Calla McFadden's butt got dangerously close to hitting her in the back of the head every time she swayed to the music, but she tried her best to ignore it.

Mike appeared out of the labyrinth of bodies to her right, doing his best to avoid bumping into people as much as possible.

"Here," he said, handing her a drink in a red plastic glass. He had a similar one, which he took a long slurp from. "Virgin Jack and Coke, on the rocks."

"That's just Coke with ice," she laughed, taking just enough to wet her lips. "You sound like a douchebag."

He laughed, fizzling cola almost coming out his nose when he did. He brought his sleeve to stop it, the edges of his smile poking up over his arm. "I

61

like it my way. Sounds important."

"What do you call an orange juice? A Virgin Screwdriver?"

"A Virgin Screwdriver is orange juice and 7Up," he said, raising an eyebrow at her.

"How do you know that?"

"How do you not know that?" he laughed, holding out a hand to her.

She rolled her eyes and took it, letting him help her to her feet. There was a short boy trying to dance with a rather tall girl in front of her, and she could see Sara and Xander again over his shoulder.

Xander was drinking his cola as though he were searching for the meaning of life at the bottom, wiping the sweat from his free hand onto his jeans as he did.

She shook her head at them and tisked.

Mike followed her gaze, then stepped into it to block her view of them. "You know in some cultures, that's considered rude."

"Stop it." She hummed playfully, bouncing on her heels to see over his shoulders and not even coming close. "I want to see."

"Yeah, I got that." He smiled. "Now stop it."

"Ugh," she huffed, folding her arms and puffing out her cheeks. "Men."

"Yes. Men get in the way of the picture show. Men drink of the beer and have of the women."

She glared at him, though she couldn't help herself from smiling. "Idiot."

ʎʎ

Tommy hoisted his camera quickly and took a shot of Cathy, just as she was smiling at something Mike had said. He examined her image on the screen of his camera, its colour-corrected vibrancy making it look more real than in the dimming light of dusk. He'd caught her just beginning to laugh, in that wonderful and rare moment photographers called a Mona Lisa smile.

He clicked off a few more rounds in quick succession, examined the latest one on the screen again, then stepped back into the crowd.

He'd loved cameras ever since he could remember. He'd owned his first one at age four, and currently owned five. This one was a Canon digital-film hybrid with a facefinder feature he found remarkable.

He brought it to his face again, using the viewfinder to peruse the crowd.

John Walker was behind Calla McFadden, not so much dancing with her as he was holding her tight and swaying with her to the music. He was sucking on her collar and had left a long line of red blotches from her ear and down her neck before he had arrived there. Her bra was undone, one strap lying loosely over her shoulder.

-click!-

Tommy shifted focus, finding Sam Reynolds as she downed the last of a beer. Copious amounts of froth billowed down her cheeks on either side, fluffy and light like clouds.

"You're wasting some!" Wes King shouted next to her, pointing at her and

62

pumping his fists radically. "Point goes to me!"

-click!-

Tommy turned and came face-to-face with Derek Smith, his boyish face and bushy eyebrows taking up the entire screen.

-click!-

"What the hell are you doing?" Derek frowned.

Tommy took the camera down from his face and smirked wide. "Documenting."

"Documenting what?"

"Everything," he replied, raising the camera high and snapping a random shot of the crowd. He examined the back of the camera and smiled, then turned to show Derek. "See?"

It captured half the yard, every face digitized and in perfect focus. The perspective was skewed, the picture taken while the lens had been tilted to the right and making everyone look like they were fighting gravity to stand on a deep slope.

"Not bad." Derek hummed, bobbing his head from side to side.

"Thank you," Tommy responded sharply, turning the camera back on Calla and John and snapping three quick shots.

-click click click!-

"Just don't aim that thing at me anymore, okay?" Derek grumbled, looking around. He saw Julie Peterson and smiled at her. She waved back.

"Why not?"

Derek turned back to him, his face serious for a moment, then grinned. "I've seen your room, with all the pictures around. I don't want you looking at me while you're stroking your moke."

"Fuck you," Tommy laughed, punching him in the arm.

Derek punched back, smirking so big that his earlobes moved. He nodded, then turned and started in the direction of the drink cooler.

Tommy turned and watched him go, then raised his camera and took another shot of him.

-click!-

Grendel stood on his balcony with his arms folded across his chest, nodding triumphantly at the amassed students. Sud sat next to him on a plastic lawn chair, his drink balanced precariously between his legs.

"This is what I wanted," Grendel said, stretching his arms out to encompass the yard. "This is what this class really needed! This party is going to go down in history!"

Sud grunted softly in response.

Grendel turned to look at him, his face drawn tight in a scowl so deep that the folds of his skin looked like cracks in the pavement after an earthquake. He shook his head, then squat down to be face-to-face with Tommy, who had his camera pressed to his face and was waiting for the opportune moment to snap a picture of Julie Peterson.

"What's his problem?" he asked, sticking his thumb over his shoulder at Sud.

"Liz Tyler kicked him in the balls after he got a little too grabby during the last song."

Grendel stood up and looked at Sud's drink, only now noticing that it was filled with ice and had no liquid in it whatsoever.

"Get up!" he barked, kicking the side of the chair and forcing Sud out of it. "You're supposed to be helping, not sitting there and licking your wounds like some --"

He stopped.

They all had, every person in attendance. Someone had even turned down the music as all eyes turned toward the orange-hued western sky.

The sun was starting to go down, and that meant one thing. Seven o'clock. They moved the party inside Grendel's house, where a lot of the first people grabbed couches to sit on.

Cathy snagged the love seat. Mike was about to sit down next to her, when a voice traveled over the crowd.

"Hey, Mike!" Sud called, unnecessarily loud. "Come help us with the speaker."

Mike's stomach turned.

You know that feeling in your side when you know something bad in going to happen? That sickness which ebbs its way up from your bowels and into your throat at the mere mention of a word? Right now, Mike was getting that feeling.

He turned and looked at Sud, Tommy and Derek from across the hall.

"Sure. Just a sec," he drawled, then turned back and looked at Cathy, sitting on the love seat. He leaned over and kissed her lightly on the lips, then stood back up and looked at her.

"I'll be back in a sec." He smiled, then walked over to help Sud and the others.

Somehow he just had to say that. That feeling... the last time he gotten it, it had almost been the last time he had ever seen her. He put his hand to his side and squeezed his stitches a little, wincing in pain.

It's just the painkillers kicking in, he assured himself as he walked over and started to pick up a speaker.

Grendel's downstairs bathroom was a large step up from the Factory's, but it was still far from the Ritz.

It was a half-bath that his father used only to shit and shave in the morning, and was fairly utilitarian. There were no pictures or candles or decorative soaps. There was just a toilet and a sink, crammed in a space so small that most people wouldn't have used it for a closet.

Sara sat on the toilet with her arms hugging into her knees. Her jeans were down around her ankles but her underpants were still up, and the toilet lid was down. It was cold against the exposed flesh of her calves and made her shiver fiercely.

She was crying in big cartoon tears, praying that the music outside was loud enough to drown it out. Every so often she let out a wretched sob, some so powerful that they made her throat feel like it was being stabbed with a large knitting needle.

She'd come in to use the bathroom, but found that once the door was closed the urge had gone away and was replaced by this new one, which was much more powerful. She could have held her pee, she thought, but the water streaming down her bright red cheeks had come out like a tsunami. She wasn't even quite sure where it had come from. She hadn't been thinking about Jamie, at least not when she'd started. She hadn't been thinking about much at all. Now his image was frozen in front of her, like he was trapped in a bubble in her mind that she couldn't shake loose.

"Oh, God..." she wailed, although if anyone had heard it they wouldn't have recognized the words.

She reached down into the crumpled pockets of her jeans pocket with her thumb and forefinger. After a moment of fishing around, she withdrew a small blue tablet with an indentation on one side.

This time she pushed it past her lips with no reservations, swallowing it back with nothing but saliva. It hurt her throat going down, but then was gone.

Feeling better almost immediately, she pulled up her pants and examined her face in the mirror. Her eyeliner was miraculously still acceptable, but there were streaks slashed in the foundation on her cheeks that made her look striped. The flesh underneath was red and blotched. She sighed, then reached into her jeans again and withdrew her compact.

Mike let out a labored breath, his cheeks puffing out comically.

"I think that's it for me, guys," he said, a smooth trail of sweat trickling down his face near his ear.

Sud looked over his shoulder and saw Cathy, still sitting alone.

"We're almost done. It won't be long now."

"Hey Cathy," Grendel said, sitting down next to her in the love seat. "How you doin'?"

She giggled at him lightly.

He smiled at her.

Sara was standing next to Joseph Townsend, laughing so hard at something he had said that she had to brace herself on the crook of his arm in order to keep herself up. She had a Coke in her other hand. It sloshed over the edges of the red plastic glass and her fingers with every giggle she made.

She wasn't standing far from the speakers, and had to lean in close to Joseph to hear him say anything. He smiled every time she got close, smelling the sweetness of her perfume that made his mouth fill with saliva.

A song by Linkin Park was playing on the stereo, and she was dancing in the barest sense of the word, bouncing on her knees and swaying her hips. She wasn't dancing to that song, though.

She was bouncing along to *Spirit in the Sky*.

Xander watched her from across the room, his own drink clutched tightly to his chest. He had yet to take a sip of it, and it had been sitting there for so long that all the fizz had gone out of it and turned it into stale sugar water. He took a deep breath, then turned around to face the wall.

"Hey Sara," he said sheepishly, fiddling with the curtain. "I don't know if you know this, but I'm-

"Stupid," he spat, forcing himself to let the fabric go. It fluttered back into place alongside the window and stayed there. "Hey Sara. I know you don't think of me like this, but I think that if you gave me a chance --

"No," he stopped again, rolling his eyes. "No, that's underselling yourself. 'Hey, this piece of meat is gangly and disgusting... buy it!' Stupid."

His throat was suddenly very dry. He took a long drink of his cola until he needed to draw breath. It was flat, and tasted like bile.

"Hey, Sara..." he started again, turning back toward the crowd. He almost bumped right into her. As it was, another great slosh of her drink splashed down onto the silver rings of her left hand.

"Hey, yourself," she smiled, steadying herself on her feet. "Enjoying the party?"

"Most definitely," Xander said enthusiastically.

She smiled at him.

He got lost in it for a moment, just staring at her. Her eyes were glossy, and he could see the brush strokes on her cheeks from where she had applied her makeup before going out.

She smiled at him again, nodding her head and waiting for him to speak.

"Oh!" he said finally, laughing humorlessly. "I had something I wanted to talk to you about."

"Okay," she chirped, still bobbing along to the song in her head. "Anything in particular?"

"Yes," he said. "No. Maybe."

"Glad we cleared that up."

"It's not any one thing. It's... look, we've know each other a long time, and --"

"Hey! You dropped one! You gotta take a shot!" she howled at someone from across the room, pointing at them wildly with her drink hand. She was still laughing when she turned back to him. "Sorry."

"That's okay."

"What were you saying?"

"Yes. What I was saying. What I was saying was -"

"This is the end of this year's flute hanger!" someone called from the next room.

Sara laughed, so hard that she almost fell over onto Xander.

"Hey, listen, you wanna go talk?" he asked, smiling as she helped herself back to her feet. "This place is a little loud."

"Yeah, sure."

He motioned toward the curtains he'd been playing with. When he pulled on the drawstring next to them, they opened and revealed a sliding glass door that lead out onto the balcony.

"Sly," she said, tossing him a playful wink. "If I didn't know better, I'd have thought you planned this."

Xander laughed.

The two of them walked out onto Grendel's balcony. The cool night air whipped at them, her light blonde hair blowing gracefully backward, exposing her neck and chest. He found himself looking at her unintentionally.

"Dear God, you're beautiful," he said finally, with the honesty of a person who had been waiting forever to say it.

She smiled at him, with those beautiful lips that she had painted sparkling platinum for the occasion. "Excuse me?"

"I said you're beautiful," he repeated, turning to look her square in the eye.

"Yeah," she laughed. "I got that. But why?"

"Because," he said, taking her hand. "You are."

He leaned in to kiss her. She looked up at him, moving in slightly herself, her lip quivering in an anticipation she hadn't even realized she had had until now. Her eyes fluttered back and forth between his lips to his eyes and his did the same, making eye contact every so often. He could smell her perfume and it overwhelmed him. He could feel the softness of her body, so close to his and yet still not touching. Slowly, they moved closer together. Closer...

"Xander," came a voice from inside.

"What?" Xander turned, angrily.

"We need you for something in here." It was Dave Marston, a jock friend of Jamie's. "It's this weird thing with Gren's computer. Some kinda net nanny keeping us off. You wanna...."

"Yeah. Just... gimmie a minute."

"Alright."

Xander looked at Sara for a long moment, smiling. "Hold that thought."

"Dammit," Grendel muttered to himself.

"What?" Cathy asked.

"I just remembered. I still didn't find that Ragnarok CD."

"The one with *Old Maid in Alaska* on it?"

"Yeah."

"Darn," she whined. "That's my favorite."

"You wanna go look for it?"

"Alright."

Xander was busy at the cluttered computer. The keyboard was literally covered in papers.

"Geez, doesn't he know how to take care of it? He's got homework from last month on here, gum wrappers ... even his new Ragnarok CD..."

Mike and Sud dropped the stereo to the floor when they were half way to the door.

Mike stretched and wiped the sweat from his brow. "Sorry I can't help more guys. My side still hurts."

"S'alright," replied Derek.

Mike glanced over into the house. Cathy wasn't on the love seat anymore. She was going upstairs with Grendel. "Hey!" he shouted, but then fell to the ground as Derek punched him in the side.

The *right* side.

He could feel a stitch split as he went down onto his knees.

"What'd ya?" he started, then got kicked in the ribs by Tommy.

"Nothing personal," Sud said in his stupid tone. He walked over and punched Mike in the back of the neck, sending him down for the count.

"It can't be here," Cathy said, lifting pillows and blankets around on Grendel's unmade bed trying to find the CD.

"I'm pretty sure it is," Grendel said as he looked around, hardly taking his eyes off Cathy.

"I'll go down and check the CD rack." She sighed as she walked over to the door and twisted the knob.

Nothing.

"It's locked," she said in a much lower tone. "Why would it be locked, Gren?"

She looked over at him.

"No way," Grendel shrugged. "Let me see."

He twisted the knob himself and got the same result. "Geez. How'd that happen?"

He turned to face her and she looked at him for a second, her eyes narrowing as she figured out what was going on. He put his hands on her hips and leaned in to kiss her. She jerked away.

"What the hell are you doing?" she screamed.

"Hey, don't be like that." He put his arms around her.

"Grendel, stop it!" She struggled against him, but he was much stronger than she was. He pushed her down onto his bed and got on top of her, kissing her forcibly.

"No!" she screamed.

He put his hand down onto her leg, the spot where she had been slashed. She winced, and he took the opportunity to begin to take off her shirt...

"See? It's really very easy to get into Windows from dos mode," Xander explained to the computer illiterate that had gathered around him. "All you have to do is type in 'win' and Windows should automatically start up, unless there's something wrong with..."

"Grendel, no!" came a cry from upstairs. He'd have recognized that voice anywhere. There was something wrong with her. It was Cathy and there was something wrong with her.

"Cathy?" Xander shouted up the stairs, jumping away from the computer. "Cathy!? Are you alright? Grendel?"

He began to wander toward the stairs, picking up speed as he went.

"Hold it," came a voice from behind him. He turned with a start and came face to face with Tommy.

"What's going on? Where's Mike?" Xander asked, staring him down. He knew something had to be wrong. He was getting that same feeling in his gut that Mike had had, but it was elating, overpowering everything else. It made his pulse quicken and his blood boil.

"Grendel, please stop..." came Cathy's voice from upstairs again. This time it had become obvious that she was crying, and what Grendel was doing to her.

"I think you ought to leave those two alone," Tommy said, giving Xander a little push.

Xander looked around, seeing the increasing amount of people gathering around. They were all staring at Xander, their brows furrowed.

Tommy folded his arms as more screams and sounds of a struggle came from upstairs.

Xander looked up the remaining stairs, then back at the people who had begun to move in on him. He broke out into an all out run for Grendel's room and made it to the top of the stairs before Sud grabbed his pant leg, causing him to tumble and fall.

The crowd parted as Xander rolled down the stairs, landing with a thump at the bottom. The crowd formed a little circle around him and he tried to get up, but Derek kicked him in the side.

There was a loud, wet snap that Xander recognized as the breaking of a rib. His left hand went immediately to his side while the other propped him up until someone stepped on it, creating an ear-shattering crack. Xander grunted in pain and he could feel tears forming in his eyes. Somebody else from the circle punched down onto his neck and he felt blood rise up into his throat. It left a coppery taste he'd always hated. He looked up, blood smearing down his face and onto the floor.

"All you had to do was nothing," Tommy scowled down at him, his arms folded.

"Go to hell," he said bluntly, the sound of his voice muffled by the blood in his mouth.

Tommy gave Xander a hard kick, knocking his head back onto a coffee table, where he finally lost consciousness.

ᚹ

"Grendel, please..." Cathy pleaded. He already had her shirt off and now he had her jeans unbuttoned. "Please, just stop."

"Shh. It'll be alright," he said, kissing her forcefully, pushing her shoulders onto the bed.

Tears ran down her soft, freckled cheeks. She sobbed and he stopped for a moment. He looked down at her, then slowly starting to pull down her jeans. But of course to do that, he had to let go of her with one hand, which meant that she had one hand free. She wracked her nails against his face, leaving four large scratch marks.

"Ow!" he exclaimed, putting his other hand up to his face.

She was free now, but the door was still locked. She ran over to the window, trying desperately to open it.

"You stupid bitch!" he shouted, punching her across the face.

She hit the floor like a ton of bricks and then started to cry once more.

"I'll teach you..." he slapped her across the face.

Through her tears she looked around the room for something, *anything* she could use as a weapon. Something to defend herself with. He sat on her and grabbed at her. In desperation, she kicked him in the groin.

He bent over in pain, then drew back and punched her again. Then he got up and tossed her clothes onto her. "Pff. You're not worth the trouble. Stupid whore."

He kicked her once as hard as he could, in the ribs, then left. He went back down to his friends to lie, to tell them what the two of them had done.

She was still crying uncontrollably. There were already bruises starting to form on her face and chest. As she got up and got dressed, she happened to glance in the mirror at her battered face and her puffy eyes. She broke into a whiny cry and walked out into the hall. When she got there, she started to feel dizzy. Her head started to hurt and then, without warning, she lost consciousness.

ᚹ

Grendel was greeted with the hoots and hollers of his friends as he walked down his stairwell. The music started to play again and everyone got back to the party. Grendel walked over to Tommy.

"Did the guys give you any trouble?" he asked, grabbing a drink from an end table and taking a long slurp.

70

"Naw, take a look for yourself." Tommy laughed, cocking his head in the general direction of the downstairs bedroom. In it, Mike and Xander lay sprawled across each other. Their faces were masks of pain as they slept off their injuries.

Grendel walked over and closed the door. "We'll have some fun with them later."

Outside, Sara was still waiting for Xander to come back. She had no idea what was going on inside the house. Out here, everything was quiet. She stood there, her head hanging over the balcony, her satin shirt swaying in the breeze behind her. She looked out at the lights of Coral Beach, sparkling along with the stars in the sky. On a night like tonight, it was hard to tell where sky ended and the earth began. Everything was quiet, still, peaceful... perfect. She closed her eyes, took a deep breath of the cool night air, thought of Xander, and felt a smile cross her lips.

-Shink-

She opened her eyes.

-Shink-

Again. A metalish sound, like Mr. Calendar desperately trying to create a spark with two pieces of metal in the physics lab.

-Shink-

Again. This time she looked around.

Nothing.

Just the cool air and the black of night.

Fidgeting and rubbing her exposed arms, she turned to look around.

There was patio furniture on the far side of the balcony, of the sort that was typically hidden from public view unless it became very necessary to have it out. It had been painted white with some sort of base that didn't agree with it and the colour chipped off in random shapes, revealing rust underneath. The vinyl strips that covered the chairs were broken in places and missing in others, creating a mishmash hammock of plastic and metal that was sure to leave its user nervous and uncomfortable.

There was a book bag sitting snugly in the lap of the chair closest to her. The plastic buckle on it had drooped down over the side and swaying lightly into the breeze, connecting with the leg every so often.

-clink-

-clink-

-clink-

She sighed, then placed the buckle onto the chair and went back to looking out onto the city.

-Shink-

She sighed again, turning to put the belt buckle back on the chair.

It hadn't moved.

-Shink-

She looked up, leaning over the rail of the balcony to see if there was anyone under her. Suddenly, there was a sharp pain in her side. Blood oozed into her shirt as the killer twisted, then pulled the knife from the mouth it had just opened. Sara let out a little sound like a dove cooing, a small tear rolling down her cheek. The killer wiped her cheek clean, then sliced her slowly across the throat. Her hand went up to her wound, and was instantly covered in blood.

The killer put a finger up to his hooded mouth. "Shh."

She opened her mouth to scream a warning to the others, but couldn't. All she felt was her blood pour out onto the wooden balcony. She lay down on the floor and her eyes rolled back into her head as a small puddle of blood began to form all around her. As the killer walked through it, he gazed into the room filled with teens. A wry smile spread across his lips.

The last thought to go through her mind was of Xander.

⋀⋎⋀

Tommy sang drunkenly on the coffee table, a small group of people incoherently singing along with him. "need to rewind myself..." Then without warning, he fell onto those gathered around him. Swears were loudly uttered by those directly in his path, but then they all started laughing. All but Tommy. He was clutching his side violently. Eventually, the laughter stopped and all eyes were on him. "...pain..."

The power went out in the house, plunging it into darkness. The music stopped playing and everyone was still.

Sud walked over to the front door and tried to open it. "It's jammed," he said.

Everyone looked at one another and around the room cautiously.

"Hold on... hold on..." Grendel mumbled as he fumbled through a junk drawer. "Geez, a fuckin' power out and all you guys turn to pansies." He pulled out an old phone book, grabbing an aged flashlight under it. "Here we go."

He turned it around for a moment before finding the switch, then turned it on. Nothing. There were a few disappointed moans from the crowd. Grendel frowned, tapping the flashlight against his palm twice. A beam of light cut through the dense darkness. "There."

He swirled the light around. What the beam found made him feel sick.

Hanging by a rope from the ceiling fan was the body of Sara Johnson. Her once vibrant and beautiful face was caked with blood. Her clothes were in shreds, barely covering her. There was a gaping hole in her right side, some of her major organs were visible. Her hands were in twisted, deformed positions, like claws. Her hair (formerly soft and lovely), which had been put up into a bun for the party, had been let down. It was matted in blood, giving it an eerie, brittle look.

One girl screamed in the crowd. However for the most part, people just stared in a silent shock as the corpse swung slightly on its rope. The slight breeze in the room made her spin just a little. Grendel looked up into her eyes. They stared blankly back at him, fixed on nothing. They used to contain light and life, but now had a smoky, glossed over look to them. He felt his lower lip begin to tremble.

Suddenly pain ripped up and down his right side. The flashlight dropped to the floor with a clunk and he strained his neck to look behind him.

The dark spectre behind him twisted the knife in its wound before pulling it from Grendel's entire body. He took the long knife to Grendel's back, driving it through until it protruded from his chest cavity.

As Grendel dropped to the floor with a thump, people in the room began to scream and run hysterically. The man threw his knife, digging it into a young girl's back. He looked down at the flashlight on the ground, stomping his foot down onto it and immersing the house in total darkness.

⋏⋏

As darkness enveloped the crowded living room, many people kept running and screaming, but one young girl stayed statuesque and still. Frozen in the shock of seeing friends killed before her very eyes or just having absolutely no idea what to do. Or maybe it was that she had come to the conclusion that there was absolutely nothing she *could* do. Whatever the case, this one girl, no older then fifteen, just sat there curled into a little ball as others pushed past her in an attempt to find an exit. She looked up from her fetal position and stared blankly into the darkness around her. She let out a long breath, the first she had taken since the house had been plunged into blackness. The breath followed the darkness' movements through the cold air before it eventually became one with it.

It's funny what goes through your mind during intense situations. All of a sudden, she realized that she had missed the latest episode of *Survivor* last night. She remembered that the Toronto Maple Leafs and the New Jersey Devils were even now playing against one another. That she had an exam next week in World History, that she had forgotten to walk the dog before leaving her house and even that she had left her television on. All of these things and more wandered through the girl's head as she stared into the total darkness surrounding her body.

Something flashed before her eyes.

She glanced about nervously, struggling to stop the sobbing that might give away her position. The moonlight shone in through the broken glass window, creating eerie silhouettes as her friends realized that there was nowhere to run and settled on hiding. There was a dead silence looming in the air.

-thunk -

The sound of a friend's body dropping to the floor after a quick, silent death.

-thunk-

-thunk-

-thunk-

Over and over again. The girl turned her head to the floor, attempting to pretend that she was a piece of furniture. The hardwood near her reflected the moon's light up into her face, as the wood was slowly enveloped by a different kind of darkness. A dark liquid rolled, and then streamed over the floor, eventually cascading lightly onto the girl's sneaker. She continued staring down at it.

73

As the moonlight reached it, the liquid took on a reddish tint.

Blood.

Suddenly, all the thoughts which had previously clouded the girls mind were erased, replaced by one word that continued to scream within the depths of her mind. *Blood. Blood. Blood...*

She looked up into the darkness again, and again she sensed movement within it. Abruptly, the moonlight caught hold of something else: a long, metal blade. Before she could react in defense or even scream, it was upon her.

She felt the blade slice clean across her throat.

She attempted to let out a cry but heard no sound despite all efforts. The killer's strike had destroyed her vocal cords. She put a hand to her neck to try and halt the blood which now flowed freely. She knew this kind of blow rendered the victim dead within seconds, so she strained her neck so that she could look her destroyer in the eye. She fully expected him to finish her, deliver a killing blow across her head, but the blow never came. Instead the slayer just stood there, watching as the girl clung to life by a thin thread, her blood staining the floor and mixing with that already there.

After a second that seemed to be an hour, she lost strength and collapsed to the floor, her skull landing on the wood with a loud crack. The killer cracked a sinister smile.

ʎ(ꞏ)ʎ

John Walker crawled slowly along the edge of the wall, trying to stay out of the path of any light. He crept along, as silent as humanly possible, attempting to get to the shattered glass the murderer had entered through. He reluctantly stepped on a shattered piece, the quiet crinkling sound it made echoing through the dark room. He stopped and looked into the darkness to see if his position had been realized, then came to the fruition that if he had been he would have to move even faster and kept going.

-thunk-

A sound from the darkness that he recognized, yet wished that he hadn't.

-thunk-

Again.

-thunk-

-thunk-

He kept going, his eyes beginning to get hazy from tears of knowing exactly what was happening in the darkness. He looked ahead and saw that the window was only a few feet away. Letting out a short, raspy gasp of excitement before becoming silent again, he listened to the sounds in the darkness.

There was some soft sobbing, followed by a slinking sound and a sharp crack.

He moved forward again, but realized that he would not be able to step over the glass without blocking light and attracting attention. He would have to crawl over it. Lifting his two hands over first, he began to pull himself along. The jagged, toothed glass stuck up from the doorframe, cutting into his abdomen as he made his way along. Blood ran freely as the sharp glass ripped and rendered the tender flesh of his chest and stomach. He bit back a yelp of pain as a piece of flesh got stuck on a small, razor-like piece of glass.

Rather than go back, he moved forward, pulling on the piece of hanging flesh. It stretched momentarily, before the glass itself broke off into the wound. With the stomach out of the way, John now stepped over the glass with one foot, lifting it high to make sure what happened to his mid-section did not happen to more sensitive areas. He lifted his other foot over in the same fashion and began a slow crawl over to the edge of the balcony where he would jump the two stories to freedom.

Suddenly, he felt a tug.

For a moment he thought that the killer had finally caught up with him. He stayed perfectly still, almost waiting for the inevitable to rain down upon him. But it didn't. He turned his head slightly, enough to see that his jeans were hooked on the glass. He turned back for a second, giving a short sigh of relief. Believing he was out of trouble, he pulled his leg forward. Riiiiiiip. The sound of fabric tearing cut through the air like a knife, and John knew that there was no chance the killer hadn't heard it.

He stopped, listening to the darkness again.

There was a dead silence, and he thought for sure that he was finished. Then he heard the sickly reassuring sound of his redemption.

-thunk-

The sound of yet another friend's body dropping to the floor. He sighed again. The fact that he was relieved, almost happy at the sound of death made him want to vomit. He sucked it back and pulled his leg forward again. His jeans pulled on the glass again, this time causing it to break. As if in slow motion, the glass flipped and spun as it cut through the air before landing on the ground and shattering with a clink that cut through the muteness. All at once it seemed as though the previous quiet had been nothing. It was as if even the silence had shut up.

It finally came to John that he had been discovered. He got up quickly, running to the edge of the balcony. He paused only for a moment, staring into the darkness behind him. Hearing the loud, heavy footsteps of his stalker behind him, John saw the glint of his blade as it swung from side to side in his back holster. He turned his eyes back to the ground below and, placing a hand over his stomach wound, jumped over to it.

His loss of blood and the couple of Budweisers that he'd had all gave him the sensation of flying, when in fact he was only falling. He didn't even do that for very long. He felt an enormous pressure on his throat as his downward momentum came to a halt, and he had a brief sensation of weightlessness.

The killer had grabbed his collar.

Throwing him onto the balcony, the killer let loose with a hard kick to the ribs. John bent over in pain as he rolled through the glass and back into the house, almost exactly where he had begun. The murderer loomed over him, the moonlit night casting the shadow of him down upon his latest victim.

He took the drawstring from a window shade and held it up to the light. There was a warning on it that advised that children could choke on it. That sinisterly evil smile once again curved his lips, showing his sharp teeth. He wrapped the string around the chandelier, then around John's neck. He picked John up with both hands and held him up for a moment, supporting his weight.

Then, smiling, he let go.

There was a loud crack as the string went taut against John's neck.

Another girl attempted to run for the exit and the killer threw his blade into her back, sending her toppling to the floor.

He twisted the blade before ripping it out with a sickening sucking noise. Bringing the blade to his thick lips, he licked some of the blood off, then wiped the rest away with his index finger.

Frightened and scared, Liz Tyler wandered from room to room trying to find one that had been left open. She could hear the sounds from the living room with crystal clarity. -thunk-, -thunk-, -thunk-, -thunk-, a weird cracking sound, followed by a loud rip and a lot of footsteps.

She tried one door after another in an attempt to escape the inevitable peril that was crashing down onto her like a wave onto the shore. Grendel's bedroom door had been barred shut, as had been the downstairs bathroom. Her only option left was the spare room. She rushed to it quickly, reaching out her long, slender arm and turning the cold metal knob.

To her immense relief, it turned freely.

She swung the door open and almost closed it again with fright. Before her were Cathy and Mike, laid down on each other, both unconscious. She stepped back for a moment. Then, hearing a wet snap in the living room she stepped in, she closed the door and locked it behind her.

She glanced around the room, and finally just curled up in a corner and started to sob as water ran down her cheeks.

She was only there a moment when she came to a realization: *Wasn't Xander supposed to have been in the room as well?*

The killer looked around at his handiwork and smiled, then walked from the living room into the hallway. He kicked down one door and looked inside.

Nothing.

The next, a bathroom. Nobody inside.

Then he found his way to the spare room.

Forcing the door open, he stepped inside...

Liz heard the latch on the door break. The door swung open and slammed against the wall. She buried her head into her arms and pretended that she was invisible. She was breathing hard, her chest near convulsing. When the killer

76

came into view, she felt her heart skip a beat. He walked over to Mike and Cathy. He turned Cathy onto her back so that he could see her face. He held it in his hand for a moment before he heard it. Heard her. He turned and stared down at her, shaking in the corner. He reached down and picked her up by the scruff of her neck, then reached to his back to draw out his sword... then stopped when he heard a new sound.

The sound of police coming.

Some concerned neighbor must have called the police.

The killer looked down at his prey for a moment before he merely threw her against the wall as if she were a rag doll, snapping her neck. He opened the large bay window and stepped out, taking his leave.

CHAPTER SIX: ZONE

Mike awoke on a stretcher. He opened his eyes then immediately closed them again, forcing them to adjust to the light. He opened them a second time, this time as he got up.

A paramedic rushed over to him. His name was Richard Dreyfus, and less than two hours ago he had asked his girlfriend of two years, Marjorie, to marry him. She'd said yes, and they'd both cried happily. Her three-year-old son had thought something was wrong at first, and had patted Richard soothingly on the back. It had been adorable. They'd all laughed, and he'd given the boy a hearty kiss on the cheek. The idea of being his father was overwhelming and good, and he hoped the feeling would never go away.

His pager had gone off just as Marjorie was calling her mother.

It seemed like a lifetime ago now.

"Easy, son," Richard said, putting Mike's arm around his shoulder. "You'll be alright if you just sit down and rest. It's over now."

"W-wha?" Mike stumbled, having trouble getting the word out. His head felt like it was in a vice. He put his hand up to it, only to discover a rather thick layer of bandages surrounding it. Suddenly, his eyes went wide. "Cathy?"

"She's fine. Would you like to see her?"

Mike nodded, and the Richard helped him to his feet and around the corner of the ambulance he had been sitting in the shadow of.

There were cars parked all over the front of Grendel's front lawn, and the lawn next door. Police cars and ghost cars and ambulances, all of them flashing their lights in different patterns and casting a stuttering red hue over everything in their path. It was like the streets had been painted in blood, and as he looked beyond this street and onto the next, he saw that it continued out into the rest of Coral Beach. Maybe even the entire world.

There were bodies lined on the grass. They didn't look like bodies, covered in zipped-up black bags that looked like the ones Mike's father took his suits to the dry cleaners in. It didn't help, though. He knew what they were, lined up seemingly forever and casting long, thin shadows with the light.

Police and paramedics and firefighters scrambled everywhere. They ran around and past each other, one somehow never hitting the other. Some people stood and just surveyed the chaos. People cried. There were more sirens far away, as well as a constant buzz of radios as reports were updated and then re-updated.

Cathy was sitting on the sidewalk with a blanket wrapped around her shoulders, her head enveloped in her arms. She looked up at the sound of approaching footsteps.

"Mike." She smiled, wiping tears from her eyes. "They wouldn't let me see you until you woke, and--"

"Shhh," he said, placing his arm around her. "It's alright now."

She broke down crying in his arms. "No. It isn't. It never will be again."

"What do you mean?" he demanded in a hushed voice. "What's happened?"

"It's Sara..."

ʎʎ

Rumors spread like a wildfire in a small town like Coral Beach. By the time Monday morning came and the exact number of the dead had been counted, that wildfire had turned into a forest fire. Especially with Xander Drew among the missing. The worst part was all of the rumors came back to Mike and Cathy.

"Now I'm sorry I have to ask you two these questions," Tim White said to Cathy and Mike from behind his desk. "I understand that you've been through a lot and if you want to do this later, that'll be fine. But I want to catch this killer."

Cathy looked at Mike.

"Now will be fine," she answered for the both of them.

"Alright," he opened his folder with a sigh. "I know this is a sensitive issue for you, but do you think... it could have been Drew?"

"Xander?!" Mike exclaimed. "No way! Never. Not in a million years. No."

Tim raised his hands in surrender. "I know it's hard, but there is substantial evidence now. The three of you were locked in that room, according to your own statements, right?"

"Yes," Mike nodded.

"Now, this killer shows up, starts murdering everyone that Xander always hated and now your boy is gone. Not only that, but the first one he killed was a girl who had turned him down repeatedly."

Cathy wiped her eyes at the mention of Sara.

"Then, the killer comes across you two. You were his friends, which is why he overlooked you. Which is why you were some of the only survivors. Then, he leaves. He realizes that he's outsmarted himself and that people like me would put two and two together, and he runs. And now he's out on the streets somewhere."

Cathy was crying.

78

Mike looked at her, then turned back to Tim with hatred in his eyes. "Okay. That's your opinion. Here's what I think happened. This killer is just another freak serial killer in a long, sad line of freak serial killers. He kills for a reason, but one that we don't fully understand yet. Anyway, before he tried to kill Tommy and Sud the other night, he heard them talking about Grendel's big party and decided to crash it. That's why he let them get away, when he probably could've killed both them and you. So, he shows up at the party and kills a lot of us. That girl, Liz you said... right? Well, she runs into the room where Xander, Cathy and I are being kept. He follows, but thinks that the three of us are already dead, when we're really just unconscious. He kills the girl and the sound wakes up Xander. So, the killer saw Xander wake and was about to kill him, when... he hears the police approaching. Rather than leave his plan undone, with no time to kill Xander in the grotesque and elaborate ways that he employs, the killer decides to take Xander with him if only for a little while. And yes, the killer is on the streets somewhere."

Tim looked thoughtful, leaning back and stroking the edges of his mouth and chin.

"That's what you think happened, huh?" he said calmly.

"That's what I know happened!" Mike shouted in response.

"Mike," Cathy said, speaking finally. She turned to Tim with a look of desperation in her eyes. "Xander didn't do it. And if he ran... you can be sure it was for a good reason."

"What reason would that be?" Tim pried, fingering his pen against the paper.

Cathy looked away, staring instead at the wall in an effort to fight back tears.

"He didn't," Mike said again, tapping a finger against the desk to elaborate.

Tim looked taken aback, then he restored himself. "Okay, son. You can go."

Mike got up, taking Cathy by the hand. "Come on, love. It's over now."

They left Tim that day with much to think about, and much to reconsider.

He bent over his desk and looked at the massive pile of files in front of him, one for each person killed during the ordeal. Jamie Dawkins. Carl Dent. That elderly couple, the Jacobies. Liz Taylor. And at least thirty other teens from Coral Beach High, including Julian Grendel.

Of all of them, Xander was their only link... except for the Jacobies.

He furrowed his brow.

"Maybe..." he thought out loud, pulling the file on the Jacobies forward. "I'm playing this the wrong way. Stop looking for what they all have in common... and look at the one that doesn't have anything in common..."

He opened the file. There was nothing there. There was the autopsy, but that was it. No birth record, no death certificate, no fingerprints, no dental or medical records... nothing.

"What the hell...." he mumbled, pushing through page after page of blank documents until he found one with something written on it. It was a copy of Salvadore Jacobies' record of employment, of which there was only one position for which he had reference.

"What the fuck is Engen?"

⋏⋏

"Coral Beach Precinct Morgue. Tuesday, the 26th. Harry Ford, mortician for this evening."

The words were once an attempt at levity and humor. Now, as they were delivered with a sad voice muffled by sobs, they just served to add to the weight of the situation.

"Come on, Harry," Lance said to his partner through tear filled eyes. "We've got a job to do."

Lance's wife had always asked how he could do this job. How he could *dissect* the bodies of his fellow human beings, even if it was in the pursuit of whatever killed them. He had always replied that there were worse jobs out there. That police and firemen often had to deal with gore *and* danger on the job. That stunt artists in movie crews lost partners on the job in grotesque ways all of the time. But right now he could not think of a single job worse than his as he stared at the thirty freezer drawers, each one containing the body of a child under the age of twenty. He fought back tears. "Come on."

He pulled a white mask over his face and asked Harry for a scalpel, then pulled back the blanket covering the chest of the first patient and began to cut into the chest cavity.

⋏⋏

"Where could he be?" Cathy said to Mike.

They were in Xander's room, which was a total mess as usual. Cathy sat on his bed, where she often had before while Xander downloaded music for her. She'd always thought of this space as warm and inviting. Now it was just cold and empty without his presence.

Mike paced about, looking for anything that might lead him to Xander's whereabouts.

Xander's mother had let them go up, but had refused to go herself. She hadn't been able to since she heard the news of his disappearance. His shirts littered the floor around his bed and his pants were strung across a chair at his desk. The drawers had been taken out of his dresser and thrown onto the floor. The room had been ransacked almost beyond recognition.

"Who would do this?"

Mike was repeatedly flicking the power switch of Xander's computer on and off, with no result.

Did this happen to the computer before, or did whoever broke in do it? he thought to himself. "Uh, I don't know. But I can take a guess."

"The killer," she said softly, a shiver running down her spine.

"He must have been looking for something. If he wasn't, he probably would

80

have killed Mr. and Mrs. Drew," Mike continued. "The question is: did he find it?"

"I don't know. But we've got to figure it out good and fast before that cop jumps to any more conclusions."

"Well," Mike muttered as he pushed aside an old bookcase. "If I know Xander, if he had something important to hide, he'd put it here." He stepped aside, revealing the ventilation duct to her. He pulled the grate off of it and reached in. His hand came out, first clutching a bundle of adult magazines.

Cathy rolled her eyes in disgust.

"I'm pretty sure that's not it," he chuckled.

"Duh. Unless our sicko is a major, um, sicko."

Mike reached in again, this time coming out with a little disk marked: ENGEN.

"What is it?" she asked, snatching it away.

"Dunno," he replied, snatching it back. He held it up to his eye. "But I'm sure as hell gonna find out."

Nothing.

And more nothing.

It seemed as though no matter what Tim did, there was nothing linking the Jacobies to existence. It was as if they had simply appeared dead in that house, out of thin air.

There was no record of them in any state, or even any country for that matter, that he could think to search. It was like they were phantom bodies.

This is it, he thought to himself, hunched over his laptop computer. *This is what I need; this is what's different. One of these things is not like the other and this is definitely it. If only I could figure out what 'it' was.*

The only thing he had to go on was the name Engen, which he could only assume was a business, but there were no records of it. Anywhere. Ever. It was like it too simply existed on that one slip of paper and nowhere else.

He let out a heaving sigh and felt the uncontrollable urge to pick up smoking again, something he hadn't done since he was a kid. His parents had told him that those things would kill him. Obviously they hadn't grown up in Coral Beach, or they'd have realized that the cigarettes would just have to wait in line for the chance.

He closed his eyes tight, realizing suddenly that he hadn't slept since Carl was killed.

When he opened them, he was looking directly at Carl's desk across the room, next to the window.

His brow crumpled as he looked up, something sparking in his mind and then fading again.

"Now what was that thought I just had..." he asked, almost begging his mind to let it return. He clicked his tongue against the roof of his mouth, staring at Carl's desk. "What are you trying to tell me, old friend?"

He sighed.

His fingers started to dance over the keyboard, as if they had a mind of their own. He went onto the national adoption agency and typed in both of the Jacobies.

No less than fifty hits came up with children they had adopted going back forty years or more, in almost every state and a few in Canada.

"Curiouser and curiouser..." he mumbled, scrolling down through the list.

Coral Beach High School Library.

They could feel the eyes on them. Somewhere in the back of their minds, they could sense it.

However, Mike and Cathy couldn't really care less right now, as they popped the disk marked ENGEN into the school's computer.

There was a little internet browser file labeled engen.com. Mike looked at it for a second, then brought the cursor up to it and clicked. Instantly, the browser popped up and began dialing in the name engen.com. When it did come up, the site was blank.

"This is what was so important?" Cathy wondered out loud.

"No. They've fixed it so that nobody will find out what was on that site," he said, then pulled the disk out of the computer and looked at it. "Whoever they are."

"Thirty-nine bodies done, one to go," Lance said aloud, with a miniature sigh of relief.

"Yeah, sigh now," Harry muttered, pointing a finger at the list of corpses. "But our murderer friend has changed his M. O. No organs were missing from any of these victims. Tim White's not gonna like hearing that this may have actually been a copycat killer."

"You're wrong. This last victim," he pointed to number forty on the sheet. "She was ravaged. She had her ovaries and the rest of her reproductive system taken."

Harry looked down through his sheets. "Sara Johnson. What's so special about her?"

"Tim?" the secretary said as she poked her head through his doorway.

Tim removed his reading glasses. "Yes, Felicia?"

"Those two children you saw earlier are here again. They say that they have some new evidence..."

"By all means, send them in," he smiled, turning off his computer screen.

Mike and Cathy walked in. Mike looked stern. He didn't like White. At all. He threw the disk onto his desk. "Have you ever been to engen.com, Mr. White?"

CHAPTER SEVEN: ENGEN

"AAARRRGHHH!" Xander screamed in pain, arching his back and pulling against the safety harnesses placed all around his body.

He could feel what they were doing, could feel them inside of him. If he turned the right way at the right time, he might even catch a glimpse of one of the doctors or the shadow of a guard. It barely registered with him. He was in too much pain to really register anything else. He screamed again, feeling a pinch deep inside his body. *Why are they doing this to me?* was all he could think. He had done nothing wrong. He hadn't hurt anybody, or anything. The last thing he remembered was actually trying to help someone. His friend, Cathy...

He screamed again. This time, finally, he got a reaction.

"Doctor?" the female shouted from somewhere above. She sounded mud-dled and dulled at first, as though she were under water, then came into clarity and was so loud that it was all he could hear. His vision was blurred and there were a lot of bright lights in his face, every so often something moving between him and them. "Can't we do something? He's in pain for god's sake!"

"No!" a male voice exclaimed. "Now, I don't like it any more then you do, but we can't put him to sleep because it'll dull his reactions. We can't administer an aesthetic to him because that'll affect..."

"Carry on," came a harsh voice from over an intercom. There was an audible click as it turned on and off.

"Right away, sir. Nurse, do something about his screaming."

A shadow fell in front of the light. The nurse bent over him, wrapping thick cloth around his mouth. He mumbled against it for a moment, then tried to scream again as the doctor went back in. They'd been at it for hours. The worst part was remembering every detail. He had been strapped down to this steel bed, his arms and legs stretched outward. He remembered the doctor telling him that everything would be all right, then asking the nurse for a scalpel. He cut right across Xander's stomach, pulling the skin away and holding it there with metal clamps. He was routinely given drugs to prevent him from blank-ing out from pain. He could feel the blood slowly pumping out of him, only to be replaced by even more. He felt the doctor pushing organs from side to side, looking for something. His arms and legs had been cut to stop him from strug-gling against the restraints. He did anyway. That pain was of little consequence in comparison. He turned his head and watched the blood trickle down the side of the table, the metallic buckles on his stirrups glistened in the intense light coming from above. He fought against the straps once more, then gave off a long sigh and gave up.

Suddenly, the doctor pinched something that made his whole body convulse without control. Xander clenched his teeth until the intense pain ceased. He was watching the doctor pull something long and yellow from him when the nurse came over and shone a miniature flashlight into his eyes. She whispered something to him. He was too out of it from anguish to actually hear the words, but the woman's calm tone soothed him. Until the doctor went back to work.

"Nurse, get away from there," the doctor said sternly. "Sponge."

An assistant handed the doctor the requested sponge, which was used to wipe some splattered blood from his brow. The assistant then faded back in the darkness that surrounded the operating table.

New entry. Tests continue. The patient has exhibited the same resistance that his mother used to employ. This slows the testing process and inevitably causes the subject great pain. A most unfortunate waste of time.

Xander cried out in torment once again. The noise was ear splitting, and would have chilled normal men to the marrow. The doctor never so much as flinched. He cut away the last part of the rib cage, his eyes getting wide. "Dear sweet mother of god..." he uttered.

"What?" the nurse reacted in fear. She looked over the doctor's shoulder and saw what had frightened this cold, hard, emotionless man so much.

Blackness. Where Xander's appendix *should* have been, there was instead a cancerous blackness. It didn't look to be attached to the appendix organ at all, but more like... *replacing* it. The doctor regained his composure. He had been briefed about all of this, but had never actually expected to find it. Never in his life would he have thought such a thing could exist.

The blackness convulsed in synch with Xander's pulse, as if it acted as a secondary heart of some kind. It had gray spots which were lumpy, unlike the jet black areas which appeared to be smooth and almost silky. Valves protruded from the blackness to other areas of the body.

It's spreading, thought the doctor.

Acting fast, he pushed the darkness aside with a gloved hand to reveal: more blackness. It had touched many major organs. The heart had tiny speckles on it. The liver was a sickly gray on one corner. One lung had been completely enveloped, while the other remained untouched. It seemed that it had even *dissolved* some of the bone structure of the rib cage, feeding off the marrow. Not only that, but the thing seemed to be beating faster now. The doctor could see where darkness was being pumped through his body at a faster rate.

"It's spreading faster," the doctor said, sounding extremely worried. "We'll have to amputate."

"NO!" came the voice over the loudspeaker again. "I will not allow it!"

"Too bad! We've waited almost twenty years for the subject to return, and

I'm not going to lose him again now!"

The doctor raised the scalpel.

All this time, Xander had been screaming like a banshee. Now, seemingly for no reason, he just... stopped.

Curious, the nurse walked over to again check the boy's eyes. She immediately dropped her little flashlight. Placing her hand over her mouth, she screamed. "His... his eyes!"

The doctor rushed over. Xander's pupils seemed to have completely taken over his eye, as they were now entirely blackened in, taking on a glossy appearance.

"It's spread to the optical nerves," he announced, going back to the blackness. He raised his scalpel once more and drove it into the dark substance.

Or at least, he attempted to.

The darkness resisted, acting sort of rubbery, bobbing whenever the doctor poked at it. Finally, he decided to cut the valves surrounding it and take it out whole. He cut a small slit in the top valve. Dark liquid spewed out onto his scalpel and hand, pulling on him. He screamed. It burned at him, scalding the flesh. The darkness was still being pumped onto him. It was sticky like tar and it seemed that the more the doctor pulled away, the more it held. The nurses and assistants crowded around. Two strong looking guards took the doctor around the waist and began to pull. With a loud snap, the doctor finally got his hand back. The flesh had been stripped away, revealing bundles of nerves, and muscle. He cried out in agony, falling to the floor and passing out. All eyes were on Xander, when something amazing happened.

From the slits made in his wrists and near his ankles, black liquid began to bubble and squirt. It first covered his hands and feet, then slowly it moved its way up his skin like waves move on a shore. Xander began to expel the substance from his mouth and within moments he was vomiting it upward, allowing it to flow back down onto him. As it did, his muscles seemed to grow exponentially, expanding as the substance touched it. His skin gained a smooth, yet scaly and shiny texture, like cohesive gel. He screamed, but all that came was the gurgle of the liquid. The experience was obviously painful. The gaps closed at his chest. He was now completely covered in the black liquid.

Three red slits formed on his face, opening to reveal two triangular bright red eyes and a glowing red mouth. Slowly, turquoise liquid filled the red of his eyes until that was all there was, making them look like pools of swamp water. The creature that was once Xander Drew broke the bonds which restrained it and stood up, much to the horror of the onlookers. It then said something in a deep, scratchy voice:

"Black Womb lives."

The creature leaped onto them, grabbing the doctor by the throat and squeezing. Blood ran from the neck down the monster's arms, but it hardly even noticed. Its eyes shone brightly in the dimly lit area surrounding the examination table. The Black Womb looked down onto it with disgust, throwing the doctor atop it. Tools and instruments flew everywhere and the scalpel which had been previously used against Xander Drew now made its final mark, digging into the chest of the doctor.

Black Womb turned its head to the assistants and nurses, who were clambering toward the exits. When it turned, its face turned first. Its face turned and then its head, something that paralyzed the nurse with fear.

There was a man outside of the door, engulfed in the shadows of the coat he wore. Only the bottom half of his face was visible, and was drawn upward in a smile. He looked down and turned something, then held up a key for the assistants to see. They began to scream angrily at the dark-suited man.

He laughed.

The creature looked at the men and women as they beat on the shiny metal door with panicked fists, swearing and uttering threats to the dark-suited man. Then they stopped and turned to Black Womb, who had not moved an inch after killing the doctor. It crouched on the steel floor, staring at the people. One by one, they all turned and locked into its eyes. Those eyes reminded one woman of a cat's eyes as it watched its prey, following them wherever they went.

It began to stand up now, as silent as a breeze, every movement without effort. As it did, it opened its mouth, revealing two rows of thick, jagged teeth. It held its hand up to the light and a look of concentration came over its face. Suddenly, four black talons unsheathed, one from each of its fingers. It crouched again, ready to pounce on the people who now stood perfectly still. A long, slender forked tongue protruded from its mouth and licked its lips before retreating. Without warning the beast pounced upward onto a wall, only long enough to kick off of it, propelling itself into an assistant. It drew back its arm, which now appeared long and elastic, pointing its clawed fingers at the man's face.

There was a slight hesitation in its posture, as the moment seemed to hang in the air. Then, with unbelievable speed, the creature slashed down across the man's face, tearing at his tender facial skin. It stuck one of its claws in its mouth and sucked a bit of blood off. The creature smiled sinisterly as the medical assistant clutched his burning face, screaming loudly. His screams were followed by those of the other workers as they realized what had happened to their fallen partner.

It sprung at them again, this time landing a few feet in front of its female target. It clenched its hand into a fist and punched her in the side of the head. She flew across the room, smashing her head against the concrete wall, leaving a trail of blood in her wake.

He turned his attention to a third victim. This one was male, somewhere in his early twenties, and was slightly overweight.

Black Womb jumped onto him. Pressing against the man's chest with his feet, it forced him forward into a wall. It wrapped its hands around to the back of the man's head, inserted its claws into his skull and *pulled*.

Looking around at the dead bodies of all the medical assistants, the creature was satisfied that it had slaughtered them all... until he heard it.

The soft rhythmic whimpering, like the gentle coo of a pigeon on a warm summer's day.

Then the monster remembered the nurse. It walked over to the metallic table that had once held the doctor's tools, flipping it aside. There, curled into a little ball, was the nurse. Her blonde hair was matted over her face, her eyes peering from between the strands in cold fright.

It looked at her and appeared sympathetic. She looked up into its aqua eyes, and seemed almost... comforted. It sheathed its claws and extended its hand, gently brushing a stray piece of hair from her face to behind her ear. Then its eyes suddenly took on an evil, triangular slant. It grabbed her head and forced it to the side, exposing her slender neck. Opening its mouth wide, it bit down on the tender flesh. Blood flowed freely as the second row of teeth sliced through her jugular vein. It sucked in hard, drinking the life giving liquid. The nurse attempted to scream in pain, but her throat had been too damaged in the attack. Her body convulsed. It grabbed her to stop it, then finally flung her aside, hurling her against the wall. It growled long and loud, tossing its blood soaked head up toward the ceiling.

The metal door slid open, and the black suited man stepped into the room. The door hissed to a close behind him. He walked over to Black Womb and smiled.

Black Womb turned its head to one side and started to claw at its own face in pain as red liquid pumped and swirled its way into its eyes. The aqua colouring was forced out, melding and conforming to the new colour with a sickening squish, looking like dye placed in water as it churned about. It took a deep breath, looking around as if confused.

Inside of it, Xander Drew gasped. He looked around at the bodies surrounding him then up at the killer standing before him, his eyes widening with fear and his mouth going slack. The Womb's face on the outside mimicked the motion, but it looked more like a hungry animal spotting a slab of meat, its mouth salivating when he opened it.

How did I get here? Xander thought feverishly, looking down at his hands and seeing the claws for the first time. *What the hell is this?*

He tried to remember how he even got off the operating table and how all these people had died. As he stared at the body of the young blonde nurse, he felt a sick memory come over him, then forgot it instantly. It reminded him of when he tried to access corrupt files on his computer. They would try to open, then fail. An ache from his head made him think that if he tried too hard, his brain might lock up.

He looked up at the killer, hatred in his glowing eyes. "You killed Jamie."

The murderer nodded silently.

"Who are you?" he demanded in the Black Womb's voice, struggling to get the words out, as if training its own throat how to utter each new syllable. The corners of his eyes began to glow aqua, then returned to red.

The killer threw away his hat and whipped off his trench coat, revealing a skintight jumpsuit. The suit was black and leather, with pointy white triangles showing along the waist and shoulders. There were two blades crossing at his back, each one double sided, curved and glinting in the dim light. The killer removed one of the blades, gripping the rubber handles. He flipped the blade in his fingers, then held it in place diagonally at his side. When he finally spoke, the words were cold and unforgiving. In a voice sick and raspy, he said:

"Call me Genblade."

CHAPTER EIGHT: GENBLADE

"Call me Genblade."

The words hung in the air for a moment. Xander looked up into the dark eyes of the killer, staring silently into his inner soul. He saw nothing but a blackness that rivaled even his own. There was a deep pain building in his side and he could feel the Black Womb's heart convulse wildly, fighting against the rib cage.

Genblade took out a small device, pressing his thumb against the switch.

"Waddaya know. This thing really does detect the Darkness," he chuckled, throwing it onto the floor next to them. "This shouldn't take too long." He was confident, and rightfully so. His muscles bulged against the black spandex as they tightened and shifted.

Then Xander realized why.

Genblade leaped almost five feet into the air from a standing position and flipped over his opponent, landing on the other side and slashing at the Womb's backside. Blackness spiraled in long slithering strands in the direction of the blade, the wounded human flesh underneath visible through the gap in the oil. The slashed strands slithered their way back, rejoining Black Womb at the hand. Within seconds the wound had closed and was followed by the gap in the blackness closing up as the strands flowed back into place.

The Womb stood up and tilted its head to one side until the calcium popped, then turned to face its attacker. "No. It shouldn't."

Genblade gritted his teeth. His eyes narrowed into little slits on either side of his pointed nose and his fingers stretched along the grip of his sword. The blade hung by his side loosely until he let it fall until it almost hit the floor, then caught it. Extending his arm slightly, he let the metal touch against the metal of the tile, creating a small sound.

-shink-

-shink-. Again.

He did it over and over, all the while keeping his eyes locked on the Black Womb's opaque pupils. The Womb stared back at Genblade, but with each -shink- the urge not to look down at the blade became unbearable. It strained, forcing itself not to comply with its reflexes. Genblade paused for a moment, the blade rising as he finished scraping the floor.

-shunk-.

Genblade had let the blade drop again. It created a louder, more intense scratch. The Womb's pupil moved down to the corner of its eye as it glanced, only briefly, at the blade. When it looked back up, Genblade was already bearing down upon it. The spiked blade ripped across Black Womb's face, briefly revealing the guise of Xander Drew underneath, writhing in agony.

Black Womb reeled backward in pain, gripping at its face with its hands. It howled as it remembered the claws too late, ripping them away and taking a large chunk of its own cheek with it. The sliver of meat dropped from the talon as it retracted and fell to the floor with a plop.

"Gah!" it hissed, staggering as it tried to steady itself on its feet.

As the brute's arms flailed, Genblade kicked it in the side and sent it teetering even more off balance. More specifically, its *right* side. The creature's mouth opened wide as it forced back a scream of pain. It looked up at its opponent standing over it, as it crashed to the ground.

Inside it, Xander's pulse began to beat so loud that it was all he could hear thumping at the base of his skull.

I'm done, he thought, gasping for air and getting a mouthful of the dark bile that covered him instead. *I may have power, but I have no idea what I'm doing. This guy has skill. He knows what he's doing and I don't. He's better than me.* He growled as he got up again, clutching at his side. *Don't know what's going on, but if I've got power I've got to use it now. Use so much of it that it won't matter how hard this guy's trained himself. None of it matters. I've got to get out of here, Cathy still needs me.*

The Womb raised its hands, palms open. It gritted its teeth as its talons unsheathed from their holding places inside of its fingers again, each one accompanied by a tiny spurt of arterial blood. It lunged at Genblade, mouth open and arms reaching out toward the murderer, aching to repay him for the flesh it had lost.

Genblade shifted his weight to the right foot casually, letting the Womb pass harmlessly by.

"This is really starting to get sad," he tisked, reaching out and grabbing the creature by the back of the throat. Bringing him up to eye level, Genblade looked at the monster and laughed, slamming its head into the hard metal floor, then raising it up again.

"Guh... tit... gug," the Womb mumbled as both red and black blood spewed from its lips, its head bobbing around on its neck as if one of the joints which held it there had come loose.

"You know what the difference is between you and me?" Genblade taunted, forcing it to crash into the floor once more, then bringing it back to eye level again.

Black Womb merely stared at his assaulter in a cold response. Xander's bruised and cut face was visible through the small gap in the oily substance, before it swallowed into itself.

"No, not about a hundred I.Q. points," he quipped, smashing his rival into the now bending metal once again, then brought it up to answer the question himself. "It's just like I whispered to that dumb blonde before I cut her."

Xander's eyes went as wide as they could while still bruised, and the Womb's followed.

"You can knock 'em down, drive skates through their hearts or shoot 'em, but one thing always stays the same."

SLAM.

"...death ALWAYS has a face."

SLAM.

"ALWAYS has a name."

SLAM.

"And today, that name is Genblade."

SLAM.

Genblade looked at his adversary for the first time since beginning his little speech. The Black Womb's healing process had obviously slowed, the blackness now looking as though it were painted on and barely clinging to the flesh beneath. About half of Xander's face was visible now, and it was in bad shape. The wounds looked to be closing, but not as fast as before. His vision was impaired by large, swollen bruises and his cheek and forehead were cut deep with gashes.

Xander's pupil turned to look at Genblade, his voice somewhere in between the Black Womb and his own. "Sara?"

"Bit the dirt like a starving earthworm."

SLAM.

SLAM.

SLAM.

Suddenly, Black Womb's eyes began to glow bright aqua again. It reached behind itself, grabbing Genblade by the wrist and digging the claws in deep to hold it there. With a quick pull of his arm, Black Womb flipped Genblade over its back, slamming him onto the blood stained floor. Black strands flew off of the Womb everywhere, healing his wounds quickly. It picked Genblade up by the neck and pushed him against the cold metal wall.

Blood ran from Genblade's nose, flowing down his chin. He smiled, licking his lips of the red liquid.

"There you are. Was wondering when you'd come back out to play," he teased.

Black Womb stared at Genblade, looking as if it wanted to say something. It opened its mouth to speak, but nothing came. After a moment it managed three words, each one sounding as though it were vomited up rather than spoken. "Black Womb lives!"

"Had a feeling you were going to say that," Genblade snickered as he started to rise to his feet.

The Womb grabbed him by the shoulder and threw him straight across the room as if he were a rag doll. He slammed into another wall, smacking into a light hanging from the ceiling as he went. The light swung around for a moment, making shadows dance and jump everywhere. It blinked several times from the impact, creating a strobe effect and made it hard to focus on anything in the room. It couldn't even focus on Genblade or where he was in the room, or even on its own hands.

When the light finally flickered out, Black Womb stared into the darkness and saw nothing. It put its clawed hands in front of it, preparing for the moment that Genblade came out of the shadows.

Suddenly, it felt an extreme rush of pain in its right side. It looked down and to its shock, he saw the end of Genblade's blade sticking out of it. It crumpled over, straining its neck to look behind him.

"It's all about skill." Genblade smiled as he withdrew the blade, flicking it toward a nearby wall to clean the blood off of it.

He picked up Black Womb, elevating him and propping him up against the wall. He took out a small, sharp blade and jammed it into Black Womb's right side. It sliced directly through the cancerous blob that the doctor had been so concerned with, and a small -shink- sound indicated that it went clean through the wall as well. Genblade let go of the Womb, letting the blade prop him up, its flesh tugging around it.

"This was absolutely pathetic. If you're gonna keep going with power over skill, there's a couple of things you should be made aware of. Number one..."

Shunk. Genblade stabbed Black Womb in the arm. The creature's head raised, fully awake for the first time in several moments and really listening now, wanting to scream but unable to make the right sound.

"...your right side is your weak spot. It's where your true self, the real Black Womb, resides. But you probably figured that out. Number two..."

Shunk. He stabbed it through the other arm.

"...That healing factor of yours'll only go so far. If you tax it too much, or if I do, it'll simply cut out. Number three..."

Shunk. He stabbed it through both feet, pinning them to each other and the wall.

"...Nobody, I repeat, NOBODY escapes death."

Genblade stepped back and admired his work. Black Womb stood there, his body pinned into a cross position.

Black Womb's mind reeled. He couldn't focus on anything, his vision was blurry, and black around the edges. He felt the healing factor cut out. He lifted his head to face his attacker.

"A crucifixion," Genblade sneered, stroking his chin as he admired his work. "It'd almost be poetic, if it wasn't so damn funny."

A voice crackled to life over a nearby intercom, just out of sight. "Excellent work, Adam... Excellent work."

⋏⋏

Black Womb stared down at the cold metal floor, now wishing that he could merely stand on it. It glared at its reflection in the blood, distorted and obtuse. It reflected how the creature felt, beaten both physically and psychologically.

Its blood mingled with that of the doctor's assistants, splattered all over the walls and the floor, making it look like a scene from a B-list horror movie. As it stared down at the reflection, its eyes swelled in shock. Its body began to convulse and throb. Slowly and painfully, it began to transform into Xander Drew again. The dark liquid that had been clinging to him ever since this nightmare began finally let go as if it had just lost its grip. It splashed to the floor, revealing his flesh starting with his feet and working its way up to its eyes where it disappeared.

All that was left was Xander, naked and pinned to the wall, blood hemorrhaging from his wounds.

His eyes remained black for a moment, but when it passed they returned to normal. His skin was still covered with a thin layer of blood, a film left over from the change. He gasped for air as sweat and blood rolled down his face. He screamed long and loud, as if he was feeling the crucifix for the first time. Blood began to flow liberally from his hands, feet and side. As the floor around him began to fill with it, he noticed a small drain under him which it was all flowing into. His body began to shake as it ran out of fluids, his eyes rolling into the back of his head.

Genblade stepped into the Womb's field of vision again, bending down and placing his hand flat into the puddle of tar-like blood. When he brought it around to look at it, it was covered completely in the shiny black liquid, and he found himself staring at it intently.

"That should be enough, Adam. I believe it time to begin phase two," came the voice behind the intercom.

Genblade stepped out of the darkness, a corrupt smile on his face.

"Engen.com. Huh."

"What is it?" Mike demanded. They had been waiting for a background check on the web site for several hours, and the exhaustion had long since started to fray at him. It was all he could do not to think about the events of the previous night. "What have you found?"

"Nothing," Tim answered, turning his screen a little. "It's just someone's home page. Aside from the animation, it's a poorly done home page. There's nothing unusual here."

Mike sighed, then turned the computer screen so that he could see. The Engen symbol danced around the window to the tune of *Minority* by Green Day. He examined it carefully, and after a second, he noticed something in the corner. "What's that?"

"What?" Cathy and Tim said simultaneously, each shifting a little in their seats.

"That spider symbol in the corner," he said, even as he clicked on it. Automatically, a single message came up onto the screen: Black Womb Lives.

"That's it? That's what you have to tell me?" Tim growled, as much at the web site as at Mike.

"Black Womb. That was written on the wall where Jamie..." Mike stopped, looking at the floor. "Where the first murder took place."

Tim frowned reluctantly. "There could be something, I guess. But it doesn't give us any leads."

Cathy sighed, turning his laptop toward her so that she could finally get a look, mouthing the words 'Black Womb lives' to herself over and over again.

"We've got nothing," Mike agreed, clenching his fist and almost punching the wall, stopping himself right before he did so.

"Like I said," Tim agreed, motioning in his direction.

Cathy frowned. "You said... the Jacobies adopted kids... right?"

"Yes," Tim answered, rubbing the bridge of his nose while he mentally calculated the hours he had gone without sleep.

She clicked her tongue against the roof of her mouth. "Then... is there any way to find out where these kids are now? Or where they were adopted from?"

Mike and Tim exchanged a look.

Tim leaned forward and opened up a web browser, typing in his user ID quickly. After only a moment of looking, he responded to her query. "I can't find out who they adopted... there's just no record... but they were all adopted from the same place. A little convent upstate."

"That's where Xander was adopted from," Mike said, leaning in and squinting at the screen. "And me."

Cathy rolled that around in her head for a minute. "Who are Xander's birth parents?"

Again, Tim typed for a moment. "No record."

"How does that happen? Is it just, like, a drop the baby on the doorstep kinda deal?"

Tim's eyes went large as he realized what she was getting at. "Yes. It would be something just like that, actually."

"So... what's to stop us from going to that place and just looking for a big building with Engen stamped across it?" Mike said, giving a nod to his girl.

Tim paused, taking a long look at each of them, trying to gauge how serious they actually were. He got up and grabbed his coat.

ʎ⟨⟩ʎ

"Interesting. Most interesting indeed," the man on the intercom said, as he observed Xander getting shocked by the electrified bars of his cell. He brought an oxygen mask to his face and sucked back air, steadying his voice before he pressed the intercom's 'On' switch so that Xander could hear him.

"Welcome home, Subject 08276," he said in an overly dramatic voice. "You probably don't remember, but this cell was once the home of you and your dear mother."

"My mother?" Xander gasped, smoke rising up from his back.

There was a slight pause on the intercom. Suddenly, the rough voice returned. "Welcome home, 08276. Welcome home, Black Womb."

The intercom switched off, leaving Xander with more questions than answers. He rose up and looked down at himself, taking note of several red stains on the paper gown he was clothed in. He looked around his cell. It was exceedingly simplistic in its nature, with three concrete walls that obviously held wiring for the electrical steel bars that covered his exit. The floor and ceiling were both metal. The room itself was only about five meters cubed, with no furniture or plumbing.

He stared at the bars.

He stared at them until they went from being solid lines dissecting his vision to watery, unfocussed slashes. There was an ache building in the centre of his chest the more he looked at them. They filled him with an anxiety that dispelled all rational thought, until for a moment all he could think was: the *bars*.

He sniffed back hard and forced his eyes to refocus. Slowly, thought returned to him.

But the anxiety remained, no matter how much he tried to bury it.

Electrified bars needed to be hollow to have wiring inside of them and to better conduct electricity, he recalled. So the only real problem was getting past the electricity. Xander frowned.

"Genius, man. Genius," he mumbled to himself.

Still, he searched his brain for something, *anything* he could use. Finding nothing, he walked over to the bars. Touching one lightly with his index finger, he pulled it away immediately as the electricity coursed through his fingertips. He touched another bar with the same result, then pulled back and stroked his chin.

He poked at the bar at the top, near the ceiling. There was still a shock, but it wasn't as potent. If there was a place to short it out, it'd be there. There was still the problem of what to do with this knowledge. He sat down on the metal floor.

"Ow!" he yelped, jumping to his feet. Something had poked at him. He examined the floor and found nothing, then reached around to his back and smiled.

Safety pins.

He pulled the top one out of the back of his gown. The top of it opened and he glanced down at his chest. To his relief, many of the wounds were healing. Except the ones from the crucifixion.

He stepped up to the bars and inserted the pin to the top. He pulled away automatically with shock, but the electricity held the pin there. As he watched the pin began to glow white hot, until finally the bar's generator exploded in an array of white and blue sparks from which he had to shield his eyes momentarily.

He stepped up to the bars again and attempted to stretch them. To his surprise, they slid open. He stepped out and looked around.

There was no one in either corridor, in any direction. Both sides seemed equally long and equally intimidating, stretching on forever. So he just went with his gut and chose right. He started to run but his body rebelled, smashing him to the floor. He looked down at his feet, which were now bleeding again from the crucifixion wounds.

"Dammit. Where's my guardian monster when I need him?" he uttered in self-pity as he began to crawl along the floor. Inwardly, he thought, *It hurts. It hurts so bad. But I can't stop. Just like Sara always said. You can never stop. I swear I'll kill that monster for what he did to you.*

ᚚ

"Just like his mother," chuckled the voice behind the intercom, before letting out a massive, hacking cough. "An admirable try, my boy. But nobody escapes from Alpha Quadrant twice in one lifetime."

He pressed a small red button on his control panel, and a buzzer began to sound throughout the facility.

Xander heard the buzzer and forced himself to his feet, despite the incredible amount of pain that it caused. He made his way to the end of the corridor already gasping for breath, then looked around for options.

Again, it was a simple choice of left or right. He thought he heard something and turned around quickly, sending shoots of pain up and down his spine. He thought that he saw something out of the corner of his eye, but he couldn't be sure. Turning back around, he decided to once again go right.

He limped to the end of that hallway, to a large yellow door. A gold plated plaque on it read: STORAGE. He opened it slowly and stepped inside.

It looked like a warehouse, but with no visible exits that he could see. Large wooden crates were stacked up almost to the ceiling and there was moving equipment everywhere. He walked to the middle of the first column.

He heard the faint sound of scuttling footsteps and turned around quickly. It was like thousands of crabs all clambering toward him at once, their tiny legs pounding against the tile. Or spiders. It could have been spiders, too.

The door that he came in through was swinging, back and forth, then came to a slow stop.

Somebody's here.

Xander turned around slowly, surveying his situation and his environment.

The crates seemed to go on for forever and ever, like a large wooden stairway. There were gaps where he could see through to the next column and when he looked out through them, all he could see was a long, slender hallway filled with more wooden crates.

He leaned on the box in front of him to get a better look. The cover rattled slightly with a clunk. He reached his nails under the lid and began to pull up. Almost instantly, pain began to shoot up his arms from his wrists. Blood poured fresh again, and he let a swear pass through his blood spattered lips. The cover finally popped off, revealing that it was filled with items that appeared to be bottles, all wrapped in a thick layer of soft gauze. Taking the prime opportunity, he unwrapped some gauze and wrapped it around his wrists. When they were done, he applied some to his heels, the cuts on which had stretched and bled with every step he'd made, and then finally to his side. The makeshift bandages almost instantly filled with blood, but they seemed to be helping.

He glanced down at what was in the jar.

It was a heart.

He jerked back with shock, dropping the jar to the floor. It shattered with an ear splitting sound that echoed throughout the entire facility. Formaldehyde splattered onto his cuts, causing a slight burning sensation as he backed into the row of crates behind him.

He felt a sudden rush of wind and turned around, but there was nobody there. He felt cold. He began to turn around and thought he saw something in the next row out of the corner of his eye and followed it. Again, nothing. He ran to the end of the column, turned the corner, and gazed down the next row. Nothing. He looked down the next. Again nothing. He kept running down the same direction, trying to trap his follower. It occurred to him that given his condition that this may not have been the wisest tactic, but he had to know.

The columns ended abruptly.

There was nobody to be seen. Then it dawned upon him: he could have easily doubled back... and followed him. He stopped dead in his tracks and slowly began to turn around. He closed his eyes, expecting that when he opened them, Genblade would be raining down hell on him. He fully believed that it would be the last thing he would ever see. Coming to a halt, he slowly opened his eyes.

Nothing.

Nothing but the bare hallway. He let out a sigh of relief.

-clunk, clunk-

The sound came from above.

Xander looked up just in time to see the crate fall.

"Get up," said the soft, soothing, feminine voice.

The voice triggered a memory deep within him. He had gotten into a fight with Grendel when he was twelve years old. He had given Grendel a black eye, but with one punch, Grendel had given him a broken nose. He had hit the ground hard and closed his eyes. The voice had come to his ears like a sweet melody that man could never hear, because no music made after would ever compare. There was a slight giggle in Sara's voice as she said the words.

"Get up."

A voice like springtime. The warm, soft... just good feeling that came with springtime. Like the sun's rays on your face.

He opened his eyes and through his blurred, painful vision, he thought he saw her standing over him with that cute smile on her face. He smiled as the voice came again, but this time there was an edge on it. He felt a sharp pain in his leg, finally opening his eyes all the way.

An athletic woman loomed over him. She was Asian, with almond eyes and a perfect, thinly honed muscular body. She had a long ponytail which swerved down and wrapped around her body. She was dressed much like Genblade was, in skintight leather, only hers was dark red with black edges.

The handles of twin katana blades protruded from holsters on her back, the straps crossing her chest with an x. She removed one of the blades and pointed it at him. It had four gold spikes coming off of the handle making the legs of a spider, with two rubies making up the body and head. "I said, get up."

He slowly rose to his feet to face her. "Mrs. Genblade, I presume."

She struck him hard and fast with the broad side of her blade.

"You may call me Spider," she said coldly. That voice was so smooth, so beautiful... it almost didn't matter. As he crumpled to the floor, she looked down at him. "What could he possibly see in the likes of you, you impotent cur?"

"What?" he stammered.

"Nothing," she smiled. She would have had a beautiful smile, if not for her eyes, which betrayed her sinister intent. "The weapon in your blood has been depleted as a result of your inexperience and carelessness. When it has healed your rather extensive wounds, it will return to you. It has not yet, which makes this a drastically unfair fight."

She unsheathed her second blade and held it out.

He stared at it for a moment, then took it from her.

She backed up from him a few feet then stood still, glaring at him. He gripped the sword in his hands, attempted to swirl it around like on TV, and dropped it immediately.

She chuckled at the foolish attempt, watching him with fascinated amusement.

He picked it up again and held it straight. His chest rising with a deep breath, he lunged at her with a force that surprised even him, striking at her with the blade.

She lifted her own to block it, creating a sudden spark as metal met metal.

"Good," she said curtly, as if she were teaching him.

They both pushed away and she jumped at him, making one clean and graceful swipe with the sword.

He tried to lift his to defend himself, but he wasn't fast enough and her blade cut at his elbow. He felt it scrape against the bone and cringed in a sudden rush of pain and adrenaline. He swung back, but she curved her body and jumped away casually. He lunged at her a second time. Again, she blocked him with her sword.

"Better," she said again, suppressing a laugh.

They pressed against each other, neither willing to give up, until she kicked him in the side and sent him into a pile of crates. The wood splintered beneath the force of his weight and he let a deep groan from his throat. Formaldehyde leaked from broken bottles inside the crate as she dashed up to him, placing the razor sharp edge of her blade against his throat.

He glared at her, hatred in his eyes. She leaned her head in and kissed him lightly, then flipped backward, landing in a fighting stance.

He hurled himself at her, slashing with his sword.

She jumped over it.

He lashed out again.

She ducked under it.

Finally, she slashed back. He pulled away, but her blade still nicked the gauze bandages. They fell to the ground, their blood slathered surface splashing the concrete floor. He looked at the palm of his hand, wiggling his fingers. No blood. Not even a scar. His wrist was healed.

He sneered, then turned back toward her. "I think it's time you saw what I'm *really* made of."

He clenched his fists until the thin pads of his fingers dug into his palms. His heart began to pump so hard that he could feel it in his ears, drowning out the mechanical cackle of the madwoman across from him. His eyes pulsed with it as

97

his breath became shallow and his veins became tight. He could feel them all, the pressure building all over his body until he felt like he was about to burst.

Nothing happened.

"Ngh," he grunted painfully, he cheeks flushed and red as his pulse began to slow again.

"What's the matter, little boy? Can't summon the demon in your blood?" Spider laughed. She thrust herself at him again.

Then he realized just what she had said. The demon in his blood... *I've got it.*

He raised his blade up to eye level and ran his wrist along it.

Spider stopped in her tracks, watching him with wide eyed interest.

As the sword slit the vein, blood poured down his arm. At first it was red, then it was suddenly blackened. His face cringed in pain as his pupils grew to envelope his entire eye. The blackness seeped from his arm to the rest of his body and then to his head. Three red slits appeared to slice through his face, each glowing. They opened to form glowering eyes and a mouth. Long, sharp teeth grew in from the top and bottom of the gaping gums.

"Black Womb lives."

Spider looked onward at the Black Womb in awe. She smiled, licking her lips. "Now I think I see what he sees in you."

She jumped at him. This time, he was the one to jump over her swing.

Her face twisted angrily as he jumped so high that he landed on a stack of crates. Doing a flip off of them, he propelled himself toward Spider and kicked her in the face.

She sprawled backward, slipped on the formaldehyde that had spilled on the floor, then turned and looked at him with hatred burning in her slanted eyes.

He was crouching across the hall, staring at her. He slowly reached over and grabbed a large chunk of wood from the shattered crate.

As Spider got up, he tackled her, sending them both flying through wood and glass. He raised the wooden stake high above his head, prepared to bring it down onto Spider. She caught it between her hands an inch in front of her face. Pushing the wood backward abruptly, she smacked Black Womb in the face with it. He took a step backward, then regained himself. He looked at her, her face a mess of small cuts and her ponytail now ragged. She wiped a spot of blood from the side of her face, then smeared it onto her blade.

She got up and swiftly threw the blade at Black Womb, who tried to jump out of the way, but was too slow.

The blade sliced through the corner of his side and his face distorted from pain. Claws protruded from each fingertip and he started whipping at the air around Spider wildly with them. She jumped high into the air, coming down onto his shoulders. He got up and turned to her, then picked up her sword and prepared to lunge at her when a burst of blue electricity ripped through his spinal column. He slammed to the floor and Genblade loomed over him, continuously stinging at him with his taser.

"That's enough playing around, Spider. The master requests an audience with our dear old friend, 08276 here."

They both laughed. Spider walked up to Genblade, kissing him passionately on the lips. She put her arms around him, then quickly snatched the taser away.

"But I want to play," she said with a pouting child's voice. She dug the taser into Xander's back and turned it on. His eyes lit up with blue.

Her smile widened.

ʎ⟨ʎ

"Okay," Tim sighed, shuffling through a pile of papers. "We have about five hundred references to something called the Black Womb in all of these files, but the first two hundred and fifty contradict the last two hundred and fifty."

He buried his head in his arms and tossed his glasses onto the table in front of him.

"Alright, but there is one continued reference," Cathy noted, staring down at her own stack of papers.

"There is?" Mike said, leaning over her shoulder, giving her a little kiss on the cheek.

"What?" Tim asked, getting up from his chair.

"A date," she said thoughtfully. "March 7th... fifteen years ago."

They all looked puzzled for a moment.

"Hey," Mike said, his eyes brightening. "That'd be around the time Xander was born."

"Quick," Tim said, walking over to her. "What document was that from?"

"Um... something called Alpha Quadrant up near the Canadian border," she replied.

"And about six miles from where the orphanage was," Mike murmured, stroking his top lip with his index finger.

"Alright then," Tim smirked, heading for the door.

ʎ⟨ʎ

Floating. He felt like he was floating. That was the first thing that Xander thought when he woke up. Every inch of his body ached. He tried to move, but pain shot up and down his spine, making him wish that he were dead. He struggled to open his eyes and when he did the light shone at him, bright and burning.

"Hi, lover," came Spider's voice, her evil cackle echoing through the stone walls.

The light was lowered and he could see Spider and Genblade looming over him, smiling. There was someone else too...

"AAAARRRGHH!" he shouted, as pain shot through his body.

"A reminder," Genblade said coldly. "Don't try and escape. Those electrical currents will eventually kill you." His teeth showed as his smile grew. They were pointed, each one sharpened to a razor's edge.

Xander's body went limp. He was covered in a thin layer of blood again, his head splitting from repeated blows. He could feel blood pumping out of his ears and down the side of his neck.

Spider reached out and took some of it onto her finger.

"Fear is so much more interesting an emotion than hope, isn't it, Adam?" she said as she put the bloodied finger into her mouth. "Tastier too."

Xander felt like throwing up. The mixture of a blood filled stomach and what she had just done causing him to have to fight back the urging of his gut.

"You look just like your mother, my child," came a voice from the darkness. It was the exact same voice that had come over the intercom before. Thick, raspy, and nearly hushed to the point of a whisper. "She fought us too, you know. But from her, we learned. Taking people from the outside leaves them with a sense of resistance. They long for the relationships, friends and lovers that the outside world brings. After your mother's death, we decided to scrap all those projects and start anew."

Xander squinted his eyes, trying to penetrate the darkness. "Who are you?"

He laughed, then let out a wracking cough. It chilled Xander to the bone. "Soon son, soon. Now, as I was saying, we learned a lot from your mother's escape. When we won the gene war, there were a few section heads that were nervous about the damage that would be done if word got out about project Black Womb. About you. It had almost happened once before in the seventies and almost led to the collapse of our entire research and development department. They were idiots, all of them. Old fogies set to their mindless ways and then bold enough to call their work a new genesis. They had to go. How else could one rise above in this world, after all? Soon I was a section head myself and one of the controlling stockholders at Engen Industries."

"Engen?" Xander murmured, the words striking a chord.

"Also known as Alpha Quadrant. You see, I believed that you and the others on the outside could be assimilated into life on the inside. But first, we had to sever all of your links to the outside. We had to end your relationships with those you love, those you hate... everyone associated with you. This would leave you susceptible to the mind tempering needed for the final step of assimilation."

Xander looked over at Genblade. "So you sent this walking militia to kill off my friends."

"No, boy. We needed to do research. I found you online after months of searching through chat sites. Finally I found you and, using a user name that was not easily traceable, I approached you and eventually gained your trust."

"Soul," Xander said, cursing inwardly.

"Precisely. Then, my dear Spider began contacting your friends via the internet, making them trust you even less."

"Spider."

"Exactly. Thinking we would never meet, you felt free to talk to me about your friends, your loved ones, and even people you didn't like much at all. We thought it wise to begin there, sending Spider to herd the cattle to a certain spot for Genblade to mow them down."

"Jamie," Xander whispered as shock ran down through his face.

"You hated him because Sara loved him. Pathetic, teenage drivel! You were bred to be better than that! Cur! But what else could I expect from you, really?

Whether you blame it on nature or nurture, you didn't really have a chance. You were made of junk DNA and raised by white trash... How could we hope for you to grow into anything but garbage?"

The thoughts crashed upon him like a wave onto the shore. It was his fault. All of this. Jamie's death, Carl Dent's death, the attacks on Mike, Cathy, Sud, Tommy... all his fault. And Sara. At the thought of her, he wanted to cry. He'd killed her. He may not have actually done the deed, but he may as well have pulled the trigger. It was his fault that she was dead. Dead.

"You fucker. You killed all these people... just to get to me?" The hatred burned in his eyes.

"No," Genblade said, his smile growing ferociously as he wrapped his hands around Spider, letting them trickle up and down her front. "I killed Jamie Dawkins. I loved it. He came apart so easily I could taste it. That old couple and your little whore, yeah I did them too. But that was it."

"Then who?!?" Xander shouted, pulling against his restraints. Electricity surged up from them, forcing him back down. "Who did it? Give me a name. I'll kill him right after I'm done with you, you sick son of a..."

"You want a name?" Genblade interrupted, laughing hysterically. "You want the name?"

"Just give me the damn name!" he shouted. This time when the electricity surged, he ignored it. The emotional pain outweighed the physical.

"Xander Drew."

CHAPTER NINE: TRUTH

All was quiet. The words sunk deep.

"What?" Xander spat, his upper lip curling.

"It was you. Or rather, the 'savior' within your veins."

"You're a liar. And a killer. Give me one good reason why *I* should believe *you*."

"Because," came the voice from the darkness. "It's true. The Black Womb's consciousness resides within you. You have remarkable skills, my boy, but not even you can control a Black Womb twenty-four hours a day. These past few months ever since you hit puberty, when you sleep and your mind is overpowered by that of the Black Womb, he escapes. It's easy to identify. When you call him, that is, when you have his body surrounding yours but you still remain in control, your eyes have a reddish tint to them. But Black Womb's consciousness is let out when you stop thinking rationally, when you get extremely emotional or when you sleep. On one of his outings, the Womb happened upon Genblade murdering Jamie Dawkins. Spider and Genblade thought it to be an extraordinary bit of luck and allowed you to watch and participate as they stripped him of his usable organs. The Black Womb's savage instincts took over. He had gotten a taste of the blood that he was meant to *bathe* in and he wanted more. There were other programming methods, of course. Engen.com filled the Womb portion of your consciousness with subliminal messages while that screen was flashing. But in the end, it was that simple act of getting blood on your hands that brought out the real you. So each time you slept, he went out to claim another. Or at least to try. It seems that your consciousness had some residual effects on Black Womb. When it came time to strike down someone you loved, Mike Harris, he could not. A pity."

"M-me?" Xander stammered, the words cutting into him worse than any of Genblade's daggers ever could. He had maimed and killed all those people. Not indirectly, but in pure form. "Kill me."

"Oh! No my boy, no," the figure laughed. "Not quite yet." Then, his captor's voice became surprisingly sympathetic. "I wanted to die once, too. Once, when I was just a security guard, waiting for death to claim me as I lay in that hospital bed..." then his voice perked up. "But you must remember, my boy. It wasn't you. It was that bloody bastard in your veins that did it. That's why I brought you here."

"What?" Xander balked, again searching the darkness. "What are you talking about?"

"I think my predecessors did a bad thing. We let you go. Out there, in countless orphanages, you didn't get the training that you needed to harness the Black Womb. You didn't know what was happening inside of your body every minute of every day. But alas, this can be remedied. You can be rid of it."

"Not sure I follow."

"If you willingly give up the Black Womb and someone else, at the same time, willingly takes it, I can surgically remove it from you. I can relieve you of your curse."

"How?"

"In the years since that lowly security guard Abner Jacobs was injured, I have become a man of science. With the help of Engen scientists, I mastered the darkness. Even found a way to purify it and all other diseases from unborn children, thus producing my genetic Adam and Eve."

"Genblade and Spider." Xander's eyes widened as he looked over at the two assassins as they kissed.

"But they were incomplete, missing organs. It created artificial ones for their use, but they were still inferior."

"So you strip mined your victims... and mine... to put their organs into these two?" He had to strain the word 'mine' out of his lips.

"Yes. My goal is to have them reproduce. To create a new, perfect society, under a new god. Me."

"You're sick."

He laughed. "You don't know the half of it," he coughed. It was sick, like he was throwing up a lung.

"Something wrong?"

Electricity jolted through the shackles. "Quiet. Anyway, I finally got the last thing I needed for my children. Or, more appropriately, for their children. Ovaries."

"Sara."

Spider smiled at him. "Mmm. I can feel how much she wanted you to touch them, Xander. To taste them."

Xander lowered his head, forcing his eyes not to well up with tears.

"Yes. You should be proud. Your friend will live on in Spider's children."

He processed this. "But, I don't understand. There were way more organs than you needed. And what do you need Black Womb for?"

"Will you give the creature up?"

Xander thought about it. Hadn't he done enough harm? Like the guy said, he couldn't control this thing. He couldn't even restrain it. This guy, whoever he was, he had already melded it into life. "Okay."

Genblade walked over and cut Xander across the stomach.

Xander's back arched and he screamed in pain. Blood flowed from the wound which had already been opened too many times this night. The blood ran down his legs, mixing with the red film the Black Womb had left behind.

Then, finally, the man came out of the darkness.

He was in pieces, no part of his form whole. His head was only half there, a line having been ripped down his nose and dug out as if somebody had taken a shovel to the left side of his head. His mouth didn't end, it just melted into the mauled flesh that was his face. There were gaping holes of ripped flesh covering his bald head, giving way to his skull. Blood poured freely from those holes. There was a hunch on his back so huge it rose slightly above his hairline. It had stretched the flesh to the near breaking point and was covered in hideous warts and boils. His ridiculously muscular arms were covered in places where skin just melted away, showing his actual muscles as they rippled. His stomach and rib cage were missing, revealing the convulsing organs within. His heart pumped so fast that there was hardly a space between beats. His legs were much the same as his arms. They were covered in torn laboratory pants, the tears revealing exposed tendons and blisters. He looked like a cross between an Ogre and a corpse.

"Christ. What are you?" Xander asked, astonished.

"Call me Alpha. You see, I needed all those extra organs for myself," he said as he inserted the Womb organ into his lower chest, easy considering it wasn't covered. "You see, I was a guard on duty the day your bitch of a mother saw fit to leave us. She also left us a parting gift. She blew our power generator, killing all of your brothers and sisters that were in stasis. She prevented Engen from ever creating a soldier capable of bringing you back. She truly loved you."

For the first time, Alpha's words felt good. He had always assumed that his mother had abandoned her child out of hatred and bitterness, not circumstance.

"But I was on duty in that sector. She literally blew half of me away. The preservatives in the goop that kept your siblings in stasis kept me alive long enough for Engen scientists to find me and rebuild me. One took me under his wing and taught me everything he knew. He became like a father to me as I became a son to him. By the time my condition was stable, I knew everything I needed to do to rise to the top of the company and get my vengeance on your mother... by killing you."

103

"I still don't get what you need Black Womb for."

"I'm falling apart," he said, gesturing toward himself. "The Womb's healing capabilities, which I saw fit to test in your battles with Genblade and Spider (hence the crucifixion), will heal me. It will meld all of my stolen body parts into one ... my own."

Even as he spoke, Alpha's face began to flow like liquid, reforming itself into a normal one. A thin covering of skin formed over his exposed stomach, then getting thicker and thicker. His muscles covered over with flesh as blood flowed from his mouth and ears. Black blood. The substance oozed over him as he laughed, deep and hysterical. When he was covered, a large jaw formed that, when opened, stretched down to his chest and displayed a full ten rows of jagged, yellow teeth. His eyes were gigantic and red, meaning that he was in complete control. "Alpha lives."

It was all Xander could do to keep from urinating in his pants. His gut was slowly closing itself as a final gift from the now absent Black Womb. His clothes were splattered in blood and vomit. His eyes were filled with tears, but more than that, they were full of hatred.

"Now you understand, boy. The cycle is complete. And I can finally offer an end to your suffering." He snapped his fingers. "Spider, do with him as you will. Genblade, you're with me."

Genblade paused, clenching a fist and stepping closer to Xander, before finally turning and obeying his master.

Spider stood over him, smiling.

Xander was fully content with letting her kill him. He had done enough damage. It was time to let him rot in hell, in peace. He lay on the floor and stared upward at Spider. He closed his eyes as she drew her sword and waited for sweet, sweet oblivion... until he heard that harsh, rough voice cut through his ears.

"You know," Genblade said as he walked toward the door. "You can't start a new, more powerful civilization without wiping out the old one. Out with the old, in with the new, and all that crap."

Alpha snapped his fingers, and Genblade followed him out the doorway.

Xander stared at the door for a moment, then let his head fall again. He clicked his burned, bleeding tongue against the roof of his mouth as Genblade's words sunk in, ignoring the pain it caused.

"So that Spider and Genblade can produce a new era in humanity, they'll have to obliterate this era," Xander whispered to himself.

There were still so many people alive that he cared about. Mike, Cathy, his Mother and Father, Derek.... They would all be wiped out. Along with everyone else on earth.

"And I just gave Alpha the power to do it."

Spider swung her sword down.

Xander felt something twitch within his brain. That tiny spark he'd kept hidden from the world from long before Alpha entered his life, the part of him that kept him after Sara and telling himself that tomorrow would be better. Even though Sara was gone and tomorrow would never be better than yesterday, that part of him was still alive. He clapped his hands together and caught the blade with his palms. "Sorry lady, but no more blood goes on my hands tonight."

He flipped up onto his feet and turned to face Spider, pointing her sword at her. She reached behind her and pulled out her second blade, then lunged forward, slicing at the air around him.

He looked down and saw she had cut the fabric of his shirt above his heart. He allowed himself a small sigh of relief, then swung back in retaliation.

She did a back flip to avoid the hit, landing on her hands. She pushed off with her palms, doing another flip and landing on her feet again, making the whole thing look effortless. Xander stood his ground.

He remembered all of the times he had fought Mike in Marble Mutant Super Heroes. He'd pick Obsidian (because he's *Obsidian*, of course) and Mike' d always pick Stone Spider. Obsidian had the claws and all of these cool moves like 'dark rage' and 'abyss x'... but he'd never get a chance to use them. As soon as he got anywhere near Mike's Stone Spider, he'd start to cream him using 'ultimate spider', where Stone Spider just whipped around the screen, hitting Obsidian hundreds of times as he went. Stone Spider's strength always relied on the fact that he was so fast and so agile, that anytime you got anywhere near him, he'd have you. Just like Spider. If he went near her in this weakened state, she'd slice him up like a sausage. He'd have to use a tactic he learned while fighting Mike: *wait for the opponent to come to you.*

He stared at her and she stared back, both of their swords ready to draw first blood.

She jumped at him again, but this time he was ready. He lifted his arms and let her pass by him. Her sword nicked his side and he cringed. It was so much more painful now, with the knowledge that without Black Womb, that one slice could be lethal. He turned around and stabbed at her. His sword punched through the skin of her thigh.

"Ahh!" she cried, buckling a little to one side. "You can't do this. You are an impotent dog waiting to be put down."

He hopped backward, widening the space between them. "In case nobody ever told you, Spider... every dog has his day."

She glared at him, applying pressure to her wound for a moment. There was hatred in her eyes as she realized he had gotten the better of her. She stood straight, raised her sword, and in one swift motion she threw it at his head.

It missed, zooming past his ear and digging itself into the pavement. He turned to watch it go and when he turned back, she was almost on top of him. He quickly raised his sword to deflect her attack, but it was too late.

Her fist smacked hard against the side of his face, causing the skin to split.

He fell to the pavement, skinning his joints. As the flesh pulled away from his knees, he ground his teeth so hard that a chunk of his left molar snapped off and bounced down his throat.

She picked up his sword and lunged at him with it. He rolled to the side, her blade slicing into the pavement. When she tried again, he rolled back to where he had started. He looked up at her as she raised her blade high above her head. He kicked out with both legs, smacking into both her kneecaps. She fell forward slightly and he ran to the wall and scooped at her sword handle, trying desperately to pull it from the concrete. He braced himself against the wall with one foot and he yanked on the sword violently, struggling against the stone that held onto it. He glanced over his shoulder and saw that she was rapidly recovering, even trying to stand. The wall finally gave and the sword slid into his hands. He gripped it firmly and turned to face her. Their swords itched for the other's flesh. He lowered his to the ground, until the very tip scraped against the blood-smeared concrete.

-tink!-

-tink-. Against the pavement. Xander smiled as Spider's eyes grew wide. She kept her focus on him, using all the training her mind had ever absorbed.

-tink-. -tink-. -tink-. -tink-.

Her eyebrow started to twitch as the instinct to look down began to over-whelm her. She calmed herself, breathing deeply. -tink-. Slow, rhythmic breath. -tink-. Her eye twitched to the side, only for a moment.

Xander smirked, enjoying the use of his enemy's tactics against them.

Finally she gave in to temptation and looked at the source of the sound.

When she looked back at Xander, he was gone.

She stared out into the darkness surrounding her. Slowly, the hatred in her eyes faded away to something else: fear. She began slashing at the darkness wildly, screaming as she did so. She stopped in the centre of the room, the light shimmering down her long hair. She stared wide-eyed into the darkness.

She twirled around, then back again - always convinced that he was behind her. Sweat dotted her brow and traveled down in itchy trails as she fought to keep it out of her eyes, scanning the darkness wildly for any motion.

"Where are you!?" she bellowed into the black, panic coming over her. As powerful as she was, she looked small and fragile now, the way a tree looks massive but a single leaf like nothing at all.

Light bathed the room for a quick moment and she thought she heard a door close.

She spun around to face it, her blade in front of her.

The window in the door stared at her like one great luminescent eye pinning her in place. Her breath was still tight in her chest and her hair clung to her face, which was now drenched in a fresh smattering of panic sweat. She didn't know where it had come from, but she could feel the chill of it on her skin and the salt of it on her lips.

She tried to hold the blade in front of her steady, but it wavered as adrenaline shook her nerves until her arm quivered. The blade wavered back and forth like a tuning fork.

And there was quiet.

She let out a slow sigh of relief and lowered the sword.

"Fuck," she cursed, then stormed toward the door after him.

-click-

She turned around and bumped right into Xander.

He plunged the sword into her. She let out a small, almost inaudible yelp.

Her head fell forward onto the nape of his neck, and he could see the sword protrude from her back.

Her mouth and eyes opened wide in a look of pure shock. He removed the sword and laid her carefully onto the pavement floor. Blood gushed from her open wound and she stared up at her killer. Her mouth opened as if she was about to say something, then closed, her lip gloss shining in the intense light. Her eyes gazed upward, then they rolled into her head.

Xander stepped into the darkness. Finding the door, he exited the room, sliding his sword along the floor as he went.

In another part of the building, Genblade and Alpha walked toward their destination. Suddenly, alarms began blaring from everywhere.

Alpha looked downward, as if briefly mourning. "You know what this means."

Genblade's eyes filled with disappointment. "That the Black Womb has bested Spider."

Alpha slammed him against the stone wall, pressing his arm against his neck. "Never! Never call him that AGAIN! I am the Black Womb now! Do you hear me?"

"Yes, Master," Genblade said quickly, avoiding angering his creator anymore. He did a small bow as Alpha let him go. "I am sorry, Master. It will not happen again."

"Go, Genblade. Stop 08276 from ruining my plans. Do whatever it takes."

"Yes, Master," Genblade replied, pulling at his shirt.

He turned and jogged back down the corridor the way they had come.

Alpha turned to face a door marked REACTOR and walked in.

Alarms ringing in his ears and electric surges shooting up his side from where Spider had cut him, Xander ran up the halls in a constant state of pain and confusion, not even knowing if he was headed in the right direction. He came to a four-way intersection and tripped, despite all his attempts to keep his steady pace. He fell to his knees. Pain shot through them as the spots where he had skinned them became irritated again. He clenched his teeth to fight back a yelp and suddenly, the alarms just... stopped. He stood up and turned slowly, looking in each of the three directions and back the way he came.

Out of the corner of his left eye, he thought he saw something.

When he looked down that hallway, it was gone. Something ran past the hallway in front of him. He felt the breeze of speed as the person passed by. A cackle of insane laughter echoed through the hallways, making it impossible to tell which direction it came from.

"Genblade," Xander said under his breath. He raised his sword to eye-level, prepared for the oncoming battle. Beads of sweat began to form on his scalp as his eyes darted from hallway to hallway, trying to catch a glimpse of his predator. Then he remembered the words Cathy once used for predators:

'They're just people, like you or me. I have this dream, where I'm supposed to be

some kind of protector. But I always fail to protect the prey from the predator. I think it had something to do with a past life.' She giggled. 'Not that I believe in that. So, anyway, the only way you could ever rise above the predator is to become the predator. Learn to think as he thinks and you'll know his move ten moves before he makes it. Just like in chess. Not that you'd know anything about chess, the way you and Mike are always wrapped up in that bloody video game. I swear by all that's holy, someday I'll take a baseball bat to that machine-'

And the answer came to him. It was cliché, but: it takes one to know one. He had to become that which he hated most: Genblade. And to his own surprise, he actually found himself thinking, *if I were a savage, disgusting, born and bred killer, where would I be?* The answer dawned upon him like the sun dawns upon the earth each morning. *I'd be behind me.*

Xander jabbed his sword under his arm without even looking. His eyes bulged with delight as it connected, producing that same subtle tug that Spider's flesh had.

He retracted it and turned around to face Genblade. "You killed the woman I loved."

Genblade glared down at him, removing his double blade from its straps. "And you killed the woman I loved."

They circled each other for a moment. The tension hung in the air as each combatant weighed what the other had said. Xander shuddered at the thought that he and Genblade might as well have been opposite sides of the same coin. He raised his sword, which was now tarnished with the blood of both Spider and Genblade. The new Adam and Eve. Sweat bubbled from each opponent, each waiting for the other to make a move. Finally, Genblade struck. He lashed out at Xander, cutting him across the chest. The sword dug deep, clawing at the bone. Within seconds, blood had soaked through the entire chest of his shirt. Shoots of pain ran up and down Xander every few seconds, but it wasn't constant, making it impossible to tune out.

He turned to retaliate, but found that he was already on top of him. Genblade's blade came across Xander's jaw like quicksilver, slicing at the mouth and causing him to bleed violently. It hurt to breathe. All the while he struggled to remember the words that Cathy had said. *To beat him, I have to become him.* Genblade put his arm around Xander's neck, embracing him in a headlock. He drew back his sword, preparing to plunge it through his trunk. *To beat him, you must become him.* Was he a killer like Genblade? He'd killed, now not only as Black Womb, but also as Xander Drew. Did that make him any better? Or worse?

No! his mind screamed. Twisting in Genblade's grip, he brought his knee to his side. Genblade doubled over, winded from the unexpected attack. Xander drew back his own sword and in one swift motion he sliced him across the shoulder. Genblade pulled back his own sword, then dropped it from pain. The shoulder wound would not allow him to lift his own weapon in defense. Xander sliced him across the chest, making a deep incision. Blood ran freely from the wound. Xander was about to make a shot to the jaw when Genblade tackled him, using what was obviously his last iota of energy. They both flew into the concrete wall and Xander bumped his head on it. He could hear his skull crack under the pressure as Genblade lay into him with a series of stabs with his dagger. He punched three holes into Xander's torso before Xander finally kicked him off, sending him flying into the other wall.

Genblade was unconscious. *Helpless.*

Xander picked up his sword and pressed it against his enemy's neck.

"You killed the woman I love. But I did the same to you. Does that make me the same as you, Genblade?" He paused for a second, twirling his blade. For a brief moment, he thought he saw Sara reaching out to him.

"No," he said, throwing the sword aside. "Nothing can bring Sara back. There's been enough blood spilled this day."

Then he gazed up the corridor that Genblade had come from.

"Almost."

๙๙

The room marked REACTOR was impossibly large and circular, like the inside of some giant dome. It was bordered by metal catwalks and stairways, some of which dropped off to nowhere or led back onto themselves, like something out of a M.C. Escher painting. In the centre of it all was a giant sphere made of metal plates of varying colours and qualities, some rusted beyond belief and others new and shimmering. One arm of the catwalk lead to it, and where they met there was a large control panel made up of gaggles of wires and turning parts. What had once been new and sophisticated was now crumbling and falling apart, patched up with stolen parts... much like the man who had done the patching. There were three car batteries wired into its side and long spirals of clear blue cable connecting one side of the terminal to the other. Dimmer switches and gearshifts had replaced buttons, and near the centre there was a CD player held tight to it with Bondo.

The centre of the sphere glowed nuclear green, so bright that it could barely be looked at.

Alpha stood in front of it and laughed quietly to himself.

"You're insane," Xander said from the doorway. "It's over. Your perfect world can't exist without your perfect mother. Give it up."

Alpha turned to face him. "It's funny that it should end this way. The same way it began nearly twenty years ago with your mother and I." Alpha raised his hand. Two long, black claws protruded from each wrist. "Interesting. It appears that the Womb's abilities vary from person to person." He lunged at Xander, claws outstretched. Xander barely managed to dodge it. "You're too late anyway," he laughed, cocking his head toward the reactor.

Xander turned and saw red numbers flashing on the control station's screen. It looked like it had been lifted from an old clock radio. They were counting down, and were fast approaching the minute mark.

"The core is set to expose itself. The Womb will allow me to survive that blast, but not you... and not anyone in that pathetic town of yours."

Alpha jumped toward Xander, propelled by powerfully elastic legs. He flew through the air, growling deep in his throat. Xander was barely able to jump out of the way. Alpha's claws tore at his flesh, causing blood to splatter onto the walls. Xander landed on a metal walkway that led to the reactor. He got up, holding his side and started a limped run for the control panel.

0:59

Alpha turned to face him and saw what he was trying to do. With one fluid motion, his body stretched so that it was in front of Xander, towering over him. He was all that stood between Xander and the timer. Alpha slashed at him again, this time ripping through his stomach. There was a gaping hole there now, he could feel it pulsing and seeping. Could feel the blood splashing down onto his legs. He drew back to punch Alpha, but he caught the attack in his palm. Alpha squeezed on Xander's fist, blood running from his knuckles. Then with one quick heave, he threw Xander back against the wall.

0:40

Blood gushed from a cut on his head as he tasted the coppery tang of it in his mouth. He spit out a tooth onto the metal floor. Beads of sweat began to roll down his face as the reactor powered up. He opened his eyes to see Alpha crouching in front of him. He opened his mouth, showing his monstrously pointed fangs. Alpha jumped at him with mouth open wide, biting down on Xander's leg. He screamed in terror as the creature's many rows of teeth acted like a chainsaw on the flesh and bone. He kicked at Alpha with his free leg and finally managed to beat him off. Alpha drew back a bit, growling.

0:20

Xander felt like giving up. Giving in to the monster before him. His guts in his arms, his blood on the ground... it was his time. He let out a final breath. Then, he thought of her. Of Sara. Of a conversation they had had once.

CHAPTER TEN: OUT

Xander lay on the ground, broken and beaten by Grendel, who was Sara's current boyfriend.

"When are you going to stop doing this?" she had asked him, using his shirt to wipe a bit of blood from his lip.

He looked up at her, smiling. "I guess when I start winning fights."

"Not that," she giggled, wiping more blood from his forehead. "This. Chasing after every boy I go out with like some... jealous father."

"Oh," Xander said, looking downward. I guess when you start going out with reasonable guys."

"What do you mean?"

"Gee, I wonder. Grendel, Derek, Sud, Tommy, Jamie, Travis, Cecil... the list goes on. Guys that are... Okay, but they don't deserve you. You deserve someone special. Someone who'll treat you right and make you feel good and... and not look at you like you're an object. You're better than you think you are, y'know. You deserve better."

She leaned in and kissed him on the cheek. That was the nicest thing anyone ever said to me." She smiled. "Make me a promise."

"Anything."

"Don't ever give up."

"Huh?"

"Don't ever stop protecting me. And when I finally do find that guy you were talking about, protect someone else. The world needs a protector, Xander."

"I promise."

"Don't ever give up

"Don't ever give up

"Don't ever give up

"Don't ever give up…"

"I won't," he said aloud. As Alpha lunged at him, Xander reached into his pocket and pulled out one of Genblade's daggers. He thrust out, giving it every ounce of raw power he had left. The blade sunk deep into Alpha's right side, then ripped across to the left. As Alpha ripped at Xander's back, Xander reached his hand into Alpha and ripped it out. The pure essence of the Black Womb. That black and gray, smoldering lump of organ.

Alpha's eyes went wide for an instant, before shrinking back into small white marbles in the middle of his face.

The blackness lost its hold on him all at once and fell from of his body, splashing through the grates of the catwalk and down into the nothingness below. His toothless, cancerous mouth took a deep gasp before he went limp and fell to the floor. His stomach, muscles and skull were all exposed again. As Xander watched, each one seemed to sputter and die on their own.

Wincing, Xander pried open the edges of the wound that Alpha had slashed across his stomach and pushed the Womb organ inside. Black tendrils spat out of its porous surface and latched onto his large intestine, pulling itself into place and pouring out so much blackness that it flowed freely from the opening in Xander's side and out onto his legs.

His heartbeat doubled, then tripled, then began to beat so fast that it sound more like static in his ears than a drum. Only it wasn't his heart, at least not his human one. He could feel it pulsing and moving in his side, bending and kneading itself to spread more and more. And, as horrific as it was, it somehow it felt... *right*.

Black liquid began to pour from his mouth and nose, falling down onto his chest and building there a quart at a time until it covered his entire body.

"Black Womb lives."

0:10

He ran across the metal walkway to the timer and opened the hatch on it, revealing the mess of wires inside. He stared at it blankly for a moment.

0:09

He pointed a claw at the red wire, then shrugged it off.

0:08

Blue wire. He inched to it with his talon, then decided against it.

0:07

Green wire. *No*, he thought, *it's never the green wire.*

0:06

Frustration built and Xander could feel Black Womb begin to take over.

111

Alpha leaned against the wall, a wry grin prying across his lips. "The blue wire!" he yelled, before finally succumbing to his wounds and slamming against the floor. Blood oozed from his lips.

Black Womb ripped at the slender cable with his hooked claw.

0:05

"Did it stop?" he wondered aloud.

0:04

"Why didn't it stop?"

0:03

He looked back in horror at Alpha, almost certain he could see the deranged man's grin, even in death.

0:02

Hope Alpha was right about Black Womb being able to survive this...

0:01

The radioactive rods in front of Xander exposed themselves, their eerie green glow filling the room. He felt his flesh start to burn as the liquid surrounding his brain boiled within his skull and his teeth rattled, trying to shake themselves free of his gums. He closed his eyes as they started to bubble and crack.

Behind him Alpha's body exploded, erupting in blue flame, then green, until eventually there was nothing left to the madman.

Here goes nothing, he thought to himself, as he felt even the Womb-skin begin to peel back, revealing the tender, weak form of Xander Drew underneath. Reaching out with both hands, he pressed down on the reactor rod.

All around him, the walls were cracking, steel and wood falling down around him as the building's foundation became weaker and weaker, getting ready to implode upon itself.

⋏⟨⋏

Outside, police cars were surrounding the building. Suddenly, it began to fall into itself, its centre crumbling away one piece at a time. There was a roar like thunder and a single wave of intense heat as the chunks of falling metal and plaster got larger and larger, crashing onto the floor inside. Long cracks started to spread their way up from the foundation, jumping from one direction to another as if they had a mind of their own.

"Oh, my God," one of the officers said in a hushed whisper, as the building started to emit a soft glow.

With a force that made the earth all around them shake, all sides of the building crumpled inward almost in unison, as if someone had crumpled it up like a ball of paper.

There were screams and hollers as officers tried desperately to shield themselves from the ensuing dust cloud it spat out in its wake. A few cars in front were hit, causing them to erupt in a blaze of fire.

Tim stopped his car and got out, shielding his eyes against the heat and dust. When it stopped, the once majestic building was nothing but rubble. He stared at it for a moment. "Damn. Too late."

Inside Tim's car, Cathy fell into Mike's arms, crying uncontrollably. He put

112

his arms around her, as he looked in hatred at the smouldering pile of rubble. Then his expression changed. He smiled. "Everyone... Look!"

A board fell over in the debris, revealing a small pocket created by the blast. Xander Drew stepped out of it. He was covered in soot, bleeding from every crevice in his body, torn both physically and mentally, limping, shocked beyond human comprehension and overall looked like grim death. It was Xander, just the same.

"Xander!" Cathy cried, getting out of the car and running toward him with Mike not far behind. They embraced him, tears of joy streaming down all three faces. They fell to the ground, kneeling on the wet soil, still embraced.

Xander leaned in and kissed Cathy on the forehead. "It's alright."

Suddenly, there was more movement from the tattered building, a loud crash.

"I'll KILL you for this!" Genblade screamed as he burst from the smelting pile of rubble. He pointed his sword at Xander and was about to throw it directly at his head, when...

-click- -click - click- click -click- -click - click-

Fifty handguns trained themselves on Genblade at once. Red laser sights dotted along Genblade's forehead and chest. The killer's eyes moved through the crowd, searching out Tim White. He found him, found the hatred in the policeman's eyes. He continued looking through the crowd, and found what he was looking for. Xander got up from the warm embrace that he, Cathy, and Mike had been sharing. He stood straight and rigid, glaring at his back at his enemy. Genblade's sneer moved slowly into a smile as he mouthed the words:

'It'll never be over.'

Xander didn't flinch.

Genblade seemed to love it. He released his grip on the double -sided blade. It fell to the ground with a final

-clink-

Genblade smiled at Xander once more as he put his hands above his head.

EPILOGUE

"Let us pray," Reverend Robert Gallagher said, overlooking the coffin.

Xander would have loved for it to be an open casket, to be able to say good-bye to her one last time, but the damage Genblade did was so extensive they had to leave it closed. The emotion of the situation nearly made the Black Womb surface, but he held it in.

The priest continued, "Lord, we gather to lay to rest your daughter, Sara. We ask that you welcome her into your heavenly kingdom and give repose to her soul. Through Christ, our lord, Amen."

I've been up all night trying to write... something *that could express what I'm feeling. Every time I tried, it kept coming out like a confession instead of a eulogy. But how can I possibly do Sara justice with just a few pages of scribbles soaked with a flood*

of tears? What can I say to these people to even remotely portray to them what Sara was and how much she meant to me?

"I've asked Alexander Drew, Sara's long time friend, to say a few words about the young woman we all held such a special place in our hearts for. Mister Drew?"

It's vulgar - playing the role of the helpless boy. I caused her death.

I feel like the worst kind of liar.

Xander got up from his seat in the second row and started toward the pulpit, a piece of paper shaking uncontrollably in his hands. He walked over to Reverend Gallagher, who put an assuring hand on his shoulder before stepping aside. The simple empathetic contact sent shivers throughout his body. Deep down inside him, the womb organ twitched once, as if to shake back.

"Hello," he started, "this may take a while." He cleared his throat, staring out into the crowd. It was filled with friends, family, classmates, relatives... "Ahem. Um... Sara was..."

He stopped.

"Sara was..."

He looked up from his paper, tears streaming down his face. *No. There are no words.* He walked over to the coffin and placed his hand upon its white surface. It felt cold and inhuman, but he still felt her in it. As if she were connected to it in some way. "I'll miss you."

There are no words.

Then he left the church with tears in his eyes.

(ʌ‿ʌ)

As soon as Xander stepped through the door into the cool night air, the Womb overpowered him, black ooze flowing over him.

I'll never live it down. Sara's death can never be justified. But this I know: I'm going to spend the rest of my life making up for it.

A few blocks away, a mugger clubbed a young girl over the head, smiling as he rolled up his sleeves, revealing a red letter 'T' tattooed on his right arm. "... come 'ere, sweet thing..."

Genblade plead guilty to all the murders, even the ones that I committed. I guess his sense of honor realized that I beat him and that I should get something for it.

"... no.... please, stop."

I'll never stop, Sara. I'll keep my promise, protect the innocent from the scum. All the scum. Be it big like Alpha or small like Grendel. They're all guilty.

"... please... just stop."

If you're innocent...

"...stop..."

You're hurt...

"...please..."

Or you're scared...

A black figure dropped from the sky and kicked the mugger in the face, sending him sprawling to the ground.

I'll be there.

BOOK TWO

TRANSFORMATIONS IN PAIN

SHE RAN

She turned the corner quickly, scraping her shoulder against the brick.

Her breath came in quick, labored pants as her feet slammed against the pavement one after the other, displacing mounds of gravel and mud as she went. It had rained the night before, and the asphalt was slick and wet beneath the soles of her feet. Fighting to maintain her balance, she turned around to see how far she had gone. Her auburn hair caught on her eyelashes as it whipped around her head, making it hard to see.

They were still back there. She couldn't see them now, but she could hear them. Could hear their puffs of breath and their own footfalls, as well as the steady stream of curses that one of them kept up in constant supply between bouts of a hacking smoker's cough. The other one was stronger, his legs pumping like pistons. The sounds of his heels slamming against the street were louder than the other one. He was closer, but it was hard to tell exactly how close because he remained deathly silent as he advanced upon her.

It had started about three blocks back. Every time she had stopped, they had stopped. Every time she sped up, they sped up. She hadn't been sure what to think at first, then she'd seen the knife sticking out of one of their belts, only partially obscured by his red-and-gold sport jacket. Her eyes had lit up and felt twice their normal size. For a moment it had been all she could do to stare at it, glimmering against the faded denim.

She turned away fast, pushing some hair out of her face to try and hide the fear in her eyes and make her exit seem casual. Whether or not they had been fooled they still followed, keeping roughly ten meters between themselves and the girl at all times.

She turned down Laird Street, the way she always did on her way home from school, then dropped her knapsack and broke into a run. When her two pursuers turned the corner a few seconds behind her they found that their ten meter buffer had become closer to thirty, and took off running after her.

Her chest heaved fire now, her stomach clenching in continuous bursts of agony as she cursed the potato chips she'd had for lunch. She could feel their jagged little edges digging into the lining of her gut, tearing at her from the inside out as her abdomen contracted with each step she forced out of her body.

She'd spent the latter part of her last semester skipping Phys Ed class in favor of hanging out with the boys in the smoking section or text-messaging her cousin. Anything to not have to be covered in sweat for the rest of the day, in a school where the air conditioners seemed to be mostly for decoration.

As a stitch developed in her lower left side and her legs began to feel numb and rubbery, she began to wish that she had been a little more health conscious.

She felt blood trickle down her arm from where she'd scraped it. She bit her lip as she pumped her arms and focused all her attention on the street corner just one building length away from her. After that, she would be on her street. Not long after that, she'd be home. She'd be safe.

She heard a loud curse close behind her, but dared not turn around to see. It was the one word she'd never say herself, even in the worst of situations, and just the sound of it curdled in her ears until it was almost all she could hear.

She tried not to think about it as she closed her eyes tight and poured on the steam, willing her legs to pump harder and faster than they ever had before. She didn't know what they wanted with her, but she knew she didn't want to find out anytime soon. She heard something in her knee pop like when her Biology teacher cracked his knuckles. Fresh pain shot up her leg and into her spine, burying in deep and making a home there.

When she opened her eyes again, she was almost at the curb. She could see her next-door neighbor's house, dissected by the wall she was about to pass. The windows were dark and the blinds were closed tight, their usually inviting porch now looking cold and desolate. Someone had taken all of the flowers inside and she realized, strangely, that they were on vacation. She didn't know why that occurred to her at that moment, only that it did.

Behind her, one of the footsteps stopped and was replaced by very loud breathing and panting. Without even turning around, she could see the thinner of her two pursuers hunched over with his hands against his knees. He was trying to catch his breath, sweat getting caught in his short brown hair. The other set of footsteps just got louder and faster, as if he had only been moving at that speed so that his friend could keep up. If they were any indication, he'd be on her in seconds.

She turned the corner, ready to dart across the road and into her driveway faster than she ever had before, hoping that there were no cars coming. Instead her nose crashed into something hard and she fell backward. Her backbone slammed against the pavement. She felt her entire body quake with the sudden impact, aching from the base of her skull right down to her ankles.

The man she had bumped into also fell to the ground and looked to have skidded out his elbow in the process.

Stunned, she wasn't fully aware of the passage of time until she felt two massive hands clamp down on her shoulders like vice grips. They brought her to her feet.

"Get the car," the man behind her said with a high-pitched voice. It was not the man that was holding her -- he was the one that had lost his breath. By the sounds of things, he still had yet to regain it.

The lanky man in front of her smirked as he rose to his feet. Then turned and looked over his shoulder at the row of houses behind him.

"No!" she screamed as the man who held her pulled her close. He forced her to walk with him toward the nearby alley. She tried to hit and kick at her capture, but it seemed to have as much effect as hitting solid stone. She continued to scream even after they dragged her away. Eventually the screaming stopped, long before her terror was over.

It occurred to her that nothing would ever be the same again. Someone had told her once that every time that happens in life, it was like a caterpillar changing into a butterfly. A transition and transformation into something different.

This time, she thought, it was a transformation... in pain.

CHAPTER ONE: CONFESSION

He awoke on the floor, his body shaking with shock as all his senses seemed to scream at him at once. At first he wasn't quite sure where he was, something that happened so often lately that he was almost getting used to not being used to anything he saw anymore.

Everything around him was red and his eyes stung terribly, like he'd gotten twigs in them as he always did as a child while running through the forest behind his house. He didn't understand why at first. He blinked several times. When the dark crimson didn't fade, he started to become afraid. Sweat dotted his brow and tears welled up behind his eyes, making them hurt even more. He reached up with his right index finger to stop the salt water from spilling onto his cheeks and was surprised to see that red goop, not unlike the type he used in his Creepy Crawlers oven as a child, had come off on his finger. It hung there for a moment, dangling and dripping a viscous fluid before he realized what it was.

It was blood.

A congealed layer of blood covering his entire body, naked beneath the covers. Now that that much was gone and he could see, his room and everything in it was clear to him again and he knew where he was. He saw his television propped up in the corner – the remote on top of it meaning his father had been upstairs watching the game again at some point yesterday afternoon. He saw his computer, which was the top of the line with all the best video capabilities and nothing to put those capabilities to good use since the screen had been blown out a week before. He was convinced that the air around it still stunk of carbon monoxide and charred plastic.

He wiggled his toes along his thick, matted carpet that reeked of a thousand odors absorbed into its fabrics, mostly from Kraft dinners and other delicacies that his mother had begged him not to eat upstairs. And he saw his window: his window that looked out upon --

He stopped, steeling himself against that direction. Angered and frustrated, he turned toward his padlock-covered door and started tearing at his face to get the congealed blood off of it. He unwrapped it in a continuous strand around his body, like his father unwrapping a meal covered in shrink-wrap. He tried to think of those meals now; badly breaded fried chicken. Steak and mashed potatoes. Or something. Or anything. Anything to get his mind off that window and what lay behind it.

Because Alexander 'Xander' Drew could pretend that he was a normal fifteen year old kid, just like any other person living in Coral Beach, Maine. He could fool himself into believing that he didn't know where he was when he woke up (and did so every day) because in truth he wanted to wake up to anything but these four walls again for the 5,567th day in a row. He could even make believe that the layer of blood that he was now tucking away was normal for him, and that it didn't really matter. He could convince himself of all these things... but for all his strengths, he could not bring himself to look out his bedroom window.

Past the moldy-green curtains, past the tall evergreen that his father had planted between his house and hers in an attempt to keep them from spying on one another late at night, that they'd climbed instead and where he told her he loved her. Past the high picket fence that he'd hopped over and past the shit-coloured shingles on one side of her house, opposite the off-white that reflected the new morning light on every other side. That was where he didn't want to look.

That was Sara Johnson's bedroom window.

Sara Johnson. The angel of light that had filled even the darkest corners of his soul with hope. That was how he had described her back when she was alive and when he thought he had a soul. When he thought he was alive and mortal. Before he had killed her. Ten days ago, two men had ripped his world apart from one end to the other: Abner Jenkins and Adam Genblade, otherwise known as Alpha and Genblade. Two people that looked as though they'd been born out of Shelly or Stevenson's minds, with their garishly filed smiles and eyes that pumped hatred into you like fuel into a tank. Then again, he couldn't say much anymore. His own face, his real face, was something much worse.

Adam and Alpha had revealed to him the truth about what he was, about what he was made for. He was a killer. A soulless, guiltless killer designed to jump start humanity's evolution by slaughtering the weak to bring about a new age. He'd been rescued at a young age and had grown up here, in a quiet place in Maine that was barely able to classify itself as a city, but was more like a not-so-small small town. Something had set him off a month back and his real face, the Black Womb, had emerged for the first time and killed everything he'd ever loved. It had killed her, taken her light away. In her place, the Womb had embedded itself, filling his heart with black and pain and blood.

He stopped walking seven inches from his door. He closed his eyes tight and made one last wish for it all to just go away, sighing a desperate prayer for it to work this time. When he opened his eyes again, it hadn't worked. Of course it hadn't worked. Sara wouldn't be shimming up the storm drain or scuffing her knees as she got in through the window to wake him up. He wouldn't have the chance to say, "You spend all your time on your knees anyway" as he often had, much to her chagrin. They wouldn't sneak downstairs and steal his mother's waffles again, and she wouldn't tell him that she loved him.

Not that they'd ever done any of those things anyway, but in the time since her death he'd allowed his mind to wander, imagining conversations that *could* very well have happened if he'd had the courage to start them while she'd been alive.

He gave her one more minute to come in, then unlocked his door with a rusted squeak, turned the handle, and walked out into the light.

Xander stared up at the bus stop in front of him, its metal dented and bent from years of beatings from the harsh Maine winters and the diligence of bored, destructive teenagers. It rattled against its pole as the wind around it picked up, sending a steady and constant rapping sound squealing through the air.

His dark auburn hair baying against the wind, Xander watched the sign fight against its bolts but never really get anywhere.

Lately, he felt much the same way.

His hands were buried deep inside his jeans pockets even though he didn't feel the chill of the breeze. He did not feel it, but he was aware of it. He gave the spearmint gum in his mouth another chew before shifting it back to its place between his cheek and his teeth, still just looking up at the sign and squinting against the rising sun behind it.

The imprint of the sunbeams stayed on his retinas for a moment, an anamorphous blob in the centre of his vision. He heard the mumble of distant speech and clicking heels, but when he turned to see who it was, the purple and yellow blob was still there and blocked his line of sight.

"Xander!" called a familiar voice, one so sweet that it almost left the taste of sugar on your lips when you heard it.

He could now clearly identify two sets of footsteps coming toward him, one keeping its regular pace and one coming at him a little bit faster. Hearing the double-click, he could tell that the faster person was wearing heels. When the wind changed, he caught the scent of orange-oil perfume cascading onto him from afar and now he knew exactly who was coming toward him. In truth, he'd known from the second she said his name.

Catherine Kennessy threw her arms around Xander, hanging off him as she held him close. She'd been doing that a lot over the last few days, ever since Sara had died. It was just another of those reminders that was meant to be pleasant but always ended with him having a bad taste in the back of his mouth.

For his part, Xander forced a smile, but did not squeeze her back or even put his arms around her. They stayed limp at his sides until she was done and she plopped back down in front of him. She had to look up at him, her eyes about a half-foot lower than his. The blurb on his eyes was gone now and he could see all of her soft beauty as it stared up at him. Her shoulder length near-black hair came down straight on either side of her porcelain face, like a frame for her large brown eyes. Her lips were small, red and always glimmering, even when there was no light for them to glimmer off of. She was wearing a black blouse and blue jeans that looked far too big for her. The jeans were fine, but he had never seen her wear black before. It had been the same blouse she had worn to the funeral. Or *funerals*, more appropriately. He hoped that it would not find its way back into her regular wardrobe rotation.

"How are you doing today?" she asked sympathetically, stroking his arm.

A million different answers flooded his mind all at the same time. After a moment he just shrugged and turned his attention back toward the bus stop, avoiding eye contact with his friend.

"I'm fine," he said, when he realized she wasn't going to look away.

She shook her head, having to accept an answer she knew wasn't true but making a mental note to bring it up later. That was what Cathy was, when you boiled away everything else. She had to make sure everyone else's life was going good, even when her own was in shambles around her ears. "What did you do last night?"

Xander got a flash of memory before it was gone again, his face wincing. Again, he didn't answer.

"Me and Mike rented some old movies and stayed up late over at my place. Have you seen Ferris Beuler's Day Off? I think it's really good, but Mike hated it. Thought it was the worst thing he'd ever seen."

Again Xander got caught in a memory, this one clearer than the last. It was of him and Sara sitting next to each other on her couch, munching on popcorn and watching Ferris Beuler riding the parade float and singing at the top of his lungs, with all of the people around him dancing and cheering. He could *see* Sara laughing as if she were the one standing in front of him instead of Cathy. "Never saw it," he said after some hesitation. His voice was almost a whisper.

Michael Harris stepped up behind his girlfriend finally, having taken his time catching up with her. He nodded curtly to Xander, who reciprocated the greeting.

"Lord," Cathy said. She rolled her eyes as she watched the both of them, then smiled. "You two would communicate with just grunts if you could, wouldn't you?"

"We'd use the occasional hand gesture, too," Mike chuckled in defense, raising his hands comically. He laughed as she gave him a little slap on the arm, then turned back to Xander. "Did she ask you to break our little tie about the movie yet?"

Xander just stared at him for a moment, as Cathy explained that he hadn't even seen it. Mike made some kind of remark about that being for the best anyway, but Xander barely heard that. It was like the voices were under water as his mind slipped into a muddy daze and the world around him was pasted on a screen of moist paper towels, ready for him to rip through at any time. There was a prickling feeling on the tips of his fingers as that thought crossed his mind, and he buried them deeper into his pockets.

Mike noticed and shot him a queer glance as he continued talking to Cathy. He stood almost over a head taller than Xander, making even the smallest such gesture have some measure of authority. His light blonde hair had been combed with his fingers that morning and still looked messy from a night spent on Cathy's couch, his clothes ruffled and creased as they clung to his muscular body. He'd been one of the star runners for the Coral Beach Cougars until he'd quit last year, something that he rarely let people forget whenever he could fit it into the conversation. His face was kind and belied the power of his arms and torso, his heart-shaped freckled cheeks always wearing a warm and inviting smile that matched his bright blue eyes. Right now that smile was gone, replaced by a look of concern as he said something to Xander.

Xander shook and snapped out of his daze.

"Dude, are you okay?" Mike repeated, placing a hand on his friend's shoulder.

Xander looked at him and really saw him for the first time in what felt like days. "Yeah," he said, looking from him to Cathy and then back again. "Yeah, I'm fine."

Mike frowned and threw a look at his girlfriend, who pouted her feelings as well. Both of them wanted to pry into what Xander was really feeling as much as he wanted to tell them, but somebody had to make that first step and no one would. "This bus is here," Mike said, settling for giving his friend a heart-felt slap on the back as he turned toward the curb.

Xander turned toward the bright yellow morning sun, finding that it was gone and that he was now in the shade of the large yellow vehicle. He zoned out again, briefly, lost in that solid yellow.

After a moment he took a step back from it, his upper lip curling with fear and disdain.

Cathy turned to him, her hand on the guardrail as she stepped onto the bus. "Xander?" she said finally, not sure of what else to say. There were so many different questions that everything seemed stupid and frivolous.

He took another step away, then turned and started to walk in the other direction. After a few paces he picked up speed. By the time he got to the corner, he was running.

Mike took a single step after him before Cathy stopped him, resting her hand gently on his shoulder. He turned to look at her and when he looked back, Xander was out of sight.

"He'll come to us on his own time," she assured him, before heading onto the bus.

ʎ⟨y⟩ʎ

Ninety minutes later Xander was staring up at two large wooden doors. They were old and at least three inches thick each. He felt dwarfed by the sheer size and magnitude of it all, the building's very presence overwhelming him. It reminded him almost instantly of Engen.

The building itself seemed to rise up out of nowhere. He hadn't really noticed until just now, but the land was perfectly flat for miles in all directions surrounding it. The land sprung up into a grassy hill just to the side of it, with a tall

123

chain-link fence encompassing both the structure and the hill. It was like even the earth was reaching for something.

Twin steeples stabbed at the clouds and had a tendency to melt into the mist on foggy afternoons. Each one was adorned by a brass cross and stain-glass images whose eyes seemed to stare directly into him from their vantage point on the brick wall. He turned and looked at the golden plaque next to the door and read it. The words The Apostle Church were carved into its gold trim.

Deep inside of him, amidst the blood and veins, the true Womb cringed. "Yeah," Xander said aloud. "You would be intimidated by a Holy place, wouldn't you, you sick son of a--"

"My son?" came a voice from behind the door. A small peephole opened and soft, caring eyes peered out. "Are you not well?"

Xander stared into those eyes for a moment. "No," he said finally after a long pause. "I'm... sorry. To disturb you. I thought you were closed this time of day."

The door opened, revealing a kind-looking balding old man smiling warmly at him. His grin complimented his eyes, both of which were accented with laugh lines. His fingers were clasped together near the centre of his chest, their knuckles thick and swollen with arthritis. A purple sash draped down from either side of his neck, the ends embroidered with golden crosses. He didn't just *look* holy, he felt it too. Holy and royal, somehow. His voice was soft and soothing, sending a cold chill through Xander when he spoke. "The doors to the Lord's house are always open, my son," the Reverend said, fanning his arms and making his robe dance. "Come."

Xander stepped inside cautiously, looking from one side of the old church to the other. Every step he made echoed back at him, making him want to cover his ears. There were even more glass people in here, their stares equally as judgmental as the ones outside. Their eyes didn't just see through him, they sliced through him. Despite that, the creepiest things by far were the pews. For all of the times he had been there, he had never seen all of the seats empty before. It looked barren and wrong and far too still.

The Reverend had walked up to an aged table set up near the back room and was currently pouring up two cups of coffee. He motioned for Xander to sit down.

"Isn't this traditionally done at a confession booth?" Xander joked, smirking at the old man.

The Reverend's bushy gray eyebrows lifted. "You have sins to confess?" he asked, almost shocked.

"I'm not what you'd call a religious man."

"That's not what I asked."

Xander sat down. He took his coffee cup in one hand and chanced a sip on the hot liquid. It burned his tongue, and he felt the Womb veer up to repair the damage instantly. His eyes darted around the church nervously, always coming back to the visage of the Son of God upon the cross, hanging dead centre in the archway. He could still feel the spikes in his wrists from his own crucifixion, and felt a new empathy for the man on that tilted x. He looked at the kind old Reverend, who was smiling back at him expectantly, patiently waiting for the young man to speak.

"I can see I'll have to start," the old man laughed. "Shouldn't you be in school?"

Xander smiled, but it was a fake smile. The smile that youth give to older people when they ask questions such as those. "That school's got too many memories. Those old walls talk, y'know?"

"Indeed." He motioned all around him. "As do these walls. Often, late at night, I can hear the echoes of a thousand spirits." He paused, staring Xander in the eye. "Recently, the voices of the dead have gotten louder."

Xander looked down toward his feet. "Yes, they have." There was a pause then while they both sipped on their respective coffees. "I'm having... problems... telling my friends about the events of these past few weeks," he admitted.

The Reverend nodded. "I take it you lost someone close to you."

"Yeah. You don't get much closer than... her."

The Reverend nodded again. "Find guidance in the Lord, my son. He will help you."

Xander took a sip of his java. "I feel like the Lord had abandoned me, Father. I feel like I'm alone."

"Have faith, my son," the man said, touching him on the hand. "The Lord exists in all things. You may not find him here, but rather in a person. A loved one."

Xander took a last sip of his coffee, then put it down onto the table. He got up and began to walk towards the door. "Thank you, Father," he said distantly.

"My son," the Reverend called after him, "do you know what you must do?"

"I do," he nodded.

ʎ×ʎ

Xander crept through the halls of Coral Beach High, trying to keep a low profile. He ducked down to avoid being seen by Principal Shnieder, then quietly made his way into the male washroom. He kept his eyes peeled and constantly on watch for the principal, who was usually on hall patrol this time of day. Toward the end of the week he gave out detention slips like a traffic cop frantically trying to make quota.

"What's up?" came a loud voice from behind a stall.

Xander nearly jumped out of his skin, turning quickly. "Derek!" he shouted, laughing at his own anxiety. He slapped his friend on the back heartily, which was returned. "It's only you."

Derek nodded, smiling. "Only me."

There was an awkward pause between the two as Xander regained his breath. "So," he drawled, pointing casually at Derek. "You got any clue where Cathy is?"

Derek smiled. "Yeah. Biology. Where I'm supposed to be."

125

Xander thought for a minute. "Shit. That's right next to Shnieder's office.

Derek waved his hand, dismissing the notion. "Naw, don't worry. He's letting people off who were friends of... y'know."

Xander nodded. "Oh."

Cathy was concentrating diligently, but if you had asked her the last word she wrote in her notebook she would not have been able to tell you if her life depended on it. She stared blankly at the page before her, and realized that she had replaced several key words in the last sentence with Sara's name. She became disgusted with herself and closed her book, then turned to gaze out the open doorway.

Xander poked his head in, grinning stupidly at her.

She responded in kind, waving her fingers and brushing some hair out of her eyes.

He motioned for her to join him.

She reluctantly looked up at the teacher. "Can I use the washroom, sir?"

He smiled at her, "I certainly hope so."

She frowned miserably as the class laughed. The humor of the situation was lost on her. He motioned for her to leave and as she did, he called after her. "Cathy?"

She turned. "Yes, sir?"

"Tell Mr. Drew that he can't go into the little girls' room with you."

She smiled. "Yes, sir."

The three of them walked down the street in near absolute silence.

Since they had gotten Mike from his physics class, Xander had barely spoken a word to either of them. He was just staring at the cracks in the sidewalk as they passed under his feet, not making eye contact with either of them.

"If we're going to The Factory, we should have brought Derek," Mike said finally, motioning to the building that was just now becoming visible around the corner. He looked disappointed and anguished that he had forgotten about his friend, but still began to pat his pockets to make sure he had some quarters.

"That's... no," Xander stammered, looking in their direction for the first time but still not making eye contact with either. "That's not why we're here."

Cathy sighed. If he had been able to look at her then, Xander would have seen pity resonating toward him from his friend's face. She could see the weight he carried, but not what it was. She knew that Sara was a big part of it... but there was something else, too. Something secret that he carried on his own and she hated him for it. She got in between the two boys, then reached out to touch Xander's chin and force him to look at her.

He jerked away, putting an extra foot between Cathy's path and his own, now walking on the faded grass beside the sidewalk.

"If you're gonna drag us out of class to talk to us, the least you could do is

126

talk to us," she huffed.

Mike chuckled at her exasperation. He leaned in and gave her a small kiss on the temple as they walked. She smiled, then let out a single puff of air by way of a laugh.

They were approaching The Factory's entrance now, its steel door shimmering brightly against the evening sun. At this distance it was easy to hear the baseline thumping over the speakers from within, sending vibrations through the entire building and the ground as well, the pebbles near the door bouncing against the gravel in tune with the beat. Xander eyed the door for a moment and licked his tongue against the front of his teeth the way he often did when he was trying to decide something. He finally turned away from the door and starting to walk around back.

Mike almost stopped in his tracks as he watched his friend move around to the other side of the building, while Cathy followed him with a movement so gracious that anyone observing would have thought that it had been her intended destination all along. After a moment, Mike followed in suit. "Why're we going back here?" he asked, shoving the quarters back down into his pocket.

Cathy turned and gave him a look that he knew from past experience meant 'shut up,' and he did so immediately.

Xander walked a few feet in front of them without so much as a word until he reached a large, smooth rock that was partly overtaken by the foundation of the building and mostly submerged underground. When they were growing up, someone had dubbed it the Old Sitting Stone. The name had stuck, to the point that now most of The Factory's staff referred to it as such. There were old cigarette butts surrounding the rock in a loose semi-circle. He wondered briefly if one of them had belonged to Sara. The thought started a domino effect of images in his mind, which he struggled to force out before turning to face Mike and Cathy. He opened his mouth to speak, then stopped with his jaw hanging open.

After a long moment of silence, Cathy finally spoke up. "Whatever it is, you can tell us," she said in a soothing voice, taking a single step towards him.

"Yeah, man," Mike echoed, trying his best to sound supportive. "You can tell us if you want."

Xander sighed, reaching deep into his jacket pocket. "I want to tell you... I just can't," he said finally, revealing a small but sharp knife and bringing it up to his wrist. "So I'll just have to show you."

Cathy's eyes went wide, her hands immediately cupping over her mouth with shock as Mike moved forward to stop his friend.

He was too late.

Thick red blood started to spew forth from the ripped flesh, some of it spurting out toward Mike but most of it running down Xander's arm and dribbling off of his elbow into a little pool on the ground. A tingly, numb feeling started in his fingertips and worked its way through his entire arm and then out into his chest. It made his whole body feel warm and fuzzy except for his heart, which ached with a cold pain. Each beat felt like trying to move a frozen limb, yet the pain it brought made the heart only beat faster.

"What are you doing?" Cathy screamed, tears starting to flow down her cheeks already. The blood was so thick it reminded her of pancake batter.

Mike batted the knife away from Xander and attempted to put pressure on the wound.

Xander pushed him away, tripping over the sitting stone and falling flat on his back as he did so. He clenched his teeth as his arm began to shake violently, sending gushes of blood everywhere in tiny droplets. "Wait," he managed to say, holding up a hand to Mike to stop him from coming at him again. He started to get dizzy and light headed. As he stared down at the redness that was still flowing out of his arm, he wondered if this had been such a good idea after all.

Then he felt it.

A rumble from the right side of his abdomen that felt very close to the vibration of the baseline coming from The Factory. The feeling cascaded throughout his body as if a small bomb had gone off there, the ripple effect making his whole body shake. He felt his heart slow as his side twitched again, then started to beat all on its own. A migraine started to build behind his eyes as he crunched over in pain, throwing a look at Mike and Cathy to try and get them to keep their distance. His veins all felt like they were going to explode, the way a balloon filled with too much air must feel. He had only experienced this twice before, yet had come to recognize it as though it had always been a part of him.

In many ways, it had been.

When he looked at his wrist again, the red liquid had stopped pouring out of his wrists -- but had been replaced by a thick black tar that didn't spurt or spray. It all flowed down over his arm, but did not drip off of his elbow. Instead it then started traveling up his arm, circling around until it had covered his entire body and was now moving onto his chest.

Mike backed away a step as Cathy's hands fell from her mouth, dangling lifelessly at her sides as she watched the black ooze take her friend over inch by inch, as if it had a mind all its own.

Xander screamed as his jaw seemed to snap free of itself and his eye sockets bent upwards, the pink meat surrounding his eyes visibly popping blood vessels as it was exposed to air. He tried to grit his teeth against the pain but couldn't, the lower row still hanging too low. After a second longer they snapped into place, but farther down than they had been a moment ago, making his face seem more angular than it had been before. The blackness had overtaken his torso almost completely by now, sticking to his body like paint or liquid latex as it began to make its way over his head. He opened his mouth in a silent scream as it finished taking over, several tendrils converging on his face all at once.

For several moments there was nothing. He looked like a statue made of used chewing tobacco, stray remnants of the ooze still sliding off of him onto the ground below his feet.

"Xander?" Cathy said, her voice a hushed whisper.

Suddenly three red slits formed on his face and they opened to reveal two triangular bright red eyes that were slanted on either side and a glowing red mouth filled with dual rows of razor sharp, yellow teeth.

When he opened his mouth to speak, the voice sounded like it were vomited up rather than simply spoken, his entire body shaking with the effort of each syllable. "Black Womb lives."

Mike and Cathy stared silently.

He started to tell them everything. The truth about what their lives had become for the last few weeks. About Adam Genblade's real agenda, about the motive behind the murders that had swept through their town and about the Black Womb. The hardest part, though, was telling them about Sara... and who was really ultimately responsible for her death, along with the deaths of many of their friends.

In the end there was silence, as all parties tried to digest the information, even Xander himself.

After the silence became too much for her to bear, Cathy sighed and walked over to Xander, once again placing her hand on the side of his face to force him to look at her. This time he did not turn away or object in any way, her touch sending a tingle through his oily black form. She traced his large eyes with her fingertips, looking deep into them. Really looked. Past the liquid hatred that covered him, somehow cutting through it all and getting past it unscathed. She squinted and bit her lip as she found what she was looking for, smiling. "It's really you in there, isn't it?"

"Yeah," he replied. "Somewhere."

ᚕ

That night, Reverend Robert Gallagher lit over forty candles in the Apostle Church, one for every life lost in the massacres. Their flames flickered, making shadows like ghosts against the stained glass visages of the saints. The darkness flowed back and forth over their faces like masks, making them laugh and scowl and cry in turn. He closed his eyes, and let the voices of the dead wash over him.

Suddenly, he opened them again.

He picked up his coffee and walked over to the window that overlooked the graveyard. He saw Xander out at a grave he recognized as belonging to Sara Johnson, just standing there.

"You will find peace, my son," he whispered softly, glancing at the steam which rose hauntingly from his cup. He sat there, watching Xander keep a silent vigil over Sara's grave, for a long, long time.

CHAPTER TWO: PICTURES

Mike wrapped his hand around the cold stainless steel knob of Coral Beach High School's front entrance and stepped inside, feeling as though it had been years since he was last there. The head of his tall frame brushed across the top of the door as he entered, dislocating several strands of his short blonde hair. He carefully patted them back into place, more out of habit than vanity. His green t-shirt itched, so he scratched it as he looked throughout the assembled students crowded around their individual lockers. Their eyes struggled to avoid him, and failed. They stared at him, like he was some kind of freak. As though he'd done something wrong, narked out on them or some other crime punishable by loner-status.

Somewhere in the back of his head, he knew that it was just his imagination. A little stray madness left over from the past few weeks, during which there had seemed to be no shortage. His sideways grin slowly returned to him, and he continued strutting down the halls the way all his Language and Lit teachers hated. He walked to his locker, number three eighty-seven, and took a moment to appreciate the gaudy orange and green sunflower sticker that Cathy had stuck there months ago. It was faded now, almost white in places, but it still caught his eye every time he went there. He opened the locker and the picture that was taped lazily at all four corners smiled back at him from inside the door. It was him, Cathy, Xander and Sara out at Coral Cove. The four of them had gone out. Grendel had been there too and had gotten completely wasted in front of everyone, somehow managing to break his ankle jumping off a small rock.

Sara had laughed at that.

Sara who was dead, now.

Sara, whom Xander had killed.

Mike pursed his lips tightly. He wasn't taking to that idea as well as Cathy had.

He shuddered at the thought of that thing that Xander had transformed into, what it had looked like. As if everything he'd ever had a nightmare about had been boiled down in a vat of hatred and bubbled onto his body from inside of him. Mike shut his eyes tight and braced himself, gripping the sharp metal of the locker door. He kept his eyes closed until painful little dots started piercing their way through his eyelids. He clamped his teeth until they made a sound like nooks of wood grinding against one another and clenched a fist until his knuckles were white with spots of burst red blood cells showing through. His breathing got hard as sweat started rolling down his face, making it glisten under the fluorescent lighting. He opened his eyes, only to find that his vision had become blurry -- fuzzy around the edges. He reached out and grabbed his Physics book, his fingers spread wide enough that he would catch it even if he had misjudged the distance. As soon as he moved, pain shot up his side, erupting up through his spinal cord and burning a hole in the back of his brain. His vision shook, as if he was the only thing on the planet that was standing still. He put the book back down and let his arm flop to his side unceremoniously. The pain slowed, decreasing from a streaming rapid to a small trickle that pumped into his mind with every beat of his heart. His ears were ringing so much so that all he could hear above it was the sound of his own heavy, labored breathing.

"What's up?" came a whiney falsetto voice. Its bearer slammed the locker door shut, nearly chopping Mike's fingers off in the process.

Mike watched the small dial on the combination lock snap back to zero as it bounced against the cold steel under the force of motion. He didn't have to look to see who it was. There were only three people he knew of that could ever be that aggravating. One was dead. The second didn't speak of his own will, it seemed. "Tommy," he said dryly, his tongue like sandpaper. He tried to moisten his lips. The word came out much harsher than he meant it to, but he found that he didn't mind.

"No, man," Tommy laughed, something that sounded for the world like a squeaky tire, sharp and in quick bursts. "I'm not up. Wish I was though... *high* up, if you know what I'm sayin'?" he grinned devilishly. When he asked the question, he reached out a hand and placed it on Mike's shoulder, unknowingly sending bursts of pain through him again.

Mike grimaced, then turned his eyes to glare briefly at the hand on his shoulder, mentally commanding it to burst into flames and then getting irritated when the event did not occur. "Yeah," he nodded curtly. "I know what you're sayin'."

"High," Sud said in the background, finally making his way over to the conversation from the male washroom. His hands were still dripping wet and his palm prints slathered across the front of his jeans.

Is it me, or did it just get stupider in here? Mike quipped to himself.

Tommy mistook that grin as encouragement, and leaned in a little closer. "Anyway, man. There's some crap I need to talk to you about. About Grendel's party."

Mike felt the hairs rise on the back of his neck. When he spoke, he didn't do a very good job of hiding the resentment in his voice. "What?" he asked, not to get the information but to make sure he was hearing right. *If this little mall-rat is actually trying to suck up to me...* His fist clenched bone-white again, but not as a result of pain. To cause it.

"Well, see, it's about Cathy."

Again, rage, he thought whimsically, as he pictured Tommy's head caving under the pressure of his balled hand.

"I think she should stop talkin' about cryin' rape on Grendel," he began with a sigh. "I don't know what went on there, but he's dead and buried with Sara and all those other fools and now it seems like all the *other* little daddy's girls with no life have started doin' it too."

Mike was about to draw back a hand and permanently implant it into Tommy's skull, when he stopped himself dead in his tracks. "What are you talking about now?"

"I can't stand this place," Cathy mumbled as she sipped her Vanilla Coke and watched Principal Shnieder pass her for the fifth time in the last twenty minutes, each time discreetly looking at her company and her chest. "And could somebody please get that man a porno?"

The short, stocky man pretended to look down at his shoe for a moment, catching the sunlight in his big out-stretched ears and balding head. He wore a green tweed suit that made him look stuffy and uptight, his face just a little pink from the warmth of the garment on the sunny fall day.

"He is in serious need of masturbation," Xander concurred, the words accompanied by a crunching sound as he popped potato chips into his mouth one after another. "His birthday is coming up, I hear. Maybe we should procure him some good lubricant."

Cathy rolled her eyes, crumpling her nose a little as she turned to him, her straw dangling just outside her pink lips. Her tongue darted out once and touched it, letting the small suction effect grab hold of it. "What is men's fixation with boobs?"

Xander frowned. "Even if I could explain that, it still doesn't shed light onto our staff's recent fixation with you."

"Excuse me?"

"Let's face it, girl, you're kinda flat," he nodded, trying to disguise his smile by shoving more chips in.

"I hate you," she growled playfully, squinting her eyes so much that her long eyelashes batted against one another.

"You're practically a carpenter's dream over there. Personally, I think I'm much sexier than you." He motioned to his own body in mock seduction.

She shook her head, tried to fight it, then finally gave up and simply burst into laughter. She hadn't wanted to laugh right then. The way everyone was looking at her since trying to convince people that Grendel had raped her the night he died was merciless. There was so much in their eyes. Hatred, pity and always a little desire with the men, no matter who was looking at her.

Except Xander.

"Thank you," she said honestly, her voice sounding like the sun. As if warm sunshine on your face could speak to you and tell you that it would empower and protect you. There was security in her voice, a place where he could make his home.

"For what?" he asked, cocking a brow at her.

"Making me laugh," she explained, those pink lips curling into a smile. His hand lingered near hers so she took it, her fingers dancing gently across his. "You know, the only other time I've smiled since Sara died was when I found out you were okay."

Xander closed his eyes at the mention of Sara, his eyes flickering toward the ground and away from her own.

"I'm sorry," she sighed apologetically. She felt it too, but she knew what it must be doing to him. He did it, after all. For all they knew, he could do it again. He could kill her, she realized with a start, and jerked her hand away from his.

He felt her touch leave him, a numb sensation of loneliness overcoming him. It fizzled throughout his body, like a slow cold-shiver. "For what?" he asked curtly, trying to avoid the topic altogether. "What's there to be sorry about?"

"Don't do this," she pleaded, feeling the tears start to come but forcing them back. Out of the corner of her eye, she saw Shnieder walk past again. With her back turned, she could only assume what he was gawking at this time.

"Do what?" he said, speaking very slowly as if she were in the 'special' class two tables over, the valedictorian of which was currently shoving his carrot sticks up his nose in a vain attempt to get the broccoli out. "What am I doing?"

She cursed and slammed her drink down on the table, tiny droplets spraying up into her face and hair. Her voice took on an accusing tone, one that made it clear she was no longer dealing with his crap. "If you're gonna keep pulling this shit out of your hat, then you don't have to be so fucking patronizing about it, okay?" she demanded, glaring into him with full feminine fury. "Because I don't need it. You think that you hold the monopoly on pain? That you're the only one who misses Sara? Guess what, you can get off that damn high horse right now, because she wouldn't have put up with it and I won't either." Her voice slowed as his had, so that his tiny masculine brain could comprehend the words. "I - don't - need - it. Okay?"

He took a long pause, meeting her gaze evenly. He reached over, picked up her drink, and took a small sip before asking, "What? What don't you need?"

"Ugh!" she screamed, her cheeks puffed out with frustration. She thrust her fingers into the air, then turned on a dime and leapt off of the table, pausing for a moment to see if Xander would try and stop her. He didn't. She walked away, trying hard to take as much swivel out of her hips as humanly possible.

Shnieder stepped out from behind a tree, his eyes behind him at the two young girls having a smoke by the corner. He bumped into Cathy, who narrowed her eyes at him in frustration.

"I... I was just..." he stammered, slowly backing away as he realized their bodies as a whole were touching.

She set her jaw, her mouth seeming to become smaller as she got even angrier. "Men," she spat finally, disgust in her voice, then shoved past him.

Shnieder, awestruck and looking very much like a small furry animal caught in the headlights of a eighteen wheeler, turned to Xander for explanation. Xander merely shrugged one shoulder lazily, maneuvering the straw of Cathy's former drink to suck up the last little bit of cola.

Mike stomped into the playground, almost knocking into Cathy and barely realizing it was her, his eyes fixed on the picnic table at the far corner which Xander occupied. "Oh!" he squirmed, trying to get around her. "Sorry, babe!"

She gave him a little shove, then made her way past him and toward the bottom floor locker room to get ready for her Biology class.

He squinted, and could have sworn he could hear her touting profanities against testosterone on her way down the stairs. He shook it off, regaining his set jaw and driven stare. *Mental note: if I ever understand that girl, commit self into nearest mental hospital.*

He made a beeline across the grounds for Xander, who watched his approach calmly. They both ignored Shnieder, who was still whimpering next to the tree after his confrontation with Cathy, rubbing his bald head and trying to wrap his mind around girls.

Some things, it seemed, didn't change as one got older.

Mike stopped a foot in front of Xander, who was now staring down into the drink cup, as if there were something in the bottom that nobody else was aware of. It was something he did when he was depressed. His mind started latching on to simple things, trying to keep itself occupied so that it wouldn't drift back -- to her. Mike knew this and often dealt with invading thoughts in the same fashion, but he found different things to grasp his thought processes. He took out a C.B.H.S yearbook of last year's date and threw it down onto the table between them, the leather binding smacking against the wood with a hard thump.

Xander ignored this, seeming very intent on discovering what lay just past the bottom of his drink cup.

Mike motioned toward the yearbook with one hand, still with no words, his jaw seemingly locked shut.

"Did you tell Cathy what a carpenter's dream was?" Xander asked finally, still ignoring the green leather book with Coral Beach High School engraved on it in golden letters.

"Open the book," Mike sighed.

"Are there bars full of chocolatey goodness inside?" Xander asked with a weird, manufactured grin. "I've got a weird case of the munchies today."

"Just open it, okay?" Mike growled, annoyed at Xander's indifference. "It's important."

"Is this for real, or is this like the time you told me my parents were dead?"

"Open. It. Why is this difficult?"

Groaning at the mere idea of movement, Xander lifted his arm and opened the front cover. He began to flip stupidly though the pages. He passed a picture of Sara with some senior at last year's grad, blowing a kiss into the camera. He turned the page quickly, then looked up at Mike. "Is there a point to this, or are we just taking a fantastic trip down memory lane?" he asked, his voice sounding tired and old. He stopped, pretending to point to a spot behind a brick wall, his voice filled with mock wonder. "Hey, look! It's that spot where I threw up after the middles threw me a beating. Good times!"

"Page seventy-four," Mike replied, disregarding his friend's crudeness.

Xander flipped open to the page Mike had said to go to. It was an eighth grade gallery from last year, with all of the students' individual shots. He shrugged. "I don't get it."

Finally, Mike sat down across from him, turning the book sideways so they could both look. After scanning the assortment again for a moment, he came upon a picture of a brunette girl with green eyes and freckles across the bridge of her nose, the kind that really showed up in sunlight. She had a nice smile, like something out of a movie. Mike tapped the picture twice. The file name next to it said Julie Peterson.

"Cute," Xander agreed, nodding.

"She was walking home from school last week, the way that she has taken for nine years. The same way we take home. Three guys, the youngest was probably twenty-eight, grabbed her and dragged her into an alley. They all raped her, and they all took a turn, and then they beat her," Mike said, leaning in closer to Xander as he spoke. "The doctors are saying her uterus is pretty much demolished. And you know what? The alley was right across the street from her house. She has to look at it now every time she-"

Xander raised a hand for him to stop, and he did. There was a long moment of silence then, as Xander traced the outline of the girl's small face with his index finger, then carefully closed the book. He pressed his elbows into the wood of the table, knotting his fingers together in front of his mouth. "What are we going to do about this?" he asked.

"I don't know," Mike admitted, slumping down onto the table. "Can we do anything? Should we? She isn't even going to press charges."

"What?!" Xander yelled in astonishment, gaining the attention of the principal. He calmed himself, then repeated: "What?"

"She won't tell anyone who did it. Most people in school are just calling her a slut."

Xander shook his head. "The ignorance of this school's student body amazes me sometimes. What about a rape test?"

"She has to give consent, and as soon as the doctor mentioned it she wouldn't let him near her again."

"Can you really blame her?" Xander reasoned. "If I'd just gone through that, I wouldn't want any cruddy old man going down there with a pair of forceps any time soon."

"Guess not."

They both sighed, just as the school bell rang. They looked up into the Science Lab as one, watching Cathy as she sat down to her Biology class. She waved to them, all the anger she'd felt moments ago having wasted away in the halls.

"I can't help but think that it could have been her."

"You don't have to tell me," Xander nodded glumly.

"Are we going to do anything?"

Xander looked up at Cathy, sadness creeping over her soft face as she started to stare into space. "Oh, you'd better believe it."

CHAPTER THREE: SUPER HERO

Cathy stared blankly out the window of room two oh three, watching a few sparrows dance and fly about. They interacted with one another playfully between the rays of sunlight that streaked across the sky in such well-defined lines that they almost looked solid. A few strands of her jet black hair fell down in front of her face again, and she considered taking the special bio-room scissors and lopping it all off. She settled for simply pushing it behind her ear for the fifth time that minute. That was okay, though. The little annoyances helped. They meant that she had something to focus on. That she could pretend she didn't hear their voices.

All around her, the rest of her Biology class was talking, most of them so loud that she couldn't have blocked them out if she'd wanted to. But every now and again, there was something worse. The quick rush of air that accompanied a whisper. Every time she turned to look in whatever direction it had come from, notes would mysteriously drop from desks and eyes would dart away to the nearest available place, many of them choosing to watch the sparrows as well.

She closed her eyes and let her chin drop until it rested against her blouse. It was white with little frills across a neck that was unusually high for her. She was also wearing pants that were higher up her stomach than she'd ever worn before in her life. She might as well been wearing overalls.

Yet still, they whispered.

Even Mr. Miles, standing at the head of the class pointing out the greater aspects of evolution and the Darwinian theories, something about birds on islands in a place she'd never heard of before. He wasn't saying a thing about her, at least not verbally. But his eyes were casting odd glances her way. At the beginning of the year, those eyes had been kind, the wrinkles around his cheeks had made him look warm, and his British accent had marked him as a kind soul. Then, after the murders, his gaze turned to pity. That one had been popular among a lot of the staff at first. They looked at her the way she looked at the children from Afghanistan in one of those telethon pledges for PBS. In the final stage of this 'face evolvement' theory of hers, it was like the dual islands of birds in Darwin's theorem. Half of the school's population had done what Miles was doing now: looking at her with a kind of suspicion that was hurtful for both of them to have on his face. The other half (a segment grossly populated with boys) were looking at her as if she were, in their own words, a 'slutty piece of tail.' She never did understand that expression, but she felt she was starting to get the gist of it now. She looked down, and realized that her bra was visible through her blouse in this light. She grabbed her jean jacket and quickly pulled it over herself, then glanced at Mr. Miles, who suddenly seemed to no longer harbor any interest toward her.

She clutched her jacket around herself and leaned her delicate head against the window, deciding it best to keep her attention focused on the sparrows.

"So how are we going to do this?" Xander asked Mike as the latter stowed his bag back into his locker, the halls wonderfully vacant at this time of day. It seemed as though Mike was very angry at the book bag, but Xander decided it best not to comment to that regard, lest he become the subject of his rage in its stead. *I swear, if my life gets any more like a Shakespearian play I'm going to start auctioning off the TV movie rights,* he groaned mentally, rolling his eyes as the bag's belt buckle kept falling out and preventing Mike from closing the locker door.

"Why don't you tell me?" he asked, his voice borderline sarcastic, just enough so that Xander couldn't make heads or tails of what he meant. He slammed the locker door shut, the lock snapping into place despite the fact that the strap was still hanging out. "You being the big time superhero and all, right?"

That time the intention of the spite-dripped words was clear. Xander closed his eyes tight, turning his head away from Mike to brush away the pain that comment had just inflicted. *Engen said they were trying to make me so that I couldn't be hurt,* he recalled, somewhere in the deep reaches of his mind. *I don't think they did a very good job.* "Well, who signed their name to her portfolio in the yearbook? Best friends and crap?"

Mike stopped, turned, and smiled at Xander, waving a finger at him. "Watch out. You were pretty close to a good idea there."

"I'm past due," Xander agreed, shrugging as the two started moving again. "What do you mean, 'almost'?"

"See, I thought of that already. But we're gonna have a hard time tracking down most of her old buddies from the last few years."

"Why's that?" Xander moaned, thinking of all the fun of sifting through yearbook photos.

"You killed them all last week," Mike replied. His tone was blunt. He did not even pause as the statement stopped Xander dead in his tracks just long enough to grimace, then move on.

"So, what else do we have going for us?" he asked, knowing that he would regret asking the question.

Mike stopped at locker three fifty eight, spreading his arms before it and making himself look like Vanna White, or one of the models on the Price is Right. The locker was burnt along the bottom edge, most likely from a lighter, and the rest of it was decorated with Metallica and Guns n' Roses stickers and decals. There was also a playing card with a naked lady on it, certain areas of which had been covered with Smurf bubble gum tattoos. "We have our ability to break and enter, and our willingness to do so."

"Is that Sud's locker?" Xander asked, raising an eyebrow in his direction and pointing to it dumbly.

"You know anyone else who would perform these indecencies to his own property?"

"True," Xander nodded, stepping up to it and giving it a good, hard look. "Now, for the fun part: why are we breaking into Sud's locker?"

"Because it's also Tommy's locker."

"Okaaaay," he sighed. "Why are we breaking into *Tommy's* locker?"

"I think the question you should really be asking is: why wouldn't we?"

Xander shot him a look.

Mike leaned his arm against the next locker, and his head upon his arm. "It's like this: Julie Peterson was at Grendel's party a few weeks ago, just like the rest of us, right? This was just after at least one of her friends was killed, and on the night that a great deal more would be. Chances are, she needed someone to talk to. Someone she felt she could tell things to..."

"Someone, should he still be alive, that she might have told her rapists' names to."

Mike grinned and fanned out a palm before Xander. "Give the man a prize."

Xander did a small bow, then returned to a more serious mindset. "I still don't see what this has to do with breaking into Tommy's locker. Not that I'm really opposed to the idea."

"Okay. Remember before everything started to go downhill at the party?"

"Vaguely. I was Mr. Concussion when things did go bad, so I wouldn't trust anything I said."

"Same here, *but*, Tommy was running around with that little camera of his snapping pictures, wasn't he?"

Xander smiled. "And one of those pictures probably caught Julie chatting it up with her newfound friend." He pointed a finger at Mike approvingly. "Nice."

"I like to think so," he complimented himself, doing his own half-bow this time.

"So, ladies first?" he said, motioning to the locker as he backed away from the metal squares, keeping an eye out for Shnieder. "We should have brought Cathy. If any of our staff comes, they'll be too busy gawking at her to notice anything we're doing."

"Don't remind me," Mike grunted, drawing back a fist and slamming it into the Metallica stickers. He kept punching until blood erupted from his knuckles, splattering against the green metal in a semi-circle from the point of impact. In spite of that, he seemed to be enjoying himself.

Xander raised a hand to stop him, and Mike pulled off. He was hunched over from exhaustion now, breathing hard.

"I think you're forgetting something," Xander said, in an annoying father-knows-best sort of tone.

"The Black Womb?" Mike gasped, from lack of oxygen, not astonishment. He'd actually expected Xander to pull that angle.

"Nope," Xander grinned, tapping his right index finger against his temple. "We're dealing with idiots here, Harris. To catch an idiot, you have to think like one. Something I'm known to be good at." He said this as if it were an accomplishment.

"A'ight. Fine. How do we get into their locker, idiot?" he asked, rolling his eyes.

Xander reached out, pulled on the lock and took it off, twirling it about in his hand.

"Are you telling me that wasn't locked?"

Xander reached out and patted his friend on the head. "That's why I'm the big time superhero, and you're the sidekick. Now grab the photos, Fallout Boy."

Officer Tim White smiled graciously at Officer Lensherr as he stepped through the revolving doors of the Coral Beach Precinct, even waving a two-fingered salute as he started to peel out of the beige trench coat he'd worn into the office today. He had already regretted taking it off of the rack. The day had turned out to be more humid than any day in September had any right being, making all of his joints feel chaffed and scratchy under the suffocating fabric.

He was a tall African-American man, broad across the shoulders and looking as though he worked out at least some of the time. Muscles that were tightly coiled and honed to perfection ten years ago had begun to sag. What he had once referred to as his six-pack abs had since been downgraded to a small keg, but he still turned a head every once in a while and that was enough for him. His black hair was neatly trimmed close enough to his head that you could see that his hairline was beginning to recede. His complexion was dark and teeth bright white, so that when he smiled it could be seen clear across the room.

Officer Lensherr smiled back and waved courteously, then grabbed a handful of files from a mail cart as it passed by and started to sort through them as he headed back to his desk, not looking up at Tim again.

Tim smirked a little, laid his jacket over the wall of his office (which was really nothing more than a cubicle) and then leaned back in his chair. He'd been getting a lot of responses like the one Lensherr just gave him lately. Mostly because he wasn't *Officer* Tim White anymore... now he was *Agent* Tim White, a fact he had to remind himself of at least twice a day. He had received the honor less than two days after apprehending Adam Genblade, the man responsible for the Coral Beach Massacre. For ten years he had been the only African-American on the force here in Coral Beach. Even though none of them had ever given him a hard time or so much as told an inappropriate limerick, he still felt a smug feeling of satisfaction at being the first one to ever be promoted out of the department.

Leaning back with his hands behind his head, he stared out the open window and watched a few cars go by, puffing air in and out of his mouth. After a moment he turned back toward his cubicle. For the first time in a decade, there was nothing on the walls but unused tacks and his phone. Usually it was adorned with different cases or elements of cases, mug shots or evidence photos. The north wall was usually reserved for ongoing cases, mostly missing children and robberies. Now the wall was empty and all of the cases had been reassigned to other officers. That redistribution of casework had made him the source of a few unhappy stares in the past few days, but most people had been more than happy to pick up the slack.

Now, for the first time in his career, he had nothing to do. It would be days or more before he was reassigned, and he felt boredom creeping over the back of his skull as he continued to stare at the gray-flecked wall of his cubicle.

A steady squeaking noise that had been present ever since he came through the front door became louder all of a sudden and he turned to see Peter coming around the corner, pushing his mail cart along at a brisk pace.

Tim moved to get up and almost fell off his chair. He grabbed his desk with both hands and pulled himself forward, the chair steadying itself back on four legs. His fourth grade teacher had always said that would happen if he kept leaning on his chair long enough, that it was Murphy's Law. He sighed with relief for a moment, wishing that he'd listened, but resigning himself to the fact that it had taken her over thirty years to prove her point, so perhaps the odds were still in his favor.

He got up successfully the second time, turning toward the cart just as it squeaked past. "Anything for me?" he asked, slyly glancing over the contents on the cart and shooting Pete that big smile of his again.

Pete's expression remained vacant as he started to thumb through a few of the yellow and orange envelopes, finally turning to Tim. "Nope," he said simply, then started to wheel past again, the left wheel proceeding with its steady shriek.

Tim laid his hand upon the cart to stop it, something on it catching his attention. "Hold on," he said as he reached out and grabbed the third yellow folder from the end and pulled it out. It had the word 'sensitive' stamped across the front of it, which was what had gotten his attention as Pete was flipping through. He checked the ledger at the bottom of the file, making sure that it wasn't assigned to anyone in particular yet, then sat on the corner of his desk and flipped the file open as Pete continued to wheel past.

The first page of the file, held down by a paperclip with rust flecks on it, was a page that had been printed off of the old printer in the back and had left ink splotches all over it. It was the generic page that was printed for almost every case that came through, with little check-boxes the initial officer on the scene had to fill out with the nature of the case, victim name and brief summary. It would also be the page faxed as a kind of cover letter should any information have to be shared with other precincts around the country. On this particular cover letter there were only two pieces of information pertaining to the case: that the victim's name was Julie Peterson, and that the check-box for sexual assault had a thick letter 'x' scrawled through it.

His phone rang once next to his head and he picked it up almost immediately, bringing it to his ear as he turned the page. "Tim White's office. Offic -- Agent White speaking."

There was a sound of ruffled fabric and a loud puff of air that hurt Tim's ear, making him cringe, and then a voice came that was fast and low, the accent had just a slight hint of New York twang on the end of the sentence. "Jeez, what were you, sitting on the phone?" The man on the other end of the receiver seemed annoyed and a little amused at how fast Tim had picked up, letting out another puff of air that made Tim's phone gargle with static.

"Next to it, actually," Tim corrected, his eyes going wide and then frowning as he saw the picture of Julie Peterson, her smile almost as vibrant as her eyes. "Who is this?"

"Duncan. Agent Duncan Taggart," he said, and somehow Tim knew that he was smiling. There was a honk in the distance, and he assumed that the man was driving. "I'm from the Bureau. They've assigned you to help me out with a case I've been working on for a few months now. Great job on the Genblade capture, by the way. Top-notch stuff, I hear. I'd really like to meet that guy before they stick him in a hole for the rest of his days. Really rare to catch a serial alive."

"Believe me, you wouldn't," Tim said as he rolled his eyes, trying his best to focus on what he was reading. There was a photo of the scene where the rape had actually taken place. One of the officers involved had circled the upstairs window of the house across the street with a red felt-tip marker and written the words 'Julie's Room.' It made him want to throw up just thinking about her having a view of that spot for the rest of her time living in her parent's house.

"Ooookay," Duncan drawled, clearing his throat. "Well listen, I don't want to brief you now, but we really have to get started as soon as possible. I've put a lot of work into this case over the last few months and I don't mind taking on someone new, but you're going to have to pick it up fast or get left behind like a high-school prom date."

Tim balked at the comment, flipping to the medical report that had been written up on Julie Peterson. He shook his head and sighed when he got to the part about her refusing the rape test, cursing to himself. There were pictures of the bruises that had been left on her arms and legs, as well as scrapes across her back and breasts that he imaged would make it impossible to sleep for at least the next month. There were worse injuries, but most were described rather than photographed.

"You still there? We've gotta get started quick, or else--"

"Sorry," Tim interrupted, closing the folder shut and tucking it under his arm. "I've already got a case." He gently placed the receiver down on its hook, then started walking toward the door, leaving his jacket draped over his cubicle wall.

ʌ⟨⟩ʌ

Mike brushed a pile of cigarette butts out from beneath him as he sat down against the solid brick wall of the school's smoking section. The air around that corner of the building smelled stale and toxic, like a sock left to soak in its owner's sweat for thirty years or so. He checked behind him once more to make sure that there were none left, then finally rested his back against the warm wall, absorbing all the heat of the sun shining down on him. "So, what should we look for?" he asked, staring at the envelope in his friend's hands.

"I'm thinking your basic couch shots. You know, Tommy running around and just taking pics of people chilling out and shit. If we pay attention to the group shots, it could be easy to go off the wrong way," Xander reasoned, flipping open the bright yellow paper and taking out the stack of photos. "Aw, God."

"What?"

Xander flipped the first photo around. It was a bedroom window taken from inside another bedroom window, most likely Tommy's. It was blurry, but it looked like he was trying to get some shots of a girl changing. "Never miss a trick, do they?"

"Dude, is that your Mom?"

"What?"

"Just kidding."

Xander grumbled something about Robin being a better sidekick, but he trailed off and moved on, flipping to the next set of photos. "And the sick-o gets sicker."

Mike leaned in and looked at the picture, a full-zoom shot of Cathy's breasts. "So, we're not giving any of these back, right?"

"Burn the negatives?"

"Uh-huh," Mike nodded, taking the negatives out of the yellow envelope and bringing a lighter to them.

Xander flipped to the next picture, a full-body shot of Sara, yelling and smiling and generally having a good time. He shoved that one into his coat pocket without another word to Mike, who was watching the negatives burn. "Those chemicals are poison, man," he said absent mindedly. "Don't breathe them in."

Mike nodded, bringing the smouldering black filmstrip over to an empty metal garbage can and tossing it in, closing the lid behind it. "Any actual photos yet?"

"Two of Grendel we can burn. One of him alone and another of him heading into the bedroom..." he trailed off.

Mike grabbed those two and ripped them to shreds without even glancing at them.

"Here we go," Xander said and Mike leaned in, both of them huddling over a shot taken from atop the dining room table of the entire party. Their eyes scanned the faces and clothes of those attending feverishly.

"Wasn't she on the red couch?"

"Don't ask me, I was on the balcony," Xander reminded him, spitting out the sentence as quickly as possible, as if not liking its taste in his mouth.

"I can't see anything. It's too wide a shot," Mike groaned, turning away and flipping through the stack to find more.

Xander kept staring at the photograph. As he did, the pupils of his eyes enlarged slightly, slowly, until they almost overtook him.

Mike finally noticed, doing a double take. "What are you doing?"

"There," Xander said finally, the slightest hint of the Womb in his voice. Mike cringed, but looked to where he was pointing. Sure enough it was young Julie Peterson, freckles and big white smile and everything. "I can't pick out the guy next to her, though," he sighed, his pupils dilating to their normal size.

Mike smiled, noticing the black plastic jacket their guy was wearing. "I know that fool."

ʎ⟨ʎ

Derek looked at Cathy from across the lab, watching her stare blankly out the window as he took down Miles' biology notes for the next class. He hated this 'theory of evolution' crap, and briefly considered asking why they were forcing it down their throats so hard. Like they'd ever really need to know about evolution, anyway. The way he saw it, whatever happened, happened. There wasn't too much he could really do about it.

Cathy still had her jean jacket wrapped around her slender body, her elbows sticking out a little through worn sleeves that added to the jacket's character. Her hair was perfectly straight, and with the way she had her head tilted he could only see her nose sticking out from beneath her bangs.

He sighed heavily, turning his attention back to the board as Miles' squeaky little red marker etched a crude diagram showing man's evolution from apes.

At the back of the class, Tommy raised a hand in question.

"Yes?" Miles responded, poking his head up to see above the taller students, the action misplacing his gold-rimmed spectacles. He re-mounted them onto his nose carefully. "Yes, Thomas?"

"If man evolved from apes, than..."

"Why are there still apes?" Miles finished for him, smiling.

Tommy nodded.

"That's a point that a lot of people bring up, Thomas, and I'm glad you did. Actually, there are over a hundred different species of ape. *One* particular species had the good sense and cunning to start to stand upright - to become men - and that particular species is now extinct. Gone from the face of the earth. Some say it's coincidence... but..."

"There are no coincidences," someone in the back quoted, remembering that it was one of the professor's favorite literary quotes.

"Exactly."

Again, Tommy raised his hand. Derek groaned, rolling his eyes and burying his forehead into his palm. He knew what was coming now.

"Yes, Thomas?" Miles asked again, smiling at the young man's thirst for knowledge on this subject.

"Will man ever evolve again, like in X-Men?"

The whole class, with the exception of Cathy and Derek, roared into a fit of laughter. Miles chuckled softly, wiping his old eyes. "No... no, not like X-Men. But, I wouldn't rule out the possibility of evolution."

Derek squinted.

Cathy piped up, speaking for the first time since class had begun. "What would be needed for evolution? For us to change again?"

Miles took off his glasses and started cleaning them with a pearly white handkerchief he always had in his coat pocket. He tilted his head to one side, carefully considering the question. "Well... there'd have to be a need to change for survival."

"There's definitely that around here," Tommy piped up.

Once again there was a class-full of laughter for something that wasn't funny. Cathy's mouth went slack, her tongue suddenly dry.

Miles coughed softly to hide his utter amazement at the vulgarity of such a comment, then continued. "Yes, well. After a time, certain members of a species will learn a behavior, or sometimes even grow an adaptation that will allow them to survive their natural or un-natural limitations and predators. These are the beings that survive, and they pass these traits onto their young, until eventually a lot of beings have it and they become a separate species. So, theoretically, if man had a strong enough reason to evolve, he would do so... yes."

"How?" Derek said finally, his brow furrowed in disbelief. "Where's the room to change?"

Miles gestured toward him briefly, giving him credit for the point he'd made. "True. But, many scientists believe that the appendix is either something we used and eventually evolved to the point of no longer needing it, or that it's something that we will grow to learn to use. To change further."

Derek shook his head and frowned, then stared down at the notes he'd made. He couldn't see any of this coming in handy on a test. "Can I go to the washroom?" he asked, seemingly out of the clear blue sky.

Mr. Miles looked at him side-on for a moment, not clearly understanding how the conversation had gone from one point to the next. "Yes, of course," he said after a moment, waving toward the door.

Derek nodded his thanks and got up, walking out the door. Before it closed, he caught a glimpse of Cathy, finally turning away from the window long enough to watch him make his exit.

ʌ˅ʌ

Derek walked through the halls, keeping a close eye out for Shnieder as he quietly made his way to the men's room. His shoes scuffing softly against the tile floor and his jacket swishing back and forth were the only things he could hear. He paused slightly as he passed the 'little girls room,' then rejected the immature notion to call inside and see who was there. He proceeded to the men's room, un-zipping his jacket and showing a *l33t me* t-shirt underneath, his own silent testament to his love of online manga. He turned the corner and stepped into the bathroom, his heels scuffing to a sudden stop.

"Hi, Derek," Xander smiled sinisterly, leaning up against the stalls.

"We've been expecting you," Mike added, stepping out from behind a corner and giving Derek a start.

Derek raised an eyebrow and smirked at the situation. "How long did you guys practice that?"

Xander heaved a sigh, then turned and looked at Mike, who did the same. "Alright," Xander said as he stepped away from the locker and loomed toward Derek. The Womb surged inside of him, forcing him to swallow hard to keep the black bile from rising up his windpipe. "I'm gonna put this into terms you can understand, pal. This is the end of Empire. You're Han and I'm Boba. This isn't going to end well for one of us."

Derek raised an eyebrow, looking from one to the other. "That's... not a great analogy. I mean sure, it was going Boba's way at the end of the movie, but Han ended up on top in the end of the trilogy. Maybe you're looking for more of a Green Goblin/Gwen Stacy reference?"

"Sure. Why not?" Mike shrugged, rubbing the bridge of his nose.

"That wouldn't really work either, though. Maybe you should just use a metaphor instead of an analogy. Or use an analogy more commonplace, like saying that I'm Bates to your Manson or something like that," he chuckled, then took another step forward. Again, the true Womb vibrated.

"Let's get to the point," Mike interrupted, rolling his eyes. "Tell us what we need to know, or that smirk'll come off your face before you can say 'Revenge of the Nerds.'"

Xander cursed and stepped forward, his tone losing all the menacing crypticness he'd tried so hard to convey throughout the exchange. "We need you to tell us about what happened with Julie Peterson," he said empathetically, pressing his lips together and looking down, obviously feeling shameful of the actual topic.

Derek shook his head. "Why? So that you can turn around and freak on her like all the other low-life scum in this place? I tell you, you guys deserve to die like the rest of them."

"Careful what you wish for," Xander said, his tone sounding like that of a wise old man. "You just might get it."

"Like it'd matter," he scoffed, discarding Xander's warning. "I'm not telling you crap so that you can ruin her any more than this shit already has."

"We don't want to hurt her, we just want the names of the people that did this," Mike spoke up, stepping toward the both of them.

"Oh yeah, why?"

"We wanna kick their heads in."

Derek stopped, looking from Xander to Mike and then back again. A sly smile extended across his face. "Okay," he said cheerfully.

CHAPTER FOUR: HEAD FIRST

The library smelled old and musty, like something between the scent of new paper and an old, smouldering cigarette. There was a dryness in the air that set it apart from everywhere else in the school. Mike kept expecting to see large clouds of dust move ominously between bookshelves, as if they had a mind of their own. It was still a welcome change from the bathroom, especially after Tommy and Sud had come in and used it. It seemed that he had been right all the years he'd said that those two were 'full of it,' and that they wasted no time expelling 'it' from their systems on a daily basis.

He frowned, putting the large, navy blue book back onto its place on the shelf. He was sure that Mrs. Richards, the old bat that they used for a librarian in this school, wouldn't react kindly to some of her books being out of place. He traced his fingers carefully over the leather bindings, each yearbook a different colour but all of them sporting the same golden lettering along the spine as the one they'd looked at earlier. All of them had the same creases of use up and down their weathered edges.

At the end of the corridor, Xander sat atop a table with his legs resting firmly upon a chair, flipping through old files. "Any luck?" he asked, not really interested as he turned another page lazily. He already knew what his friend's response would be anyway.

"No," Mike responded, his voice taking the high-toned pitch it did whenever he was truly annoyed. "I don't think we're doing this right," he admitted as he took out another yearbook, this one dating back ten years, and flipped it open to the index. "Shouldn't we have found that clue everyone else had overlooked yet?"

"I think you'll find it's rarely that simple. Plus, we're the only ones looking for clues, in case you haven't realized that yet," Xander responded bitterly, muttering something incomprehensible about this town's population. He stopped a moment, slamming down one stack of counsellor files and scooping up another. "I've been through all these a thousand times. Our guys aren't in here."

"Are you sure they went to school here?" Mike asked under his breath, scrolling his finger down through the index.

"That's what Derek said, anyway. We're taking a lot on his word, and he's taking a lot on Julie's. I'm not entirely certain we can trust third-hand knowledge, man. You know the way gossip in this hole works."

"True," Mike nodded, handing him the yearbook. "But we've got nothing else to go on."

Xander shook his head in dismay. "I thought you said there were three guys?"

"There were. She only told Derek about two of them."

"Christ. Remind me to stay away from this girl. If I met anyone whose logic was that screwed up, I'd have to reconsider whether or not they deserved saving."

"Same goes for Cathy, then?" Mike asked without looking up, his tone even and very hurtful.

Pain shot through Xander, as he realized that was the same way he'd spoken to Cathy earlier. "I didn't mean--"

Mike raised a hand to dismiss the thought, then abruptly changed the topic. "Is it just me, or does the fact that these two have gang connections unsettling?"

"Tell me about it. I didn't even know there was a real gang, outside of the Godfather films anyway."

"Not what I meant," Mike said quietly. "I mean, these two guys are probably sitting around with twenty other guys, laughing it up about what they did to that girl."

Xander grimaced, flipping the black leather book open to the index and began to scan through it. "Shouldn't this all be computerized?" he asked in exasperation.

"The last few years, yes. But nobody's bothered to go back and type in *all* the old files yet since we got the new systems in. Threw out all the old comps, remember?"

Xander smirked mischievously. "I remember the four of us fishing through the dumpster out back so that I could salvage some of the parts into a PC."

"Good times," Mike nodded, the both of them falling into a short, uncomfortable silence. Both of them trying not to dwell on Xander's slip of tongue when he had said 'the four of them.' Because that would have implied Sara. Therefore, it was never actually said.

"Got it," Xander said, turning his yearbook around so that Mike could see.

He pointed down to the side-by-side pictures as Mike leaned in, putting his own book back on the shelf. "Allan Bishop and Bram Raine. Their last year was about ten years ago, before they got kicked out."

The pages were yellowed a little even though they shouldn't have been, their edges curling and cracking as Xander thumbed through them. The photos themselves looked like twisted black and white images from the twilight zone. He wasn't sure if it was just the knowledge of what they had done, but something about the two yearbook photos seemed eerily sinister... As if they could see him through the old book. The first guy had shoulder-length brown hair and some bad acne, along with braces that shone with the reflection of the camera's flash. The other man was thinner but looked wirier, his mouth the only one on the page not curled up into a smile. His expression was blank and devoid of emotion, and Xander didn't need a colour photo to know that his eyes were red.

"I didn't think Shnieder kicked people out," Mike said, his voice a mixture of surprise and newfound respect for the sniveling weasel that had been gawking at his girlfriend earlier today.

Xander cocked his head to one side. "Back in the day he did, when he first got here. And it wasn't just him; these two had a recommendation for expulsion from the guidance counsellor and everything."

"Phillips?"

"Before his time. This was Dr. August O'Grady," Xander corrected, pointing to a picture of the woman. She looked as though she'd seen a great deal of pain walk through her doors in her tenure, every cry of suffering taking its toll upon her face. Even her mouth hung open on one side, which would have given her an almost comical expression if not for the menacing glare of her eyes.

"I remember the stories the seniors used to tell about her," Mike recalled with a start, pointing at the picture. "She was a witch!"

"I don't know about that, but I think they should put that picture up in prisons. It'd start scaring people straight," Xander smirked.

"No, you don't understand," Mike chuckled. "She kept permanent records on *everybody*. She'd give out detention slips for chewing gum. She even had one of those canes mounted on her wall. I heard she even used it once or twice."

Xander slammed the book shut, a cloud of stale dust rising up as he did so. He turned and pointed to the files on his desk. "If she kept records on everything, then why isn't there a single word about either of our two offenders in those?" he asked, his tone gravely serious.

༺༻

Cathy sat in Math class, staring at the empty chair next to her. It was one of many throughout campus. As Mrs. Green babbled on and on about logarithmic functions and their practical use in today's society - none whatsoever, by the way - Cathy sat in the fourth row with her back uncomfortably shoved against her wooden chair, a loose screw digging into her behind. As much as it bothered her, her attention was still focused on the seat adjacent to her. It was the seat that until a few days ago had belonged to Sara Johnson. She remembered all of the times the two of them had sat there gossiping about Jamie, Mike, and Grendel. How she'd tried to convince Sara over and over again to go out on a date with Xander, much to the blonde's disdain.

Neither of them had ever done exceptionally well in Math... but it wasn't like it was their fault, they reasoned. *What kind of moron sticks Math on the third period slot anyway?* Sara would often contest, usually just after Mrs. Green had handed out the results of their latest pop quiz. *Right between Recess and Lunch was not a good time to start logarithmic functions, in my mind.* It seemed to go against nature and puppies, as the perky little blonde next to her used to quote six times a period. Cathy never did understand what that meant, but she was certain it was a compliment to the puppy population of the world.

But she'd never do that again. She'd never sit there and talk about how the teacher looked like a troglodyte and how she was growing whiskers. She'd never go to the mall and watch the new Stephen King movies even though she hated to be scared and usually jumped into either Mike or Xander's arms -- and depending on which she chose, Cathy would either get jealous or excited. She'd never eat a birthday cake again, the kind that's two days old with little bits of candle wax melted into the icing. The kind that you eat with your best friend while you talk about boys and the biggest worry you have is whether each other's hair was done right. Sara would never have a milkshake again either. Come to think of it, Sara had always disliked milkshakes and would only get them upon Cathy's demand that it was a 'girl thing.'

Cathy felt the sadness start to bring moisture to her eyes, then she wiped it away stubbornly.

Sara would never have chocolate, or kiss a guy, or fall in love, or watch Power Puff Girls re-runs, or sit there in Math class and yap about how the men in this school were adolescent perverts except for the one that she was gunning for *this* week, and -

"Miss Kennessy?" Mrs. Green said for the third time, her voice taking a much more annoyed tone.

Cathy jumped in her seat, dazed and confused that the teacher had not been where she thought she'd be. She scanned the room quickly and located her at the door, talking to a balding man with large, round glasses and a cheap blue suit. "I'm sorry, Miss," Cathy apologized earnestly. "It won't happen again, I swear."

Mrs. Green smiled, shaking her head kindly and speaking as one spoke to a kitten. "No, no, Catherine," she chided warmly, motioning to the man behind the door again. "It's not that. Mr. Phillips would like to see you now."

"Who?" Cathy asked as she got her things together, shoving textbooks unceremoniously into her book bag. "Who is that?"

Green smiled again, as did many of the students around the room. "The Guidance Counsellor, Miss. Kennessy."

Cathy huffed, throwing the heavy bag over her back and starting towards the door.

The office was stuffy and stupid, reminding her of the inside of a shoebox. It was so humid that she could practically see all the air in the room creating wavy lines in her field of vision. It made her feel like the room was closing in on her, her breath becoming short from the moment she walked in.

The only thing in the room that did not make her feel uncomfortable was the man sitting behind the desk in front of her, his hands laced together and his thumbs twiddling each other. He was waiting for her to say something first, a typical tactic of his it seemed.

Her eyes darted around the room, everything in there seemingly out of place with the rest of the school for some reason. For instance, the rugged old cross on the wall to her right that her pupils kept itching for in her peripheral vision. It was just a standard brown wooden cross with Jesus slung upon it, but something about it was different. Something about the tilt of it, as if Christ were trying to turn the entire rig so that he could stare her right in the face and tell her that she was doing wrong just by being here.

The colours in the room did not match, and in fact clashed drastically, leaving her disoriented as her pupils made their way from one side of the room to the other. She wanted to get those guys from that decorating show on TV in here right now and remodel the whole place. Maybe a fireplace and something else rustic...

"The colours were like this when I started, I've been lobbying for paint for a year and a half," he informed her with a smirk, as if reading her mind.

She shifted in her chair, moving her purse so that it covered her crotch and making sure that her jacket was zipped all the way up for the fifth time that minute. "Uh," she started finally, and his eyebrows rose to hear what she had to say. "Why am I here again?"

He chuckled softly at her unease, doing his best to assure her that it was unwarranted. "You're here for the same reason that everyone else in the school has been here over and over again for the past week. I want to make sure that you're all okay. That everything's fine."

She shrugged, then slapped her hands down onto her knees and smirked her best fake-smirk. "Well, I don't know about you, but I'm fine. So... I don't *have* to be here, right?"

He spread a hand toward the door in casual defeat, glancing down at her file as he did so. "What about Sara and Julian?" he asked, not even bothering to look at her as her entire body ceased into a complete halt. His voice was even-toned and icy cold. "Are they alright?"

She stopped, the only movement her pupils as they slowly turned away from the door to finally meet his gaze. He wasn't looking at her blouse as it hung out of her jean jacket, and he wasn't trying to catch a glimpse of her pants as she moved her purse to her side. He was meeting her gaze with his own, waiting for a response like a stone statue. "Excuse me?" she demanded, her voice slicing through the air like a knife.

"I asked you how your friends Sara and Julian were... although I believe the latter went by the name Grendel, is that correct?" he asked, but his voice wasn't cold anymore. He sounded like a computer talking... like an android on that damn Star Trek show that Xander loved so much. She wondered how anyone could say these things without the slightest hint of sympathy.

She sat back down, but didn't really notice the chair beneath her. Her entire body was numb, and she looked around as if she'd forgotten where she was. "Why are you saying these things?" she asked. She gripped her purse now, digging her fingers into the black imitation leather.

"What have I said?" he shrugged, pouting his bottom lip out momentarily. "What do you think about when I say these things, Cathy?"

Still in shock, Cathy looked back and forth across Dr. Phillips's desk, answering the questions absent-mindedly. "Frozen yogurt," she said truthfully, only meeting his eye for a fraction of a second.

Now it was his turn to be totally confused. "What?"

"I think about how much I like frozen yogurt -- in cones, not dishes -- and how I used to like to eat it with Sara. But Sara won't ever get to eat frozen yogurt ever again. Or have coffee, or go out by the door and have a smoke. She won't get to do anything anymore," she sobbed, tears finally streaming down her hot, pink cheeks. "And nobody will tell me why," she whispered, so softly that Phillips had to struggle to hear her.

"And what about Mr. Grendel?" he asked, still holding both fists against his mouth with his thumbs riding the waddle of his neck. "What do you think about when I say his name?"

She buried her head deep into her hands, gazing down at the floor from between her knees. She sucked back the mucus that was in danger of streaming out of her nose and tried hard to control her mouth, stop it from quivering. But it didn't stop; it spread until she felt as though her entire body were shaking. Until she couldn't feel her legs. "I wasn't worth it," she said softly, holding her shoulders with her hands.

"What does that mean?" he asked, his voice taking on a little more compassion now.

She swallowed hard. "He took me up into his bedroom..." Her eyes were burning a hole into some point on the far wall and it was hard to understand her, with her mouth refusing to work and her sinuses wet with tears trying to force their way out of her body. "... and he forced me down onto the floor. He got on top and started... started..." She sobbed uncontrollably.

"I know," he soothed, reaching out and touching her hair softly. His touch calmed her slightly. "Believe me, I know."

"He stopped," Cathy sobbed, her chest feeling as though it were going to collapse in on itself. "He didn't finish."

"He said you weren't good enough," Phillips nodded, pursing his lips and fighting the urge to curse. "Cathy, what do you think of when you hear things like... like what happened to poor Julie Peterson?"

Cathy stopped sobbing a little then, slowly raising her head to look into his eyes. "I don't care," she said, with the same lapse of emotion he had employed only moments ago. "I'm sorry, but I -- can't think that it's happening to other people. I'll--"

"It's okay," he assured her, and she started to cry again.

Outside the door, Mike watched the girl he loved break down crying again. He raised his hand, wishing that he could reach out and touch her. Wished that he could tell her everything was all right. That he wasn't going to let it happen again, that he wouldn't let it happen to anyone again. Slowly, that hand clenched into a fist as he stared down at the address in his opposite hand. *Then again, why tell you when I can show you?* he asked her mentally, then turned and walked toward the exit, careful to keep a lookout for Shnieder's hall-monitors.

ʎʏʎ

It was three o'clock by the time Mike arrived at the address on the sheet of paper he still clutched in his hands, and that gave him a sense of relief. Now he was actually supposed to be off school, as opposed to simply not being there for no reason. It also meant that Xander would be walking Cathy home, so he didn't have to worry about where either of them were. Besides, there were plenty of other things for him to worry about. Like if he had any sweet clue what he was doing, like if she was as mean as all the kids at school said she was, like what he was going to do with the knowledge he was after should he get it... plenty of things to keep his mind active.

So why was it that I keep thinking about Cathy and Xander? he grumbled softly, wiping a layer of sweat from his freckled cheeks as the warm sun beat down on his face as it had the entire way here. The sidewalk was boiling now and every time he chanced a glance at it, his vision got wavy, making it hard to focus on anything. His hair was sticking to the top of his head, so he ruffled his hands through it to try and make it presentable as he looked up at the mammoth house that jutted up from the soil before him.

It was a two-story house that was pretty much shaped like a square. The main entrance was on the second floor -- not the ground level -- so there was a veranda and a winding set of stairs leading from it down to the driveway, where there was a small yellow Beetle parked. The siding was painted white, with a navy trim on it that gave it an almost royal air. Those colours inspired a sense of awe, except here that wasn't a good thing. Mike had been hoping for some quiet little condo with lawn-ornaments depicting cats scattered across the lawn, may-be even a large wooden sign hanging from the mail box that read 'welcome.'

He took one last look up at the house. As he stood there, he couldn't help but feel as though the asphalt driveway was melting into his sneakers. Shifting his feet slightly to test the theory, he found that there was an odd sticky feeling beneath his sweaty feet, which supported his hypothesis.

He turned, shoving the small piece of paper down into his pocket and began to walk back down the driveway, his frown weighing down his face like an anchor.

"Young man?" came a squawky, parrot-like voice from behind him. He

151

stopped in his tracks, all of the colour draining from his face until he looked like the paper he'd just shoved into his pocket.

He turned slowly and saw an elderly woman's head sticking out through the front door of the house, looking at him. Her face looked for the world like melted wax, drawn out as far as it could go. There was still some up-lift around the eyes, giving her friendly cheekbones. Her eyes were black and sunk deep into her withered head, but there was still a mischievous twinkle in them, a gleam of youth left in her. She had curly, thin silver hair that Mike thought was the standard for all little old ladies, wondering if somewhere they were cloning that hairstyle and sending it to them by mail. "I'm sorry," he said finally, realizing that he'd been staring. "I didn't mean to disturb you."

"You didn't," she said bluntly. She looked as though she might slam the door tight right then and there, but then a smile spread across her face, revealing false teeth that couldn't have been properly glued in. "But I was wondering if you were going to stand out there all day, or if you were going to come in?"

Mike smiled, then hopped up the stairs to the entrance two by two.

She poured the coffee into a small cup for him right next to hers and offered him the sugar bowl, which he refused. He added a splash of milk for colour, then brought the liquid up to his lips. "This is a beautiful home you have, Miss O'Grady," Mike said politely, the hot liquid burning his lips and making him put it back down onto its saucer.

"Liar," she said simply, but that smile gave her away again. "I've been trying to get around to changing the colour for years, but I can't find the time. I think I'd like it yellow. Or pink, maybe," she rambled, her voice very nasal to the point that Mike almost needed to rub his ears to alleviate the pressure. "And it's August. Nobody has called me Miss O' Grady since I was back at the school,"

Mike nodded. "Thank you, August," he said honestly, gazing about at the little white doylies that were thrown about everywhere. "Actually, that's kind of what I needed to talk to you about, your old days at Coral Beach High--"

"Horrible place," she interrupted, her voice shaken and unsettling. "I'll never go back there again. Horrible things happen in those halls, Michael. I didn't condone absence back in my day... but after what I've seen in my tenure, I wouldn't dare make a child step foot through those doors if they had the strength of mind not to."

Mike nodded knowingly, then spotted anti-psychotic medication resting on her kitchen counter. The pill bottle was almost behind her microwave, leaning against the plug with its childproof cap. *Still, a crazy woman who is right is still right, isn't she?* he thought, turning back to meet her eyes. "I know."

"Those deaths. They wouldn't have happened anywhere else."

"I know," Mike agreed, ever more readily, his eyes taking on a darker shade. "Something happened to one of the young girls there the other day -- and I think you might know the two boys responsible for it."

"Me?" August asked, a puzzled looked coming over her. "Why in heavens would I know them?"

"I think they spent time with you, a lot of it. Allan Bishop and Bram Raine?"

She turned ghostly white, staring at him for a long moment. "Is this some kind of sick joke?" she accused, her voice bitter and having lost some of its nasal attribute.

"N-no... I..." he stammered, setting down his coffee and standing, backing up a pace. "They did something. Something horrible. There's no mention of them in any of your old files, so I -"

"No mention?" she repeated, and her menacing attitude melted into a hysterical laughter. "My boy, you had me plum fooled! But there were stacks of paperwork on those two. It was enough for a small novel! We even started filing them together, so that it'd save time during their daily visits to me!" She stopped laughing abruptly. When she spoke again, her voice sounded dead, her eyes void of emotion. "What would anyone ever want with those boys? You run along now..." She got up and shooed Mike toward the door.

He stepped outside, huffing the entire way. When she was about to slam the door on his nose, he quickly reached inside of his coat pocket and pulled out the picture of Julie Peterson that he had torn from the yearbook. "I don't give a shit about them, lady. Or you, for that matter. I care about what happened to this girl."

She shook her head and continued to close the door.

"Look at the picture!" he shouted. The sound startled her, forcing her to see the image for the first time. "They say that she'll never have children now. That's how badly they messed her up. That's what they *did* to her *body*." He stopped yelling and looked down at the ground, then tucked the photo back inside his pocket. He looked around anxiously, pressing his lips together and shrugging wide in desperation. "Doesn't anybody care?"

August looked at him for a long while, then took a slip of paper out of her blouse and wrote an address on it. "That's where the police told me they used to hang out. It's an old building, should've been torn down years ago."

"I know it," Mike nodded thankfully. "Bless you."

"Don't turn your back on them. Those two will kill you, boy. They're what *started* the evil in that school."

The thought sent shivers rushing up and down his spine, that there were things out there worse than all he'd seen already. The worst part was that somewhere inside him, he knew it to be true.

Cathy had been waiting for Mike and Xander for over an hour, and now it was starting to get cold on the picnic table where she sat. All the teachers were long gone by now, even that troll Shnieder had called it an early day and gone home to eat cheezies and spaghetti-o's, or whatever the hell he did at home. She took another look around, sending her hair into another swirl of motion as the wind picked up. She tried for a moment to straighten it, then gave up. Her feet hurt already just looking at the road that stretched out before her, the thought of walking it alone not all that appealing. She wanted to take off her jean jacket. She'd been huddled up into it all day and had made it all warm and sweaty, and it still stank of smoke from Grendel's party. Her dark eyes danced along the tree line one last time, trying to see if either of the boys were coming even though she knew that they weren't. She sighed, slapped her palms against her knees, and got up.

Where the hell did they go? she wondered, sighing heavily. Both of her feet feeling like lead weights. *Men. Why do they all have to be so stupid? Is testosterone some kind of I.Q. retardant or something?* Her book bag straps pressed against her shoulders, making sweat pool there. It itched and made her uncomfortable, as she glared evilly at the setting sun, daring it to come back up. *I hate the night. I used to love it, once. Before the crash a few years back, before all this stupidity started. Xander is being such an idiot, bottling up all of his feelings the way he does. No wonder he goes out and kills things in his sleep... I probably would too, if I was that overly repressed.* The trees loomed around her, their old branches whining in defiance to the motion that the draft was making them participate in. Their groans started to get to her, her pupils darting to the corners of their sockets every few moments to catch a glimpse of them.

She heard something behind her and turned swiftly on her heels, almost falling to the curb when she did so.

Her eyes darted along a patch of leafy green foliage on the side of the road, only partially obscured by an old metal gate. Even though the sun was still bright, it was dark inside, the leaves creating a blanket of shadow that made everything underneath them look homogeneous.

"Hello?" she called out into the shadows. It was damp here, and she couldn't help but wonder if this is what it would be like after her and Julie... jumping at every sound in the dusk-hours, waiting for some pervert to jump you.

There was another sound, very faint.

She had to strain to hear it, leaning her ear towards the bushes but keeping them in her field of vision at the same time. It took her a moment to recognize it, but when she did a thousand memories came back to her all at once, as if it had been someone saying her own name.

-click-

The slow, rhythmic tapping of metal upon metal.

"Xander?" she mouthed softly, taking a step back from the trees without even realizing it. Her hands came up to her mouth as she stared into the darkness. Only now instead of seeing nothing, she saw everything. Every misshaped branch was a shoulder, every ragged red leaf was a slanted eye.

She turned and ran, hearing the click of her heels as she did. She listened carefully to the rhythm as she heard each step once, then again as it echoed back at her. Every few seconds, like clockwork, there was an extra click.

Like a hum or tap in your car that you know doesn't belong, it stood out amongst all the other similar sounds. Her mind processed the information a million times between each pump of her legs as she ran down the street, beads of sweat pouring from her forehead and falling to the ground somewhere behind her. These sounds were so familiar to her she could have recognized them from a mile away.

But they're not a mile away, she thought as she closed her eyes briefly, the cold fall air stinging at them as she ran. *In fact they're gaining on me. Each one's closer then the last.*

She bit her lip out of nervous frustration and ended up pushing her tooth into it from the force of her footfalls. She was close now. She still hadn't turned around. She knew that if she turned around and saw the Womb, she wouldn't be able to run anymore. Her legs would melt right then and there and it would be on her like a wolf.

She turned sharply into Xander's driveway, pouring on the steam for those last few strides along his shale walkway. She opened his front door and slammed it shut behind her. She paused for a moment, let out a breath, then turned the deadbolt almost as an afterthought.

She leaned against the door like that for a minute or two, trying to give her mind a chance to catch up with the rest of her body. Both her hands were shaking, the adrenaline in her body working itself off via involuntary spasms now that her legs didn't need the extra energy anymore.

She turned her head and pulled back the blind to check outside.

A black hand burst through the glass, grabbing her by the mouth and all she could see with her wide eyes were the long, yellow teeth behind it.

She jumped, opening her eyes and slowly letting her head rest back against the door. Sighing, she turned her head and pulled back the blind to check outside. A leaf blew across Xander's front yard into the Johnson's, but other than that there was no movement.

She laughed at herself, then took a step toward the stairs.

She stopped after one step and listened, her ears perking. The house was as silent as a tomb, without so much as a heater hum or a vent rustling. For a moment she thought she heard something, but at the same instant she thought that the more rational side of her brain was arguing the difference.

She took another step onto the stairs, then another. Her pace got faster and faster until one of them finally squeaked under the pressure of her weight and she bolted into an all out run. She ran into his bedroom, taking only a moment to regard the shattered computer screen and general shambles of the room, then collapsed onto the bed. She didn't cry, she didn't even sob. She just wrapped his warm covers around her body, then slowly drifted off to sleep.

Again, Mike Harris looked up at the building before him.

This time, however, it was distressingly less inviting. It was charred on the outside, a victim of many careless bonfires, and the heat had left the plastic siding melted and black. The stench of marijuana was thick in the air and made him want to vomit onto the step as he assumed many other people had done before. This area of town wasn't known for being good... Still, it was by no means the 'bad part' of town either. That was what made its presence here even more gut wrenching to him. All around him were quiet suburbs painted in tranquil greens and off-whites. Places where you'd expect to see little girls and boys running around their lawns, playing baseball and climbing trees and not worrying about anything. But they couldn't. That slowly dawned upon Mike as he glared at the black door that must have once been red, judging by the chipped paint between graffiti, Tee gang symbols and profanities involving the reader's female ancestry. The kids in those houses couldn't do what they were supposed to be allowed to. They couldn't play hide-and-seek so late that their parents would have to come find them, or splash in the mud by the road, or even stop to admire the ravishing brunette that just moved in across the way, as he had at that age. They had to stay inside, away from the gaping maw of hatred that was this house, and more specifically the morons that resided there. Morons that didn't think twice about what they did to Julie Peterson. They did it like it was a part of everyday life, a step in the routine, and would probably do it again, maybe to any one of the little girls and boys that they found playing outside 'their' neighborhood.

It's not right, he thought bitterly, clenching his teeth. *Children shouldn't have to be afraid in their homes, around their friends... at school.* He took a step toward the ramshackle house, then another, until finally he was on the concrete stairs and only inches from the door. *I won't have it.*

"And just what do you think you're doing?" came a voice from behind him.

Mike closed his eyes and sighed. He didn't even have to turn and look. The sheer anger and frivolousness of the statement, the way he said it as casually as though he were asking someone to check the mail for him. The almost child-like joy he took in the danger of the situation. It could only be one person. "Get out of here, Xander,"Mike said with a cold voice, then turned around to face his friend.

"Why would I go and do a thing like that?" Xander asked. He leaned carefully against a rotting fencepost, one knee half-bent, and looked up at Mike. His face was cut through the middle, it seemed, with his eyes deadly serious and ready to kill, but a sly grin spreading its way across his face like butter onto hot bread.

"This isn't your fight," Mike argued. "How'd you get here, anyway? I've got the lead."

"True," he nodded. "But I have something better."

"Oh yeah, what's that?"

"A friend who has a lead and doesn't know enough to know when he's being tailed," he quipped, stepping up next to Mike and pushing his index finger into the taller man's chest. "You're not going in there to get yourself killed, you got that? I don't care if you feel the need to crack open rapist skulls after what happened to Cathy. I *respect* and *understand* it, but I really don't care. You wanna get killed? Fine. Go grab my dad's handgun. Feel free to blow your own head off," Xander said, meeting his friend's angry gaze with equal amounts of fury. "But don't expect me to let you go in there and let the enemy do it for you."

"There's only one problem with that statement, Xander," Mike spat, his voice like venom.

"What's that?" Xander asked, mimicking the way his friend had said it a moment ago.

Mike pushed his own index finger into Xander's chest, giving him a little shove. "You are the enemy."

Xander took a deep breath, letting the words cut as deep as they could. It didn't matter. There was nothing Mike could say that he hadn't already told the person in the mirror. "I'm going in. If anything happens, I need you to bail me out," he reasoned.

"Why can't we do it the other way?" Mike shot back.

"Because if something happens to you, I'll lose my cool and probably finish you off myself," Xander reminded them both.

Mike stepped away from the door, curtsying toward it. "Ladies first," he snapped in conceit.

CHAPTER FIVE: TRANSFORMATIONS IN PAIN

Xander opened the door carefully as it felt about ready to snap off of its hinges. A stream of light bled from beneath his feet, melting back into darkness about three yards from where he stood. He couldn't see anything of the walls or floor from here, save for a few shards of broken glass strewn about in front of him. The smell of cheap beer and cheaper drugs assaulted his senses, along with a musty aftershave that he was sure he'd smelled somewhere before. He squinted, trying to force his eyes to adjust to the light as the floor groaned beneath him. Something deep inside of him cringed, like your stomach when you haven't eaten in days, or organs addicted to nicotine and convulsing from withdrawal. He realized too late that it was the true Black Womb warning him of danger.

There was a sound like a firecracker going off right next to his head, something big slamming into it at the same spot. Pain shot through his skull, like shockwaves in a calm pool. The agony exploded out the other side of his brain, trying to find some place to escape. The pain was followed closely by numbness, a tingly feeling that crept over his skin, as though someone were tickling him from the inside out. His ears were ringing. What was worse was the harder he tried to concentrate on the sounds now coming at him, the more he heard the ringing. He clenched his teeth as figures started to emerge from the darkness. There were more than twenty at first, but Xander soon realized that there were really only two. His vision was failing him as well it seemed, the figures before him doubling and then tripling in a shimmering haze. It was as if he'd just gotten off the Twister roller coaster at Wonder World, the one that Sara was always so afraid of. *Sara*, he echoed, the thought shrieking high inside his skull. It cleared away the cloudiness brought on by the blow, his own personal lighthouse shining to bring him back to port.

The first man stepped out of the darkness, and his form expelled all of the shadows that were left in the room. His shoulders were broad and packed tight with muscles, the sheer width of him surely reminding onlookers of tractor trailers coming towards them full-steam. His nostrils flared, making deep huffing sounds to support that hypothesis. He was powerfully built. Beyond powerfully built, actually. His muscles seemed to defy all laws of human anatomy, Xander thought as his eyes caught some of the glare off of the man's sweat-covered skin. It wasn't hard to see a lot of that skin either, as the man wore a simple white wife beater that looked three sizes too small and was clinging to him for dear life. His eyes bulged with rage, but the most striking thing about him was his hair. Long brown hair that hadn't been combed or styled particularly in his yearbook photos but was now drawn back into a pony tail with a blonde tip, revealing that it had been dyed not too long ago. His hair danced along the edge of his black denim jeans, nearly invisible against the shadows, except for the gleaming belt-buckle in its centre that was shaped like the state of Texas for some reason. His brow furrowed, making his face shrink into itself and his slightly elongated jaw seem even larger, like Jay Leno's. He patted the piece of two-by-four he'd just used to strike Xander, ready to use it again if the boy moved. Xander recognized him as Bram Raine.

Which made the second man Allan Bishop, a theory that was proven when the slimmer man lumbered out of the shadows. His heels tapped softly against the rotten, moldy floor, hardly making a sound as he descended toward Xander. He seemed to be the source of the scent of cheap drugs, amplified by the fact that his eyes were bloodshot and bugging, seemingly beyond the man's ability to control them. His pupils darted around aimlessly and his fists were clenched into small balls that moved so fast it was hard to tell if those blurry lines were in fact fingers. His hair was short and wiry, looking like something an army general might have, and was the polar opposite of Raine's. He had a small mustache which looked like an earwig crawling over his upper lip that he was obviously too proud to shave. However, his face was trim and there didn't seem to be any fat on his body. He was toned, even if he wasn't overly muscular. He was breathing hard, making his loose t-shirt wave slightly as his chest heaved. It also made his sweatpants drop about an inch only to rise again the next time he inhaled. "Jesus," he said, his voice coming in quick bursts of air. His lips barely moved when he spoke, a trait that was typically learned in the harsher prisons. "He's a friggin' kid. Just some stupid kid."

"Don't matter," Raine barked, his voice was low and commanding with a heavy New York accent. That made about as much sense as his Texan belt-buckle, and Xander decided that he was just faking such things as gimmicks to make himself look tough. "Kid's still got a mouth, hasn't he? He can still talk. We gotta shut him up."

Xander coughed, slowly rising to his feet. It was like watching smoke billow upwards from a blast. He seemed to just keep rising and rising, until he stood at eye-level with both men. "I'm not here to talk," Xander said quietly, bringing both fists up into a jabbing position. "I'm here to--"

SMACK!

158

The chuck of wood that Raine had swung at Xander from the darkness came around again, this time planting itself into his jaw. He felt splinters make their way into his mouth and gums as his neck twisted and nearly snapped, the muscle tendons in his shoulders straining then breaking. "Guh," he said simply, forcing his aching skull back around just in time to see the wood get pushed forward again, catching him head-on between the eyes. He fell backward, but Allan caught him before he could hit the ground, the boy's limp body as heavy as a sack of potatoes in his thin arms.

Raine chuckled softly as he looked down at Xander, coppery blood that seemed just a bit too orange (but about as far from black as a colour could get) leaking from the boy's mouth and ears, which were already starting to swell. "Hey, lookit man," he laughed, pointing at the battered teen. "It's that Xander Drew freak!"

Allan careened his head around to look in the bloodied face. "Yeah, so it is. Little punk," he giggled, and he sounded more than a little nuts. He was probably just high, though. "We should make him wear his ass as a hat," he laughed again, and that time Raine chuckled too.

Come on, Xander thought, fighting unconsciousness as more blood dripped from the growing crack in the roof of his mouth down onto his tongue. *You can do this, Drew. Just think of... of...* but all he could think of was that metallic-tasting liquid that was pooling in all of his facial orifices. *Sara!* he realized suddenly, and he felt the true Womb twitch a little. *Think of Sara. Concentrate on her*, he thought, coaxing his 'other side' out of its shell. *Think of her, lying there in that coffin...* he continued, tears welling up from the memories and the pain.

"Look, he's crying," Allan said with mock sympathy. "Poor baby."

Julie, lying in an alleyway across from her bedroom window, that smile ruined, trying to find enough shards of clothing to get her home without her perv neighbors catching too much skin... Still, the Womb just fizzed. It was like trying to start a cold engine in the dead of winter. In Antarctica. It just wasn't happening, a fact that slowly grew in the back of his mind as he watched the red liquid from his nose seep into the soaking-wet plywood flooring.

I can't transform, he realized, just as the wood again jabbed at him, catching him square in the left eye and knocking him back, his brain beating around inside his head until it stopped making noise. Stopped thinking.

Allan kicked him, laughing as the comatose boy's body tossed and turned under the pressure. Then Raine joined in. As Mike watched from a window in horror, they beat Xander's chest in until he thought it was going to cave his rib cage onto his lungs. They slammed their heels against his face and his crotch, laughing heartily at the wet snap of flesh being loosened from bone. Then Raine pulled something from his pocket and showed it to Allan. They both smiled and walked out the back door, and left Xander for dead.

Mike opened the front door and hurried in. He leaned down into Xander's face, his own wrought with terror. He slapped him on the cheek to wake him, and was horrified when the impact made blood shoot up from his lips like a geyser.

He grabbed him by the arms and started hauling him out of the house, using all the strength he could muster to command the dead weight.

It was dark.

He knew that much, but everything else was more than a little fuzzy. He couldn't remember anything much outside of 'pain' and, of course, 'it was dark.' So, all said, he didn't know very much about what was happening.

In the distance, there was an odd humming. He recognized the tune, his mother used to sing it to him when he was little. When he was a baby. God, that seemed like such a long time ago now. What must it have been like for her? Little mama Drew holding her baby against her nipple, never thinking that this would be how her son would die. Alone in some dingy burned-out house, blood coming out of every hole in his body, ending up being a waste of time for everyone around him.

Then again, it wasn't that surprising.

"Oh, stop whining!" came a voice from out in the darkness. It was thick and raspy, and it spoke with an ill demeanor. The person speaking didn't want Xander to stop complaining. He wanted him to keep going so that they'd have an excuse to beat him down more than he already was.

Xander groaned, rolled over onto his gut and took a look around, struggling to prop himself up. Blood gushed from his lip, black and oozing, dripping into the darkness where he lost sight of it. "Where am I?" he called out, the echo of each word returning to him before he had even finished it. He barely recognized his own voice; it was like he was underwater.

The person humming stopped long enough to chuckle-- more like a cackle, really. It seemed like a contradiction to their... no, her voice. It was so evil now, laughing at him as he stared out into the world blindly. It had been so gentle only a moment ago. Soft and warm on the breeze, wrapping around him like a blanket. The humming had started again now, and it reminded him of lying on his back on a grassy knoll not far from his house, with Sara only a few feet away. Looking up at the sky and picking shapes out of the clouds. The way the wind used to whistle in the hollow tree branches. Birds in their nests, chirping as they fed worms to the eager mouths of their young. It reminded him of... springtime.

Suddenly, he knew. The blackness was all too familiar now, and he fought to get up. He managed to scramble to his feet, draw his sliced hands into aching fists and get up the energy to glare into the darkness as best he could.

SLAP!

His feet were knocked out from under him and he fell backwards, beating his head off of the shadows. He felt his brain rock in its casing and his teeth crammed shut onto his tongue for a second. He coughed, laying there on his back and looking around for the person that did it. "Am I... dead?" he asked, gulping back spit.

"No," came the humming, springtime voice. A face became visible in the darkness, pale and chalky at first. Dark circles around the eyes and jet black hair matted in front of her face gave her the brief approximation of an albino skeleton. Or of a ghost. It floated, as if bodiless, up into a height that meant it was standing and then slowly started com-

ing toward him. As it got closer, its features became more and more defined, until Eve Spider stepped out in front of him. There was an odd glow around her. An ambience that was welcomed, the first light he'd seen since coming to this dreadful place. "But I am. You killed me, remember?" she teased, her fingers dancing around the stab wound in her silken robes sexually. She rubbed her gut, tracing the lines of it with her index finger, then bringing it up to her mouth. "It's okay. It doesn't hurt anymore... only sometimes. When I sleep." She smiled at him, and it was surprisingly warm. Her slanted eastern eyes held a tint of mischievousness and glee to them, but there was kindness there too. You had to look deep, but it was definitely there. "Get up," she laughed, and it was no longer that of an evil mastermind. It was that of a friend laughing at someone who'd just tripped over their own feet, and he felt the strange urge to laugh with her.

He repressed it.

"What am I doing here?" Xander asked, sitting up and rubbing the bridge of his nose. "I have to get back to Coral Beach. Mike needs my help, he can't fight those assholes alone," he pleaded with her, as if she were somehow holding him here.

"I know, sweetie," she chided gently, reaching out and stroking the side of his face. "That's what I said too, when I first got here. But for me, it was a one-way ticket." She smirked. "There wasn't even an in-flight movie." She dug her nails into the side of his face, raking them across his cheeks.

Xander coiled back, rushing to his feet. He brought a hand up to his ripped flesh, but found there was none. No marks, not even a scar. Just a chubby little cheek with not enough facial hair on it. "What the hell are you talking about? Where am I?" he demanded, pointing a finger at her. "Tell me, now!"

"Yeah, that'll work," came a second voice, the one who'd told him to stop whining a moment ago. Only this time Xander recognized it. All of the colour drained from his face and the blood coming out of him ran cold as ice. His lower lip quivered. He did not want to turn around to face the man behind him. "'Tell me... now!'" The voice chuckled again. "You sound real intimidating. I almost soiled myself, really. You didn't sound at all like some scared little teenager wishing he could go home, watch Adam Sandler movies and try to look down his girlfriend's bra." Again, laughter.

The lights came on, finally, and he was there again. "Home sweet home," he mumbled under his breath, trying to mask his fear at the solid metal room they were in the centre of, with a drain for blood directly beneath his feet in the middle of the semi-circle. His remark did not sound fearless, as his voice quivered past the point of comprehension.

They were back at Engen.

He heard the second speaker's lips open again, the tongue snapping against those sharp, jagged teeth as he prepared to speak. "This is absolutely pathetic," Genblade spat, and Xander felt tiny driblets of saliva splatter against the back of his neck. "You might as well let me kill you now, and do yourself a favor."

"Oh, but you mustn't do that, dear Adam," Spider said, humming that song again and speaking to the tune. "Ruin all the fun, it would. All the daisies would die and the sun would go all pink." She spread her legs slightly, looking past Xander to Genblade, a hint of seduction in her face. "Take away from all the other good things that are pink, I say."

Xander's brow furrowed as Genblade bumped past him, nearly knocking him over as he made his way over to his wife. His hand slid up her leg and he kissed her passionately, their tongues darting in and out of the space between their mouths. It made Xander wish that the lights were out again. They wished it, too.

Spider's silks were draped over her body just the way they'd been the day they met. The day she died. She wore them loose and they blew hauntingly in the breeze, just enough so that he couldn't get a glimpse of anything. He found himself staring at her, until he saw a scar on her right thigh. A surgical scar. The spot where Alpha had put Sara's ovaries into her.

They stopped kissing, and Genblade glowered at him. "Is this your dream, or mine?" he hissed wickedly.

"Beats me," Xander replied honestly, shrugging one shoulder.

Genblade whipped out the Spider-Sword as though it were an extension of his own body, its smooth metal gleaming against the fluorescent lights. The two gems that made up its handle sparkled like a thousand eyes, making up the head and body of a spider and giving the blade its name. "That's the best idea you've ever had," he snarled menacingly.

Spider brought a hand up to his chest, stopping him as she stroked the area over his heart. "There now," she said helpfully, giving her lover a little pat. "Can't kill him yet," she hummed a gleeful tone. "That'll spoil the surprise." She broke away from him, but still held his hands tightly. For a moment they looked like two normal people out for a walk in the park. "The birds will chirp on that day," she started to sing the song, and her voice was odd. Still Asian, but now it had a British accent as well. "'Your vows you've broken, like my heart...Oh, why did you so enrapture me... Now I remain in a world apart... But my heart remains in captivity!'" Then she broke off into her normal voice again, still singing the words to her own song. "The Cheshire Cat and the White Rabbit, all lined up together... all six of them lined up in a row. And the bad man... and the right switch... and we'll all be home for supper before you know it!"

Xander raised an eyebrow at her, stepping back slightly. "You... realize you don't make any sense, right?"

"Sorry, scar tissue," she smiled, nodding apologetically. She waved a hand over her face, and for a moment it became bruised and beaten in, full of holes. Like she'd been in... an explosion. And her robes... they were filled with blood, coming from the hole he'd put into the right of her abdomen.

Xander felt a pang of sympathy when he saw that. His lower lip quivered as he reached out, touching the stab wound tenderly and getting some of the blood on his fingertips. "Will you be alright?"

She smiled. "It's alright. It fades, it all fades," she assured him, reached out and stroking her fingers through his matted hair. "Just like the pain."

He looked down at the ground, and suddenly he didn't feel in danger anymore. He felt like... like he was in his mother's arms. "I want the pain to stop."

"Pain..."Genblade cursed, as he stroked his blade alone in the corner.

Spider turned and hushed him, then went back to Xander. "The pain is the key. It's only begun, but you have to use it. You have to see it. It can help you, if you let it. Like today."

162

Xander shook his head defiantly, cursing. "I didn't need pain today. I needed power. My power."

She shook her head in dismay, looking deep into him. "Pain is your power," she told him with some amount of regret, then leaned in and kissed him, softly, on the lips.

His eyes snapped open and he lunged upwards in bed, gasping for breath. He reached up to pull the layer of blood from his face, but found that there was none there. He closed his eyes, the bright light assaulting his pupils and forcing them to dilate beyond the realm of human comprehension. His teeth hurt, but he didn't quite understand why until he reached up and found that his jaw was still dislocated. He snapped it back into place with a quick twist, and felt the soft tickle in the back of his neck indicate that his healing factor had, in fact, finally kicked back in to repair it. Every bone in Xander's body ached, and he welcomed the feeling of coolness that came when she dabbed a cold, damp cloth onto his forehead.

She was humming something, and for a moment he thought he was with Spider again, trapped in Engen. That maybe all this had been the dream and that he'd never really left that horrible place. He opened his eyelids again slowly and saw the face of Cathy Kennessy staring down at him, her beautiful features encompassing his vision. Her long black hair tickled the sides of his face as she leaned in and looked into his eyes... then snapped her fingers twice to see if he was alive.

"Cathy?" he groaned wearily, bringing a hand up to the bridge of his nose and rubbing it rhythmically. She said something in return, and he felt her warm candy-scented breath on his face, but the words weren't audible. They came out as a low hum, sounding very much like one of the teachers on Charlie Brown. He furrowed his brow in utter confusion. "What?" he called out, even his voice sounding far away and underwater.

Holding his throat, he sat up. He felt an immense pressure deep inside each of his ears, and then a pop so loud he was sure someone had fired off a gun next to his head. "Ow," he said more clearly, bringing a finger to one of the lobes and caressing the tender cartilage gingerly. He hissed in pain when he did, an electric surge coursing throughout his face. When he brought his hand back, there was condensed black blood dripping from his fingers onto his sheets.

"You okay?" Cathy asked, taking the damp cloth that she held in one hand to both his ears, dabbing them gently.

"Yes," he replied sarcastically. "I always bleed from the ears when I'm okay."

Her eyes looked down, scanning the sheets as more drops of blood started to fall and it became obvious that her efforts were futile. "You should lay back down," she said, stroking the cloth along his sweat laden face.

He reached up to stop her, his hand missing her arm once and then jutting out quickly to grab it.

Her eyes rose up again to meet his and they let the gaze linger on for a minute.

"That tickles," he said finally, tossing the cloth down on his night table. He heard it land with a loud plop, glancing at it just long enough to see just how much blood there was on it. More than enough to cause alarm, at least until he figured out what was wrong with his powers. He looked at her and couldn't help the smile from beginning to twitch at the corners of his mouth, even though the motion hurt his bruised face. "What happened to me?" he asked, trying to talk above the pounding coming from both his temples.

"You were an idiot," she said simply. She reached out and forced him to lie down completely. He was surprised when her pressure felt like a ton of bricks on his chest, as if everything was more sensitive. He felt weaker than he ever had been before. "Mike got you out of there before anything else could've --"

He jumped up again, sending the covers flying. "Mike!" he said, startled. "I've got to --"

"Lie back down," she finished for him as she wrapped the lost sheets around him again, her arms around his body for a moment, sending an odd sensation up through his body. "Excellent idea. I agree completely."

"No!" Xander shook his head defiantly, making his brain slosh around inside his skull. "You don't understand! I have to--"

"Re-*lax*," she finished again, putting a little more punch into the words as she shoved him down, just to let him know that she was serious. He tried to get up again, so she lay down on him. She wrapped her arms around his upper torso and cuddled in until she was on his entire right side, resting her head comfortably into the nape of his neck.

He tried to protest again, but found that he couldn't bring himself to. Like his limbs had temporarily stopped listening to his brain and were instead concentrating on what his heart was telling him to do. "Where *is* Mike?" he asked, clearing his throat.

"He went home late last night. Somebody had to do the round robin thing."

"Round robin?"

"Yeah," she said matter-of-factly, adjusting her head a little to get comfortable. She wrapped one of her arms up around his head without looking, playfully stroking the hairs behind his ears. "You know, that's when he calls my parents to tell them that I'm over there, so that they don't worry, then he calls your parents to tell them the same thing, so they don't come in here and find the two of us..." she paused, looking over at the trashed computer. "...or anything else, for that matter."

"Yeah. I really need to clean that up," he admitted.

"Yeah, you really do," she agreed, in a tone of voice that let him know this was one of those things that should have gone without saying.

He leaned in slightly, until his lips were right next to her ear. Her cheek was infinitely tweak-able, so he tweaked it as he whispered, "I really have to get up, you know."

She rubbed her cheek softly, shifting her head so that she could see him. "The only way you're getting out of this bed is with your claws inside my body."

He paused and leaned in a little. "Be careful. That sentence could be taken the wrong way..."

She reached out and pinched his cheek with her nails and he winced, proving he was still in need of being bedridden. "Don't be a jerk," she whispered without realizing it.

"Very funny," he shot back, but it wasn't a whisper now. As they both had drawn closer, it had become more hushed. Like lovers taking in slight gasps for fear of being caught.

"Look very... very... closely," she instructed him, and he took it as encouragement to get even closer. "You'll see that I'm not joking."

They both stopped, opening their eyes to their fullest. They both realized at once just how close they'd allowed their two faces to become. They shuffled apart, slowly at first and then with increasing speed, as he looked around for his shirt. He coughed away his discomfort, clearing his throat, then turned to her. "So, time to get up now?"

"Definitely," she responded happily, without actually turning to look at him.

He watched her get up, watched how her white blouse stuck to her slim body like glue. Not super-model slim, the kind that you'd be afraid to hug in case you'd break a rib, but just the right size. The way her hips swiveled when she walked over to the window facing Sara's house, just standing there and looking out at it. "My parents are gone then?" he asked, the typically casual conversation losing all of its calm atmospheric qualities.

"Yep," she said, a perky word. But her voice wasn't perky, it was distant now. Her hand played with a few strands of her hair that had gotten tangled between her teeth. She turned then, as if finally acknowledging that they had spoken. "Why?" she asked, and there was a mischief in her voice that he couldn't quite put his finger on.

He smiled.

ʎ⟨ʎ

Tim gave the door to The Factory one final shove, steadying himself as it finally jerked open. He hadn't been to the teenage arcade/club/pool hall very often while he lived in Coral Beach, but he had never had that much trouble opening the door before. He suspected it had something to do with the heat from the sun beating down almost directly onto the rust-splotched door, the same heat that had small circles of sweat gathering at the nape of his neck and the armpits of his blue striped shirt. He closed the door behind him quickly, trapping the heat outside and breathing in the cool air-conditioned atmosphere inside. He smirked at himself, his hand still on the door, as he turned to enter the main part of the club.

The place was all but empty except for a couple of kids skipping school, one waitress, and the back of house cook (who was just barely visible through a window behind the cash register). The building used to be used for storage and you could still see the concrete walls behind the posters of The Who and Jefferson Airplane that were pinned up on the walls with sticky tack and tape, most of them skewed sideways or flapping in the breeze from the air conditioner. What had started out as two arcade games and a few vending machines had grown in the last few years to become an establishment featuring a full eat-in and take-out menu, five pool tables, a wide assortment of arcade games and a lounge. There was even a small stage where local bands played every Friday night until recently.

Tim glared at the two kids playing pool, laughing on the inside. He recognized the girl as Calla McFadden, a girl he'd caught smoking pot behind the post office twice late last year. He wasn't sure, but he thought the other was Randy Owchar. Randy looked more relaxed, but the sweat on his forehead despite the cool air proved he had something to hide. Tim gave them one extra huff of his nostrils just for the fun on it, then walked over to the bar.

When he leaned up against the countertop, he felt as though he'd been hit in the face with the smell of pine cleaner. As much of it as there was, there was still a slight scent of mold underlying it that came with the old building. Shaking off the sudden dizziness that the cleanser had given him, he forced a smile at the girl behind the counter.

Roxanne Carpenter was about thirty-six years old according to the file Tim had pulled on her, but she didn't look a day over twenty-nine. Except her eyes. Long hours had run circles around her eyes that she had tried hard to conceal with just a little too much eyeliner. Other than that her face was clear. Her short, curly red hair had been combed out on either side to points by her ears, bobbing a little each time she moved. She was wearing a jean-jacket over her apron right now, and had probably just come in from a smoke. She looked up from counting out the skim in the cash register, but did not return the smile. Instead she turned her dark green eyes back to counting all of the five dollar bills, leaving only five of them in the register and adding the rest to a pile that she had made on the windowsill between the front and back of house. After a moment, an unseen person reached a hairy hand out and shoveled them forward, then closed the window. She checked the back counter to make sure all the money was accounted for, then sighed with displeasure as she finally turned her attention back to Tim. "What do you want?" she asked, her voice even and devoid of emotion. She spoke as though she didn't really care about the answer to the question.

Tim smiled, grabbed a toothpick from the small canister on the bar and twiddling it between his fingers. He almost laughed, not knowing quite what to say. "Did you hear about Julie Peterson?"

Roxanne tried hard to keep her eyes as devoid of sentiment as her speech had been a moment ago, but couldn't keep the slight twinkle of acknowledgment out. She reached down and tied off the top of a garbage bag beneath the cash register, her lips drawing up in a bow. "Only what the kids have been saying."

"Then you know what's happened to her?" he prodded, realizing that he was dancing around the issue but unsure of how to stop.

She nodded, not even so much as looking at him when she did, still finding things around the cash to busy herself with.

"Listen, this type of thing doesn't happen around here very often-" he started, trying to help his words find their footing.

She rolled her eyes and cut him off before he had the chance. "No, it doesn't get reported very often. There is a difference," she corrected, pointing a glossy red fingernail at him.

"Fair enough," he conceded, raising his palms in defeat. "Either way, the only other person I know of that's filed an official sexual assault report in the last two years is--"

"Me," she said, cutting him off again. She was smiling now, but it wasn't a happy one. It was a smug smile as she proved her initial suspicions about Tim's visit correct.

"Well, yes. I was wondering if you knew anything about this case. I know it's a long shot, but could it be the same person?" He was trying his best to sound sympathetic and sound authoritative at the same time, to mixed results. At best it made his voice uneven, having to clear his throat often.

"Persons. Plural," she corrected, even the fake smile fading slowly.

"Yes, there were two or three men working in conjuncture," he nodded, admitting that Peterson had fallen victim to more than one man.

"Not what I meant," she snapped, shaking her head. Her eyes were distant for a moment as she pictured Julie in that way, then forced the image from her brain. "I meant with me. Not at once, but a couple of times... a couple of different guys."

"I'm... sorry," he stuttered, wishing he had the file he had left back in the car. "I was only aware of the one time, back in May of last year."

"No, they go back a while," she informed him, snorting a little unamused laugh. "The first few times I called it in. Carl Dent or one of his rent-a-cop flunkies would come down and take my statement and a description. They'd take pictures of the scene and dust for prints and tell me where to send the doctor's reports to... and then I'd wait. And wait. About four weeks in each time, it'd finally sink in that they weren't going to actually do anything."

"Well, I can't speak for the other officers, but- "

She sneered at him, no longer attempting to hide her contempt. "And the *second* it happens some cute little blonde haired, blue eyed thing, a damn *federal agent* is down here asking me questions. Typical."

"Actually, Miss Peterson had brown hair and green eyes, I believe," he corrected, but his voice was nothing more than a whisper. He felt about one inch tall.

"Well, whatever," she said, rolling her eyes at him again. "I don't think it's the same guys, to answer your question. All of mine were out-of-towners, and I don't suppose you'd be here asking if you thought that was the story with these ones."

Tim shook his head sheepishly.

"Didn't think so," she mumbled, grabbing a cloth and starting to wipe down the back counter. Her elbow pumped fiercely as she did it, as if she were pouring all her anger and frustration into her work.

Tim tapped his knuckle on the counter twice then turned to leave without a word, unsure of what to say.

As he neared the door, she called out to him without looking up from her work. "Hope you catch them."

"Me too," he agreed, pushing the door open and letting the heat hit him in the face. He turned and watched her for a moment, her face red with rage but not at him. There was a time that someone could have said she was mad at the men that had wronged her. Then at the police that had ignored her. Now she was just… angry. It became a part of who she was despite her efforts to hide it, but was obvious now as the countertop vibrated and rocked under her constant pressure. "I don't like thinking about what happens when we don't," he finished in a much lower voice, then closed the door behind him.

It was a bright, sunny Coral Beach day.

Actually that statement was misleading, as Greer Donaldson told everyone who informed her of such a thing. Her fresh, fourteen year-old mind had thought it a disgusting paradox why people would call it that. It made a day like today sound ordinary, or run-of-the-mill. Such was not the case, however. Coral Beach, Maine was subject to a vast majority of hurricane-level storms, rain, sleet, mid-summer snow and (at least once a month, it seemed to her) the temperature would drop so freakishly low that it might actually hail. That wasn't even counting obscene murders and odd disappearances, things that often made days like today considerably less bright, even a little gray. As if the shared mood of this town's inhabitants affected the forecast, making the poor weatherman consistently wrong.

But that was what made it even more important to appreciate days like today. Her young, republican-raised mind hated to be so cliché, but the sun was bathing her face in warm rays and the birds were filling her ears with a happy, relaxing tune. She didn't care if she was late, she simply *had* to walk to school today.

Greer's long blonde hair flowed behind her, catching rays of sunlight as they passed her. Her lips were full and red, a clear contrast to her pearly white teeth. Her skin was milky white, with the exception of a few freckles across her upper cheeks and the bridge of her nose. Large blue eyes shone brightly with a light that came from inside and threatened to outdo the sun in sheer radiance. She was wearing a loose orange top and a pair of faded blue jeans that were pretty well white at the bottom. She was truly a vision, young and beautiful and innocent.

That was why they picked her.

Allan Bishop and Bram Raine leapt from the shadows as one, each of them grabbing her by either of her small, round shoulders. She tried to scream but one of Allan's hands was already over her mouth, the other firmly planted in the small of her back for the moment. She made a small noise, but it escaped through his thick fingers as nothing more than a whistle. He jerked her head to one side as Raine picked up her kicking feet, forcing her onto the pile of rotting, rat infested garbage at the back end of the space between two houses. Her neighbors' houses, to be specific.

She resisted, trying hard to get at least one of her weak limbs free, but they were by far too much for her alone. She could see another man approaching, though she could not see who. He was laughing, she knew that much. It was a sick sound. Allan jerked her head to the side again, the calcium in the bone cracking from the stress, sending a sudden jolt of pain through her cranium. He brought his disgusting, rough tongue down to her skin and tasted it as the three men began to rip the clothes off of her, the threads snapping and cutting against her flesh as they did so, nearly taking it off of the bone.

She started to cry. But, that was all right. As far as they were concerned, it wasn't worth it unless they cried. The tears were hot and Raine kissed them off of her cheeks, the taste of salt making his mouth dry. He made his way down her neck, hungry for more and grunting like some depraved animal.

They took *turns*. Two of them holding her down, beating her if she started to struggle, the other climbing on. By the end, she couldn't even cry anymore. Her sobs came as dry heaves, and she wanted very much to vomit.

Then they urinated on her. It stung at the cuts that laced her tiny body.

She looked up, barely able to see out of her bruised and swollen eyes, and she saw him. The third man. More than that, she *recognized* him.

The third man looked down on her. He drew back a hand and slapped her, the sound echoing off of the nearby homes. She fell to the ground, her face splashing into a puddle of coke and ketchup that had spilled from a torn garbage bag. She was unconscious, a fact that made him roar with long-repressed anger. He continued to beat her as Allan and Raine watched, snickering the entire time.

When her face was no longer recognizable as that of a human being, they emptied out a Glad bag full of garbage and stuffed her naked, bloody body inside, leaving it there with all the other trash that they had no more use for.

"Get out of here," the third man said to Allan and Raine. "Go find that goddamn kid that came to the house last night. Xander Drew." He nodded, then repeated, "Find him."

He walked the five feet to his car, casually got in and drove away, whistling that damned song from Alice in Wonderland, without a care in the world.

Raine had a car as well and offered to give Allan a ride, but he chose to walk.

Because it really was *such* a nice day.

He looked into the mirror that hung lopsided in his bathroom, the tiles on the walls gleaming the fixtureless light into his eyes and making them all red, the veins in them bulging to the point of rupturing. His face was flushed and glossy from sweat. Suddenly his features contorted in anguish and concentration, trying desperately to force something upon itself. He closed his eyes in strain and when he opened them again, Xander Drew was infinitely disappointed by the fact that the exact same face stared back at him. Only now it was breathing much harder, sending foggy streaks across the reflective surface mere inches from his face.

"Maybe you're just tense?" Cathy offered helpfully, faking a smile as she sat with her hands between her knees on the nearby toilet.

He gave her a look filled with tension. "Now why would you say that?" he said gruffly, a bead of sweat dripping from his chin into the faded yellow sink. "This never happens to me. During the Genblade thing, I transformed all the time."

"But that was just the one time," she reasoned, something that brought immense disappointment to him. She frowned at her incompetence and general stupidity on the subject, but how was she supposed to know anything about transforming, anyway? "Maybe you're nervous?" she tried again, only to be hailed with another look from Xander. She hated that look. It sank into her, and made her feel like nothing. Less than nothing... less than human. Like the way Grendel and the boys at school would look at her and make her feel.

"I need to get this down," he said flatly, ending the argument. "I have to learn to transform if I'm ever going to do anything about those idiots Al and Raine. If anyone deserves to see the true me, it's those two." He paused and stared himself down in the mirror. "Spider said pain was my power..." he whispered to himself.

"Was that before or after you killed her?" Cathy asked, confusion apparent in her dark eyes.

"After," he said, slapping a hand against the sink as if that were obvious.

"Oh," Cathy nodded. Then she stopped, thought about it, and crumpled her nose a little. "What?"

He waved her off and continued to concentrate on the mirror. He thought of Sara, and the funeral, and those rapist bastards, and Grendel and Tommy and Sud... all of them. He let all the rage and hate and anger and sorrow fill up inside him, waiting for the Womb to fire up and let him reform. Into *something*. *Anything*. Even the slightest change controlled by his will would be a good start; if he was able to change his appearance like the Womb could, he wouldn't have to worry about being recognized when he went out at night. *That's if I'm gonna keep this damn hero thing up*, he thought doubtfully in the back of his mind, as he examined the bruised skin that was healing nicely around his eye. *And it doesn't seem like I can keep myself out of trouble.*

He felt the true Womb twitch again, then surge. What had he been thinking about? What had triggered it? It started to fade down again, as he struggled to find the right train of thought to jump aboard. *Christ*, he thought sickeningly. *Sometimes I can't stop this shit for overtaking me, but now I can't seem to coax it out of its damned hole. What is with it?*

Cathy just watched him from her ice cold seat and twiddling her fingers. She glanced over at the tub curiously, seeing baby bath shampoo and toys there even though Xander had no siblings. The normally humorous sight did not help her now though, a barrage of images running through her head. "I try, y'know," she said as she gazed down at the dark green floor tiles. They reflected her face in them, staring right back up at her. "I try to be good, and to think the happy thoughts, and to do whatever the hell else my parents, the guidance counsellor, and the frigging TeleTubbies say to do." She buried her face into her palms, fighting to regain her composure as she forced the words out. "I haven't been sleeping. That's why I came over here last night, I needed to get away from my own bed. It doesn't feel safe there anymore, y'know? Just knowing that Raine and Genblade and all the others know where it is... and Grendel, too." She sighed. "I know he's dead. Just like all the others. But I have these dreams... nightmares really, where he slips into my room late at night and..." She stifled a sob. "... Well, you know. And when I wake up, I'm never sure if I'm really awake. Like maybe, the real world is where I'm just his plaything and this is all just some stupid dream from my naive head. God knows, our lives lately aren't realistic. They read like a comic book, for christsakes." She paused for a long time then, staring at the yellow duck next to the soap on the edge of the tub. "He took it all away, Xander. The safety. I don't feel safe here anymore. Not even around Mike. I'm just afraid that he'll do it, too. I can't even feel safe around you, and not just because of the Womb. Because you're a man too and that makes me sound awful, and the fact that I don't give a shit about Julie Peterson and her problems makes me sound awful and I am awful but I just don't give a fuck!" she cursed, tears streaming down like rain now. "The worst part is knowing that it could all happen again, y' know? That it will." She stopped crying, becoming deathly quiet for a moment. "People don't die all at once, y' know. I'll never believe that, no matter how many friends I bury. I think you die bit by bit over the years, each pain and loss slowly chipping away at your heart until there's nothing left -- and then you just can't take it anymore -- *and then you die.*" She stopped. She was looking at Xander's feet, unable to bring herself to look into his eyes when she said this next part. She didn't even want to say it, for it was a horrible thing to ask. But she simply couldn't stop her lips from moving. "Well, if this isn't what kills me... I don't want to stick around and find out what does. I want to die, Xander. Kill me. Why not, you killed everything else..." she stopped and pursed her parched lips. "I'm sorry. I didn't mean that."

He turned away from the mirror. "Sorry about what?" he asked coldly. "You say something?"

Shock filled her eyes, as she realized he had not heard a word she had just said.

"Be quiet a minute," he said, raising a finger to her. "I think I almost got it."

Xander stared into the mirror, horrible thoughts filling his mind. His blood was pumping hard and it felt like it was too thick for his veins. Like the black blood.

It was as if he was there -- that's how vivid the memory of Engen was. He knew that was the key, it had to be. He could feel the heat of the reactor on his face as he raced against the clock to disarm it, Abner Jenkins -- The Alpha -- dying on the floor not far from where Xander stood, the murdering devil's organs splattered out across the cold grates, blood filtering down through and landing on hot heating vents, creating a disgusting smell. He remembered the madman's cries, and suddenly he could feel it. He could feel the change coming over him, the power.

He opened his eyes again, trying not to lose the image of Alpha, his surrogate 'father.' He focused on a particular point on his face -- the upper cheek under his right eye -- where a scar had been ever since he was a child. When he focused on that area, it got very hot all of a sudden, as if he were burning a hole into it with his eyes. The skin seemed to boil, large bubbles forming there. It shrunk down until it disappeared into his face again, skin folding over the spot where the scar had been. The place where it no longer was.

When he smiled, the skin quickly shifted back to the way it had been. Xander grunted impatiently, then tried again.

This time, he felt something different. His entire face felt like it was on fire, smouldering with tiny boils that were popping up everywhere, covering his features.

Cathy screamed as he fell to the floor, clutching at his face. He tried to withdraw his claws, but they would not come either, so he scratched at his face with his bare nails. When the boils finally stopped coming, they stayed. They'd reformed and folded his mouth and nose away, along with his left eye and both ears. His face was turning blue, and Cathy shook him by the shoulders, realizing suddenly that he could not breathe. She ran out into his room across the hall, grabbing a small blade that he had always kept there for god knows what reason. By the time she got back to the washroom he was going from blue to purple, with a little aquamarine around the corners of where his lips would be. She drew the blade back and stabbed him in the gut, right where his appendix would have been. The boils turned black then and melted off of him, leaving the same thin layer of congealed blood that accompanied every transformation.

Pain is your power.

He gasped for air, clutching his chest as breath filled his lungs and colour started to come back into his cheeks. For a moment it was all he could do not to have a heart attack, then he turned and grasped Cathy, bringing her into a hug. "Thank you," he said honestly, kissing her neck softly. "I love you. Thank you."

She smiled, wrapping her arms around him gently and rocking him back and forth, his sweat dripping onto her shoulders and down her back again.

"I know," he said finally. He pushed her away and she saw that he was wide-eyed and looked crazed. "I know!" he shouted again, shaking her slightly.

"Know what?" she demanded, palming both sides of his face and forcing him to look into her eyes. "What do you know?"

"Why... I can't," he said in short gasps. "The explosion at Engen. I shouldn't have survived that, the Womb's still healing my body from it... it's burnt out still, no power there. Not yet."

She nodded slowly. "That makes sense. How'd you figure that out?"

"Spider told me, Cathy," he said again, the sweat still pouring down and mixing with the blood now. "Spider told me that, and she said: pain is my power." He crumpled his brow. "What does that mean?"

Cathy shrugged solemnly, wishing she could help her friend more. "I don't know."

There was a knock at the door.

Then there was a knocking sound as the door was kicked in.

"Get in the tub," he said quietly, staring at the bathroom door. It was hanging open and swaying still from the force Cathy had used to open it. There was no lock on it; his mother had been bugging his father to get it fixed for weeks. All that was left was a few scraps of twisted metal where the lock had been. He looked across the hall at his bedroom door, and all the locks on that door. But the stairs were between the two and he could already hear their heavy, drunken footsteps on them.

"What?" she whispered harshly, glancing over at the tub which simple age had stained a dark yellow. Her head seemed to be on a swivel. She wanted to look at the tub, but every time one of the criminal's feet fell, her head snapped back in the direction of the door. Sweat was lining the edge of her hair now, making her bangs soak against her forehead. It did so in spirals, and if you looked at her the exact right way, she looked like an alien from Farscape or something like that. "No!" she blurted out, finally realizing his 'master plan'. She grabbed his face and forced him to look at her. "I won't let you."

He grabbed her by the wrist, giving her a little shove in the general direction he wanted her to go. She nearly toppled over the side of the tub and beat her head off of the faucet. "Go," he mouthed slowly. By this time, Xander could see Al and Raine's shadows on his bedroom wall. It was unmistakable now; there was no question. Cathy still hadn't moved, so he reached over and gave her a little nudge into the tub, pulling the curtain shut and hiding her presence.

Xander crouched down, preparing himself. As soon as he saw their laughing, maniacal forms start to make their way up over the stairs, he bolted for his room. His feet flew along the floor he knew so well like wings, each impact sending a vibration through his body that irritated his bruises. That was alright, he knew there would be plenty more where they came from. As he passed by them he reached out and gave Raine a quick shove, nearly sending him toppling over the stairs. But the rapist steadied himself on the railing, and Al helped him regain balance from behind.

Xander cursed softly to himself. His cheeks red and puffy from the sudden effort as he made his way to his bedroom door and opened it. He slammed it shut behind him, hearing their screams and protests, then quickly reached up and started to fiddle with the lock.

Too late.

They slammed on the door, forcing it into the young man's face. Xander tumbled back, landing the arch of his back against the corner of his computer desk, of all places. *Damn*, he cursed again as he tried desperately to catch his wind and regain his footing. Unable to move, he watched both men enter the room like locusts, taking their places on either side of him. It was abundantly clear that, unlike in the movies, these two would not be coming at him one at a time and waiting for him to assure himself a victory.

They lunged forward as one, each grabbing him by a shoulder just as they had done to Greer Donaldson, and probably Julie Peterson as well. Probably god only knew how many other people. They forced him down onto the floor and started slamming their fists and heels into his lower neck and jaw.

"I'll teach you, you son of a bitch!" Al laughed, as he picked up Xander's wooden chair and slammed it across the boy's face. Blood flew from Xander's mouth and splattered against the wall, making a long red streak there. They were coming at him from both sides, with nary a space between blows. His head was so rattled he thought he could actually hear his brain bouncing around inside it, barely protected by the fluid therein. "Bastard!" Al screamed again, planting the sole of his boot squarely into Xander's face.

"Try to ruin our fun!" Raine chimed in, snatching up the knife that Xander had dropped and driving it deep into the child's mid-section, puncturing a lung and coming a little too close to his heart for anybody's comfort. "I know you did!"

They finally slacked off, but Xander did not fight back. He fell to the floor in a heap, looking as dead as one could, blood seeping out of a swollen face that was so puffy in wasn't recognizable as his own.

Al laughed and cocked his head toward the hall. Raine got the idea and started to laugh as well. They both grabbed Xander by the shoulders again and carried him out of the room.

The two of them dragged him into the bathroom, where Cathy watched in horror through the slits in the shower curtain as they started to dunk his head in the toilet, over and over again. They were trying to drown him, and were obviously very disappointed when they held him under for a full minute to little effect. Raine scooped up a bottle of Mr. Clean and shoved the nozzle into Xander's battered mouth, then put as much pressure on the bottle as he could. The vile chemicals filled his lungs, burning them from the inside out.

"No," Cathy mouthed softly as she shifted back, watching her friend get beaten to what would surely be his death. She brought a hand to her mouth to stop from screaming, a hand that had been propping her up. She slipped a little on the slick porcelain, then caught herself... on the yellow rubber duck Xander had had since he was a child.

-SQUEAK!-

Everything stopped. Everything was silent. The only sounds were that of a few, solitary drops of blue liquid coming out of Xander's nose, the only motion Al and Raine exchanging glances. Raine stared at the shower curtain for a long moment... then shrugged. Smiling at Al, the both of them again got Xander up, carried him to the stairs, and hurled him out over with all their combined might. He flew for just a moment, his eyes barely open, then he landed on his face with an earth-shattering *crack!* and flipped over onto his shoulder, which popped out of joint with a wet snap.

Upstairs, Cathy stayed in the bathtub, huddled into herself until long after she was sure that Al and Raine were gone. *Long after.* When she started to hear the sounds of people taking their lunch breaks, which must have been hours after it had all begun, she decided to move. When she started down the stairs, Xander was still there. A pool of blood had grown around him in a roughly circular pattern. He didn't seem to be breathing well. She ran to his side, wrapping her arms around him and forcing his head up onto her lap. He grunted in dismay, but said nothing else. She leaned down and kissed him on the forehead, stroking his blood-caked hair out of his eyes. And she cried.

Because it's not worth it unless they cry.

And still, all that Xander could think were those four, simple words:

Pain is your power.

CHAPTER SIX: REAL EVIL

Tim White marched down the hallway of Coral Beach High School, ignoring the frustrated rambling of Principal Shnieder beside him. He hated having to do this, but despite him loathing being back in these walls and the memories that they brought for him, he still couldn't help but keep a certain swagger in his hips. There was a certain amount of joy in such a desperate situation, for he knew that he'd be gone soon. Gone far away from this horrid little town and all the cretins and weirdness that seemed to make their home here, and going all the way up to the hallowed halls of the FBI. He smiled when he thought of his badge, wondering when they would actually give it to him. He hoped that there would be a ceremony of some kind.

"...don't like this," Shnieder continued in his high-pitched voice, the lights gleaming off of his bald head as they strode throughout the halls. Tim could no longer tune it out, like a growing itch in the back of your mind. "Really don't like this. Every time anything happens in this town, I'm the one who gets the brunt of the weight. I'm the one who gets his school turned upside down. I'm the one who -- "

"Shnieder, you little worm," Tim cut off, stopping dead and turning to stare the troll in the eye. He had to look down to do so, and from this distance Shnieder looked to be about three feet high and shrinking. "I used to have to actually listen to this crap back when I was a P.D., but now I've been alleviated of your gross incompetence that got a good portion of this school's student population killed less than a month ago, moron." He reached deep into his pocket, taking only a second to appreciate the sound of the cowering man's gulp as it echoed through the halls. He pulled forth a picture of a girl with bright, long blonde hair and a series of freckles in a line across her face. "Greer Donaldson. She in school today, by any chance?" he asked, though clearly the question was rhetorical.

At least, it was clear to anyone with an IQ over ten. Sadly, Shnieder did not qualify. "No, she isn't. How did you know that?"

Tim frowned. "Because I just watched her parents identify her body."

All of the colour drained from Shnieder's face. "She's dead?" he asked, mortified by the notion. "She's only fourteen."

"She's comatose, actually," Tim admitted as he placed one hand on the shorter man's wiry shoulder. "They're still doing the rape tests, but it's fairly obvious what happened... There was a lot of bleeding."

Shnieder looked about ready to throw up. "I helped that girl study once or twice, back in my teaching days. Such a sweet child. What can I do to help?"

Tim put the picture back into his pocket, withdrawing his hand again with a small slip of paper. "I want all the people on this list in interviews with me. I don't care how stupid or inconvenient it may sound."

Shnieder took the list and went down it, reading it aloud and furrowing his brow at some of Tim's choices. "Peterson? Harris? Smith? Thomas and Frederick I can understand, but what do you want with those first three children? It doesn't make sense, man," he said, trying to reason with him.

"The Drew kid, too. I've been trying to get hold of him since the Genblade capture."

"Mr. Drew is not in school today," Shnieder mumbled absent-mindedly, trying to recall where each of those students would be at this time of day.

"Isn't that convenient," Tim mumbled, putting a toothpick into his mouth and beginning to chew on it as the gears started to grind inside his head.

He couldn't wait for that reassignment.

ᚨᚤᚪ

Mike had been in Chemistry class with Mr. Howards when the intercom had buzzed to life and hailed him to the library. He'd been picking a hole in the wall next to him, trying to appear interested in what the teacher was saying about some new theorem he should know by now. The truth was he just couldn't concentrate anymore. His mind was elsewhere, understandably. As it turned out, it had been in the library, where he now sat across from Tim White, a man whom he admired a great deal and yet despised for the memories that he wrenched up. He'd been expecting a conference with Dr. Phillips, so the African American federal agent sitting across from him, running thick fingers through his short wiry hair, was a welcome surprise.

"How have you been, Tim?" Mike asked, remembering how frustrated the cop had been after he and Cathy had called him 'Officer White' or 'Sir' for the hundredth time. "You look good."

Tim smiled genuinely at Mike, who was an extraordinary young man in his eyes. "Looks can be deceiving," he chuckled. "You should know that. I've been better, though. The precinct saddled me with this damned case a week before I was scheduled to leave." He turned to Mike, looking at him as an equal. "Do you have any idea how fun a rape case is?"

"None at all?" Mike hazarded.

"None at all," Tim repeated, nodding.

176

"Then why are you talking to me, Tim? Am I a suspect?"

Tim chuckled. "No. I'm talking to you cause you're like me."

Mike looked puzzled, leaning his head to one side.

Tim leaned forward, stroked his goatee, then lay his hands out before him as if laying out his points. "I'm sitting here complaining about being stuck with this case, when they didn't force me. Couldn't. I out-rank them all now. I took it willingly, because I just can't seem to keep my nose out of this stuff." He gestured towards Mike. "Like you."

"Again, why am I here?" Mike asked, throwing a suspicious eye toward the cop.

"Because you know things I don't. You can get into places and have access to information that I never could, simply because of your age, not to mention other factors. We've both seen you play street hockey."

Mike smirked.

"So I'm coming to you for information. What do you know?"

Mike swallowed. "Have you been talking to Julie?"

"Right before you came in, why?"

"What did she tell you?"

Tim coughed, lowering his voice considerably to tell Mike exactly how much trouble he could get into for repeating something of this nature. "Nothing she didn't tell her doctor. Rape, three guys, and not so much as a physical description. And now she refuses to accept that this second rape is probably her fault for not being more helpful."

Mike let that information stew in his head for a moment. "Two of the men you're looking for are Allan Bishop and Bram Raine, they used to go - "

"I know those two," Tim nodded, suddenly looking very tired and rubbing his eyes. "They're bad news."

"I know," Mike sighed, "You think after you bust them, you can get the third..."

"I can't arrest anyone yet, Harris," Tim sighed.

"What? But we know it's them!" Mike shouted, jumping out of his chair and glaring down at Tim.

"No, we don't. Not legally, anyway. You have a third hand high-school rumor that could have originated anywhere," Tim explained, trying to keep his tone even.

"So, what?" Mike yelled, "You don't trust me now?"

"No, I believe you," Tim nodded, waving for Mike to sit back down, which he did. "But that information isn't applicable in court unless it's from a first-hand witness. In other words: unless Julie says it herself, or another victim."

"The only other victim is in a coma, according to you."

"And there is the second point. It is *illegal* for me to have given you any information in this setting whatsoever," he said, his voice becoming grave. "We go back to HQ now, and we're both screwed. Not only that, the sons of bitches themselves 'll get off because *we're* guilty of obstruction, see? Then, we'd also never get hold of the third party and this whole mess would start again... only now we'd be able to do shit all. See?" He slapped the table to bring Mike back to reality. "That's how it works in the real world, kid. Unless we can bring those yahoos in on a lesser charge, the girls in this town are gonna have to start wearing padlocks on their panties."

Mike shook his head, scratching the back of it. He scooped up his book bag and started for the door. As he left, he bumped into Tim's next appointment: Derek Smith. Mike squinted at Derek, the wheels within his own head beginning to grind.

ᴧᐧᴧ

By the time Bram Raine got home, it was long past dinner. That was all right, though. There was always plenty of food in the fridge in the form of leftovers and sandwich meats. He walked over to a small cooler that rested comfortably by the kitchen table and flipped open the lid, grabbing a beer out of the half-melted ice it floated in. Cracking it open and letting a certain amount of the head flow out onto his hand, he sighed and strolled over to his reclining easy chair, kicked up his feet and closed his eyes.

The living room was small and oddly shaped, with seven different 'corners' at odd places along the wall. A rustic stone fireplace took up most of the eastern wall, but could never be lit because the sparks always managed to catch something else ablaze in the cramped space. Most of the furniture had been found at flea markets or liberated from the side of the road when neighbors moved out of the area. The coffee table was actually a windshield from an old Chevy that he had fitted with legs.

As small as it was, the living room was still one of the larger rooms in the house. The kitchen did not even have enough room in it to open the oven door all the way, and most of the bedrooms were about the same size. As bad as it was, it was cheap, which was what he needed in a home more than anything else at this point in his life.

He looked down at his knuckle and saw a long scrape going from the base of his index finger almost straight down to his wrist, wondering how he had gotten the injury. He got a sudden flash of a wire mesh fence near Julie Peterson's home and remembering slicing himself on it. Sighing heavily, he took another sip of his beer.

"Bram?" he heard a voice call out uncertainly, nearly making him jump out of his skin. He dropped his beer onto the carpet and it immediately started to soak into the coarse fibers. He cursed softly as he scooped up the Budweiser, then turned towards the hall that led towards the bedrooms.

She was absolutely beautiful. Maria Raine was by far the most delicate butterfly on the face of the planet, graceful and sweet. Even as she stumbled, her hands fumbling along the stucco walls of their familiar house, she still contained within her the motions of an expert ballet dancer. A pink, fluffy robe was clutched around her thinning body, only her wrinkled face and ankles exposed. Her features were haggard and frail, her face looking as though it were melting slowly in the fires of time. Even so, it wasn't hard to tell that she had been beau-

178

tiful once. Her friends had often said that her eyes were possessed of a constant sparkle, preserving her youthful exuberance.

Now her eyes were a chalky white all over, their pupils faded into obscurity. There were small scars along the bridge of her nose, burn marks that were the only other souvenir from the day she lost her sight. Everyone was very careful to tell her that she looked perfectly normal, even lovely at times, knowing that such words eased her mind and she would never know the difference. Her silver hair flew in all directions, all of the bangs falling in front of her face, concealing it slightly. "Bram, is that you?" she called out again, her voice quavering with fear. Her face darted around the room expectantly, looking towards each place that she heard a new sound. "Is somebody there?"

As soon as he saw her, Bram forgot about the beer. He left it chugging liquid onto the floor and went to her side, taking her hand and hip gently to guide her to a chair. "It's me, Mama. It's only me."

A warm smile spread across the old woman's lips, as she reached up and stroked him along his rough-hewn face. That tactile contact was all she knew of her son anymore, and it always brought her great joy. "Oh, Bram. You gave me such a start. I thought it was that Allan boy again, so rude. I don't like him, Bramwell."

"I know, Mama," Bram nodded softly, fixing her hair with his thick fingers. "It's okay." He reached deep within his jacket pocket and withdrew a tape. There were words scribbled across the cover in indecipherable handwriting... but one supposed that didn't make much difference to Maria. "I got you something today."

The old woman smiled thinly, trying to conceal her excitement. "Is it what I think it is?" she asked coyly, tilting her head in his direction to hear better. She was starting to go deaf too, something she feared ever so deeply.

He placed the tape in her palm, carefully closing her hand around it. "It's the audio transcript from last week's 'Mystery Theatre', complete with description of action," he smiled.

She beamed wildly. "Oh, thank you," she laughed, clutching the tape deck to keep it from getting away. She leaned over and gave him a kiss on the cheek, which he graciously returned. "I'll go have a listen right --"

There was a moan in the background, interrupting their happy moment. Bram turned back toward the hall that his mother had come through and started towards it without a word. Maria said nothing, for she was quite used to this behavior from him. There was nothing else on his mind at the moment, no thought for his manners.

The third door on the right was covered with get-well cards and posters of the Backstreet Boys, a band that everyone but the bearer thought was a dead band. She knew better. Bram opened up the door and there she was, his little Mercedes Raine. The little girl sat upon the bed, her knees crossed Indian-style underneath her Tinkerbell comforter. Her face was tilted downward and her long, jet black hair covered the majority of her face in two straight lines. Tears dripped from her gray eyes, streaming down her cheeks like tiny waterfalls, collecting in a small pool on her faded yellow nightgown. She was no more than nine years old, but looked much closer to seven.

He walked to her, taking note of the ripped posters of Nick Carter and Winnie the Pooh that scattered her walls, their shreds flapping in the warm air current coming from a heating duct. Bram took her in his arms, leaning her head against his powerful chest and heart. "Shhh," he cooed, the same word that had caused so much fear in Greer Donaldson. Now, an onlooker would never recognize it as the same sound. "What's the matter, baby?" he asked, stroking her hair down the back of her head.

She sniffed back tears, mushing her nose into him and covering the front of his shirt with mucus. He really didn't care. "It h-hurts…" she stammered and sobbed, trying desperately to force the words out.

Bram put a finger to her lips gently. "No more tears, baby," he coaxed her. "No more cry. You be alright, soon. You see." He wasn't sure if he was trying to convince her or himself, but it seemed to calm his child. It had been the same cancer that had killed his ex-wife a few years before, landing him with custody of Mercedes. That much, he didn't mind. Only good thing his stupid ex had ever done for him anyway. But if Al didn't get the money from the boss soon, he wouldn't get his daughter the operation in time. And if he didn't get the operation in time, then every bitch in this city was going to find out exactly what he could do.

༺༻

Derek Smith walked out of the Library and slammed the door behind him, half expecting Mrs. Richards to give him a verbal scolding for it. He glared at her and waited for it, but she saw a malevolence in his eyes that chilled her deeply and she decided against prying any deeper. She turned back to organizing her card catalog. Derek breathed heavily, his knuckles white with the need to bury them into something. Anything. Specifically, Tim White's soft facial flesh. His face was livid with anger as he stared down at the cuts his nails had made in his palm, blood bubbling to the surface.

"He can have that effect on people," came Mike's voice from the corner. The tall blonde leaned against the coat racks and lockers that lined the walls, his black shirt and jeans hiding him in the shadows. His milky-white complexion stood out though, making Derek wonder how he had missed it. Mike stood up and took a few casual steps towards Derek, smirking a little at the teen's rage. "Lemme guess, he kept pushing buttons until he found one that hurt you, then he kept pushing it?"

Derek actually laughed at that, waving a finger at Mike. "Something like that," he reasoned, "Jeez, don't you just wanna rip that guy's head off?"

"Sometimes," he nodded, then re-thought the response. "Actually, all of the time. Tact isn't his strong suit, I'm afraid. One of these days, he's going to break his neck jumping to conclusions."

"Yeah," Derek snarled, "He actually accused me of helping Al and Raine do this shit to Julie. Me! I mean, she's probably the one person in this school that I *wouldn't* take a machete to…" his voice trailed off for a second, eyeing Mike's right side sheepishly. "…Present company excluded, of course."

180

Mike laughed, an act that stretched his stitches painfully. "Think nothing of it," he replied, trying to keep the agony out of his voice. He didn't do a very good job of it. "But that's not really what I wanted to talk to you about."

Derek squinted, backing up a pace. He hadn't realized that there was an agenda to this conversation. The revelation did not bode well with him. He felt his fists clench tight again, almost without his knowledge. "What *did* you want to talk to me about, Harris?" he asked accusingly. "You come here to give me the third degree too? Guilty by association, right? I've got a dick so that makes me a rapist?"

"No," Mike stated evenly, careful to sap all of the emotion from his voice. "I think we need to have a little talk... about what to do about the way things are in this city."

Derek smiled. He was beginning to like Mike.

Xander felt Cathy dab another cotton swab onto the gash on his brow, feeling some of the fibers get stuck there by the half-congealed blood. He was beginning to get used to waking up covered in various bodily fluids with a cute brunette leaning over his face. He stared blankly at his computer until his eyes began to hurt, then stared some more. He felt something plop onto his cheek, something moist. He turned and looked at Cathy, who was still crying far more than she would have believed herself able.

Her throat bled, pumping redness into her mouth every few seconds. Her entire face shone from tears and sweat from dragging Xander over the stairs and into his room, which had made her feel even more warm and clammy than she already had. The air around her was humid, making it difficult to move as she dabbed the swabs all over her friend's body in an effort to halt the bleeding that only seemed to be accelerating. Cathy struggled to see where the two of them had found humor in this only a few hours before... even some small degree of romance. She watched him, his tight skin splitting from mere movement and creating more cuts for her to tend to, and she couldn't help but think of him as the loser that had sat across from her in tech class all last year. He'd barely paid any attention to her while they were in school, or her to him for that matter. There wasn't any need to; their social lives were so different. She'd always felt like they were on two different planets... But even that was better than how she felt now. It was as though her world had been destroyed and she'd been thrust into the hell that was Planet Drew. A place of pain and constant suffering, where she was just some stupid secondary character in a story that was all about him and his new life. When night fell on that planet, she went from the tortured to the hunted... and if you've never experienced both, you simply can't appreciate the difference. At least she could see who was torturing her. When she felt hunted, there were only glimpses in the darkness, shadows that haunted her dreams and made her wake feeling cold no matter how many covers she piled onto herself. They stalked her through the night, but she never once saw them. She could only trust that she knew who they were. Tommy, Sud, Grendel... Black Womb. Yes, in this world even Xander was different come nightfall. Yet in so many ways, he was still the same. That's what frightened her most about the killer living inside of her best friend. It wasn't the differences... but the similarities.

"Xander?" she whispered softly.

His eyes kept staring forward at some unknown spot on the wall, and he never even blinked to acknowledge her presence.

"Xander," Spider repeated, deep within his sub-conscious. She smiled as she looked down at his beaten body, stroking her fingers along Genblade's chest. His hands were all over her, and she motioned for him to stop. Instead, he got up and slammed her to the ground, sucking on her neck hungrily. An obscene look of pleasure filled her face, a small moan escaping from quivering lips. She turned her head to the beaten teen about ten feet away from her, speaking to him even as Genblade persisted in slowly working her clothing off of her. "You'll have to pardon Adam," she said to Xander. "He hasn't had a go since you locked him away, and I think he's suffering from withdrawal." She paused, and for a moment the old, evil Eve was back again. "It's Sara's reproductive organs that are shimmering with pleasure for him now, remember. She's still inside of me, telling me how much she loves him. How he's a better lover then you could ever be..."

Pain filled Xander's eyes, his pupils shifted a little from their fixed position. Just enough that Cathy thought he was acknowledging her, finally.

"When I was in the tub, I don't think I was scared," she blurted out finally. "I think I was hopeful. I hoped that Al and Raine would come in and find me, and maybe they'd want me. Maybe somebody would finally want me. All these years, I've been watching you and Mike and Derek fawn over Sara. Since the party, Mike will barely touch me anymore, and I wasn't even good enough for Grendel to rape." She paused, nodded as the tears began again, then repeated herself. "Not good enough to rape."

"...but then, I'm crazy," Spider reasoned, the words muffled slightly as she bit on Genblade's ear. Her expression grew serious then, as she just let Genblade do his thing and no longer paid him any attention. "It's all coming, you know boy. Even now, you'll start to see it. The explosion at Engen may have dulled your senses for a time, but they still hear the firing of the guns, hmm? The war is coming, Drew. Those that you call allies today will destroy you come the morrow. Those we count amongst our allies today will have betrayed us yesterday, and themselves in the morrow. The actions you take now lead you not to peace, but to bloodshed. To pain. And you will love it, for that is your power."

Xander rose, confused. "I don't understand," he said, and Cathy sighed.

"What?" Genblade snarled as he used his nose to fondle Spider's breasts. "Isn't she being direct *enough for you?"*

"There are trails ahead, the stars are singing it so," Spider said musically to Xander, her body again racked with pleasure from her husband. "But the man in the moon is terrible jealous, for he has no voice. Only eyes. He can't sing and make the girls love him, but he can watch. Oh, yes he can. He watches everything."

Finally, Xander began to clue in. The third rapist could see them. The victims, he'd seen them all before, known about their problems and lives. He knew them, somehow.

Spider laughed, as Genblade ripped off the last shreds of her jumpsuit. "Now you're starting to think like a Womb."

"What's not to understand?" Cathy asked. "Nobody wants me, they just want my body. And it's getting to the point where that's going to be good enough. I'll let them have it. They can take it away so that I don't have to deal with it anymore," she sobbed, collapsing onto her friend's chest. "I don't want it anymore, Xander," she convulsed. Her hand reached up to brush against his lips, to have him kiss her hand. To have her feel as if someone wanted her for something other than a cheap lay.

Xander grabbed her hand out of the air and looked down at her, his mind snapping back to reality. "How did you get here?" he asked, his voice almost accusatory. "Why are you crying?"

Her lower lip shook violently. She snatched her hand away from him, her moist eyes becoming even more so. She shook her head, jutting a palm towards him to shut him up. She realized that again, he hadn't been listening. That not even *he* cared. "I can't..." she started, but couldn't even finish before she left the room and the house completely, leaving Xander in a well of his own tears, feeling completely useless.

᛭

-BEEP-
-BEEP-
-BEEP-

Tim sighed as he peered in through the doorway to Greer Donaldson's hospital room, listening to the tones emitted by the machine next to her as it coldly kept track of her heart rhythm. He was only vaguely aware of the woman next to him who had been going on for almost ten minutes about stats and hospital regulations and medical jargon, none of which he found particularly useful.

What he had come to see was in there.

Past the forest green door propped open with a rubber peg and behind all the equipment dedicated to keeping her breathing, was what he needed more than anything else in the world right now: motivation.

If his conversation with Roxanne that morning hadn't made him feel bad enough, his one with Mike had sunken his heart even further. He had left the boy with a feeling of uselessness caked on him so hard that he didn't even think a shower would get it all off. The worst part was the knowledge that it wasn't completely ill deserved. Derek had almost been the worst of the lot, giving him no information and very little to go on. He felt like he was grasping at straws.

"--rated as a nine on the Glasgow Coma Scale. She makes no movements and cannot open her eyes, even upon application of painful stimuli. She does make the occasional sound, but they're mostly just incomprehensible grunts and moans," the nurse continued, Tim's attention snapping back to her suddenly.

For a moment he didn't really understand what she was saying, until his brain caught up with him and he remembered what they had been talking about. "Nine. That sounds pretty bad, Miss..."

"Reilly," she said, but did not smile. She stared through the door at Greer for a moment just as Tim had, her dark red lips turning into a frown against the tan complexion of her face. She did not get as lost in it as Tim had, though, turning back to the conversation after only a moment. "And it's not as bad as it sounds. The Glasgow Coma Scale goes up to fourteen, not ten. If I had to put it into simple terms, it is a very 'moderate' coma."

"Will she recover?" he asked, again glancing toward the girl. It could have been anyone in that bed, really. The bruises and swollen welts that covered her head and upper body made it hard to distinguish her as female, let alone as Greer Donaldson.

Nurse Reilly sighed, pushing her brown bangs out of her eyes. "It's hard to say, really. At this point she could recover... or she could recess deeper into the coma. A person's place on the Coma Scale isn't stagnate. It can change daily in the first few months... but with every day, the chances get less and less that she'll wake up."

Tim frowned. It occurred to him, and not for the first time, that there was another problem in this whole mess. Greer Donaldson's attackers could only be charged with murder if she died within a year of the attack. After that it would be deemed as 'natural causes,' a thought that sickened him. Not that he didn't want her to get better... But with every day the chances of that would get less and less likely. If she wasn't going to wake up, he hoped that she would pass on in time to really get back at her assailants.

- BEEP BEEP!-

Nurse Reilly jumped back, her face startled as she looked into Greer's room to see what was the matter.

Tim raised a hand to stop her, then withdrew his cell phone from his pocket. "Sorry," he said quickly, his open palm changing to a single finger in a motion everyone understood as 'give me a minute.'

"Well, that's not the least of the reasons we don't allow cellular telephones to be active while you're inside the hospital, Mr. White," she huffed, still regaining herself from the momentary start she'd been given.

It was the first time since beginning his conversation with her that Tim would have honestly described her as anything but mechanical. Now she shuffled her feet and let out several exasperated puffs of air, reminding him of the hens on his grandmother's farm after the cat had given them a scare. The association made his lips curl into a smile, even though he knew it would only make her madder. Regardless, he brought the phone to his ear. "Hello?"

"Jeez, you are fucking impossible to get hold of," came the agitated male voice from the other end.

Once again, despite the words being said, Tim got the distinct impression that the man was smiling. "Duncan," he said, running a hand through his hair as he felt a migraine coming on.

"How'd you know? Anyway, hope you don't mind me using th' personal number and all, but you haven't been in the office all day."

"No, I've been out working my case all day, which I happen to be doing right now. So, if you don't mind..."

"We don't know our perp yet, but we think he's a male age thirty to thirty-five. That could be wrong, but it's coming from a reliable place," Duncan continued, as if White hadn't even spoken. "He likes to use things he finds at the scene on his victims, I'll tell you that much now. Has made for some nasty autopsies.

But listen, I'm on my way to pick you up. I'll brief you more then, but --"

Tim tried to find a spot to break into the conversation, but Duncan Taggart just kept talking. After a full minute of this, White simply closed the cell phone, hanging up on his overzealous partner.

"If you're going to keep that thing on, you're going to have to leave," Nurse Reilly said sternly, her hands again folded in front of her.

Tim sighed, pocketing the cell phone. Turning toward the dark green doors, he took one last look at the battered face of Greer Donaldson, then turned to leave.

The Factory was in a rare state of emptiness, something that looked almost foreign and alien. Seeing it this way produced the same sort of uneasiness as seeing an empty dance club in the daytime, or returning to your old Kindergarten classroom and feeling everything was out of place.

The arcade games against the back wall still rung out taunts and chimes to its absent audience, the bells and whistles only slightly dulled by the sound-proofed walls. The fighting games were the worst, spewing out sound effect after sound effect as battle waged on upon their screens, like some sort of auditory regurgitation.

One game flashed blue light in rapid strobes, casting odd and disjointed shadows on the pool table not far away. The shape of the sticks leaned against it were projected onto the wall with such intensity that if left in that position for a long amount of time, they might get burned there like the shadows of the unlucky souls that stood near ground zero at Hiroshima.

That's what Roxanne had decided Coral Beach and the surrounding towns felt like lately: Hiroshima. The atomic blast that was Adam Genblade had killed a lot of people, but they were almost the lucky ones. In the past few weeks the fallout of those events had begun to take its toll on her and the children she catered to. Depression was a popular reaction, but so too was anger, hostility, disbelief and paranoia. It was the same way she pictured the aftermath of a massive attack of any scale, large or small. The only difference was that the people of Coral Beach wouldn't discover radioactivity in their breast milk in fifty years, although according to the rumors she had heard about the building they found north of town that might not be out of the question either.

She ran her hands through her curly red hair, raking her press-on nails against her scalp in a desperate effort to keep the thoughts that were stalking her out. She was leaning over the bar of The Factory on her elbows, staring down into an untouched cup of tea that wafted the sugary sweet scent of orange pekoe up into her face. The heat from the drink made her forehead and upper lip dot with sweat after only a moment, but she found she liked the way it tingled against her face.

An image flashed across the top of her brain like a strobe light. The memory produced a smell like ammonia and spit that made her nose curl even though it wasn't really there. The recollection of it was more than enough. Gritting her teeth and digging in her nails until she thought she might be bleeding, Roxanne forced the image from her mind as she had many times on sleepless nights in the past two years. Nights when she'd woken up screaming and not remembered why at first. Nights after which no amount of showers and soaps could make her feel clean again.

But it was gone again now, and she could turn her attention back to the muddied and distorted visage of herself in her tea. She could force those images out for as long as it took. She'd had a lot of practice. It had taken some time, but she has started to think of it as a movie that had happened to someone else. The illusion was so complete that her memories of what had been done to her no longer had colour, and were grainy with cigarette burns the way old movies from the thirties were. Once she'd managed to convince her mind that it was just a movie, all she needed to do was turn off the projector.

The new things coming at her weren't so easy. These weren't memories she was fighting now but thought processes, her own mind working overtime against her.

"Yes, there were two or three men working in conjuncture."

The federal agent's voice had been so cold when he'd said that. It was just a fact to him, something with no emotional weight to it other than the loosest sense of empathy. To her it was the gateway that made the plight of that young girl real to Roxanne, a point of reference that could be used to extrapolate her experiences to fit this new scenario.

There would be more of that smell with three of them, she thought, even as she ground her molars together and tried to turn off the switch to the projector only to find that it was broken.

More of that same ammonia and saliva smell but not as much as she initially thought. Not three times as much, by any stretch. Scent was one of those odd things that reached a ceiling fairly quickly and no matter how much more you piled in, the smell would get no worse. Other things would get worse though. The smell of sweat with one of them was bad enough. With three of them, the B.O. would reach tsunami levels. It was so bad it almost made her throw up into her tea thinking about it. Cologne, too. Nothing expensive, something that an idiot would pick up with a sailboat on the bottle that smelled like her Uncle Chris's moonshine.

That was just the smells. As her tea stopped sending wave after wave of heat at her face and became cool, she started to *feel* it. Again she tried desperately to turn off the movie playing in her head, but this was something her mind was creating. Once started it was like trying to stop an avalanche of thought. It simply couldn't happen.

It started as a memory of the hands gripping her shoulders and her breasts. They were rough and pulled on her flesh as though they wanted it off like her clothes already were. Most people do not understand that rape is more about violence than it is about sex. She understood all too well. As she took the teacup in her shivering hand and brought it to her lips, her thoughts deviated from memory into their own tangent. There were three of them, after all. She'd never had that experience, but it wasn't hard for her mind to fabricate. While the pressure was still tugging hard on her chest and shoulder, more was added at her hips and legs and hair. Before long she felt as though she had been tied to three different cars and they had begun pulling her in all directions at once.

The pressure was soon joined by weight. The sum total of the first one's entire body was upon her and within her all at once. It would have been a thousand times worse than the pressure of their hands all on its own, but the hands had never really stopped their steady grope. The pain was unbelievable. What was worse, her scientific mind instantly named and explained all of the sensations she was experiencing. Somehow it made it all the more real as the second one started.

Even though it wasn't real.

Warm tea sloshing against her open-toed shoes brought her back to reality with a snap, the movie reel fading away for a moment. She breathed a sigh of relief, but did not smile. The thoughts were leaving fast, but not nearly fast enough. She still thought she could smell the mold of the garbage in the alley she had found herself in.

Huffing angrily, she took one last look out at the empty Factory. Glaring it down, she grabbed her red leather purse and opened it to make sure there was still a pack of Camels and a light inside, then buttoned it again and headed for the door, her left shoe leaving footprints of tea all the way to the door.

ʎ⟨ʎ

Roxanne cursed when she stepped in a puddle as she rounded the corner, her smoke already smouldering in her hand. She took a quick puff from between her ruby lips then brought the smoke away, holding it off to the side of her head the way she had seen women do in old movies from the fifties.

The back wall of The Factory looked the same as it always had, even before it was an arcade. None of her patrons really remembered this except for those that had seen it, but back in the day it had been a gymnasium. For a while, Coral Beach had been a boomtown as industrialists flocked there looking for coal and oil. The coal was gone now and the oil had never even existed, and most modern industrialists couldn't find Coral Beach on a map of Maine even if their lives depended on it. Around the time when it was a 'boomtown', it had attracted many of the prosperity and the problems that came with larger communities. When the success waned as it always does, the prosperity left but the problems remained. The gym had been closed within a month of the mine shutting down. It had sat there gaining rot for three years before Joan had bought it, slowly transforming it into what it was today.

Through all the paint jobs and reconstruction, the back wall was still just as she remembered it. Long and white with the paint still flecking in the same places no matter how many times they went over it again, a large mound of smooth rock jutting up half way through the foundation and combining with the concrete wall to create a makeshift seat.

Nowadays kids called this the 'old sitting stone.' She'd heard Tommy and Derek refer to it as that more than once while heading outside to have a smoke, much as she was now. Although she thought 'old kissing stone' would have been much more appropriate, as many kids had had their first kiss sitting on that stone after a concert or a game of pool.

Back when she was that age and before she'd gotten her first kiss, the smooth mound of granite was known by the more sinister moniker of The Devil's Chair.

She didn't know who named it that. She supposed nobody really knew who named such things around towns all over the world, only that it happened. Unlike 'The Old Sitting Stone' (which was, in itself, self-explanatory), The Devil's Chair had started out as a ghost story. A kind of urban legend of her youth that everyone passes off as rubbish until they were staring it right in the face.

It was a fairly simple tale. One of those 'heard it from a friend of a friend of mine' stories that always make it into heritage books and television shows like The Twilight Zone. Legend had it that if one sat in that chair when alone, that the Devil himself would come out to get you. He would rise up from hell and eat your heart before sending your soul down to hell, taking over your body and using it to walk around the earth unabated until it started to rot and fall apart. Then he'd go back to his chair and wait for some other person foolhardy or suicidal enough to climb up on it.

Roxanne chuckled a bit as she took another puff of her smoke, letting it curl out of her mouth and into her hair slowly. The memory of the legend had managed to distract her from her life for a few minutes, which she was grateful for. She recalled how that story had terrified her as a child, how she used to stare at the rock as she passed by the gym on her way to school every day, wary of Satan coming to get her. Once in third grade she'd seen her older brother back there eating a sandwich and wouldn't go near him for a week, afraid that he had been possessed.

But she wasn't scared of urban legends anymore. Urban reality was frightening enough. So when her legs began to buckle at the knees from being on her feet all day bussing tables and cleaning the back of house, she walked out and plunked herself down on the stone, taking another draw of her smoke from between two yellowed fingers.

It was an odd feeling for her, sitting on the stone slab. It was like being in the darkness of your room and thinking that you'd seen the image of a ghost in the darkness. You could tell yourself over and over again that ghosts didn't exist, but in the end you'd have to turn on the light to make sure before your overactive imagination would let you get any sleep.

From her current point of view, though it was only a few feet from where she had stood a moment ago, the fall leaves that had been orange, yellow, and inviting a moment ago now seemed a more visceral red. The trees hung lifelessly, their branches forming sagging faces that stared at her with woe and despair, as if to say, "Look at this poor soul. She doesn't even know what she's gotten herself into."

The toes on her left foot felt like they were fusing together as they rubbed against each other. She glanced down and saw that the tea was sticking there on her foot and tisked at herself, taking a napkin from her breast pocket and wetting it on her tongue, then bent over and cleaned off her foot.

When she turned her head back up towards the trees, they stopped moving.

They hadn't been moving when she'd been staring at them and they were still again now, but clearly they had been even though Roxanne had felt no breeze. It was like walking into a room where people were talking about you and they all shut up at once. The shrubs seemed to have joined the trees in staring at her now, as if the trees had let them in on the joke.

There was a silence in the air so thick that she was tempted to poke her fake nails forward to see if she could jab a hole in it. There were no birds chirping. There were no sounds of rats at the garbage around the corner. There were no voices fading in and out as people walked down the street. When the trees moved they rustled, but they weren't right now. Right now the only sound that happened was made by her when she took a puff of her smoke, hearing the paper tube crackle and pop as it burned.

The smell on the air was the crisp clean that came with fall, dew, and condensation weighing down every leaf until they couldn't hold on anymore and fell to earth. She drew in breath hard, half expecting to get a nose full of fire and brimstone. When she did not, she laughed at herself for being so silly, allowing a smile to caress her lips. If nothing else, this non-adventure had taken her mind off the conversation she had had with Tim White.

She felt heat on her fingers. She looked at her hand and realized the cigarette was almost down to the butt. She brought it to her lips quickly for one last puff before turning around to doubt it against the cement wall.

As soon as she turned, she heard the familiar rustle of branches she had a moment ago. Dropping her smoke immediately, she turned back around towards the trees, again watching them as they stopped moving. This time it was the bushes, still waving a little bit before halting completely.

"Hello?" she called out, her voice cracking slightly.

There was no response, just the silence and motionlessness of the trees.

She hissed in pain and jumped off of the rock as her smoke burnt though the fabric of her pants and onto her leg, swatting at it with her hands and sending embers flying everywhere. The trees and shrubs seemed to go insane as she did this, like they were laughing at the punch line they hadn't bothered sharing with her. When she looked up this time they continued to move, finally coming to rest after a few moments. She raised one of her carefully plucked eyebrows in curiosity. Checking her leg quickly to make sure it wasn't burned, she took a step towards the tree line.

The shrubs in the far right of her vision moved. She turned her head towards them and they stopped, with the only hint the event had really happened being the steady vibration of the leaves. One fell from its branch finally, twirling and baying until finally hitting the ground. Now that it was gone Roxanne could see into the shrub a little more than she could a moment ago.

It was hard to focus, but whatever was in there looked... white. White and glimmering dully in the low light inside the foliage. It was in the rough shape of a half moon with the fat side down. As it slowly came into clear view, she saw that the crescent-shaped object was further divided, sectioned off in tiny squares.

It was the Devil's smile.

Her hand was at her mouth with instant shock. The second she saw the teeth and gums of the smile, it was impossible not to see the whites of the beady green eyes locked onto her own, burning with hatred and bloodshot.

A fist shot out through the shrub and caught her in the chin even as she pulled away, trying to remember the self-defense training she'd taken a few weeks ago and coming up empty. She stumbled to the ground even as the Devil rose out of the orange and red leaves. Once again she was reminded of Hiroshima, the man being the mushroom cloud that rose up into the sky and towered above her.

He didn't have red skin or a pointed nose or a tail, but he was the Devil all the same. He was slim and toned, smelling of cheap drugs so strongly that she didn't know how she hadn't gotten a whiff while sitting on the stone having her smoke. His hair was short and wiry, looking like the crew cuts that had been very popular a few years back. He had a small mustache that looked like it had been scribbled on with a pencil. His face was trim and there didn't seem to be any fat on his body. There was a stench of B.O. and cologne. Not expensive cologne, but the type with a sailboat on the bottle. Roxanne's quick-witted mind wondered instantly if it was to hide the stench of brimstone.

Because she didn't care that the man in front of her looked just like Allan Bishop. She knew without a shadow of a doubt that she was looking square into the eyes of the Devil.

He laughed wickedly as he descended upon her, grabbing for her breast and ripping off a chunk of her blouse instead.

Mike started to walk home from school early, and none of the teachers or administrators did bugger-all about him skipping fifth period. It was Family Education, a subject that he found positively mundane. He only went to see Cathy, and with her gone his attendance seemed moot.

What was it Sara had said? "You know society's going down the shitter when you need a class on how to not hit your kids."

That one had always made he and Cathy laugh. Not so much Xander, though. He had found the whole subject of domestic violence appalling while growing up. Surprising, considering he'd grow to become the poster-child for abusive tendencies. He grunted to himself, pushing the idea aside. He hadn't realized that he was thinking about Sara until long after the fact and it wasn't an avenue he particularly enjoyed exploring. *Traveling down memory lane is like traveling on Baltic,* he mused, thinking of the popular board game; *both are completely useless.*

His train of thought kept defaulting back to Julie and Greer. He couldn't tear his mind away from those poor girls, or what had been done to them. Now Greer was in a coma, but the lumps and scrapes told the story pretty well for Tim and his forensics department. Julie wasn't talking, and it didn't seem like she ever would. Unless something happened quick, those assholes would get away with everything they'd done. He kept seeing poor, young Julie Peterson being held down as they each climbed on, beating her and calling her vulgar names. Making her feel as though they were doing it to her, just like Grendel had. *Argh!*

he screamed inwardly, grabbing at his hair with one hand while clenching the other into a fist. The knuckles ached, still sore from trying to punch in Tommy's locker yesterday. At that precise moment, he would have given anything for something to hit.

Then he heard it. Down by The Factory, right around the old sitting rock where he and Cathy had made-out for the first time. Cathy and Xander always acted weird when they went down there, though he didn't know why. He couldn't see the actual stone from where he was standing, but the sounds of struggle were clear. He peeked his head around the gray slate corner of The Factory and saw Allan Bishop slamming Roxanne's back against the rock, choking her and riding his free hand up her skirt. Mike barred his teeth as he stepped around the corner. Suddenly his hand didn't hurt anymore. *That'll do just fine.*

Roxanne was crying, her shirt ripped in several places and a clump of her hair blowing about in the wind. Mike could see the blood rising to her scalp where it had been ripped out. Her purse had been thrown aside, makeup and pictures spilt out everywhere. Allan was huffing something sensually disturbing about how he knew she liked it. Mike grimaced. *Give me Adam Genblade any day of the week*, he joked inwardly, then he thought better of it and simply got ready to fight.

Carefully, he snuck up behind Al, then shoved him as hard as he could. Al flew over Roxanne, who seemed just as surprised as the would-be rapist. It was only then that Mike noticed her leg had been sliced near the pelvis and her underwear was dangling lazily around one ankle. The hole for the other leg had been ripped off. The image provided more fuel for his rage as she turned to run, not bothering to look back at either of them. That was fine by Mike, who had wanted nothing more than five minutes alone with this creep for well over twenty-four hours now.

Al started to rise to his feet, blood gushing from his nose and cheek from where he'd skidded across the ground. Grass stained the front of his white Yankees shirt as well, and his jacket had been ripped. The man suddenly seemed to grow, as if he'd gained a foot in every direction since Mike had shoved him. Mike gulped loudly, starting to feel the sweat dot his brow randomly.

"First the brunette," Mike observed as he clenched his fists and got prepared for an attack. "Then the blonde and now a redhead. What next? Some silver haired old lady? Geriatrics style, sponge-bath rape? Am I close?" Mike kept quipping, mostly just to keep from wetting himself. The insults made him smarter than Al, made him braver.

"You're close to death," the rapist replied, and there was no humor in his tone. No anything, actually. It was like a teacher reading from a textbook. He wrote Mike's death sentence as if it were a god-given fact.

It stripped Mike's bravery away in an instant. "Um..." he started. He didn't have time to crack wise again. Instead, he felt Al's fist against his face before he even saw the killer move to strike. He felt his teeth chatter and one come loose, slithers of blood being unleashed into his mouth. His eye was swelling before he even hit the ground, which he did at twenty miles an hour. His other eye jammed against the sitting stone, snapping his head back to the sound of a large snap. When he tried to open his eyes again he found that he could not, bruises having already formed over them. Blood dribbled from his mouth and nose. Pain shot into his scalp as Al picked him up by the hair, slamming the child's face into the concrete wall of The Factory. Blood splattered in all directions, and something in Mike's cheek cracked.

With every ounce of energy that was still inside of him, he drew back and punched Al, breaking the child abuser's nose and quite possibly his own hand. The cracking sound was amazingly loud, echoing several times before fading completely. It didn't matter. It disoriented Al long enough that Mike could make a mad-dash back to Xander's house.

"Soon," Mike promised himself, trying to stop the blood that poured from his face.

He thought he heard a scream, then realized that Al must have entered The Factory, where Roxanne would be alone... He kept running for Xander's, cursing himself and trying not to think of what that monster might do to her.

When the bell to end fifth period rang, most of the kids in Coral Beach High were bolting out through the large double doors that welcomed children into their halls each and every day. They were all running to get home to their warm little houses, safe from all the bad things that went bump in the night. Not Cathy Kennessy. She was going up those stairs, her shoulders bumping and being shoved by the unmannerly teens that were racing to get home and play Nintendo. A few of the senior males were looking at her backside -- she could feel it. Feel their eyes moving over her. She bit her lip spitefully, then continued into the school. The halls were bare, her every movement echoing off of the tiled walls. There were splotches on each one of the doors where students had ripped the numbers off of classrooms, many of which ended up decorating lockers or bedrooms. Trophies proving that these few managed to get back at this school in some small way. Mr. Larkin, the school custodian, wheeled his squeaky pail and mop down the hall opposite her, no doubt heading to see what mess of graffiti Tommy and Sud had left in the men's room today. His eyes fluttered over her as she walked past, an obscene smile playing over his lips. For a moment, she actually thought she saw him reach out to grab her, fear swelling up inside her. But it was just the mop handle he was reaching for, and he went about his business whistling the theme to Gilligan's Island.

Cathy could faintly remember feeling safe here, once upon a time. She remembered not having to worry about everything around her as if even the walls would try to kill her, when she would not have had to do what she was about to. If things had been the same, she would have been able to talk to Xander or Mike. More importantly, she wouldn't have had to. She would have still had Sara, her best friend in the entire world. Three seconds in a secluded bathroom stall with that blonde would have melted all of Cathy's fear and doubt away. Minutes later, they would have been laughing at Julian Grendel and plotting an equally devious way to get him back. But she was dead, and so was Grendel. Cathy had been robbed of her chance to get even on more than one occasion, and

192

it was getting to the point that she could not even hate their killer. After all, he was her best friend.

Still, with nobody else to turn to, she had to talk to somebody. Even if it didn't solve anything, she could still find more solace here than with Xander. At least the man behind those doors would pretend to listen. To fain interest. The letters on this door had been left untouched, and read: Dr. Phillips, school counsellor.

When she reached out for the doorknob, her hand began to shake violently. She closed her eyes tight, making one last wish to wake up and have all of this been a dream. When she opened them, she caught Shnieder out of the corner of her right eye, pretending to pick up a pencil to get a better look at her. She huffed loudly, then opened the door to Phillips' office. The door closed with a click and she leaned up against it, as if wanting to stay as far away from the man as possible.

Phillips looked up from the papers that he was working on and smiled warmly at Cathy. "Hello, Catherine," he said politely, using her full name as he did with all students until they asked him not to. "Is there something I can do for you today?"

She felt instantly safe. Or at least, safer then she had out there. His eyes were not wandering. In fact, they seemed to want to go back to his work. He wasn't mentally pulling her jean jacket off of her, the comfort she felt in that making her realize just how *uncomfortable* she really had been before. "Yes," she sighed, then brought a hand to her head to stop it from pounding, "No," she corrected, then fell into his chair. "I don't know," she decided on finally, ducking her head between her knees and wrapping her arms around it.

"Hey, hey," he said soothingly, getting up and then sitting on the edge of his desk. He laced his fingers together, resting both hands on his kneecap. "What's the matter here? What's going on?" His voice was so peaceful. It took you out of yourself, made you feel as though you were telling somebody else's sad story instead of your own.

"There's nobody else I can talk to," she said, trying not to make the words come out as a dry heave.

Phillips actually chuckled softly at this. "That doesn't really surprise me, Catherine. This may shock you, but I'm typically not a student's first choice for a person to come talk to. Now, what has happened to you?"

She sniffed. Then she opened her mouth to speak, but it came out as another sniff. Finally, she managed to force a word out. Once that first one came, it was as though she couldn't stop. "I don't want to be here anymore. This town, it's just too much. First Julie, now Greer in a coma, and I just can't take not feeling safe anymore. I picture them laying there and feeling so helpless... and it's easy, because it happened to me once." She paused for him to say something, her hands shaking. When he didn't, she kept going. "It was a few weeks ago, at the party where all those kids... where they died. Grendel he... he and his friends tricked me into going upstairs. He locked the door behind us and trying... trying to *make* me... His hands were everywhere. It was like they were everywhere. Every time I thought I could stop him, could get him off of me, his fingers were already there, stopping me. It was like he could read my mind, like I was stupid... Guess I was..." Again, she paused for words. Again, none came. "I can still feel his greedy palms. They were sweaty, forcing my clothes off of me, pulling at it. He..." she stopped, feeling that she'd gone on long enough. "I just needed someone to talk to, that's all."

Phillips was silent for a long moment, just tapping a finger against his chin and squinting his eyes, as if mentally saving this information into the correct folder in his mind. She'd seen Xander make that same expression many times before. It was like these computer nerds had some CPU in their brains. When he finally spoke, his voice was clear and still wonderfully calming. A contradiction to what was being said. "That is the biggest lie I have ever heard," he remarked, careful to punctuate every syllable.

"What?" Cathy asked, her tears suddenly visible again.

"I mean seriously, how much denial can one little girl be in? Please, Catherine. Your case-file says that you always have to be the centre of attention, but this just goes beyond anything I've ever encountered before. Really, I expected more from you."

Her brow furrowed, and she shook her head in disbelief. "What are you saying?"

"Oh, it's obvious. Painfully so. Julie and Greer become victims and suddenly everyone in school is talking about them, thinking about them. They're not looking at you anymore, in your tight little outfit that only a whore would think to wear. Do you tell them you're a virgin, Cathy? Do you? Is that what you tell the men right before you let them in, you filthy thing?"

Now it was her turn to be speechless.

"So, you couldn't handle these poor, sad girls getting all your precious attention, so you made up a story where you got raped, right? Some sick story from a delusional mind. Worse yet, you used a dead boy in it, a sweet young man who can't even defend himself," Phillips shook his head, then grew very angry. "Well, my dear. If you wanted it that bad, believe me, there are plenty of people out there willing to help you out. Give you what you need."

She looked up, knowledge sparkling in her eyes too late. "What did you-?"

He lashed out with one leg, kicking her between her breasts and knocking all of the air from her lungs. Her back pressed against the soft cushions of the chair, her head knocking back onto the wooden frame. Pain shot through her skull, the jolt forcing her to close her eyes. By the time she opened them again, he was on top of her. His hands gripped her blouse viciously, grabbing her skin whenever he could. He ripped it, sending buttons flying in all directions.

CHAPTER SEVEN: FEVER DREAM

For a moment, everything felt disjointed. Her mind tried desperately to catch up to what was happening in the room around her, taking great leaps of logic from one revelation to the other. She was confused and her brain felt groggy as her hands went up, instinctively pushing back on his face to keep him away from her. She tried to kick him but barely managed to twitch her leg under his weight as he struggled with her and attempted to keep her pinned down.

Pain brought her mind back to crystal clarity as he slapped her across the face hard enough to rattle a molar. Her head jerked awkwardly to the side and sent a v-shaped stream of saliva streaking across the floor. The red print of his hand stayed on her flesh and she smelled copper as a small tendril of blood escaped from her left nostril.

He grabbed her forcefully by both shoulders and shook her, slamming her head back against the floor. Each impact made her vision go completely white for a moment. When it returned, he was never in quite the same position where she had left him. When her mind snapped back the last time, he was mauling her breasts under her bra with his nubby fingers. His other hand gripped her chin and forced it to look up, stretching her neck to the point that she thought she could feel tendons snapping in her shoulders. His thumb was riding her throat, making it choke for air more and more with every failed breath she tried to take. She felt his lips on her collarbone and wanted to vomit.

Unable to move without extreme pain, Cathy stared up at the cross that hung lop-sided on the wall. On it, Jesus writhed in pain as well with blood streaming down his forehead from the crown of thorns. His eyes were turned up in his head, as though the agony had driven him mad.

She felt the clammy flesh of his palm leave her chest and got the impression that he was trying to unbutton his pants. Suddenly his grip got tighter and she could barely get any oxygen at all, her lips turning blue the way Xander's had earlier that same day. Her body made the convulsions of a cough but the sound never actually came, choked off at her windpipe by hands that smelled like copy toner and bleach. Now her vision was starting to go black around the rims and her throat was as dry as a lint trap. She felt like her head was going to explode, her every thought screaming relentlessly for air.

Bracing herself she turned her head quickly, feeling something she didn't want to think about in her neck pull free. The pain was enormous, but she didn't care. Given what had happened to Greer Donaldson, there was no alternative. She clamped down hard on his thumb, the stale taste of toner caking her tongue for just a moment before she pressed down and pulled, replacing the taste with that of copper almost immediately.

Phillips howled in pain and thrust his head up towards the ceiling as he tried to shake free of her mouth.

She felt the molar he had loosened chip, a small chunk of enamel traveling down her throat and slicing her tonsils along the way, but did not let go. Tears ran down her face and she thought the taste of blood was going to make her throw up, but she did not let go.

"Bitch!" he yelled, finally bringing his other hand up from the crotch of his gray dress-pants and raising it high, hoping that the threat of him bringing his fist down on her nose would be enough to make her stop. He didn't want to have her unconscious just yet, let alone dead.

As soon as she saw his hand she shot up her knee, burrowing it in between his legs as hard as she could. His eyes went wide with shock and his fist unclenched into trembling fingers as his entire form started to curl into the fetal position on top of her, wracked with pain.

Hot tears still streamed down her face as she finally let go of his thumb, her mouth curling up in disgust. The expression on her face was an impressionist's version of emotion, her features unable to decide whether to cry out in horror and sadness or to curdle in disgust and anger. In the end, it settled for a little of both as eyes filled with hate still soaked her cheeks with salt water.

She brought her knee up again and again, paddling faster than she used to when she and Sara used to swim in the creek as kids. She felt whatever she was kicking (she didn't really want to think about the specifics) maul and contort themselves under the pressure and stopped. His eyes were rolled up into his head. His hands, one still gushing blood, cupped his penis gently as he fell to the floor and off of her.

"Come... back..." he ordered in a faint voice, taking long gasps between each syllable.

She scrambled to her feet, still spitting foamy mouthfuls of blood as she reached for the door handle and ran out of the room faster than she ever had in recent memory. She ran so fast her legs felt like melted rubber and she thought her heart was going to explode in her chest.

"Come back, you bitch!" she heard him yell furiously when she reached the end of the hall, the embittered command echoing off the walls of the empty school until it sounded like it was coming at her from all directions.

She could still feel his hands on her. She had to turn around once or twice as she ran, just to make sure he hadn't really caught up with her. Never once did she see him, but nothing could convince her that he wasn't there as she pushed her body past the point where her lungs ached for air.

Finally her legs gave out and she collapsed on the gravel sidewalk halfway between the school and The Factory. Her eyes belted out tears more readily now and she sobbed out a constant string of sounds that she didn't think the human throat could even make, all of the pain and hurt and anger crashing down on her all at once as the adrenalin slowly seeped its way from her bloodstream.

Half naked and bleeding, she lay against a tree just a few feet from the road and cried in agony until she felt like she could walk again. All the while, she would have sworn that she could still hear Phillips screaming out at her, ordering her to come back.

ʌ˅ʌ

"What do you mean, you don't know where she is?" Mike demanded angrily, slamming his fist down onto Xander's computer table.

Xander frowned, unable to meet his friend's gaze. "Oddly enough, when I said that, I actually meant that I don't know where Cathy is."

"How could you *not* know where she is?" Mike groaned through clenched teeth, gripping his right temple and rubbing it. "She was here. You were here with her. Why don't you know where she is?"

"She left without telling me!" Xander snapped, more than a little angry him-

196

self. "Why don't you know where she is? What's so important that you left your girlfriend all alone, huh, big time superhero?" He thrust an accusing finger at Mike. "What, you going off to play lone wolf again? You'll get yourself killed, you moronic--" he paused, then stopped completely as the womb surged up within him. Despite the beatings his body was taking, the damn thing was actually *healing*, albeit slowly. "I don't know where she is," he repeated, trying desperately to calm himself.

Mike sighed, slumping down in the chair next to Xander's ruined computer. "I just don't like her striking off on her own, man. Not now."

Xander nodded, but it wasn't quite in agreement. "You should talk," he said finally, pointing out the gashes that lined Mike's face. His nose had finally stopped bleeding for the moment, until he accidentally tried to breathe through it again. "You look like a walking piñata, idiot. And that was just Allan, I took on them both remember."

"Thank you for recapping the last two days," Mike replied sarcastically. "But I was already there, hence I already knew. Dumbass. And at least I can say I was conscious for most of it, unlike you." He paused, punctuating his sentence by stabbing at the air with his index finger, then added: "Again, dumbass."

Xander groaned, thinking back on all that Spider had said. "The man in the moon..." he mumbled, stroking his chin.

"What?" Mike asked, squinting his frustration into his bedridden friend.

Xander looked up, as if suddenly realizing that Mike was still there. "Something Spider said. She said that he's watching. Watching the girls, watching us... watching everything. He doesn't speak, he just listens... and watches."

"Who?"

"The third rapist. He knows these girls somehow. He knows us. We need to find a common link, a thread that can bind them... tie it all together... before he gets into our heads too, like he did poor Julie Peterson."

Mike nodded, not fully understanding how the dead bride of Adam Genblade had managed to tell him all of this, but deciding that now was not the best time to ask. "What else did Spider say?"

Xander looked thoughtful then, trying to remember the exact wording. "She said that 'those we count amongst our allies today will have betrayed us yesterday, and themselves in the morrow.'" He stopped, mouthing the words again to try and comprehend them better. "Does that make any sense at all?"

Mike shook his head. "Not really. But she's crazy and she's dead and I'm not entirely sure it isn't all in your head, so I'll hold off on passing judgement just yet."

Xander looked as though he were about to object, then began to nod. It was true, all of it. Even if the vision of Spider had been real, she was a less than reliable source.

Suddenly, his bedroom door swung open and Xander jumped to shield his wounds from the eyes of his parents... Instead he saw Cathy, clothes ripped and blood seeping slowly from her left hip.

Her hair was matted, mascara running and lipstick smudged. Forcing herself not to cry for once today, she held herself up until both of her men rushed to her side as one, taking her into their arms.

"Something bad happened at school today," she whispered, collapsing onto the floor. She laughed at her own little joke, and it chilled both boys to the bone. For it was a hollow laugh, devoid of humor or emotion, as they feared she might now be.

ᚳ᚜ᚦ

She cried herself the sleep on Xander's bed, not letting either of them cuddle up next to her or even touch her. Gazing at her one last time, Mike closed the door and left her to hopefully sleep it off in the darkness. Some things didn't fade so easily. Her body convulsed with fear as she dreamt and he was tempted to rush in and wake her, to hold her in his arms and tell her that everything is all right. But he knew that that wouldn't help, knew that he had to give her time... And in that time, he could make things right.

As soon as the door closed, his expression changed. He was no longer hurt or scared for the woman he loved, but was now something to be scared of. The transformation was every bit as real and opposite as Xander to the Black Womb, his eyes narrowing and becoming evil. Bloodlust entered his every feature, and a thirst for vengeance made his lips bone dry.

"Come on," Xander said from behind him, rubbing one of his shoulders. "We've got some work to do."

Mike nodded, both of them starting down the stairs towards the living room.

The old couch had a pattern on it that spoke of its age, and cigarette burns that told of its use. The entire room was a decorator's nightmare, with colours that clashed no matter what direction you turned your head in. It made Mike almost glad that at the moment his eyes were almost too swollen to notice, otherwise this vertigo-inducing room might have pushed his nausea to the edge. Or beyond. He feared that if he vomited in here, it might blend in and they'd never find it. He sat all the same, leaning his head back onto the cushions and rubbing his bruised eyelids gently. Xander sat in the loveseat across from him, his hands folding together at his lip as his eyes bulged with fear, aimed down at some unknown direction.

"Phillips," Xander cursed himself softly. He'd been there. He'd been next to him and not realized it. "There must have been a thousand and one ways I could have taken him out, if only I'd--"

"None of us saw it," Mike cut him off, staring at the ceiling. "None of us could see it," he mumbled near the end, sighing once more.

Xander nodded, but not in agreement. Suddenly, he came to an understanding. "This is what Spider meant. The person that listens to us, watches us... It's Phillips. He waits for girls that he thinks are unstable... vulnerable..." Their minds filled in the gap, every dirty little possibility they were trying desperately to contain leaping in.

"Gets Al and Raine to cover his tracks, while he covers theirs." Mike shook his head in consternation.

"That's why we couldn't find the old files on those two low-lifes... Phillips

198

destroyed them all when he started here... probably his own, too. I find it hard to believe that he just woke up last week and decided that he was going to be a serial rapist."

Mike was still shaking his head. "Man... These guys are exactly what you refer to when you say 'a real piece of work.'"

All was silent for a long time then, as both boys struggled to assimilate this new information into their systems. Xander seemed to be having more trouble with it than Mike. Up until now, everyone he'd fought had been bad because they were... well, evil. Genblade, Spider, Alpha... They all just seemed to be that way. Born into the role. Now Phillips had come along and he seemed to be making the choice to do so, even going out of his way to avoid doing the right thing. "What are we going to do?" he asked Mike finally, the desperation showing through in his voice.

Casually, Mike picked up the phone next to him and dangled it by its cord slowly, letting the dial tone ring through the air. He grinned sheepishly at Xander, letting the thought linger. Then he pulled a business card from his jeans pocket and chucked it to his friend. The breeze from the open window caught it and forced it to veer left, but Drew snatched it out of the air with inhumanly quick reflexes. Mike regarded this with some degree of amazement, remembering that the Alexander Drew of less than a year ago that couldn't catch a baseball to save his life.

But Xander had winced from the effort, still not healing the way he should. Far faster than Mike would heal, but still not fast enough for his liking. A spot of blood appeared on the card from his swollen knuckles. He tried desperately to hide it as he flipped the piece of cardboard over. In standard newsletter print was the simple, all-American name of Tim White, FBI. Xander stared blankly at the card for a moment, flicking the corner with one finger until it was dog-eared. "No," he said dryly, calmly placing the card face down onto the table between them and sliding it across.

Mike nearly dropped the phone, along with his jaw. "What? Why?" he asked in astonishment. "It's kind of his department more so then ours."

"I can do this on my own," he responded, his pride visibly wounded.

"No, you can't," Mike replied matter-of-factly, picking up the card as he leered his eyes at his friend.

"Give me one good reason why not," Xander reasoned, with a touch of sarcasm in his voice as he began to rise.

Mike tossed the card at him again, this time putting a backspin on it. It shot high, making Xander reach to get it. Xander cringed as he felt the movement rip the tender, scabbed flesh across his abdomen. Bits of blood stained his shirt, expanding in circular motions. "I don't know," Mike shrugged. "You've done a bang-up job so far."

"Like you're doing so great," Xander retorted, finally letting the charade fall away to childish name calling, as it always eventually did between the two.

"Which is why we need *help*," Mike emphasized, pointing to the card again.

Xander grunted, passing the small paper square back and forth from one hand to the other. He sighed once or twice, each time looking to give in to Mike's inarguable logic, but did not. Finally, the third time, he handed the card back to Mike. "Make the call," he said quickly and without looking up, shamed at being defeated.

Mike smiled, dialing the seven digits into the off-white phone, its fluorescent numbers glowing back at him and reflecting off his eyes. It made him look sinister. Evil, even. Especially with that victorious smile across his lips, the one slowly fading with each number he dialed.

The phone rang three times before someone picked up, and the voice on the other end sounded tired despite the fact that it was four-thirty in the afternoon. "Hello?" There were the sounds of traffic and car horns outside. The sounds of many people walking on concrete. The sounds were of downtown Coral Beach, where most of the cops would be anyway. The noise muffled the sound of Tim's voice, making him even harder to understand.

"Hello," Mike responded, fighting to keep his tone even.

"Hello?" Suddenly, there was the sound of shuffling as White seemed to realize where he was. "Tim White's office, Agent White speaking," he said suddenly, wishing he could have taken back the previous thirty seconds.

"Catch you at a bad time?" Mike asked, cocking an eyebrow at Xander.

Xander smiled wryly, picturing Tim asleep at his desk with papers stuck to his face. Then he thought about how those papers would contain the word rape, and that smile disappeared.

"No, no of course not..." Tim trailed off, snapping his fingers and trying desperately to place the voice. Finally, he simply scrambled for his caller I.D. "... Brian Drew?"

"No," Mike responded without humor, balking at being compared to Xander's adoptive father. "No, this would be Mike Harris."

"Harris," White breathed. Mike could almost hear his lips curl in embarrassment. "What do you have?"

Mike careened his head, checking up over the stairs to make sure that Cathy had not made her way out of bed to listen. Taking the cue, Xander got up from the chair and walked to the bottom of the stairs, playing lookout. "Don't quote me, but we have a fourth rape. Attempted rape, I should say."

"Who was the third?" Tim asked, audibly confused.

"Roxanne didn't check in with you?" Mike asked, clicking his tongue against his mouth. "Well, you may want to get some info out of her. Allan did it; I was there. Tried to stop it, even."

"Don't get your hopes up. She's The Factory waitress? Not the first time she called in about some drunken patron forcing her into things. We couldn't pin anything, and eventually she stopped wasting her time calling."

Mike didn't know how to respond to that, so he just didn't. "Well, the new-and-attempted victim happens to be Cathy Kennessy, and she actually got a very good look at the third rapist."

"Who is?"

"Dr. Phillips, school Guidance Counsellor at Coral Beach High School," Mike said triumphantly.

Tim sighed.

"What?" Mike asked, the colour draining from his face. "What is it?"

"What did I tell you today?" Tim asked him impatiently. "Haven't you been paying any attention at all? That isn't your information to give. It isn't, I'm sorry. You have *another* third-hand story that I can't admit into a court of law as evidence."

"Are you saying you don't believe me?" Mike asked, getting Xander's attention.

"Oh, Mike. If you said that the Pope was the third rapist I'd believe you. Because I know you. That doesn't make you a witness I can credit." Tim sounded more tired now.

"What if Cathy--" Mike began desperately.

Tim cut him off abruptly. "I'm sorry to have to tell you this Mike, but the testimony of an emotional fifteen year old girl who is known for crying rape isn't worth a whole lot to us."

"Fine!" Mike yelled, angered beyond anything he'd ever thought possible. He slammed the phone back down onto the receiver, then picked it up and slammed it again just to be sure the message got across.

ʎ∀ʎ

On the other end of the line, Tim let the phone drop to the floor. He buried his forehead into his palms and shook it, now both mentally and physically exhausted. "Those're the breaks, kid," he sighed solemnly, then picked up his shiny new Federal badge and wondered exactly what it was good for.

ʎ∀ʎ

"We goin' down like that?" Xander grumbled to Mike as they both slipped into their jackets. He was clearly pissed at Tim, all past aid the man had given him pushed aside. This was Cathy they were talking about.

"No fucking way," Mike spat, a rare curse coming from his lips to punctuate the sentence. "I got a lead I'll have to go clear across town for. Could take awhile."

"Need help?" Xander asked, even though he knew Mike would never accept it.

"Naw, no knuckle-bustin' this time. Strictly recon," Mike had thrown 80's street lingo and military speak into that sentence at once. Either of which separately didn't quite hit the mark coming from him. Together, it was just plain wrong.

"Good," Xander nodded. "I'm going after Phillips." His expression was grim, even as he held up the ripped out telephone page for P in Coral Beach.

Mike looked about to protest, then thought better of it. Hopefully, he'd catch the old pervert alone. Should be an easy tag for either of them. "What about Cathy?" he asked, concern finally seeping through his lips.

Xander's stone gaze softened as he peered up the stairs to where his poor friend slept, no doubt plagued by nightmares of the events of the past days, weeks, and months. He glanced around again, then sighed. "She'll be fine."

201

6020 Temple Ridge Drive, just a thirty-minute sprint to the high school. The home of Dr. Darren Phillips, his name engraved deep into the seeder sign outside.

He stood in his living room, calmly placing orders into the phone that touched his lips. "Yes, she got away. I know, Bram. I know. We need her to be shut up, like the Donaldson girl and that waitress bitch. What do you mean you? Alright, I'll do it. Just get Allan and bring her here. If she's not at her place, then she'll be at Drew's. Yes, fine. Do what you have to with him.

"We're going to kill them both anyway."

The sky had become a dark pink and most of the trees had turned their leaves a bright orange in the past few weeks. The combination of colours looked absolutely gorgeous together, as if someone had taken a paintbrush and a meticulous eye to it. The air all around the buildings practically glowed with the dusk light, from the quaint houses lining each side to the small purple convenience store on the corner that was the only thing that ruined the picture, yet made it real all the same. Let the viewer know that this beauty was completely natural. It was lost on him. Xander hardly even noticed it as he leaned against one of those trees, leaves slowly falling down around him as if he were in some magical, gigantic snow globe. He took a moment to glance at the page in his hand and verify Phillips' address, then let it go and ignored it as it flapped away in the wind. He glared at the front door expectantly, waiting for something to happen. Wishing for it, too. Silently daring it to burst open in a cloud of smoke and for Phillips, Al and Raine to scramble out of there with guns blazing. Guns that would have little effect on him save to piss him off.

Yeah.

It was exactly that type of fairy tale that he kept telling himself before he even got out of bed in the morning now... And before he went, for that matter. The illusion that he was a twenty-something superhero instead of a fifteen year old with no life who'd barely even kissed a girl. Who cried himself to sleep every night, then woke up to see the blood on his hands and then cried again.

He washed all of those thoughts away, letting the fear swell up inside of him. Like an actor with stage fright, the fear would fuel him. Feed him. Drive him to do what had to be done. For Cathy. For Sara.

If you're innocent, you're hurt, or you're scared: I'll be there.

He remembered those words from the other night. Somehow they transformed the fear into courage just as the sun went down and he walked over, opening the door to the rapist's home and delving deep into the belly of the beast.

He expected the door to creak open. The doors always creep open and then a ray of light shines from the door, slitting a line straight through the darkness, where his three opponents would be waiting to take him on one at a time. That was just the way it worked.

In actuality, the doors hinges were quite well oiled. When he opened the front door and stepped quietly into the main hallway, he found that it was actually very well lit, showing off the leaf-green coloured interior. Off to each side was a different section of Dr. Darren Phillips' living room, each carpeted teal with a nice, homely feeling to it. Xander stepped in slowly, finding that the walls were lined with traditional American paintings. One from every state, in fact. There was even the old-fashioned forty-eight-star American flag hung over a fireplace and a gun display case, all three of which were antiques and looked like they'd been military issue. All this plus the fishing and hunting trophies on the far wall lead Xander to believe that this was the den. The only thing throwing it off was the closet that seemed out of place here. Obviously, renovating had been done. Xander took another step in. In the previously hidden corner of the room he saw Phillips.

He was standing casually, his suede overcoat draped over one shoulder, snapping his fingers as he listened to an old *Neil Young - Harvest Moon* record. There was a lot of distortion.

Phillips looked up, giving Xander a big smile when he noticed the boy. "How are you?" he asked pleasantly, his nice-guy routine still firmly in place. The same smile he used to lull the girls into the dark now charming Xander.

"Been better," Xander admitted, unable to hide the cuts around his eyes and cheeks.

"Pity," Philips said. "You know, a kid your age getting hurt like that, it could lead to some real violence building up in you over time. Cause some real psychological damage. Maybe anger management would be in order..." he trailed off as the record played on, tapping the side of his temple contemplatively.

Wide-eyed, Xander began to wonder if the nice guy act wasn't an act. If he really was a kind hearted man who'd apparently just gotten up one day and decided that he was going to be a rapist. To commit horrible acts on young girls. He kept the images of Cathy and Julie and Greer in his mind, kept thinking about how they must have cried. How they suffered. "Sir --" Xander started.

Phillips cut him off, closing his eyes and listening to the music, "I love this part," he explained. He turned it up slightly, the music blaring, as he started to hum along. "When we were strangers, I watched you from afar...When we were lovers, I loved you with all my heart..."

Usually the song was wonderful, but now the words seemed to hold a near freakish meaning. As if the bastard thought his victims loved him. Without even so much as opening his eyes, Philips pulled a series ten revolver from behind his back and fired once, piercing Xander through the right breast with an ear-shattering bang. Xander fell to the ground, crashing through an end table as he slammed down. Chips of ashwood twirled in all directions at once, some of them sticking into the back of his head. Immediately he felt hard to breathe. His lungs were filling up with blood and he could feel the wound becoming infected already. He coughed, gangrene coming up his throat in a sick burp. Phillips walked over to Xander, the music still playing.

"Because I'm still in love with you, I want to see you dance again... Because I'm still in love with you, on this harvest moon."

-BANG!-

He shot Xander directly through the central plexus of his chest. The young man's body jumped slightly from the sudden impact, but did not move afterwards. Phillips grabbed him by the arms and dragged him into the closet, hoping that the blood would not stain his carpet.

"Well, isn't this absolutely pathetic?" Genblade asked rhetorically, gazing down through the darkness as a pool of blood seeped from Xander's open wounds. "That dude busted more holes in you then he did that brunette." He laughed, then his brow crumpled and he seemed contemplative. "Why didn't I ever think of that?"

Spider stepped out of the darkness, smiling warmly. It was a smile one would expect from a mother after a three year-old scrapes their knee. "I'm sure you will eventually, darling," she assured him.

He smiled seductively in response.

"Not now," she scolded him. "I have to tend to the boy-womb. Run along, Adam... You can let your Eve tempt you later."

He smiled, glancing down at Xander with something mixing jealousy and fear. Then he walked away, fading into the darkness that surrounded them like a bad memory.

Spider leaned over Xander, touching his two throbbing chest wounds softly. It stung at first, but only at first. After that, it felt good. It felt as though he were healing. Without warning, she dug her nails inside of the bullet hole. Xander screamed wildly, thrashing about until she withdrew them again. Her fingers were almost completely covered in blood, but now held a thick banded golden ring which was spotlessly shimmering.

Xander looked up, confused. "Where did that come from?" he asked, his voice hoarse from the pain.

"Inside of you," she said simply and truthfully as she stuck her thumb into her mouth, sucking some of his blood off. "It's a ring, Xander. More than that, it's a circle. See, circle," she spoke to him as if he were a baby. There wasn't much he could do about it. "Are you paying attention, little Abel?" she asked, using the Biblical references that her creators were so fond of. "Pain and power are both on a circle, Abel. Just like this one. And it doesn't matter where you start when you begin your traveling. If you start at pain, it will lead to power. If you start at power, it will lead to pain."

He kicked the door where the deadbolt was, shattering the wood around it. He thought there would be something more than that somehow, given whose house it was.

Mike walked into the hall of the cheap, low-rent home. It was really just a door that led directly into their kitchen/family room, but they called it a hall for lack of a better term. He stomped a boot down onto the slick tile. Most of the house's interior was either off-white or simply not painted at all, some furniture homemade from other things that had broken. He'd heard rumors that the family had just gone through a tough divorce. Which had given her a reason to see the school counsellor every day. Which in turn had given Phillips the perfect opportunity to choose her for his first victim.

Julie Peterson jumped up from her kitchen table, the wooden chair falling back off its legs. The poor girl's face was still bruised, so much so that her freckles were barely visible. Her amazing smile that had shone with youthful innocence in her yearbook picture was gone now, and if anyone had asked, they would have said this girl was not capable of such an angelic display. She looked old and tired, so much so that Mike had a hard time believing that she was only fourteen.

"Hello," Mike said, faking a bit of cheer. *I hate doing this*, he thought, but the image of Phillips looming over Cathy's ripped and torn body kept his charade going. *At least for a little while longer.*

"W-What are you doing here?" she asked, stammering with fear as she backed herself up until she was against the wall. She jumped when the cold boards touched her back, as if she had thought someone was behind her. She was covering herself very well, wearing a fluffy pink pair of pajamas with flowers on them. They seemed seasoned and shabby, like she had been wearing them all day. Beneath the frills of the shirt a white undershirt was visible, but only until she pulled the top a little tighter.

It occurred to Mike what this sad child must think. *Why else would we be here?* Hating himself, he carried on. "I'd like to have us a little chat," he smiled, the malevolence in his own words frightening him.

Her expression was anger now, her face turning blood red as she struggled to point an accusing finger at him while holding the pajama top together. "How did you get--"

Julie Peterson's words stopped in mid sentence, as her cute little pointed nose and triangular chin both seeming to quiver. In reality, it was her body that was shaking. "No..." she whispered silently, her bottom lip no longer under her control. Those magnificent green eyes filled with unholy fear, something that went far beyond anything Mike had seen before. He didn't pretend to understand. "Gawd, no--" she continued, no longer shouting at them. It was just a frightened whisper now, like someone slowly praying in the darkness during one of those slasher movies.

Derek Smith finished walking into the door, closing it behind him with a soft click. "I let him in," he said flatly, no trace of emotion or grief anywhere in his voice. He smiled though... but somehow it was an emotionless smile. Like it was a photograph pasted onto his lips.

"Your Mom still went out to the Clarksburg wedding reception with you home like this?" Mike asked, trying to sound menacing instead of absolutely shocked. "Tisk tisk."

"That won't do, will it?" Derek laughed, his fingers dancing wildly along a nearby wall.

"Don't hurt me..." Julie pleaded, huddling into a little ball on the floor now, rocking back and forth but never taking her eyes off of them. "Please--"

"We won't," Mike cut off, a bit too quickly, then added. "As long as you give us what we want."

Tears jerked down the girl's face, and a series of dry sobs escaped from her lips. "What do you want?" she asked, very afraid of the answer.

Mike turned and looked at Derek.

The both of them smiled wickedly.

ʎʎ

"You're crazed," Xander said finally, a small dribble of blood rising to his lips with the words. The pool of blood that surrounded him had grown exponentially, spreading out in all directions. It was glowing with an ethereal presence, because the dark life-liquid should not have been visible there, in the darkness of his mind.

Spider grabbed him by a handful of hair, throwing him. His body turned for the first time since he arrived, and he slammed his back against the floor. Again, blood came to his lips. It made him gag, wishing that he could force himself to throw up. "Ingrate," she spat, her upper lip curling in disgust and her eyes narrowing in contempt. After a moment her lips lost all their emotion. Her slanted eyes remained narrow, but abandoned the anger that they had readily embraced seconds ago and replaced it with something that could only be described as hunger. She sat on his gut, her legs tucking around either side of his head and her dress curling about on his chest. The red gown was slit up both legs, making him feel like there was nothing separating the two of them at all. Her long black hair swung about wildly as she looked down upon him with an almost sensual desire. Suddenly, her features softened. Her body became warm onto his and she leaned down and kissed him, lightly, on the lips. "She always loved you, you know," she informed him, her expression growing sad. Her hands fluttered over her abdomen, as if Sara was talking to the madwoman through stolen ovaries. "She loved you, but she didn't know how to love you. You were so much more to her than a boyfriend, Xander. They all used her, her body at least. I don't think one of them much cared about her mind. You were so wonderfully different. She simply did not know how to react to it." She paused and glanced down at him. Her fingers slid down her own legs and then onto his chest and neck, nails punctuating every word. "The night she died, when you were about to kiss her... that's when she knew she loved you, Xander. She did. I can feel it."

Xander looked hurt and confused. He brought his hands up to shrug and Spider took each of them in her own, placing them on her waist. She was warm all over, comfortable. As if he could snuggle into her and sleep safely until he died. Like Sara had felt on the nights they'd sit at her house watching stupid movies until the TV turned white. Spider leaned back into the shadows slightly. When he squinted to see her in the darkness, it was Sara.

"Hello," she said softly, her lips moist and good.

ʎʎ

Cathy stirred, her arm reaching over across the bed instinctively. She opened her eyes suddenly when she realized that there was no Mike there. All she saw was the old, ratted Led Zeppelin poster that had hung on that wall for years, for a moment becoming very scared and forgetting where she was. She rose, then realized that she was in Xander's room. She sighed with relief, her chest still rising and falling with the panic that had overcome her. Slowly, she began to remember.

206

"Have a nice sleep?"

She turned in the direction of the voice, and Al slapped her alongside the face. She went back down onto the bed, the entire mattress shaking from her sudden impact. He climbed on again, straddling the poor girl in her best friend's house. She screamed, hoping for Mike or anyone to hear her. No one did. Al drew back and slammed his hand across her mouth, her jaw taking a queer shape momentarily, then he drew back to do it again.

This time when he moved to strike, his hands floating over her thin body as though he owned it, his fist was caught in mid air. He stopped and turned, coming face-to-face with his partner's stone-cold resolve. "What?" Al asked, but got no response. He chuckled. "I'll save a bit of skin for you, don't worry. You went first last time, pig."

For what seemed like hours, Bram Raine just stood there, staring at his partner. "We're taking her back to Phillips, like he told us to," he said flatly.

"Aw, come on!" Al laughed. "I'm just having a little fun," he reached over and grabbed Cathy by the face the way a grandmother might, but with more lethal force. "You like it, don't you? Don't youuuu," he babied her, then pushed her back onto the bed and slammed her shoulders down, slowly caressing her blouse downwards.

Again, there was a pressure on his shoulder. "We're takin' her to Phillips and gettin' our paycheck."

Al grimaced in pain, then relented. "Yeah," he agreed finally, turning and slapping Cathy once more. "We'll let him take first crack at the bitch."

ʎϒʎ

"Hello."

Her voice echoed off of the darkness as if it were solid, bouncing back and assaulting his senses from all around him. Slowly, the darkness began to close in and the blood around him faded into the ground. He turned and looked away from her, staring instead into the deep beyond.

"What's the matter?" she asked, her voice almost tired. Her voice was always tired when she asked that question, because she knew that he was just in one of his moods. She reached over with her index finger and stroked the side of his cheek. It sent chills throughout him, because it felt so much like her.

"You're not her," he responded dryly, turning to look at her. She was so amazing, her blonde hair wet with sweat and sticking to her head. She sat on him with her fingers all over his neck and face, wearing Spider's uniform loosely over her perfectly shaped, hourglass like body. She bounced a little, and it made him melt. He shouldn't have been looking, but he couldn't help it. Had to treat himself to these last few seconds with her again, for he hadn't realized the first time around that those were his last moments alive with her.

She smiled devilishly at him, the way she'd done a million times before. The smile that knew she had control over him and liked it. The smile that had forced him to run ten blocks just to get her a Kit Kat bar more than once over the years. She bit her lips slightly, the white contrasting the perfect ruby red of those slivers of soft flesh. "Of course I am, Xander," she pleaded, her big blue eyes growing sad all of a sudden. Her face was the

207

shape of a heart, and he wanted to take it in his hands. As if reading his mind, she gripped both his palms and slid them over her body, working their way up to her neck. She leaned in and kissed him lovingly on the lips, her small tongue darting between their two mouths. He heard the faint sound of their teeth clicking together, but did not feel it. She tasted like strawberries, just like she had on the night of her death. With that thought, the kiss slowly broke off. She leaned back up into her sitting position atop him, staring down at him as if she never wanted to take her eyes away.

Somewhere, he heard a door close. No, slam.

"I love you, Xander Drew," she assured him. He tried to speak, but she brought a finger to his lips. "I have always loved you. Ever since we were kids and I used to catch you carving our initials into wood, I knew that you were the one person who could love me. Who I, in turn, could love back. Someone who wouldn't use me, like so many have been used now."

A tear rolled down Xander's cheek as he remembered the kiss, wanting so much to stay.

"She looks much tastier than I remembered..." Phillips said, the voice cutting through the darkness.

Xander looked around, searching for the madman that had shot him. Still, he found only black.

Sara reached down and held his face, bringing it around to look at her. "I will always love you, now." She started to cry tears of blood, and they dripped down onto his shirt. Her voice became uneven. "Don't forget," she demanded, shaking her head defiantly at him.

"Let's have us a taste, then?"

"No..."

"Promise me you won't forget," she whispered, leaning in again slowly.

"I promise," he said softly, yet somehow each lover heard the other's hushed words above Cathy's screaming.

Sara leaned in and kissed him, and her features melted and tucked away to become Spider. The blood tears Sara had been shedding had been pressing onto each of Xander's cheeks, and the Asian assassin broke off the kiss and looked at him. "Don't forget. Pain is your power."

He opened his eyes and could hear the struggle just outside the closet door. Heard Cathy's body being thrust around as though it were a rag doll. He reached up to his cheeks and felt Sara's blood was still there somehow. As his vision slowly adjusted to the low light and Cathy's screams got louder, he looked upon himself and realized that he was covered in blood. Black blood that was oozing over his entire body from the duel gunshot wounds in his torso.

"Black Womb lives."

CHAPTER EIGHT: POWER

"Black Womb lives."

All three men stopped what they were doing instantly, their hands frozen in mid-air on or around Cathy Kennessy's body. Al had been clutching her by the shoulder and had began to shake so violently that pain shot in and out of the muscle from where she'd hurt it fighting off Phillips earlier. He hadn't turned around yet and already she could feel goosebumps traveling over his body and into hers at merely the sound of that rough, scratchy voice. It didn't even sound like speech that could come from human lips. The closest approximation he could think of was someone vomiting out words one syllable at a time, rather than simply speaking them.

Raine was the first to really regain his motor function and turn around, his hand dropping from where it had been next to Cathy's head, clutching her dark hair and getting ready to yank as hard as he could. For the briefest of moments when he faced the closet, he lost all sensation in his body. It took a moment for even basic bodily functions to restore themselves and let him blink and draw a small gasp. In that short interim he had lost control of his urethra and hot yellow liquid now dribbled down his leg. He barely even noticed. He tried hard to swallow but found that he couldn't get any saliva going no matter how hard he tried.

Phillips had barely even noticed. He stopped an instant or two after the other two, only because they had. He was still smiling so wide all his gums were visible and gripping the hot flesh of her left breast in his pale, thin fingers again. They felt cold against her flesh, like skeleton bones. He was about to bark something at them when something told him not too. There was a still in the air that hadn't been there before. *Shouldn't* have been there, really. With Julie and Greer there had been enough electricity in the air to light a city block, an excitement that had overwhelmed and enchanted him instantly. It was the carnal knowledge that his ancestors had known and he never could. Raising an eyebrow and keeping a wary eye on Cathy, he raised his head to follow the gaze of his two underlings.

It was black. Completely ink black, something Phillips knew was next to impossible in nature. It was so thin that its ribs almost stuck out of its scaly hide and every breath it took was accompanied by its chest heaving under huge muscles. Though its skin looked hard it also looked thin, as though its lungs and heart were just out of sight but their vibrations present as they rippled through its flesh with every beat. There was another spot creating shockwaves as well, in its lower right side. It beat out of sync with the others, as if its function wasn't tied to the rest.

Dark navy veins popped out of its arms and legs, its biceps and triceps seeming to grow and expand with every throb of its heart. Even as they watched, its knee snapped itself forward of its own power, sending a spurt of ebony blood onto the carpet as it seemed to make itself double jointed.

Its hands hung open-palmed at its sides, dangling and ready to strike at any moment, like a cowboy in a western shootout movie. The fingers were distorted and angular. At the tip of each finger was a talon, each one a few inches long and the clear, pale yellow of enamel. They came to points so sharp they could barely be seen, with each middle finger claw slightly longer than the rest. The index of its left hand dripped a dark substance that looked like Jell-O mixed with printing ink. Only after it landed on the floor with a plop was it identifiable as a chunk of flesh.

Its head looked normal until it opened its mouth again, its bottom lip lowering almost to its collarbone when it did. A joint in the back of its mouth snapped just as its knee had, as if it had to make room for all the teeth in its head. Dual rows of serrated teeth lined sore and bloodied gums. Each one was at least an inch long with the same yellow tinge that the claws had had, only they were dotted with slithering tendrils of blood as well. The meat of its mouth was coral red and seemed to glow when compared to the rest of it. Between the teeth and the colour, neither man present could keep their eyes off of it. A forked, saliva covered tongue darted in and out before it closed its mouth again, like a reptile tasting the air for familiar scents. Which made sense, as it appeared to have no nostrils, just a hump on its face where the nose should have been.

Now the only colour on its face came from its eyes. Small slits that curved upwards on the outside and downward inside, like a letter S on its side. They glowed the greenish-blue of the sea with a little red in the corners at first, but that faded away in an instant as it narrowed the triangular eyes to needlepoints, staring down the men in front of it with a pupil-less glare.

It seemed to focus on Raine's hand, still clutching a large tuft of Cathy's hair between his plump fingers. He let go as soon as he realized this, but the creature's gaze seemed fixated on him now, its claws twitching with anticipation. A growl emanated from deep within the beast, its lip curling in tune with it. It sounded like a kettle full of water boiling, that deep hatred bubbling up from inside it as it stood poised to extend upon them at any given moment.

Cathy lay on the floor in the centre of them. There was a gash traveling along the right edge of her jaw that was bleeding down onto her neck, along with a red spotty patch of skin on her forehead and shoulder from where Al and Bram had dragged her across the carpet. Her clothes were ripped and torn, but other than that were still on her. Her eyes had still been closed tight shut, but now started to open as she looked up in the direction that the snarling voice had come from.

A smile spread across her lips. *You're fucked now,* she thought to herself, as the last of her assailants' hands left her body.

Phillips turned back toward his record player, eyeing the gun that lay upon it, loaded with four bullets still.

Slowly, it crouched down onto all fours until its claws danced along the floor, tearing up tiny shards of fabric as it did. Raine raised his eyebrow quizzically, regarding its actions with fascination even as perspiration began to bead and dot his brow.

All at once its legs extended again, catapulting the creature forward almost too fast for Raine to see. Its arms rose high above its head and its feet bent up to shoulder level, each big toe sprouting a claw of its own that was easily twice as long as the ones on its fingers. Raine let out a high pitched wail as the monstrosity landed against his chest like that, its arm coming down hard and plunging themselves into the doughy flesh of his back. Blood forced its way out from between each nail, drawing long red lines down his back and making it look striped as the blood seeped out into his shirt. There was an audible hiss as each of the middle claws punctured a lung, as Bram suddenly found it very hard to gather the air to power his screams.

Phillips and Al each dove to either side away from the creature. Phillips scrambled toward his record player, while Al started backing up toward the door, afraid to turn and run or do anything that would take his eyes off of the creature for even an instant.

Raine stopped screaming, his eyes growing so wide he thought his eyeballs might fall out as he stared into the creature's aqua eyes. He could tell now that they were scaled too. Made up of millions of little octagons that glimmered against the light from the street, like the eyes of an insect. They seemed to look directly into his soul with their unblinking, remorseless stare. Then, for a brief instant, he thought he saw something else in the demonic stare. For a moment, he could have sworn he saw a glimmer of happiness. Then the long claws at the end of each foot dug into each of the pectoral muscles on either side of his chest. His eyes bulged further still and his mouth drew into an o-shape as the creature continued to stare at him. All at once, it brought its hands up and kicked its legs down, opening up Raine's chest and back wide with one smooth motion. It kept kicking over and over again, sending shards of skin flying and spattering blood in all directions. Raine found his breath again and began to scream anew, the creature digging its teeth into the trapezius muscle at the left of his neck, the skin having already peeled away under the force of its claws. As it dug its yellowed teeth into the muscle, the milky protective sack punctured and tore itself off, the muscle pulling free of its tendons and snapping from the bone like a rubber band, sending more dark crimson sloshing against the wall, smattering over a painting of Kansas and turning the Sunflower on it a dark orange. By this time Raine was bellowing out words that didn't even make sense together, the pain having driven him nearly out of his mind as it overloaded his brain's ability to process it.

-BANG-

The sound rang out like thunder as the creature's neck seemed to explode, sending black tendrils flying in all directions. A few feet away, Cathy's eyes went wide as she turned in shock to see Phillips, again standing next to his record collection, holding his smouldering pistol in his quivering hands.

The creature's body slammed against the floor next to where Raine lay, the claws on its feet retracting almost instantly. It lay there for a moment and all was still.

With the gun still aimed at it, Phillips took another step closer. Still, the demon did not budge.

Al took a step forward as well. He took off his hat and scratched his head, sending large flakes of dandruff down onto his shoulders. He stood on his toes to see the creature's face, now devoid of any colour at all. It was simply a blank black tablet, with no features to speak of except for the lump where its nose should have been. "What the fuck was that?" he asked finally, his voice squeaking in a way it hadn't done since he was thirteen.

Suddenly, its eyes snapped open again and it rose up quickly, the blackness flowing around the wound on its neck until it was no longer visible where it had been. Its green eyes were like headlights for a moment, then dulled as it got to its feet again.

"Argh-guh!" Phillips yelled, his lower lip trembling in fear as he shot again. This time the splash of black liquid came as the bullet seared its shoulder muscle. The small piece of lead passed right through and the creature did not even seem to register that something had happened this time.

Phillips shot twice more as the creature loomed ever closer, its hands clenched into fists that dug the claws into his own palms, sending tiny bits of blood onto the carpet before the wounds got a chance to heal. Each shot connected with the centre of its chest and went ignored, the pale flesh of Xander Drew visible through each hole for a moment before the darkness slithered in to cover it up, like the rush of water after a stone is thrown into it.

-click-

The creature grew stiff and ridged, its face showing the closest thing to emotion it had since it had appeared at the closet door. Its eyes grew wider, as though it recognized the tiny sound of metal on metal that had rung out towards it. It turned, its eyes narrowing again as it saw Al with one hand on the knob to the front door, and one still on the deadbolt he had just unlocked.

"Maaanah!" the creature roared at the top of its lungs, turning its body so fast that its kneecaps snapped in the wrong direction, his femur breaking the skin and healing itself seconds later, leaving only the spurt of black blood as any evidence it had been there. It charged at Al, leaping onto its hands and feet and pouncing, its mouth opening half way through the motion to show all of those teeth again.

Al screamed, bringing his arms up to block his face.

A moment later, one of those arms slammed against the door, leaving a circular red splotch that ran down towards the floor.

Tears coursing down his cheeks, he stared at the stub of mangled flesh and bone, clutching it with his other hand as blood sprayed out and onto his face and the ceiling, dripping back down on both of them. "Fuck!" he screamed, clenching his teeth so hard that one in the front that was decayed actually cracked and popped out, rolling along the floor and coming to a stop next to a shoe.

The monster brought its hand upwards quickly, giving Al an uppercut with its palm open and its claws outstretched. The long one and the end of its middle finger caught the loose flesh where Al's cheek met his jawbone and an instant later it was gone, along with all the skin on that side of his face right up to his receding hairline. When he opened his mouth to scream, his jaw came loose, falling slack against his chest. The creature reached up its hand again, shoving it forward after a second's pause as if to aim. Its arm jutted forward, the talon-less thumb digging into Al's lidless eye. Clear gelatinous goop came out as it wrapped its remaining digits around the back of the rapist's head, then slammed him against the metal door with such force that his skull caved in, tiny bits of it sticking out of his hair as he slid lifelessly to the floor.

The creature sunk its teeth deep into Al's chest as the body lay on the floor, gnawing and gnashing about wickedly. There was a sick slurping sound as the dead man's wet muscles contracted reflexively around their killer's chin. Finally it reached what it wanted, withdrawing its head with the young man's heart resting comfortably between its jaws. After a moment it clamped down hard, sending fountains of blood in all directions, before swallowing its prize.

The black beast turned, its hands dripping with blood and brain matter, towards Phillips. Between the two, Cathy still sat on the floor unsure of whether to be happy or sad about what the Black Womb was doing all around her. The entire altercation had taken place in less than three minutes.

It took a step forward. When it stepped out of the hall where Al's remains were and into the light of the living room, Cathy could see redness pumping its way into the corners of its eyes. After a moment it went away, then came back again as the Womb took another silent step forward. It ground its teeth as if in pain, closing its eyes and clawing at its own skull with its claws. In her mind's eye, Cathy could almost see the mental tug-of-war going on between Xander's consciousness and the Womb's. After a moment its eyelids split open again... revealing eyes that were a deep green aqua as the creature opened its mouth in what could only to perceived as a smile.

"Black Womb lives!"

"Oh, god," Cathy gasped, kicking herself back against the carpet. Scrambling to her feet, she took off towards the door to the kitchen so fast that she almost tripped on a record that had been tossed out onto the floor.

The creature watched her for a moment, looking at her the same way at cat looks at a mouse before giving chase, the light reflecting off of the opaque lenses it had for eyes. As soon as she reached the door to the kitchen, it leapt, landing next to the couch on all fours before standing up straight and walking in.

Quivering and shaking as he used the record player to prop himself up, Phillips turned and ran towards the door and didn't look back.

The Womb stared into the small kitchen. The lights were off and the lenses over his eyes inverted and expanded to take in all the light possible, allowing him to see Cathy as she pushed a chair between herself and it on her way out the other door and into the back hallway.

It growled like an engine revving, jumping onto the table and watching her run as his claws dug into its wooden surface. It jumped again, landing in the hall just behind her and slashing out with its claws, three of them catching her back and making long narrow lines there. The shallow cuts were already bleeding as she fell forward, slamming her head against an end table and knocking over the potted plant on it. Soil and mud fell into her hair as she hit the hardwood, the sky blue vase shattering right next to her. She turned to face it as it loomed over her, its face emotionless and barren.

"Please..." she begged, her hands before her in defense just as Al's had been. Tears streamed down her face, mixing with the blood and dirt on her cheeks.

"Please, Xander... not you."

The creature stopped in its tracks, its eyes narrowing at her.

Cathy sighed and walked over to the Womb, placing her hand on the side of its face to force it to look at her. This time it did not turn away or object in any way, her touch sending a tingle through his oily black form. She traced its large eyes with her fingertips, looking deep into them. Really looked. Past the liquid hatred that covered him, somehow cutting through it all and getting past it unscathed. She squinted and bit her lip as she found what she was looking for, smiling. "It's really you in there, isn't it?"

Redness poked its way along the corner of its retinas, until it twitched its head and the colour changed back to green again. It raised its arm high, extending the talons on it to their fullest.

Pulling herself to her feet once more, Cathy darted into the closest door and slammed it behind her. It was dark, but there was enough light coming in through a shaded window to tell where she was. She had come into Phillips' bedroom. She grabbed a hamper quickly, moving it in front of the door as best she could before darting into the closet and closing the door behind her.

For a long moment there was nothing. She wondered if it had forgotten about her the second she was out of sight and had gone back to deal with the third rapist. The closet was damp and musty. It smelled of moldy laundry and a sterile smell that stung her nostrils and reminded her of hospitals.

There was a crash as the door opened, followed quickly by another as the hamper slammed against the far wall of the room.

Her lips shaking, she cast her eyes down and watched the tiny ray of light coming in from beneath the doorway. After a second, part of it turned dark with shadow as the Black Womb stepped into the room. She cupped her hand over her mouth to try and contain the whimpering sound that her mucus-ridden throat was making without her knowledge, pressing so tightly she might have cut off her own air flow.

From outside the closet, she heard it growl. There was a ripping sound, and she could almost picture it crouched down on the floor and ripping at the carpet with its claws as it surveyed the room. It seemed like it was always doing something with its hands. Just like Xander. The thought scared her even more, a shudder escaping from her despite her efforts to stop it as she peered something under a pile of bloody towels out of the corner of her eye, almost obscured by her wet lashes.

In the bedroom, the creature stopped scratching at the carpet and was immediately still and silent when it heard the shudder from somewhere in the room, followed by a sudden rush of air. Its eyes became small slits in its head as it stuck its tongue out, tasting the air for scents. Its head turned so quickly that it pulled a muscle, which healed even as it happened. It stared at the closet door, watching it as though it was supposed to do something other than what it was.

Slowly, the creature crept towards it, its claws ready to strike at a moment's notice as its head bobbed from side to side.

Cathy watched as the shadow under the door became bigger and bigger, biting her lip so hard it drew blood.

"Xander!" Cathy cried, getting out of the car and running towards him, with Mike not far behind. They embraced him, tears of joy streaming down all three faces. They fell to the ground, kneeling on the wet soil, still embraced. Xander leaned in and kissed Cathy on the forehead. "It's alright."

She shook her head, trying to fight it, then finally gave up and simply burst into laughter. She hadn't wanted to laugh right then. The way everyone was looking at her since trying to convince people that Grendel had raped her the night he died was merciless. There was so much in their eyes. Hatred, pity and always a little desire with the men, no matter who.

Except Xander.

"Thank you," she said honestly, her voice sounding like the sun. As if warm sunshine on your face could speak to you and tell you that it would empower and protect you. There was security in her voice, a place where he could make his home.

"For what?" he asked, cocking a brow at her.

"Making me laugh," she explained, those pink lips curling into a smile. His hand lingered near hers so she took it, her fingers dancing gently across his.

Again it twitched, grinding its long teeth against its gums.

The closet door flung open as Cathy pushed her arm forward with something in it, a bottle whose contents were now surging towards the creature as it was distracted.

Rubbing alcohol spewed into the Womb's eyes and was immediately absorbed by the retina. They turned pitch black around the edges as the blood vessels in them exploded, sending the tar the monster used for blood into its pupils. It thrust its head backward and screamed something that couldn't be described in human terms, though it was clear it was the creature's version of a vile curse. Its hands went to its face instinctively, which only resulted in it tearing at its own eyes with its talons. "Ma-gda!" it bellowed, finally opening its eyes again in time to see Cathy bolting towards the door.

It screamed longer and louder than she had ever heard it. Although it wasn't English, it sounded like Phillips screaming for her return in the school. As she re-entered the hallway, it occurred to her that she had managed to piss it off.

She stepped on the shattered remains of the vase, a large chunk sticking through her shoe and into her foot. Hissing in pain, she tumbled to the floor again, this time catching herself. When she tried to get up again, she felt a weight on her back and looked over her shoulder to see that face of the Black Womb through clumps of her dark hair, its piercing eyes like greenish-blue spotlights. "No!" she cried, even as it raised its hand again.

"She looks much tastier than I remembered..." Phillips said, the voice cutting through the darkness. "Let's have us a taste, then?"

"No..." Cathy protested, trying in vain to get her attackers off of her.

Spider broke off she and Xander's kiss and looked at him. "Don't forget. Pain is your power."

Pain is your power.

215

From somewhere deep inside, the consciousness of Xander Drew let loose with one final push for freedom. The creature's eyes began to glow red as it brought its talons up and again started to tear at its own face, falling backward off of Cathy and screaming. Then, without any other warning the black ooze fell from his body as if it suddenly lost the ability to cling there, splashing against the floor and leaving a thin layer of blood surrounding Xander's naked form. He pushed back a scream, falling to the floor and shuddering. He was cold, even though it was quite humid here in the house. Slowly, he crawled over to Cathy and held her close to him.

She pulled away from him, her eyes filled with uncertainty and fear as her lip curled slightly in disgust.

"It's alright," he said softly. "It's alllll right."

Her body shaking as she finally let go of everything she'd been holding onto, she collapsed into his arms and pressed her face against his naked, blood-drenched chest and started to cry in massive heaves, wrapping her arms around him. He stroked her hair as best he could, making a soft shushing sound to try and calm her.

There, alone and naked with her in the dark as her clothes hung off of her, he realized what Spider had been trying to tell him all along. *Pain is my power*, he thought, his eyes growing so wide that he was physically unable to shut them. His hand began to shake. It wasn't his pain that had triggered the Womb and saved them both, or the transformation back. It wasn't his suffering. The thing that had triggered it at Sara's wake, in the fever dream and just now was emotion. The desire to protect his friends. It was *their* pain. He looked down at Cathy, shivering in his arms. *Her pain.*

He found this information sick, twisted, and absolutely no help at all.

Dr. Darren Phillips walked down the hall of Coral Beach High School towards his office the next day, a broad smile across his lips. He was confident of his own immortality and had even enjoyed the fifteen-minute walk to work today, just as Greer Donaldson had attempted to do not long before. The thought brought a smile to his face and a song to his heart as he skipped over the stairs, waving to Tommy, Sud and some girl he hadn't seen much of. Then he waved to Randy, the young man smiling back at him.

He was humming the Cheshire Cat song from Alice in Wonderland without a care in the world. Those kids couldn't pin anything on him, he'd made sure of it. Cathy was known for crying rape and Drew was long suspected of being a gang member and a killer. The police wouldn't believe anything they said, if that... thing hadn't killed them anyway. He hadn't found a trace of either of them when he ventured home to dispose of Al and Raine's bodies. It was no matter anyway. He'd kill them soon enough.

He twirled a key around his index finger, the tag on it saying something about how life was unpredictable. It was a line from that song by that guy in that band. Everyone knew it. Phillips stopped the key where it was and tried to shove it into the keyhole of his office. That was when he noticed that his door was open, just a little. *Curiouser and curiouser*. He chuckled inwardly, pushing the door open to see who was inside.

Mike and Derek both sat casually on Phillips' desk, sifting through files on Allan Bishop and Bram Raine at their leisure, not even bothering to look up when he came in. Both had a satisfied smile on their faces. Tim White was in front of them, holding up a third file. It was on a one Phillip Masters, but they all knew him as Dr. Darren Phillips... Before he got his name changed, of course.

"What is this?" Phillips demanded, trying to play innocent. His face gave him away though. Innocent men didn't get their faces covered with sweat that quickly, nor could the blood have drained from his face that fast on shock value alone.

"This is your criminal record, Mr. Masters," Tim informed him, and Derek could not help but chuckle at his own private joke. Mike wondered if Smith would ever clue him in on exactly what that joke was. "And this," Tim continued, holding up a small sheet of paper with a police header on it, "is a signed statement from Julie Peterson pinning you as the third rapist to attack her." Tim smiled, visibly enjoying this. He wasn't done yet. "And finally, this," he teased, handing up a third sheet. This one had a Federal border along the top. "This is a warrant for your arrest."

Phillips said nothing, his keys dropping to the floor with a clang as he lost motor control.

Tim smiled. "You're going back to Cleveland, Phil. Where I'm sure there will be plenty of big, nice, friendly men that'll show you exactly how a rape victim feels."

EPILOGUE

Agent Tim White walked through the revolving doors of the Coral Beach Police Department, immediately starting to peel out of the beige trench coat he'd worn into the office. He stopped in his tracks just past the door, his eyes bulging slightly as he looked toward his desk.

"Not a bad day," the man leaning against his cubicle said, running a hand through his auburn hair and flashing Tim a quick smile. It was the type of smile a used car salesman gave when you knew he was about to sell you the bridge, but you liked him anyway for it. He flipped the page of the police file he was holding, glancing only briefly at the pages. "Phillip Masters was wanted on eight counts of sexual misconduct back in Cleveland. They'll be happy to have him back."

"Not as happy as we'll be to be rid of him," Tim growled as he marched over to his desk and tossed his jacket upon it. "Duncan Taggart, I presume?"

The man smiled, shooting Tim a little two-fingered salute. "That's me," he chimed, giving Tim the once over and smiling.

217

"What?" Tim asked, raising an eyebrow.

"Your name's Tim *White*. And you're *black*. Please don't tell me I'm the first person to point out the irony in that."

"To my face, yes," Tim sighed, rubbing the bridge of his nose. "Is there something I can help you with? I've hung up on you twice, what more can I say?"

Duncan closed the folder and waved it in front of Tim's face. The red-stamped word 'CLOSED' shimmering back and forth in front of him, its ink still wet. "You did great work here, White. And with the Genblade case, but I told you that before."

Tim nodded, tapping his index finger on the rail that ran across the top of his desk.

"But let me ask you this: how much fun is it doing a rape case?"

Tim stopped, thinking back to when he'd asked Mike that very same question only a few days before. It felt like months. "None at all," he said finally, his voice hushed.

"That's what I thought," Duncan said, his mischievous grin returning. "Now, are you ready to get to work?"

Tim raised his head again to meet Duncan's gaze, feeling a smile spread over his lips as the both of them started to walk towards the exit.

ʎʞ

After fifth period, Xander, Mike, Derek and Cathy all sat around the picnic table in the back lot of the school, where this had all started mere days before. It felt like years. Horrible years spent tortured in hell, where not even the crows could peck at their eyes.

They knew by now that Bram Raine had been paid for his part in everything. That he'd been a hard case in high school, but had tried to turn himself around... Until his wife and daughter had been diagnosed with cancer.

The daughter wasn't expected to last much longer, and Xander wished that she could have maintained her image of her father for her final weeks.

It made the victory sour, neither of them feeling much like celebrating as they licked their respective wounds.

Derek shuffled slightly, uncomfortable with the dragged out silence. He frowned as he looked to each of them, all of whom were avoiding eye contact with one another. The pain was too great, too much of it to simply smooth over like a hot knife would butter. His black shirt ruffled slightly in the wind and made him cold. They all felt it, but he was the only one to wrap his jacket around his arms. The rest of them felt they deserved the cold, for one reason or another. Finally, Derek asked the question on all of their minds: "What now?"

They all glanced at one another's faces for a split second, then found their way back into the separation again. This time Derek joined them, resting his head on his knees. After a few more minutes, Cathy got up and walked away without so much as regarding either of her men, going home to lie down on her bed and cry.

Somewhere, Xander thought he could hear Spider laughing at him.

BOOK THREE

SMOKE & MIRRORS

SHE RAN

Lawrence Hogan leaned his head back against the concrete step he was sitting on, the sharp stone digging into the back of his skull. "Ow," he said to himself in a dry, dull voice. He made no attempt to move or shift into a more comfortable position, choosing to sprawl his thin, lanky form across the stairs in every direction.

"Well, if it hurts that much, don't do it," Julie Peterson sniped, rolling her eyes around her freckled face as she turned away from him and back toward the three girls she was standing with. "So anyway, I call up my cousin and she's dating this guy named Walter. She said that she tried to call him the night before, but that she couldn't get through because she said he said he was in a no call zone. What an idiot, right? Only no call zone is out with the trailer trash on the TR. Might as well just admit to..."

Lawrence let the conversation fade into the background, slowly dissipating into a dull mumble as he let his gaze flitter up and over the girls with his big brown eyes, a slow smirk growing to the left of his mouth.

Julie's light brown hair fell down onto her thin shoulders, just touching the top of the pink shirt she wore. It looked to be about two sizes too small for her, and he thanked heaven for growth spurts as he examined the small, heart-shaped emblem on the center of her chest. Her jeans clung tightly to her diminutive hips, so form fitting that they didn't even have pockets, just smooth denim travelling down her long legs and withdrawing into the black leather cowboy boots she'd taken to wearing lately. She shifted her weight from foot to foot as she spoke, trying to find a comfortable position to stand on the cracked, shattered sidewalk as she continued with her story.

Jesse Newhook nodded along, smiling politely as she listened to Julie. She had short black hair that had been braided on the back and sides, yet gelled into spikes on the front. Her eyeliner was a deep purple and had been layered on thick, offset by shimmering pink lip-gloss that winked at him every time she moved her head. It was an odd combination that somehow managed to work for her. She wore a Coral Beach Cougars sweatshirt so big that it didn't stop until it reached her knees, hiding even the shorts underneath it and showing only her bare, shivering legs. His eyes lingered on them for a moment, then travelled back up until they met with hers before moving on.

Nancy Kelly was a strawberry blonde with hair that went straight down to the base of her spine, moving and flowing with her when she laughed. Her smile seemed too bright for the size of her petite, heart-shaped face, with the sides of it almost touching her eyes at times. Her nose was cute and turned upward, even though from what he'd seen of her so far, her attitude was anything but. She was still wearing the dull brown, grease-smelling uniform from the restaurant she worked at, not even caring how she looked and somehow looking beautiful all the same. His gaze focused on her and stayed there, watching her as his mind drifted slowly into fantasy.

"Ahem," Julie coughed dramatically, tapping her foot as she glared down at him. "Got comfortable, did we?"

He raised an eyebrow to her, then sat back up and placed his hands in his lap. "Um... Yeah." He blushed, tossing a smirk at Nancy.

She smiled back, regarding him for only a moment before she resumed her conversation with Jesse.

Julie scoffed at Nancy, then turned her scowl back towards Lawrence. "Why're you here again?"

"Free country," he shrugged, running a hand through his long, black hair.

Julie shot him a look.

"Relaxing before my Chem test," he amended quickly, pushing off the stairs and getting to his feet. "But I get the feeling I may be able to do that someplace else."

"You must be psychic," she drawled sarcastically, sticking out her tongue at him as she turned back toward her friends.

He stepped forward to say something else, then stopped himself and let out a sigh. Frowning as his shoulders drooped, he turned and started walking toward the corner, kicking stones off the sidewalk as he went.

Nancy's gaze followed him for a second, the smile fading from her lips until Julie began to talk again.

"So, anyway, I'm there at home and then there's this knock on my door and it's them, and I'm like, what the hell? What are you doing in my house?"

Nancy nodded, not really hearing what was being said anymore.

Jesse looked from Nancy to Julie and then back again, cursing softly to herself. "I gotta hit the washroom," she said under her breath, stepping between the two and heading around the corner.

"Whatev," Julie piped, making a little 'w' with the thumb and forefinger of each hand without even realizing she was doing it, then continuing on with her story.

Jesse jogged around the corner, seeing Lawrence just up the street. When she thought she was a safe distance from the girls, she called out to him. "Hogan!"

He stopped, turning around quickly. His hands were up as if to block something, but he loosened quickly upon seeing the semi-gothic brunette stepping up towards him, almost out of breath already. "Jesse? What's goin' on?"

She stopped a foot shy of him, pausing to consider her words. After a moment, she bit her bottom lip, realizing she had no idea what she wanted to say. Huffing, she grabbed him by the arm of his shirt and pulled him between two buildings. "Look... she likes you. Okay? She won't say she likes you, but she likes you."

He raised an eyebrow at her, brushing the tip of his nose and smirking to himself.

Her dark eyes darted around in their sockets, looking everywhere in the dust-filled alley but at him. "And you like her. Just because Julie's a bitch doesn't mean you should leave. Just, come back. We'll figure out something to talk about with her and you'll get to know her and it'll be cool."

He leaned forward into her lips, bringing his hands up to cup either side of her face. His rough fingertips grazed the ends of her hair and her earlobes lightly before he moved his hands down, squeezing both of her arms firmly just before the kiss ended, her pink lip balm making a smacking sound as their lips parted. "Don't like her. Sorry if it seemed that way."

She blushed so much that her cheeks turned bright red, still refusing to make eye contact with him and instead picking a spot on the nearby fire escape to stare at. She brought her hand up, twirling the ends of her hair nervously before responding. "Oh," she said finally, her voice small and sheepish.

"Listen," he smiled, touching his hand to hers. "I really do gotta go cram a bit more before that test, but maybe after we could get a bite to eat? I hear good things about that Deli down on Fifth but never go there."

"Um, yeah." She nodded, finding it hard to catch her breath again. "Yes. Absolutely."

"'Kay." He smiled. Reaching into his pocket and pulling out a pen, he gently scrawled his number onto the palm of her hand. "Give me a call in about three hours, and be hungry," he laughed, before turning to walk out the other side of the alley.

"'Kay," she said happily, waiting for him to leave the alley before letting out a squeal. She turned around the corner and started back the way she'd come, her heart beating faster than it ever had while running as she tried to figure out what she was going to tell Nancy and Julie and came up with a blank. She took a deep breath and rounded the corner to greet them, trying to hide the smile pasted across her lips.

The sidewalk was bare except for the small stones Lawrence had kicked up while he was leaving. "Guys?" she called out, raising a pierced eyebrow suspiciously. "Nancy?"

There was no answer and nobody on the street, period. Not even the sound of people close by. "Frig," she huffed, shoving her hands down into the pockets of her sweater as she started to trudge down the sidewalk towards home.

Her scowl faded after only a few steps, the memory of the kiss coming back to her and making every inch of her skin tickle. His lips had been so smooth and warm, her face still scratchy from the patches of stubble that dotted his angular cheeks. She could almost feel his fingertips as they just barely touched the tips of her ears, wondering if he'd done that on purpose or not.

Her stomach growled, but she wouldn't let herself get hungry before she went out with him... or maybe she should, so that she wouldn't eat too much while she was out? She sighed, turning the corner by the courthouse and taking one hand out of her pocket, sliding it along the wire mesh fence that stood along the side of the road.

-tink!-

She stopped a moment, looping her fingers through the fence and turning to look past it and into the salvage yard. There were old tires and engine parts scattered everywhere, their rusted out frames casting weird shadows against the ground. She let out a long sigh, smiled, and then sighed again as she leaned her head forward against the fence. "Frig," she said again, gripping the fence tighter and tighter until she felt the cold metal start to dig into her flesh.

-tink!-

Pushing back from the fence and backing up a pace, she looked down at herself. She grabbed at the sweater, tugging in out until she could see the entirety of the letter C printed across its torso. She almost gagged, then turned and started walking again. "I can't *believe* this was what I was wearing for my first kiss," she moaned, letting her head fall back and looking up at the sky. She almost laughed at the words, the concept itself still foreign to her. First kiss. She'd just had her first kiss.

-tink!-

She turned down the alley behind Claire's Video, making a smooching sound towards a kitten as she did so. Suddenly, and without her even realizing she was doing it... she began to skip. Had she noticed what she was doing at all, she would have stopped immediately. Never before would she have thought of herself as the type of girl who *skipped*, even as a child. Yet she bounded down the dark, slimy alley as happily as if it were a yellow brick road, her short hair bobbing each time she landed.

-tink!-

-tink!-

She stopped, skidding to a halt just shy of a puddle as she finally noticed the sound. Furrowing her brow, she turned around with her mouth already open and her tongue forming a defiant curse.

Her head hit the wall before even the first syllable came. She was unconscious before her body even splashed into the puddle.

CHAPTER ONE: WHERE THERE'S SMOKE

"Okay class, shall we pick up right from where we left off last time?" Professor Miles smiled, turning from the board to face his class.

He was greeted with twenty-three blank faces staring back at him, their eyes vacant and dead. Randy Owchar sat in the back row tapping his pen against his desk, making the only sound in the room.

"Oh, for God's sake," he sighed in his thick British accent, taking off his gold-rimmed glasses and rubbing the bridge of his nose before addressing them again. "We were discussing *evolution*. That little thing that gives us opposable thumbs and straight spines. Ring any bells?"

Near the front, a cute, chubby girl opened her mouth to speak, then stopped.

"Yes, Calla?" Miles coaxed, smiling warmly again.

"I just don't understand it, I guess. I just don't see it. I mean, no matter what you do to a dog... it's still going to be a dog. It's not going to change."

Leaning his chair against the back wall, Derek frowned and rolled his eyes dramatically. He closed his notebook and dropped his pen back into his bag, realizing that nothing said over the next few minutes was going to be particularly helpful on an exam.

"You're right, Calla," Miles agreed, nodding.

Derek squinting, leaning forward until his chair was back on all four legs.

"Animals do not simply change their behaviour, unless some external source forces them to. It is the one key difference between human beings and animals that we have found. Humans change their behaviour, animals don't." He paused, wiping some gook off his glasses before continuing. "Now, those changes are the first steps to evolution. If the change in behaviour results in that particular animal surviving whatever oppresses it, then it will pass on that knowledge to its offspring until *many* creatures know it. Once the creatures that did not learn this die off, it becomes something that all members of the species inherently know."

Calla scribbled furiously, the side of her hand black as it rubbed the ink off the page behind it.

"What about that dog?" Derek drawled, calling out from the back of the room. "With the bell?"

"Good point. Excellent," Miles agreed, pointing at him heartily. "Pavlov's dog was one of the first experiments in purposefully altering animal behavior. He would ring a bell every day just before feeding his dog. After so long with this routine, the dog would begin to salivate at the sound of the bell alone, even if the food was nowhere in sight. It was a behaviour learned by human machinations, the first steps toward controlling evolution, albeit on a very small scale."

"What could that be used for, though?" Randy scoffed, smirking as he dusted off his red baseball cap and then placed it back onto his head. "What could controlling drool do?"

"Well, nothing," Miles admitted, smirking as he nodded his head. "But, it has been attempted successfully with more practical results. In 1993, a scientist named Bill Lishman used a bird's natural tendency to imprint on the first thing it sees to get a flock of Canada Geese to follow him and his small aircraft from Ontario to Northern Virginia. The geese still follow the same flight pattern to this day on their own, and are now effectively a self-sustaining flock. He used his knowledge of bird instinct of Pavlov's theories to alter their behaviour, taking them out of the flight path of poachers and predators... effectively changing the outcome of their species as a whole."

"Cool," Derek said, smiling. "Crazy that he even thought to do that."

"'We can see further than ever, because we stand on the shoulders of giants.'"

"What?"

"It's a quote. From Albert Einstein. It means that we can accomplish more today because we already know what people before had to work to find out. In our own way, we ourselves are evolving."

Derek frowned, then grabbed his notebook and got up from his desk. "Can I go to the bathroom?"

Miles frowned, gazing from Derek to the rows of empty chairs in his classroom. "If you must."

He walked out from between the rows, giving the teacher a small salute before heading for the door.

"How will you ever evolve?" Miles called after him, a wry smile on his face. "If you don't know what those who came before you found out on their own?"

Derek turned, squinting at the man over his shoulder for a moment. He opened his mouth to say something, then shut it again and left.

Miles frowned, shaking his head as he turned back to the rest of the class. "Now then, can any of you think of any examples where this type of species education has been seen in human history?"

ᚠᚡᚷ

If you're innocent, you're hurt, or you're scared... I'll be there.

He brought the gun to his head and put first pressure on the trigger.

A shiver ran through him as he felt the metal against the edge of his temple, jerking away instantly and instinctively before settling back down. He closed his eyes, took a deep breath, then slowly exhaled. The sudden rush of air blew a layer of dust off the wall beside him, sending it spinning outward like a miniature tornado. He opened his eyes just in time to see the last of it swirl about, caught in the light streaming in through his bedroom window.

His fingers slipped from their grip on the gun, the skin hot and sweaty against the smooth wood grain of the gun. With an annoyed grunt, he stretched them, feeling the calcium in the joints crack before they resumed their position, index finger poised and ready to fire.

There were no tears. He thought there would have been, had been each and every time he thought about it over the past few weeks. No there was just the grim certainty that came with the realization of an awful truth. The only liquid running down his face was a small dribble of whiskey from one corner of his mouth. He picked up the bottle once more, grabbing for it twice before his fingers actually found it, and brought it to his lips one last time. The putrid brown liquid burned its way down his throat as he let the bottle fall to the floor carelessly, its remnants pushing their way out and soaking into the floor.

He laughed a little, watching as the puddle of alcohol grew slowly, expanding ever outwards until it consumed everything it could.

Like a cancer.

Like grief.

Like him.

Xander Drew lowered the gun onto his lap, leaning forward on the rough carpet.

He sat cross-legged, resting his arms against his knees as his eyes fluttered feverishly over the collage of items laid out before him.

His floor was covered in things of Sara.

A shirt she left when she slept over, just after her dad had gotten sick. Pictures of the two of them at the junior prom last spring. A pamphlet from her funeral. His comb she'd used only once and yet still carried her scent. And photos. Dozens of photos of her, clipped from yearbooks and newsletters and albums. One of them she'd taken herself, holding the camera out in front of her as far as she could. In it, her eyebrow was cocked up comically, a fraudulent scowl smeared across her face.

It looked right through him.

If you're innocent, you're hurt, or you're scared... I'll be there.

The words rang through his head again, followed immediately by the memory of all the times he'd tried to live up to that promise and failed, like cars following a train.

"It'll never stop. Never be over," he said to himself, his voice calm and steady all but for a slight waver at the end.

This is the choice you made, he reminded himself inwardly. *To take either that road... or this one.*

He stared down at the gun again.

Composing himself, he wiped the sweat from his palm onto his shirt and picked it up again. He brought it to the side of his head again with only a second's pause, bracing himself as he started to pull the trigger.

Put it down.

"Excuse me?"

"You heard me, Xander Drew, put it down," Sara Johnson said, echoing her own words. She sounded like springtime. "Are you going to? Or are you going to make me repeat myself again?"

Xander looked at her with surprise and puzzlement, not for the first (or the last) time. "And again I say, excuse me?"

"You have been at those damn Chemistry books for ten hours straight. You need to relax, and something tells me that I'm just the person to help you." Her back was arched, making her even sexier then Xander could've ever thought possible. She wore cut-off jeans with a sleeveless pink tube top, a modified fishnet stocking providing a sleeve for one arm, which held a smoldering cigarette in it. The summer sun beat against the back of her head, creating a halo effect around her blonde hair. She looked like an angel.

"I can't. I really can't. I'd love to, really... but I can't."

"Give it up," she huffed, smacking his books to the floor. "Come outside. Have fun. For me?"

He looked at her for a moment, raising one eyebrow suspiciously.

She tipped her head to one side, batting her eyelashes extravagantly. She didn't say another word.

"Let me get my coat," he sighed.

"Yay!" she chimed happily, thrusting her hands up into the air and making V's with both of her hands for 'victory'. She bounced as she walked with him into the main hallway of his house, barely able to contain her excitement. As he was putting on his sneakers, she bent over quickly, giving him a tiny kiss on the top of his head. "Love you, Xander," she chirped, then opened the door and walked to the end of the porch to finish her smoke, giving him a cute little two-fingered wave as the door closed between them.

He watched the spot where she had been in bewilderment, smiling as he finished lacing up. Even though he knew she was just being playful, something in her eyes had been serious. Had made it seem like even though it was a joke, it was still true. "I love you too," he replied with a happy sigh, as he opened his front door and followed her.

"I love you, too," Xander said aloud.

The gun fell to the floor with a dull thud.

He clenched his fists until the knuckles turned white, the skin stretching so tightly over the bone that it became transparent. Grunting angrily, he squeezed even harder, falling to his knees amongst the small shrine he'd built for her on his floor. The skin split, causing blood to flow down his arms and fingers, tracing the familiar contours of his flesh.

After a moment, it began to flow a deep black.

"No," he pled with himself, bending over and rocking back and forth until the growling, pounding feeling in his right side faded away. It didn't leave completely though. It never did. Never.

When he opened his eyes again, he was staring directly into the picture of Sara, only inches in front of his face. He made a sound that was so wrought with grief that it didn't even sound human.

The tears came now, making his eyelids bulge and his cheeks get hot. He slammed his fist against the floor three times, each one harder than the one before.

"Fuck!" he screamed, getting to his feet and grabbing the chair that sat next to his computer and hurling it at the wall with all his strength. It shattered into splinters, one leg driving into the cheap plaster and remaining there like a bony finger pointing at him accusingly. The splinters flipped and tumbled everywhere, bouncing off his chest and getting caught in his hair, the tiny sound each one of them made becoming an earsplitting chaotic cacophony of white noise when heard together. His face red with tears and rage, he picked up his whiskey bottle by its stubby glass neck and threw it blindly. It crashed into a clear lamp filled with seashells, both shattering upon contact with each other and adding a rain of tinkling, sharp shards of glass to the wood that peppered the floor. Both halves of the lamp fell in separate arcs, banging against the wall on their way down. The bulb shattered, its filament shining brightly before going out completely, like a star going dead. It sent sparks splashing upwards, making small semicircles as they spun away from their source, losing heat with each passing instant. He did not notice, turning and driving his fist into his computer screen, the glass slicing into his flesh as blue sparks singed his fingertips, each one creating shadows that cast over his face and made him look even more menacingly demonic than he already did.

"Ag," he grunted, retracting his hand quickly and watching as the blood dribbled down the back of it, forming a small pool at the tips of his fingers before falling away. Sneering down at it, his pupils tiny and focused, he spun around and planted the heel of his boot into his television. Once again, hot sparks cascaded out of the fragmented box, tumbling downward like rainwater, the embers they created dancing about wildly. The sparks shimmered down toward the broken whiskey bottle. There was a sound like the rush of air as the rank brown liquid ignited, becoming flame almost immediately. The fire swept over the floor, traveling along the drops made by the alcohol until it was everywhere. It reached the pictures and papers in the center of the room, their edges beginning to curl as they were lit aflame and consumed.

Xander's eyes went wide, reflecting the fire as it sprang up all around him, its red and blue and yellow fingers reaching out to enclose around him like a fist.

He grabbed a small black throw pillow off of his bed and started slamming it down against the flames, each beat stomping out a small section as the impact snuffed the air out of the area and smothered it. Smoke billowed toward the ceiling as he wailed harder, his mouth contorted, blending desperation and anger as the last of the fire went out with feathers and smoke still hanging in the air but slowly settling to normal.

He started to sob the way a child sobs as he looked down upon the destroyed items, charred and blackened beyond recognition. He gripped both edges of the pillow and was about to pull it apart, then buried his face into it instead. His tears soaked into the smooth fabric as it rubbed soot off onto his cheeks. His whole body shook and convulsed, urging several times from the pit of his stomach as though he were about to vomit, but instead just bringing more tears and a fresh bout of sobs. He stayed that way for thirty minutes, until all the smoke had cleared out of the room and the smell of alcohol had started to fade.

When he looked up and opened his eyes, he saw the one thing that had escaped the fire intact: a picture of her, all dressed up to go to the prom that he had clipped from an old yearbook.

When are you going to stop?

Xander lay on the ground, broken and beaten by Sara's current boyfriend, Julian Grendel. Blood seeped from his upper lip, making the bottom of his face warm and wet.

"When are you going to stop doing this?" she had asked him, using his shirt to wipe a bit of the blood away.

He looked up at her and smiled, the motion stinging the tender flesh around his mouth. "I guess when I start winning fights."

"Not that," she giggled, wiping more blood from his forehead. "This. Chasing after every boy I go out with like some ... jealous father."

"Oh," Xander said, looking downward. "I guess when you start going out with reasonable guys."

"What do you mean?"

"Gee, I wonder. Grendel, Derek, Sud, Tommy, Randy, Travis, Cecil... the list goes

on. Cathy always says that you go through them like popcorn at a chick-flick. Serial boy-friends, I think she called them. Guys that are... Okay, but they don't deserve you. You deserve someone special. Someone who'll treat you right and make you feel good and... and not look at you like you're an object. You're better then you think you are, y' know. You deserve better than you think you do."

She leaned in and kissed him on the cheek. "That was the nicest thing anyone ever said to me." She smiled. "Make me a promise."

"Anything."

"Don't ever give up."

"Huh?"

"Don't ever stop protecting me. And when I finally do find that guy you were talk-ing about, protect someone else. This world needs a protector, Xander."

"I promise."

"Don't ever give up."

"I won't," he said, emptying the bullets from the gun onto the floor with a series of metallic clinks. Tears streamed down his face as his eyes turned black, his heart pounding in his chest as he felt his blood pressure climb to levels nor-mally fatal. This time he made no effort to halt it.

The skin on his wrists began to swell as the pressure built there, growing more and more with each passing second.

Through his open mouth, his teeth could plainly be seen grinding together as he tried not to scream, every cell in his body trying to fight for its life, fail-ing, and then being re-written. His gums started to bleed as new teeth were cut again, the old ones cutting long rivets in the roof of his mouth as they were forced aside. After a moment only the new were visible, over two inches long each and the yellow of putrid urine.

His jaw popped out on one side all on its own, hanging on a few inches be-low where it had been by a tedious strand of flesh and tenue. After a moment, it healed itself, the muscle weaving its way down to meet in as the other side of his face fractured itself as well, making room for the massive set of jowls he would soon possess.

There was a pounding in his skull as it became thicker and broader across the forehead, reshaping his face until his dark eyes seemed to be travelling back, becoming something beady and unseen beneath his scowl.

The veins in his hands finally burst, opening up his wrists so fiercely that the holes it left looked as though they had been made with shotguns shells. The blackness clung to him as it spewed forth from the open wounds, powered by each and every beat of his powerful heart. It took on a life of its own, crawling over him like a million black worms. It had already encompassed both his arms and most of his chest when he felt his kneecaps shatter, his legs painfully bend-ing back in the opposite direction.

The blood kept flowing, sticking to him until it became a second flesh. He felt like he was sinking into it, *drowning* in it, rather than it coming over him.

Long nails formed over his toes as it finished covering his body, the worms moving upwards towards his head in an open defiance of gravity. His lips started to turn blue as he held his breath, thrusting his head skyward to belay the darkness as long as possible. He closed his eyes and spoke with a voice not his own, just as the blackness finally closed in around him.

"I won't."

Mike stroked his thumb back and forth along his upper lip, staring off into space from his perch atop a high barstool. His legs were tucked up beneath him and his back was as straight as he could make it, making him feel high above the floor below him. The teetering of the uneven chair even made him feel a little dizzy as he swayed back and forth.

All around him arcade games and pinball machines buzzed and chimed, calling out in a jumble of bells and sirens. Some had spinning lights on the top of them that flashed whenever the computer-controlled characters on the screens scored a point, dominating his vision in sporadic beams of red and blue. They made it hard to see the vintage posters of Zeppelin and Petty that lined the walls, but he still knew what they looked like. Could have seen them with his eyes closed if he had wanted to.

Just a few inches to his right, Cathy was leaning over the bar and taking a long sip of her drink. She twirled her hair around her finger as she always did, humming a tune he couldn't quite recognize between gulps.

As cute and endearing as he found it, he tuned it out. He closed his eyes for a moment, mentally willing himself not to hear any of the things he didn't want to. He got rid of Cathy's sweet humming first. Then the clink of a soda machine in the kitchen. Then the bass beat of a car passing by. What was left was the chime of the video games combined with the sharp crack of pool balls hitting each other and the buzz of the fluorescent lights above it all. He opened his eyes to see the Stones poster bathed in blue light, the putrid smell of cigarette smoke filling his nostrils until he thought he was actually at a concert.

He smiled.

This was The Factory.

It was a local arcade club where almost every teenager in Coral Beach could be found at some point or another in the day. Located in the scenic downtown of Coral Beach, the Factory jutted up out of the otherwise calm rural Maine landscape, always loud and exciting and neon. This had been where Mike had learned everything he really knew in his life. His first real fight was just outside the back entrance (followed almost immediately by his first nosebleed). His first date had started here, with some pool before a long midsummer walk. This was the place where he had uttered his first curse in anger and heard his first dirty joke. This was home.

It hadn't felt like it in weeks, not since the murders. There was something about being here that reminded him of that period in his life a little too much. Even though the building itself had nothing to do with it, this whole street was as much a part of the horrors that had happened, as they were a part of this town. More like a vein running through a living organism than a street running through a city. Like any living thing, it could be damaged. It could be hurt. But if he tried hard enough, like now... he could look past the scars and be home again.

"Mike, I'm worried about Xander," Cathy said, taking a long sip of her slush-puppy and snapping him out of his trance. She pushed a strand of her long black hair out of her face, its darkness a complete contrast to her pale complexion, then slid her straw in and out of her paper cup to mush up her slush.

Mike sighed as all the sights and sounds that he'd fought so hard to block out came screaming back to him with all the subtlety of an oncoming train. He winced as he heard Jennifer Bradley rip into the green fabric of the pool table, feeling his chest grow tight as though he had felt it too. "Yeah," he agreed, ruffling a hand through his short blonde hair. He shifted into a more comfortable position on the stool, letting his legs dangle a little more than they had been. He felt the skin along his right side pull tight when he moved, sending a burning pain up his side and into his rib cage. A few weeks ago he'd been stabbed there. By Xander. His appendix had ruptured and had shot poison and bile throughout his system, until the doctors had removed it. It was mostly healed, but when he turned it a certain way, it still hurt. Still felt like it was going to rip. Maybe that was why he reacted so intensely when the table ripped. He did know exactly how it felt. "I know. I thought things would get better after a while, but he's just been keeping himself up in his room all the time. It's like he doesn't even want to see the light of day."

"I guess we can't really blame him," she reasoned, allowing her head to tilt to one side. She always did that, as if her neck were somehow attached to the scales within her mind weighing the outcomes of every situation. "Even we've been acting a little odd, trying to adjust to life without her." Her hair fell back in front of her face again.

This time, he pushed it back for her. As he did, his finger caressed her round, pale face, making her quiver. He looked down into her eyes, his height and her lack thereof making him almost have to bend down to do so. "It'll be okay. It's over now. Things can only get better."

"Yeah, right," she said bitterly as she rolled her eyes, turning away from his touch. "Things can only get better. It's always darkest before the dawn. The glass is half full. That and countless other clichés that I've heard a billion times a day for the last month." She huffed, plopping her slush down beside her, sending pink liquid sloshing over the sides. "I am just so sick of everyone telling me that things can only get better. Things aren't really that great and they're not getting any better, in case you haven't noticed."

Mike cast his eyes downward. "I'm sorry."

She said nothing, barely even making eye contact with him as she stared blankly at a Beatles poster that always managed to catch her eye.

"I know things are bad. Xander's trying his best to get control of this thing and I don't know if he can or not. I don't know what it means if he can't. What we're supposed to do. But you know all that. I shouldn't sugar coat it for you. It's patronizing and I'm sorry." He paused, running his tongue over the front of

232

his gums. "I just don't like to see you hurting."

She felt a grin twitch at both sides of her mouth even though she didn't want it to, then turned back to face him with a full-fledged smile. She tilted her head up and gave him a kiss, light with levity, on the lips. "I'm sorry too. I know you're trying to help; it's just that, when everybody tries to help, it only reminds me that I need the help, which makes things worse." She sighed, taking a moment to go over what she had just said, her lips moving a little as she did. "Did that make any sense?"

"Not really, but I think I got the gist." Mike smiled, leaning his forehead against hers so that their noses touched. "But - -"

His sentence cut short as the front door opened with a bang, letting a fresh gust of fall air in for the space heaters to combat.

"How's it going, guys?" Derek Smith said cheerfully as he walked in, making his presence known to the room as usual. His spirit was amazing. He had lost nearly everyone he was close to in the 'party massacre', yet he'd kept his morale high. He was a person all the other kids looked up to now, wishing that they could have even a percentage of his strength. His beady eyes, which were almost always holed up into a squint, had an exuberance to them that was only added by a childish grin and long, sloppy brown hair. There was an excitement and an energy to his every word and action, like a kid on Christmas morning. He scanned the room quickly, nodding politely to Jennifer and Randy before laying eyes on Mike. He snapped his fingers instantly, pointing at him from across the room. "Dude, just snuck out of Miles' class and need to get it off me. Wanna have a game of Granite Gladiators?"

Mike chuckled to himself. He had been wrong before. This was The Factory. No matter what was going on outside these walls or in your own life, it all stayed outside. It was like a bomb-shelter for stress more than a club. He turned his head towards Cathy, his eyes as big as he could make them.

She laughed at him. "Begone," she said dramatically, tapping him twice on the chest and then waving him away. "Just don't beat him too bad, sweetheart."

"Okay, man. How'd you wanna play?" he smiled, getting up and walking over to the game.

"Tag team, not as enemies," Derek announced, wrapping his index and middle finger around one another in a gesture Mike could only assume reflected their partnership.

"Cool," Mike nodded, fishing a quarter out from deep inside of his pocket and inserting it into the game. The CHOOSE CHARACTER screen came up onto the display, filled with colourful, mean looking animations. "I pick Stonehenge."

"Don't you find him hard to use? His moves are so slow."

"Not once you get used to it. What was so bad about class?"

"I'll pick... Chip. Nothin' really, just bullshit. Talking about how animals don't change what they do, humans do. How you can make it change, blah blah blah."

"You keep notes?"

"Yeah, I'll get 'em to ya."

The battle screen appeared, basking both of their faces in a multicoloured glow.

From her chair over at the bar, Cathy picked up her slush-puppy again, sulking briefly over the bit that she had spilt. As she watched, a smile spread over Mike's face. It was the first real smile she'd seen on him in almost a month. He was even showing teeth.

She grinned to herself as she watched, then gazed past her straw and into her cup, deciding it might be half-full after all.

CHAPTER TWO: REFLECTION

"Ugh," Mike grunted, the tip of his tongue sticking out the side of his mouth as his hands bobbed and spun on the red control stick. His character hit the large stone hand on the screen one last time, sending it slowly crumbling into pebbles, until there was nothing left but a gem in its center. Mike smiled to himself as he finally let go of the joystick, feeling the tendons in his hand cramp as he did.

"Man, that was cool!" Derek laughed hysterically, giving his friend a congratulatory slap on the back. "I've never beaten the whole game before. What happens now?"

"Well, since I won, now I have to fight your character. So, Chip. Hey, you've never beaten the game before?" Mike said, astonished.

Derek shot him a look, grinning. "Sorry to disappoint. Guess I just don't have as much free time on my hands as you do."

"Heh. Yeah, sorry. Once you've moved on to Metal Minions over there, it's hard to believe you ever had trouble with this one," he thought, nodding his head toward another game in the corner of the room. "If it makes you feel any better, you're way better at all this than Xander is. When I tag with him, I usually can't get past the forth stage." Mike tensed his hand again as the loading screen started to fade away. Even though he couldn't say it out loud to Derek, he couldn't help but think how ironic it was that he could beat Xander at any game. He felt a pang deep inside his gut as that thought crossed his mind. He tried to shove the thought away, but it lingered. *I am happy with my life,* he reminded himself. *With Cathy. Happier than I ever thought I was capable of being.*

Sometimes he thought he'd never truly be happy again. In the past few weeks, he had seen things that could not be unseen and done things he would regret to his dying days. Some days he thought he would never have peace.

On days like that, it was usually Cathy who brought him back up for air.

The way she thought and the things she did drove him wild. His skin tingled at her touch and always gave him a drunken, half-hungry feeling deep in the pit of his stomach. When he held her, he felt like he never had before she entered his life. Like a man. He was truly, deeply, madly in love.

234

"Are you done *yet?*" Cathy whined. She didn't usually use that tone with her boyfriend, but he'd been playing that game for the better part of an hour. "I'm really bored." Her tone of voice was a playful one. She outstretched her arms to him like a little girl, pouting her lower lip. It was irresistibly cute.

Mike let go of the joystick. "You've never finished the game, Derek?"

Derek nodded.

"Here's yer chance," he said, walking over to Cathy. Grinning mischievously, he started to tickle her and then lifted her up into his arms as she squealed in defiance. "I, on the other hand, have a prior engagement."

"Wow," Cathy said, kissing his lips lightly. "You actually said the 'E' word without breaking out into hives. I'm impressed."

He laughed, kissing her. After a moment, his neck began to itch and he resisted the urge to scratch it.

"Waddaya sayin', boys and girls?" came a new voice from the doorway, followed quickly by a second.

"Girls. Huh."

Mike broke off the kiss and stood up straight, his body automatically becoming hard and ridged. All of the hairs on the back of his neck stood on end and he found his arms covered in gooseflesh. Adrenaline started leaking into his system and he found himself ready to get into something fierce right then and there.

Cathy yanked on his jacket to bring him back down next to her. She held him close. "Don't do it, Mike," she said sternly.

"Guess it's obvious who wears the pants in this relationship, huh Mike?" Tommy Irons said, smiling slyly as Sud came in behind, the front door to the Factory closing behind them. He was a tall boy, easily a few inches higher than Mike (and seemed even taller with his hair spiked up as it was), but he was lanky and frail, his arms and legs flopped around him like a rag doll's. This was emphasized by the baggy clothes he always seemed to wear, including the denim shirt that was always on him and open, with a ripped 'Hello Nasty' T-shirt underneath. He smirked devilishly as he watched discomfort sweep over Mike's face, thoroughly enjoying every moment of it.

"Yeah, pants," Sud chuckled in his usual incoherent manner. Sud was shorter, about Cathy's height. His head was shaved clean, except for some excessive stubble around the hard-to-reach areas like the ears. His brow was slanted and thick, making him look like a Neanderthal hunched over the way he was now, his sweater making him look furry and his large knuckles hanging down past his knees. He spoke rarely, but when he did, his deep voice and short sentences made him sound like a grunting ape. Alone, the appearance of either was a source of much amusement. Together, they were downright comical. It was as if they'd stepped straight from a Saturday morning cartoon show.

Mike clenched his jaw. The both of them had gotten off scot free for their part helping Grendel do those things to Cathy during the maelstrom that had claimed so many lives. In Mike's eyes, Tommy and Sud were worse than Genblade himself, the beast who had brought the Womb out in Xander, and given the monster its first taste of blood. They had helped an evil man rape a beautiful young girl, then they had the gall to still attempt to hang around with them. As if nothing had happened.

"Come on, Cathy," Mike said, pulling the woman he loved to her feet by the hands. "Let's get out of here."

"Sure, lover," she said softly, trying to sound as happy as she could to help keep him calm.

They both moved to grab their coats. Tommy stopped Mike halfway to the door, pushing his hand against Mike's chest. "Why ya goin' so fast, brud? Something I said?"

Mike clenched his fists, ready to strike. Cathy took his hands and the fists uncoiled, entwining in hers reflexively. He loosened up and merely brushed past Tommy and Sud.

"I'll get our coats," Cathy said, walking into the coat checkroom. "You boys play nicely."

She was gone. For the first time in weeks, Mike and Tommy's eyes met. They both squinted, cracking their knuckles.

"So," Tommy said, finally breaking the tension of the silence with his shrill, annoying voice. "Do you always do what your bitch tells ya to?"

Mike drew back his fist to hit Tommy.

Tommy winced, closing his eyes tight and snapping his hands up to cover his face. After a moment with no impact, he opened them again.

Mike had lowered his hand and now stared at Tommy, forcing himself not to smirk. He stepped up closer to Tommy until they were nose to nose. "Listen to me, you little freak. One of these days, Cathy's not going to be around to stop me, okay? And when that day comes, we are going to have a go. You think what that Adam Genblade guy did to Grendel was bad? You ain't seen the half of it. Then, when you're all nice and dead, I'll find a plot of ground for you right next to Grendel. And I'll have one steaming hot piss on you both," he spat, his teeth grinding more and more with each word. "Do we understand each other, you motherfucker?"

"Got 'em!" Cathy said, tossing Mike his coat, who caught it without even looking in her direction, never breaking eye contact with Tommy. "What's going on?" she added.

Tommy shuffled his feet uncomfortably. Sud did the same, but Mike wasn't sure if he was actually uncomfortable, or if he was just mimicking Tommy's movements again.

"Nothing," Mike said calmly, finally turning away from the boy. He put on his coat and opened the door for Cathy. When she left, he glanced at Tommy before leaving himself. "Another time."

When Mike and Cathy left, Tommy punched the table with surprising strength, sending splinters everywhere and startling everyone else in the club.

He sat cross-legged on the cold concrete floor, his expression stern and unmoving as he stared down at the floor in front of him, the muscles in his arms twitching violently of their own accord. He'd been naked for roughly an hour, and now sweat glistened off of every inch of his flesh, seeping its putrid stench from every pore.

His palms lay flat against the floor in front of him, its rough texture digging into the tender skin and making it itch. His fingers wriggled at the ends of each hand, forcing the blood to flow through them as he felt the tingle of numbness at their tips. He let out a long sigh through both nostrils, keeping his lips sealed tight as he surveyed what he had done.

On the floor between his two hands was a sketch drawn out in the dirt and dust that lined the bottom of his cell. The lines were jagged and wavy, each one punctuated with grease stained fingerprints dotting along their sides, and yet were clear all the same.

They were men.

Small, simplistic stick men made up of a circle for the head and single line each for the torso and arms. All lined up in a row, one following the other until there were ten all together looking back at him with glazed faces. He reached out with one long nail and scratched over the head of the sixth one in line, making it a little more round before pulling back and clasping his chin in his hand.

He let out a long huff, staring down each of the men he'd created one at a time. His pupils moved from one to the next in short bursts so synchronized that they might have been timed rather than spontaneous.

Bringing a finger to his lips, he squeezed his long, yellowed nails between his sharpened teeth until he heard it crack. When he took it out, the nail had split and was now seeping redness out from between the cartilage. He swished the remainder of the nail around in his mouth for a moment before turning his head to one side and spitting it out, bouncing it off the far wall and onto the floor. Reaching his hand out over the first figure, he squeezed the wound between his thumb and middle finger until two small drops of crimson came out, landing in the middle of the circle. Now it had eyes. Two gaping, red eyes that burned back at him in hate.

Smiling, he sucked the excess blood from the tip of his finger. He turned his attention to the third man from the back then, drawing a small loop on it that remained open at both ends, like a ribbon or an infinity symbol left incomplete. He then drew a quick line through the centre. He smiled a little, then drew a large circle around the next figure to the left.

His grin faded away as he turned his attention back to the second man in line. He ran his hand over his chest and forehead, wiping off the copious amounts of sweat that had accumulated since he'd started his project. He squeezed his fist together over the drawing, dripping the rank-smelling liquid onto the second man. He squinted at it for a moment, then nodded.

Turning his gaze to the third man in line, he let his grin grow so large that it showed off all his sharp, filed teeth. He reached down and clutched his penis from where it had been resting quietly in its tuft of pubic hair, wrapping his fingers around it tightly. He squeezed, pulling upwards a little until the tiniest droplet of moisture secreted from its tip. He wiped it off with his thumb, immediately transferred the liquid to its rightful place smeared against the torso of the third man in line.

Finally, he turned to the forth. His smile waned for a moment before vanishing completely, staring down at the crude sketch on the floor. His arms had been made too long, and he almost appeared to be holding hands with the previous figure. He sighed, leaning forward onto his palms again until he was almost exactly the same position he'd been in when he started, staring down at his work. He swished saliva back and forth through his mouth as he thought, then raised his eyes to the small window near the ceiling of his cell. The air outside was thick with fog, some of it swirling in and dancing with him before turning into nothing in the air-conditioned room.

"Not over." He smiled, letting himself lean back as the sweat rolled off of him into a puddle on the floor.

⋏⋎

"Mike, honey, are you okay?" Cathy asked her boyfriend, using her 'prying' voice. He had described it once as combining a pouting lip, soulful eyes, a sad voice and the slightest tip of her head, adding all these ingredients to a jar, and mixing well.

He stared blankly for a moment, his eyes solemnly focused on the road ahead. He began to pick up speed slightly, forcing Cathy to speed up as well to keep up with him.

"Mike, talk to me," she said, tripping over a rock and skipping for two steps to keep from falling onto the cold hard pavement. "Please."

He turned around and looked at her for a moment. There was anger in his eyes at first, but it quickly twisted to frustration under her influence, then finally to calmness. Her face always did that to him. No matter how angry he was, the second he looked at her eyes, her hair, her lips... it was like his heart melted inside his chest. "There's nothing to talk about."

"Bull. You've been acting like this for weeks, Mike. You're angry like I've never seen you angry before." The grimness of the situation rang true in her beautiful voice. Her eyes stared deep into his, cutting through the barriers he had erected and into his very soul. "This isn't like you."

He broke, but that didn't mean that he wasn't mad. "Why do you do it?" he asked with a raised voice. He cleared his throat, then started again with a calmer tone. "Why do you do it?"

Cathy's eyes opened wide. Her eyes went from one corner of her eye to the next, as if she was searching for an answer. "Do what?"

"'Do what?' What do you think? Why do you defend those two creeps, Tommy and Sud? Do you realize what they did? What they helped Grendel do to you?"

Cathy started to tear up almost instantly. Ever since it had happened, she spent nearly every waking moment trying *not* to think about what had been done to her. Whenever someone else brought it up, she had no defense against the memories that came flooding back. It was like the pinprick that broke the

238

dam. Every dream she had since that night was a nightmare reliving what Grendel had done to her.

"It wasn't like it was some random thing. The guys say that the three of them had been planning it. They convinced everyone at the party that Xander was the killer so they'd take care of him. Tommy and Sud *attacked* me, damn near fractured my fucking skull when I saw what was happening inside and then Grendel... he... well, I think you know what he did, even if you won't say it."

Her make-up was running down her cheeks and onto her blouse now. Her eyes were red and puffy.

Mike sighed. "I can understand that it might be hard for you to talk about what happened, but that doesn't mean that you should just... forget about it. Y'know? You shouldn't let them get away with the shit they pull all the time, the things they call you. You're better than they are. You shouldn't have to take it."

"Well, what exactly do you think I *should* do?" she stammered, wiping her eyes.

"You shouldn't have to do anything," he said, squinting and shaking his head as though that were obvious. "Don't you get that? You shouldn't have to lift a finger against creeps like them. Nobody should. All I'm asking is that you let *me* handle it when- -"

He stopped in mid sentence when she slapped him across the arm, her face curled into bitter contempt for a moment. "I do not need you to save me, Mike, so you can give up the damn hero act because I'm getting sick of it. *Sick*. Everyone's lining up to choose everything for me. Tommy and Sud think I'm a slut, you and Xander think I'm a saint... and the only thing all four of you have in common is that not one of you asks me what I think I am."

He let out a puff of air, turning away from her angrily. His lower lip curled up as her words swarmed around in his mind, forcing him to look at his encounter with Tommy a different way even though he didn't want to. Like a gear being forced to turn in the wrong direction, his train of thought came to a screeching halt, then slowly started to chug along its new path.

Slowly, her face lost its intensity as she watched him be at war with himself, knowing how much her words must have been cutting into him. She reached out and laid her hand in the crook of his arm, smiling gently.

He turned back, gentler now for having been touched by her. "I just wanna make sure that they know what they do --" He paused again, making sure to get the words just right. "...that they know what they do is not gonna fly anytime soon. I love you, Cat. I can't stand the thought of them thinking they're righteous for the way they act."

She pulled him into a hug, squeezing him tight, then lifted her head off his shoulder with a massive smile on her face as she looked him in the eye. "And I love you, Mike."

He leaned down and kissed her, all thought lost as his heart started to race faster and faster with each movement of her silky lips.

She pulled back a little, ending the kiss with her lips still only millimeters from his. "But if you ever raise your voice to me like that again, I'll punch you right in the throat."

"Yes, dear," he said, smirking.

She leaned back into the kiss.

There was a moment at the beginning of every kiss where the act didn't feel quite right to her. He'd move one way when she moved the other, their lips bending into odd directions and their teeth sometimes clacking together. Yet somehow, a few moments in, they each seemed to succumb to the other's will and move as one, the warm moisture of their lips bringing heat to the rest of their bodies.

Mike opened his eyes.

"What?" Cathy asked as she pulled on his arm, only to be met with restraint. The cool night air whipped about the fog created by the bay around them. "Come on. If we're late, my parents will kill me."

"Bad choice of words," he said, his voice low and almost angry. But not at her. "Look at where we are."

She turned her head from side to side. She was confused at first, seeing only alleys and corners. Then it hit her like a punch in the gut. Her eyes widened. "This is where we were attacked."

"Yeah," Mike muttered, pacing slightly, spitting onto the curb in disgust.

They'd always chosen another route to get to Cathy's, just to avoid this spot. The spot where they lost the carefree nature of childhood and gained the hardness of reality. The death of their innocence and very nearly their lives as well.

"You feel that?" Mike said.

"What?" she asked, her eyes bulging as she leaned in close to him. After a moment, she forced a laugh, giving him a little slap on the arm. "Do *not* do that, Mike! You know how much this spot creeps me out... even in the daytime."

"No, really. This is exactly the type of night it was when it happened. And..."

"What?" Cathy exclaimed, clutching his arm tightly, "What is it?"

"Déjà Vu."

"That's not something that I wanna hear right now."

Mike paused for a second and looked around. All the hairs on his body were on end. "Let's get out of here."

"Yeah," she agreed.

They began walking, not overly fast at first, then began to pick up speed after a few seconds. They crossed the street in a hurry even though it was devoid of traffic, Mike dragging her by the hand. This had been the spot where they'd kissed. It had seemed like the perfect end to the perfect night. But the night had been far from over, and its true end would be far from perfect. Mike and Cathy kept walking, the street lamplight illuminating their jackets. Cathy began to walk a little faster, as did Mike, dragging each other along. They were at the spot now, where they'd first heard it, that ear-shattering sound of metal on metal.

Mike stopped moving.

"What is it?" Cathy asked, putting her hand on her boyfriend's shoulder. "What's wrong now?"

Mike was silent for a moment, as if waiting for something. "There!" he finally exclaimed. "Did you hear that?"

Cathy's eyes suddenly went wide. "That's not funny, Mike," she said quickly. But as she leaned in close to him and held his hand, she could feel the clammy sweat pouring off him. Nervous sweat.

"Just listen," he told her, holding her close to his chest.

They both perked their ears. The streets were silent tonight. The slightest footfall could have been heard for miles. At this moment, Cathy and Mike strained their ears to hear even the slightest sound to indicate that they were wrong. That Mike had been mistaken. A rat or a pair of teenagers, even a police car would be welcomed. He didn't want to be right, possibly for the first time in his life.

Then, from out of the darkness, it finally came:

- click -

The sound of metal striking briefly against metal. It echoed off of the brick street corners, making it impossible to tell exactly where it was coming from. It came once again,

-click-

Without so much as taking the time to look at one another, Mike and Cathy burst into a run, trotting past street lamps and garbage cans. They couldn't tell which direction the sound was coming from and they realized that the sound could have been coming from any direction. For all they knew, they could've been running straight into their follower's arms. They didn't really care. They just had to run. Because if they were dealing with what they both secretly thought they were dealing with, then they'd have no chance either way.

The Black Womb.

Mike turned around to see if it was following them. He couldn't see anything, but he knew that didn't mean nothing was there. Not if it was Xander.

-click-

It was closer now. Louder, too. Mike wondered if indeed they were running into a waiting trap set by their opponent. Then he banished the thought from his mind. If it was Xander, under the influence of the Black Womb, then the creature would know their next moves like the back of its hand. Nobody knew them better than Xander. Nobody.

Mike stopped running again.

"Mike, are you alright?" Cathy asked, remembering the horrors of the last time this had happened.

"The last time we crossed this corner, he almost killed me," he replied grimly.

They both stared silently at it. It was only stone and mortar, but it held so many beastly memories for the both of them. All at once, Mike could feel it again. That sharp pain as something long and jagged punctured his skin and ripped through his body. He could feel the redness trickling down his side and into a little pool on the bench next to Cathy's house. He could see the blood and saliva being hurled from his mouth, staining the cold stone sidewalks. All at once, he was there again. He was dying again.

-click-

This time, the sound felt like it had been coming from both the front and the behind, and he shivered in raw, primal fear. This night, these circumstances, they were all too familiar; too familiar to be a coincidence. Someone had planned this. Planned it perfectly.

-click-

The sound was right next to them, but it still came from all directions. The two lovers stood perfectly still for a moment. She looked at him, her eyes blurred by tears of fear. She tried to say the word 'go' to him, but her throat was too parched and it ended up just being the silent moving of her lips. Still, he got the message. He grabbed her arm and they ran around the corner.

There was nothing there and Cathy's home was now in sight.

They ran before their brains could even process what had happened, their legs moving of their own fruition rather than by choice. The arches of their feet ached with every step they made, the calloused flesh turning a light red from the pressure. Cathy felt the back of her heel rub raw against her shoe, tiny trickles of blood seeping out into her sock.

She tripped a hundred feet into the sprint to her house, falling to her knees. They both bounced off the pavement in awkward, misshapen half-circles, her flesh tearing away as though it were silk to let the crimson cascade into her jeans. She felt her kneecap bend out of place and then snap itself back in. She opened her mouth to curse, but her jaw slammed against the ground before she could, twisting sharply to the right without the rest of her head following. A tooth in the back of her mouth came loose and flushed down her throat when she gasped for air, ripping and tearing at her esophagus as blood washed it down. "Fuck," she swore finally, spitting blood onto the curb.

Mike grabbed her by both shoulders and pulled her to her feet, her legs already moving to run before her soles were even touching the ground. When he thought she was balanced enough, he let her go, turning briefly to glance at the windows they were passing. There were no lights on, not even the faint blue flicker of televisions glowing. It was like Coral Beach had turned into a ghost town in an Old West movie, the streets deserted and awaiting a visceral showdown. When he turned around, he thought he saw something behind him duck behind a light pole, its lanky frame completely obscured by the wooden shaft. Still, he knew what it was. Could almost see the opaque aquamarine eyes as they glared at him with their pupil-less stare. The sharp row of yellowed, germ-ridden teeth that came down over the normal ones, rendering them obsolete. The claws that danced about gracefully on the air around the creature until it chose to use them in movements so quick you wouldn't even know that they had occurred until you felt your own intestines splatter against your feet. He could *see* the Black Womb, even if he couldn't. In fact the invisibility of whatever was behind them only added to his certainty of what was coming.

Cathy turned in front of him, making him spin his head back around to the front and pulled him onto the concrete stairs of her house.

242

He slipped once on the smooth cement, then steadied himself against the black metal guardrail as they both caught their breath. "Made it," he said between gasps, almost laughing a little as he kept an eye trained over one shoulder.

Cathy did not respond, but he heard a soft plop from in front of him as a small drop of salt water fell from her round chin onto her porch step.

Mike turned, finally pulling his vision away from the street as he felt his heart skip several beats, the color draining quickly from his face.

The lock on the door had been kicked in, with enough ferocity to splinter the frame.

They both stood staring for a moment, feeling their salvation slip away.

-click-

The door creaked in the wind, but did not open.

"Come on Cathy," Mike whispered. "Let's get to a neighbour's house and call the cops."

Cathy's eyes darted from the door to Mike. "But Mike," she stammered, "What about my parents?"

Mike froze in his tracks. The Kennessy's had always been good to him. They'd supported him and Cathy's relationship from the very beginning, even when his own parents did not. Her father had been the one to help him the night that Xander had first attacked him and Cathy. He couldn't just leave them to the Black Womb. As he considered the force that must have gone into kicking a hole into the Kennessy's *metal* door, Mike didn't figure it could be anybody else. "Go to your neighbour's, Cathy."

"What? We can't just leave..." she started.

Mike cut her off, touching the side of her face. "*We* aren't. Just you."

"I can't leave you again," she whispered, pulling him close. "The last time... I won't leave you."

Turning his back on the door for only a fraction of a second, he pulled her head into his by the small of her neck, kissing her quickly, but passionately. "You never do," he assured her. He'd always wanted to play hero, ever since he was little and saw the first episodes of Saturday morning cartoons, or heard those weird news stories from Atlanta. But when it was her, no matter how hard he tried, he couldn't be the hero. Couldn't think of the world or the town or even himself. It was just fear, the fear of losing her that drove every choice he made. "Go."

Forcing herself to listen, she turned and ran.

He watched her go, making sure she actually got into the house safely, his backside still facing her front door until her neighbours' closed shut behind her.

Then he turned to the real problem. A million and one scenarios bounced around in his mind. Even though not one of them ended with them living, he had to try.

He stepped back a bit, then rammed the door. It had already been partially off of its hinges and now ripped off of them, slammed to the hardwood floor with a loud thud. There was no need for stealth. He knew that whatever waited in there was expecting him. He reached to his left without taking his eyes off of the gaping darkness that now surrounded him, jiggling the light switch. No effect. If Black Womb was hidden here, he had made sure that he would stay hidden.

Mike stepped into the darkness surrounding him until it was all he could see. In the absence of shapes, his mind created its own images that danced about and lunged at him haphazardly. One looked so real that he almost jumped back a pace when it came at him. Shaking with fear, he bit his lip and closed his eyes as tight as he could, until small dots began spotting along his eyelids. When he opened them again, they had adjusted to the low-light and he could see. He almost wished he couldn't.

He could see a blue-ish outline of many objects now. There was a chair a few metres in front of him that he moved to avoid, along with a Math textbook. Cathy's computer and desk were there, off from the living room. The moonlight shone through a nearby window, bouncing off the desk and into his eyes.

The desk's surface glimmered with a thick dark gel turned light purple in the blue glow of the moon. It dribbled down the sides of the desk in long, slow paths, turning this way and that every time it became obstructed by a nook or hole. The more he looked at it, the less it looked like blood. It looked like melted plastic, poured perfectly over the surface of the desk without any bumps or bubbles, just smooth and perfect. But the smell was unmistakable, that coppery vomit stench mixed in with putrid B.O. It was blood, enough to have almost covered the desk completely.

He gazed around the room once more. The lamp in the corner seemed to move suspiciously, rocking back and forth on its base. He'd noticed it once or twice before, even discussing it with Cathy's father more than once, an optical illusion created by the feng shui of the room. Now, no matter how many times he told himself that it always seemed to be moving, he couldn't take his eyes off of it. There was a long couch between him and the lamp where anything could be lurking, waiting. A shawl that Cathy's mother had knit years ago was draped over it, filled with little black holes that could have easily been fingers gripping the top of the couch from behind it. Or claws. No matter how much he strained his ears, he could not hear anything, not even the sounds of the pipes or the house settling.

Forcing his foot forward, he took a step toward the table. Then another. He felt his foot collide with something on the floor, lifting to get over it as he walked toward the desk. When he reached it, he ran his finger over the desk, the path creating a long streak wherever it went. A small cascading wave preceded his finger by a few millimeters, but did not ripple through the surface of the liquid like it would have if it had been water. He squished it between his thumb and forefinger before wiping it against the leg of his pants until the skin on the tips hurt. Even when he knew it was gone, he could still feel it there, clinging to him. The blood was thick and had already begun to coagulate, and had been sitting there for some time waiting for him to discover it. That meant something, but he wasn't sure what, his train of thought moving along at a snail's pace as he watched the pool of blood seep into the gap he had made in it with his finger, swallowing the space whole until he didn't even know where it had been.

-cree

A sound from behind him stopped all thought immediately. It was a long, deliberate creek that seemed to cut itself off the moment he twitched. It had been no more than two feet behind him and he could already smell the rancid blackness that covered the Womb. It smelled like all the sweaty orifices of the body rolled up into one.

Sweat rolled down Mike's brow as he waited, knowing how close it must be. Knowing that if he tried hard enough he might be able to feel the creature's breath on his neck even now.

-eek

He spun the second the sound finished, fists coiled and flailing in a wide upward arch to cover as much ground as possible. They connected with nothing, sailing through the cool air with such force that he almost tipped over. There was nothing there except the gaping darkness leading out the doorway and into the street beyond. He could see the neighbors' lights on now, wishing that they would shut them off before someone noticed. There was a shadow in the window partially obscured by the doorframe. He moved a step closer to try and see, his toe hitting something on the floor again. This time it moved to avoid him, and he heard the floorboards creek again.

His face went white, his mouth filling up with cotton balls as his stomach started to flutter. He'd almost managed to purge the memory of what this felt like from his mind in the past month, but now it all came flooding back to him.

"Fuh," he huffed. It had been intended to be a much fouler word, but he found he did not have the breath with which to finish it.

Suddenly his throat became tight and there was a sharp pain in his right side as something slid into him. He could feel the creature's iron grip on his neck, its long nails each making their own mark. Pressure seemed to build to the breaking point in his side, but the blood didn't flow. Whatever had made the hole also plugged it, letting the tension build and build, like water behind a dam. All at once, they pulled out, so fast that the muscle and tendons in its way threatened to pull themselves free and come with them, effectively turning him inside out. A rush of blood came as well, seeming to hang suspended in the air for a moment as Mike's neck was released. He hit the floor at the same time as the large pool of blood, the both of them landing on the collapsed body of Cathy's Dad.

Fighting to keep pressure on the wound, Mike turned around to face the creature. Again there was nothing, just the soft glow of moonlight on the desk. His blood had begun to get into the tracts between tiles of hardwood floor already, making long grids as it pooled outward quickly. He already felt lightheaded as he reached his free hand, still covered in his own sticky fluid, and grabbed Mr. Kennessy by the face, forcing him to look at him.

His face was slack and lifeless, but the eyes looked right at him and were very much alive.

"Mr. Kennessy?" he asked, gulping back saliva and blood, then wishing he hadn't. He felt like he was saying every word with a large bubble wedged between his teeth. "David?! David, can you hear me?"

The man's throat moved, his Adams' apple bobbing three times in rapid succession before his lips parted, ever so slightly. His eyes did not move in unison, one continuously trying to roll back into his head and then snapping back in quick spasms. "Cat..." he managed, then coughed up a great heap of blood.

"She's fine," Mike assured him in a hushed voice. He could hear his own heartbeat all the way up inside his throat, making it hard to hear anything else. He had to resist the impulse to shout above it. "She's at the neighbors. We have to go, David, can you walk?"

The man seemed to try to move, but the muscles barely twitched.

Mike reached out and touched his shoulder to move him, then decided not to. There was no telling what the Womb had done to him and he might do more harm than good.

His throat bobbed a few times again and Mike pulled his ear close to try and hear what the man was saying. "Martha?"

Mike's eyes lit up with fright. Summoning all his courage, he turned back toward the darkness and saw... nothing, everything appearing clear and danger-free. There were no more bloodied lumps of the floor. The lamp had stopped moving. "I can't see her. Where is she? And Trina, where's..."

"Kitchen," he managed, his eyes getting a little wide. They looked sympathetic and grateful all at the same time somehow, and Mike nodded before turning to spit out a mouthful of blood. Trina wasn't here, the eyes were telling him, and he thanked his blessings no matter how small they were.

He placed a hand on the side of David Kennessy's face, forcing him to maintain eye contact. "I am coming back, okay? Just hold on and we'll go to Cathy."

At the sound of his daughter's name, Kennessy let out a long sigh of relief. His little girl was safe.

Mike crawled across the hardwood, ignoring the searing hurt which erupted from his heel every second or so. His blood left long streaks behind him, lopping every few feet when he switched sides to crawl on.

-clink-

He heard the sound with amazing clarity, coming from his side this time. He started to hurry despite the pain, allowing it to feed him rather than hinder him. Each pump of agony acted as a whip, forcing him forward with every jolt.

There was a lump lying dead against the kitchen tiles and his heart sank instantly. He rushed over to her, grunting with pain. He stretched his arm out to her, grabbing her shoulder and rolling her over. She looked at him. Her arm had been cut, but it was nothing serious. It could have been a lot worse.

She looked away, but didn't speak. Suddenly, her eyes moved from Mike, to behind him. They became wide with fear, her mouth opened to speak, but no words came. Slowly, Mike turned around.

Something cold and metal slammed against his face, sending him back against Cathy's mother. Blood streamed down into his eyes from a cut on his

246

forehead. For a moment, when he felt blood trickle down his neck and chest, he thought that the monster had cut his neck. Red, coppery liquid streamed from his nose into his mouth. Mike squinted into the darkness surrounding him. First his vision doubled, then everything to the left tilted to the left until he wasn't sure what he was seeing anymore. He saw a sharp edge gleam against the faded blue light. It was curved and stained with red. For a moment it was all he could see. He still couldn't see the Black Womb, but he didn't have to see it to know that it was there. The sounds of scuttled, hurried steps and the clicking of that tongue of his as it thought were as good as fingerprints to him. It was Xander. It was the Black Womb.

That clinched it for Mike. It could only be the Black Womb, not that it mattered now. The blade came down faster than Mike could see and he closed his eyes, waiting for the sharp pain before death. Nothing. He opened his eyes to see the killer had lowered his weapon.

"You have already been harvested," he said. The voice sounded exactly like Black Womb's, rough and gritty. Mike blinked once and the monster disappeared into the darkness.

He heard a sound from Mrs. Kennessy, but before he could react, Black Womb had him in his strong grasp. The Womb forced Mike into a pantry and pushed a large table up against the door with ease, vanishing again.

Mike slammed his body into the door to little effect, then tried again. All the while, Black Womb's words kept ringing in his ears: *already been harvested.*

Suddenly, as if a light went on his head, he realized. *My appendix. That freakshow's already got a piece out of me, so now he's after... Cathy.*

He started banging harder.

Cathy shivered violently against Sandra Davis' breast, sobbing despite all her best efforts to stop. Her heart still pounded so hard that it made her chest twitch with every beat, pumping enough fear through her body to give her a migraine. She had known the woman holding her for as long as she could remember, used to stay at her house as a child when her parents went out of town. Her cinnamon-scented perfume brought her back in time nearly a decade and reminded her of a place where she felt safe. It did not make her feel better, but instead proved how different her life was now compared to then. The contrast between the two made her want to throw up even more than she already did.

Sandra stroked Cathy's long black hair, her nails tickling against her scalp as she made soft shushing sounds like those made by softly flowing waves. Under different circumstances, they might have put Cathy right to sleep. "It'll all be okay," the old woman said in a hushed voice.

Cathy turned her head up briefly and examined her woman's face. Her silvery hair was dull in the glow of the forty-watt lamp in the corner, and her lips that were always ruby red stood out so much from her milky white complexion that they might have been fake. The nightgown she wore was sky blue and had flowers printed all over it, just like every other piece of clothing she owned.

Everything about her spoke to her sweetness and honesty... but her eyes shone with tearful pity, giving her away. Her lip quivering, Cathy buried her face into her blouse again.

Across the room in a rickety wheelchair that looked as though it had been manufactured during the first World War, John Davis glanced at Cathy and frowned before turning back toward the window. He poked apart the plastic strips of his blinds so that the Kennessy's blackened doorway was just visible, squinting to try and see any movement that might be going on inside. He thought he saw something flash, then quickly flutter about, but wasn't sure. His eyes weren't as good as they used to be and his doctor thought it might be glaucoma, but they were still waiting to get the tests back. His old service revolver lay on his deadened lap and he brought his hand to it every few minutes, as if to make sure it were still there.

"Is he there yet?" Cathy sobbed, stammering out every syllable as bubbles of mucus joined the tears on her face. She held Sandra in close, making her ribs hurt. She didn't complain.

Cathy's voice was so wracked with tears and adrenalin that it took John a moment to process what she had said. When he did, he nodded at her solemnly, forcing a smile onto his thin, heart-shaped face. It made his large ears wiggle a little, something that had always made her giggle as a child. "Not yet honey, but I can hear the sirens coming."

She sniffed twice, then continued the same broken moan she'd been making for the last ten minutes, mumbling something about Xander in a voice so inhuman neither of them understood a word of it.

John checked the safety on his revolver to make sure it was off, then turned back toward the window. His chair squeaked from the sudden motion, the pin on each wheel making a soft clicking sound as they snapped into place and prevented him from rolling involuntarily.

There were no sirens, of course. He knew better than most that the only police in Coral Beach would be all the way on the other side of town at this time of night, patrolling the stretch of highway between here and Coral Cove. He pushed the palm of one strong hand against the worn rubber wheel, moving a little closer to the window. Again it made the same clicking sound, a little louder this time.

Cathy nearly jumped out of her skin, pulled Sandra closer and forcing the wind out of the older woman's lungs in one quick huff.

"Just the chair," John smirked, winking at her from over his shoulder. "The police will be here soon."

The soft-glowing lamp in the corner flickered twice, sending sprawling, sputtering shadows across the walls before it went out entirely, along with every other light in the Davis' home.

"Not soon enough," Cathy said quietly in a dead voice, sitting up in Sandra Davis' lap as the last memories of light faded from her retinas.

There was another metallic click as John pulled back the hammer of his revolver, bringing it to eye level as he wheeled away from the window and closer to the girls. His unseen face had become taut and expressionless, his lips becoming invisible thin lines across the bottom of his face. In his mind, he was instantly twenty years younger, could walk and see perfectly, and could still fire off three rounds in less than a second.

-click-

It came again, with no reason this time. He glanced from the girls to the kitchen, searching for some explanation for the sound and finding none. Swallowing hard, he pushed his chair another inch forward, his palms sweaty and shaking.

Something slammed against the front door and he spun the chair on a dime, aiming the pistol at it. Whatever it was had been so hard and violent that it continued to shake the walls of the house almost ten seconds later.

Cathy nudged away Sandra's attempt to pull her closer again, swallowing back a mouthful of moisture before she could speak. "Mike?" she said finally, her voice small and wet.

John raised a bushy eyebrow towards the door, tapping his tongue against the back of his teeth for a moment contemplatively. "Mike?" he called out, his voice loud and authoritative in a way Cathy had never heard before.

There was another thud, louder than the first. Light was seen as the door moved in for a split second then settled back into its frame.

"Mike, if that's you say something or knock normal, son," John yelled again, closing one eye to aim as he raised the gun again.

There was a long, tense moment when nobody breathed. Cathy refused to blink as she awaited some response from Mike.

There was another thud. This one so hard it cracked the wood around the deadbolt.

John fired the gun twice, creating two forty-five-millimeter holes in the door instantly. The light from the street shone in in two long lines as burnt gunpowder wafted its way out of the barrel, floating into the atmosphere and dissipating slowly. For a moment their ears rang loudly, then there was no sound. His hand throbbed with a dull ache. He'd forgotten how much the gun kicked, as well as how his heart raced with every shot fired. When he was sure this was over he'd have to take one of his pills to slow it back down before his angina acted up. Even now he felt that pain in his chest, like the world's worst case of indigestion just a few inches too high to actually be that.

He turned his head back towards the girls again, smiling at them even though he knew they couldn't see him through the darkness.

-click-

John's eyes went wide as all the hairs on Cathy's body stood on end. She could almost see his opaque yellow claws tapping against the door.

He turned back around and pulled back the hammer again, willing the joints in his trigger finger to bend again.

-clink-

-clink- -clink-

Sandra stared into the darkness, pulling on Cathy's shoulder again. This time the girl relented, laying her head against her throbbing heart, and for a moment Sandra forgot who was comforting whom.

Cathy didn't sob or moan now, made no sound at all. She willed her eyes to take in more of the light, trying to see what she already knew was there. Her head twitched from one side to the other every few moments, her mind continuously tricking her into thinking she saw the aquamarine eyes of the Black Womb in her peripheral vision.

John lowered his revolver slightly, turning his chair so that he faced the girls while keeping his eyes trained on the hallway that led down to the basement entrance. That was where the killer had come in through, he was sure of it. He lowered his gun slightly, the hand that held it shaking. It stopped after a moment as he turned away from the hall toward Sandra and Cathy. His heart-shaped face drew down in a frown that seemed to melt his features, his eyes small and dark underneath his bushy eyebrows.

"What is it, John?" Sandra whispered, leaning in slightly to make sure she was heard.

He opened his mouth to respond, blood dripping from it in a long trail into his lap as his gun dropped to the floor and slid underneath the couch. The blood looked as black as the Womb's in the moonlight as more spewed out, his mouth still moving without a sound as he tried to tell them something. "Run," he managed to force out, as a shadowy figure stood up from behind his chair.

Cathy's eyes went wide in paralyzed fear as she looked at it, backlit and powerful behind John's body.

It shoved something forward from behind the chairs brown leatherback and John's chest exploded outward, spraying Cathy and Sandra with hundreds of tiny droplets of blood spatter.

Sandra screamed as they both scrambled to their feet, running past the killer and into the hallway, bumping her shin into the end table as they went.

The killer made no movement to intercept them, the blackened head turning only slightly to watch as they went.

John finally fell to the floor in a heap, the thud of his form shaking the house. Blood still oozed slowly from his mouth as he forced his head up, feeling his energy ebb slowly out of the hole the killer had made in his lower back. Somewhere deep inside him, the spiteful cop who enjoyed Gallows Humor chuckled at the monster that had cut into him. *Joke's on you, flyboy. Ain't been able to feel anything that low for fifteen years or more.*

He could see the brown grip of his gun poking out from under the couch just a few feet away, the gleam of the engraving on its base shimmering out like a beacon. Grunting through gritted teeth, he thrust a hand forward, grabbing onto the coarse fibers of his carpet and pulling himself forward. Every inch was agony, each leg providing thirty pounds of dead and useless weight.

The killer stepped out from around the chair without a sound, walking over to where John crawled. The murderer lifted a heavy heel and brought it down into the center of John's back with slow, deliberate pressure.

John tried his best to stay up but buckled quickly under the force. "Bastard," he grunted.

There was a deep, animalistic grunt from the shadows as the killer twisted his heel quickly.

John screamed so loud his ears blocked out the sound as he felt something in his back twist and then snap. His eyes stared at the barrel on his weapon, his fingers literally touching its smooth material. Tears began to roll down his cheeks as he realized he could not close his grasp as the numbness he'd lived with for almost two decades seeped its way up from his waist and into the rest of his body, from his neck on down.

With bony fingers, the killer grabbed him by one shoulder and whipped him around, leaning in until their faces almost touched.

He wanted to scream, to close his eyes and never open them again until it was over... but found he couldn't. Couldn't move at all to even swallow the nervous sweat growing in his mouth. He watched with unblinking eyes as the killer went to work slicing a long gash in his right side. Saw as the cold, sharp-nailed hand sunk into him and started to rummage about his intestines, feeling nothing, not even the warm blood that came out of him in buckets.

He felt nothing for the next few minutes, until a drowsy feeling came upon him and he drifted off to sleep with his eyes still open. He was thankful for it.

Sandra pulled Cathy into the master bedroom, trying hard to ignore the sounds she heard in the living room as she slammed the door shut.

"Whatdowedowhatdowedowhatdowedo..." Cathy repeated continuously, her voice back to that low, wet moan it had been while she'd been pressed against Sandra's flower-covered blouse. Her hands were cupped over her nose and mouth as she breathed in and out too fast to ever get a real lungful of air. She was trying not to pass out, but the top of her head had that floaty feeling that usually came a few moments before it happened and her eyelids had started becoming heavy.

Sandra grabbed her by the shoulders, giving the girl one good shake to bring her back to reality. "We're going to get out of here and help John." she said, not even convincing herself as tears tumbled across her withered features. "We're going to help John and everything's going to be okay, okay?"

Cathy sniffed, then nodded quickly.

There was a loud thud at the door to the bedroom and Sandra turned to face it, both girls backing up until they were against the far wall. The room was dark and black except for the edges of the king-size bed that Sandra and her husband had shared for more than forty years and the smooth pink wall, turned a weird eggplant color when mixed with the light from the window. There was a square panel on the wall that Cathy didn't recognize but wasn't even really looking at, her eyes glued to the door.

Sandra took a step forward.

There was another thud, shaking the door as well as the room.

She backed back against the wall, swallowed, then repeated the same step again. Grabbing Cathy by the wrist, she pulled her toward the square frame on the wall. "Come on, child!" she said in a hushed voice.

Cathy stepped along with her. The square looked like a picture frame at first in the low light, though there was no picture in it. There was a small knob at the bottom that Sandra grabbed now and thrust upward, revealing a small compartment with two lengths of rope coming out of the ceiling and passing through the floor. It was a laundry chute.

"Get in, Catherine," Sandra whispered, motioning her head toward the hole.

Cathy shook her head, almost letting herself laugh. "It won't matter," she said in that same, dead voice as before. "Not against him."

"Who, child?" Sandra asked, squinting as she tilted her head to one side.

"Black Womb," Cathy answered, her eyelids rising and then falling again when she said the name. "Xander."

Sandra shook her head in confusion, motioning towards the chute again.

Relenting and getting some of her energy back, Cathy grabbed both sides of the frame and pulled herself in. Her chin was down past her knees by the time she got herself completely inside. Sandra leaned forward and kissed her softly, then slammed the shaft shut.

For what seemed like an eternity, Cathy listened intently to the silence that surrounded her, almost surrendering herself to it. Then after a forever of eavesdropping, waiting, knowing what was coming even though it never seemed to, it happened. The heavy thuds of a large frame tossing itself against a wooden door as it gave way under the pressure. The sound of heavy feet on carpet floors.

-thump-

-thu–thump-

She could picture it, standing in the middle of the room and looking around with those opaque eyes like swamp-water, waiting for something in the room to move so that it could pounce on it.

There was a heavy thunk followed by hundreds and squeaks all in unison as the killer turned over the mattress, staring down at Sandra through the bars of the bedframe.

She stared back, her eyes first filled with intense fear and then anger as she stared into the emotionless eyes of her killer. "You fucking tart," she said bitterly.

Cathy didn't think she'd ever heard Sandra swear before in all the years she'd known her. It had always been 'sugar' or 'fudge' in place of more offensive language.

There was a sharp sound, followed by a squish. It was the all-too-familiar sound of flesh giving way under pressure. It continued for a moment, its wet sucking sound filling Cathy's head with an all-too-accurate image of what was being done to Sandra just a few feet away.

The footsteps started again, their heavy thunks moving further and further away from her. Smiling weakly, Cathy allowed herself a sigh of relief.

The footsteps stopped.

252

Cathy put her hand over her mouth, realizing her falter.

Now the footsteps came closer again, faster and heavier than before. They sounded determined and ready, more sure of themselves then they ever had.

Cursing, she moved forward to brace her hand against the chute's door, hoping she could stop it from being opened. The thumb of her right hand brushed up against something rough and tight. She stopped, grabbing onto it. It was one of the ropes dissecting the box. A lightbulb went off in her head, her eyes glimmering with hope as she gripped the rope with both hands and pulled.

The entire box slid up in the shaft half a foot, the pulleys screaming from use but working all the same. She smiled, sticking her tongue out one side of her mouth as she pulled again, moving even further and more freely this time.

She heard the swift -shunk!- as the chute's door was slid open again down below her. She could almost see the Womb's emotionlessly shocked expression now, its head tilted to one side as it found the empty shaft. It made her grin.

-shhhaut-

It was a quick sound, lasting little more than half a second and so faint she barely heard it, but it made something in the back of her head twitch.

-shhhaut-

She pulled the rope again, feeling its fibers burn red marks into her palms and not caring. She could see a line of light at the top of her box coming from the second floor window. She pulled upwards again and the room came into view, dusty and dank.

-shhau- -tick!-

Too late Cathy realized what the sound was as the rope vibrated in her hands and then became loose. There was a split second where she felt weightless, reaching towards the opening with every ounce of speed she could muster. It lasted only moments before the compartment lost its battle with gravity, the rope slicing through the middle, and she began to plummet back down the chute. She screamed as the box shot downward, the draft catching her hair and whipping it up around her head. She braced both palms against either wall as she plummeted past the master bedroom, continuing down for another few seconds until she crashed into its base, creating a mushroom cloud of dust and mold. Her tiny form rocked about the small space as violently as a dice in a cup. Her head slammed against the top of the box at the same time her butt beat against the bottom, making her entire form feel squished as she bit down on her tongue so hard she felt her teeth connect with one another. Blood oozed from the soft flesh into her mouth as she jolted forward, mashing her nose against the door and twisting her arm the wrong way, hearing the bone break easily. The sound echoed off the closed-in walls and made it ten times worse than it actually was. Pain shot up and down her spine like fire. She couldn't think, couldn't move. Her head throbbed along with everything else in her body as warm urine trickled from her crotch onto her leg, then into a small puddle in the center of the shaft.

She sat still for a long moment, focusing on her own breathing as though without her concentration it would stop completely. Something sharp dug into her side that she didn't want to think about, bringing even more blood out and mixing with the yellow liquid in the middle.

A black arm burst into the chute, grabbing at her neck with its sharp, bony fingers. They wrapped around her carefully and fully as she yelped in fright, then pulled her through the wall. She screamed as shards of molding and plaster ripped at her skin, the sound muffled by the pile of clothes she was thrown into face first. Crying and whimpering like a beaten pup, she tried to scramble to her feet. She lay her hand against the floor to brace herself. "Agh!" she winced, feeling the bone break even more as it scraped against itself. The monster stepped into the small of her back just as he had John Davis, pinning her down with his foot as something sliced across her arm and drew blood. She screamed and sobbed all at the same time, the type of sound only those new to this world and those about to leave it can make.

The same sharpness touched the right side of her stomach, pressing into the tender flesh just over the appendix and denting it inward until it was just beyond the breaking point.

She sobbed again, long and hard. "...please, don't..." she begged, her voice a whisper. Her shirt and arm were cut, revealing the bruises left by Grendel and other men like him. They would fade eventually, but the emotional bruises would stay for years. She cried as this, her friend's touch, brought back those memories in ways she didn't think it ever could, his fingers hungry for her flesh in a way much the same yet very different from those that had hurt her before.

The killer began to lean in, causing the skin to puncture.

He withdrew it before it went in any great distance, then began to walk back toward the basement door and into the night air. As he did, he turned and looked at her.

"You're not even worth the trouble," he said, in a voice so angry that it wasn't human.

Cathy turned to face the Womb, to look Xander in the eyes after what he'd just said. There was nothing there but darkness and moonlight, and the stench of blood that was already seeping down from the two dead bodies upstairs.

She turned back into the pile of dirty, sweaty, flower-printed laundry, crying as she finally heard the sirens approaching the house.

Don Smith clenched both his hands in his hair as he stared down at the stack of papers in front of him, pulling until he could feel the tug against his roots.

The rest of the halls and offices of *Beach News Daily* were dark that night. He was the only staff member working late, something he'd gotten used to in his years of service.

It was a small office located in Coral Beach's lone strip mall, with its own glass-door entrance that was shattered on a monthly basis by idiotic teens looking for cash and finding only bound copies of old newspapers. Once they'd taken a computer. The space had three offices and four employees, making it constantly obvious who resided at the bottom of the pecking order. The editor, the ad salesman and the head reporter, Drake, each got their own.

Drake had the corner one with windows that opened up to the forest behind the mall. Don had a cubicle-sized storage room with a computer made in 1991 and a printer that constantly spewed toner.

On the wall were small-press awards the paper had won, along with many empty spots for more plaques and certificates to go. They had not been filled in some time, something the editor made them aware of constantly.

Don worked day and night trying to find that one good story that might point his career in the right direction. Then, he and his son could move out of that junk house in the crap part of town and into the city, where he could get the big stories, lead a real life and make his son proud of him for the first time since his mother died.

He brushed a hand through his thinning brown hair, displacing the comb over he'd long since stopped believing was anything close to convincing. Staring down at the pile of papers, contacts and photos on his desk, he saw the stories that had consumed his life and career. 'Mayor cuts ribbon at new hospital wing.' 'Summer Games in Full Swing.' 'Less Youth Voting.' Stories that he thought proved the theory that if you put enough monkeys in a room with a typewriter, eventually they would produce Shakespeare... or at the very least, reasonably competent journalism.

A month ago, he thought he had written that ticket with a series of stories on the 'Midnight Massacre'. Detective Carl Dent had given him full access to police files and profiles that had been worked up on the murderer. What he'd found in them had sent chills down his spine and brought a smirk to his lips as he thought of the public's reaction to such a story. Dent's forensic psychiatrists had the killer pegged as being somewhere in his late teens to early twenties, around his own son's age. In fact could have been one of his son's *friends*, a notion which he'd forced himself not to consider at the time. They were male and Caucasian, most likely from a broken home (although Dent had focused on an adoptee as a good candidate). They were non-smokers and had real upper-body power. More than that, they had control. Up until each victims last breath every strike had been perfect and pristine. There had been no hesitation lines along any of the wound tracts. It was only *after* each person died that they got the attention that had turned them each into grotesquely mutilated works of anger. The killer never seemed to really cut loose until after the kill had been made.

The material had spoken for itself. It almost needed no work or dramatization. He could have simply stuck a by-line on it and sent it to the editor, but instead he had worked it into a piece of journalistic gold then started planning his vacation to Cuba.

Less than forty-eight hours after the story had gone to print, Genblade had been arrested. *Not* in his late teens or early twenties. *Not* from a broken home. *Not* anywhere close to his profile. The editor had almost torn him a new asshole... and Drake had gotten the story of Genblade's capture –a story that had attracted national publicity and been run on almost every news outlet, all of which Drake had received royalty checks for.

He glared past the old-fashioned typewriter he kept on his desk for show and at the computer screen, its harsh artificial glow stinging at his eyes. It was the page that the editor had asked him to lay out and no matter what he did, he could not make the Blockbuster ad fit with his story. Which meant, incidentally, that the story would probably have to be cut down. He thought briefly that he could add some space by removing his by-line. He didn't particularly want his name on anything he wrote lately anyway.

Out in the lobby, he heard the fax machine buzz to life and start to churn out paper. Frowning, he looked at his watch, shaking it twice to make sure it was right.

"The hell sends a fax at this hour?" he grumbled, stepping out into the main office and switching on the light. After a moment's pause, the lights hummed to life and burned his eyes. He stopped at the receptionist's desk to rub them, gazing over it at the fax to see if it was another offer to win a free trip to Hawaii.

It was an All Points Bulletin, to all media outlets.

He hopped around the desk and snatched the paper off the press, just as it finished printing.

Across the top in big, bold letters were the words 'Midnight Massacres Return'.

He stared at it for a long moment, his face moving from horror to shock... and finally to something resembling glee. He walked back into his office, paper in hand, and opened up the file folder that had been collecting dust on his desk for almost a month now. Inside was the profile he'd printed. If the killer was back... so was the profile.

Don couldn't hide his smile.

This was it.

He could feel it.

He was going to break this story wide open.

Lance Berkshire felt a chill that had nothing to do with the air conditioners as he entered the basement level of the Coral Beach Police Department.

The metallic room shone a dull blue, its sad sterility making him feel sad and emotionally impotent. The walls of the room were lined with drawers and cabinets, some large and some small. Roughly half the drawers on the wall still had names taped lazily to them from when they had been the final home to so many people weeks ago. In the center of the room were two identical steel tables, each standing at waist height and bolted down to the floor. He walked over to them in a daze, his head swimmy with thoughts he kept trying to force out. There was a body on each table, their mulched flesh ruining the otherwise clean environment. Their skin was white and powdery and even though he had seen it a million times before, he felt his gloved hand move up to touch it. His fingers shook violently, the nervous quakes felt all the way up to his shoulder.

"Coral Beach Precinct Morgue. My name is Harry Ford. I'll be your mortician for this evening."

Lance Berkshire looked up from the two corpses lined on the tables. He hadn't even noticed that Harry was there. Snapping out of the trance he'd slipped into, he lowered his hand and swallowed hard to try and get his bearings.

"Lance? You all right?" Harry asked. It was moments like this that Harry wondered if his job had desensitized him to gore and death. Looking down at the bodies laid not two feet away, fighting off vomiting, he was almost glad. Glad that he *wasn't* desensitized. "You up for this tonight, pal? We can reschedule..."

"Naw, Harry. I'll be fine," he lied, staring at the slain people once more before turning his attention to Harry again. "Besides, the papers are already on our backs to release statements about the deceased..."

It was obscene, referring to them as merely 'deceased.' It made it sound like a heart attack, or maybe some word some grieving widow might use to calm he children. These people were dead, plain and simple. You don't see people with holes in them that big that are alive.

"Which one do we start with?" Harry asked, breaking the silence.

"Um, the male, I guess," Lance replied, lifting the cloth over the body's head, revealing its torn face. He turned on his recorder. "Name: John Davis. Weight: 170 lbs. Height: 5 feet 11". Cause of death:... stab wound through the trunk." He clicked off the recorder for a moment, then continued. "Subject's blood was found throughout the scene of the murder, indicating it came from behind as he was sitting at the time. To add to this theory, we have found traces of leather from the recliner he was sitting on, embedded into his body cavity next to his left lung and kidneys..."

CHAPTER THREE: POWERLESS

Warm red light shone in through Xander's eyelids as his mind slowly seeped back to reality, the soft fuzzy feeling of sleep slowly fading from him. Even though the sunlight on his face was warm and bright, he still shivered from head to toe, making the springs of his mattress cry out from the sudden effort. Moaning, he turned over and opened his eyes. It took considerable effort, the lids feeling like they were swollen and fused shut with gook. Grumbling, he reached up and rubbed them with the knuckle of his right hand. It stung fiercely. When he opened his eyes and looked at it, the skin across all four knuckles had been ripped off.

Across the room his curtain billowed and flailed in the midmorning draft, the cold fall breeze taking away some of the rank stench left by the whiskey and the fire. The odd scent of burnt air still lingered though, refusing to go away like the last guest of a party that went dreadfully wrong.

He rose up and sat on the edge of his bed for a moment, stretching both of his arms back until he felt the stiff vertebra in the center of his back pop, releasing the pressure that the night's activities had stored there. It radiated over his entire backside for a second before shimmering away in a hail of gooseflesh encouraged

257

by the chill on the air, the wind feeling good against his naked skin.

It stared at the gaping black rectangle that had been a door a moment ago, watching the shadows inside dance about like puppets in a play. They excited it wonderfully; their movements could not have been more perfect if they'd been planned.

Xander stopped, his eyes growing wide as his head jutted forward in shock as though he had lunged forward but was held back by invisible seatbelts. He tried hard to hold onto the flash of dream or memory, but it was gone. Locked away deep inside a subconscious that wasn't his own and would not let him see the rest. Every time he tried to access the information, he felt a migraine start to build in the top-right corner of his brain. He looked up at his reflection in the broken black glass of his computer screen and saw darkness slowly fade from his eyes as the normal white reestablished itself. The rest of his face looked dried and splintered and dusty, much like the glass itself.

Sighing gruffly, he reached under the computer desk and pulled a black T-shirt out from under the wheel of his chair, snapping it in the air twice to get some of the wrinkles out. Holding it up in front of him, he examined it for stains or smears and, finding none, stretched it over his head and body, wincing as the soft fabric grazed his abdomen.

He looked down and saw a few deep cuts across his stomach. They were healing even as he examined them, shriveling into little black dots, until they finally disappeared altogether. He grimaced slightly when they closed. It had always been an odd sight, watching his own wounds heal. It was almost like saying he could watch grass grow. He rubbed his hand over his stomach and pulled his shirt the rest of the way down.

"Stupid frigging thing," he mumbled to himself as he grabbed a pair of faded denim jeans off the foot of the bed and started pulling them on. "Think you'd know how not to get yourself sliced open by now."

Frowning, he unlocked the door to his room quickly and swung it open hard enough that it slammed against the corner of his desk. The crack of the wood echoed through his splitting skull, making him grit his teeth.

To his right along the wall were family photos that were taken every year. In each and every one his parents wore the same plastic smiles, as though they'd been cut and pasted from one to the other. In each one he had on his meek little smile, the best he could force out at the time with the hot lights of the supermarket photo-hut glaring down at him, more families waiting in the hall. There was one near the end from around three years back that made him grin every time he saw it. His parents still had those same Barbie-and-Ken smiles mashed onto their faces, but in this one, his was real. His smile was big and genuine, his eyes sparkling with life in a way he'd never seen in a photo before or since. That day, the next family waiting in line to get their pictures taken was Sara Johnson and her parents. She'd looked at him and smiled and waved and he'd smiled back, just as the shutter snapped open.

He looked at it only briefly before starting down the stairs, hopping down over them two at a time until he reached the bottom. He started to reach for his sneakers when something caught his eye off to the right in the living room.

Nobody should have been here this time of day, yet his mother's purse had been tossed onto the couch and his father's pipe smoked with freshly-lit tobacco. Raising an eyebrow, he dropped his shoe and stood up straight before walking around the corner until the room was in full view.

His mother sat on the love seat in the far side of the room, tears billowing down her red and puffy cheeks as she held a doily close to her face, using it to wipe the moisture away every few seconds. Her body shook with sobs as his father knelt beside her, one hand laid on her palm and one rubbing her shoulder rhythmically. He turned toward Xander and frowned with his steely cold gaze. The one that Xander recognized his eyes took on when he stopped caring about whatever was going on and expecting everyone else to, too.

Xander lost the feeling in his fingers, the tingling sensation rising slowly until it was almost at his elbows. He'd seen them like this before, right before the start of one of the worst chapters in his entire life... one that didn't seem to want to end.

"What's happened?" he asked, in a voice too low to be heard. He stopped, then took a step forward and cleared his throat. "What happened?" he repeated, making no effort to hide the desperation in his voice.

His mother started to sob again, unable to make eye contact with him.

Tell me it's Aunt Sue, he thought, the pit in his stomach growing larger with every passing instant. *Tell me her heart finally gave out from all the sweetened-condensed milk she eats. Or tell me Principal Shnieder hung himself in his office after last week's PTA meeting. Tell me anything except what I know you're going to.*

"Son," his father said, his voice gravely and stern. "Here's how it happened."

He knew it was bad now. That was the phrase his Dad had always used when delivering bad news. According to his Nanna Drew, it'd been that way ever since he was a kid. The first time he'd been caught stealing it was that exact phrase which had preceded the explanation he gave his mother.

"No," Xander demanded, but his voice was only a whisper.

"It's Mike and Cathy."

He listened to everything his father had to say, along with the sobs of his mother that punctuated every sentence perfectly. But inside the words curdled and gargled in his ears, staying there until he was ready to process them. The only things his mind had heard were their names, Mike and Cathy.

It stared at the gaping black rectangle that had been a door a moment ago, watching the shadows inside dance about like puppets in a play. They excited it wonderfully, their movements could not have been more perfect if they'd been planned.

It had been the Kennessy's door, he was sure of it now. The greyish-blue siding matched perfectly, as did the black metal spirals they used on their railing on either side of the stairs. The Womb had been there last night.

Eventually his father finished speaking. He said nothing for a full minute, still nodding every few seconds as he pretended to listen.

"Son?" his father asked, lowering his wild, stringy eyebrows down over his tiny sunken eyes.

259

"Alex?" his mother called, speaking finally.

The sound snapped him out of his trance and he turned towards them, giving them one final, curt nod. "Yes," he said, trying hard to keep all emotion out of his voice. He didn't think he had it in him to fake anything at the moment, like he had in all the pictures upstairs. He knew that if he pretended to be okay or happy, the real thing would come pouring out and he didn't want that, not now. "I have to go."

"Maybe we should - -"

"Have to go," he said quietly again as he turned and grabbed his shoes, avoiding eye contact with both of them the entire time.

He closed the door behind him and the second he did his mother began to cry again, burying her head into the crook of her husband's neck.

Xander tripped on the chipped concrete stair leading up to his front door, tumbling face first into the purple shale walkway leading up to it. The brittle stone broke on impact, sending tiny shards of it into his hands and chin as friction ripped the skin raw once more.

He stayed there for over a minute, staring at the shadow image that the morning sun had made. In it he couldn't see the outline of his short-cut hair, and his muscles looked more defined, his jaw slightly squarer. He looked bald and made of darkness, like a demon sprung from a child's nightmare. Blood dripped from his chin and fell to the ground, looking like two beady red eyes in the center of the shadow-demon's head.

"You son of a bitch," he whispered, sweat gleaming off his moist lips. He drew back and punched it right between the 'eyes,' shattered the shale and digging more of it into his hand. Gritting his teeth as his face became livid with anger, he drew back and slammed down again, creating an eruption of blood from the open wound. "You son of a bitch!" he screamed louder, raising both hands high into the air now and hammer-fisting his shadow. He felt his voice crackle with the vomit-like urge that came with the Womb. Curling his lip as he recognized it, he punched himself in the jaw.

Something in his mouth snapped and then righted itself almost instantly. He felt the top of his jaw split, blood and spit streaming down his throat until the wound knitted itself back together. He laughed at himself as blood started to drool from his mouth and down his chin, tapping onto the ground. If anyone had walked by or seen, they might have called the men in the clean white coats to come and take him away.

His heart started to pump harder and faster, his blood starting to feel hot. Like it was boiling in his veins. Letting out a bubbly laugh as he started to wind down, he peered down at the shadow puppet version of the Womb he'd been so angry at a moment ago.

It was bleeding black ooze, just the way the creature did in real life, the blood-red colored eyes squinting into a long, angry scowl at him.

He stared back at it, afraid and confused with the excitement and grief and pain. He looked down at his hands and saw that they were no longer forcing pulses of red-celled blood from between the spikes of purple rock, but was now producing a thick black substance that stuck to his hands like stringy tar.

"What'd you do?" he spat, reaching a palm over the shadow-womb's face to rub out the eyes completely. Even now, he could still feel them burning holes into his face. He tried to stand up, wreathing over in pain as the blood vessels inside him exploded again and again, at war with themselves, until finally the veins in his neck and wrists sprang open through the skin. Bending over in pain, he hobbled to the small space under a tree where he and Sara used to play as children between their two houses, where nobody could see. Where he'd imagined kissing her since before he'd even really *wanted* to kiss girls. To his surprise, he found himself laughing a little again, though nothing was funny. He fell to the ground next to that old oak, his eyes rolled back in his head as black blood squirted upward in tiny splashes and slowly covered his entire body, hardening quickly into a second skin.

One last bit of black blood threw itself out of his mouth, his taste buds singing a brief celebration at being rid of it. He felt the adrenalin push him to anger but not take over. "Black Womb lives," he heard himself say as he stood, almost choking on the words. His red eyes slit open. As tenuous as the hold might be, he had the driver's seat for the moment.

He popped all eight of his claws, then clenched his fists, digging them into his own palm. *What have I done?*

ʎ⟨⟩ʎ

Cathy stared at the fleckled white wall of her hospital room, her eyes focusing on random clumps of stucco. Each time, an image almost appeared out of the wall and then slipped away just as it was coming into view. Trains of thought kept occurring to her and then drifted off, but one remained as constant as her heartbeat.

Not good enough. Not worth it. Too much trouble. Not worth the trouble. Not worth the trouble.

The words had been ringing in her head ever since the police found her unconscious, clinging to the lifeless form of Sandra Davis. Those words cut deep. Deeper than any of Genblade or Spider's blades ever could. The words sliced to the very depths of Cathy Kennessy's soul. Grendel had said it. Xander had said it, as Black Womb. Two people who were very close to her had hurt her, had come close to killing her, and then stopped... because she wasn't even worth the effort that it would take to deliver a killing blow. Neither Grendel nor Black Womb had killed her physically, but emotionally they had both succeeding in shattering her.

There was a sound from the window like a small, stunted tap. Her eye twitched when she heard it, joined a moment later by her mouth as well. Her eyelids droned up and down lazily as she tried to find the energy just to move her head. When she finally lolled it into a flopish turn, her eyes sprang open with new energy. Her hands clamped down against the bed, crumpling the sheets as she pushed herself to the far edge of the mattress. Her hair fell over the side as her throat made a small, whimpering sound.

The Womb put one foot down onto the floor, the black ooze that covered it masking all its toes and making it look cloven. Its other leg remained on the sill, bent at the knee as the drapes fell lifelessly around its toned, dark frame. There had been a breeze a moment ago, she was sure of it, but the creature had taken it right from the air as easily as it took the breath from people's lungs.

Its emotionless triangle eyes looked at her, the light of the white room turning them into scaly pools of red swamp water. It opened its mouth slowly, its lower lip quivering as it unveiled duel rows of jagged yellow teeth. One in the top right was starting to rot away, a large hole in it surrounded by dark green decay. Soon it would snap off and be replaced by another, but from the way its tongue lashed at her, she assumed she wouldn't be around long enough to see that happen.

"No!" she screamed, finally falling off of the bed. Tubes tangled around her arm as she fell, yanking them from the IV drip that had been fed into her arm the night before. She kicked her feet and threw her hands about wildly, trying to get away from the tubes the same way a dog would try to kick free of a tangled leash. Her hair swiveled in front of her face, masking her fear and anger in a tangled mess of knots and curls until she didn't even look human.

"Hey," Xander soothed from deep inside the beast. His soft, caring words turned to a gravelly vomited urge when passed through the Womb's lips, shredding any of their original intent along the way. It came closer to her, one hand outstretched and ready to pop its claws as it stepped down off the windowsill.

"Nono NO!" she howled, still pushing at the floor to back herself up even though she was up against the wall. The rational part of her mind had shut down, replaced with the pure animal instinct to run.

"It's just me," it pleaded, its eyes turning upwards into what passed for sadness on its face. Its teeth barred as its fingers curled up into a small fist, its knuckles protruding like little mountains across the bridge of it.

"No!" she cried again, her eyes burning with hate. When it got to close to her she lashed out, slamming her white-knuckled fists against its chest and raking her nails across its face as she screamed.

The Womb brought its hands up to try and grab her and stop her, grunting something incomprehensible as she started kicking it in the gut as well.

"Mmmmnnno!" she wailed as loud as she could, worming away from its grip and continuing to smack at it, digging her nails into its eyes.

Closing its mouth bitterly, it brought its hand up quickly and pressed it to her mouth. It brought its own face in until they were nose-to-nose. Her wide brown eyes stared into the red gelatinous pools of the Womb, watching as tiny chunks of black flesh floated around in them.

Her eyes still burned at him, fiery hate behind them that would have caught him on fire if they could have. Her voice was muffled, every syllable sounding like the letter 'M' in succession. She tried to bite the Womb's hand once, her mouth filling with the moldy-ash taste that was its flesh.

Growling, the Womb closed its eyes. It stayed there for a long moment, without any movement between either of them. Suddenly, the darkness around him seemed to lose its ability to hold itself together and came crashing down onto the floor, revealing the bloodstained form of Xander Drew underneath.

"It's just me," he said, the sadness in his voice finally audible for what it was.

She squinted at him as he took his hand away. He could see sanity flooding back into her face along with recognition. "Xander?" she whispered, rising to her feet.

He nodded sheepishly as he backed away. There was a tiny slice in her cheek from where his claws must have poked out. He couldn't take his eyes away from the redness there as much as he tried.

"What the hell do you think you're doing here?" she asked, more out of astonishment than spite as she moved back towards her bed.

"Checking up on some friends, I thought," he said as the oil oozed its way off of his body. He got on his knees next to her bed and took her hand. She pulled away at first, to his obvious sadness, then let him take it. His touch was tender, nothing like it had been last night. His thumb stroked her fingers, paying equal loving attention to each one. "What happened?"

She tried to hide her anger at the posing of the question. She knew, somewhere in the back of her mind, that it wasn't his fault. But it would be so easy to blame him. "You did," she spat.

He closed his eyes tight, forcing Black Womb not to surface despite the impassioned pain this caused him. He could barely stand to see her, this woman he loved as much as life itself, in this condition. It didn't help that he knew that he was responsible.

"Tell me exactly what happened," he reiterated, hiding the pain in his voice. He did not deserve her pity for this.

Cathy looked at him for a moment, astonished that he didn't know. Even though she knew that he could neither control nor remember what he did as the Womb, she would never truly understand it.

He reached up and pulled back her hospital gown a bit at the sleeve, revealing her bruised and cut shoulder. He leaned over and kissed her cut, which was now stitched. Blood smattered the hospital gown where it had bled. He held her hand again. "I am so sorry," he said. He felt like he'd been saying that far too much lately.

"I know," she answered, sighing, her eyes cast downward.

He squeezed her hand. "I love you, y' know."

She smiled. "I know. And I love you too. It's the other part I'm not so crazy about."

They both laughed nervously, but she could hear it in his chuckle that he was faking the light-hearted expression.

"Now, what happened to you?"

She sighed again. "I didn't see much, but it started off just like the last time. The clicking in the background, that smell, like mouldy oranges. Mike and I ran into my house, but realized that the kill... that Black Womb was inside. So, he went in to save my parents and sent me to some neighbours. After about ten minutes, Black Womb showed up at the Davis' home. He slaughtered the Davis' and tried to kill me. But he didn't... he said... he said that I wasn't worth it."

He felt his heart sink again, immediately moving into an embrace that was as much for his benefit as it was for hers. "God, I'm sorry. You are worth it."

"I'm worth killing?"

They both laughed again as he used his thumb to discreetly wipe a teardrop from the corner of his eye. "No."

He paused for a moment, scuffing his feet against the tile floor anxiously and causing long black streaks of rubber.

"There were people killed?"

She tilted her head to one side, her eyes filling full of sympathy and regret as her hair tumbled out onto her shoulders. She almost didn't want to actually respond, but knew that he needed for her to. Needed for her to make it real for him. "Yeah."

"Dammit," he spat, pounding his fist against the bed table as he bit down on his lip and turned away from her. He had more words, worse words, but dared not say them now. Not in front of her. "Where's Mike?" he asked finally, trying to get his mind off the fact she'd just laid on him.

"He's five rooms over. He should be waking up soon and they say I'll be able to see him when he does."

"That's great. Uh, if you don't mind, what'd I do to him?"

"You slit his heel, scratched his face up a bit. Thing is, the heel cut was in the *exact* place as the last one. I'm sorry, Xander, but I only know one person who could do that."

He put his head down on her hands. Then raised it again after a moment, blackness whipping at his eyes. When he spoke his voice was filled with knowledge, like a light had just flickered to life inside his head. "I know two."

Cathy looked confused, hearing the difference from *too* to *two*. "Who's the other?" He glared at her in anger for a moment, but soon she realized he wasn't angry at her. His grip tightened around her hand, until she had to pull it away. "Xander?"

"Adam Genblade," he said finally between clenched teeth, slapping his knees and jumping to his feet.

"Xander!" she called after him. "Where are you going?"

"I'm gonna check on Mike and then I'm going to pay a visit to the penitentiary."

"Xander..."

He walked to the door and opened it, and was immediately bombarded with bright flashes and loud voices. The shock almost made the Womb surge, his pupils expanding rather than dilating, but he kept it under control. Reporters bombarded him with questions, as he tried to force the door closed again. One, wearing a classic looking beige trench coat and a less-traditional black baseball cap, slipped thru and ran over to Cathy.

"Miss Kennessy!" he shouted from lips that were entirely too big for the rest of his head. "Is it true that this was a gang related attack, as the late Carl Dent suspected?"

"What?!" she said, obviously floored by the question.

"Do you think that this is a copycat killer?..."

"Excuse..."

"... or that Genblade was innocent of his crimes?"

"...huh?"

At the mere mention of Genblade's name, Xander felt his blood rush to his cheeks. He walked over and grabbed the reporter by the scruff of his jacket. "That's just about enough, buddy."

"Hey," said the reporter, shrugging Xander off of him. "I've got first amendment rights here."

"Who the hell do you think you are?"

"Xander, this really isn't..." Cathy started.

"Thomas Drake. Beach News Daily." he said, wedging an open palm between he and Xander.

"Interesting," Xander nodded sarcastically, pulling Drake toward the door with enough force that his feet beat against the tile.

Drake slapped Xander's arms away from him, a haughty look of disgust sneering onto his face. Smirking smugly, he turned back toward Cathy.

Xander shoved him, hard. He hit the wall, then slipped and fell on his ass, his head knocking back into the stucco. He reached back, pushing the strands of his thinning hair aside and feeling the tiny droplets of blood that were rising to the surface of his dandruff-ridden skin. "Xander, huh? I remember you. You're that kid Dent thought was behind all the murders. Apparently it all came back to you."

Xander smirked. "Good thing Genblade confessed."

"Yeah," he smiled, dragging out each syllable. "Weren't you even at the crime scene when White arrested him?"

"I was kidnapped by Genblade."

"That's what they say," he whispered, leaning in close. "But maybe... just maybe... we aren't looking at a copycat after all. Maybe we're looking at the real deal that just never got caught."

Xander laughed, trying to hide his nervousness. "Then why would Genblade admit guilt?" His eyes kept darting to the floor, instinctively avoiding Drake's.

"Because Dent was right. It is a gang, and you're the leader. Genblade said what he said to protect your ass," he said it in a way that was half mocking, half serious, and Xander wasn't sure exactly how he meant it. His was annoying and had a high-pitched voice, and reminded him of Mr. McGee from *The Incredible Hulk*.

"Okay, that's enough," he said, grabbing Drake by the shirt collar again and throwing him out the door. Xander heard him utter a swear as all of the cameras again snapped away.

265

"Hey Mike," Xander said, entering through the window, having decided it was the best way to avoid the media vultures outside. As bleak as Cathy's room had been, Mike's was worse. There was no color, only a few glow-in-the-dark stars tacked on the ceiling by some previous tenant, and even their arrangement seemed somehow depressing.

Mike stayed tight lipped and looked away.

"I'm sorry. You know I didn't try it."

"But," Mike interrupted. "It had to come from somewhere, didn't it? You had to have had some hidden desire to hurt me, or Cathy, right?"

"No, it doesn't work like..."

"How can we be sure?" he interrupted, his voice angry and wet. "Or how can Cathy and I even be sure that if it was true that you'd tell us?"

"Mike, I..."

He tried to continue, but it was like his mind wouldn't create words. Mike opened his mouth to interject, but no sound came from there either. After a moment, they both sighed in unison.

"Fuck," Xander said after a few minutes of awkward silence, rubbing the bridge of his nose and willing his tear ducts not to fill.

"Look," Mike sighed, flapping down his hand as though he were literally laying down the grudge he'd been carrying for almost a month. "I know that you - -"

"Stop," Xander said in his cold, blunt voice, raising a hand to punctuate his words. "I don't deserve forgiveness. Not from you."

Mike frowned, shooting him a look. "Wasn't going to. It's just frustrating to know what's doing this and not be able to do anything about it. It's like trying to hit a target that vanishes every time your finger touches the trigger."

"Tell me about it," he nodded, collapsing into the chair next to him as his mind ventured back to think of his father's revolver, still laying on his bedroom floor amidst the charred carpet.

There was a long silence.

"So what's the plan?" Mike asked after a minute or two.

"I'm going to make sure Genblade had nothing to do with this."

"And if he did?"

Xander paused, looking down at the floor. When he turned back and met his friends' gaze his eyes were so cold and full of hate that it was no longer hard for him to see the connection between him and the Black Womb. "If he did I'm going to undo the mistake I made back at Engen when I *didn't* rip his heart out."

Thomas Drake gripped the leather steering wheel of his bright red Porsche until the joints of his fingers ached, his trimmed nails leaving eight tiny half-moon indentations in the Suede. This car was the only thing his ex-wife had let him keep when they'd gotten a divorce and the only thing he had *wanted* to keep. She'd told him that he'd bought the car to make up for his penis and now she didn't have any use for either, something that rang in his ears every time he slid the key into the ignition, making it harder to enjoy the fall rides with the windows down that he used to crave to-and-from assignments. Right now the memory only served to agitate him further than he already was, his loose cheeks turning a bright, livid red.

He glared at the entrance to the hospital as the other journalists slowly started to trickle out, some alone and some getting into their cars in pairs, breaking his gaze only once to glance at the fuzzy white die that hung from his rearview mirror. Some of them were laughing, the smiles on their faces big enough to see all their teeth as they slapped each other heartily, one howling so hard that he looked like he was having trouble catching his breath.

At our most paranoid and vulnerable moments we think that everyone's talking about us. From his vantage point at the other side of the parking lot, Drake could not hear what his colleagues were saying, but he could guess. When someone got even a little bit of an edge on the competition in any field, it immediately made you a target for every half-assed remark or jeer people thought of, even if there wasn't a good reason for them.

Being tossed out of a hospital room by a teenage boy was a good reason.

He could still hear them chuckling as he had gotten to his feet, and the way that sound had grown by the time he had gotten to the end of the hall. He could feel Xander's thin, steely fingers wrapped around his collar before shoving him into the door. Could see a wide-eyed insanity that scared him lying just beyond the anger he'd been expecting to see in the boy's bluish-green eyes. He grimaced when he remembered the tiny smear of blood that had been on his fingers when he'd touched the back of his head. The stain from where he'd wiped it was still a dark crimson line on the leg of his pants.

Fuck! he cursed inwardly, gritting his teeth as he slammed his palm against the wheel. The horn sounded briefly from the sudden impact, but nobody seemed to notice. He let out a sigh, then slammed the wheel at least thirty more times. "Fuck!" he said out loud, forcing himself to re-grip the wheel before he did damage to it. He let out a long breath, his cheeks shaking back and forth violently as his fat lower lip made a sputtering sound like a small motor revving.

He leaned his head forward until his forehead rested between his two hands against the wheel, taking another deep breath as some of the scarlet started to drain from his cheeks. *That God-damned kid*, he thought, reminding himself of one of the over-the-top villains from Scooby Doo. The image of himself in a large Halloween mask being confronted by four hippies and their dog brought a smile to his face and helped him relax a little. *One quote from Kennessy would have made this story soar. Would have made it jerk at the heartstrings of every teenage girl and little old lady from here to Timbuktu. She's the perfect little victim. Sticking a knife through Miss America wouldn't get as many results; it's perfect. 'Crazed killer tried to take a slice out of American Sweetie-Pie'. It's the thing Pulitzer was made for. The type of thing that movie studios would bend-over backwards to take off your hands. Without her input, it doesn't have that same tug. Like the kid on the milk carton. Everyone feels bad for the kid whose picture's on the milk carton. But if they just told you about the miss-ing kid, people wouldn't even read it. You need their picture, their words... something to make the idiots reading it think they know this person. That it could have been someone they know. Their daughter, their sister, their...*

He pictures Xander's stubborn gaze again as he slammed Drake into the wall. It interrupted all other thought and made him jolt back off of the wheel as though he'd just awoken from some nightmare. Wincing, he reached around and felt the back of his head again. It was still moist, the hair around the bump pointed and hard like it had been gelled. A stinging sensation throbbed through his skull as his fingers connected with something damp and when he brought his hand back around, there was more blood on it. Less than the first time, but it was still there.

He stared at it for a minute, looking too watery to be the blood he was used to seeing in the movies, before wiping it into his pants. Squinting, he tried to think of another angle to go from now that his story lacked a quote from Ken-nessy.

Once again, Xander's blue eyes flashed over his memory like a strobe light. How the boy's lips had curled when he'd forced him into the wall. He was so full of hate, even though he hadn't done anything *that* bad. It was like that hate was always there, just waiting to come out.

A slow smile started to spread over Drake's face, as a new story started to fall into place inside his mind. Bracing himself against the wheel, he took a quick glance around and then slammed his head back against the seat, hissing as sharp pain pinched at him and his ears started to ring. He bit his lip to muffle the grunts, then slammed his head back again against the firm leather. And again. And again. He did it eight more times before stopping, when he couldn't take the constant throbbing anymore and his brain felt like mush.

Again he brought his hand to the back of his head and when he brought it back there was more blood then there had been even when the wound was fresh. He thought he even felt a tiny trickle tickling its way down his spine. Smiling, he wiped the blood away again then started the car and pulled out of the park-ing lot.

After all, he couldn't go back to his editor with nothing.

"Genblade, you got a visitor," the guard said in a gruff voice, one hand resting nervously on the revolver strapped to his side. Behind him, four other guards stood at attention against the wall. Beads of sweat rolled down their fore-heads into their eyes and made them itch, but they did not move. Did not twitch. Didn't do anything except watch Genblade.

When he'd first arrived a few weeks ago, he'd tried to escape. Genblade had pulled a guard's head through the bars of his cell and twisted it off. Then he'd kept the head in the cell with him and used it for a toilet for two hours until the guards shot him full of drugs in order to retrieve it while he was in an uncon-scious stupor.

After that, the warden had moved Genblade to a special needs cell and had requested extra guards. Billing finally approved it from the fall budget. Now he was under constant supervision by five full-time guards twenty-four hours a day.

His room had been padded until recently, everything having been stripped from it so that nothing could be used as a weapon. His bathroom was a hole in the center of his floor that dropped eight feet before becoming pipes. His bed was a spring-less mattress that had been bolted to the floor from the underside. He was fed from outside the cage by a bowl welded to a ten foot long pole.

For a moment Genblade did not move, just stared blankly at the wall of his cell as he almost always did.

The guard frowned, shuffling his feet and getting ready to join the others against the wall when Genblade did not respond.

Finally, he acknowledged that the guard had spoken, turning his head toward him. The motion was slow and unnatural, turning just a little further than any normal person should have been able to. His eyes were wild and crazy. "A visitor? For li'l ol' me?" he exclaimed in a mock-southern accent. He smiled wide and sinister, showing all of his teeth. It chilled all the guards to the marrow, each one of them sharpened to needlepoint. "Well, I wonder who it could be?"

⋏⋏

Xander heard the stuttered rapping of his nails against the desk he sat behind, gnawing at the inside of his cheek as he stared into the glare of the plate glass. On some level he was aware of the sound his nails were making, but could not have stopped it if he had tried. In fact, he had all but lost motor control in his right hand from the elbow down.

His eyes were locked on the vault-like steel door that stood a few feet beyond the other side of the glass. It stuck out like a postulant sore against the cracked plaster and chipped paint that dotted the walls around it.

Shunk. Genblade stabbed Xander in the arm. The creature's head raised, fully awake for the first time in several moments and really listening now, wanting to scream but unable to make the right sound.

Shunk. He stabbed it through the other arm.

Shunk. He stabbed it through both feet, pinning them to each other and the wall.

"... Nobody, I repeat, nobody escapes death."

Genblade stepped back and admired his work. Black Womb stood there, his body pinned into a cross position.

Xander's mind reeled. He couldn't focus on anything, his vision was blurry, and black around the edges. He felt the healing factor cut out. He lifted his head to face his attacker.

"A crucifixion," Genblade sneered, stroking his chin as he admired his work. "It'd almost be poetic, if it wasn't so damn funny."

Xander winced, slamming his open palm flat against the table to stop it from shaking.

As if on cue, something heavy slid to one side inside the door, then it began

269

to creek open. It seemed to move unbelievably slow, as though he'd stepped out of reality and into some pivotal scene within a movie. He wasn't sure if it was actually happening that way or if it was all in his head, but either way it gave him chills.

Genblade stepped out of the bright light that illuminated from beyond the door, shimmering off the shoulders of his prison jumpsuit as he was led to his chair on the other side of the glass from Xander. Chains bound his hands and feet close together, an extra one holding both sets together so that he could not raise his hands over his head to strike.

At the sight of his twisted smile, pointed nose and wild blue eyes, Xander's skin set on edge as though it were ready to leap from the chair and flee at any given moment, with or without the rest of his body in tow. Deep in his right side, the mass of grey flesh and black ooze that made up the Womb organ surged and convulsed until it felt like it had jumped up into his throat. It sent hormones and testosterone shooting throughout his system, screaming at him to smash through the inch-thick glass and rip Genblade's head from his shoulders. Despite his urge to end it now, he swallowed it back.

Genblade smiled, his shoulders moving up and down in a snicker rendered soundless by the glass. It was unendingly creepy. He stared at Xander through the glass with those pale blue eyes, sizing him up. Smirking, he picked up the white stained phone alongside his cubicle and put it to his ear.

For a moment, it occurred to Xander that he could just turn, leave, and not look back. Forcing control, he picked up the phone and clenched it against the side of his face.

"How ya been, buddy?" Genblade said in a shrill, condescendingly cruel voice. "Long time no see."

At the sound of his voice Xander was there again. He was nailed to the stainless steel walls of Alpha Quadrant, blood pouring out of his veins into a drain in the center of the floor. He could smell the coppery tang as it overtook him. He could feel Genblade driving knives through his wrists, legs and stomach.

"So," Genblade said, taking pleasure in the pained look on Xander's face, "to what do I owe the pleasure?"

Xander stared silently into the glass, squinting in contempt. He clamped the phone tight until he heard the plastic crack.

Genblade heard the snap on the other end of the line and smiled. "So, how's the family? Mike... Cathy... Sara?"

Xander furrowed his brow even more, his eyes barely visible as he stared down the person who had haunted his memories for weeks now.

"Oh, wait, that's right," Genblade chuckled, pantomiming slapping himself on the forehead. "You're down to a threesome now. Sorry."

"You won't get to me like that, Genblade," Xander drawled, finally speaking.

"Sure. Why your pupils getting so bulgy, then? Light bothering you?"

Xander turned away for a moment, swallowing hard to force the Womb away. He could control it, at least for now. After a second he looked back, his eyes returned to normal. "What can you tell me about the Black Womb?"

270

Genblade tilted his head to one side, grinning slightly as he tried to figure out why his sparring partner was here. After a moment his eyes became wide and his smile grew. "I don't know anything you don't already know. We done?"

Xander rolled his eyes, then leaned in close to the glass. He forced a cruel grin onto his face and whispered into the phone. "The itsy bitsy *Spider* went up the water spout..."

Now Genblade clutched the phone, clicking his tongue against the roof of his mouth. "You never did answer my question," he said after a second's pause, changing the topic with only the slightest trace of frustration. "To what do I owe the pleasure?"

"Some weird shit happened last night," he answered finally, leaning back against his chair and doing his best to appear casual. "The cops say we're looking at a copycat killer, but I wasn't as sure. Came to make sure the man I put behind bars was still there."

Genblade harked out an honest laugh, slapping himself against the knee and making his chains rattle. "Ha! I wish I were out. Man, that'd be a good time." He leaned in close to the glass just as Xander had a moment ago. "First I'd go up to good-old Coral Beach Square and paint the town *red* with your blood. Really see how good that healing power of yours is. Then I'd finally off that loser friend of yours. And Cathy... well, it'd be fun, lemme tell ya. I am a widower now, after all. I think she could provide hours of comfort... days even."

Xander felt hot blood rush to his face even as he tried to block out the visuals Genblade was making for him. "So you had absolutely nothing to do with last night?"

"Sorry, pal," he remarked slyly. "Wish I could tell you different."

"Thanks," Xander snapped sarcastically, rolling his eyes.

"Hey," Genblade cut in, his tone deadly serious for the first time since the call began. "Don't take that tone here. You think you're better than me because I'm a killer? That's rich, from you."

"Not the same."

"Everyone's a killer, kid. Every person on this planet, their first act of life is to out swim ten thousand other sperm, all for a fucking woman. Just living means you've already killed thousands. So don't act like you're better than me."

Xander looked as though he were about to respond, then stopped, unable to think of anything to say that would combat Genblade's warped logic. Frowning, he took the phone away from his ear and started to place it on the receiver.

"Hey!" Genblade screamed, his voice ringing out over the line. "Don't worry about me, buddy! I'll be out of here in no time!"

Eyes wide with shock, Xander slowly brought the phone back to his face. "What do you mean? They can't let you out."

"Sure can. Pretty soon I'll never have to see this place again. Ain'tcha heard? I've been given the death penalty for 'my' crimes," he spat harshly, his voice thick with sarcasm as he hung up the line.

The glass door slammed shut behind Xander, its dull thud echoing around his head as he stepped out into the fall air. The sun shone directly onto his face as a cool breeze ripped at him. He barely noticed either. His eyes were wide and unblinking as he started to walk down the gravel trail to the main drag, feeling each step resonate through his body like a shockwave. Everything felt harder, sharper... more *real* than it had before he'd gone in. For the first few feet he was completely devoid of any thought at all, his brain refusing to do anything else until it processed what it had just heard.

Genblade is going to die, he thought as soon as he was able to. He was almost in the parking lot now and already his legs ached from the movement. Just the act of filing the information away had exhausted him, body and soul.

"Genblade - - is going to die," he said aloud, shifting the emphasis of the sentence around to try and force it to make sense. It didn't work well.

He spun around suddenly on the asphalt of the lot, slamming his fist down on the hood of a nearby car before even he knew what he was doing. The white metal hood of the police cruiser compacted in under the weight of his fist. He stared at it for a moment, his eyes singeing with fury, before he finally blinked and let sanity return to his face. Looking around to make sure nobody had seen him, he turned and walked quickly toward Laird Street.

Goddamn it, he cursed inwardly, his train of thought finally beginning to chug down the tracks again. *God fucking damn it!*

His hand still throbbed violently and he ground his teeth together to steel against the pain.

Genblade was the one thing I still have to cling to in all this mess. As long as he's alive I can say that I didn't *kill him back at Engen. That I still had some small touch of humanity, whatever that meant.* He paused, gazing down at his open-palmed hand. Slits slowly appeared on the tips of each finger, dribbling blood trails as dark talons poked their way out. *I can say that I'm not a monster.*

Now that's changed, he thought bitterly, shoving his hand back into his pocket. *If Genblade's killed for my crimes, then I may as well have done the deed myself. It'll be another death on my hands.*

I can't have that.

The worst part is Genblade probably doesn't even deserve the death penalty. Locked away forever, maybe, but not death. I should probably be the one getting the chair. I'm the one with the double-digit death count.

He paused and waited for a large truck to pass, then started walking down Laird Street. Genblade's words still rang in his ears as if they'd just been spoken, no matter how hard he tried to block them out. *Fuck. Much as I hate to say it, I need Genblade. Alive. With everything that's happened in the past few weeks, he may well be the only person who understands what's happening to me. He may be all I have left. God help me, that sick son-of-a-bitch is all I have left.*

He stopped again as he saw a red dress that looked like the one Sara had worn to the prom. It captivated his attention momentarily, until he forced himself to look away.

The only question now is: what am I going to do about it?

Don Smith got up from his desk and hurried over to the city room photocopier. He put a sheet on it and pressed on. Several sheets spat out of the already failing machine before it made a loud, grinding noise. Don looked at the old control panel. It said *toner low*. But then, it always said that. He re-opened the top and took his sheet out. He'd just take it down to his editor manually. The sheet read 'WHO IS THE CORAL BEACH MURDERER?' and was followed by a long article showing police suspects from the original massacre that were still alive today, quotes from various psychiatrists around the city that specialized in the criminal mind, and other tidbits of information. Don thought this was it. His provocative analysis of the criminal psyche and their motives would win him the editor's attention.

If not a Pulitzer.

He marched across the office and approached Tom Drake's desk. He always dreaded this. Drake always looked at him, his smile wide and fake. He'd ask, "How's everything buddy? About to uncover that big story?" - as if he was a little kid on his mother's old typewriter. He slowly turned his head to look in the office, preparing himself for Drake's grossly sarcastic attitude. He turned to face him, preparing a fake smile to rival even his. The cubical was empty. If Don knew Drake (and he wished that he didn't), at this time of day he was always either in his cubical... or in the editor's office giving a pitch.

Don ran through the rest of his cubical, waving his paper high above his head like a flag as he went. He got to the editor's office at the end of the hall. He opened the door only a crack when he heard it.

"...and then he threw me out of her hospital room! I'm sure I'm close, John! We've got a solid lead here."

Don's head hung. Drake had beaten him to the punch once again. He opened the door regardless. "Sir!" he said, trying his best to inspire enthusiasm in his employer. "I've got a list of possible suspects and professionally credited motives to the murders!"

John Tyler looked up from his desk, snatching the paper from Don's hands and read through it. "This is great, Don!"

"Really, sir?" Don repeated, astonished.

"Yeah. This'll make a great add-on to Drake's story. It even supports his theory. Good work, Smith!"

"Yeah, good work," Drake mimicked, closing the door in Don's stunned face. When the door was closed, he turned to John and rolled his eyes. "You may have broken this story wide open," he laughed, grabbing the paper and tossing it to one side.

CHAPTER FOUR: HOSPITAL FOOD

Mike Harris had always hated hospital food.

It came in lumps or squares and it never tasted exactly like it was supposed to. The food had a texture and a taste like styrofoam, as though it had been partially dehydrated. The worst part was, most of the time he didn't even get what he wanted. If he circled meal 'A', they'd give him meal 'B'. Once or twice he'd tried to cheat this jinx by ordering meal B... It had been the one and only time they had actually given him what had been circled. As revolting as the meal in front of him was, at the moment it didn't matter.

Cathy Kennessy lifted the grey plastic cover off of her desert dish, revealing a lime green substance. "You know what's really interesting about hospital Jell-O?" she asked as she chewed on her chicken, which was probably the only thing on her dinner plate that *didn't* taste like chicken, including the Jell-O itself.

"This is Jell-O?" Mike replied, poking at the green jiggling food. "Dear God."

"Yes, it is. The weird thing is, you're never really sure which fruit is inside it. Unless its banana, which I think is quite universal." She lifted her dish and brought the green cubes up to eye-level, poking them to make them jiggle about like blubber. The more she stared at it, the more convinced she became that these were not bananas. It looked more like a malformed cross between pineapple and peaches. It may have been kiwi.

"Yeah, I think maybe it's peach. But that isn't the point," he said, finishing off the last of his mashed potatoes.

"What is it then?" she asked in response, tilting her head back and dropping a cube past her ruby lips.

"How is that *Jell-O*? I thought for sure frozen applesauce, but *Jell-O*? ..."

"Hush," she said, picking up a cube of Jell-O between her thumb and forefinger. "Taste."

He opened his mouth and she carefully placed it onto his tongue. He swished it around in his mouth for a moment before finally swallowing with a gulp. "Uh-huh," he said, nodding his head once.

"What?" she asked, grinning. "It's definitely peach."

They both laughed and she pinched at his sides playfully. He winced, laughing through the slight nipping pain.

She leaned in quickly and kissed him.

He kissed her back, laughing.

ᚳᚹ

The Factory was dead that night, vacant of the usual chaotic and constant spin of teenagers coming and going. There were still sights and sounds in every corner and against every wall, but they all tended to drone into white noise and go unnoticed.

Without the buzz of life, it seemed a much more depressing place than Xander remembered. When he, Mike and Cathy would stay up until 3am playing video games and talk about what they'd done all day. Now they only served to remind him of what he was and what he had done to them and everyone else around him.

"Lord, you're depressing," Sara said, walking over to him with an orange tray loaded down with a large plate of fries. To some, fries were just a snack food, but to her they were a full-course meal. They were loaded down with cheese, bacon bits, green onion, onion and sour cream. The sight of it made Xander urge every time she took a bite, washing it down with a large slurp of watered-down cola. "What the hell do I have to do to get you out of this funk?"

Xander smiled at the memory just as he had at the time, a sly grin twitching at the left side of his face. "I can think of a few things," he whispered aloud, leering playfully at the vacant seat across from him.

She tossed a cheese-spattered fry at him and he moved quickly to dodge the gooey projectile, letting it sail into someone else's table. "Jerk," she said simply as she continued her meal, a spiteful look on her face.

His grin widened.

"Seriously though, whatever's wrong, do you really think that sitting here with me moping about it is going to fix anything?" she asked, staring at him knowingly from beneath her blonde bangs.

"Might," he said aloud again, keeping his voice low. He could almost see her in his minds eye now. Could smell the rotten mess that she called food. "I'm scared. Scared to move, scared to think... feel like no matter what I do'll be the wrong answer."

"Probably true," she nodded, frowning at him.

He shot her a quizzical look, but did not respond.

"But that's a good thing. I mean, if every answer is going to end up bad anyway, it takes the pressure off. You can just do what you feel. Sure you'll get beat down, but no more than you would if you didn't do what you feel... gotta take your satisfactions somewhere, y'know."

He nodded, stroking his chin with his thumb and index finger as he did. No matter how he thought about it, Genblade was just as much a link to his sanity as Mike and Cathy were. He had made the choice not to kill him, despite what he had done to Sara. *I chose to let him live. That's not something I can back away from now.* He thought, the memory of Sara still playing out before him as she lifted her head up to get all of the cheese literally melting off the fry she was holding. "Thanks," he said finally, his smile more genuine now.

"No problem. If I can patch up Grendel and Peterson, I can- -"

"Hey, Drew," came a voice from behind Xander, just as a heavy hand fell onto his shoulder.

He jumped in his chair, almost falling off it as he lost the memory and snapped back to reality, his mind momentarily fizzed by the jolt in perception. All at once the sounds of The Factory that he'd been sifting out into white noise came crashing back, like an avalanche of commotion. He turned around bitterly, his face drawled up in a scowl. "What?" he snapped at the person behind him, standing up as he did so.

Derek raised his hands in the air and backed up a pace, his thin eyebrows shooting upwards and his mouth curling into a letter O. "Sorry, man. Didn't mean to interrupt your teatime there."

Xander stopped, closed his eyes, then sighed. Slowly, he let a smile perk back onto his lips. "Sorry. M'in a mood, it's a thing. Not your fault."

Derek grinned, his shocked expression mellowing down to his usual stoic eyes and comedic grin. "What's got your panties in a bunch? I thought I heard Mike and Cat were gonna be okay?"

He nodded slowly, the smell of the poutine that hadn't even really existed still fresh in his nostrils. "Yeah," he said finally, forcing a smile. "Yeah, I guess you're right. Probably nothing."

Derek's grin grew so wide that it didn't seem natural, as though someone had sliced it onto his face. "Good," he said, slapping his hand down onto the man's shoulder again and giving it a friendly squeeze. "Saw you comin' in here from across the street," he said, jutting his thumb over his shoulder in the direction of his house. "Couldn't figure why you were comin' over all by your lonesome. Thought you might wanna get some food or something?"

His smile was contagious, and after a moment Xander didn't have to fake his own anymore. "Sure," he said, chuckling as he motioned to Roxanne that he wanted to place an order. "Let's get a couple of fries with everything. On me."

"Thought you hated those," Derek shrugged as the two of them walked towards the counter.

"They grow on you."

Two-hundred and forty-eight dollars.

That was the take-home amount that Clarence Fisher drew every week for thirty-eight hours work as a security guard at Coral Beach Penitentiary. Thirty-eight hours, not forty. If he worked just two hours more a week, he would be eligible for medical benefits, insurance and be guaranteed a raise once every six months. Even though two hours didn't sound like much to him, it apparently made all the difference to the people that signed his paychecks because he'd never managed to get any more than an extra hour out of them. If he complained too much, he often found his hours slightly reduced for the next week and had learned to just leave well enough alone.

He contemplated leaving more than once, usually after pulling the short straw and having to do janitorial duties on the cells. Overall though, he was happy enough at his job. He got to pick his start times most of the time, got every second weekend off and got to chat with other guards all day. Most of the time, the job involved just sitting and waiting for nothing to happen. He'd caught up on a lot of reading since he started here and if worse came to worse, he always had his Gameboy. Sometimes, when he got really fed up with the job, his friends would remind him that he'd be doing a lot more for a lot less at any shopping mall or fast-food joint around. All in all, the minuscule pay seemed worth it.

Last month, that changed.

The Pen had been assigned a new inmate, a high profile one at that, forcing shifts to change and more staff to be hired on to accommodate the extra manpower needed to deal with him. Clarence had even finally been offered his much-coveted full time position, but had turned it down almost instantly. Suddenly, the risk no longer seemed worth the reward.

Clarence stared vacantly into Adam Genblade's cell, watching his shoulders rise and fall every time he took a deep breath. A shiver ran down his back as he watched, even though he felt warm and there were great circles of nervous sweat forming under each of his arms, staining his bright blue uniform a deep navy. He didn't want to look at him, yet couldn't turn away even when he focused all his energies on it. Wiping a speck of drool from the corner of his mouth, he waited anxiously for Genblade to move. To do something.

Genblade sat cross-legged on his mattress, the cold from the concrete floor making it one of the most unbearable places to sleep imaginable. He stared at the wall with a blank look in his eyes, just as he had been for hours ever since that visitor had come to see him. He seemed to fixate on one point on the wall, burning a hole into it with his eyes. A small sliver of warm drool oozed its way past his jagged teeth and onto his chin, rolling down his face, then hanging for a moment before finally dropping onto the floor with a quiet plop.

From out here he looked harmless, or even helpless. If Clarence hadn't seen the photos of what he had done himself, he wouldn't have believed it. This monster had killed children. Dozens of them, resulting in almost eight liters of blood on the walls at the Grendel home, so much that the family had to move. He had read once that serial killers as demented as this were often cold and emotionless. That, at least, he could have understood if not condoned. But this monster, when he did choose to speak, was filled with a kind of gleeful fascination. Like a child playing a new game.

"What the fuck is that guy doing?" a skinny guard with blonde hair remarked, stroking his unshaven chin as he eyed the inmate.

Clarence nearly jumped out of his skin, his hand immediately clutching his heart as it started to throb violently. After a moment he let out a sigh of relief, forcing a jittery smirk.

"A little high-strung are we?"

"Forgot you were there, Rudy," Clarence laughed, taking a deep breath. "What were you saying?"

Rudy motioned towards Adam Genblade again, his upper lip curling noticeably when he did. "This fuck in here. The whole goddamn departments bending over backwards to make sure he don't move a muscle. All the men we hired on and now I can't pick shifts anymore. Had to hire someone to look after T.J. when Janet's working. All because of that fuck in there."

Clarence's gaze went from Rudy to Genblade (who had just taken another of those large lungfuls of air) and then back again. "He's a child killer, Rudy. What do you expect?"

"Oh, for god's sake!" he scoffed, leaning in for a better look at the killer. His fingers weren't even moving like they had been an hour ago. "He looks like he hasn't had a coherent thought in hours. How in god's name does a loser like that rate all these guards?"

"Rud - -"

"Watch," Rudy interjected, raising a finger for pause before bending down and picking up two small pebbles from the floor. Craning his head around Clarence to make sure nobody was coming, he leaned in close to the cell, holding one of the small stones between his thumb and forefinger. He tossed it, watching as it bounced harmlessly off of the mattress and onto the floor.

"Come on, Rudy," Clarence urged, nudging his friend's shoulder, "Give it a rest."

"No, watch," Rudy chuckled, fingering the second stone. "I'm gonna prove to you how bullshit this is. Watch." He closed one eye as he aimed, the tip of his tongue sticking out the side of his mouth ever so slightly. After a few phantom swings he let the tiny projectile go, flying through the air in a wide arch and bouncing off of Adam Genblade's right cheek.

Both men watched with anticipation as they waited for some sign of movement or reaction.

After a few seconds, another glob of saliva dripped from his chin and plopped into the puddle on the floor.

"Fuck," Clarence sighed, allowing himself a laugh as he started breathing again.

"See? What'd I tell you?" Rudy grinned, turning toward his friend and shrugging childishly.

"Still man, it does look like the D.A. is gonna be pushing for death row. Never know what someone that desperate might do."

"If he's that bad then someone should just take him out back and shoot him. Solve all our -"

Rudy stopped in mid-sentence, his lower jaw trembling.

It took less than a second for Clarence's mind to process what had happened.

Genblade gripped Rudy's wrist from inside the cell, slowly pressing his palm against Rudy's elbow until it snapped back the opposite way. The sound of cartilage cracking echoed through the halls for a brief moment before being drowned out by Rudy's screams.

"Jesus!" Clarence screamed, jumping backwards eight paces before reaching for his Taser.

Genblade smiled, licking his jagged teeth and then squirting the blood from his tongue out from between pale, cracked lips. He pulled on the guard's arm more, making him to scream loudly as tears started to roll down his face. His mouth was opened so wide that Clarence could barely see anything else on his face.

Genblade closed his eyes, as if enjoying the sound. He looked like some aristocrat listening to old vinyl's of Beethoven or Chopin. A warm smile spread across his lips as he opened his eyes, locking them with Clarence's.

Clarence pressed his back further against the wall. The Taser still trembled in his hands, but he would not move close enough to use it. Could not have even if he had wanted to. His legs felt like they had bags of cement tied to them. The only things he could feel were those eyes that had been burning a hole into the wall of the cell for the past three hours now burning a hole deep into his soul.

More guards came running down the corridor, training their rifles on Genblade's head.

He barely noticed them at first, instead staring directly at Clarence as he pulled on Rudy's fractured limb once more, eliciting another high-pitched wail and causing Rudy's shoulder to squeeze in through the tightly spaced bars. He watched as Clarence's face winced but did not blink or turn away, even though the man did nothing to stop it.

It was like he was testing his limits.

Rudy's skin began to split at the shoulder as it pulled itself out of socket, blood staining his clean uniform. The guards prepared to fire, aiming at the grinning gargoyle that was Genblade. He caught the glimmer of a shotgun barrel in his peripheral vision, then turned toward them as if only now noticing their presence. He gave Rudy one final, powerful tug before letting go and retreating to the corner.

Rudy fell limp against the bars and one of the guards rushed to him, placing two fingers against the nape of his neck to get a pulse.

"I think he'll be okay," he said, hoisting him to his feet as they helped him towards the infirmary.

Clarence stayed pressed against the wall, finally letting his Taser slip from his fingers and clamber to the ground.

Genblade curled into a ball facing the corner, rocking back and forth like a small child being punished by a teacher with a dunce cap on. Suddenly he burst into an insane fit of laughter, turning to face Clarence. His cobalt eyes seeming to glow under the flourescent lights. The hairs of Clarence's neck stood on end as he slowly moved away from the cell, his back still against the wall until it was out of view. He felt another cold shiver, even as Genblade's hysterical laughter echoed throughout the building, his smile wide and fierce.

He decided working at the mall would be worth the pay cut.

Roxanne watched Xander leave the Factory as she wiped their table of gravy and melted cheese with a rag she'd pulled from her apron. It was closing in on dusk now and she guessed that she'd seen the last of the teenage crowd for the night, not that there had been many of them anyway. Randy Owchar and Calla McFadden had stumbled in stoned and loaded while Xander and Derek had been playing video games, but they'd sucked down their burgers in a heartbeat before leaving again. Calla had gazed at her with paranoid fear in her eyes more than once.

She'd felt like telling the child that in this town, getting caught being stoned was the least of your worries if you were out after dark.

She glanced at her watch and frowned. In about an hour and thirty minutes the college crowd would show up. They'd order pretentious drinks and throw things around when they were watching the game on the big screen and start fights. She sighed, her smile fading into a frown as she wondered if she'd have to call the cops on any of them again tonight. Last week had been like that, when one girl wouldn't stop causing a fuss over someone hitting on her boyfriend. Or it could have been the other way around, she wasn't completely sure.

Grinding her teeth, she started to pump her arm faster to try and work a glob of hardened cheese out of the porous plastic table.

"Sorry about that," came a friendly sounding voice from ahead of her. That didn't matter much around here though, she'd found the best-sounding of the college crew were often the worst-tempered.

She looked up and saw Derek grinning down at her, one hand shoved into his jean pocket.

She didn't smile back, just let out a huff as she pushed a lock of her curly red hair from her face.

"You need any help?" he asked, gesturing toward the table.

She rolled her eyes at him, allowing herself a brief smirk before wiping it away. She couldn't let herself be smiling when the older crowd came in. With them, a smile just made you a target. "Thanks hun, but I'm fine. Been doing this a long while."

"Yea," Derek chuckled, nodding. "Ever since I've lived across the way, at least five years."

"Six," she said with an air of cynicism, getting the last of the cheese off the table and shoving the rag back into the belt of her apron. "Took it figuring it'd help me pay my way through University... but you know how that goes."

Derek nodded, then stopped and grinned. "Actually, no, not really."

"Right," she grinned, waving a finger at him. "High school."

"Sadly," he responded, even as he started picking up dirty plates from the table closest to him and stacking them in a little tower. "What were you going to do?"

"Hmm?"

"In University. What were you going to do?"

She paused a moment, a dirty glass still in her hand as she piled them into a grey bin. "A kindergarten teacher, actually. I don't know why, I just always loved kids."

Derek bobbed his head as he listened, bringing his leaning tower of plates over and laying them carefully in the bin.

"I like how eager they are to learn at that age... you know? No offense, but kids your age would rather be anywhere than in the classroom. I don't envy the teachers who have to deal with it."

"Me either," he agreed, thinking of the number of times he'd given Mr. Miles a hard time in the past few years. He was actually fairly certain that he was the reason the old Brit was growing grey. "So, what happened?"

"Well, you know," she shrugged. "Bills, really. First it was full-time school with a part-time job. Then I needed more money, so it became part-time school with a full-time job. Then I started missing classes because I was so tired, or I'd be embarrassed to go with the same assholes I'd been serving the night before...

you get the picture."

Derek sighed, putting the last of the dishes away. "Maybe someday."

The brief smile she had worn faded as she stared off into nothingness for a moment. She thought of the 'night crowd' that would be slowly pouring in. Somewhere in the back of her mind she got the impression that tonight wouldn't be a good night for tips. The college folk weren't likely to tip big unless they were trying to get a girl in bed. More than once, before she'd trained herself to hide her smile, that girl had been her. But she'd found that the guys actually worth going home with had a tendency to forget her name the next time they came in. She eyed Derek up and down, realizing that for all his sweetness he'd probably be another one of them in just a few short years.

"Thanks for your help, Derek," she said in a faraway voice as she picked up the plastic bin and walked behind the counter.

Derek watched her go with a solemn look on his face, then turned and walked towards the exit.

⚔

Robert Miles ran a hand through his thinning chestnut hair, struggling to see the paper in front of him as more and more light was sapped from the room by the setting sun. The words scrawled onto the white, lined paper had become so hazy and moist that he had a hard time seeing them at all, let alone read them. Frowning, he grabbed his glasses by their golden rims and brought them into the light from the lamp, examining the tiny flecks of dirt and grime on them and wondering, not for the first time, how they had gotten there to begin with. He pulled a bright red handkerchief from the breast pocket of his suede jacket and started to rub the lenses with it vigorously, stopping once to examine the glass before wiping at it one more time and sliding them back onto his face. It was a little better, but no amount of cleaning, no matter how vigorous, could run out the effects of exhaustion and hunger.

He turned back to the paper in front of him, taking a sip from the long-cold coffee next to him on the desk as he did so. There was a slow tapping sound at the other end of the vacant classroom that made him stir his eyes away from it for a moment, gazing out upon the empty desks that stood silently in the shadows like soldiers ready to open fire on a condemned man. He watched them for a moment, then turned back to the page.

His eyes darted along the words for a moment, a smile slowly growing over his lips.

"*The Elmbert-Eaton Dynasty*," he read aloud, scanning down over the page. "Felix Mason turned on his clock radio with a sudden switch of the dial. He liked this song, had ever since he could remember, and turned the volume up... to eleven."

He wasn't sure if 'to eleven' was supposed to have been a dramatic moment in the story, but when he read it aloud he did so with a deep, monotone voice that made it sound dire. He chuckled again at the passage, skimming down through the rest and then laying it aside.

281

- tak -tapptapp- tak -

There was the sound again from just beyond the veil of shadows cutting him off from the rest of the classroom, like the old electric heaters cutting in or a drape flapping in the breeze from an open window.

But he didn't feel either the warm soothing flow of heat or the bitter chill that usually came with night air.

Miles stared into the darkness for a moment, then frowned and picked up the next sheet, and book report on *Faust* by Sara Johnson. He smiled, reaching for his red pen and circling her last name as a spelling error. For some reason the act itself made him sad, the word acting as a weight attached to his chest and bringing down his entire body.

-tak!-

"Hello?" he called out finally, standing up abruptly and letting the page fall back onto the desk.

The darkness just loomed back at him, only the desks and chairs from the first few rows visible before they became entrenched in darkness.

"Is someone there?" he called again in his thick British accent, stepping out from behind his desk with his head cocked to one side and one eyebrow thrust up into the air.

Again, there was nothing but silence in response.

Squinting his wrinkled eyes knowingly, he stopped himself from taking another step. Without removing his eyes from the dark, he reached his hand around behind him until he felt the hot plastic of the lamp, turning it quickly to shoot out a beam into the shadows.

Nothing. Nothing but the desks and chairs and one knapsack that had been left after everyone else had gone, slumped against the back wall lazily. Its strap hung out over the side, swaying back and forth gently in a breeze that Miles couldn't feel but obviously was there, making it touch the metal leg of the chair.

Miles chuckled to himself, turning away from the rest of the room when the lights came on.

"Christ," he jumped, bringing one hand to his chest. "Don't do that."

"Sorry," Principal Shnieder said gravely, visibly annoyed by the reaction. He was a short man with almost no hair and a large, red nose that Miles had always attributed to years of alcohol abuse, something that had been confirmed at last year's Christmas party when he'd gotten so plastered on Southern Comfort that he'd passed out in the host's front yard cradling a lawn gnome. "Didn't realize there was anyone else here."

"Me neither," Miles admitted, returning to his chair and trying to settle in.

"Grading papers?" Shnieder asked, stepping inside and leaning his head up a little to see what the other man was up to.

"No, not grading," he mumbled, waving Shnieder away with a flick of his hand. "Looking through some old papers."

"Why? Do we suspect the seniors are selling their old papers again?"

"No, no. Nothing like that," Miles frowned, finally picking up Sara's report

282

again. "I wanted to find a good example of each student's work. Maybe put it with their flowers at the memorial O'Toole has planned. You know, then the parents could look at what their child had achieved, maybe bring back a good memory or two."

Shnieder opened his mouth to retort, then eyed the large pile of papers just to the side of Miles' elbow. "I think that's a lovely idea," he said finally, giving his friend a curt nod.

He nodded in return, not even looking up.

"I'm going home. Be sure to lock up when you're done."

This time he did not even respond, his pupils darting over each word of the report.

- tak -tapptapp- tak -

He looked up at the bag again, staring it down for a long moment as he waited for it to make the sound again. Wanted to see it make the sound, just to quell the paranoid itch in the back of his mind. After a moment, the sway of the strap slowed... and then stopped.

He stared at it one moment longer, then started shoving papers into his briefcase one by one.

There was no reason he couldn't do this at home.

The house was quiet and empty, even though it didn't feel like it.

It never felt empty anymore, not as far as he was concerned. There was always the sound of skittering or a creaking pipe that wouldn't have been audible to anyone else in the house but was nearly deafening to him. He was never really sure if the sounds were even real or if they were all in his head, especially around this time in the evening, with his eyelids already getting heavy. He'd been sleeping more lately, and he wasn't sure if it was because his body didn't rest when the Womb ran around at night... or if the Womb was simply fighting for more of their timeshare.

Xander closed the door and slid off his sneakers and jacket, letting them fall unceremoniously to the floor before walking past the archway leading into the kitchen. There was a plate on the counter top between the fridge and the stove with a piece of paper stuck to it with scotch tape. On it was a few hunks of garlic bread and leftover chicken, the barbecue sauce on it forming a small, sticky stain in the center of the plate.

His mouth watered at the scent of it, even as he turned and looked around to make sure nobody else was home. There was an ashtray on the table that smelled like it hadn't been fed a fresh butt in hours, meaning that wherever his parents had gotten to, it wasn't close by.

Smiling, he scooped up the plate and the note attached and sat at the table in the dark of evening and started to pick at his chicken, able to see his plate less and less with every passing moment as the sun ducked down below the tree line.

Chewing the rubbery but flavorful strips of breast meat, he picked up the note between his sauce-covered fingers and brought it close to his face so that he could read it in the low-light:

Alex,

Your father and I have gone down to the hospital to visit the Kennessy's. They mentioned that you went there too, maybe see you there. If not eat the chicken and the bread, more in the fridge if you want it. Take off foil before heating. We'll probably be out late so go to bed at a decent hour, you have class tomorrow.

-Love, Mom:)

xxx ooo

He allowed himself a smile, shaking his head at the note as he laid it down on the table next to his plate. She was the only person in the world who still called him Alex.

After a moment, he ripped a chunk off of the garlic bread and popped it into his mouth, the smile fading from his lips. The room was dark now, except for the sad blue glow of twilight that touched everything with a lover's gentleness. He lay the chicken back down onto the flower-patterned plate as he started to feel the tug of that sadness, like a hook with a weight attached poked through the meat of his heart.

That tug was joined by another, more virile one from his right side. It felt like the way he imagined a baby kicking from inside you, that sudden, solid bump coming from the wrong side out. His eyes went wide as he realized that the Womb was reacting to what he was feeling.

He closed his eyes and started to think 'happy thoughts' to try and balance himself out again. He thought of Mike, Cathy and Sara and how the four of them used to have fun together late at night at the Factory before all of the Black Womb crap had started.

He remembered the way Sara had looked at him from across the pool tables, speaking volumes with her eyes. Some people spoke with their hands, some with their whole bodies... Sara Johnson talked with her eyes. One look this way or that could convey the ultimate in sadness, happiness, confusion, disbelief, or any one of a hundred other things. He remembered the way they had looked out of the balcony the night she died, right before they'd almost had their first kiss. She'd looked at him as though he was the only person in the room, and for once he'd felt like it, too. It made his lips quiver, even now.

The way Mike and Cathy would spend all night making-out when the four of them went out on Fridays, making it incredibly awkward for him and Sara if they were sitting on the other side of a booth. He remembered the way each of them had looked in the hospital, with stitches and bandages on to keep their insides from spilling out onto their outsides.

Because of *him*.

Wincing, he started to feel like he was choking, or drowning on his own blood as the black ooze worked its way up into his throat. The Womb hadn't slowed down, it had pounded harder and harder as every thought of every friend he'd ever had led to something horrible. Some terrible thing that he himself had done. The pain was twisting and grinding within the womb organ and becoming his power, the way food was turned into energy in a normal person.

For a moment, his entire world turned black as the darkness shrouded his eyes through the veins in his corneas. Then everything was illuminated with light and he could see not only the normal dim blue that he had a moment ago, but also the infrared and ultraviolet portions of the spectrum. He tried to fight it, clutching his fingers into his scalp and trying to push away the thoughts that were running through his head. He imagined the blackness turning in on itself, being crumpled into a little ball and hurled back into the depths of his bowels, willing it not to pop out into the open air.

Suddenly, as quickly as it had come over him, it recessed back to whatever hell inside him that it had come from. The blackness in his eyes faded to grey before disappearing completely and his throat was clear again.

He opened his eyes and let out a sigh of relief, then noticed the half-plate of food still in front of him. He snarled at it, picking it up and bringing it over to the trash compactor and scraped it in.

He placed the plate in the dishwasher before leaving the kitchen and heading up the stairs two at a time, casting his gaze down and away from the portraits on the wall as he did. He opened the door to his room and closed it behind him, turning each lock along the frame and then giving the door one last tug just to be sure.

His eyelids felt heavy again as he sat on the edge of the bed and started to peel off his clothes. He took off his shirt and looked down himself.

There was a long, thin line over where his appendix should have been and the Womb now was, a tiny scar on an otherwise smooth surface. Engen's scientists had given it to him while the Womb was out of him, the only one it couldn't repair quite right. He ran his finger along the bumps of it, feeling the bizarre folds of skin just beneath the surface. *The scar Alpha put there will always be on my torso, but the cuts Genblade inflicted haven't even closed yet,* he thought, glancing down at the picture of Sara in her prom dress. *They haven't even started.*

Suddenly he felt too tired to even finish undressing. He lay down on his bed and closed his eyes, his head barely even touching the pillow before he was out. Just before he lost consciousness completely, he felt that telltale kick in his right side, as if something were trying to get out through the scar he'd just touched.

The rusted metal door of The Factory slammed behind her, letting out one final gust of warm air before the cool fall night surrounded her. She barely even heard it. Roxanne had walked this stretch of unpaved parking lot so many times in the past few years that she did it on autopilot now, not even conscious of her own dazed movements as she allowed herself to slip into her everyday routine.

Her fingers slid up her jeans, finding a malformed lump just below her hips. She fiddled with it, bouncing it in the cup of her palm. The keys inside clinked and jingled against one another, the sharp ridges of her surfboard-shaped key chain digging into the smooth flesh of her leg.

She let out a long sigh, running her nails through her hair and across her scalp as she took out the buckle that had held it up for at least the last twelve hours. It might have been longer than that, but she couldn't remember if it had still been in when she woke up that morning.

She shut her eyes tight as she turned slightly, something in the back of her mind reminding her that she hadn't parked where she usually did today. Like a post-it note on her subconscious.

The car was in sight now, its chipped off-white paint standing out like a beacon in the dark night surrounding it. It was a 1993 Rover 400 series that had seen better days. The driver's side window shook as though it was about to fall out every time it was hit by a stern gust of wind and the original hood had been replaced by a deep forest green one. There were already nine hundred thousand clicks on it when she bought it a year ago for two hundred dollars and since then it had been in the shop three times and cost her almost double what she'd paid for it. Moreover, it ate gas like it was going out of style.

She reached her forefinger into her pocket and found her keyless remote in the jumble of the tips change and keys. Holding it high, she pressed the green button on it once.

The car chirped to life with a two identical beeps as she got closer to it, slowing down a little as her heels started to scream out with the pain she'd managed to ignore for most of the day. The keys still clinked, swaying back and forth as she pulled them out of her pocket, sending pennies and other loose change scattering to the ground with more ringing clicks. The sharp, metallic sounds were beginning to annoy her after listening to the band practice their solos for the last few hours, so she reached out suddenly and grabbed her keys together into one big lump. She almost cursed as one of the pointy pieces of metal poked at her palm, but deemed it to be worth the pain if the noise would stop.

The clicking continued.

-clink-

-clink- -clink-.

"Hello?" she called out, wrinkling her brow as she squinted into the sheet of blackness all around her.

She stopped walking, the sound of her heels no longer pulsing out into the night air. A second later, one last echo came back to her from the side of the Factory, then there was nothing. She waited, her green eyes looking all around even though she couldn't see anything except her car, as bright as a ghost compared to everything else. She couldn't even see the ground.

A gust of wind blew her hair back and the clicking continued, this time even more rapid and clambering than before. It was louder, now, and sharper too. The cold sound of metal on metal, something she remembered from all the stories Mike had told her about the night he and Cathy were attacked. *But Genblade's in prison, now,* she reminded herself. Somehow, it offered her very little comfort.

She listened to the sound, her eyes growing wider in their sockets with each passing note.

The stone bricks on either side of her ricocheted and amplified the sound, making its source impossible to locate.

The wind gusted and she thought she felt something pass along next to her shoulder, yelping. She spun quickly to see who was there, almost tripping and falling on her ass as she did, swearing that this would be the last time she wore heels to work.

Nothing.

There was nothing behind her and the more she strained her ears, the less she heard the metallic sound that had been driving her insane since leaving the club. Still, she refused to move. Somewhere inside her, she knew that the second she turned around, she would feel the metal that she had spent the last few minutes listening to.

Finally, a smirk spread across her lips as a thought occurred to her. She moved her thumb over the keyless remote she still clutched in her right hand, applying pressure to the yellow button in its centre. The old Rover's bright headlights flashed on, illuminating the alley and banishing all shadows into the darkest corners of the alley.

She took a good look around, inspecting every nook and cranny of the stone walls. Satisfied, she turned around and walked toward her car, raising one hand to shield her eyes against the light.

The front door nearly fell off when she pulled on the handle, but she pulled it up and slammed it quickly. She was almost already back into her routine daze again now, her mind already starting to relay the band's cover of a song by Matchbox Twenty. She started to bob her head to the beat in her head even as the car started with a hacking roar and she pulled out of the parking lot.

As she picked up speed, for no reason that she could see, the clicking started again as she hit Main Street. It was faster now, each click almost indistinguishable from the next. She glanced up into her rearview mirror, seeing nothing but empty streets and light poles that whizzed by. She looked at all the lights and dials on the dashboard, making sure the check engine light wasn't on. She'd heard the car make sounds like this before, but these didn't sound like they were coming from the engine.

The more she listened and looked around, the more she became convinced that they weren't even coming from in front of her. She bit her lip, glancing away from the road long enough to see her cell phone laying on the far side of the passenger seat. Gripping the wheel tightly, she leaned over and grabbed it, flipping it open to make sure the battery wasn't dead.

When she turned her attention back toward the street, the red light that intersected Laird Street glowered down at her like one evil, demonic eye.

"Fuck!" she yelled as she slammed on the breaks, forcing the car to skid to a sudden stop and slamming her chest against the steering wheel. The hard rubber thrust into her breasts, knocking the wind from her lungs violently. She stopped, both hands clutching the wheel just to keep from shaking as she tried to catch her breath. The light changed to green and then back to red again before she even realized what was going on.

You're such a fucking flake, she chided herself when she regained the ability to think reasonably, putting the cell phone back down in her lap. The back of her neck ached already and she knew that if she didn't get home and get some ice on it soon, it'd be too swollen for her to work again by morning. She almost considered that a reason *not* to do it.

Summoning all her courage, she released the brake and let the car roll through the intersection, hoping to get home before too late. Maybe in time to get a decent night's sleep for once.

No sooner was the car past the light and starting to speed up again when the clinking started again, resuming its persistent tack on her last nerve. It wasn't just the clicking itself that nagged at her, but the annoying sense that something wasn't right that she couldn't quite pin down. Making sure to keep one eye on the road again, she re-surveyed the dashboard indicator lights, turning off the heater to make sure it wasn't something blowing up against it. The sound continued unabated. Frowning, last glanced up into the rear view mirror.

Her eyes went wide.

There was someone in the backseat.

She felt an enormous pain on her chest as something ripped out of the seat from behind her, travelling through her midsection. She couldn't see what it was but it felt cold at first, then slowly got warmer and warmer. The moist heat spread throughout her body as she slumped against her steering wheel, rapidly losing consciousness. Her body jolted violently as the killer tried hard to remove the appendage, jerking it from side to side, ripping it across Roxanne's chest sending spurts of blood from the wound as well as from her mouth.

The car slammed head on into a fire hydrant, thrusting both bodies forward again. Her air bag puffed open, leaking deadly fumes out where from it had been punctured. The gas burned at her nose and throat, making her last few breaths sheer agony. Water splashed down onto her face. Her eyes began to roll into the back of her head as blood poured from her open wound and down into the street, the red liquid so thick that it dropped to the bottom of the puddles it fell into.

The monster calmly opened the door, letting her battered body slump out onto the pavement.

Her vision was fuzzy and she couldn't quite understand what she was seeing, but she heard the click and recognized it. She opened her eyes wide, tears clearing the blood out of them for her, and saw the metal buckle from the back seatbelt clang against the side of the car. There was a scrape there from where it had happened so many times and when the wind picked up it got more rapid again.

-clink-

-clink- -clink-.

The back door opened and the winch that held the belt finally kicked in, sucking the buckle back into the car in a flash so fast that her tired mind did not even register it. All she knew was that the sound had finally stopped.

The shadowed monster once more brought itself down across Roxanne's once beautiful face.

Blood mixed with water and gushed down into the sewer grate, falling through pipes and earth as it went.

Natasha Mercer popped two Tylenol into her mouth with an open palm, their stale taste filling her mouth for a moment before she knocked her head back and forced them down her throat without the benefit of water. She closed her eyes for a long moment, feeling nothing except the steady thud in the back of her head and cursing. She knew the pills weren't supposed to work for at least fifteen minutes, but sometimes just the act of taking them was enough to will the aches and pains away.

She considered herself a strong woman. Anyone would after what she'd gone through in her time on this world.

She had never known her father. As a child she'd always dreamed that her conception had been some royal scandal. That she'd been the love child of a prince or a king, and that someday the real daughter would die and some handsome prince would sweep her off her feet and bring her to England or France to be his second duchess.

Those dreams had faded in her twenties, reserved for romantic thoughts in the minutes just before sleep. Thirty had brought an end to them completely, save for the odd reminiscing on them while she watched her own daughter play.

Her once vibrant and beautiful appearance had shifted into a haggard form of a woman at the very end of a very slender rope. She realized now that her origins didn't involve kings or queens, but it did involve riches, ironically. Simply put, her father's family didn't deem her mother 'good enough' to enter into the family. They had cast her pregnant mother out onto the streets with no child support or means of finance. When she'd learned that, Natasha had sworn she'd prove her father's family wrong. That she would *make* herself good enough, in her own eyes if not in theirs.

For a short time, she had actually dared to hope that she would succeed.

She looked up from the large desk covered in scattered papers she sat behind. Her gaze moved over the open suitcase on the floor and then on to the suede love-seat beneath the large bay window where her daughter slept, her knees curled up to her chubby little chin as she slept. A light orange afghan was draped over her, making her look warm and snug as she smiled in her sleep.

She cursed her ex-husband for not taking her to his apartment again. He was supposed to take her twice a week but rarely did, though she never seemed to lose hope. Every time her eyes would light up and she'd spend the day jumping around the motel room, screaming and laughing. Then seven o'clock would come and he wouldn't be there, and slowly she'd get the picture again.

Bastard, Natasha thought bitterly, shaking her head as she turned back toward the papers on her desk.

A year ago she'd made partner in the law firm of Mayer, Summers and Soul. It hadn't been terribly long after that that the third partner had left, along with two corporate backers and the majority of the firm's funding. There had been layoffs and pay cuts galore, so much that she couldn't even afford a steady apartment anymore. She and Gwen rented a motel room most nights, though on the two nights that Paul was supposed to have her, she just slept in the office to save a little money.

Tonight they'd both be sleeping there.

She let out a heavy sigh as the drum in the back of her head began to fade away, but the tightly-coiled knot in each shoulder remained. She bit her lip as she reached up and began to kneed her own muscles, staring back down at the files and folders that were scattered across her desk.

There were blood tests, psyche analysis reports, IQ test scores, weight classifications, legal documents, all on one man: Adam Genblade.

The files had been faxed to the office the day before, though nobody had been quite sure why at the time. A few of the kids in accounting had been ruffling through it for fun when she'd walked in and seen it and if Gwen hadn't been with her she might have chewed them a new asshole. Even as it was, they knew they'd been dressed down and were still walking around with their tails between their legs today.

She'd read the original stories in the report Tom Drake had done on them. She'd even gotten a look at Tim White's police report on it before he'd been promoted, albeit briefly. She'd picked up the file assuming it had been sent by the family of the guard that had been mutilated by Genblade at Coral Beach Pen. They'd decided to sue and rightly so, from what she'd read of what had happened to him. But nobody from either the guard's family or the prison had sent the file.

It had sat on her desk for only an hour before she began to thumb through it.

She'd thought it would be clear-cut murder story, but the more she read into his case, the more oddities appeared to perk her curiosity. The police still had no idea who he was, besides the name Adam that was believed to merely be an alias. He had no record of birth, no passport... no fingerprints, even. A few people had suggested CIA, but Genblade himself had debunked that claim almost instantly.

Not that that meant it wasn't true anyway.

The oddest thing by far though was that he had maintained his guilt for the duration of his arrest and in early interviews, but had always maintained his innocence to the guards. Had teased them with it, one of them had said, used to even *sing* about it when they sprayed him down for his shower. It was only after the D.A. had insisted on his receiving the death penalty that he had changed his tune and publicly claimed his innocence, turning what would have been a no-contest case into a circus.

Frowning, she picked up the transcript of the last psyche evaluation that the penitentiary's clinical therapist had done and skipped down to the center of the second page.

WO: Are you saying you aren't responsible for the deaths in Coral Beach,

Adam?

AG: Responsible?

WO: Did you kill those children, Adam?

AG: (*laughter*). Ain't ya heard? It's a funny, funny story. I'm innocent.

WO: Who is responsible, Adam?

AG: Directly responsible?

Natasha repeated those words in her head as she stared at Genblade's black and white file photo. His cold, piercing eyes seemed to stare right at her and follow her no matter where she was sitting. They didn't just look at you, or even through you. They dissected you, cut you open in his mind until you were nothing but a shriveling worm of rendered flesh. She shivered, covering up the photo with another sheet of paper.

The door to her office swung open, tapping off of the far wall with a thud. She slammed the file down to the desk like a child caught doing something wrong, her breath shallow for just that one moment. She laughed at herself, realizing that she was on a coffee high and had no sleep these past few days, as her partner, Nate Summers, strolled into the room.

Nate was a tall, skinny man with silver hair and a rough, unshaven chin. He smiled at Natasha as he entered, a playful swagger in his step as he walked.

He looked her up and down, pursing his lips together tightly. She was tall and thin herself, coming in an inch or two above him when she was wearing her heels. Her hair was short and brown and usually pulled back in a bun, though today it draped in front of her eyes every few moments as she examined the papers. Her cheeks were covered in freckles and her eyes were just a little red, though he wasn't sure if it was from being tired or sad or both. He let his eyes move over her slender frame for a moment before stopping himself, hoping that she hadn't noticed.

He handed her a tan file folder, then let his eyes wander to all of the photos and written reports scattered across her desk. He sighed, shaking his head. "This goes way beyond taking your work home, Natasha."

She grabbed the folder from his hand. "When you live at work, it's hard not to take your work home."

He chuckled.

She didn't.

She opened the folder and looked into it. Inside were more photos from crime scenes all over Downtown Coral Beach. One was of a blood spattered prison cell and a security guard lying limp, but not dead, against the bars. The next photo was profoundly more disturbing, but it still intrigued her. He still intrigued her. It was Genblade, laughing hysterically, showing off his jagged teeth. His lips were lined with redness. His eyes were there again, such a light blue that they were almost white in the black and white photo, cutting through to her soul.

She shivered.

Following the pictures was the request from the D.A. that Genblade be executed as soon as humanly possible, by act of the state. Following that was a letter, the toner of which still smelled fresh. It was ragged and tattered, its corners lined with redness. One eyebrow moving upward, she glanced at Nate from over the top of the letterhead.

He shrugged dramatically, then turned to watch Gwen and smiled.

Frowning, she turned back toward the document and started to scan through it.

Kind representative of Mayer, Summers and Soul;

It has come to my attention recently that a person/ persons at your firm has come into contact with my case file after my information was sent to you via the District Attorney.

Lavish as it is for me to have a fan, I feel it necessary to inform you that I have plead guilty to the majority of the crimes to which I am accused.

Likewise I am sure you are aware that I am expected to spend the remainder of my short life in a maximum security upstate while awaiting execution.

You above anyone understand how unacceptable this is. I have grown to regard Coral Beach and this place with fondness and do not wish to leave any more than I wish for my life to end.

Ordinarily I would be appalled at admitting this, but I find myself overcome with fear at the idea of my death. I do not want to die, sir or madame. I wish to live and to learn of the world around me, albeit through the bars of a gilded cage. I wish to fight the death penalty sentence as well as my conviction. As such, I will require the services of a lawyer.

Understand that despite all accounts, I do have the means with which to compensate you handsomely.

Sincerely, Adam Genblade.

Natasha stared at the ledger for a moment, then looked over it at Gwen as Nate moved a strand of her dark hair out of her face.

In her mind's eye she could see it. She watched her own tears dry up in an instant. She saw her ex-husband finally being forced to pay child support and give his daughter the attention she deserved. The attention she never got. She saw the firm becoming one of the most influential in all of Maine again. She saw herself buying away her rich father's family's land and kicking *them* onto the streets with no resources to call their own. Most of all though, she saw a real future for Gwen. A future where life's disappointments all happened to miss her, rather than hit her head on as they had been.

She saw all this in an instant, as clearly as if she were looking into a crystal ball. This was her chance to do it. To prove once and for all that she was good enough.

"I'll take it," she mumbled, already forming a defense for Genblade in her head.

Mike watched Cathy's tiny nose tilt up a little with every breath she took, displacing hairs and making them fall into her face. His nose was millimeters from hers, moving back and forth in tune with her as she breathed in and out.

In, out.

A smile perked along his freckled cheeks as he carefully pushed her dark hair away from her eyelashes with one finger. She frowned once, squeezing her eyes closed as she adjusted herself in her sleep, then quickly fell back into her calm, steady rhythm. The movement shifted her hair, making it messy and tangled as it doubled over onto itself.

He stifled a laugh, turning away and bringing his fist to his mouth. She stirred again and he cursed himself, holding his breath until she settled again.

She hadn't gotten any sleep all day. He, at least, had been drifting back and forth because of the painkillers the nurses had dosed him with. Medicated sleep wasn't good sleep, but it was better than none. She'd just lain there, staring at the wall all day until she'd come into his room. She had been laying in his arms only eleven minutes before she was sound asleep.

His arm tingled painfully, a pinching burn shooting up from his fingertips whenever he tried to move them. He grunted in discomfort but dared not move. As long as she was sleeping, he could deal with his appendages doing the same.

She sniffled once, her nose twitching from side to side like a rabbit, and then she resumed her slow, intense breaths.

Grinning, he turned away from her and stared up at the ceiling. There was an odd, circular blue light staring back down at him attached to a crane-neck that was bolted to his headboard, the screws of which were currently burrowing into the back of his skull. Beyond it a small drip of condensation had formed on the white tile ceiling close to his window, moving up and down in a tug-o-war between gravity and the ceiling. He watched it for about twenty minutes until finally it fell to the floor with a soft pit, leaving him nothing to distract himself with.

A television was secured to the wall a few feet from the foot of the bed, the remote for which was just out of reach on the bedside table. If he stretched, he might be able to reach it and turn it on mute. Reaching as far as he could, his fingertip narrowly missed the edge of the remote's black plastic.

Cathy stirred, a small moan passing through her lips.

He frowned, then settled back down into place. There was a line of drool seeping out of her small mouth and onto her chin. Once again he had to turn away from her to keep from laughing out loud.

Seconds passed. After a few minutes with nothing to occupy his mind, thoughts started coming into his head like clockwork. Thoughts that he had known were there but had been trying so hard not to be conscious of, like a bad song stuck in your head.

Fucker, he thought bitterly, his lip curling as he thought of Xander's face grinning back at him from somewhere just in front of him. The memory-Xander laughed at something, no sound coming from his lips. *She's so scared. She's so scared that you're coming back that she couldn't even sleep and then you have the nerve to traipse in and out of here whenever you want. Talking about getting answers to things that you already know. Just because you don't like the answers doesn't mean they aren't true. Doesn't mean that you get to come in here and pretend everything all right when it's not.*

His head started to hurt and he became aware that his face had gotten hot. Although he couldn't see it, he knew that he was turning red, his freckles fading away in the anger. Every muscle and joint in his body had become stiff. Next to him, Cathy cooed softly as her brow crumpled for an instant before turning back to its natural, perfectly smooth state. He wondered briefly what she was dreaming of, if it was him or something weird... or the Womb.

He sighed, flopping his fist down onto the bed. His knuckles had been clenched so tight that they had turned bright white, the color now bleeding back into them slowly. He felt helpless and scared and useless all at the same time.

Slowly, a sparkle grew in his eyes and he looked up, a smile brimming across his thin lips. "Maybe I can get the answers you're afraid to," he whispered to himself before turning to give Cathy a small kiss on the head.

⋔

"Okay people, I know it's getting late but it's going to be a busy week here and I need to know what we've got. Go," John Tyler said quickly as he sat behind the massive oak desk that dominated the majority of his office, popping a handful of Rolaids into his mouth as he did. Don and Drake sat across from him, the former trying to stack his papers so that the tops all lined up and the latter checking under his nails for grit.

"Got some new stuff on the murders," Don offered, flipping over the page of his clipboard and scanning down it, one finger lifted into the air. "Ah, an angle that they might have been racially motivated."

Drake slowly turned his head toward him, his left eyebrow raising a little more with every degree. "How in Christ's name do you figure that?"

"Well, there were no Blacks or Asians killed, just Caucasians."

"Racially motivated crimes are racially motivated because they're *against* minorities or *by* minorities. White is not a minority. It's barely a race."

"But the killer could be a racist."

"Could also be Jewish! All people killed were Christians, too!" Drake yelled, running a hand through his hair.

"The murders have been done to death," John interrupted finally, just loud enough to shut them both up. "Pardon the pun. There's gonna be lots on them, we don't need to reach. Any luck on the Genblade interview yet?"

"No," Drake answered, a small growl accompanying the word from deep within his throat. "Insane prick keeps saying we did this. Won't talk to us. Even told the secretary at the Pen not to bother forwarding the messages anymore."

"Son of a bitch," John sighed. "You know if he gets moved to state we'll never get our hands on him again, right? I'm surprised Newsweek and Time aren't camping on our front lawn as it is."

"They're not gonna move him to state," Drake scoffed.

"What makes you so sure?" Don mumbled, almost under his breath as he thumbed through the rest of his notes.

Drake snarled at him, his cheeks turning read. "They got half their staff going round the clock just to keep him in that cage as is. You think they're gonna try to *move* him, fucknuts?"

Don did not respond, turning back to his notes. "Some follow up on the Phillip Masters case, needs an interview or two and maybe an extra source, but I can have it for this weeks."

"Good. Get it," John nodded, scrabbling something onto the large paper calendar that doubled as a placemat over his desk. He paused a moment, then looked up at the both of them. "What else, people, the pages aren't going to fill themselves."

"Someone should cover the Memorial coming up at the high school this week."

"Fuck it," John rebuffed, waving the idea away distastefully. "It's sidebar to the trial story. Don't need to be there, just need to know it happened."

"Been some gang violence again lately," Drake piped up, cocking his head to annunciate his point. "Been seeing a lot of graffiti the last few months. Most of it Omegas, some of it Snakes. Might be escalating."

"Look into it, but try and not be too dickish," John said, pointing a finger at him. "Last time you went at them hardball, we were cleaning the graffiti off the panes for a month."

"Girl went missing a few days ago," Don said, raising his hand again.

"It's a runaway," Drake almost whined, lolling his head dramatically.

"She's not a runaway," Don said again, his tone the same. "Same grid of the city that the killer likes to strike in."

"How do you know where she was taken from if she's a runaway?"

"We know where she was last seen."

"Yea, well those two things are often very different. Either way, she's a runaway. Killer hasn't been takin' many prisoners, in case you ain't noticed."

"Just because it's not related to the killer, doesn't mean it--"

"No body, no ransom: runaway."

"The crimes could be sexually - -"

"Enough," John barked, stopping the both of them. He turned to Don, smacking his lips together thoughtfully as his fiddled the Rolaids wrapper between his fingers. "You don't have enough to run with it as a feature, but do it up. If nothing else, it might help get the girl found, and if the paper helps with that, *then* we've got a story."

"Done and done."

"Anything else?"

"I hear the Mayor farted last week," Drake scoffed under his breath. "Maybe you'd like to do a story on that, too."

Don dropped his pad, waving his hand before him as though to open the field for him. "I suppose you've got better?"

"Abuse charges against Xander Drew," he said smugly, tossing his open pad onto the Editor's desk and leaning back.

"What?" Don said, leaning forward to read the notes even as John did.

"Where are you getting this from?"

"Personal experience," Drake smiled, tapping himself on the head. "Little bastard clocked me so hard I bled almost ten minutes. Had to go get it checked out and everything. That cute nurse at CBG thought I had a concussion. Riley."

"This is good stuff, Tom," John said, almost drooling from the mouth as he looked over Drake's story notes.

"Please," Don sneered, rubbing his head for a moment before sitting back down. "Its bloody Wow journalism and you know it, John. If I'd known we were working for a tabloid I would've brought in a few more stories about Elvis' new love child."

John stopped reading and looked up, his mouth open as he lay the pad back down.

"I think you've stepped out, boyo," Drake chuckled a little, swirling finger around his head once before giving Don a hearty slap on the back.

"Get off me," Don snapped, pulling away at the moment of contact. "And how'd him hitting you give you a lump on the back of your head, anyway? But go ahead, go after the kid that Tim White found broken and bruised up where they caught Genblade. A kid not even the Feds will go near for God-only-knows what reason, because if I were them, I think I would've asked what went on up there by now, wouldn't you? So try it, see what happens. When you go missing, I'll be sure and tell the cops you're a runaway."

Drake paused, opening his mouth to retort. After a moment he closed it again, turning away from Don and back to the desk.

"He's... right, Tom," John frowned, handing back the folder sadly. "It's sensationalism. We all know it's sensationalism. As much as I'd love to, we can't print it."

"Sure," Drake nodded, picking the pad back up and closing it.

"All right, you guys know what to do. Get to it," he said, waving them both toward the door as he unrolled another white capsule and shoved it into his mouth.

Both men got up and headed for the door, Don's eyes cast downward and his free hand rubbing his temple again.

"Everything okay, Don?" John asked, leaning forward onto the desk just as Drake left the room.

"Hmm?" Don groaned, almost not even hearing it at first. "Oh, yes sir. Sorry, sir. I didn't mean to go off like that."

"It's okay. You were right."

"Shouldn't have gone off."

"Even so," he shrugged. "Have you been feeling all right? We're a little busy now, but you could go on leave after the trial if its - -"

"Not that," Don sighed, rubbing the bridge of his nose. "Got *no* sleep last night. Pipes kept me up at all hours."

"Pipes?"

"Yeah, they thump and crack and make all kinds of weird shit noises. Happens every fall."

"Hmm. Well, get it looked after," John nodded, turning back to his computer and visibly having been tuned out for at least half of the sentence Don had said. "Sleeps important."

"Yes, sir," Don heaved again, turning to walk away as he started to yawn.

"Neocitran. Does it for me every time."

"Yes, sir."

ﾊ⟨⟩ﾊ

Garfield Samson smiled softly to himself, the smirk spreading tenuously over his aged, angular face as he spotted a small patch of tulips growing just outside the Peterson's fence. They were colored a milky white and were just starting to shrivel back from their summer bloom as the cold of fall got to them. He bent over to pick one, pausing only slightly when his right hip didn't seem to move with the rest of his body. He clutched the stem tightly, sawing the nail of his thumb back and forth on it until it snapped loose of the rest of the bush. Grinning like a gargoyle, he turned toward his companion and presented it to her theatrically. "For you, my love."

Linda Samson turned away for a moment, blushing. She took the flower from him without meeting his gaze, knowing that she would start to laugh the moment she saw the sun caught in his large ears, making them glow like candles in the night. "Flatterer," she chided him, holding out her arm for him as they started to walk again.

He took it gently, keeping stride with her even though his back now ached fiercely. "Isn't that how I won you to begin with? It certainly wasn't my looks."

"Certainly not," she agreed, hiding her smile as best she could.

He raised a single bushy eyebrow at her, then chuckled softly.

She laughed too, squeezing herself a little closer.

Black Womb landed on the chimney of the Peterson home, sending soot and grime toppling over the side. It leaned forward as far as he could, its body standing at an angle almost impossible for bipeds, digging its claws into the red bricks for support. The early morning sun reflected off of its opaque, green eyes as it stared down at the old couple walking on the sidewalk. Its mouth was practically invisible while closed, its large catlike eyes following their every moment as emotionless as a statue.

Garfield winced as his right leg gave a little in mid-step, forcing him to limp.

The Womb's head turned slightly at the sight of this, watching the way the impairment affected the man's step. It leaned a little closer, then finally let go of the chimney and slammed chest first onto the roof, grabbing onto the rain gutter. It swung its legs underneath itself until it found balance, then continued to stare.

Usually the beast would be heading home about now, but for whatever reason, it didn't. Its aqua eyes shone in the twilight, giving eerie images to those who passed. Daylight now loomed along the outskirts of mountains, creating a beautiful orange glow. Black Womb stared up at it, its eyes changing slightly, adjusting to the light. The creature looked at its hands. They were splattered with blood that was nearly impossible to see in the low light, appearing so black that it blended in with his skin. It licked them, then turned its vision back down towards the couple. Extending one claw to its fullest, he started tapping the rain gutter rhythmically.

-click-

-click-

-click-

"Do you hear that?" Garfield asked, those huge ears twitching with every sharp sound. He stopped in mid-step, craning his head up to look around. Nothing surrounded him but more shrubbery and the Peterson home. A car passed them quickly and was out of sight before he even really saw it.

Linda stopped, tilting her head to one side and straining her ears. "I don't hear anything."

"Oh, you're deaf anyway," he laughed, poking her arm playfully.

-click-

"There," he said again, turning and taking a step back the way they'd come.

Even though it was almost impossible to tell one emotion apart from the next on the Womb's face, the creature's eyes sharpened and turned upwards in a way that could only ever be described as delight. Licking its lips, it glanced at the incoming sun again. Its head twitched painfully to one side and it let out a low growl, deep inside its throat. It could feel the other awakening... like being stuck half way between dreaming and alertness. Its jaw dislocated like a snakes, stretching down to its lower chest and revealing two rows of jagged teeth. Its fingers elongated into freakish claws. It squatted, preparing to pounce down at Linda Samson, who was now admiring tulips just beneath where it was perched.

"Arrgh!" the creature bellowed, clutching its gut as it exploded in pain. Desperate, it turned the talons on itself, slashing at the black scales that covered its abdomen. It brought its hands up to its face as the sun shone across Coral Beach, burning at its eyes until all it could see was white and all it could feel was pain.

Garfield and Linda both backed up a pace from the home, their eyes wide with fright. They stood paralyzed for a moment, then turned and ran back the way they had come, towards home. Half way there, Garfield felt something snap deep inside his side but kept going anyway. As bad as it hurt, he had the impression it was nothing compared to what would happen if whatever had made that sound caught him. Besides, they had coverage.

Shivering violently, the Black Womb watched them disappear around the corner with regret. Its pupils finally adjusted to the new light, making at least part of the pain stop. The rest only got worse, the cuts it had sliced on its stomach spreading and opening like hungry mouths, recessing to reveal pink flesh and red blood underneath.

Its eyes turned red for a moment, then black as the darkness seeped into the creature's open mouth. The darkness that surrounded him seemed to lose its

ability to maintain itself, flowing off of him and onto the Peterson's roof, leaving only a thin layer of congealed blood behind.

Xander Drew fell to the shingles with a wet thud.

Groaning, he reached up and peeled the layer of blood off of his face. It resisted slightly, like plastic wrap trying to come free from a piece of meat.

He felt a breeze, then finally opened his eyes with a small click and looked around. "What the hell?" he whispered softly into the air. He looked down at his bleeding, naked body and almost fainted again, then steadied himself before tumbling off the roof. Pausing to make sure he was balanced, he tried to get some sense of where he was.

"Great," he muttered, turning toward the Peterson's back yard. There was a clothesline there filled with jeans and shirts. They were damp and cold, not to mention all meant to be worn by girls, but they were clothes and that trumped any other argument at this point. He shouldn't get cold. He shouldn't be *able* to feel cold. Yet still he felt... cold, somehow. Like it was coming from something other than the elements.

Pausing cautiously, he dropped into the yard and waited to hear a high-pitched scream. When one did not occur, he started grabbing clothes that looked like they would fit off of the line, tossing the wooden pins to the ground.

As he got dressed, he couldn't help but wonder why things like this had actually started to become natural to him. Normal even, he thought. *Just a few weeks ago, attempting something like this would have caused me more embarrassment than I would have ever wanted to remember, but would anyway. Why, now, would the Black Womb decide that it didn't want to come in tonight?*

The answer to his question was ready in his mind. Too ready, as if it wasn't even his.

It's thinking.

Dr. Dennis Marx stopped just shy of room 1013, glancing down at the clipboard he had cradled in his arms. His eyes darted over the ink-smudged photocopy for a moment before he licked his fingers and turned the page, then kept reading. The second page was scrawled in handwriting that was legible only to him, along with a few crude diagrams of wound tracks with arrows going from them to equally crude stick figures to indicate their placement on his patient's body.

He ran a hand over his bald head, then through the greasy remains of his black hair that exploded from his neck like wild grass. Finally he stuck his pinky finger into his ear, subconsciously rooting around as he read down through the file before him until he found an obstruction to pry out by the nails.

He glanced to one side and saw Nurse Riley staring at him, one of her eyebrows raised upwards suspiciously. Frowning, his cheeks turning red, he wiped his hand in the waist of his otherwise white lab coat and then turned around the corner, entering the room.

Mike lay silently in his bed, his eyelids fluttering wildly as the eyes inside them darted back and forth. His breathing was slow and constant, his toned chest rising and falling every few seconds as he lay on his back. His mouth was open, but he did not snore.

Cathy entered the room from the bathroom just to Marx's right, in the middle of bringing her hair back into a ponytail. There was a bobby pin clasped between her pink lips for a moment as she gave the Doctor a look that said 'just a minute'. After a moment she removed the black strip of metal and slid it gracefully into her hair to keep it in place, then smiled at him. "Sorry, hospital-head bugs me."

"Hospital-head?" Marx asked, raising one of his bushy eyebrows. His voice was very small and weak, a smokers wheeze of the end of every word.

"It's like bed-head only worse," she explained, cocking her head in the direction of the paper sheets.

"Ah," he smiled, nodding as he chuckled loudly. "I don't think I've ever heard that one before."

Cathy winced at the surprising level of the man's laughter, walking past him to close the privacy curtain around Mike's bed. "He didn't get much sleep last night, you mind?" she huffed impatiently, though not without her usual air of kindness.

He nodded in apology. "Sorry."

"S'okay. What can I do to help you?" she asked, her face returning to her normal, soft demeanor.

"I just need someone to sign the both of your release forms. You're both making great progress. Usually we'd keep you an extra day or two to watch you, but the hospital's all booked up and we have new patients that need the rooms."

"Patients?" Cathy asked, her eyes growing wide. "More victims?"

"No... no," the doctor mumbled, ruffling through his paperwork to find the forms. "Nothing like that. A lot of children have been getting ill lately. Haven't really been able to put my finger on the cause."

"Oh. Good," Cathy sighed in relief.

He shot her a glance from above his clipboard.

"Well, not good... you know what I mean."

"Mm-Hmm," he hummed dismissively.

"So, um, do you need to be a relative to sign those?" Cathy asked, making a big and fake smile as she tried to segway from the topic.

"Um..." he mumbled, thumbing through a few of the pages looking for a document labeled parent/guardian, finding none. "No. We've already contacted both of your parents, so you can sign your consent forms yourselves on your own. It only says that you checked out of your own accord."

Cathy sucked on her teeth a second, getting the last bit of milt-flavoured toothpaste off of them. "I'll sign," she said, then took the forms out of the doctor's hands. He gave her a black ballpoint pen with golden stripes to sign with. She did so hastily, scribbling her name where the 'x' indicated.

"Thank you," he said curtly, folding his arm back over the clipboard.

"You too. And good luck with that kid... thing."

He did not respond, simply turned away from her and left the rom.

"Tool," she uttered to herself, frowning as she turned back toward the room. She smiled then, tip-toeing until she reached the yellow curtain he had pulled across. "Mike?" she cooed softly as she stepped forward in an exaggerated manner she had only ever seen used on Saturday morning cartoon shows.

There was no response from beyond the curtain.

"Miiikey," she sung musically, her arm out in front of her and ready to pull the yellow plastic aside at a moments notice. She waited for a beat, then yanked the curtain aside, the rings that held it up scraping sharply along the pole they rode on.

Mike looked up at her as he finished buttoning up his shirt, his face devoid of almost all expression.

"Oh," she said, pouting a little. "Thought maybe you'd still be asleep."

"Dr. Mumbles woke me," he said simply, fastening the clasps on either sleeve.

She looked him up and down suspiciously. His shirt was red with white stripes and fit him very well. It somehow made him look older than he was, or at the very least nicer. His jeans were pressed and had no holes or burns in them, not even along the cuff. He was even wearing a belt, one that looked to be real leather. "You're dressed up today," she said.

"Not really," he scowled, shaking his head. He paused, then looked her up and down and smiled. "I don't think I've ever seen you with a ponytail. Not since we were kids, anyway."

She blushed a little, her small mouth drawing up in a smile. "Don't try and weasel out of the subject. Who are you all dressed up for?"

"You caught me," he said with fake exasperation, letting his hands fall to his sides in defeat. "There's another woman. She's much better than you. I have to dress up around her to fit in."

"Nobody better than me would take you," she giggled, moving in close to him and giving his bottom lip a kiss. "I shouldn't even have."

He laughed again, kissing her back. "You're probably right."

"Always am."

He moved her gently to one side, then stepped past her and scooped up his sneakers off the floor and began to slide them on.

She watched him for a moment, unsure of what to say for one of the first times in their relationship. "Seriously Mike, where are you going?"

He stopped tying immediately, turning around to face her. "I've just got somewhere I got to be. It's nothing to be worried about."

Cathy forced herself to smile. "Any room for me?" she chimed innocently.

He sighed, tilting his head to one side.

"Guess not," she said in response to her own question, casting her eyes downward.

He took two steps to close the distance between them, resting a hand on each shoulder and kissing her softly on the head.

301

When she looked up again, he was gone.

Frowning, she walked over to the phone next to the bed and picked it up. She let it hang next to her ear for a moment, its tone ringing in her ear, then put it back down. She sucked in her bottom lip and chewed on it for a moment, tapping her chin as she stared down at the plastic buttons. Cursing, she picked it up again and hit redial.

The phone rang twice as she tapped her nails against the plywood table it rested on. Halfway through the third ring, a very bored sounding woman with a nasal voice picked up the line. "Coral Beach Pen, how may I direct your call?"

"He wouldn't," she said aloud, before hanging up the call.

ʎ૮ʎ

A row of candles flickered and danced in unison, the only source of light in the room as they bathed the walls of the Factory in their ethereal glow. It made the entire place look foreign and somehow eerily romantic, the scent of burning wax and matches filling the air.

Xander gazed into the flames until he thought they were burning his retinas, casting his eyes down toward a photo of Roxanne that had been framed and propped up in the center of the miniature shrine. The picture had been from her graduation and the girl in the picture didn't look remotely like the Roxanne he had known. They shared the same curly red hair and dark green eyes, but the girl in the photo was bright and smiling and full of existence. While the Roxanne he had come to regard as a friend was still all those things, you had to dig deep to find them. For the most part, she'd been cold and bitter, especially toward males.

He heard someone walk up behind him, along with the steady, wet clack as they chewed on a large wad of gum. He turned just enough to look over his shoulder, his face shadowed in the candlelight.

Joan Delft stepped up beside him, rubbing her hands with a cloth that he thought had started off white but hadn't been in quite some time. Her hair was grey and her wrinkled face seemed to want to cave in upon itself, with its brow furrowed downward and its chin pointing up. Joan had bought the Factory years ago and turned it into something worthwhile, with Roxanne's help.

"News traveled fast," she said. Her voice was calm and desolate, free of the sadness that was weighing her down so much that she slouched. Only someone who knew her well would recognize the slight West-Virginia accent that she only reverted to when she was truly upset as being a giveaway of her true feelings.

"Bad news always does," Xander nodded. "Guess that says something about our society that we obsess over the bad things like that."

"Like vultures over the dead," she spat, her eyes reflecting the candlelight back toward him. After a moment she forced herself to look away from it, turning to Xander. "Foods all free today, 'un. Should get yourself something."

Xander waved a hand in dismissal, smiling. The thought of food made his stomach do a back-flip, though he wasn't exactly sure why.

"Suit yourself," she shrugged, taking one last look back at Roxanne's photo before turning away completely. "It's there if'n you want it."

Xander sighed as he watched her until she disappeared behind the counter, smutting her face with the rag as she used it to wipe her eyes, before he turned back toward the display. *If you're innocent, you're hurt, or you're scared... I'll be there. What a joke,* he snorted, reaching out and laying a finger gently on the top of the picture frame. *Starting to think I had the right idea with the gun.*

"Don't ever give up," his memory screamed at him in her soft, mellow voice. It was so vivid that he could almost hear it.

I'm sorry, Sara. I promised to do good in your name, that I'd never let you down again, but now... it's starting to look like I do more harm to the world than good. Maybe the best thing would be to just off myself and be done with it. I just -

"What's all this shit?" came a loud, obnoxious voice from the doorway. "We haven a friggin' power ootage or somethin'?"

"Huh. Power out," came the echo.

He didn't even have to turn around this time to know who was there. He fought back the Black Womb, but actually had to remind himself why he didn't want to sick it on the duo that had entered. They were the only two people in the world who could annoy him that much that quickly, and he caught himself thinking that if Tommy and Sud were the ones on death row, he wouldn't have wasted a second thought on letting them fry.

"Hey Xand," Tommy said, his voice slightly mocking as he pulled up a chair next to Xander. "Geez, all this for that bitch, huh?"

"Bitch," Sud repeated, grinning at the use of the curse.

Xander's shoulders twitched into a knot as he fought the blackness, turning to be parallel with Tommy. Despite all instincts, he choked the Womb back. He wanted to do this himself. "Tom, you just picked the worst possible opening line..." he said, even as he cracked the knuckles on each of his fists.

"What's the matter with you? Were you puttin' it to that one, too?" Tommy snickered, running his fingers through the bangs of his spiked hair to make sure it stuck out properly. The spikes made the already tall boy somehow seem even larger. As Xander's nostrils flared, he could smell the odor of the cheap gel and dandruff.

Xander turned over the table Tommy sat at, sending a glass flying. Before either of the crude punks could move, he rushed his hands out and grabbed Tommy's shirt collar.

"What the hell?" Tommy screamed at Xander, pressing both his palms against Xander's face and forcing him off, scrambling to his feet as Sud backed up a pace or two in shock. "What the fuck is the matter with you?" he spat angrily as he quickly fixed his collar, although it still stuck off. "The way that bitch touch you remind you of your mommy, or what?"

That was it. Even though Xander still wouldn't let Black Womb out, it still pumped adrenaline furiously throughout his system, strengthening his muscles. He grabbed Tommy by the shirt and pulled him toward the door at the far side of the Factory, the boy's feet literally dragging at one point while he regained his balance.

"Jesus fuck, Drew. Piss off, ya Goddam techno freak."

He pulled Tommy out in front of himself and gave him a shove, sending him into the door with such force that it cracked the knob. He kept going until his back connected with the brick wall across from the door, his head slamming back hard. He hissed sharply as he got to his feet, Xander and Sud not far behind.

Xander drew back and punched Tommy square in the nose. Hard.

Tommy twisted as he fell again, slamming into an old metal garbage can with a loud crash. Blood gushed from his nose when he got up, his eyes burning.

"Get 'em," Sud shouted as he stood off to one side, his feet dancing back and forth nervously as he watched the fight.

Tommy put up both of his fists, clenching his jaw tightly as blood ran down it in two trails. He never took his eyes off of Xander for a second as the two men circled each other in the cramped alleyway.

Xander put up his own fists as well, feeling four tiny pricks in each palm as his claws tried to poke their way out, eager to join in the fray.

"You've had this comin' a long time." Tommy grunted, his voice devoid of the usual wit and whimsy it carried.

"I was about to say the -"

Tommy lunged forward, his fist outstretched. Had it connected, it would've hurt something incredible for a guy of Tommy's size.

If it had connected.

Xander dodged to the left, turning his body to the side and giving him a much thinner target to hit. Tommy fell to the ground and kissed pavement, breaking the blood vessels in both his kneecaps and bringing more speed to the blood from his nose that covered the lower half of his face now. Xander reached out and grabbed Tommy by the collar of his denim shirt, pulling the arrogant child back to his feet. He turned and lunged out again, this time grabbing Xander by the throat and pressing his thumb against his Adam's apple.

Xander's eyes went wide as he felt the thyroid cartilage in his neck be forced in, gagging back vomit.

With one hand holding Xander and one hand free, Tommy jerked back his fist again and jutted it forward. It connected this time, mashing in the features of Xander's face. He drew back again, slamming Xander's torso and causing ripples of flesh at his side as he tried to squirm away from it.

His right side.

The vibrations agitated the true womb organ, once again sending blackness to Xander's eyes.

How is he this fast?

Xander fought the rising blackness with everything he had, concentrating more on it than the person who had him gripped by the neck.

Tommy let go of Xander's throat, bringing his arm around and slamming it into the back of Xander's head where his neck met his spine. A drop of blood dripped from Xander's nose and hit the ground. It was a deep black, though neither Tommy nor Sud noticed.

Xander filled with horror as he felt his control slip away as though it had been covered in soap. His pupils had grown wide and he got up as fast as lightning.

Tommy lunged at him again with both fists cupped together, his teeth ground together angrily.

Xander dodged to the left, then to the right when he lunged again.

"Rrrrah!" Tommy grunted, enraged. He lunged again, tripping over himself and taking a moment to get his feet back in place. His teeth were stained a dark pink from all the blood.

Xander backhanded Tommy's fist as he attempted to strike out again, and the boy felt the power of the simple motion tug at the ligament in his shoulder.

Shocked and desperate, Tommy punched at him again.

Glaring through him, Xander finally remained. He reached out his open palm and let the fist hit it, clutching down quickly to stop it in mid-swing. He squeezed, slowly, dragging out the pain as long as he could as he heard the bones in Tommy's hand snap, crackle and pop like cereal. Blood streamed out from between Tommy's fingers and he started to scream, tears forming in his eyes. Something in his hand made a wet snap.

"Hey, man stop!" came a new voice from the road.

Xander turned with a bitter look on his face, ready to tear this new person in half as well. His eyes were completely black.

Derek ran toward them, out of breath from sprinting across the street from his house. He pushed Xander and Tommy apart, placing a hand on both their chests.

Tommy immediately fell to the ground and curled into the fetal position, clutching his maimed appendage as Sud rushed to his side.

Xander drew back a fist and was about to hit Derek, then he stopped and blinked. His pupils shrunk back to normal as he realized what he was doing, the primal urge inside him still pushed him to go for his friend's throat. He looked down at his hands, trembling and shaking off droplets of Tommy's blood. "Thanks, man," he said humbly to Derek, his voice gruff and distant as he continued to stare at the blood on his hands.

"Yeah," Derek replied, squeezing Xander's shoulder. "You wanna grab a game or a drink, cool off?"

"Okay," Xander said, between deep breaths. "Okay."

Derek nodded and walked ahead, thinking that Xander was right behind. When he entered the Factory, Xander bent down to come face to face with the whimpering Tommy. "You ever talk about a woman like that, or if you even look at Cathy like I've been seeing you," he paused, grabbing Tommy's shirt collar again, forcing him to look him in the eyes. Xander licked his dry lips, "... I'll kill you."

"Genblade. You got a visitor. Keep it short, eh?" Tom Lensherr said, step-

305

ping away from his guard post for the first time in hours. He'd made a vow to himself to be nice to Genblade these next few weeks. After all, after that he'd be dead and they'd all be a lot happier.

It wasn't an easy truce.

"A visitor?" Genblade perked, his face lit up with an eerie smile. His lips were still smattered with the blood of the guard that he had attacked. They couldn't risk giving him a cloth. The last time they had, he'd used it to slowly strangle a young guard. Anything was a weapon in his hands. Every so often, Genblade would moisten the blood with his tongue, forcing it not to coagulate. It chilled the other guards to their core.

Tom had seen Genblade's work first hand. He had been the officer who'd discovered the body of Jamie Dawkins, the first victim of Genblade's massacre. He remembered the night clearly, the image burned into his mind no matter how much he wanted to root it out and never think of it again.

He glared down at Genblade, a look of disgust coming over him. "Just get up, will ya?"

ʌɣʌ

Genblade walked into the visitor's room they had made especially for him, his chains clinking steadily with every step he took.

His eyes sparkled wide when he saw his visitor, his evil grin widening from ear to ear. He sat down and stared through the glass, his pale blue eyes running over the man over and over as his warped mind tried to figure out what his purpose here was. After a few moments of curious anticipation, he picked up the phone and put the fractured receiver to his ear.

Mike picked up his phone, holding it near his face without ever actually making contact with his skin. It felt dirty to him, somehow. "Hello, Genblade," he said flatly, revealing neither the anger nor the fear that the killer's presence had stirred in him.

Genblade squinted a confused look at him, but he still grinned wide. "Hi-ya Mikey! How ya been?"

"Yeah, okay," Mike said dismissively, rolling his eyes and glancing away from the glass to his side.

"How's the woman?" Genblade smiled profusely.

Mike grew silent for a long moment. When he finally got his nerves together and spoke, his voice wavered slightly with anger and made Genblade smile. "You know that judge will never actually let you live, right? You're gonna fry, you smoldering sack of crap."

Genblade's smile faded into an amused sneer.

"I figure, the least you can do is give us the information floating around in that... thing you call an excuse for a mind, before it boils under a couple thousand volts, right?" Mike said with false lightheartedness, shrugging his shoulders nonchalantly.

Genblade stared back at Mike through the plate glass. He reached out a finger and tapped on it, bringing the phone close enough to catch it. - click-. -click-.

306

-click-.

Mike laughed. "You don't seriously think you can psyche me out with those parlor tricks, do you?"

Genblade smiled, leaning against the small ledge of the sill on both elbows. "They had such plans for you, you know... Still do. I think they really could've made something of you."

"Who?" Mike asked, raising an eyebrow before realizing that Genblade had lulled him out of the tough-as-nails persona he'd spent twenty minutes in the bathroom practicing before telling the guard he was ready.

Genblade smiled. "Had some plans of my own, though. I think you'd make just as good a playmate as Xander... better even. Might even stand a chance against Zy-"

"How's the woman?" Mike spat, cutting Genblade off in mid wisecrack.

There was another long pause from Genblade as he slowly closed his mouth, electing not to finish the sentence as he gripped the phone.

Suddenly, Mike's eyes went wide with mock shock. "Oh! That's right! She'd dead. But don't worry, you'll be seeing her again real soon."

Genblade's brow furrowed. "Kid," he started, taking a deep breath, "I'm gonna tell you the same thing I tell your idiot friend every time he comes in here, looking for trouble: All I know is what Alpha told me. I trust that what he told me was true. You don't have to."

Mike smirked. "Heard we had a bit of rain a few weeks ago. It came down and washed the Spider out."

Genblade merely grunted in response.

It took Mike aback. He wondered he'd actually scored a direct hit on the beast. He hoped so.

"So, you know a weakness and you've exploited it, can we move on now?" Genblade said, cutting the tension of what they were both thinking.

Mike's voice lowered, his eyes narrowed. "Only you would think of love as a weakness."

There was another long silence as their eyes met, and they stared at one another coldly.

Genblade reached up a hand and wiped blood from the side of his cheek with his index finger. He smudged it against the glass where the image of Mike's neck was reflected, making it look like he was bleeding from the jugular. "Another time, then," he said in a soft, musical voice as he got up and started to hang up the phone.

Mike got up, startled. "Wait!"

Genblade's eyebrows rose. He sat back down and re-lifted the receiver. "There's more?" he said with sarcastic interest, his tone venomous. "What, think of a new crack to make of my dead wife? By the way, how's Sara?"

Mike flinched, letting the small twinge of guilt he felt show. Genblade may be deranged, but he wasn't trying to say that what he and Spider had wasn't love. He knew better than anyone that you just didn't do that. Mike sighed, turning away from the phone again and cursing softly to himself. When he looked back, his eyes were softer and larger, pleading with Genblade through the glass. "Cathy was hurt in the attack. Genblade, you're gonna die anyway, now. I'm begging you, as someone who lost a person they loved, give me something I can use."

Genblade looked thoughtful. He swallowed hard. "If you're here, I think you already know what the answer is."

"Yeah. Had to hear it first," Mike said, letting his emotions show. He sat a moment, letting that dwell in his mind. "But not from you. You don't know what I need to, either. That's why Xander couldn't get any answers out of you. You don't have any. You're just some stupid muscle Engen used to get under Xander's skin, and now you're going on about their plans as if you knew any of them. But thanks, I know what I've gotta do now."

"What you've gotta do is think good and hard before you turn a blind eye to -"

Mike slammed the phone down. He turned to go, then made his hands into a spider - shape and crawled it across the window.

Genblade jumped up and began pounding against the glass. It shattered again, the cracks spreading out into the shape of a web.

Mike saw it and laughed.

Even though he couldn't hear it, Genblade stopped what he was doing and watched Mike's silent chuckle as he left. His pupils shrank and his face stretched out as he watched the boy through the shattered glass, rage slowly building inside him.

Tom Lensherr ran over and restrained Genblade, clasping the killer's chains and giving them a hard tug. He struggled against the cop, screaming wildly, the echoes travelling throughout the building.

CHAPTER FIVE: SMOKING GUN

Roxanne Carpenter stared up at Lance Berkshire with a face she hadn't used in almost ten years. It was devoid of emotion, with no spiteful sneer or pasted-on smile, no quirky tilt of her head. Her skin was pasty and white, all the makeup gone down the drain long ago. It wasn't until all of the eyeliner and eye-shadow had been washed away that Lance had even noticed that her eyes were green.

Her breasts were small and perfect, but didn't look at all right as his eyes passed over them. Somehow, breasts looked very different when they weren't moving the way they should when their owner was breathing. He knew that sounded ridiculous. That the breasts in the magazines he'd spent hours gushing over as a teen hadn't been moving either... but somehow it was still true.

Her lips and hair had dried out long ago, looking as though she'd been pulled out of the Sahara instead of a ditch. He'd managed to get all of the gunk out of the curly red locks, collecting it into an evidence bag for Detective Andrews. He didn't think any of it would be helpful, but then that wasn't his call to make.

For a moment, she looked so lifelike that he almost expected her to get up off the table.

"Coral Beach Precinct Morgue, my name is Harry Ford. I'll be your mortician for this evening," Harry said, throwing a grin at his partner as he twiddled his scalpel between his fingers.

"That's really getting old, Har," Lance breathed impatiently, barely throwing a glance Harry's way.

Harry stopped, standing up straight. "Sorry," he said in a small voice, then clicked on the tape recorder and handing it to his friend. "Your turn, anyway."

Lance frowned, taking the small, square device away from him and then bringing the mic to his face. "Berkshire, Lance MD. Preliminary autopsy for Carpenter, Roxanne M. Thirty-six years of age. Weight approximately one-hundred and ten pounds, height five three."

He paused, laying the recorder down onto the table to free up both his hands as he leaned over her body. There were several holes in her chest, the skin bulging out around each. Puss had started to form before her immune system had shut completely down, turning into putrid gangrene in the hours before her body was discovered. It multiplied the stench of the decomposition a thousand fold. "Two... three exit wounds in the chest made by sharp low-velocity object. One additional slice vertically along the torso beginning at the naval and ending at the solar plexus."

"Jesus," Harry muttered, bringing a hand to his mouth.

Lance ignored him, moving up to her face and forcing her eyelids wide with his fingertips. "Pupils are fixed, no signs of asphyxiation... I think she was conscious while he did this to her. It was definitely pari-mortem. There's bruising around each wound, so blood was flowing through her veins and her immune system was active as this was done." He stopped, nodding at Harry.

Harry grabbed the sheet which had been up to her waist by both corners and pulled it down as far as her ankles, then spread her legs apart just enough just enough so that Lance could examine her genitals.

"Bruising at seven and five..." he mumbled, spreading her legs apart a little more. "Definitely evidence of sexual assault, but nothing within the last few days. I'd say this is at least two weeks old, but I'll check her vaginal vault for semen in any case."

"Dump and go, maybe?" Harry said, a little too much hope in his voice to be asking what he was. "Bastard boyfriend gets tired of raping his girl, so he kills her and trades her in for a newer model?"

Lance shot him a look.

"Just tell me we're not dealing with the same guy here, Berk," Harry said, his eyes nearly pleading.

Lance sighed, prying open her mouth with both hands. When he did, Harry saw that the entire front row of teeth were missing, gum and all. What was left was a bloody, postulant maw of what had once been a very inviting smile. "Can't say that, Har," he sighed, picking up his camera to take a picture of the grotesque smirk.

Harry turned around and threw up onto the next table over.

Derek grunted angrily as he spun his joystick around in a quick half-moon shape, tapping red and blue keys as he desperately tried to get the tiny digital character on the screen to do something - *anything* - that might save him as his health bar throbbed a painful looking maroon. For his part, Xander was trying his best not to laugh as he mashed down all three red buttons at once, making his rocky sprite shoot boulders from his eyes and into the opponent. Derek cursed, pushing against Xander with his hip to try and throw him off or get him to release the controls.

"Die, die, die," Xander smirked, his tongue sticking out of the side of his mouth as he spun the control stick 180 degrees and slammed the keys just as Derek had been trying to do, successfully executing the finishing move.

"Fuck!" Derek spat, slamming his hand against his own controller. He stepped away from the machine for a moment and ran his fingers over his scalp, then laughed. "That was nice," he said, pointing a finger at Xander and shooting him a sly smile.

"Thank you, thank you," Xander said in a voice that was supposed to be aristocratic but came off as just being whiney, taking a few dramatically overdone bows as he did. When he straightened back up, his smile was so wide that even his molars were showing.

It faded instantly when he saw what was over Derek's left shoulder.

Mike stood in the doorway; his blonde hair turned a dark golden with sweat and matted down against his forehead. His chest heaved up and down under the shirt he was wearing, which had been clean and pressed only hours ago but now had large circular stains under each armpit. His mouth was open and breathing hard and his eyes were barely visible under the shadow of his brow.

"Hey, you're out of the hospital!" Xander said cheerfully, his arms spread out before him. After a moment with no response his smile faded more and his arms lowered. "Are you all right?" he asked, taking a step closer.

"Ran," Mike said simply. He scratched at his wrist where there was still an oozing red bump from where the IV had been taken out.

Derek looked from one of them to the other, smirking. "How's Cathy? She doing all right, too?"

Mike nodded, gasping hard for air but never once taking his eyes off of Xander.

Xander still had a smile perking at the corners of his lips, taking a step or two toward his friend. "That's great. That's really great."

Again, Mike nodded. Even his freckles seemed to be sweating.

"Cool, cool," Derek continued, patting Xander on the back heartily. "I'll be sure'n let Julie know. She's been asking."

"Kay," Mike said finally, his voice hoarse from all the running. "Xander, can I talk to you alone for a minute."

"Sure, buddy," Xander replied, raising an eyebrow quizzically. He turned and gestured to Derek.

The taller boy nodded briefly, then watched as Xander hopped up the stairs to join Mike without another word before they both walked out the front door. He frowned so far that it stretched the sides of his face, then sighed and turned back toward the video game.

Mike and Xander walked around to the back of The Factory, their feet kicking up loose pebbles and cigarette butts with every step they took. The grass here was always a little darker and sickly looking than anywhere else in town, always caught in the shadow of either the building or the trees behind it. There was a large, grey rock half submerged by the concrete foundation of the hall. Its smooth surface had acted like a chair for anyone who wanted to use it for as long as Xander had been alive. It was also the most popular spot in town for teens to get drunk or stoned when they didn't want to be noticed, but that was one of its less-advertised virtues.

Xander had heard rumours that before The Factory had been here there had been urban legends about that stone and how it had been the seat of the Devil before men had moved to Coral Beach. Now it was just 'the old sitting stone', as Cathy had childishly named it once.

Sometimes he'd end up there on his nights out as Black Womb. He'd wake up covered in blood and vomit and semen with his head propped up against the stone, unable to catch his breath. He'd wondered more than once if somehow the Womb could sense his connection to this place, or if it was just some random coincidence like everything else seemed to be.

Xander smirked, a memory tickling at the back of his mind. Even when he was here after a transformation, it always came to him, and he couldn't help but smile.

Cathy shifted slightly. The stone beneath her was rough like sandpaper, but it was the only place for her to sit. Squirming uncomfortably, she cursed Xander for making her come out here for no reason she could discern other than his need to be outside on a warm day. She glared menacingly at the back of his head as he walked around aimlessly, his shoes kicking up dirt and dust. She was only burning the hole into his head for a moment when her gaze shifted and a smile spread across her lips. "Oh, look Xander." she said, scooting to the edge of the stone.

"What?" Xander said, grinning as he turned on his heels to see her. Her long auburn hair tumbling over her shoulders. Mike, Sara and Julie had gone inside for some drinks and left the two of them alone on the stone. Mike and Cathy had just started going out a few months ago. Independence day, actually, and Xander had spent the next few months joking that that had been the day that Mike had lost his independence. But he always said it with a smile on his face.

"A squirrel," she replied, her lower lip pouting slightly at the cute sight.

"What?" Xander repeated, a puzzled and skeptical look passing over his face. He thought this would be another of her childish 'made you look' gags, but turned his head anyway. Sure enough, there it was, a little baby squirrel, no more than a few weeks old.

"Oh."

"Oh my gawd, he is the cutest thing," she said in a whiney voice, like a child that wanted a toy she knew she could never have. She turned and hit him on the chest suddenly, so excited that she blurted all her words out at once. "Let's name it!"

"Okaaaaay," Xander sighed, pretending to be too mature for her antics. "How about 'squirrel'?"

She tisked and gave him a little slap on the arm. "No! A real name."

"It's a squirrel, Cat. That's why it doesn't have a real name. If your brain's the size of a pea, you don't get a name. It's in the Bible."

"Then why do you get one?" she shot, brow furrowed angrily. "You're just saying that because you can't think of a name anyway."

Xander rolled his eyes, taking a single step forward cautiously until they were shoulder to shoulder. "How about Alvin?"

"It's cliché."

"So is Cathy."

She shot him a look. "Besides, Alvin was a chipmunk."

Xander opened his mouth to respond, then closed it and nodded.

As suddenly as before, she turned and backhanded him across the chest.

"Ow," he winced, though she didn't notice.

"Let's name him Bob," she blurted.

"Bob the squirrel," Xander stated bluntly, raising an eyebrow at her.

"Yes. Bob the squirrel," she smiled at him with her big brown eyes and ruby red lips. She knew he was way too uptight to actually get the joke there, which just made it that much more funny. The squirrel gazed up at them, and in the blink of an eye was down on all fours, examining them. "Oh, you little cutie. Come here, Bob."

"He could have rabies," Xander said in caution, gently grabbing Cathy's shoulder to keep her from getting closer.

"Ew. I didn't know squirrels could carry scabies," she said, crinkling her nose as she recoiled from it a little.

Xander burst in laughter, frightening the little animal, although it didn't run.

"What?" Cathy smiled.

He kept laughing, turning his face away from her as he tried to stop.

"What?" she demanded again, pinching his sides to get the answer.

"I said rabies, not scabies," he said, laughing through the words.

"Oh," she said quietly, her face losing all expression for a moment as she filed that away. She shrugged, stepping in close to Bob again. "I don't care about that."

Smiling warmly and making little clucking sounds with her tongue, she reached her hand out slowly and tried to pet him on the head. It looked up at her with large, black eyes as though it were trying to figure her out just as much as she was it. It inched closer to her, its nose twitching and whiskers turning this way and that until finally it turned and bolted back into the woods as quickly as it had appeared. "Oh," she said sadly, as if she'd just lost her best friend. "Bye Bob."

He choked back a laugh at her expense.

She slapped him lightly again, tisking.

That seemed to only make him laugh more as he stumbled back a step away from her, his face growing red now.

She shook her head as she looked at him, and before she knew it, she was laughing as well.

When he could stop laughing long enough to get his eyes open he looked at her, the smile on his face as broad as it had ever been. She looked back at him with one even brighter, the morning sun glistening off her cherry lip balm and her eyes. After a moment her smile faded completely and so did his, and then they were just... looking at each other.

She had a truly fair face. There were lots of girls prettier, but very few that were as beautiful. There was an innocence and a softness about her that put the people around her at rest. Like a human sedative walking around infecting people with peace. Big eyes, thick lips, cute freckles across the bridge of her small nose.

He leaned in without really even knowing what he was doing, as though his body had been disconnected from his brain and now acted on its own instincts.

She leaned in, too. Her lips parted slightly as they got close, showing just a smidgen of her small, white teeth and the tongue that rested on them.

They both smiled again as their lips met, her hand coming up and stroking the side of his face and pulling it in closer. He didn't move. It was all he could do to stop himself from shaking as he felt the warmth of her body mix with his.

Her fingers traced the outline of his familiar, rough-hewn features and then suddenly pushed away from him.

They both gasped, both for air and for words

"Sorry, I... I'm-- " Xander stammered, his mind going a mile-a-minute after its temporary rest.

"No, it's --"

"Hi guys," Sara said in her bubbly voice, rounding the corner with Mike carrying five drinks. "What are ya doin'?"

"Nothing!" they both said simultaneously.

Sara raised an eyebrow suspiciously, throwing a smirk at Xander as Cathy went to Mike and kissed him.

They never spoke of it again.

Mike walked forward with the determination and posture of a drill sergeant until his toes were almost touching the stone. He came to a dead halt and turned around to face Xander, but would not meet him with his eyes. Instead he stared down at the bar wrappers and trash on the ground in front of him, his face at war with itself.

Xander stared at him for almost a full minute, rubbing his tongue back and forth against the roof of his mouth as he tried to figure out what was going on.

"I need to talk to someone," Mike said finally, still unable to meet Xander's gaze as he clenched both his fists so tightly that his nails made tiny semicircle indents in his palms.

"Okay," Xander said, stepping forward and forcing a smile. Awkwardly, he reached out and lay a hand on the taller man's shoulder. "What about?"

Clenching his jaw, Mike drew back fast and punched Xander square in the mouth.

Long, slithering spurts of blood and saliva spewed out of his mouth from either side of the impact as he fell backward. Two pink-tinted teeth hit the ground even before he did, getting lost amongst the stones and gravel. There was an electric pain as the bones in the bottom half of his face realigned themselves with the top. "What the hell?" he screamed, the words mumbled and distorted from the mauling his mouth had taken. "I thought you said you needed to talk?"

"I do," Mike nodded honestly, his voice full of regret as he took another step forward. He loomed over his friend, the sun hot on his back making his features unreadable. He drew back again, as far as his arm could go. "Just not to you."

Xander tried to get up, but before he could even summon the will to move Mike's hand had connected with his skull at the eyebrow. It knocked him back down again, almost falling into himself as dirt and dust kicked up in all directions. The skin over his eye split, sending blood gushing down into his eye. It was as though all the blood in his body had been there, waiting to come out like a raging river held back by a frail dam. It came in great spouting bursts, turning his whole world red.

Mike pushed him down again when he tried to scamper to his feet, pinning his friend's shoulders down with his knees. His felt his fist connect with the soft meat on the side of Xander's face, the only audible sound within earshot the wet smack of flesh against flesh. He pulled back, his lips stiff and resolute while his eyes were floating in a half-inch of saltwater.

Xander's face looked and felt like ground beef. His lips looked like a shirt that had been twisted and bunched to one side, showing not enough of his teeth on one side and too much on the other. The skin along his left cheek was missing, replaced instead with muscle bone barely hidden behind a veil of crimson. His mouth filled with a sweet, coppery taste as his head fell back onto the ground with a soft thud. His eyelids fluttered.

"Get up," Mike said softly, wriggling the fingers of his tightly-wound fists. His pinky cried out to him in agony when he did, broken during one of the impact tremors along Xander's skull. He punched Xander again, hammering down onto his nose. "Get up!" he said again, barking.

The peachy pink that had been Xander's flesh was gone. Some of it had flown off all of its own accord, some of it hid behind a layer of thick, slick blood; but all of it was gone. It was so dark a red that it might as well have been *black*. All the vessels of his eyes had ruptured and broken, leaving only glossy black circles to stare up at Mike from red pools that were indistinguishable from the flesh around. He looked as close to the Womb as Xander ever had. The *Crimson Womb* opened its mouth to speak and for a moment there was only a wet, suckling sound as it tried to force its own lips apart. "Why?" he said finally, salt from his tears mixing in with the splits in his face and making them burn. "Don't... guh... don't wanna fight you."

For a moment, pity won the war for emotional control over Mike's face. His eyes softened and his lower lip became wrinkled and trembled as he looked down at his friend. He reached out and touched the side of Xander's head, running his nails over his scalp gently. "I know. I don't want to fight you, either," he nodded. His fist closed around Xander's hair, holding his head steady as his other hand came up between them one final time, connecting to the side of Xander's face and shattering it from ear the ear. "But like I said, I've gotta talk to someone."

When Xander opened his eyes again they were a deep aquatic blue, the pupils long since faded away as the edges of them turned upwards like a villain's mustache in a thirties movie. His mouth opened wide to reveal that the missing teeth had been replaced with longer, sharper ones that came down from his gums as though they were on lifts, sliding out and locking into place naturally. From somewhere deep inside his throat, there was a dull hiss like he'd swallowed a python and when Mike looked hard enough, he swore he could see bones resetting and righting themselves in the back of his friend's mouth.

Slowly, Mike let go of the back of Xander's head and got off of him, watching as the oily crimson that covered his face slowly got darker and darker. It was like watching two similar shades of paint mix together in an automatic stirrer, the blackness swirling around on the surface until it was everywhere, matting down his hair until it looked like he was bald. It travelled down his neck and over his body, soaking into his clothes layer by layer until it wasn't visible anymore. It was just blackness held so tightly to his skin that it might as well have been skin.

It got up, its neck hunched as it lowered its steely, slanted eyes at Mike. Its hands hung loosely at its sides, like a cowboy itching to drawn his gun. Slowly and discreetly, a black-tinted claw slid out from each fingertip as the last of its red blood fell from the corner of its lip. "Black Womb lives," it barked, its voice low and menacing as though it had just uttered some horrible curse at Mike.

"Just the person I wanted to see," Mike said, his voice quavering only slightly as he forced a smile and licked his lips.

The Womb lunged forward, slamming both its palms into Mike's shoulders.

He nearly bit down on his own tongue as his head slammed against the ground before he even realized he was falling, his jaw snapping shut upon impact. The Womb sat on his chest, its feet rested on either side of his head. Long talons had unsheathed themselves from his toes as well, tapping contemplatively on the gravel next to his ear. He could feel them brushing alongside the hair of his neck. "You don't scare me," he said, curling his lip in disgust.

The Womb bent down slowly until the sides of its head were roughly level with its ankles, although Mike knew full well Xander couldn't even touch his toes. The thing was nose-to-nose with him now, the stench of old vomit that came on its blood overpowering Mike. It gawked at him with eyes twice the size they should have been, small scraps of leftover flesh floating in their greenish pools. It blinked slowly, then tilted its head to one side. It remained that way for a full ten seconds before blinking again, then tilting in the other direction.

"What's so confusing?" Mike said bitterly, his voice almost a whisper. "You not used to people fighting back?"

Its long tongue came out of its mouth and licked its lips, showing off long duel rows of jagged, yellowed teeth at the same time. It clacked its tongue against them just as Xander did when he thought, making a loud hollow sound that echoed off its gaping mouth. Its eyes glowed, light flickering across them from the sun. It closed its mouth again and made a sound that was almost purring as it continued to stare at Mike.

"What do you want from us? Huh?" Mike yelled, squirming under the creature's weight. "Come on! You come and you come every chance you get, well *I'm right here!*" he bellowed, so loud that his voice didn't even sound human. Each syllable was a roar, cracking and rising again before the next. Hot tears streamed down his livid face as he finally got his arms free and shoved the Womb off him.

It backed up a pace, staying squat near the ground.

Fuelled by rage and without any conscious thought, Mike struggled to his feet and then let loose one punch that amassed all the anger and hate that he had let well up inside him for weeks, as though his fist had been a cannon and he had fired his heart upon it.

The Womb's head jolted sideways, the black flesh that clung so tediously to it coming loose for a split second. It turned back toward him quickly, not moving its hands or position at all. Its eyes turned up in their sockets in the closest thing to confusion that its blank tableau of a face could accomplish. It looked shocked, then snorted the air through nearly invisible nostrils. It almost looked hurt.

"What?" Mike yelled again, thrusting his arms out to either side of him. "You can't kill me here? Excuse me! I didn't know that your priorities were so damn high!" He drew back and nailed the Womb in the face, shattering the knuckle of his middle finger as he did.

It stared back at him, unmoving, its head ducked down a little now as it looked up at Mike with large eyes.

"Why us? Why me, why Cathy? Why Sara? What could we have possibly done to you, you piece of crap?" he screamed, his words barely making sense anymore. He lashed out again despite the throbbing sensation in his hand, this time getting the creature in one of its massive eyes.

"⌊_ac!" it snarled, snapping at him as it brought one hand up in a motion so fast it made a long, black blur in the air behind it as it went. It struck Mike in the side, stretching the stitches there and sending him tumbling to the ground again, his head beating off a rock. When he opened his eyes again, the Womb was standing over him, looming back and forth as its clawed fingers twitched over and over again, preparing to strike.

It stopped moving at all then, but for the narrowing of its eyes again. When they were almost too slender to be seen, it stopped moving them as well, staying as still as a statue as it watched Mike leak salt water, blood, and mucus from his mouth.

The blackness covering the creature lost consistency, splashing down to the ground as Xander fell as well, his clothes soaked through and through. The stench of blood, sweat, and BO that came with the sudden loss of the tar-like skin was like pennies that had been rubbed with friend chicken.

Xander gasped at the air as his lungs started to work again, churning to force all the darkness out of them before he drowned.

Mike stared at him, squinting, before slowly bringing himself up to a sitting position. He groaned as his bones cracked, his hands shaking violently as adrenaline wore off and he started to feel what he had done to his hand. He didn't realize he was breathing hard until he noticed he was doing it at the same pace Xander was.

"So what... did that accomplish?" Xander said after a moment, still gasping for breath. He put his head between his knees and hacked up black blood and saliva, spitting it out in a long, dangling wad as he massaged the back of his own head.

"Not what I hoped," Mike said, getting up off the ground and dusting himself off before extending his hand to his friend. "Felt better than punching a wall, though."

Xander raised an eyebrow as he took his hand, pulling himself to his feet.

"I do have one thing we didn't have before I did that," he added, waving a finger as if he were displaying his saving point.

"What's that?"

"More questions."

CHAPTER SIX: HUMANITY

Tommy slammed his hands against the sink, feeling a hot pain course through his palms as he did. His lips curled up in a snarl as he stared at his own reflection with large, dark rings around his eyes.

Sud looked over his shoulder from where he stood at the urinal, frowning as he zipped up and walked over. His mouth hung open as though he had something to say, though he just continued to stare blankly at Tommy's reflection.

"That fuckin' little bastard thinks he can treat me like that," Tommy growled, wetting his hand under the faucet and then splashing it up onto his face. "Little fucker."

Sud nodded once, then grunted a single-syllable agreement.

"Doesn't know who I am. Doesn't know what I'm capable of. *Isn't even worth* the air he *breathes*, little frigging psycho," he mumbled, standing back up and wiping water away as it dribbled from his chin. "Dude belongs in a god-damned mental institution, I'm tellin' ya."

"Like on *The Secret of NIMH*," chuckled Sud.

"Huh?" Tommy said, raising one of his pointed eyebrows.

"The National Institute of Mental Health. You know, with the talking mice and that wacky crow that liked shiny things..."

"Shut up," Tommy dismissed, glaring at him.

"I like shiny things."

"Man, shut up!" Tommy said, angry now. He punched the wall of the washroom, then irked in pain as he realized that he had done so with the hand Xander had nearly broken. He let out a small yelp before grunting his frustration. "Fuck. Who does that fucker think he is? That little nerd loses his bitch lover and suddenly he's some cool shit?" He shook his head, his eyes growing small and thoughtful. After a moment, he started to wave his finger in front of him as though a light had gone on in his head, then turned back to Sud. "We gotta teach him a lesson, man. He cannot get away with this shit. There's that memorial service thing coming up soon... and I think I got just the right idea for what to do."

𝕸𝕽

Cathy slurped on her cherry cola, her small red lips pursed around it tightly.

Xander stared at those lips without really even noticing them, his eyes looking sunken and far away, as though he were lost somewhere within his own head.

They sat at a table in the Factory that they'd long ago claimed as *their* table. Neither of them owned it separately, and they only sat in it when the both of them were there. Three seats from top and four from left, the spot where all the noise in the building seemed to collide together and cancel each other out, created a kind of soundless vacuum. Once, when the four of them had come in and other people had been sitting there, Roxanne had actually asked them to get up. When they'd refused, she'd asked them to leave completely.

On the other side of the room, Mike grunted harshly as he skidded his already-sore knuckles against the side of the arcade game he was playing while trying to pull off a combo. He still swiveled the joystick relentlessly, no matter how much it hurt, tapping the buttons so fast that one tap couldn't be heard before the next happened.

Cathy grinned at him, almost getting soda up her nose as she did. "Never met a boy who could take out *all* his frustrations on a stupid game before," she giggled, turned back toward Xander.

His gaze had dropped several inches from staring at her lips, resting on the smooth, white skin over her collarbone.

She raised an eyebrow at him, a small smile perking over her face as she leaned her head back from her straw. "Ahem," she grunted, clearing her throat.

Xander continued to stare straight ahead, the shadow from his brow making his eyes nearly invisible.

"Daydream much?" she said finally, a slight hint of annoyance in her voice even though she was smiling.

He *still* did not respond.

She reached out to where his hand lay upon the table and put hers on it, her soft skin like velvet on his dry knuckles.

He finally looked up at her, the light from the candles all around the room dancing across her face and shimmering in her hair, making her look like an angel. "Hmm?" he hummed, coming back to reality at once.

"You still with us?" she asked warmly, looking up at him with a soothing smile on her mouth.

"Yeah," he said, looking off into space again for a moment before shaking it off again. "Yes. Sorry, just thinking too much, I guess."

"Anything in particular?" she asked, taking her hand from his and grabbing her drink with it, bringing it back to her lips. "Or do I even wanna know, the way you were looking at my chest?"

He did not respond to that last bit, his eyes every bit as distant as they had been a moment ago, even though he was looking at her now. "Just the way things are, I guess. They way life is. Mike got me thinking with that stunt he pulled."

"How so?"

His mouth fidgeted, as if physically uncomfortable as he tried to find his thoughts. When he spoke again, his voice was hushed and distant. "When I was a kid, I always thought that everything would work itself out. I stuck to the shadows like some stupid wallflower, knowing that all the pieces to the puzzle would just fall into place for me. That I would eventually get the girl and grow up and live happily ever after."

She didn't speak, laying down her drink to give him her full attention.

"But it didn't, and I won't. I thought I learned my lesson when Sara died... but here I am, making the same mistakes again. Sitting around and letting things happen around me to my life, my friends. Hoping that the puzzle will just work itself out. Not taking *control*."

There was a silence then as both of them waited for the other to speak. After a moment, Cathy squirmed in her seat and then spoke. "How did Mike beating the crap out of you make you think of that?"

Xander smiled, looking up and really acknowledging her for the first time since the conversation had begun. "He did something. He tried *something*. It was a stupid thing to try, but at least he did something instead of sitting around on his ass. Made me realize that it's time to start pressing buttons. That this might not work out unless I make it."

She nodded, her hair bobbing along with her.

Mike pulled a chair from the next table over and slid it over to theirs, flopping down on it backwards. His face was flushed and showing the first signs of sweat as he flashed a large smile at Cathy, then nodded curtly at Xander.

Xander nodded back.

Mike placed an arm around Cathy, giving her a kiss on the cheek and smiling. "You putting the moves on my woman again, Drew?" he said, a mischievous grin playing over his face.

A slow grin spread over Xander's face as he looked from one to the other.

"What?" Cathy asked, snickering.

"Bob the squirrel," he said, in as even a tone as he could muster.

Cathy burst into laughter with Xander not far behind, both of them leaning forward onto the table to catch their breath. Cola finally began running out of Cathy's nose and when she tried to wipe it away with her sleeve, she rolled off of her chair. Xander's face turned red, sitting back on his chair and holding his breath to try and stop.

"What?" Mike asked, looking from one to the other, a stupid grin on his face. "What?"

"Nothing, honey," Cathy said as she got up and kissed him, still giggling a bit.

Mike rolled his eyes, then leaned in and gave her a quick kiss that turned into an extended one, as theirs tended to do.

Xander watched them for a moment, the shuffled in his seat and got up.

Cathy hummed, pulling away from Mike even though his lips kept making the kissing motion for a moment. "Mmmhey, where you going?"

"Something I gotta see to," he said, both his eyes and voice having gained their far away quality in the interim between speeches.

"If there's anything you need..."

"Actually there is something," Xander said, stopping for a second as he walked away.

"Name it."

"Drop up to the house tonight."

"Okay."

"Around dark."

Both Mike and Cathy turned to look at him when he said that, but he was already gone.

Megan Greene sifted through the files cluttering her desk, the large oak surface covered in carefully stacked piles of paper. She picked the top sheet off the pile just to her right, making a tiny red mark on the next page, then laid it back down. Her eyes fluttered over the piles again and she repeated the maneuver with a pile near the top, scribbling something along the margin in dark red ink.

She sighed as she laid the sheet back down, rummaging her perfectly manicured nails through her bright red hair. After scuttling it about and then fixing it again, she stopped and smiled at herself.

It wasn't as though she wasn't prepared.

Some would make a case that she was overly prepared, actually. She was in line to be the District Attorney for the whole area and she was going up against a lawyer who was apparently living out of her offices. She'd researched every part of Natasha Mayer's personal and district history to make sure she knew exactly what she was up against. Had gone so far as to find out what teachers she'd studied under in University to try and extrapolate what kind of defense she might work out for Genblade. She'd researched all the pros – of which there were many –of sending Genblade to his death. She'd even researched the cons, which were few and far between. She'd spoken with doctors and psychiatrists that worked with the criminally insane. Gotten sworn statements from reputable sources that stated that Adam Genblade was unequivocally in control of his functions when he killed those children.

She was ready.

She repeated that in her mind several times, leaning back in her chair and letting out a long sigh. She was ready. After only a moment she rose again, bringing her pen to the page in front of her and scratching out a line near its middle.

Ever since she'd been a child, she'd been nervous this way when it came to preparing. Writing notes out for a test a hundred times to make sure it was memorized, even long after she'd tossed the book away and written it from memory. Reciting particularly hard passages over and over again until her tongue went numb. Once, in college, she'd stayed up studying for thirty-six hours on nothing but cold pizza and Red Bull.

The pages in front of her blurred together and then separated back apart, bulging in and out as if they were breathing. Groaning, she rubbed the bridge of her nose as she examined the empty cup of espresso next to her and tried to recall when the last pot had been brewed. Despite rumours to the contrary, coffee did in fact have an expiration date. Anything over an hour old was like drinking tar.

A tall man poked his head in through the window, his hair slicked back neatly and a charming smile pasted across his face. The smile would almost have been creepy but for the small sparkle in his eyes that somehow made it okay and made it more honest. The suit he wore had looked pressed and magnificent a few hours ago when he'd put it on, but was already showing signs of daily wear and tear from the day's labours. "Anthony Jones paging Megan Greene, please pick up Megan Greene."

She tried to glare up at him from her papers, but couldn't help the smile that was slowly spreading across her lips as he entered the room. "That's getting old."

"No it's not," he responded in a chipper tone, sitting down in the chair across from her and laying a steaming cup of coffee on the desk before her. "Here. Thought you could use a break."

"You're sweet," she said, taking the cup to her lips and blowing the steam away before taking a cautious sip, then downing a massive gulp.

He watched her for a moment until she noticed him.

She hummed a small laugh, then put down the cup and smirked at him. "Sorry. Thank you."

"Hmm?" he said, looking up at her. "Oh. No big deal, I was on my way up. So, you ready for the big Genblade hearing?"

She rolled her eyes and was about to make a snide comment when she stopped herself just as her mouth opened. "I think so," she said instead, tapping her finger against her desk.

"That doesn't sound good. There's a lot riding on this. I'm sure I don't need to tell you. This could be your ticket to assistant DA. You sure you don't need a hand with the research?"

She smiled, waving the notion away with a gesture. "I got it covered. It should be fairly open and shut. Even if he won't confess on the stand, we'll just read his prior statement into evidence and get him on purgery as well."

He grinned. "That's a bit of overkill when you're going for the death sentence, don't you think?"

"Why go at him with a pistol when you've got a cannon right there?" She smiled, shrugging as she leaned back in her chair again, crossing her arms in front of her. "I'm gonna see this through to the end, Tony... and I really do pity anyone who tries to get in my way."

ʌ⟨ʌ

"Ow," Natasha said as she clunked her head onto the cluttered table in front of her, feeling the impact reverberate through her skull.

She closed her eyes tightly to try and force the floor beneath her back into focus, finding it very difficult to convince her eyes to open again. Each of her lashes felt like lead weights and the bags under her eyes got bigger every time she looked in the mirror. She tried to remember the last thought to go through her head and get the train rolling again, when to her horror she discovered she was so tired that she'd actually lost the ability to *think* for a moment.

For the briefest of serene moments, she felt sleep nipping at her and began to fall into it.

A knock at the door jolted her up suddenly, scattering the papers on her desk even more than they already were.

"Sorry to interrupt," Xander said, unable to hide his bemused grin as he stepped into the office, pushing papers with the door as he went.

"No, I just... dropped my pen," she lied, sitting up completely and pretending to stack papers. She kept up the charade for only a minute before sighing and dropping them back onto the desk. "What can I do to help you?"

"Ah, I'm looking for a--" he paused, pulling a crumpled up business card out of his front pocket and examining it. "--Natasha Mayer. Any chance you know where she is?"

"That's me," she smiled, motioning for him to come in. "I am she, I'm... how can I help you?"

"Huh," Xander said, sizing her up for a moment as he flicked the card between his hands. After a moment he silently accepted her invitation and stepped inside. "Sorry, pictured you a little different."

She cocked her head to one side, squinting at him a little. "Do I... know you from somewhere? You look very familiar."

"I'm sorry," he chuckled, extending a hand toward her. "My name is Alexander Drew. Most people call me Xander."

She ignored his hand, turning back to the papers on her desk and shuffling through them quickly until she found the one she was looking for. She scanned down through it quickly, her eyes darting back and forth in her head until she found what she was looking for. "Drew, Alexander. Jesus, you're the kid Genblade kidnapped."

Xander gave a short, forced laugh as he looked down at his feet and clicked his tongue against the backs of his teeth. "Yeah, yeah that would be me."

Natasha rolled her eyes, flopping the papers aside. "Listen, kid, I'll tell you

322

the same thing I've been telling the parents who won't stop calling: everyone deserves a good defense. It's one of the backbones of our justice system and if you don't like it, you can take it up with your senator, not with me."

Xander laughed, flicking his top lip. "Okay, two things. First, do you still call them parents if their kids are all dead?"

Natasha shot him a look, then shifted her gaze towards the door.

"Okay, okay. Second, I... really wasn't here to complain."

She raised an eyebrow at him, leaning forward onto her desk and lacing her fingers together. She tried to appear collected and calm for a moment, but her face eventually turned upward in a confused drawl. "What?"

Frowning, Xander moved forward until he was standing right across the table from her. "I want to help you with the Genblade case. Be a witness, help with how to approach him in court... whatever. I want to be as involved as you'll have me."

"Think you're confused," she coughed, switching back to pretending to stacking papers again. "I'm with Genblade's *defense.* Maybe you should be speaking with--"

"I know," he grinned, taking a small folder out of his jacket and laying it down on the table. "I think I can help."

҄〈〉҄

"How do you spell *proliferate*?" Cathy asked, chewing on the end of her pen.

Mike let the magazine he was reading flop onto his chest, turning to stare at her from his place snuggled between the mountains of pillows on her bed. "Why?"

"Hmm?" she hummed, finally looking away from the rose scented piece of pink paper in front of her, the blue words upon it written in extravagant, cursive loops that she marked as one of her only true artistic talents. "It's... nothing. Just something I'm doing for the memorial."

Mike frowned, stopping to think for a moment. "P-R-O-L-I-F-E - -"

"Thanks."

He stopped, shooting her a look.

"Wasn't sure if it was an A or an E after the F."

"Proliferate. A phase of wound healing. Means getting better at a steady rate. Pro Life Rate. That's... how I remembered."

"That's a pretty weird way to remember that."

He sat up on the bed and tossed the magazine aside as he watched her hunch back over her desk, carefully making the loops and swirls of every word. "May I ask why you'd need that word for a memorial letter?"

She finished the word she was working on, then lay down her pen before turning around on her chair. "Sara couldn't pronounce it. Tried like hell, never could. Not even if someone else said it first. Same thing with authentication."

"Still doesn't explain why you're putting it in a memorial letter."

She sighed, her shoulders slumping a little. Grimacing, she picked up the

323

paper and started to crumple it up.

"Hey!" Mike snapped, snatching it away from her. "Just because I don't get it doesn't make it bad. Just means I don't get it. That's why I'm asking."

"People... seem like they're remembering everyone through rose-colored glasses."

"Through what?" he asked, smoothing out the paper against the wall.

"You know what proliferate means, but you've never heard the phrase rose-colored glasses?"

"Discovery Channel," he said meekly in his own defense.

She rolled her eyes, smiling at him. "People have been remembering every-one at their best. Like they were flawless or something. For me it was the stupid little things that irked me that I'm going to miss now."

"Like how she couldn't pronounce proliferate?"

"Or, how she didn't put toothpaste on her toothbrush, she squirted it into her mouth and used the toothbrush to scrub it around. Or the way she ate her peas one at a time. All that stuff. That's... what I'm trying to say."

He nodded, pursing his lips.

"You think it's stupid."

"No," he smiled, passing her back the sheet of paper. "I think it's great. I think her parents'll love it."

She smiled, straightening the paper as she continued to write.

He grabbed a slinky from her desk and started wobbling it back and forth between his hands as he walked back toward the bed, keeping his eyes trained on the shimmering metal in the center of the arch. "What do you think Xander wants?"

"I... don't know. I rarely ever know what Xander wants, in fact."

"I meant with us. Tonight."

"I know what you meant, I just don't know."

He paused, letting the spring slump into his right hand. He walked over next to her and laid it down on the paper, forcing her to stop.

"What are you doing?"

"You don't have to be dead to have someone that only ever sees the best in you." he said blankly, avoiding eye contact with her.

"What are you - -"

"He's got a problem. Unless we figure out what's going on soon or whether or not he can get a handle on it... we're going to have to do it for him. Are you ready to do that?"

Cathy narrowed her eyes, then turned away from him and pushed the slinky aside, continuing to write.

Natasha fixed her blouse, making sure the top button was fastened tightly as she sat down in the cold, orange chair. She twitched nervously, rapping her nails along the edge of the burgundy notebook she carried pressed against her breasts as she squirmed and tried to get comfortable.

Her usually short hair had been allowed to grow out just a little too long and tickled the tips of her ears and eyelashes. Her mouth had gone dry the second she'd walked into the glass doors of the huge stone building, and she hadn't been able to work up any moisture yet, except to sweat. The arm of her blouse was already translucent from wiping the sweat from her brow every few minutes.

The ceilings were high and all the walls painted stark white. It was as quiet and still as a church on Saturday, the only movement coming from the blinking light attached to the side of each camera; their lenses seeming to be trained directly on her no matter where she looked.

Directly in front of her was a glass wall that seemed to go up forever. It was so thick that everything viewed through it became distorted like a funhouse mirror. There were small cracks in it from the other side that made her squirm again.

There was a loud, metallic snap as the door on the other side of the glass unlocked itself. She swallowed hard as Adam Genblade walked out from behind it and into the visitor's area. His head was down and covered in shadow, yet somehow she could tell that he was smiling. Smiling so wide that it could barely even be contained by the confines of his slender face. After a few steps he looked up, his eyes so light a blue that they might well have been white, locking eyes with her instantly through the pain.

He stopped walking for a brief instant when he saw her. If it had been from surprise he did not show it on his face, calmly sitting down in the chair opposite her and hoisting up his chains enough to reach the foam-covered phone and bring it to his ear.

She did the same, her hand shaking a little as she touched the receiver. She stopped herself from checking her blouse again, even though something in the back of her head was telling her it was undone again. For a moment there was no sound, apart from the moist sickle of Genblade cleaning the front of his blood-stained teeth with his tongue.

"Hubba," he said finally, his eyes moving over her as though he owned her. "You're not the brunette I was expecting... but you'll definitely do. You charge by the hour, sweetie?"

"Actually, yes," Natasha responded in a steely voice, trying her best to sound civil. "My name is Natasha Mayer of Mayer, Summers and Soul, Mr. Genblade."

Genblade cocked his head to one side and smirked, but did not respond.

"I believe you addressed me in your letter requesting legal aid."

There was another long silence as he looked her up and down, though now he appeared to be measuring her metal instead of her brass. After a second or two he seemed satisfied, snorting into the phone. "Never thought in a million years you'd actually show. Not now."

"It's a high-profile case," she informed him, pinning the phone between her head and shoulder as she took a few pieces of paper out of her folder and began to scribble on one of them. "Win or lose, the publicity will be unimaginable. Just look at Johnnie Cochran's career."

"Who?" Genblade snarled, raising an eyebrow.

Natasha pasted on a fake, warm smile as she brushed the thought notion aside with a sweeping gesture. "Never mind. What's important is that we get started on your case, Mr. Genblade."

"You don't actually think you'll win, do you?"

Natasha tapped her folder again in silence, looking from one sheet of paper to another. "No. But with me behind you, I think you've got a much better chance."

"That's not exactly the position I had in mind for you... but we'll start out that way for now."

Again, Natasha shifted. "I'm afraid there isn't much to offer a case like this in the long run, however," she continued, as if he hadn't spoken. "The fact that you admitted guilt previously hampers my ability to undermine that. It shouldn't be too hard to claim insanity for your actions. See, if your crimes are the result of mental impairment then it's considered inhumane to put you to death for them."

"Darwin never was a judge," he scoffed under his breath.

"Excuse me?" she said, almost without thinking about it.

"Darwin, Charles. Kinda pioneered the whole 'strongest will survive' theory of evolution. He would have hated what western society has become, catering to the mentally unfit the way you do."

"Comments like that could also seriously undermine my efforts," Natasha said in an informative way, snapping her folder shut. "Also, if you would refrain from killing any more people during the duration of the trial, that would help a great deal."

"No promises," he said, staring at her through the glass.

Her eyes remained locked on his for a moment, pupils shrinking to the size of pinheads as sweat slowly dripped into them. She squirmed again, breaking the contact and placing the papers back into their place. "There's really not much more I can say. If you get another psyche evaluation I'd appreciate it if you turned down the violence and turned up the crazy... would help with our process a little. Other than that, the only news I have is that - -"

"You know how cute you are, in your little white blouse and your well-done hair?" he interrupted, slamming his palm against the glass as he spoke in hushed tones. "You look downright edible. But your red nails and dark eyeliner make you look like something I wouldn't have given a second stab at on the corner downtown. You know what? You look like such a good cross between a professional and a whore that you might as well just be a Professional Whore."

She shifted again, looking down as she opened her mouth to speak.

"And I see the way you wiggle and worm every time I open my mouth. I make you so uncomfortable you can't sit still, like a straight man watching gay porn on cable. But deep down inside, there's a reason he stopped there when he was flicking through, and it wasn't because he was hoping for bush like he tells his wife. Deep down, what really makes him uncomfortable is how much he *likes* it... same as you. Squirming around in your chair, half-dressed up... can't hide the fact that every time I speak you get just a little moist." He stopped, looking her up and down one final time and smiling. "You must really have some Daddy issues."

She winced at that last part, her eyes closed when she heard Genblade chuckle. After a moment to prepare herself, she turned back toward the glass and continued to speak, although her voice wavered heavily now. "I've actually gotten an offer for aid in your case. While I'm not sure how much help it'll actually be, it'll definitely look good."

Genblade's brow furrowed as he squinted at her, tilting his head from one side to the other. "Can't be who I think it is. Can't be anyone I can think of."

"Hmm? Oh, yes. He's a young man from town named Alexander Drew. I believe you have some acquaintance with him."

Genblade's face went white and seemed to drag downward, as if held down by some invisible weight.

"Well, if there's nothing else, I'm going to get ready for court."

Still, Genblade said nothing, his eyes as small as peas.

Natasha swallowed hard, her mouth parched and sore. "Good day then, Mr. Genblade," she said, hanging up the phone and turning away. She glanced over her shoulder when she got close to the door to see if he was watching her, but he was still sitting blank-eyed with the phone up to his ear. She shook her head and walked away.

"Time to go, Genblade," a tall guard said from his place against the wall a few minutes later.

Genblade still did not move, his face almost the same shade as the walls around him.

"Genblade, I said it's time to go," he repeated in a frustrated tone, laying a heavy hand on the inmate's shoulder.

He woke up three days later in a hospital bed with half his jaw missing and a hole in his neck that he would have to breathe through for the rest of his life.

ʎʞʎ

Xander sat at the edge of his stairs, gazing at the doorway in the dark. Only thirty minutes ago the room had been brightly lit just from outside, but now there was just the slow orange ebb of dusk fading into complete darkness.

His knee bounced a little as he waited, the sound of it tapping against the rail matching the sound of his heart, beat for beat. He took a deep breath through the fingers that were cupped together tightly over his mouth, then exhaled slowly, listening to the whistling whine as air passed between them.

He heard the scuffing and shuffling of feet outside, followed quickly by a low, deep voice talking to a louder, feminine one. Both were mumbled when heard through the wooden door. He briefly remembered a dream he had once while he was sick as a child, sitting in the dark while voices came at him. It agitated him enough that he finally got up and walked to the door. He placed his hand on the knob, forced his best fake-smile onto his lips, then opened the door with one quick painless motion.

Mike shot a raised eyebrow at him, his fist hanging in mid-air and about to knock on the door.

Smirking, Xander raised his fist the same way. "Exist extensively, and flourish," he said in a deep, monotone voice.

"What?"

"Thought that was just how your people greeted one another," he mumbled, stepping aside to let Mike and Cathy in.

Mike stepped inside cautiously, never once really taking his eyes off of Xander as he took off his sneakers.

Cathy stepped in quickly behind him, slipping off her shoes with two quick motions and then giving Xander a kiss on the cheek. "How are you?" she asked, her head leaning to one side sympathetically.

"Exactly when did that become such a loaded question?" he chuckled in response. "I remember when you used to ask me that during a movie or something... now it's like the end of the world every time you do."

Mike snorted.

Cathy pinched him in the ribs, hard, then shot him a look. "No reason," she replied, but it sounded more like an order than a response.

"Cool. Well, ah, I've got a few movies rented and some popcorn. Dad bought some poker chips last week that haven't been deflowered, so we could do that --"

"I don't know how to play poker," Cathy cut in as she hung up her coat.

"You know how, you just always lose," Mike retorted, rolling his eyes.

"That would be the definition of not knowing how to play."

"-- I was also thinking we could order a pizza later. Kay's delivers all night, right?"

Cathy paused, frowning from Xander to Mike and then back again. "Sweety --"

"Hey, if you don't like pizza either, that's your own damage. You can have the garlic fingers."

"Xander," she started again, fighting to keep her voice neutral. "Why are we here?"

The smile ran away from his face then, his eyes cast downward almost instantly. He watched his foot kick the mat back and forth for a second, then turned back to them. "I like to think I don't need your help, but I do," he said so low that it was almost silent.

"Help with what, exactly?" Mike asked, taking a look around the house.

He sighed. "It's like I was saying to Cathy earlier. I need to get a lid on this whole situation. Need to get some of my humanity back, stop the Womb from doing whatever it does. I know it's not a permanent solution, but right now I'm just not going to sleep tonight. Was kind of hoping you guys might be able to help me with that."

Cathy tisked, stepping forward to give him another hug. "Of course, that's... of course."

"I was worried you'd say no. You have every right."

"Of course we'll help. That's what family's for."

"That's it?" Mike laughed, placing his hand on Xander's shoulder and smiling. "That's the big deal for tonight? I didn't make that big a deal when I beat the crap out of you earlier."

"That's later," Xander smiled, nodding as he and Cathy started toward the kitchen.

Mike paused a moment, then walked in behind them.

There were two party-sized bags of chips laid against one another on the kitchen table, the dip between them both like a man squat down inside a teepee. There was a two-litre bottle of Cherry Cola there as well, which made Cathy smile.

"You're a doll," she said, fighting back a yawn. "But I think we should start with the coffee. Been a long couple of days."

Xander nodded, flipping a switch on the side of the auto-perk.

"There enough coffee for two cups?" Mike chimed in, sitting down at the table across from Cathy.

"There's enough for ten thousand," Xander said, shooting him a sly look. "Let it never be said that I don't know how to pull an all-nighter."

Mike smiled. "Remember the last one?"

Laughter rumbled out of Xander's mouth and he slapped his knee, almost tipping over the mugs he'd laid out.

"What?" Cathy asked, looking from one to the other and shrugging. "What am I missing?"

Mike kept laughing.

"What is it?" she demanded again, pinching him on the arm.

"Ow. Okay, it was back in grade seven. We were all gone camping, the lot of us, and there was this bet to see--"

"Whoa, whoa," Xander interjected, smiling and waving both hands out in front of him like an air-traffic controller for his friend to stop. "You're telling it wrong."

"You just don't like where the story goes."

"No, you always fuck up the story. You always fuck up every story," he drawled, coming over and sitting between them. "It was in grade eight."

"Grade *seven*."

"It was the summer between grades seven and eight."

Mike stopped, doing some quick Math in his head. "Yeah. Yeah, okay."

"Anyway, that little guy from Canada was down to visit. Keenan. Calla's cousin."

"Right," Cathy smiled nodding. "Little guy, freckles, used to hit on Julie a lot?"

"Yea. Anyway, he was down from Canada for a few weeks and we were really making the best of it. You know, every day it wouldn't just be *one* fun thing... it'd be ten. Go swimming out in the cove, playing street hockey, staying up late, having barbeques... everything we could think to do."

"It takes you so long to tell this story," Mike sighed, leaning back on his chair.

Xander shot him a look as the auto-perk clicked off and he got up to get the coffee. "It takes a long time to tell it."

"It wouldn't take this long to go back in time and *experience* it."

"I'm building mood."

Mike crumpled his brow. "Who are you?"

Xander shook his head, walking back with a cup each for Mike and Cathy and then going back for his own. "Anyway, Keenan and the whole gang were around that summer. So this one night we decide to go camping, only our parents won't let us go out into the forest alone."

"So, what?" Cathy stopped him, laughing. "Don't tell me you just camped out on the front lawn or something."

"No, that'd be lame. We went up to the park and camped there."

"What park?"

"Remember off of Laird there used to be this big outdoor wooden basketball court with a wire fence all the way around and one part gated off for when people wanted to watch?"

"Oh, yeah. I loved that place."

"Up there. We set up our tents in the place where people were supposed to watch games."

"Hilarious," Cathy snickered, rolling her eyes as she took a sip of her coffee.

"No, see the funny part was Keenan," Mike said, leaning forward and motioning off to one side as if he were actually pointing to Keenan in his mind's eye. "That kid was just the most annoying little pervert I have ever met. I think he was touching himself before the rest of us even realized there was a difference between guys and girls."

"Wow."

"Yeah. So he makes up this rule that nobody can go to sleep."

"I think there was some kind of reason... I just can't think of it," Xander interjected.

Mike waved him aside. "He made up this rule. So Xander, being the brain-trust that he is, decides to make a rule that the first person to fall asleep gets punched by every other guy there."

"So... how many people were there?" Cathy asked, a broad smile slowly going as she realized where this was going.

"Oh, me, Xander, him, Derek, Jamie, Grendel, Randy, Tommy, Sud, Trevor, Sheldon... everyone. Whole gang."

"Wow. So, he'd get like... ten punches."

"Not just punches, Charlie Horses. You'd want to cut off your own leg to get rid of the pain after the tenth one. So that's all well and good, but around six a.m. everyone's starting to doze off... except Keenan."

"Think he was still on Canada time or something," Xander added, squinting.

"Whatever. Every time I started to doze, he'd come over and clock me in the

330

jaw and then just run away!" Mike laughed, making his fingers scamper away as he did. "Just like that! The fucking monkey would just sneak up, slam me in the face and then run around the court!"

Xander tapped Cathy, his eyes wet with tears. "He'd always catch him and hit him once or twice in the arm and be like 'you better not do that again'... then five minutes later, it would happen all over again."

"Where were Trevor and Randy for that part?"

"They went fishing, I think. Said it was best in the morning, we called them crazy, they came back with thirty or so fish."

"Right." Mike nodded, pointing at Xander. He could only remain serious a moment before starting to laugh. "God, was that the night we played twenty-ones?"

Xander smiled.

"Forget I asked," Mike said quickly, raising both hands for Xander to stop.

"Why?" Cathy smiled, looking from one to the other. "What else happened?"

Xander turned to her, still smiling. "He didn't beat me at a single game that night. Nothing."

Cathy raised an eyebrow to Mike, who had turned away from the both of them.

"We were playing twenty-ones and I was on a streak. He had, like, one basket."

"Two," he chirped in a low voice.

"That one doesn't count and you know why, don't make me say it." He waited for Mike's retort.

There was none.

"Anyway," he continued, leaning in closer to Cathy as if the exclude Mike from comment. "I was up fifteen from him, and that *never* happens, so he and the guys started trying to come up with ways to distract me whenever it was my turn to shoot."

Her eyes bulged slightly. "Like what?"

"We mooned him," Mike said, his hands over his eyes.

"You started making dirty jokes." Xander added, listing off things on his fingers.

"We farted on you."

"None of it fazed me," Xander said triumphantly.

"What was it that eventually got to you?" Cathy asked, taking a sip of her coffee.

Xander answered, trying to choke back a laugh. "He kept telling me to picture Sara nude. I didn't get another shot in all day."

They all laughed, then it died down for a moment and they all took a sip of their drinks, almost simultaneously.

Cathy smirked. "Does anyone remember that stuff you guys used for non-alcoholic shots one night when we were playing pass the ace?"

"*Wake up juice!*" Mike and Xander both shouted simultaneously. They both burst into laughter.

Mike swished his tongue around in his mouth. "Man, that stuff was sour."

"Not that Keenan would ever say so," Xander scoffed. "After every shot: 'That's not sour'... meanwhile, his lips were sucked back far enough to taste his own tonsils."

"I remember Grendel got out of the game before his lips even touched the stuff," Cathy sneered at the mention of that name.

Xander kept his eye on the fridge in the corner, tossing each of them a sly look. "Remember ... how to make it?"

Mike grinned.

"Got a pen?" Cathy giggled, grabbing a sheet of paper from under the fruit basket.

Xander handed her one as he rubbed the bridge of his nose, trying to remember. "Pure lemon juice, one bottle," he said finally.

Mike piped up. "The water solution of dissolved sour candies."

"Sour kool-aid mix. Seven varieties," Cathy nodded, scrunching her nose as she wrote.

"That was your idea back in the day," Xander said accusingly. "We hated you for it then and we'll hate you for it now. Pepsi. One litre."

"Milk, I think," Mike added tentatively.

"Old milk, actually," she corrected as she jotted it down.

He nodded in thanks.

"And finally, vanilla extract," Xander smiled, rubbing his hands together as he snatched the list from Cathy and skipped to the fridge, peering in.

"How much do we have?" Cathy called after a minute.

"Only one type of kool-aid," he fake frowned.

"I'm going to check myself."

"Fine. There are two. Witch. Also, any limit on how old the milk can be?"

Mike and Cathy both exchanged looks. "No?" Mike asked, leaning forward.

"Good, cause I think this one's so old it's actually meat now," he shrugged as he began pouring the contents of the list into the blender. When he was done he set it to liquefy for a moment, the chunky liquid becoming a blur as it mixed together into a weird shade of brown. "Lord, it's more disgusting looking than I remember."

"Hold on," Cathy chirped, getting up and walking over. She grabbed the rest of the pot of coffee and poured it in on top of the mixture, then turned and smiled at them both. "*Now* it's wake-up juice."

Xander laughed, grabbing three glasses and pouring equal amounts into each until the blender was empty. He brought them over to the table and lay one in front of each of them, and for a long moment they just stared at it.

It bubbled and fizzed from the cola mixed with kool-aid, threatening to overflow from its glass at any point in time but always stopping shy of actually doing so. The coffee had turned it a deep brown that neither of them had seen before in nature, only as siding on houses or as colours in paintings. It made sounds as the different parts reacted with each other, as if each different type of liquid were fighting for control of the glass, and the coffee made it steam. It looked like something that had just come out of a witches brew or a mad scientists lair, even though it smelled like fruit-punch soda.

Xander made a small clicking sound with his tongue. "Ladies first," he said casually, glancing at Cathy.

She gave him a look, then took a deep breath and downed the whole glass so fast that she couldn't have even tasted it. She stood for a minute, her eyes tearing from the bitterness of it, then she knelt down of one knee and started gaging, gasping for air.

She held her right hand to her throat as Mike and Xander started laughing.

She punched Mike in the shoulder and he fell to the floor in mock pain, laughing even harder. "So you drink it!" Cathy shouted, beginning to laugh herself.

Xander and Mike looked at each other. With a grin, they clinked their glasses together in a toast and simultaneously said: "Bottom's Up!" They both chugged the drinks as fast as they could, and when they stopped, they both slammed their glasses onto the counter. They stared at one another, trying to see which one would give first. Both of their eyes began to well up, and Mike kept licking his lips, trying to scrape the taste off of his tongue. Finally, Mike broke down gagging, and as soon as the competition was over, Xander did as well. Cathy burst into laughter.

Mike and Xander both got to their feet laughing over one another. Xander went straight for the fridge and downed a bottle of orange juice, Mike and Cathy were not far behind.

They went back into the living room and sat down, still gasping. Cathy laid down on Mike and they both looked very tired. Xander glanced at his watch. It was now close to midnight. "I think it's time for one of you to take your shift," he said, licking his tongue across his teeth. "Who's first?"

Cathy spoke up immediately. "I'd like to stay up first, thank you very much," she stated bluntly. Giving Mike a little kiss, she said, "Time for bed now, hon."

Mike gave her a look, but started up into the guest bedroom.

Cathy turned and leaned back as far as she could on her chair, watching as Mike slowly scaled the steep stairwell leading up to the spare bedroom. They'd all slept in that room at one point or another since they were kids. She and her sister had called it home for a week once while her parents went on a second honeymoon. She vaguely recalled Trina getting sick during that week and bathing most of the walls in puke.

Xander raised an eyebrow as he watched her almost stumble from her chair, downing the remainder of his coffee and then getting up to get a fresh cup. "Enjoying the view?"

"Hmm?" she hummed, turning around with a sleepy, dazed look in her eyes. After a moment she snapped out of it and blushed, but did not respond. "So what do you wanna do now? It's been a while since I beat you in canasta, but I think I still know how."

Xander smirked. "Not quite what I had in mind."

"Really?" Cathy drawled, mimicking the same sly grin back at him. "You have plans? Do tell. We have ways of making you talk."

She said the last bit in a very bad Russian accent and Xander almost bubbled over with laughter when she did. "Naw, no big plans or secret trysts or anything like that... not after Bob."

She rolled her eyes.

"I was actually hoping we could just talk, y'know? I feel like we haven't really had a chance to do that since that night at the party. Everything since then has been so crazy that I feel like this is the first chance I've gotten to catch a breath."

Cathy smiled and nodded, standing up from the table. "Okies, but if this is gonna be another one of those kinds of talks, I'm gonna have to visit the ladies room first."

"I see coffee still has the same effect on you."

"Shut up," she sneered playfully, turning and walking up the stairs.

ᚱᚤᚤ

Trial.wmb - Smith, D. 20600084. Don wrote at the top of the word document he'd opened as he spread several files out on his desk before him like playing cards. On the far left was an eight-by-ten glossy promotional photo of Megan Greene, on the far right was a smaller photo of Natasha Mayer in the top left hand corner of her letterhead. Buried at the bottom of the papers was a blown-up mug shot of Adam Genblade. He'd only kept it in view for a moment or two before the killer's cold stare had made him shuffle it away.

He sighed, turning his neck in a semicircle to try and work the kinks out of his neck. He strained far to one side until he felt the calcium pop, letting out a small gasp of relief as he turned around and stared into the open vastness of his living room. At some point it had gotten dark, the still eeriness of the room staring back at him for a moment until he turned his eyes back toward the harsh blue glow of his screen.

Summers, Mayer and Soul, once one of the leading law firms in the North East, agreed today to take the case of accused killer Adam Genblade, with the trial to be headed by senior partner Natasha Mayer.

Genblade was arrested in late September of the murder of more than thirty people; among them Detective Carl Dent and local high-school football star Jamie Dawkins. Genblade originally pled guilty to the charge of murder in the first degree, but has since officially recounted his confession.

"Adam Genblade may deserve many things, but murder is not one of them," said Natasha Mayer, in her official press release upon taking the case. "He is a sick man who needs our help, not our judgment. It is my greatest hope that the judge appointed will see reason and remand him into the custody of a state sanctioned mental institution."

When approached for comment, prosecutor Megan Greene had this to say:

"The opposition is a joke. Insanity is a joke. I submit that Genblade knew exactly what he was doing when he killed those children and would willingly do so again if allowed. I will personally not rest until he has a needle in his arm or a mask on his face."

Local police have said that while the evidence mounted against Genblade is insurmountable, a large portion of it is circumstantial and resides with the attorney's ability to sway the jury.

Megan Greene made headlines last July when she had three-time murder suspect Ian Char arrested on gang-related charges, leading to the capture and seizure of almost eighty kilograms of cocaine.

When questioned, local high-school student Calla McFadden said that she was looking forward to the prosecutor's victory. "I've never been happier in my life. He killed so many people I know that I can't even sleep most nights. I can't wait to see him fry."

Advocates opposing the death penalty have begun vigils in the town hall away from the penitentiary out of respect for those who lost family members in the past few months.

Don sighed, leaning back on his chair and running his fingers through his hair. His head ached above both temples, and something in the back of his left eye throbbed. Each word had been agonizing to force out. Something about it just seemed wrong. He licked his lips as he re-read it, deciding that it was fine enough... it just lacked that pop. That thing that would really grab the attention of the people.

-thunk-

He turned around in his chair and gazed back out into the still silence if his home. Light from upstairs made halos around the couch and the basement door handle, the only sources of light in the shadowed room. His eyes moved around the darkness for a moment before he frowned and turned back to the screen. The light burned at his retinas even more after getting used to the darkness for a moment, and he cursed.

Scowling, he turned back toward his notes and looked for something he could add to give the story more weight. He'd been trying for hours to reach a protestor of the death penalty that would give a quote, but nobody would. Even people staunchly against capital punishment didn't want to be seen as allied with Adam Genblade. He had also wished there was a little more information on Natasha Mayer to give the story a slightly more evened feel, but her legal career had been less flashy than Greene's. He picked up her press release and scanned down through it once more.

pleased to represent... is murder like any other... needs our help not our judgment... personally responsible.

Defense attorney - Natasha Mayer
Legal Aid - Nathan Summers
Legal Aid - David Chow
Legal Aid - Alexander Drew
Legal Aid - Thomas Shirk

Don stopped, blinking once as his eyes did a double-take, scanning back up the list. Legal Aid - Alexander Drew.

He raised an eyebrow and smiled, placing the release on a paper stand next to the keyboard. This was going to break this story wide open. He could feel it.

⋏⟨⟩⋏

Cathy closed the bathroom door behind her as she walked back out into the hall, switching off the light and wiping the last few drops of water on her hands into her jeans. She tiptoed down the hallway as quietly as she could, her teeth on edge with every step she made as she passed by the spare bedroom. The door was open just a crack and she peered in, watching as Mike shuffled happily in his sleep.

"That'd better be me you're dreaming about, Harris," she whispered to herself playfully, watching for just another moment before continuing on.

She turned and looked at each of the family photos that lined the wall as she went. She'd seen them all before of course, even had smaller versions of one or two of them at home. There was one that she'd always loved of Xander smiling big and bright that she'd scanned it and cropped on her computer so that it was just a bust of him. She'd always thought it to be the best picture of him ever taken.

She turned to go down the stairs when she stopped. Her nose twitched slightly when it caught a strange smell, like tin cans getting scorched in a fire. "Xander?" she called out in a hushed voice, stepping back off of the stairs.

She turned toward his bedroom door and saw that it was open, just a little. Squinting, she stepped closer. With every inch closer she got the smell seemed to get thicker and thicker, until it was like she was swimming in it instead of walking through it. Biting her lip, she placed the palm of her hand flat against the door and gave it one hard shove.

⋏⟨⟩⋏

"This is not healthy," Cathy said, tossing the broken leg of Xander's chair down onto the kitchen table. It rolled until it hit the stack of potato chips and stopped.

Xander looked down at it for a long moment, his face devoid of any emotion. He shrugged slightly, then took another chug of his coffee.

"You don't have anything to say about this? Thought you wanted to talk."

"Kind of speaks for itself," he frowned, reaching out and picking up the leg gently. Splinters fell from the shattered end onto the table as he brought it closer to his face and examined it.

"Your room is a war zone, Xander."

"Yes, Mom."

"I'm serious," she huffed, her eyes filled to the brim with sympathy. "No small wonder the Womb's been acting the way it has with everything you've got pent up inside. You've got to find a way to let it out."

"This *is* how I let it out," he growled, gripping the wooden shaft hard until

336

he felt the grains give slightly. "What else can I do? Nothing we say or do is going to bring her back."

Cathy squinted at him, shaking her head. "You'd want to?" she said after a moment, her voice full of disgust.

He looked back at her, his face twisted into a confused snarl. "What?"

She moved forward, pulling out her chair at the table and sitting across from him. "You'd bring her back if you could? Because I wouldn't. Not in a million, billion years would I wish Sara back."

He did not respond, turning away only slightly at the mention of her name.

"She's somewhere now where the Grendels and the Genblades can't get her. Can *never* get her, no matter how hard they try. I miss her like hell... but I'd never be so cruel or so selfish as to bring her back from wherever she is now. Sometimes if you love something, you have to let it go, Xander."

"Dammit, that's not fucking good enough!" Xander shouted, throwing the leg across the room and denting the wall.

She jumped back in shock, standing up from the table again.

He drew back and punched her again, then got up, tossing her clothes onto her. "Pff. You're not worth the trouble. Stupid whore," And with that, he left. Went back down to his friends to lie and brag about what he'd done.

The killer began to lean on the blade, causing it to puncture the skin. Then, he withdrew it before it went in any great distance. He began to walk out the door. As he did, he turned and looked at her.

"You're not even worth the trouble," *he said before he left.*

Cathy lay on the floor in a pool of blood, crying, as she heard sirens approaching the house.

Not good enough.

Cathy twitched, her hands raised halfway to her face and seemingly stuck there. The words bounced around her mind like a rubber ball inside a small glass box, threatening to crack it at any point. After a moment, she turned from Xander but didn't go anywhere, looking as though she wasn't even completely sure where she was for a second.

Xander squinted, his nostrils still flaring and anger slowly melting from his eyes as he watched her shift uncomfortably. After a moment, his short, heavy breaths began to taper off and his features softened as he started to think again. He took one step forward.

She winced, then steadied herself. "Stay the fuck over there," she barked, though her voice quivered slightly.

He stopped in mid-step, trying to piece together what had just happened. After a moment he turned back to her, his eyes turned up in pity. "God... fuck... god, Cathy, I'm so sorry," Xander started, reaching out his arms to hug her.

She took another step backward, biting the edge of her finger nervously before she leaned forward and almost fell into him. Her lips quivered and shook as she tried to hold her tears in. It lasted only a moment before the memory of Grendel's icy stare or the Womb's raspy voice came screaming back again and hot tears started streaming down her face. After a second she pushed away from him, falling to her knees and still sobbing with a fierceness usually reserved for toddlers.

"Oh, Cathy," Xander cooed, scrunching down and wrapping his arms around her. She resisted at first, then buried her head into the nape of his neck. "Oh, my beautiful Cathy. I am so sorry, I didn't..." he stopped himself from apologizing, realizing that would only make him feel better about what he had just said. He pulled her head off his shoulder and forced her to look at him, holding her face in his hands as tears began to trickle down his face as well. "I love you, Cathy."

She choked slightly, each breath coming in short gasps. She tried to move her head away from him, but he held firmly.

"I do. And you are good enough. More than. You're one of the greatest people I've ever met. Anyone who says anything but is an idiot."

"But *you* said," she spat finally, her brow furrowing as the tears made her eyelids red and puffy. "You said it twice now, as the Womb and now. You *said* it."

"I'm an idiot, too," he countered, forcing a smirk onto his face. "I don't think I've ever claimed otherwise."

She laughed a little.

He took his hands away from her face, the clammy skin almost sticking to his own.

She did not turn away, just kept looking at him as she tried to stop her chest from quivering between breaths. "It shouldn't be this hard to get over this," she whispered finally, mentally stopping herself from getting worked up again.

"No, it shouldn't. It shouldn't have happened to begin with."

"I think it happens more than we think," she said, locking eyes with him. "And once it does you see the world different. Like when you go in a dark room and your eyes adjust, then you can see all the things in the dark. I think what Grendel did made me go into that dark place in the world... and now I can see all the things in the dark."

He nodded after a moment, letting that sink in for a moment. He reached out and touched her hand, gently stroking the back of it with his index finger. "At least you'll have some company," he said hoarsely.

Despite herself, she smiled a little smile, then wrapped her arms around him again.

⋏⟨⟩⋏

"What the hell is the matter with you anyway?" Cathy scoffed, bending over and picking the whiskey bottle up from Xander's scorched bedroom floor. She brought it to her nose and sniffed the remnants of its contents, curling her nose as the harsh alcoholic residue burned her nostrils.

338

Xander watched her do this with a bemused look on his face as he picked up another piece of shattered, curved glass from his computer monitor. "Truth is, I just wanted an excuse to go LCD," he smirked, giving the plastic case of the screen a friendly slap. "This old girl's seen better days."

"You're weird," she said, tossing the bottle into a small blue trash bin along-side his dresser. "Why were you trying to get drunk? Can't imagine it'd work very well on you anyway."

"Would've a few weeks ago. Guess I haven't worked out the kinks yet," he mumbled in response, standing on his toes to look over the edge of his trash bin at the liquor bottle inside. When he was sure it was empty, he flattened his feet back out, frowning. "What do you care anyway? Not like you haven't been drunk before."

She spun around quickly, her hair spinning around her, angrily whipping at the air around it. "I have not," she said in disgust, annunciating every word carefully for maximum impact.

"Ha."

"Okay, when?" she sneered, pointing a finger at him as if to physically put him on the spot.

"Randy Owchar's birthday. You and Sara and Calla went out back and Calla got stoned and Sara was smoking and drinking. When Calla offered you a joint, you took Sara's drink instead. Got loaded from sipping on half a cooler," he smiled.

Her face turned red and her feet came together quickly. She turned away from him as her face got even more red, trying to hide. "Mike said he wouldn't tell anyone."

Xander raised an eyebrow. "Sara did, you goon."

Cathy smiled. "That figures."

The clock downstairs chimed once, and then again. "Two already. Time flies. By the way, she told to keep me from spilling dirt on her."

Cathy turned slightly to glare at him from over her shoulder. "What?"

Xander grinned, pulling his fingers across his lips to pantomime a zipper.

She sneered playfully in response, turning away from him again. Immediately her features softened as she realized for the first time that she was standing directly in front of Xander's bedroom window, looking out onto Sara's bedroom window.

He watched her muscles stiffen and tense, her hands coming up to rub her arms even though there wasn't even a hint of a breeze in the room. Without asking, without even seeing her face he knew what she was thinking and feeling. "She aced all the subjects last term," he said finally, having trouble finding his voice. "Didn't want you to know. Said you're supposed to be the smart one."

She didn't respond or move, just kept staring out the window.

He watched her hair rise and fall with every breath she took, waving with even the slightest motion of her body like ripples over a calm lake.

"I can't stand this," she said finally, so low he could barely even hear her. "I can't stand this and it's only been thirty seconds. I can't imagine what it must be like for you to see this every day."

He put down the glass shards he'd been collecting, leaning against his table on his knuckles. He let out several long sighs before responding. "The Womb makes it worse," he said finally. "Lets me see things there I've got no business knowing. Her parents haven't touched it since she died. There's still a juice box against her computer waiting from her to get home from the party."

"She did get thirsty after parties."

"There are toys I didn't even realize she had lined up on the far wall with an empty spot on the middle. I think the missing one's actually on her bed. Don't know why, but I'd like to think it was bad dreams."

"What makes you think that?"

"Her dream-catcher's not hanging, it's resting on her windowsill. I caught her 'shaking it out' once or twice outside the window. Think she did it before she left for the party."

"Didn't realize she bought stuff like that."

"I don't think she did. I think she did it just in case it was true... even if she didn't believe," he smiled, looking down at the circles in his wooden desk. "The Womb lets me see all that. Makes it seem like she could come back any minute... like she's not even gone."

There was silence for a moment. When Cathy spoke again, her voice was different. It was no longer hushed and intimate, but moist with shock and even fear. "I can see all that, too."

"What?" he almost barked, getting up and walking over next to her. His scowl widened into shock as he looked out just in time to see the second of Sara's two bedroom lights flicker on.

"Her folks aren't there, are they?" Cathy asked, her voice like ice as her eyes scanned the window relentlessly for any sign of movement.

"No," Xander said, clicking his tongue against his teeth and stroking his chin. After a moment, he stepped away from her side back to where he'd come from by the shattered remains of his computer.

A shadow fell across the wall quickly as she watched, followed by another, larger one. "There are two people there, I think," she said, leaning up against the window know. "I can't see who. Xander, should we call the -"

Her words fell short as she turned around. She wanted to scream but couldn't, something deep inside her stopping the sound and beating it to death within her before it could escape from her lips.

Xander's wrists were already bathed in stringy red blood that ebbed its way against gravity up his arm, getting blacker and blacker as it went. He finished his slow slice with the thick chunk of polarized glass he'd taken off his desk, gritting his teeth together even as the larger, sharper one's forced their way down. His eyes began to bleed tar as the vessels inside them burst, sending even more darkness surging over his body.

He took a step toward her as it dropped the glass to the floor, landing in the charred circle he'd made days ago.

"Xander, no," Cathy tried to say sternly, backing up a pace and falling against the wall, then trying to get back on her feet quickly. "Xander... this is the opposite of why you brought me here!" she screamed, pleading with him.

If he looked at her, she couldn't tell. His eyes were completely black now, like most of his face.

"Black Womb lives," the creature stated as it walked past Cathy, as though she were not even there.

She had to look and make sure its eyes were red just to be sure that Xander was in control, because right now she really couldn't tell the difference as she sat on the bed and watched it go through the window. Somehow that single, blurred line was more terrifying than anything on either side of it had ever been.

She couldn't help but think that she had failed her friend.

Tommy slid open the drawer with a hard thud, several patches of grey dust rubbing off onto his knuckles as he let go of the handles. He stared down at the treasure-trove before him, rubbing his thumbs against the edges of his enclosed fists for a moment before diving in, shoving great heaps of socks and underwear aside with great sweeping motions.

A few feet away, Sud stood at the vanity, looking into the mirror with a somewhat quizzical expression on his face, not unlike a chimp upon first discovering such an object. Slowly, his eyes cast downward onto the dozens of small boxes and cases that lined the bottom of the mirror. He reached out carefully with one finger and opened a varnished, caramel-coloured box that looked like it might have contained jewelry, instead finding only its red velvet lining. He frowned, battling a tiny bell held by a small ceramic pig wearing a top hat before opening another box. This one was filled with earrings, but most of them were just the dime-store metal hoops that Sara had worn almost every day. "Pff," he huffed, closing the lid unceremoniously.

"Hey," Tommy barked, smirking over his shoulder at Sud to get his attention. He turned around, holding a pair of white cotton panties stretched between his thumbs.

Sud laughed, turning away from the mirror.

Tommy turned them around, taking note of the small embroidered long-stem rose on the front. Smiling wickedly, he brought them to his face and took in a long breath through his nose before balling them up and throwing them at Sud, laughing. As Sud did the same, he turned and started rummaging through the drawer again. "You finding anything over there?"

Sud looked up, letting the underwear fall to the floor as he turned back toward the vanity and opened a third box. "Nope," he said simply, trying to act as though he hadn't been distracted.

"Fuck," Tommy cursed, slamming the drawer shut and then pulling the next one all the way out, letting it fall to the floor with a crash. He had to back up quickly to make sure it didn't smash his toes, then dug in and tossed anything he deemed unnecessary aside. "There's gotta be something in here we can use to get under Xander's skin. I don't frigging care what it is, just so long as it makes that memorial memorable."

Sud chuckled.

Tommy rolled his eyes, grabbing a large clump of bras at once and tossing them aside.

Sud opened another jewelry box on her dresser, this one sterling silver. He was pleased to find it packed full of things, even though most of them looked ridiculous or campy at first glance. He picked up a little piece of wood from it, immediately cracking it in two and tossing it behind his shoulder. He picked up a necklace, wrapping it around his wrist and snapping its chain.

Tommy took out a pair of silk panties and ran his finders along the front, feeling how soft they were. "I bet Grendel saw these a few times before he bought it," he laughed at Sud, without turning towards him.

Sud grunted in agreement as he shoved a small gold locket into his pant pocket.

"Not to mention that skank Cathy. You just *know* they did it the night of his party, right? Just know it. Everyone knows it," he grinned, waving a cautious finger at his friend. "I'll have her one of these days, too. Just you wait."

Sud rolled his eyes, a small grin growing on his rubbery face.

"What? You don't think I could?" Tommy almost laughed, turning back away from Sud and continuing to sort through the drawer.

Sud let out a short, snort-like laugh.

"Keep it up, chuckle-brain. I'll let you smell my fingers when I'm done."

There was a loud crash and a blinding flash as the light above them snapped out, leaving both men in the dark. Sud didn't even have time to yell before polarized glass before the bulb overhead came crashing down on him, making dozens over tiny cuts and gashes along his bald scalp that started to bleed immediately.

"Jesus!" Tommy yelled, jumping to his feet immediately. His eyes went wide with panic as he searched the darkness for any sign of movement.

There was none, just the shadowy grey of the room and the imprint of the bulbs last bright flash on his retinas.

He swallowed hard, his Adam's apple throbbing up and down as he tried hard to catch his breath. "Sud, man, you okay?" he asked when he finally found his voice, turning in the direction he'd last seen his friend.

There was no response. Not even a grunt of recognition, just the calm, stale sound of the wind blowing its way up from an open window downstairs, its draft making him break out in gooseflesh.

"Dude," Tommy said, forcing a nervous chuckle. "I can't see you nod your head in the dark, you idiot."

Still there was nothing but the darkness.

Biting his lower lip, he took a step forward and waved his hand around the air where Sud had been. It passed through the thick, dusty air unabated. Frowning, he let his hand drop back to his side as he looked around the darkness of the room again.

He thought he saw something move out of the corner of his eye, turning toward it quickly. He sighed and almost laughed when he looked at his own shadowed reflection in his mirror, his features black and obscured.

Behind his mirror-image, two red eyes opened.

They were large and catlike, their rims glowing and shimmering like thousands of tiny chinks of scaly armor. They curled up at both the outside edges and down on the inside ones, unlike anything Tommy had ever seen before in his life. The shadows seemed like they passed right through it, as though it were just two eyes hanging in the air on their own.

Until he saw the mouth open.

Tommy went rigid, closing his eyes tight for a moment and wishing for it to go away. When he opened them it was still there, standing less than a foot behind him in the mirror. He couldn't feel it behind him at all, and that somehow made it even worse. If there were even a hint of its presence; an exhaled breath, a small sound; he could convince himself that he could get out of this.

Steeling his jaw, Tommy spun around on his heels.

Again, there was nothing but the darkness.

Shivering, even though sweat was now pouring off him, he looked around the room once more. There were no eyes or mouths looking back at him, not even a hint to where they might be. He swallowed hard, then took two quick steps forward again until his knee hit the dresser. Fumbling clumsily and letting out a long string of small whines, his fingers found the lamp on the top of it and switched it on. He spun around quickly, eyes open and ready to face whatever was there.

The room was empty. The drawer he had thrown onto the floor had been shoved back into place without his knowing and without a sound, all of the clothes shoved back in. The necklace that Sud had pocketed lay in a small, coiled heap on the vanity in the centre of the row of boxes, each one of which were spaced and lined perfectly against the mirror. There were no monsters with glowing red eyes.

There was also no Sud.

"Man?" Tommy called weakly, then cleared his throat and tried again. "Hey, Sud?"

He frowned, then started tip-toeing his way to the door. He stopped when he got to the bedroom window, squinting as he turned to face it. Across the pathway was Xander's bedroom window, dark and vacant. It looked so black that the windows might as well have been painted, but he still thought he could make out a figure there looking back at him. Gears started to turn in his head as he stepped closer to the open window, bending over and poking his head out to try and get a better view.

There was an enormous pressure on his neck as something grabbed him. Something sharp touched his neck but didn't cut him, but was only there for a moment before it hauled him out through the window, leaving his shoe behind in the room.

There was a brief feeling of weightlessness, followed by a sharp tug as gravity took hold and flung him to earth where he landed gut-first onto Sud's leg, the air rushing out of him as his face smacked into the lawn.

Pulling himself back up onto the ledge, Xander squinted at them on the ground below through the Womb's eyes as both men scrambled to their feet and took off for the road. Frowning, he turned back toward the bedroom and looked the mess that still remained. Sara's room had once stood as a silent memorial to the beautiful person she had been. It was tidier than they would have left it, but a few things had been broken. He made a note to himself to sneak back in and try to fix them before Sara's mother came in and found them that way.

He opened the dresser drawer that Tommy had pulled out, the bras and underpants inside forced in un-glamorously. Glancing out the window briefly, he started picking through it and folding it neatly back the way it had been, until it looked at least a little closer to the way she would have left it. "Best I can do," he said, as much to Sara as to himself.

He opened the top dresser to make sure nothing was too out of place there as well, noticing a tiny chunk of wood along the edge that was a slightly lighter tint than the rest. Curious, he placed one of his claws against it to try and pry it loose. It separated from the rest of the drawer easily, leaning against a pair of socks. He recognized it as soon as he picked it up, his touch as delicate as he could make it to try not to damage it.

He remembered his lush, green lawn where she had found out how they felt when they were twelve. He had had a huge crush on her that summer and had been sitting on the sidewalk, burning their initials into a piece of wood. She started toward him on roller blades and he dropped the wood and ran into the house. She had picked it up, looked at it, and thrown it into the trees on her way down the street, never actually bringing it up to him.

She kept it, he thought to himself. Smiling, he bent over and reached under the bed, producing a photo-album he'd given her for her birthday last year. They'd picked out the pictures to go in it together. He placed the wood safely in the album, then walked back toward the window and climbed out onto the ledge before dropping away into the shadows.

Cathy squirmed on the couch as she waited, huffing as a rigid piece of lumber dug into her side from somewhere inside the arm of it. She grabbed the pillow from the other side and from the love seat and added it to her own, making it poof out in comedic fashion before she threw herself back onto it.

She stared at the ceiling for a moment, watching the spot where the reflection from the lamp burned the brightest. Slowly, she reached out and danced her fingers along the light trail, making odd but elegant shadows.

"Shadow puppets?" came a thick, raspy voice from the hall as Xander came around the corner, rubbing a towel into his hair violently.

Cathy jumped back up to sit, clutching her pillow close to her chest. "Jesus Christ. Don't do that," she said, letting out a long breath.

"Sorry," he smirked, rolling his eyes at her. He rubbed the towel one last time until he was convinced that he was clean, then laid it across the opposite arm of the couch before flopping onto it.

She bounced up a little from his weight, making her pillows shift back into an uncomfortable position. She turned, glaring at him, then drew back and slapped him on the arm.

"Ow," he frowned, touching the spot with his hand. "What was that for?"

"What the fuck is wrong with you? Sic'ing the Womb on those two idiots like that?"

"They had it coming. And I do not just mean lately."

"You can't do this. They could have seen you, or--"

"What would they have seen? Darkness? Shadows? At most, a pair of eyes in the dark? Come on, Cat," he snorted.

She reached over and took his face between her thumb and forefinger, forcing him to look at her. "You can't do this. You can't use the Womb like this. We've seen what happens when you try. Jesus, Xander, you're acting like you're high."

He wrenched his face away from her, sneering slightly as he leaned back against the stiff wooden arm of the couch. He twitched slightly, then lifted one foot and laid it on the coffee table. He turned and stared at the fabric of the couch, watching her only out of the corner of his eye.

After a moment she frowned and got up, walking toward the stairs. "I think it's Mike's turn," she said bitterly, slapping his arm again as she walked by. "And it was shadow dancing, by the way."

He didn't turn and watch her go, and winced when he heard the door upstairs slam shut.

"Why the hell does she stick up for those two?" Xander huffed, stuffing a handful of potato chips into his mouth. At first there were too many for him to even get his lips closed, crunching down on them slowly and swallowing what he could. He turned the page of the folder he was looking at, taking a long sip of his cola as he did. He gasped, spitting it back into the glass along with several waterlogged sour-cream and onion chips. "What in Christ's name is this?"

Mike looked up from his own folder. "Cherry Cola," he said, then turned back toward the document. He frowned and tossed it aside, grabbing for another in a green folder. "When are people going to learn that cherries don't go in soft drinks?"

Xander frowned, putting the glass down on the table and then slowly nudging it away from him with one finger, as if afraid to touch it again.

"And I don't know why she sticks up for those jerks," Mike admitted, scanning down through the cover-sheet of his folder and then closing it again, deciding there was nothing of relevance there. He threw it onto an ever-growing stack of papers that they had deemed the 'nothing useful' pile. "But to be fair, I don't know why you torture yourself day and night, I don't know why you eat and drink when you probably don't have to, and I really don't know why you've got me going through the most boring literature in the world to help Adam Genblade, of all people."

Xander held up a finger, waiting until he was done swallowing. "I do it to keep myself sane. To keep some humanity in all this mess."

"Maybe it's the same for her," he shrugged, grabbing three or four chips himself and dropping one into his mouth.

Xander did not respond right away, his brow coming down thoughtfully.

"Personally, I think you're both nuts. But that's just me," he sighed, running his fingers through his hair. "Where the hell did you get these, anyway?"

"Hmm?" Xander hummed, not even looking up from his document. "Mm. That lawyer's office today. Wanted to see what we were up against."

Mike watched Xander read his file, his pupils moving faster and faster in his sockets with every line he read. "What you got there?"

"The answer to my question. We're fucking screwed. My law career is over before it even starts. Just listen to this shit:

"...found traces of steroids, barbiturates and methamphetamine in his system at time of arrest. Side-effects of long term use present, including damage to synapse of brain tissue. There is significant scarring on the surface of the brain both from drug use as well of a volatile strain of syphilis that was present at the time of his capture, but has since recessed. Psyche analysis indicates, though does not confirm, that he is the clinical definition of a true sociopath, whose morals are so skewed from the social norm that his definitions of right and wrong are unclear, perhaps even to himself. At times he is seen referring to himself in the third person, the first person and, on rare occasion, in the second person. He seems to be aware of the passage of time but also experiences shifts where he seems to forget or misplace events chronologically. Physically he is the peak of human stamina and endurance, though there are concerns that major muscles will start to throw clots soon after a long period of inactivity...

"I mean, really," Xander huffed, closing the folder. "How do you argue with that? That's just... I have no case. I don't even know why I'm trying."

"You think that's bad?" Mike frowned, picking up the green folder again. "Give this a listen:

"...Drew, Xander. Found at the wreckage of what police had dubbed 'Engen', Drew was once believed to have had ties in the mob by the late agent Carl Dent. Although Tim White has ordered these charges dropped, they are still speculated upon. It seemed that the only victims were people that had gotten in his way, and now the same pattern has started again. Even though Drew was completely exonerated for the crimes because of Genblade's confession, now that Genblade wishes not to die, it seems he may yet reveal that he was working for Drew...

"...Unbelievable." Mike sighed, throwing that folder on the table next to the first.

"Yeah," Xander agreed, "But sadly not that far from the truth."

Mike put a hand on his friend's shoulder. "Hey, before I forget. About today..."

Xander raised a hand to stop him. "S'okay."

"No, I - -"

"Really. It is."

Mike nodded, then snickered to himself a little. "I still don't know why the Womb didn't kill me. I mean seriously, of all the dumbfuck things to do, right?"

Xander chuckled forcefully, the sound slowly dying down as his face grew taught. His eyes become hollow and vacant for a brief instant, then sparked to life as he tilted his head to meet Mike's gaze.

"What is it?" Mike frowned, laying down his folder.

"What was it the Womb said to you?"

"Huh?"

"It said something. What did it say?"

"It didn't say anything. It just kind of stood there and looked... weird."

"Not today, the other night. It said something to you, didn't it?"

"Yeah. Said I'd already been harvested, or some such thing. Why? What difference - -"

"And he told Cathy she wasn't good enough, right?"

"Right," Mike nodded, dragging out the 'i' as long as possible.

Xander was silent for a moment, stroking his chin. "It never did that before."

"What?"

"Spoken. It's never spoken before."

"Sure it has," Mike scowled, rolling his eyes.

"When? What has *The Womb* ever spoken, except for the words 'Black Womb lives'?"

Mike opened his mouth to answer, then paused, and closed it again.

"Any time. Ever?"

Mike leaned forward, rubbing the sides of his nose with his thumbs. "No. No, it's never talked before."

Xander brought the nail of his thumb to his lower lip, picking at it obsessively as he thought. His eyes were locked on some random spot on the wall, not looking at anything but refusing to look anywhere else all the same. "Why would it change?" he huffed, thinking back to the day that Genblade had been captured. He'd almost smiled at Xander from across the mounds of rubble and police between them, and said 'it's not over'. "Is this what he meant?"

"What?" Mike moaned, looking up.

"Nothing, just... nothing." He ran a hand through his hair, a few strands shaking loose as he tugged on it. "This whole thing just keeps getting worse and worse."

"Makes you wonder, really," Mike mumbled, almost to himself.

"Wonder what?"

"Humans change their behaviour. Animals don't. Animals hunt the same way, day in and day out, until something forces them to change. Even then, not really. So if the Womb's changed the way it does things, that' d make it - -"

"Human," Xander finished, a bitter taste in his mouth.

347

CHAPTER SEVEN: CRANE

Joan scrubbed the tables of the Factory, the tiles sparkling clean.

The chairs and booths were empty now, the harsh light of dawn shimmering in through the cracked and broken windows near the ceiling.

She pumped her arm fiercely for one more moment before looking down at her reflection in the table. It frowned back at her with almost perfect clarity, marred only by the brown tint of the varnished wood. She'd been polishing the same table for nearly three hours, ever since the last customer left.

She heaved a sigh, casting a glance over her shoulder at the front door. It hung open just an inch, letting cool fall air into the humid steel box that made up the building. It moved just a little in the wind, shuddering on its steel bolts for a moment before settling back down into place. She turned away from it quickly, closing her eyes and biting her bottom lip so hard that it drew a faint sliver of blood. After a moment, she gripped the sides of the table so hard that her nails left indents on the other side, then opened her eyes and stared down at her reflection.

She could not bring herself to leave.

She was too afraid. Too afraid to walk out her own doorway. Her mouth went dry and scratchy with unshed tears and her joints seized up every time she tried. Once she'd made it as far as the door, but could not bring herself to open it.

After a moment of staring herself down, she turned away from the table and started to march toward the door. She made it three paces before she collapsed onto the linoleum floor and began to cry.

ﬁ︿ﬂ

Xander opened his front door and stuck his head out, taking a long whiff of the fresh morning air and smiling from ear to ear.

"You look happy," Mike said sardonically, stepping up behind him and admiring the eastern sun for a moment himself.

"Understatement," Xander replied, waving a finger at his friend without even turning around. "I don't even feel tired anymore. I think I got a second wind or something, but I feel like I got a full night's sleep last night."

"Sometimes I hate you," Mike snarled, pressing his palm against one of his throbbing, bloodshot eyes.

"Sometimes I hate your Mom, but then we make up and that's my favourite part."

"What?"

"Nuthin'."

"Seriously, what'd you just say about my Mom?"

Xander turned to look at him, rolling his eyes. "Oh, like you've never heard a joke about your Mom befo- -" he stopped, his mouth remaining locked in the circular position it had been in to make the 'o' sound but with no sound coming out. His gaze had shifted past Mike and back into the shadowed hallway of the house, his pupils shrinking to the size of pins as he did.

Mike turned back, one eyebrow cocked in the air and he followed his friend's line of sight.

Cathy stood in the doorway, her hair still a ragged and tangled mess atop her head. The T-shirt she was wearing was slumped loosely to one side, exposing her freckled, pale shoulder. There were bags under her eyes, bloodshot with tears that she was trying with all her might to hold back. Cradled carefully in her hands was a dull grey .38 caliber revolver. "Xander, what's this?" she asked softly, her voice staggering on each syllable.

Xander closed his mouth promptly, then opened it again to respond. When no words came out, he tore his gaze away from her, looking at some random spot on his lawn.

Mike turned back to Xander, his eyes narrow and hard. "What's the gun for, man?" he said, his voice firm and even, with the sour tint of anger on only the last word.

Xander turned back toward them, his gaze shifting from one to the other, and then finally looked back at the grass.

"Oh my god!" Cathy yelled, so loud and so angry that her voice shrieked to the highest pitch he'd ever heard. She took both of her hands out from under the gun, dropping it to the lawn as though it were something dirty. Mike turned toward her, moving to place his arm around her, but she twisted away. Her face seemed to be at war with itself, the top half bubbling over with tears and the bottom half curled into a rueful snarl. She took two slow, deliberate steps to close the distance between herself and Xander, burning her glare into his head the entire time. When she was close enough to him, she waited.

After a moment, he looked up to meet her gaze.

Her lip curled, she slapped him across the face.

He winced, but still did not say a word.

"Fucker!" she screamed, pushing on his shoulders until he fell to the ground and then hitting him again. Then again. Her hands ached, but she kept pounding at him with her small fists until Mike finally stepped up beside her and placed a hand on her shoulder. "How could you?" she screamed, her face as red as he'd ever seen it now.

He still didn't speak, staring up at her from his seat on the dew-laden grass. The moisture soaked into his pants and made him uncomfortable, but he didn't so much as shift.

"How could you?" Mike asked, his voice still calm if nothing else as Cathy turned and finally rested her head on his shoulder. "How could you even think it?"

Xander's mouth opened and closed again, the suckle of the dry skin of his lips sticking together palatable in the quiet of the early morning hours. When he finally spoke, his voice was parched and pleading. "I was confused."

"Bull shit," Mike snapped, almost stepping forward and then restrained himself. "When?"

Xander stared blankly for a second, as Cathy pulled herself up off of Mike's shoulder.

"When?" Mike repeated, his voice growing forceful.

"Right before the murders started again," he replied finally, his voice almost a whisper. "And I swear to fuck, I almost wish I had because then none of this would be happening right now."

"Don't talk like that," Cathy said, shaking her head from side to side. "Don't even think like that. What's wrong with you?"

"What's wrong with me?" Xander spat, finally scrambling to his feet, his hands gesturing wildly. "What's wrong with me? Nothing, Cathy... just fucking nothing. I have no control over anything in my life. I never have, really, only I'm just now realizing it."

"What're you talking about?" Mike asked, brow furrowed and taking a step forward.

"I can't control this thing inside me. I can't control it. Its almost killed Cathy three fucking times now. I couldn't control what happened to Sara, and now she's gone. I can't control this shit that's going on with Genblade, with my parents, with those idiots at school, any of it!" He stopped, pausing a moment and then looking down again. "So I decided to take some control."

"By killing yourself," Mike finished.

"Good a place to start as any," he said, almost under his breath.

"No," Cathy said firmly, closing the gap between them again. She grabbed his chin between her thumb and forefinger and forced it to turn toward her, staring him square in the eye. "You've got more control than you think. You've *got* more than you think."

"Like what?"

"Me," she said, turning briefly back to Mike and then back again. "*Us.* But maybe that's not enough. Like the Womb said the other night, maybe we're not good enough."

He looked away again, frowning. Tears began to shine in his eyes now, but he didn't shed them.

"Do you have any idea how much I love you?" she asked, almost sarcastically as she continued to stare him down, her face filled with every emotion nameable. "How much we both love you? We loved Sara too, okay? Do you have any idea what that would have done to us, if you'd fucking killed yourself?"

"Well, what do you think stopped me?" he yelled, turning back toward them. He was angry suddenly, though he wasn't quite sure why. "I didn't do it, because of you two. And now I'm killing again, people are dying again!"

"Are we all that stopped you?" Mike asked, stroking his chin as he watched his friend.

Xander calmed instantly, his shoulders slumping. It was like gravity had reaffirmed its hold, dragging his face, body and tears down toward earth. "That, and a promise I made. To not give up."

All three of them stood silently for a minute, taking deep breaths.

"You need more reason than that to stay here," Cathy said finally. "You can't live for other people. If you're doing this, you have to do it for yourself and know that things are going to get better."

Xander winced, then turned away from them both and walked back into the house.

After a moment, Cathy followed.

Mike stayed outside, then slowly walked to where the gun still lay on the grass. He reached down gently and picked it up, sliding the chamber out to reveal all six rounds loaded and ready to go. He broke down crying for the first time since the confrontation had begun, and made sure he'd stopped before he went back inside.

ʎ૮ʎ

John stared at the picture on his desk, tapping his pencil - just about worn down to the nub - against the surface of his desk.

The focus of the picture was soft, as though whoever had been operating the camera hadn't quite been sure of its function. It made everything in it looked watered down and gentle, as though it had been painted onto the paper rather than imprinted on it. The girl in the picture had soft, chestnut-colored hair that fell to her shoulders. Even though the image was forever stagnate, it always looked like it was bouncing. The sun on her face showed the freckles that dotted both her cheeks. Her smile took up most of her face as she turned to one side, something sweet or funny catching her eye. He hadn't been there when the picture was taken and had wondered exactly what it had been more than once in the past month. There was a heart-shaped silver pendant around her neck with a ruby in its center that looked so real that he thought he could just reach out and grab it.

"Got that quote from the Mayor like you said for the water supply story," Don said, opening the door. He slid a pen into his pocket and smiled at his boss, giving him a little nod. "Didn't have much to say, but at least we can say he said it."

"Good," John nodded, turning away from the picture and clasping his hands together.

"I put it on the S drive if you want to take a look at it before it goes to print," he elaborated, motioning toward the monitor on John's desk.

"I will."

There was a silence for a moment. Don stood in the doorway with one foot in the office and one foot out, the doorknob teetering back and forth between his fingertips.

"Anything else?"

"Yes, actually," Don laughed, his cheeks flushed. "I put another story in there as well. I was hoping we could find some space in it for tomorrow's edition."

"What's the copy?" he asked, mildly interested as he giggled the mouse to make the screen turn on.

"It's about Xander Drew, sir."

John stopped, taking his hand off the mouse and clasping them before him again as he turned back to face Don. "Weren't you the one tearing down Drake earlier because you didn't think that kid was printable?"

"Not the same story. He's helping the Genblade defense, sir. It's worth printing. I really believe there's something going on here that they're not telling us. If nothing else, it's a good human interest piece."

John's head snapped up from where it had lolled to, meeting Don's excited gaze. "Human interest?" he scoffed.

"Yes, sir," Don replied, oblivious to his editor's tone as he sat down across from him, his hands shaking with excitement as he explained. "I think Xander Drew has more to do with this then he lets on. Something happened out there with Genblade that he's not saying... something big. I don't know what it was, but Drew wants to keep Genblade alive when he should be - -"

"*Human interest?*" John repeated again, slamming one hand against his desk and making Don jump in his chair. "Do you know who that girl is?" he asked, lowering his voice as he turned the photograph toward Don.

"No, sir, I don't."

"That's my daughter, Don. That's my Liz. She was killed a month ago. Do you know who she was killed by?"

Don did not speak, swallowing hard.

"You know, Don. You were here when we got the call. Who was she killed by?"

"By Genblade, sir," he said sheepishly.

"By Genblade," John spat, clenching his fists. "So, no, we will not be running any stories about how Xander Drew wants to help Genblade. Or any stories about anyone but Genblade being the killer. We will not be doing *anything* that poses even the slightest doubt onto his guilt. And for the record, any interest, even a passing one, in that monster should not be called anything remotely human."

"Yes sir," Don nodded, standing. "I'm sorry, sir. I just... I guess I just thought..."

"What?" the older man huffed, letting his palms fall to the desk. "What did you think?"

"I thought maybe I could help. That we could break this open."

John laughed, wiping his mouth with his sweat-covered palm.

"What?"

"Even if I let this story go to print, which I am not, there is no way that it will result in the vindication of Genblade or Xander, or the downfall of anyone else. The information isn't relevant to anything. It barely even qualifies as information. Leave the investigative reporting to the investigative reporters."

"Sir, I can be a - -"

"No, you can't," John yelled, standing up as Don took a pace back. "You

352

know what investigative reports do, Don? They *investigate* things. They do not sit around the office, waiting for a story to come over the fax machine," he said, waving his hands toward the machine. "They go out and look into things. They *leave the office* from time to time. You take useless information and try to build a story around it. Worse, it's information everybody already knows. Seriously, it's not like Drew's involvement is a state secret or something."

Don sighed, turning away from the desk and heading toward the door. When his hand touched the brass knob he stopped, turning his head slightly to look at his editor. "If I'm as bad as all that, then why hire me?"

"Because you're good at all the other stuff," he drawled, sitting back down and straightening the picture of his daughter. "You're good at getting the quote from the Mayor and getting just the right photo to go with our lead story. You excel at all the things that Drake can't be bothered with."

Don nodded, closing the door behind him with a soft click.

John double-clicked on the S drive and found the story Don had placed there, deleting it without even opening it. Nothing like that was going to break a story like this open.

ʎⵉʎ

Natasha Mayer walked with a power in her step.

Courthouses, especially this one, had always scared her, ever since she had been a little girl. Her mother had been called to it more than once during her childhood and she'd learned to associate with bad feelings from a point very early in her life. In the years since she had learned to put on the brave face, censuring which emotions that she let others see. Now, as she strode down the lime marble hallways carrying her opening statements in hand, she made sure that the only one she displayed was calm. Inside, her stomach still fluttered at the sight of the large stone pillars and gothic moldings that made up the antiquated Coral Beach courthouse.

A statue of the blind justice stood looming at her at the end of the hall, holding the scales out in front of her and pointing them directly at Natasha. As a child she remembered thinking that the statue was mad at her, somehow. The sculptor had made its gaze too stern and instead of the tempered frown, the woman's head was forever drawn back in a subdued scowl. Now she almost pitied the woman holding the scales, forced to carry the weight of either side for eternity, no matter which way the scales tipped. "Justice isn't only blind. She's enslaved," she mumbled to herself as she passed by the tall stone figure. Composing herself again, she stuck her nose into the air and continued her strut down the hallway towards the courtroom.

She past the massive doors of petrified wood and nodded to the bailiff, her heels clacking all the way up through the center of the gallery, finding her way to the defense desk. She placed her briefcase upon it gently, maneuvering it tediously until it was in just the right position. When she was done, she turned back to the rows of empty seats behind her and let out a sigh, the first signs of real emotion she'd let pass since entering the building.

Soon the seats behind her would be filled with the loved ones of those Genblade had killed, media, legal students and just about anyone that would fit from the citizenry of Coral Beach. In her mind's eye, she could almost see three rings forming in the colors of the seats to make it a real circus.

"Nervous?" asked the bailiff, stroking his thick goatee as the sweat stains beneath each of his armpits grew to immense proportions.

"How am I supposed to look at them?" she asked, smiling at him as best she could. "I'm defending the person who killed their children. The person that destroyed all their lives."

"That's why the judge is up front, Miss," he responded, pointing toward the head of the courtroom. "So you don't have to face them."

I hope Xander comes soon, she thought to herself, turning back toward the table.

The doors behind her swung open, startling her to the point that her composure fell and she let out a little squeal.

Megan Greene strode into the courtroom, her walk strong and confident. Her red hair flowed behind her as she walked, catching the sunlight that shone in through the large stain glass windows. Three men, each of whom looked very lanky and weak, walked silently behind her. Everything about her entrance, from the way she walked down to those little lackeys who were no doubt nothing but yes men, was perfect. Everything was set up to make her seem like the biggest and most powerful person in the room.

Which, Natasha realized quickly, she probably was.

Her suit was cut off at the waist, leaving way to her white blouse. She wore a thigh-length black skirt, which flowed in unison with her hair, as if they were somehow attached. She was beautiful and she knew it, or at least she should have.

Megan walked over to Natasha. "Hello Miss. Mayer." she said, flashing an obviously fake smile. "Feeling jumpy?"

"Two nights without sleep and staring at psyche reports on a convicted serial killer would make anyone jumpy," Natasha reasoned, extended a hand.

Megan looked down at the hand, smiled, then ignored it and turned back to Natasha. "Weird. I stayed up with them, and I feel just fine."

Natasha looked down at her files. She didn't have half as many as Megan, and Megan had a much stronger case. She frowned, sitting down and staring at the files in front of her. *I hope Xander gets here soon,* she thought, beginning to organize them.

CHAPTER EIGHT: TRIALS AHEAD

Xander fumbled with the top button of his shirt, his mouth contorting awkwardly as he fastened it. He stormed down the concrete steps of the police station, one foot following the other, tapping constantly. The shoes were tight and uncomfortable, pressing against either side of his feet until he could feel every ounce of blood that passed through them. Cathy had picked them out the night before. She'd said they made him look smart.

He paused at the street, rapping his fingers against the side of his leg as he waited for a car to pass and then crossed, nodding politely to a blonde woman pushing a stroller as he did.

The courthouse seemed to have grown out of the streets of the city. As if pavement were a living thing like plants and could grow its own buildings out of the earth. Its rough, textured grey was almost exactly like the weathered streets all around it, like a living, breathing part of his city. Massive stone pillars held up the high ceilings of the entrance, with each and every inch carved and decorated with pictographs so small and fine that you didn't even notice them until you got up close. In the center of the archway was a large, oval clock made of ivory back when ivory was still legal. Animal rights activists had been trying to get the face replaced for years, but right now it shimmered in the mid-afternoon sun for all its glory.

Setting his jaw, he stepped inside, walking briskly down the hall until he reached the large wooden doors of the main docket.

The second he walked into the courtroom, the warm air trapped within hit him as though he'd walked into a wall of solid heat. He felt his own head jerk back a bit at the smell of sweat mixed with the Pine-Sol that had obviously been used to clean the room. The courtroom smelled like an old library. That scent of old wood, paper, and dust. It was a smell he'd long associated with knowledge and felt very much in place here, with its long marble floors and towering bench at the opposite side.

"Xander Drew?" came a deep voice to his right.

He turned quickly and saw the bailiff looking down at him, his arms crossed in front of his chest. "That's me."

"She's waiting for you," he replied gruffly, nodding his head toward the front.

"Thank you," he replied without giving the man another glance, turning to walk down the hall towards the head of the courtroom.

The gallery was packed full. Every seat was taken, every corner where a person could be shoved occupied. Parents clutched pictures of children that Genblade had taken from them. Students talked amongst themselves. Journalists sat with their thumbs pressed against the record button of their tape decks, just in case.

From the first step he took, all those eyes locked onto Xander Drew.

Trying his best to keep his eyes facing forward, he marched to the last row and took a seat right behind Natasha Mayer's desk.

Deep inside him, the true womb twitched. Something deep inside itched at him, *begged* him to turn just a little to his right, but he would not.

Natasha turned around in her chair, leaning one arm over the back to see him as she moved a strand of hair behind her ear. "Beginning to think you wouldn't show," she said with relief.

"Wouldn't miss it for the world," he said, tapping his foot anxiously as beads of sweat started to form on his brow. "So, how do you wanna do this?"

"We'll play it by ear," she smiled, showing off duel rows of perfectly white teeth. "Just let me know if something becomes important, and be sure to try and be as positive as possible when I call you as a witness."

"Today?"

"No, lord no. That'll be a few days at least. They may not even want to hear from you now. This is just the hearing to decide - -"

"All rise," the bailiff barked loudly, bringing Natasha's sentence to a halt. She turned around in her chair swiftly and stood, smoothing out the wrinkles in her suit as she did so.

Xander stood as well, along with everyone else in the courtroom as the judge entered through a door just to the left of the bench. In the corner of his eye, he noticed one person who did not rise. Sweat itched at the corners of his eye, making the lashes twitch. Pretending to scratch his nose, he finally succumbed to the temptation and turned to look at the person just to Natasha's right.

Adam Genblade stared back at Xander, tight-lipped at first, then opening his mouth in a crocked smile to reveal rows of sharpened teeth. His orange prison jumpsuit did little to hide the rippling physique that lay just underneath, his muscles tensing and flexing mockingly as he stared Xander down, his eyes so blue they were nearly white. For the first time in weeks, there was nothing but space between the two of them. No plate glass, no steel walls, and no smoke and mirrors. Just the thick, hot air of the courtroom and the tension.

Xander felt his fingers tighten into fists so tight that it felt like the skin on his knuckles might rupture. His heart pumped hard and fast, sending heat coursing through his body and into his face as he imagined simply walking over there and ending Genblade, once and for all. He peeled his gaze away from Genblade's for a moment, looking from the three guards stationed near him, hands on their holsters, to the thick shackles clamped around his wrists and feet. He couldn't help but smile. He turned away from the killer altogether as the judge took a seat at the head of the courtroom, taking stock of the people gathered. Suddenly, he felt more anxious than ever, but he wasn't nervous anymore.

The journalist from the hospital was there, scribbling something fiercely into his notepad. Mr. Miles was there too, cleaning smut off of his glasses with the tail of his shirt. As his eyes shifted through the masses, he caught a glimpse of Mike and Cathy. They were both shifting their eyes from him to Genblade, trying to figure out whom they should keep their eyes on more. Xander looked back at Genblade, who was still smiling fiercely at him. There was a bruise going up the left side of his face, something that made Xander beam.

"Case number 28654 on the docket," the bailiff continued as everyone rose. "The honourable Judge Pike presiding."

The judge sat down, her long black robe flowing behind her. Her curly blonde hair tumbled over her shoulders and down her back. She had full, pink lips and a tight chin. Her eyes were big and blue, with long lashes. Xander inhaled suddenly when he saw her. She looked exactly like Sara would have at that age. If Sara had made it to that age. He quickly pushed the thoughts out of his mind as he felt Black Womb stirring. *Focus, dammit,* he chided himself, praying that nobody noticed. His gaze once again fell on Genblade, who grinned at him viciously now. He mouthed something that Xander couldn't quite pick out, but knew what it was anyway.

Strawberries.

Genblade smirked at Xander sinisterly, nodding slightly, as if he knew exactly what Xander was thinking.

Xander shivered, the notion that Genblade knew what was going on in his head sending chills up and down his spine.

"You may sit," the judge said, in a voice that was hard, haggard, and nothing like Sara's, bringing him back to reality. She sat down herself, leaning out over the high table and looking down at the people below. She glared down at Adam Genblade with contempt.

Adam laughed hysterically, turning and throwing a glance at Xander.

Xander frowned, rubbing the bridge of his nose between his fingers. "I'd hoped at least the judge would be impartial," he grumbled to himself softly, letting out a short sigh.

"Adam Genblade," the judge said, her voice venomous as she said his name. "You have been charged with ten counts of first degree murder, eight counts of second degree murder, kidnapping, conspiracy to commit murder and crimes against humanity. Defense, how does the accused plead?"

Natasha stood again, swallowing twice and still unable to get enough moisture into her mouth to create sound. She turned towards Megan before she spoke, the redhead lawyer beaming happily at her. "Not guilty, your Honour," she said finally, with all the confidence she could muster.

The judge raised one eyebrow. "Alright," she said flatly, checking some papers hidden by her desk. "Hearings will begin at exactly one fifteen tomorrow afternoon. Have your opening statements prepared, councils."

The judge banged on her gavel with a loud clang. Just as the gavel hit its wooden holster, Genblade leapt from his seat, planting both feet onto the defense's table next to Natasha and sending her glass water-jug smashing to the floor. "I object!" he shouted, breaking into hysterical laughter at the wide-eyed judge.

Xander jumped to his feet so fast it sent his chair back into the person behind him. Leaping over the rail between the gallery and the court, he lunged at Genblade's legs.

Genblade leaped down from the table, allowing Xander to crash through it. The wood splintered and fragmented into hundreds of sharp spikes, digging into his side as he hit the hard marble floor. "Not this time!" Genblade squealed in a half-giddy voice.

One of the three guards posted around Genblade pulled his gun from its holster and shot at Genblade, pumping off one bullet after another. Genblade vaulted into the air as if from nowhere, spinning and twisting in midair as the bullets whizzed past him. He landed just a few feet from Xander, unharmed.

The other two guards took out their guns as well and took aim.

"No," Xander whispered to himself as he looked up from the shattered remains of the table, seeing what was about to happen.

All three guards began firing, filling the air with lead.

Once again, Genblade bent his legs and effortlessly extended them, sending his body thrusting into a twisting backspin in the air.

There was the unmistakable sound of metal meeting metal, and then again as Genblade slowly fell back to earth.

He landed safely on the ground, like a circus acrobat just finishing some amazing trick.

A moment later, his shackles hit the ground as well, a smoldering bullet hole still warm in the center of the shattered chain.

Genblade smiled.

He snatched up the broken water jug and hurled it at one of the guards. The broken glass dug into the skin of his chest, ripping away at it as if it were nothing. Blood and flesh splattered out onto the floor rapidly as the jagged glass cut through one of the man's main arteries. He let out a small sound as he hit the floor, the arterial spray almost reaching all the way to the top of the judge's bench.

"It's time for a little *dis*order in the court, if you get my drift!" Genblade taunted to the other guards as he jumped onto the bar separating him from the gallery, hopping down into the hall and running for the door. Grinning wildly, he placed his hand against the knob... and locked it, then broke it off.

He turned around slowly, watching as panic began to set in and the people who were too scared to move got in the way of those who were so scared they ran, the court threatening to tear itself apart even without his help. After a moment, they all stopped and stared at him, wondering what he would do next.

Genblade smiled, his tongue rolled across his lips. As he did, his own jagged teeth cut his tongue, blood oozing down his chin. He didn't notice, just smiled wider as the coppery taste filled his mouth.

At the other side of the courtroom, Xander looked on in absolute horror. His mouth opened wide and fell slack, and his eyes felt as though they might pop out of his head. His breathing was so quick and hard that he thought he was going to pass out. It was all he could do to repress Black Womb from coming out right then and there. He couldn't move. He could only let two words pass through his dry lips.

"Genblade's free."

CHAPTER NINE: REMATCH

The words hung in the air as Genblade shifted his gaze from one frightened person to the next, taking in all of their fear and awe. He smiled grimly at all the horrified eyes which were trained on him, the pupils following even his most minute movement as he swayed back and forth. He took a deep breath through his nostrils and then sighed happily, as if he could smell the fright in the air. Blood and saliva mixed together in his mouth, mingling together to form a thick, bubbly liquid that seeped from between his lips and ran slowly down his chin before finally falling onto his jumpsuit.

"Genblade's free."

Xander felt his own words pass through his lips, not even realizing that he had spoken them. Every muscle in his body had locked in place, holding him in place through sheer force of instinct. He watched Genblade move one foot closer to the exit, rubbing the red rings around each of his wrists.

The two remaining guards kept their guns trained on Genblade, their hands shaking so fiercely that they probably couldn't have squeezed the triggers even if they wanted to, Xander guessed. One kept mumbling something out of the corner of his mouth, seemingly without realizing it. Only after he started again was it recognizable as the Our Father.

Genblade ran his eyes from face to face, lingering on some as he scanned the crowd. Like a wave, each person shuddered or curled into themselves and those around them as his eyes locked with their own. More than one started to cry, if they hadn't already. Finally, his gaze arrived on Mike and Cathy.

Cathy turned into the nape of Mike's neck, yet her eyes still bulged and stared out at him from behind her hair.

Mike glared at him wickedly, wishing with every thought he had that Genblade would simply drop dead where he stood, but at the same time unable to control the vibrations of his lower lip.

Genblade's smile grew mischievously. Letting out a small, happy squeal, he turned around and bent over so that he was eye-to-eye with Xander. "Well, well. The gangs almost all here," he chuckled. "Time to get out the party favours."

"Stop it," Xander whispered through pursed lips, his eyes darting from Genblade to Mike and then back again. "You're the only one who can stop this."

"Hoho, now that's not true," Genblade grinned, his fingers wriggling back and forth as though he could not contain the excitement coursing through his veins. "The real killer could stop this fairly quickly, don't you think?"

Deep inside Xander, the Womb organ nudged itself against Xander's gut, kicking in the same way an unborn child would. Already it started pumping to the beat of his heart, racing to get its black ooze through his veins. His head felt like it was going to explode.

"I mean, think of all that's happened here. All that's going to happen," Genblade laughed, standing up and spinning around, thrusting out one of his legs straight from his body. It connected solid against Xander's chest, making him stumble back and smash his head against the judge's bench.

Xander's head crashed into the fragile, thin wood that cracked into splinters, gouging the flesh off the side of Xander's face before he could pull away. Warm liquid oozed out of Xander's head, and he brought a hand to it immediately. His fingers were soaked almost instantly, but they were thankfully red rather than deep black. As he turned back to face Genblade, his vision became dark and hazy around the corners, closing in slowly like the black circle at the end of a cartoon before returning to normal. No, he thought to himself, swallowing back hard and feeling that taste of sour limes and copper travel down his throat. Not now.

Xander staggered slightly, one hand on his stomach. To most of the people watching at the edge of their seats, it looked as though Genblade's blow had seriously injured him.

As Mike watched in horror, he realized that the Black Womb was fighting its way up into his friend's throat. Slowly, he tore his gaze away from the fight and looked at all the people around. "He doesn't want to kill us," he said, so softly and with so much fear that only Cathy could hear.

"What?" she almost snapped, not looking away from Xander and Genblade to see how the color had drained from her lover's face.

"He wants *Xander* to kill us," he said, taking one more look at the crowd of mourners that had gathered in the gallery.

Cathy turned and looked at him, then at all the people around as well. "Oh my God," she breathed, as she realized quickly what was about to happen.

Xander glared up at Genblade, who towered over him with a great, toothy grin pasted across his lips. The red had gushed down over the right side of Xander's face, cutting it almost evenly down the middle.

Slowly, Genblade reached out and touched his cheek with the tip of his index finger, getting just the slightest dot of blood on its tip. He put his finger into his mouth until his lips touched the knuckle, swishing it around and coating as much of the inside of his mouth with it as he possibly could. He made a small, joyful sound in the back of his throat and then turned back toward the desk he'd sat behind a moment ago.

Natasha Mayer still stood behind it, stepping back in utter fright as Genblade locked eyes with her.

Genblade grinned, a deep pleasure in his eyes. "Now, Miss Mayer; now do you admire my work?" he said, snickering at his own joke.

She stepped back again, almost jumping out of her skin as her back touched the cold of the wooden bar. She shook all over like a tiny voice, letting out a small whimper as she turned away from him.

Suddenly Genblade broke out into a hysterical laughter, throwing his head back and then bringing his arm back to strike her. Before he could follow through with the blow, his entire body thrust itself to one side, his head slamming against the defense table. He went through it, sending splintered shards in all directions. One scraped the side of his face a little as all the air in his lungs forced its way out through his mouth.

"It wasn't that funny!" Xander shouted, standing back up. Every word he spoke spat deep hatred. His fists clenched so tightly that the knuckles turned white, the veins in the back of each hand looking as though they were ready to pop out. Each of them was running black.

Genblade glared up at Xander, rubbing the back of his head with one palm. "Impudent little brat," he grumbled harshly, the smile gone from his face for a moment. He reached back and ripped a long, pointed splinter off of the table, spinning it slightly in his hand until he found a good grip.

"What's the matter?" Xander retorted, letting himself smirk. "You lose your sense of humor?"

Genblade lunged at Xander, the stake slashing at the air around him in a giant, sweeping cross as he went.

Xander leapt to one side, the weapon coming so close to his face that he felt the smooth finish of the varnish wipe against his temple. The makeshift blade continued down, digging into his leg.

Xander screamed, his mouth open wide as he felt the wooden spike connect with his bone, ripping away flesh from it as it did. The sound it made was like pulling meat from the leg of a chicken, that long slurp followed by a small, polite snap.

Genblade slammed Xander in the face with his elbow, the force on the open jaw making it snap to one side as the rest of his head stayed put.

He felt the joint on the side of his face shatter like a plate as he hit the floor, rolling away from Genblade with the impact and sending him crashing into a row of chairs that shattered under his weight. He groaned, looking down at his leg. It had a large chunk of wood sticking out near the kneecap, making it impossible to bend. Biting his lip, he wrapped his fingers around it and pulled up hard. There was a sick, sucking sound as the wet, supple meat of his leg clung to the wood. He almost bit his lip off between his teeth as he watched clear, viscous juice come out of the wound from around the spike. He felt the womb organ surge inside his side, then stopped. He couldn't take it out without setting it off. *Fuck.*

Genblade glowered at Xander from across the room, bringing the remaining sharp stake to his lips and licking a bit of Xander's blood off of it. "Revenge is a dish that tastes good," he smiled.

Xander scowled, trying his best to climb to his feet and slipping in his own blood, crashing back into the chairs.

Bringing the stake up to a striking position, Genblade started to march toward Xander.

"Stop!" came a loud, booming voice.

Genblade turned just in time to see one of the guards finally gain control of their senses and began pumping off a hail of bullets at Genblade. He leapt and twisted, letting the ammunition whizz past him before he landed and then leapt again.

"Bout damn time," Xander mumbled under his breath, glancing around to see where everyone was. Megan Greene and her associates were cowering under the table, but while her associates kept their heads between their arms, Megan seemed to be taking it all in, unable to tear her eyes away from the swarm of shots and blood drops that seemed to hang in the air forever before splashing to the floor. "Bet this'll help your case," he grumbled, shifting his gaze to Natasha. She seemed to be all right, still shaking from her confrontation with Genblade. Her eyes were wide but weren't seeing anything that was happening around her, just staring off into nothing and wondering what she'd done to him to deserve this. Cursing, Xander turned and searched for Mike and Cathy. The crowd was flowing this way and that, like water tossed about in a glass jar, trying to escape both the line of fire and Genblade himself. Through all the motion, Xander had lost track of Mike and Cathy.

The bullet fire continued, as now both officers tried in vain to force Genblade into the corner of the courtroom and pin him. Neither had yet to land a shot. He kept his eyes trained on the barrels of each gun so he knew exactly where each slug was headed, twisting and contorting in ways no human should have been able to do to avoid being there when the bullet sped past. He jumped and flipped until he heard the sound he'd come to love more than anything else in this world.

-click-

The sharp, fast sound of metal tapping against metal as the hammer of the guns came down and connected with nothing but an empty shell case. He smiled, his feet landing solid against the floor for the first time since the barrage of metal had begun. He smiled at them both of them, showing off his long row of pointed teeth.

The guard that had begun firing lowered his weapon now, staring up at Genblade with pure terror as the monster loomed ever closer until all he could see were the stark shadows of his backlit face. Suddenly, something else flashed into his field of vision as the light behind Genblade blinked away and a chair smashed into the side of his head, its leg creating a loud crack against Genblade's skull.

"Fuck!" Genblade screamed, spinning around as he fell to the floor.

Quickly, the second guard raised his weapon and fired the three remaining shots that waited in his chamber.

Genblade's eyes went wide as three bullets burrowed holes into his side.

He hit the floor hard, his blood already soaking into the creases of the hardwood. His hands pressed against the holes to try and stop the blood. He turned his head as his vision throbbed in and out and saliva drooled from his mouth, and looked up into the crowd to find the face of the person who'd done this to him. He found the clenched jaw of Mike Harris, still holding the broken leg on the chair, with Cathy Kennessy standing behind him. His eyes rolled back to see the guards reloading their weapons and Xander finally climb to his feet. Finally, he cast his gaze towards Natasha.

He took a step forward.

Staggering, Xander lunged at Genblade, his fingers outstretched trying to grab at the orange jumpsuit. His vision was almost black now, the tunnel he seemed to be looking through getting smaller and smaller with every beat of his heart. He saw his hand touch Genblade's shoulder... but felt it pass through the air and continue downward. He blinked once, and Genblade instantly seemed an extra foot away, his legs curling and letting go as he dove at Natasha, snagging her neck with his hand and wrapping his fingers around it.

She let out a small yelp of fright, like the squeak of a terrified little mouse.

He looked at her, panic-stricken beyond human comprehension and probably on the verge of a heart attack. He breathed in through his nose, smelling the fear off of her. It made him smile.

The guards retrained their weapons of him, the soft click of the shells being loaded into their chambers bringing him back to the battle he'd lost to Xander at Alpha Quadrant. His light blue eyes circled around his surroundings, shifting from the exit, to the guard, to Xander and then finally back to Natasha.

As the guards raised their guns again, he jumped backwards, taking Natasha with him as he sliced the stake through the air in front of him again, letting go halfway and hurling it towards one of the two remaining guards. It spun through the air spinning from sharp end to dull and back again before connecting and embedding itself into the guard's lower chest. It all seemed to happen in slow motion until the sound of snapping ribs filled the air, speeding everything into fast forward.

Genblade threw Natasha to the floor and then dove after her, her body sliding to a stop next to the first guard, still gasping for breath as glass made its way closer and closer to his windpipe. He landed almost on top of her, knocking her head back as she let out a wet yelp, the blood from the bullet holes in his side cascading down her face and into her nose and mouth. He reached for the dying guard's gun, his hands slippery and wet on the grip before standing and turning just as the last guard was putting first pressure on his own trigger to take Genblade down.

-BANG!-

Both the guard and Genblade stood still for a moment. After what felt like an eternity, Xander watched a wave of blood splash out from the side of the guard's throat as he brought his hands up to try and stop it. He feinted after only a moment, and was dead before he hit the ground. Xander's eyes narrowed across the room as Genblade pulled Natasha in close to his chest, smiling at him. "Let me go before I kill the girl, Womby. I would if I were you."

Xander just glowered in response, not giving Genblade the satisfaction of replying. His feet tipped back and forth, wanting so badly to just jump at Genblade but forcing himself to hold back.

"You ever wonder what life would be like if we were in each other's place?" he asked, stroking the tender flesh of Natasha's neck, making her yelp softly as he smelled her hair.

"No," Xander said, never breaking the steely gaze between them.

"Oh, I do," he hissed through clenched teeth, pulling Natasha even closer to him as he inched his way toward the door. "Got all the time in the world up in that cell, and I think of nothing but that. You know what I figured out?"

Xander did not respond, and in fact could barely even hear Genblade over the roar of his own veins.

"It wouldn't be no different," he snarled, throwing Natasha at Xander with such force that she rose up off the ground. He turned and bolted toward the courtroom's exit, the crowd parting for him as he went as if through Devine intervention.

Xander eyes went wide as he lunged forward to catch Natasha, his eyes breaking from Genblade for the first time in what seemed like forever. He felt his hands connect with her armpits as the force of her weight made his leg want to buckle and snap all over again, but did not.

Their faces within inches of each other, Natasha looked at him and almost smiled as their forward momentum finally stopped and she heard the sound of the large wooden doors of the courtroom opening. "Well, that was--"

-BANG!-

Xander felt the bullet rip through him and out the other side, jolting forward from the sudden impact and sending him into the crook of Natasha's neck. He didn't see the look on her face, but her felt the tiny pat of two tears as they hit his shoulder almost simultaneously, and he saw her blood force its way out through the hole that had been torn in the dark blue suit that her daughter had said looked perfect on her that morning. He felt her entire body shudder as her last breath shook its way from her lungs, her body not fighting death as it barreled down and overtook her.

He looked up and saw Genblade standing with his hand on the door, the smoking gun still pointed at the spot where Natasha had been. "Lied," he said simply, before disappearing outside. The door slammed shut behind him, its sound echoing throughout the courtroom.

Xander lay Natasha down on the floor before him, the weight off his leg a welcome relief. Her brown eyes stared up at him lifelessly, blood spatter covering her face. The exit would on her chest was massive and had showered his shirt and neck in thousands of tiny droplets of blood, bone and pieces of her lung. For a brief second, she almost looked like she was still alive... but then that was gone too, and there was nothing but her and the hole in her that didn't even look real under the harsh incandescent lights.

"Xander?" Mike called out from across the courtroom, Cathy standing beside him but turned away from the grisly sight.

Xander stood up, shaking his head slightly as he started walking toward the door, his leg pulsating with pain and making him limp, though not as badly as he had been.

"Where do you think you're - -" Mike started, then stopped when Xander turned to glare at him.

His eyes were completely black, so much that they looked like dark holes in his face instead of gel-filled balls. The womb pumped with such ferociousness that he cried black tar, making his face look like his mother's did when she cried with mascara on. He didn't stop walking, brushing past people as he headed for the doors.

Mike stepped back and watched his friend go, then turned and looked at the still-warm body of Natasha Mayer. After a moment, Megan Greene popped up from behind the bar and into his field of vision, rubbing her fingers through her curly red hair.

"What the hell happened?" she asked, unable to turn away from the corpse.

"What always happens when people get too interested in death," Mike said, turning just in time to see the door close behind Xander. "They find it."

人(人

The courtroom doors slammed behind Xander, the sound echoing off the empty marble floors and stone walls until it felt like it was coming at him from all directions. The halls seemed to stretch on forever in front and behind him, with nothing in sight but eerie reflections and shadows.

"I know you're here," Xander breathed, his eyes darting one way and then the other, always seeing something in his peripheral vision. "Come out and face me, you coward."

"Coward?" came Genblade's voice from somewhere in front of him, though with all the echoing it was impossible to tell from where. "What makes me a coward?"

Xander raised an eyebrow slightly, then started walking down the corridor in the direction of the voice. He stepped lightly, trying to make as little sound as possible for Genblade to hear. As he looked around, the gothic mouldings and images that danced along the ceiling of the courthouse mocked him now, like grinning gargoyles laughing at his efforts. Though he tried to fight it, the feeling of the cold floor beneath his feet couldn't help but remind him of their fight at Engen. "You said you wouldn't kill Natasha," he answered finally, keeping his eyes peeled for any movement. "You're a liar, Genblade."

"Said no such thing," the voice chuckled. "Said you should let me go *before* I killed her, and that's the order it happened in."

Xander growled deep in the back of his throat, but did not respond as Genblade's laughter filled the hall. He stepped out into the main foyer now, with its gaping stone pillars and magnificent statues. There was a painting on the wall he hadn't noticed before of Judge Pike that now had blood smeared over her neck and eyes, making her appear ghostly and as dead as the bodies back in the courtroom.

-BANG!-

A bullet ricocheted off the metal frame of the painting, making it fall to the floor. Xander backed up quickly to avoid being hit by it as it fell forward onto its face, showing the grey-brown matting behind it. The wall was discoloured around the area where the painting had hung, the rest of it faded from years of sun exposure.

"You think you'll ever be rid of this?" the voice came again, as Xander spun around looking for its source and finding nothing. "You think that if you save enough, if you forgive enough, that maybe someone will save and forgive you?"

-BANG!-

The clay moulding directly above Xander's head erupted in gunfire, showering him with bits of silt and dust as he ran forward to get away from it, desperately trying to get the tiny stones out of his eyes. He stumbled forward until his hands felt something sturdy for him to lean against, his palms flat against the cool, hard surface. His eyes watered and cried until all the dust was out of them, the grey marble square in front of him slowly coming into view, as well as the equally grey foot that stood still on it. He looked up at the justice statue again, water still streaming down his face. "That's not what this is about," he said, locking eyes with the veiled ones of the statue for a moment before turning around. "That's not what this is about!"

There was a long, odd creek from close by, but it stopped before he could get a read on it.

"No?" the voice laughed, and Xander could almost see his head rocking back in his mind's eye. "And how would you know? You don't even know why you're fighting, let alone what you're fighting for."

The sound started again, much more sudden, and louder than before. There was a sudden weight on him so immense and heavy that it forced him to the floor. There was a loud crash, and more dust and dirt erupted all around him as he tried to turn around, making it impossible to see. When his eyes were clear again, he was nose-to-nose with the lady holding the scales.

Genblade got back up off of the floor where the statue had stood and dusted himself off as he hopped up onto her back, walking casually over the beautifully carved stone until he stood directly on top of Xander. He crouched down to get closer, watching the boy squirm and wince under the incredible weight, then took aim with the gun. "Justice is a hard weight to carry, isn't it Womb?" he whispered mockingly, licking his lips. "That's why nobody ever said doing the right thing was easy."

"How would you know?" Xander grunted, forcing out each syllable more and more as his lungs refused to fill with air a little more with each breath. His eyes bulged, large and black.

"How indeed," Genblade smirked. "But I tell you, I'd rather be this good at doing the wrong thing... than suck at doing the right thing as much as you do."

Xander opened his mouth to respond, but before he could, Genblade pulled the trigger and pumped off one final shot that literally blew off his shoulder. He screamed, his hands slamming against the statue as they tried to reach up and hold the damaged flesh but were unable to do so.

As Genblade watched, he saw that the blood that seeped out of the gaping red maw was a thick, congealed black. He smiled, reaching down and grabbing Xander by the face, forcing his mouth to close and the screams to stop. "Time to continue your education, son. I think you'll like today's lesson. Round one to me."

Xander tried to respond, but the black liquid boiling up in his throat, searing the lining of his esophagus as it went, drowned out the words. In the distance, sirens finally began to blare to life as squad cars came into range. Before the blackness completely enveloped his lips... a smile started over them.

Genblade leapt from the statue and onto the floor, bolting for the doors as fast as he could.

As the blackness overwhelmed him, devouring his body until there was nothing left, Xander felt a sick, gurgling laugh build up in his throat, though he

366

wasn't quite sure from where.

"Black Womb lives."

He heard himself say in the creature's horrible, gagging voice as his eyes opened, revealing the red, opaque lenses that saw every last detail the room had to offer. The mouth gaped open, its forked tongue whipping out and tasting the air. The scent it grabbed was so familiar that Xander could almost *see* it floating in the air and disappearing at the door. It gripped the statue by the hips with his clawed hands, rolling it to one side and then breaking into a run before it had even finished climbing to his feet.

It burst through the front doors of the courthouse, landing on all fours.

There was nothing. No people, no cars and most of all, no Genblade. For one single, horrifying moment, it occurred to Xander that he'd lost the killer already.

Then the truck hit him.

The Womb slammed against the concrete steps, feeling the sharp stone dig into his back.

Smiling, Genblade leaned out of the cab of the blue pickup and watched the Womb scramble back to his feet. Laughing, he pulled out onto the road and sped away. It drove a hundred feet and then turned sharply, spinning around one-hundred-and-eighty degrees until its dented grill again faced the Black Womb.

The sun blaring in its eyes, the Womb could only stand and watch as Genblade revved the car's engine, then finally put his foot to the floor and started speeding toward the creature again.

Inside the Womb, Xander watched as the truck barreled down upon him, waiting for just the right moment. He felt the muscles in his legs filled with black blood and become tense, his taloned fingers dangling at his sides.

The vehicle was almost on top of him when he leapt, crashing through the windshield and into the cab. He landed square in the empty driver's seat, the polarized glass raining down on him as he saw the cruise control locked on.

Then the truck hit the courthouse.

It erupted in a brilliant, fiery blaze, shooting up and out until nothing of the truck could even be seen anymore. After a moment, it settled, still burning as Genblade walked over and reached past the shattered driver's side window and pulled out Black Womb by the neck. His taunting smile was gone now, replaced by a curling nose and hate-filled scowl.

"Didn't learn anything about distraction, did we?" he screamed, bringing back his fist and slamming it into the Womb's face. Its teeth grazed and cut his knuckles, but he barely even noticed. He hammered his fist down again, splashing the black tar onto the streets as he did.

The Womb tried to say something, but again its mouth was filled with blood.

"Shut your face!" Genblade screamed, bringing down his fist again. "You think I care about anything you have to say, you little shit? You killed my fucking wife!" he brought his fist down again, and this time the Womb's teeth gave under the force of Genblade's knuckles, cracking off and falling to the pavement.

367

"I'll fucking end you, you little piece of trash!"

The Womb brought up its legs and pushed Genblade off of itself, scrambling to its feet again as it vomited up the blood that had been rising up from its lungs and stomach. "She was going to kill me," it said finally, the harsh, gritty voice sounding off when mixed with the sympathetic pang of Xander's.

"I don't care!" Genblade spat, drool and mucus huffing from his nose and mouth now. He lunged forward again, hitting the Womb in the throat.

The impact made it stagger backwards again, the flames from the burning truck right behind it.

Genblade leaned in slowly, again licking those pointed teeth of his. "You still got plenty to learn, but there's one thing you're gonna have to learn fast... and there's only one way I know to teach you."

"What's that?" the Womb scoffed, even as it started to rise to its feet.

Genblade drove his hand forward, shoving the Womb's long, serrated tooth into its gut and then swiping it all the way across.

The Womb's eyes grew wide as the blackness covering it almost immediately began to lose its consistency, hanging off of Xander like wrinkled skin for a moment before losing its hold altogether and melting to the floor. Xander gasped for air and got a mouthful of the layer of blood that covered his body, his natural, blue eyes staring up at Genblade in horror as the killer twisted the tooth again, smiling.

Genblade wriggled the makeshift blade around one last time, snickering at the soft, wet sound it made before finally hauling it back out. "The lesson'll come on its own time."

"So will yours," Xander spat, jumping at Genblade's waist and forcing him to the ground. "Don't fucking care about your lessons!" he screamed, bringing back his fist and slamming it into Genblade's face as hard as he could.   " O r your distractions!" he screamed again, right before landing another blow. Blood spattered up onto his face, but he didn't notice. "Or your wife!" he brought both fists into the air at once, hammering them down simultaneously.

SLAM.

"I don't care Genblade! Nobody does!"

SLAM!

"Mike doesn't care, Cathy doesn't care... Alpha *never* cared!"

SLAM!

"Nobody cares about you Genblade. Nobody - -"

"Xander!" Mike yelled, grabbing his friend's wrist before he could bring his fists down again.

Xander struggled for a moment, turning to glare at his friend without even seeing him. Then he turned back to Genblade, and noticed the swollen, red piece of meat that had replaced his opponent's face. There was so little white left to his skin that he was barely even recognizable, having been bruised into blacks, blues and yellows. His face seeped blood from almost every conceivable hole plus several newly created ones, and one gash on his forehead was so bad that a vicious white fluid with the consistency of an egg seemed to be coming out of it.

"Jesus," Xander whispered, stepping away from Genblade.

Mike crouched down, placing two fingers on the side of Genblade's throat. "Is he alive?"

"Yes. Get out of here," Mike snapped, not even bothering to turn around.

"But I can - -"

"Get out of here, Xander," he said again, his voice a little more stern.

As the rest of the crowd approached, Xander ducked into an alleyway and was gone.

"You finish that research yet?"

Don looked up from his desk, pushing his hair back into place as his eyes adjusted to the light, trying his best to pretend that he hadn't been asleep. "Um," he stammered, gazing from Drake's frowning, impatient face to the pile of papers covering his desk, looking for some clue to jog his memory of what he had been doing before he'd passed out. "Ah, just about."

Thomas Drake cocked an eyebrow at him, his mouth never twitching to show any sign of amusement if he felt any. "The victims list, Don. I need a full, up-to-date victims list. Then I need you to contact the next of kin of each of them and see if they plan on suing the town for this crap."

"Suing?" Don repeated, furrowing his brow. "I haven't heard anything about any suit?"

"There isn't anything," Drake snapped. "And there won't be if you don't get off your ass and start asking people if they *plan* on suing for all the mental anguish the city's putting them through with this farce of a trial. And they'll sue. And then we'll report on the suit."

Don looked at him with a face that perfectly mixed both amazement and horror at the same time.

"You get all that, or do I need to write it down for you?"

"No, got it," Don nodded, finally gathering up the right stack of papers. "There was one I was having issue with. Jesse... Jesse... Jesse Something. She went missing a while back but they haven't found the body yet. Parents are still pretty hopeful, but with all the cops focused in on the Genblade case and the murders, I think they're just clinging."

"And?"

"Well, until there's a body we can't even say for sure she's dead. Should I include her in all this?"

"She young?"

"Yeah."

"She cute?"

"Yeah... yes."

"Put a picture of her front a centre with the story. If anything sells better than hot young ass, it's *dead* hot young ass."

Don winced, then turned to reply, but Drake had already vanished from his doorway. He sighed, his grip on the page he'd been looking at tightening as he felt the urge to just rip it apart... then eventually stopped, letting it fall back to his desk. Taking a deep breath, he pushed himself back from his desk and got up, his lips pursed and white.

He was going to break this story wide open.

Drake slid the key to the glass doors of the strip mall out of their lock, pulling twice on the handle to make sure it was sturdy as the setting sun offered one last glimmer of light from its reflection in the glass before ducking behind a row of trees and bathing Coral Beach in darkness. A mist had rolled in from the bay in the last few hours of twilight. The air in some areas of town would be thicker than molasses on a night like tonight, but here in the central city it just formed a neat little fog close to the ground, making it hard to see where you stepped as your feet paced along the sidewalks.

He turned around and looked out over the bare parking lot, not seeing one sign of movement in the dim of twilight. He shook his head and chuckled a little. There weren't many people who still tempted fate by walking the roads at night. Beaming to himself as he started to walk toward his car, he took it as a compliment to his writing. His briefcase swung casually by his side, his collar was unbuttoned as an uncharacteristic heat whipped relentlessly at his skin. He took four swaggering, self-confident steps before his pace began to slow and his eyes began to study the deepening darkness a little more quickly. There was a group of teenagers huddled together on a corner a few streets over, neither of them paying him much heed as he shuffled by. Beads of sweat dripped down his forehead and neck. He picked up the pace, his briefcase swinging much more rapidly now.

-TSSSH-TNK-TNK!-

He stopped, turning around quickly and running back to the mall entrance. He sighed as he came back around the corner and saw one of the glass doors he'd locked so carefully had been smashed in, the sound of heavy footfalls already fading into the distance.

"Fucking kids," he cursed, bending over and picking up a brick wrapped in a newspaper. He unfolded it, letting the brick fall to the floor with a thud as he examined the crumpled, ripped remains of the paper. It was his front-page stories from a few weeks back about the deaths of two rapists that used to attend school at Coral Beach. There were two large photos of each of the men lifted from their high-school yearbook in the center, and a good eight columns worth of story. Along the side bar was a small, unaccredited insert on reaction from the different students involved. He recognized it quickly as one of Don's, glancing down over it for the first time. "Kind of idiot uses his son as a source?" he scoffed, crumpling the paper back up into a ball and tossing it into the trash.

Cursing again, he tried to shake the glass from the bottom of his boot before walking back in the direction of his car. A few shards fell to the fog-covered sidewalk, bouncing along the pavement's edge with a series of soft little -tinks-.

The teenagers that had been across the way were gone now, even though he hadn't heard them leave. For some reason that made him nervous as the tail end of his car came into sight around the next corner, more sweat forming quickly on his neck and staining the collar of his shirt.

"Fucking kids," he said again, huddling into himself as he began to walk faster, his legs blurring back and forth in the fog.

-tink-

He frowned, shaking more glass from the bottom of his shoe.

-tink-

Huffing in frustration, he sat down against the moist curb and lifted his shoe up so that he could see the bottom. There was nothing there but a cigarette butt stuck to an old wad of chewing gum – no glass. Still, he could see the glass all around him now from where it had fallen to his feet. There were three pieces right next to him, shimmering up at him like specs of gold in a prospector's sift.

-tink!-

Suddenly, a forth piece of glass joined the other three, bouncing in from somewhere behind him. He stared at it for a moment, not having time to form any thoughts one way or the other before there was a blinding pain on the side of his face.

He brought his hand up to his ear quickly, and found that it wasn't there anymore. When he brought his hand back he couldn't even see his own skin, it was so laden with his own blood, dark crimson in the low light.

"Christ!" he yelled, trying to get up, but succeeding only in falling forward, falling face-first into the pavement. The tiny shards of glass that had been little more than an annoyance a moment ago dug into his face and gums, making his mouth fill with that coppery tang that overpowered everything. He tried to turn around, but there was almost instantly a weight on his back, digging into his spine. He let out a long wail when he looked at the ground beneath his face and saw the very large pool of his blood that had already formed there. His reflection stared back at him in horror, as did the dark, menacing figure that loomed behind him. As he watched, the shadow-figure drew back and let out one vicious blow to the side of Drakes' head.

When he opened his eyes again to look at his reflection, half of it was missing. That half had formed a wet, clumpy pink mound a few inches away from the puddle. He felt something sharp dig into the nape of his neck and as he lost consciousness, he couldn't help but think of the victim list that he'd had Don Smith working so hard on.

Nathan Summers sat in the office of Mayer, Summers and Soul; his head buried into his short, silvery hair as he fought back the urge to vomit. Sniffing, he wiped down his face with the cuff of his grey pinstripe suit as he forced himself to turn away from the picture that stared at him from the corner of the desk.

Natasha and her daughter stared back at him, the sun behind them giving their hair a shimmering, halo-like quality.

He took a deep breath, in through his nose and out through his mouth, then repeated several times as he tried to compose himself. Gathering his will, he reached up and lay his hand on the top of the silver frame that he'd given her for her birthday and pushed it down so that it faced downward. Their happy, contented eyes no longer haunting him, he turned his attention to the box between his legs and the pile of papers surrounding it.

"Loved that girl," he thought to himself, grabbing a handful of papers and shoving them down into the box. "But it wouldn't have killed her to be organized."

He reached over with both arms, spreading them to gather one sweeping armful and throw it into the box. It nearly buckled under the weight of the faxes and printouts, so much that he had to force it down with the heel of his shoe. Three pieces fell out when he pulled back his foot, their crumpled remains falling and rolling along the floor. He sighed, bending over despite the cries from his back and picking them up. On the one that had been closest to him, he saw a familiar name in dark printers ink: Natasha Mayer.

He paused, staring down at the paper in his hand for a moment before unfolding it and reading down through the document.

Kind representative of Mayer, Summers and Soul;

It has come to my attention recently that a person/ persons at your firm has come into contact with my case file after my information was sent to you via the District Attorney.

Lavish as it is for me to have a fan, I feel it necessary to inform you that I have plead guilty to the majority of the crimes to which I am accused.

Likewise I am sure you are aware that I am expected to spend the remainder of my short life in a maximum security upstate while awaiting execution.

You above anyone understand how unacceptable this is. I have grown to regard Coral Beach and this place with fondness and do not wish to leave any more than I wish for my life to end.

Ordinarily I would be appalled at admitting this, but I find   myself overcome with fear at the idea of my death. I do not want to die, sir or madame. I wish to live and to learn of the world around me, albeit through the bars of a gilded cage. I wish to fight the death penalty sentence as well as my conviction. As such, I will require the services of a lawyer.

Understand that despite all accounts, I do have the means with which to compensate you handsomely.

Sincerely, Adam Genblade.

He stared at it for a moment, his eyebrows getting lower and lower as something in the back of his mind ached at him. His lower lip quivering, he lay the letter flat against Natasha's desk and grabbed a blank sheet of paper, laying it over the top so that it covered all but the first letter of every paragraph and then read it again.

"KILL YOU.

Sincerely, Adam Genblade."

Balking, he stepped back from the desk and grabbed the box by both sides, getting his head back over it just in time before he started to vomit again.

Megan Greene sat in her office, head buried in her hands. She'd been a lawyer for a long time and had come up against some of the hardest killers in this country. She had taken pride in the fact that she had put them all behind bars, without remorse or a second thought.

Now she sat at her desk wringing her hair between her fingers, questioning the innocence and guilt of them all. Questioning a promise she had made nearly a decade ago.

There's a school of thought you learn in law school. It's an emotional void that each lawyer must find to defend a client that you may not believe is completely innocent, or maybe even just flat-out guilty. Or in Megan's case, accusing someone she'd believed innocent. She'd made a promise to her best friend ten years ago that she would never let the 'emotional void' consume her. She kept reliving the conversation she'd had with her friend, one of their last. He'd told her to live life with 'no regrets'. To never look back, and to always approach the future with a positive spin on the past. Come to think of it, that was the last time she'd seen him before he died. She'd wondered more than once since why no one had ever tried to put cancer to death.

But this young man, this Xander Drew, had lost everything to the madman known only as Genblade... and yet he forgave. Defended, even. As she struggled to wrap her mind around that, she also started to see things differently. Something twitched in the back of her mind and wouldn't let go. She saw a way that Genblade might not be guilty.

"Hello?" came a familiar voice from the doorway. She looked up at the door, even though she didn't need to to know that it was Tony. "How you holding up?"

"I've been better," Megan revealed, frowning.

"Don't stay in too early tonight, okay?"

"You mean too late."

"No, too early. It's past midnight."

Megan stared down at her watch in shock, then re-buried her face in her hands and pretended to scream. She raised her head again to see Tony about to leave. "Tony?" Megan asked, her voice following him.

"Yes?" he turned, opening the door again.

She paused, turning from him and then looking over the files and folders and documents she spent weeks preparing for Genblade's prosecution. "I can't do this anymore."

He frowned. "Megan, you've had a rough day. Every lawyer wants to quit after what you've just gone through. It's perfectly normal. You'll be fine in the morning."

"I don't want to quit being a lawyer," Megan blurted, saying the words before she realized what she was saying.

A puzzled look came over Tony. "What do you mean then?"

"I want off the case. Genblade's innocent."

Mike held Cathy close to him, rocking her back and forth. It had taken hours, but he had finally gotten her to go to sleep.

Her parents had called to tell him that she was at her grandparent's home, hoping that maybe he'd be able to sooth her. She lay with her head on his lap, still sobbing in her sleep. His jeans were soaked with two little puddles from where she had cried herself to sleep again, but since then she'd tapered off.

As he watched, he wondered what she was dreaming of. He saw her expressions change rapidly, guessing that they weren't happy dreams. *So,* his sleepless mind thought, *it's official. Genblade has infested every aspect of our lives, right down to our nightmares.*

He forced his mind to stray from Genblade, wondering if Xander had been able to keep the Black Womb at bay for another night. He guessed that they would find out in a few short hours. At that moment, the sleeping form of Cathy Kennessy outstretched her arms and wrapped them around Mike, squeezing him tightly. He smiled, brushed her hair back behind her ear, and kissed her.

"I'm coming!" Xander growled angrily as the knocking at his front door continued, groggily walking down the stairs. His eyes were bloodshot and baggy, his hair poofing off on either side so much so that it almost stood on end. He was wearing an old, loose T-shirt over pajamas that he'd had since he was in grade six, with ruts in the knees and that only came down to his shins.

The knocking continued even after he shouted, a steady rap of knuckles against wood.

"I swear by all that's fucking holy, Mike, this had better be good after the shit I've - -" he opened the door fast, and as soon as he did his scowl loosened.

Megan Greene raised an eyebrow at him, a small smile twitching along the side of her mouth.

Xander squinted at her, leaning his head out the door to see if there was anyone else there.

"May I come in?" she asked finally, clutching her briefcase close to her chest. She looked him up and down, smiling again at his appearance.

Xander frowned, then stepped out of the way. He waited for her to enter and then closed the door behind her, turning on the hall light. "To what do I owe the pleasure?"

"Wanted you to know I quit the prosecution after today," she said, taking a quick scan of the home before turning to meet Xander's gaze head-on, smiling her very best smile.

Xander tilted his head, unsure what to make of the information. "The case against Genblade is being put on hold?"

"No, the D.A.'s taking over. I quit the office after that mess at the courtroom today."

"Can't say I blame you. I'd quit if I could."

"Why?" she asked quizzically, unable to hide her grin.

"Today was just ridiculous. That was probably the worst day I've had in a long time. Maybe ever," he said, almost smiling himself. "I mean, besides the fight, just sitting next to him is like some kind of slow, nagging torture. Well, you must know. You're quitting."

"Not quitting," she said, handing him the briefcase. "Switching sides."

Xander stood dumbfounded for a moment, looking from her to the briefcase and then back again several times before reaching out and taking it. "You wanna run that one by me again?"

"I think you're right. I think he's innocent."

He raised an eyebrow. "You think he's innocent."

"Yes."

"Based on *today*."

"Yes."

He looked at her for a moment, then started to laugh. He laid the briefcase down on the floor and walked over to the stairs and sat, burying his head in his palms to try and hide the sound.

"Something funny?" she asked, taking a step closer to him.

"Life," he said, stroking his rough-hewn face for a moment before taking his hands away. "Life is funny. And, apparently, insanity is contagious. You've obviously got it."

"You're one to talk, he's done the most to you and you've been defending him from the get-go," she reminded him, pointing one of her brightly-coloured nails at him.

"Defending him and believing in him are two different things," he said, looking down at the floor. His side still ached from the battle with Genblade earlier, the skin over the wound barely formed and threatening to break at any time.

"Why do it, then?"

Xander paused, looking up at her for a moment and then straight at the wall in front of him. "Honestly, I can't even remember anymore. I think I thought that if I helped him, if I proved myself that much better than him, then I could get past this. That life would become something different than... this," he paused, then turned to her. "What's got you so convinced he's innocent?"

"Gut, mostly," she admitted, but opened up the briefcase anyway and handed him the folder. "But there was some stuff that bugged me while I was researching the case. I got all I could so I'd be prepared if the defense brought it up..."

"But now we are the defense," he finished.

She looked at him, smiling warmly and honestly. "Yes, *we* are."

He grinned at her, sighing as he felt himself get into the conversation. He took a picture from the briefcase that had been blown up from a coroner report so that a stab wound took over the entire picture. "What am I looking at?"

"Knife work," she said simply. "It's not exact, but it can be like a fingerprint for a killer if you know what to look for. Just like you can tell a lot about a person from how their handwriting looks... you can tell a lot about a person from how they use a blade, too."

"You're a sick lady," he stated playfully.

"The victims from a month ago and the ones from this week have the same pattern of wound," she continued, as if he hadn't spoken. "They're angry, quick and rapid, repeating over and over again... eager. Intense."

"And?"

"Today in the courtroom when Genblade was coming at you with that piece of wood, it was different. No matter how angry he got, his slices were all planned and perfect. The strokes were calm and effortless... happy even."

"Yeah," Xander said, touching his leg where Genblade had stabbed him. "I'm sure that's the word I'd use to describe it."

"At no point did he lose control of his attack. Ever. It was like the weapon was an extension of his body, even if it was just a hunk of wood."

Xander frowned, looking at the pictures and then thinking about today. "So the killer from now is the same killer from a few weeks ago?"

"Definitely."

He frowned, looking down at the floor again.

"Something wrong?" Megan asked, her face concerned when she saw the look on his.

"No, it's... it's nothing. Nothing at all. Let's get to work."

"We start in a few hours," she reminded him as she started sifting down through the rest of her papers. "We've haven't got much time to prepare. Believe me, we're up against the best."

ᚱᚢᚱ

"All rise," the bailiff said, loud and clear, his voice echoing throughout the courtroom.

The judge entered from the side as the bailiff continued, then stated to the court: "You may sit." She eyed the room, and found no trace of Adam Genblade. She breathed a small sigh of relief. She also noticed, raising a hairy eyebrow, that Megan Greene had switched sides and that the D.A., Tony Jones, was now the accuser. She turned to Megan. "Despite yesterday's... events... the two of you have decided to continue with this... defense. I'm not even going to pretend that I understand why. We'll hear witness statements now."

Xander leaned forward into Megan's ear. "Why aren't we doing statements?"

Megan twitched him away, putting on a fake smile as she rose from her chair. "The defense calls Harry Ford to the stand."

Both the judge and Tony raised an eyebrow at this.

Harry got up from the gallery and made his way up to the stand, sweating bullets even though it was relatively cool in the courtroom.

The bailiff walked over to him. "Raise your right hand and put your left on your heart, please."

Harry did so, gulping hard.

"Do you swear to tell the truth, the whole truth, and nothing but the truth, so help you god?"

"I – I do," Harry said nervously. He sat down quickly, almost falling off the chair and then righting himself, folding his arms on his lap.

Megan rose from her chair, took a sip of her water, and then approached Harry. She smiled warmly at him. "Mr. Ford," she began, trying to sound as kind as possible, "where do you currently work?"

"I'm the chief coroner at the Coral Beach Morgue."

"And your duties as such?"

"I perform or oversee every autopsy for the town."

"Then you've had a busy month."

"Yes."

She smiled. "Do you know what the Holy Trinity is, Mr. Ford?"

He nodded enthusiastically. "Of course. I help out at my church every Sunday."

"No, no," she corrected, raising a hand. "I meant in criminal law. The Holy Trinity in criminal law."

"Objection," came Tony's voice, before Harry could answer. "Relevance, Your Honour?"

"I'm getting to it, Your Honour," Megan assured her, casting her gaze up towards the bench.

Frowning, the Judge nodded.

"No," Harry said finally. "I don't know what that is."

"It's basically the three things we use to see if there's enough evidence to try someone for a crime. We need the weapon, the motivation and the opportunity. Now we knew Genblade had the opportunity to commit these murders, but did the Sheriff's office ever have you check a weapon?"

"No."

"Ever ask you about knife patterns?"

"No."

Megan turned back toward her desk, scooping up the enlarged photos on the knife wounds. One was marked clearly; the other was not. "Can you tell me what these are, Dr. Ford?"

He studied them carefully, adjusting his glasses as he did. "They appear to be autopsy photographs."

"Taken by you?"

"No, no. More than likely by my associate, Lance."

"Can you tell me who these people are, based solely on the wounds?"

He picked up each, looking carefully from one to the other. "No, I'm afraid not. There've been too many, I couldn't."

"Do they appear consistent with one another?"

"Y... Yes," he said, taking a moment to look at them again before answering.

Megan picked up both photos and showed them to the court, then laid them on the judge's bench for her to see. "The photograph on the left is of a lethal blow sustained to Liz Taylor, the other a superficial wound photographed by a nurse when Cathy Kennessy was brought to the emergency room several nights ago."

"Objection," Tony piped. "Your Honour, she's bringing in evidence that isn't even for this case."

"It will be," Megan said, her voice low and self-assured.

"Overruled," the Judge said, looking from one photo to the other.

Megan smiled again. "Now, for the third part... was there a motive behind the murders that took place last month, in your opinion Dr. Ford?"

Harry didn't need to think about that, as it had been the subject of he and Lance's conversations of the past few days. "No, there was none..."

"Careful!" Megan interrupted, raising a finger to Harry. "Are you sure?"

"Well, you asked for my opinion."

"Yes," she admitted, "because it is an informed one. But just because we don't know the motive, doesn't mean there isn't one."

"Objection," Tony said again, a slight bit of annoyance in his tone and he looked not at the proceedings, but at his nails, studying them carefully for grit.

"Sustained," the Judge said, banging her gavel. "You can't make the witness say something he won't, Ms. Greene."

"Thank you, Your Honour," Megan said, nodding once to her before turning back to Harry. "No further questions, Dr. Ford."

Harry smiled and nodded at her, watching her intently as she walked back to her desk.

The judge appeared to actually take this entire interaction in. "Cross?"

"What's going on?" Xander whispered to Megan, even as he watched Tony get up and smooth out his suit out of the corner of his eye. "What's happening?"

"Tony questions him now," Megan whispered back. "Don't you watch T.V.?"

Xander frowned, leaning back onto his chair.

Tony stepped up, walking casually toward Harry. He carried a folder in his hand. He held it up to Harry. "Dr. Ford, the defense asked you about the knife wounds on the victims... do you know what the relevance of that is?"

Harry squinted, looking from Tony to Megan and then back again. "I can't imagine."

"Do you believe those marks were made by the same killer?" Tony asked, turning to smile at Megan. A shiver ran down her spine as that smile turned to a grimace.

"Objection," Megan said, standing back up. "The witness, while educated, is not trained in knife-wound analysis."

"He's your witness," Tony smiled, shrugging.

"Over ruled," the judge barked. "Watch yourself, Jones," she warned.

Jones nodded. "Nothing further."

Megan snapped a pencil.

"Did he just get you to discredit our own witness?" Xander asked, leaning against the bar.

"Not one word," Megan hissed.

"Your next witness?" the judge asked, politely.

"The defense calls Adam Genblade," Megan said, rising to make the brief statement.

Xander's eyes grew wide. "Here we go," he huffed to himself.

The bailiff moved out a side door. He wheeled in Adam Genblade, who was now strapped to a specially made wheelchair, with metal clamps securing every joint and a steel muzzle over his mouth. The swelling on his face had gone back down to normal, but was still tattered with cuts and scrapes from his encounter with Xander the day before. He was moved next to the witness box, where the bailiff swore him in. The poor man had to fight back snickering as Genblade swore to tell the truth.

Megan turned and gave Xander a look before standing up, playing with the ends of her skirt until it was just perfect. She walked toward Genblade, getting closer than she would have liked to have as his eyes danced over her longingly. "Mr. Genblade," she began.

"Please, Adam," he smiled devilishly.

Xander rolled his eyes.

"Adam, do you know the man seated behind me?" she asked, turning away from Genblade and glancing over her shoulder at Xander.

"His name is Xander Drew," Genblade stated, snarling.

"Correct. And how do you know him?"

"We... studied together," Genblade smiled, glaring menacingly at Xander.

Megan raised an eyebrow, casting a glance up to the judge. "Really? Where?"

"At the Church of Smoke and Mirrors, of course," he laughed, unable to lean into it as much as he wanted to because of his restraints.

Megan forced herself to smile, cracking the calcium in one of her knuckles as she kept her eyes locked with Genblade. "But how do you know him, really?"

Genblade leaned his head to one side, staring at her for a long moment as he rolled his tongue around the inside of his mouth. His eyes danced down over her body briefly, then travelled back up to her face. "Well, he is the Black Womb," he whispered finally, smiling.

Megan nodded her head. "Of course he is. And what is that exactly?"

"A manifestation of a genetic disorder which resulted from meticulous breeding for decades by Engen's top scientific minds."

"What does it look like?"

"It covers your body in a dark, black film with red eyes and mouth," he said bluntly.

"Why can't we see it?" Megan continued, turning from Genblade to face the rest of the court, and Tony, as she spoke.

"It exists inside him until blood loss or lack of consciousness or emotional stimulation forces it out."

A few chuckles had started to work their way through the courtroom, the judge banging her gavel against its mount to hush them.

Megan smiled at Tony, then turned back towards the Judge's bench. "Your Honour, given the accused's testimony here and the psyche reports gathered by the CBPD, I don't know how we can lawfully continue with this trial under the assumption that it will end with the death penalty. Maine law clearly states that if the defendant is considered or found to be mentally ill, then a death sentence cannot be reached as he is partially not responsible for his own - -"

"I'm not insane," Genblade interrupted, drawing the attention of the entire courtroom. "Not."

Megan almost rolled her eyes, then restrained herself. She walked back to her desk and retrieved another photograph from her briefcase, holding it up to the court. It looked to have been blown up from a driver's license photo, some of the sheen from the reflective material still visible in the copy. "Do you recognize this man, Adam?" she barked, holding up the picture for him to see.

"That's Thomas Drake."

Xander furrowed his brow, leaning his head to one side as he watched.

"And how do you know him?"

"He... is... a reporter. He's a reporter with the local paper."

"Are you aware that he was killed last night?"

Xander's mouth twitched, and he almost stood up in his seat. Instead, he reached into his jacket pocket and pulled out the small, dragon-handled blade he kept there, his eyes still locked on Genblade.

"No... no, I wasn't aware of *that*."

"Were you responsible for the death of Thomas Drake, Adam?"

Genblade paused, locking eyes with Xander before letting a large grin spread over his face. "Yes."

Again, the courtroom bustled with energy as everyone in the gallery turned to the person next to them.

Megan sighed. "In my briefcase, I have screen captures from the security cameras that monitor your room from last night, one every fifteen minutes. I can personally guarantee you never left your cell last night. Care to try your answer again? If not, Your Honour, it's reasonable to assume we can't rely on anything this man admits - -"

"Didn't say I killed them," Genblade snapped, interrupting Megan and making her jump along with half the courtroom. "I said that I was *responsible* for it."

Here we go, Xander frowned, looking down at the knife.

Megan stopped, taking another step toward Genblade. "How are you responsible for the deaths you're accused of, Adam?"

Everyone in the courtroom, including Judge Pike, leaned forward on their seats. "Misdirection. I killed them with misdirection and distraction."

Xander twitched.

"Didn't learn anything about distraction, did we?" he screamed, bringing back his fist and slamming it into the Womb's face. Its teeth grazed and cut his knuckles, but he barely even noticed. He hammered his fist down again, splashing the black tar onto the streets as he did.

"You stated in one of your interrogations with police that you used certain sounds to distract and elicit responses from your victims, herding them to a predetermined 'kill zone' you'd selected. Is that what you're referring to, Mr. Genblade?"

"Sure," Genblade smirked, nodding.

Megan let out a breath, finally turning away from Genblade.

"You know what your problem is?" Genblade started again, looking from Megan to lock eyes with Xander, and then back again. "You'll never be able to figure it out all on your own. You'll never be able to make that leap because you can't think that way. You people hire good men to hunt killers... you can't do that. Your brains can't think the way theirs do," he stopped, looking at Xander again. "But his can."

Xander squinted at him again.

Genblade leaned in slowly, again licking those pointed teeth of his. "You still got plenty to learn, but there's one thing you're gonna have to learn fast... and there's only one way I know to teach you." Genblade drove his hand forward, shoving the Womb's long, serrated tooth into its gut and then swiping it all the way across.

Slowly, Xander wrapped the fingers of his left hand around the blade until he could feel the cold metal begin to piece his skin.

"Well, we managed to catch you," Megan piped up, her voice audibly annoyed with Genblade now.

"It ain't nothin to catch a killer you were looking for," he hissed. "Try catching one you weren't."

"This was absolutely pathetic," Genblade snarled, leaning over the Womb's broken body as the lights of Engen glared down from above. "If you're gonna keep going with power over skill, there's a couple of things you should be made aware of. Number one, your right side is your weak spot. It's where your true self... the real Black Womb... resides. But you probably figured that out."

Xander pulled the blade down, slicing a line through his palm so deep that he could see the meat of the muscle. He sucked air through his teeth at the sudden pressure, then opened his fingers and let the blood dribble down. He waited a moment, letting several drops fall to the floor. No blackness came.

The radioactive rods in front of Xander exposed themselves, their eerie green glow filling the room. He felt his flesh start to burn as the liquid surrounding his brain boiled within his skull and his teeth rattled, trying to shake themselves free of his gums. He closed his eyes as they started to bubble and crack.

SMACK!

The chuck of wood that Raine had swung at Drew from the darkness came around again, this time planting itself into his jaw. He felt splinters make their way into his mouth and gums as his neck twisted and nearly snapped, the muscle tendons in his shoulders straining then breaking. "Guh," he said simply, forcing his aching skull back around just in time to see the wood get pushed forward again, catching him head-on between the eyes. He fell backwards, but Al caught him before he could hit the ground, the boy's limp body as heavy as a sack of potatoes in his thin arms.

Raine chuckled softly as he looked down at Xander, coppery blood that seemed just a bit too orange (but about as far from black as a color could get) leaking from the boy's mouth and ears, which were already starting to swell. "Hey, look'it man," he laughed, pointing at the battered teen. "It's that Xander Drew freak!"

Allan careened his head around to look in the bloodied face. "Yea, so it is. Little punk," he giggled, and he sounded more than a little nuts. He was probably just high, though. "We should make him wear his ass as a hat," he laughed again, and that time Raine chuckled too.

Come on, Xander thought, fighting unconsciousness as more blood dripped from the growing crack in the roof of his mouth down onto his tongue. You can do this, Drew. Just think of... of... but all he could think of was that almost metallic-tasting liquid that was pooling in all of his facial orifices. Sara! He realized suddenly, and he felt the true Womb twitch a little. Think of Sara. Concentrate on her, he thought, coaxing his 'other side' out of its shell. Think of her, lying there in that coffin... he continued, tears welling up from the memories and the pain.

"Look, he's crying," Allan said with mock sympathy. "Poor baby."

Julie, lying in an alleyway across from her bedroom window, that smile ruined, trying to find enough shards of clothing to get her home without her perverted neighbors catching too much skin... still, the Womb just fizzed. It was like trying to start a cold engine in the dead of winter. In Antarctica. It just wasn't happening, a fact that slowly grew in the back of his mind as he watched the red liquid from his nose seep into the soaking-wet plywood flooring.

I can't transform, he realized with horror.

Xander stared at the little pool of blood forming on the floor between his feet. "I can't transform," he whispered to himself, feeling how the rip that Genblade had put in his side still ached as it healed. "The Womb burns out. Burnt

382

out at Engen, couldn't transform for a week to stop those rapists... burns out when Genblade stabs me..."

Drake brought his hand up to his ear quickly, and found that it wasn't there anymore. When he brought his hand back he couldn't even see his own skin, it was so laden with his own blood, dark crimson in the low light.

Genblade locked eyes with Xander for a long moment, then finally smiled the first honest smile he'd ever had in the boy's presence, nodding graciously.

"Is the killer in this room?" Xander yelled, jumping to his feet.

"Order!" the judge yelled, slamming her gavel against its mount again.

Genblade grinned.

"Genblade, is the killer in this room, here, one of us?"

"Order! Young man, sit down or - -"

"Forgive the child, Your Honor," Genblade said apologetically, his voice laden with a thick accent that wasn't quite anything. "He just hasn't learned how to be *direct* yet."

Xander stopped, cocking his head to one side. "What?"

"Xander, sit down!" Megan hissed, finally stepping away from Genblade and towards the boy.

"But don't worry," Genblade assured them. "We'll teach him."

"Just say it!" Xander screamed, shoving away someone next to him.

"I'm sorry, Xander, but you're not being very... *direct.*"

"Direct," Xander repeated, and immediately his head began to cascade with thoughts that he hadn't even realized were there. "*Direct.*"

"What has The Womb ever spoken, except for the words 'Black Womb lives'?" Xander posed, raising a finger to his friend.

Mike opened his mouth to answer, then paused, and closed it again.

"Any time. Ever?"

Mike leaned forward, rubbing the sides of his nose with his thumbs. "No. No, it's never talked before."

Xander brought the nail of his thumb to his lower lip, picking at it obsessively as he thought. His eyes were locked on some random spot on the wall, not looking at anything but refusing to look anywhere else all the same. "Why would it change?" he huffed, thinking back to the day that Genblade had been captured. He'd almost smiled at Xander from across the mounds of rubble and police between them, and said 'it's not over'. "Is this what he meant?"

"What?" Mike moaned, looking up.

"Nothing, just... nothing." He ran a hand through his hair, a few strands shaking loose as he tugged on it. "This whole thing just keeps getting worse and worse."

"Makes you wonder, really," Mike mumbled, almost to himself.

"Wonder what?"

"Humans change their behaviour. Animals don't. Animals hunt the same way, day

in and day out, until something forces them to change. Even then, not really. So if the Womb's changed the way it does things, that'd make it - -"

"Human," Xander finished, a bitter taste in his mouth.

Xander's mouth went dry, as he looked from Genblade to the hand that still hung bleeding at his side. "It wasn't me," he said finally, his voice hushed and low.

CHAPTER TEN: SEE

Xander spun on his heels, leaping over the row of chairs behind him and heading for the courthouse doors.

"Xander!" Megan called after him, though he didn't even look back at her.

"It's all been said before..." Genblade laughed, as the bailiff came over and began to wheel him away.

"Where are you going?"

"... just nobody pays attention, so we've got to say it all over again."

Darkness covered Coral Beach that night. And when it came, the city closed its doors. Roadblocks were set up. Police were even borrowed from nearby towns to patrol the streets, which were like vacant lots, giving the entire town a ghostly tranquility. Everything was silent and still. The only place still open was, naturally, the Factory. Its musicians had gone home and many of its workers wouldn't have stayed there for a million dollars, but the four owners and three of the customers still remained. Sud, Tommy and Derek.

"You guys could come in a while if you wanted," Derek offered. "Call your 'rents, ask them to come and pick you up."

"Naw, man," Tommy shrugged. "We'll be fine."

Sud nodded in agreement.

"You sure?" Derek pushed, taking a quick glance around the street. "It's not safe out there, man."

Tommy and Sud ran into the Factory, the killer tight on their heels as they slammed the door behind them.

Xander nearly jumped out of his skin, turning quickly. "Derek!" he shouted, laughing at his own jumpiness. He slapped his friend on the back heartily, which was returned. "It's only you."

Derek nodded, smiling. "Only me."

Derek Smith walked out of the Library and slammed the door behind him.

"He can have that effect on people," came Mike's voice from the corner. "Lemme guess, he kept pushing buttons 'till he found one that hurt you, then he kept pushing it?"

Derek actually laughed at that, waving a finger at Mike. "Something like that," he reasoned, "Jeez, don't you just wanna rip that guy's head off?"

"Sometimes," he nodded. "Actually, all of the time. Tact isn't his strong suit, I'm afraid. One of these days, he's going to break his neck jumping to conclusions."

"Yeah," Derek snarled. "He actually accused me of helping Al and Raine do this shit to Julie. Me! I mean, she's probably the one person in this school that I wouldn't take a machete to..." his voice trailed off for a second, eyeing Mike's right side sheepishly. "...present company excluded, of course."

Mike laughed, an act that stretched his stitches painfully. "Think nothing of it," he replied, trying to keep the agony out of his voice. He didn't do a very good job of it. "But that's not really what I wanted to talk to you about."

"Well," Sara started, smirking to herself proudly, "I heard from Julie Peterson today that the reason Derek has been so on edge lately is because Theresa had to take the test."

"Yeah," Xander nodded. "That Family Living test was bad news. I think I must have only gotten an eighty-five or something..."

She turned and gave him a little slap on the arm, "Not that test, you half-wit. A pregnancy test."

Xander's eyes went wide for a moment as he held open the front door for her, which she barely acknowledged. "Oh."

"Yeah."

"Why would Derek be messed up over that?" he asked naively.

She shot him a look.

"Ah. Forget I asked."

"Done."

"Wasn't she supposed to be with Jamie?"

"They broke up."

"Why? I mean, besides the 'she may be pregnant from another man', thing?"

"That's just a rumor. The real reason was because he cheated on her," she smirked to herself coyly.

"With who?" he moaned, feeling a 'relationship' headache coming on.

"Me," she said proudly, and he realized that this would become a migraine before it was over.

Jamie turned the corner and bumped immediately into a large, dark figure. The person was covered in a trench coat and looked like it was made out of shadows. The thing's eyes burned bright with hatred as it made a move towards him menacingly. Jamie

385

screamed loudly and took off in the other direction, but his stitch got the better of him again, this time right away. The shadow-figure grabbed him, pulling him into the darkness. He took a dagger from his coat and jabbed it into Jamie's right side. Blood gushed immediately from the treads etched into the sides of the blade, splattering onto the street with a sickening splashing sound.

As Jamie's vision because hazy and he realized it was over, he stopped struggling against the man's iron grip. He fell to the ground, and the last thought to run through his head was that maybe if he had given up smoking just a little earlier, he might have been able to run just that little bit further.

⋏⊻⋏

Blood oozed into Sara's dress as the killer twisted, then pulled the knife from the mouth it had just opened. Sara let out a little sound like a dove cooing, a small tear rolling down her cheek. The killer wiped her cheek clean, then sliced her slowly across the throat. Her hand went up to her wound, and was instantly covered in blood. The killer put a finger up to his hooded mouth. "Shh."

She opened her mouth to scream a warning to the others, but couldn't. All she felt was her blood pour out onto the wooden balcony. She lay down on the floor and her eyes rolled back into her head. A small puddle of blood began to form all around her. As the killer walked through it, he gazed into the room filled with teens. A wry smile spread across his lips.

The last thought to go through her mind was of Xander.

⋏⊻⋏

Tommy Irons stepped into the auditorium, bringing a hand up to his squinted eyes to block some of the harsh orange light that bombarded him when he did so. The room was filled with candles, each one shimmering and dancing and casting its own set of shadows onto the walls and the people that had gathered there, packed tightly into the tiny gymnasium. He turned as Sud came in behind him, throwing his friend a smirk. "Think they're ready?"

Sud patted the breast pocket of the dingy jacket he wore, nodding once as a grin spread over his face as well.

Snickering, Tommy's eyes floated over the gathered crowd until he found the person he was looing for.

Mike reached out and touched the pewter frame before him, the physical contact sending goose pimples up and down his arm and into his spine. Somehow, touching it made it different. Made an otherwise surreal experience a little more grounded and real.

It was a picture of Sara, laughing at the camera as her body jutted in one direction and her hair in the other, dancing at The Factory. Her smile seemed to transcend the boundaries of the frame, spreading far beyond the paltry limitations offered by the eight-by-ten cage. It came out and took a light all of its own, so good and full of life.

The candle beneath next to her picture flared up, almost touching his palm and making him flex back. The sensation was gone instantly, the image instantly

386

becoming just another picture among the dozens lined up in the gym. Each had their own candle and their own space on the table for friends and loved ones to leave poems, cards, flowers and whatever else they wanted.

"Hard to believe," came a voice from his side, sweet and soft.

He turned toward Cathy, having almost forgotten she was there while in the trance of the picture. "What is?"

She laid a folded white letter next to Sara's photo, her name scribbled into it in purple ink. She stared at the image for a long moment just as he had, then turned back to him, brushing her hair back behind her shoulders. "Everything."

He paused, nodding as he took her hand in his own, gently guiding her away from the photo as more people started to come close.

"Xander should be here," she said suddenly, letting out a small sigh.

"No. He shouldn't," Mike replied, casting his gaze over the more than forty framed photos mounted around the room. His eyes landed finally on Tommy, walking from the other side of the room with Sud close in tow. He stopped dead in his tracks, followed by Cathy a moment later.

"What?" she said, almost tripping. She followed his glare to Tommy, coming down upon them with that gangly, determined strut of his. "Oh, no."

"Hey, you guys all right?" came a high-pitched voice from behind them.

Cathy jumped a little, her heart racing before she turned and took a sigh of relief. "We're fine, Derek."

"Yeah," Mike swallowed, keeping one eye trained on Tommy as he greeted his friend. "Just trying to avoid some trouble. Know what I mean?"

Derek laughed, leaning forward and clapping Mike on the back heartily. "I can honestly say I don't, friend."

CHAPTER ELEVEN: AN ENDING

"Hey," Tommy grunted, spinning Mike around by the shoulder until their noses were only inches apart. "We need to talk."

Mike scoffed, gritting his teeth as he looked Tommy up and down, paying close attention to how the boy's fingers twitched over his right jeans pocket. "I'm not in the mood, Tommy," he said, starting to turn away again.

"Don't you turn away from me!" Tommy snarled, grabbing Mike by the wrist and twisting.

"Get off him, Tom!" Cathy cried as she pushed the taller man against the shoulder, making him step to one side.

Derek stepped forward, hitting Tommy's hand away.

Tommy backed up a pace, checking over his shoulder to make sure Sud was still behind him. "What the fuck's your problem, Smith? Why you gotta get involved in this?"

"My Pop used to say things about men like you out on the farm," Derek smirked, chuckling a little to himself. "'Bad stock of corn's not even worth

387

trouble'a harvesting.'"

Tommy frowned, his shoulders falling slightly.

Derek nodded, turning back toward Mike and Cathy.

They stared at him with ghostly white faces, Mike stepping out in front of Cathy but otherwise staying perfectly still.

Derek looked at them for a long moment, clicking his tongue against the back of his teeth. "Gramp's not really a farmer," he admitted after a moment, smiling.

Mike tried to bring his hand up. He imagined plowing it into Derek, the boy's skull collapsing under the force of his fist... but for the life of him, he couldn't even summon the strength to make his fingers twitch. Cathy quivered and shook, her legs turning into rubber rods that were barely able to hold her weight. A quiet, hushing sound came from her lips every few moments and someone would have had to have their ear right next to her ruby lips to have recognized it as the world's quietest scream.

"Would it help if I said I was sorry?" Derek laughed, slowly moving his hand into his pocket.

"How could you?" Mike said after a moment, finally finding his voice. "Why *would* you?"

"What the fuck are you talking about?" Tommy huffed, stepping forward to come between them again.

"Probably this," Derek piped, swiping his blade clean across the back of Tommy's head.

Tommy fell forward as Mike and Cathy backed up quickly to get out of the way, the back of his head streaming blood as his nose hit the concrete floor of the gym and produced still more of it. The crowd let out one scream after another as a circle parted itself around the five of them, all eyes glued on the knife that now spun lightly between Derek's fingers, reflecting the glimmering light of the candles and sending it off in different directions.

The color returned to Mike's face slowly as Tommy groaned, trying half-heartedly to get up.

"How can I?" Derek smirked, bringing the knife around and pointing it at Mike. "*How can I?* How can I not? This town's been begging for it for years. Every time anything bad happens, you all gobble it up like pigs. Newspapers and terrorists and horror novels and video games... how 'bout a little good news? How 'bout, someone finally gives these people," he paused, waving the knife at the crowd. "What they *really* deserve?"

"You killed them? All of them?" Cathy gasped, her eyes fluttering briefly from Derek to all the pictures that stood around them. To Sara.

"Not *all*," he laughed, spinning the blade again as he took a step to one side, the crowd shifting to accommodate. "'We can see further than ever, because we stand on the shoulders of giants'... I just expanded on what another man started. Turned it from function... to art. No, I didn't kill *all* those people." he grinned, letting his gaze shift to the crowd. "I'm going to kill all *those* people."

Mike lunged forward, bringing his fist up from where it hung to connect with Derek's jaw, sending him sprawling to the floor. Derek spread his fingers wide, grabbing his shirt as he fell and bringing him down as well, both of them tumbling down and sliding on the slick court.

Mike felt his knee twist, gritting his teeth as he tried to ignore it and get back to his feet. He rose only an inch before he felt cold steel against the nape of his neck.

"I've been wondering about the ending," Derek said cheerfully, his voice wet with anticipation as he ran the fingers of his free hand through Mike's hair, straddling him from behind. "There's this thing that burns out in a person right before they go to that big slaughterhouse in the sky, and try as I might, I can't see it in me..." He pulled back on Mike's hair until he could look him in the eye. "Do you think you have it too?"

"You could have killed me, and you didn't," Mike reminded him, trying not to swallow as he felt the sharp blade against his adam's apple.

"You weren't ready," he laughed, bouncing up and down a little. "Now, though... I think you're nice and plu--"

Sud shoved forward with his fist, brass knuckles clenched tightly over them as they connected with Derek's cheekbone and sent him over Mike's back and onto the floor. "Plump," Sud finished, spitting onto the concrete as he brought his hands back up into striking position.

Derek clutched onto the table, scrambling to his feet. He laughed a little under his breath, feeling his mouth fill up with blood from the large crack now forming in the roof of it. He lunged at Tommy, still clutching his head on the floor, then stopped midway and stepped back to where he had been against the table.

"Give it up, man," Mike pled, slowly rising to his feet.

"Oh, no," he smirked, looking from Mike to Tommy and then back again. "You haven't even seen the best part."

Mike clenched, waiting for Derek to move.

Derek looked from Mike to Tommy and then back again, smiling wide as Mike watched his every move. "Shall we dance?" he coaxed, before lunging at Tommy once more.

Mike dove forward, fists clenched hard as he came to his knees just over Tommy, ready to lash out at Derek and finish it.

He wasn't there.

For one stunned, silent moment; Mike stared at the empty floor in front of him with his blood boiling before turning to see Derek's hand wrapped around Cathy's throat, his knife pressed so hard against her side that even the slightest movement would send it coursing through.

"You see?" Derek laughed, spitting blood from his mouth onto Cathy's shoulder. "That's what happens when you forget who leads."

Mike stared at them, Cathy biting her lip and trying her best not to whine as she felt the sharp point of the steel blade press into her.

"You ever get to be inside her, Mike?" Derek taunted, taking a long whiff of Cathy's hair and then nodding toward the blade. "Because I'm about to be."

"Please," Mike began to plead, tears rolling down his cheeks. "Please, not her. Not - -"

"Oh, but I have to," Derek smiled, nodding feverishly. "Nothing sells papers like dead hot, young ass after all."

"Please," Mike repeated, as he watched Cathy cry more and more.

"Please?" Derek spat, taking a step closer and pulling Cathy along with him. "Please? That's all you can say is *please*? You're about to watch the woman you love get gutted like a fish and the most you can say is please?" he screamed, taking the blade away long enough to slam Mike across the face with the handle, breaking his nose with one loud, wet snap. "Tell her you love her! Tell her how sad it'll be when she's gone! Don't just sit there like a bump on a log and cry!" He lashed out with the dull end of the blade again, the sharp corner digging a gouge into Mike's forehead near the temple and bringing more blood to the surface.

"I love you," Mike said, his voice barely recognizable through the tears and the pain.

"I love you, too," Cathy screamed, her voice shaking and blubbery as water streamed down her face from every orifice.

"Tell her how you want her to stay. How you'll be better. Because in a minute..." he smiled, the blade piercing the tender flesh of her stomach and drawing blood. "You won't be able--"

Xander grabbed Derek by the shoulders and pulled him backward, the knife coming back from Cathy's side. He grabbed the killer by the throat and pressed hard, digging his thumb as far into his windpipe as he could.

Derek tried to say something, a large grin spread across his lips, but couldn't get enough wind to speak. His lips were already turning blue as he met Xander's dutiful glare, not even bringing his hand up to try and pry his away, instead keeping his fingers gripped around Cathy's slender neck.

"I'm going to rip you in two," Xander said finally, his upper lip curling as he watched Derek smile, his teeth stained with red.

He tried to speak again, but couldn't.

"What?" Xander asked finally, not loosening his grip.

Derek spat a long tendril of blood from between his two front teeth, hitting Xander right in the eye. Xander's grip loosened on Derek's throat and he slipped through it, the blood that covered him providing just the right amount of lubricant to wrestle free. "Can't a guy finish a sentence around here?" he said, bringing the knife back to Cathy's gut. "We're outta here, girl. Fun's fun, but I don't like these odds anymore, so you're my ticket out and then you're my ticket in, got me?" he said, backing her towards the door.

She did not respond.

He jabbed her again with the knife, his teeth gritting together in the first sign of real anger since the ordeal had begun.

"Yes!" she wailed, feeling the cold of the metal mix with the warmth of that small sliver of blood.

Xander glared up at them, Derek's blood still running down his face as Mike struggled to stay conscious at his side, trying to climb to his feet.

390

Derek locked eyes with him, smiled, then smelled Cathy's hair again. "Tell them you want to come with me."

Cathy sobbed. "I want to come with you."

"Good. Then we're all gonna play nice," he said, giving her a small peck on the nape of her neck as he kicked the gymnasium door open behind him. As the door closed behind them, Derek looked at Xander one last time. "Tootles."

Xander bolted for the door as soon as it closed, reaching it in seconds and flinging it open again. He paused once, looking from left to right, and was running again before the door closed.

Mike watched his friend go, trying to get up but feeling his brain cry out in agony every time he tried, the altitude making his skull want to implode.

Beside him, Tommy finally made his way to his feet. "What the Christ was that about?"

Mike turned to say something to him, then stopped and forced himself to his feet.

ʎ⟨λ

Don Smith sat at his keyboard, his fingers hovering uselessly over it as he stared blankly at the blinking curser. He'd been watching the black line mock him for the last thirty-two minutes, to the point that he could almost hear a robotic laugh every time it disappeared and reappeared.

The house was deathly quiet; there wasn't even noise coming in from the breeze of the open window a few feet away. Even so, as blocked as he was, even the slightest sound was grating. Even the beating of his heart felt like a drum bellowing out, its vibrations echoing into the base of his skull.

-thunk-

He stopped, turning around in his chair. The rest of the living room was bare, the faded chairs and table casting long shadows on the wooden floors. The patterns in the couch seemed to laugh at him for a moment, the swirls in the dusty-rose colored fabric churning until they were eyes that glared out at him and teeth that dripped with rabid anticipation, waiting for the sweet taste of flesh.

A shiver ran down his back as he turned away from the vacant room and back toward his screen. The notes he had pinned up next to it had been crossed out line by line, each one sounding stupid and insipid upon a second read. None of it had any spark or flare, and that seemed to make to curser's laugh even louder. The grandfather clock on the wall beside him started to grind at him now, the steady switch of its pendulum tocking back and forth until he ground his fingernails into his palms.

-thunk-

"Fuck off!" he screamed finally, turning around fast to yell at the room. Immediately the frustration poured out of him, leaving him a frail-looking slump swiveling slowly in his chair. He sighed, running his fingers through his hair and scratching his scalp as he tried in vain to make his mind be quiet long enough for him to think.

-thunk!-

"Christ," he grumbled, getting up from his chair and walking around the corner into the kitchen. He paused, looking around for a moment until he saw the drawstring from the window teetering against the heater. He grabbed at it, holding it in his hand and waited. After a moment of silence, he smiled.

-thunk-

"Dammit," he cursed, letting the string fall as he walked back into the living room, following the source of the sound. It had been softer that time, which meant he'd been closer to it before he'd moved. It didn't sound like it was coming from above, but could have come from...

-thunk!-

His vision stopped on the door to the basement, right next to the clock. It was small and looked more like a closet than anything else. He smiled victoriously, grabbing the crystal knob and pulling it open even as he flicked on the switch hidden behind the frame of the clock and started to walk down.

※

Xander turned the corner from Laird Street, catching the glimmer out of the corner of his eye. He turned swiftly and saw them on the next corner, staying there for just a moment before disappearing out of sight. *Fucker's fast,* he thought, taking off after them, cutting through yards and over fences.

He killed them. Not Genblade, not Spider, not Alpha... and not me. He growled, pouring on the steam as his legs thrust like pistons, churning power and propelling him forward as he turned the corner onto Main Street, the blood pumping fiercely in his veins. He still bled from his wrist, leaving a small trail of droplets every few feet behind him. They were as red as aged rose pedals, without the slightest hint of black in them again. He could see Derek and Cathy in front of him now, a good hundred metres ahead and gaining, as they turned down Xander's street.

For that, I'll kill him.

※

"Derek?" Don yelled, brushing some cobwebs aside as he walked down the whining, moaning stairs that led to the basement. "Son, are you down here?"

There was a light on near the far wall that he hadn't noticed before, craning over a desk he used to use all the time for building swing sets or crafting Christmas ornaments. It was still covered with sawdust and loose screws from his last project, whatever it had been. His tool chest still sat firmly against the wall, glistening in the stark light. As he got closer, he saw handprints in the dust that were too small to be his.

He ducked under a low hanging beam, pushing a piece of cloth out of his way. He squinted his eyes in the light as he finally reached the table. He ran a finger along its surface, making a line in the dust before rubbing it between his fingers and frowning.

His foot connected with something hard; a metal, making him hiss and hop

392

back a pace. He grabbed the neck of the light, turning it down to see under the table.

It was his hacksaw. And his hammer, multiple screwdrivers, a tape measure and a utility knife. All of his tools were under the desk.

He paused, standing back up straight and returning the light to its previous position. All the color drained from his cheeks as he stared at the shiny red toolbox in the middle of his desk, relatively untouched by the dust that covered everything else in the basement. He could hear his heart louder than ever now, louder than he ever had before.

Slowly, he reached out and laid his palm upon the metal box, his thumb releasing its lock. He kept it there for a moment, took a deep breath, then pulled it open.

There was nothing. The box had been filled with nails, each of their dull metal shafts diffusing the light that struck it.

Don sighed, then laughed as he turned back around to go upstairs.

His face connected immediately with the large strip of flesh that hung from the ceiling.

He screamed, stepping back in horror until the small of his back connected with the table, rocking it and showering sawdust everywhere.

It was dry and cracked, but still instantly recognizable as the peach color of flesh. It was held up by two nails that pinned it to the beam he'd just walked past, their impacts making the skin sunken and wrinkled. There was hair around the edge that had become coarse and haggard, falling off one at a time and falling to the floor.

Next to it was a large chunk of curly red hair, still matted together with blood and sludge.

A large, pink mass had been stretched out over a varnished slab of wood that had previously displayed a salmon he'd caught on a vacation in Illinois, but now was a pin cushion for thirty-one teeth, each one stuck into the flabby pink puss with its own sharp edge. It took him a moment to recognize the small pustules along the rosy surface as cysts on a human lung.

A large, pointed chunk of bone sat atop the beam, its chalky white surface stained around the edges with crimson. It had been smoothed off at the edge to near perfection, the cut that had detached it clean and precise. Below it, hanging from a nail that had been plunged lazily into the mould-covered wood, was a silver, heart-shaped pendant... just like the one in the photograph of John Tyler's daughter.

Don balked, feeling vomit rise up in his throat. He lunged forward and threw up, the apples he'd had for lunch ripping their way back up through his esophagus and spattering onto the floor. He stared down at it for a moment, unable to look up at the room. The vomit had landed on the tattered remains of a newspaper article he'd written almost a month ago:

Coral Beach Killer: CAUGHT.

He felt his stomach churn again, grabbing a nearby bucket and throwing up inside it, groaning loudly as he did. When he opened his eyes, he saw the chunks of noodle that had been inside him a moment ago mixed with the litre of blood that had already been there. He screamed, hitting the bucket away and spilling its contents all over the floor as he scrambled to his feet and ran for the stairs.

He fell against them, closing his eyes and laying his head against the sharp wood as tears started to stream down his face. He could smell the blood now, the metallic tinge so virulent he didn't know how he'd missed it before. It made him turn more and more green with every sobbing breath he took.

"Jesus," he sighed, and mucus and salt water fell from the tip of his nose, making a small puddle on the stair below him. He stared at it for a moment from over the edge of the one he was laid upon, the cloudy liquid reflecting his eyes right back at him. Four fingers crept their way around the stair he was on, the blood caked on them smearing the wood.

"Christ!" he gasped, his head snapping forward and locking with another set, staring out at him from between the stairs.

"Help," the feminine voice said, dry and weak and crackling from unshed tears and dehydration.

Don brought one quivering, shaking hand up to his lips as the girl grabbed at the sleeve of the other, tugging at it fiercely. She came into the light a little, both her eyes dark with bruises and almost swollen shut. The bottom half of her face was smattered in blood, some of it new and some of it long since dried there. There were large clumps missing from her short, black hair that still held one or two braids on the right side. She was shirtless and covered with cuts and long, red marks from her navel to her neck, which had duel handprints permanently pressed into them. Handprints that were too small to be his.

As beaten and ravaged as she was, he still recognized her immediately as he fell to the floor in shock and fear.

"Please, help me," Jesse Newhook repeated, finally finding her voice she started to sob, letting go of Don's shirt and letting her arm fall limp against the stair.

Don stayed curled up against the cold concrete floor for a moment. No matter how hard the girl screamed and sobbed, it could not overpower the voice in the back of his head that screamed the undeniable truth of the situation at him:

He'd broken this story wide open.

"Come on!" Derek yelled, giving Cathy's arm another hard tug as his feet pounded against the pavement and he brought his sleeve to his face, wiping away blood and sweat.

"Ah!" she wailed, as she felt something in her arm stretch and then snap and threaten to dislocate altogether. She hissed back the pain as he pulled her forward again, and she tried to run along with him as the houses sped by in her peripheral vision.

Derek spun around, glancing quickly over Cathy's shoulder and then spinning back. "Hurry up, you fat whore!" he bellowed, forcing her to pick up speed as he did.

Cathy turned, seeing what Derek had seen as Xander came around the corner after them. She turned back, seeing a tree along the side of the road that she'd seen many times before. It stood in between Xander and Sara's houses, and had since long before either of them had been born. Suddenly she fell to the sidewalk, the skin on both her knees ripping against the pavement and exposing the meat underneath to the harsh air and rocks that found their way in almost immediately.

"Fuck!" Derek screamed, letting her arm go and bringing the knife back to point at her. Licking his lips, he calmed himself and stepped close to her. "You know, I'm beginning to think you're more of a hindrance than an asset," he mused, stroking her hair with the flat end of the blade. "Maybe it's time we ended our arrangement."

Cathy drove her head forward, pushing off the sidewalk with her heels and sending her forehead straight into Derek's crotch.

His eyes went wide as she scrambled to her feet, running over the lawn and away from him. Hissing as he fell to his knees, he closed his eyes tightly and tried to will the pain away. "Oh, you little bitch," he whispered. "Oh, you're gonna pay for that."

"Doubt it," Xander quipped, his knee connecting with Derek's eye just as the killer opened his eyes.

Derek's head knocked backward, sending him onto his ass. "Fucker!" he cried out, lunging forward and grabbing Xander across the waist, forcing them both to the ground. "Can't I ever be rid of you?"

Xander only growled in response, reaching up and grabbed Derek by the face, sticking his fingers into the boy's eyes and mouth as he tried to pry him off. "I'll kill you," he snarled, one beat at a time, his pupils locked on Derek's.

Face searing with anger, Derek brought the knife around, connecting it with Xander's throat.

Xander's eyes went wide as he felt his jugular rupture, sending warm, sticky fluid bathing out onto Derek's hand. He tried to speak, but no words would come. They continued to look at each other for a long moment before Derek took out the blade, helping the blood flow more freely.

"I doubt it," Derek whispered finally, bringing the knife down again and sticking it right through Xander's shoulder.

He felt his right arm go numb, that tingly feeling like when your foot falls asleep crawling up and down it. Derek pulled the knife out again, bringing it down a third time near where Xander's neck met his chest. Blood spurted up in a large gush, the impact from one blow forcing it out through all the others. His vision became dark around the corners, though not the way it did when he was transforming. It was something he'd felt once before, very briefly, during his first fight with Genblade.

He closed his eyes and Sara leaned over, kissing him gently on the lips.

-BANG!-

His eyes burst open again, watching as Derek's shoulder erupted in a spread of flesh and blood, spraying pink and yellow and red in all directions.

Derek opened his mouth to say something to Xander, finally dropping his knife to bring his hand up to the throbbing wound that had opened up half his arm. Blood gurgled from his lips again as he tried to form a fist, then fell flat onto the concrete, mashing his nose into three pieces in the process.

Cathy dropped the still smoldering handgun that had belonged to Xander's father, letting it fall to the grass as though it were something disgusting to touch. Her lip was still curled and contorted into hatred as she fell to her knees on his front lawn, her lip shaking but no tears coming down her face. "That'll teach you to call me worthless," she said to Derek's bleeding backside, her face contorting in contempt.

Xander rose to his feet and walked over to her, lingering at her side for a moment. He reached out to touch her face, but she pulled away. He reached out again, her face jerking away. Finally, he touched her soft cheek and she immediately began to sob, grabbing his arms and forcing her head into his shoulder as he wrapped them around her.

EPILOGUE

Xander sat hunched against the large wooden bar, twirling his half-empty glass around his index finger as quickly as he could, watching it shimmer like crystal. He let it go and it continued spinning on its own for a moment before he caught it, bringing it to his lips and downing a large mouthful.

Behind the bar, the baldheaded bartender stopped pouring beer from his tap and shot a suspicious glare at Xander, raising one bushy eyebrow.

"Keep 'em coming," Xander nodded, taking one last glug and then waving the empty glass at him before turning it upside down on his coaster.

The man frowned, but turned back toward the cooler anyway.

"This is your idea of celebrating?" Megan remarked dryly, laying her purse on the bar as she took up the stool beside him.

"You're late," Xander smiled, winking at her as the bartender slid him another glass, filled to its brim with black, bubbling liquid. "If you hadn't been, you'd know it was cola."

She smiled, rolling her eyes at him as she leaned in and gave him a quick hug hello. "I don't even understand how you got in here to begin with."

"I have my ways."

"Whatever," she laughed, smirking at him as the bartender walked over to her. "Water, no ice. How've you been? Haven't seen much of you this past week."

"Genblade's not getting the death penalty," Xander shrugged, staring at the bubbles that popped and fizzed in his glass. "I did what I set out to do, no need to drag it out."

"But how do you *feel*?" she pried, poking him in the chest near his heart as the bartender slid her bottled water in front of her.

He sat silent for a moment, letting out a long sigh... and then smiled. "I feel like a great weight's been lifted off of me. I feel like I've found something that I thought I'd lost forever."

"That sounds like a good thing," she said, smiling.

"Yes, it is," he replied, sipping his coke.

"But..." she pried.

"But, there's still that one thing."

"Sara."

"Yeah."

Megan giggled, pointing at him as she took a sip of her water. "You're just like him. Right down to that damn guilt."

Xander raised an eyebrow, looking her up and down.

"When I was young, I had this friend, like you... always obsessing over everything, trying to make sure everyone was happy, that he was making them happy, that he didn't do anything wrong... right up until he died."

Xander winced, but continued to listen.

"He used to give me all this advice. Made me promise to 'live life with no regrets' and 'focus on the positive'... I never really bought into it before. Even after he died. It all just seemed like a pretty contrived way to live, I guess."

Xander stopped, clicking his tongue against the roof of his mouth. "Wow. That's a great moral, Megan," he nodded sarcastically.

"Not done. Anyway, I've been doing fine like that since..." she paused, staring off at the line of bottles behind the bartender. "...and then I met you, and kinda saw the way you lived. The way he probably would have, at least in practice. It kinda made me think... 'No regrets', 'focus on the positive'... if I *didn't* want to live like that, what did it say about me?"

"You're doing okay to me."

She held up her bare palm. "See this ring finger? It's not empty because I'm agnostic."

"Ag-what?"

"Never mind. The point is, seeing you fight for Genblade... made me reevaluate some things. Maybe you should, too."

"What? You're saying I should forget what happened? Forget... her?"

"Not forget. Forgive. Forgive yourself." She touched his hand. "It's not your fault."

There was a long pause, then he squinted in thought and turned away.

"Look," she continued, squeezing his hand. "Sara wouldn't want you to focus on the negative of her death, but on the positive of her life. Just like my friend wouldn't have wanted me to focus on the bad either. Realize that she's still somewhere, and that it makes her sad to see what you're doing to yourself. I did, and it's how I've come to terms with my friend's death." She paused. "No regrets, alright?"

Xander smiled. "She used to say that, too."

"Then take her advice." she leaned in and kissed him lightly on the cheek.

The door to the bar opened again, and Anthony Jones stepped into the bar.

He walked over and put his arm around Megan. They kissed, ever so briefly, then she turned and smiled at Xander. "I gotta go. But, I'll see you around, okay?" she said smiling at him.

He smiled back. "Not if I see you first."

"Remember what I've said. You're a good man, Xander. And a good friend." She kissed his cheek again, then walked out of the bar with Tony.

Xander finished his drink and got up.

ʎʎ

"Hello, Genblade," Xander said, sitting down in the uncomfortable plastic chair opposite Genblade.

"Hey, pal," Genblade replied, smiling with his jagged teeth from the other side of the thick glass. "How you healing up?"

"Pretty good," he nodded, leaning the chair back on two legs as he held the phone lazily next to his ear. "You?"

"Oh, you know me," Genblade laughed, thrusting his head in the direction of the gash on his forehead. "Only the good die young."

To his surprise, Xander found himself laughing as well.

"How's the rest of the family doing? Good, I assume."

"Mike's on the mend. Cathy's actually doing all right now... she doesn't feel like she's nothing anymore. If it wasn't Mike and me that convinced her, then all the media attention definitely did. They're treating her like the hero of all this."

"Not you?" Genblade grinned. "She always was a show-stealer."

"Nah, it's good," Xander smirked, dismissing the notion with a wave of his hand. "I don't feel much like a hero right now, anyway."

"But you beat the bad guy," Genblade mocked happily, switching the phone from one ear to the other. "Put him away in a cell so deep and dark that not even the devil'll come looking for him. They can hold him, can't they?"

"Oh, yeah," Xander nodded, the smile fading from his lips. "If your word and the stunt he pulled at the memorial weren't enough, his Dad found a bunch of souvenirs and a living person in his basement. You don't get much more clear-cut than that."

"Good, good," Genblade nodded honestly, pursing his lips. "One thing I never did know: did he ever give up why he did it?"

Xander shifted again, visibly uncomfortable. "He told some prison shrink that he did it for his Dad. That he wanted him to have something worthwhile to report on in this worthless little town so that maybe they could make it big and get out."

"You don't believe him?"

Xander paused, dwelling on the question a moment. "I don't think there was a reason. I think expecting reason out of someone that far gone is like expecting blood from a stone. It's just not going to happen."

"Now you're learning," Genblade smirked, waving a finger at him.

Xander nodded, his lips locked tightly.

After a moment of silence, Genblade squirmed a little in his chains, leaning

398

in a little closer to the glass to squint at his visitor. "Why're you here, Xander?"

Xander chuckled, shrugging a little. "Partly because I wanted to look you in the eye one last time before they put you away for... what was it again?"

"Twelve consecutive life sentences," he laughed.

"Twelve consecutive life sentences," Xander repeated, unable to hide his grin.

"They say with good behaviour, I'll be out in ten."

Xander raised an eyebrow. "You have any intention of behaving?"

Genblade snorted. "Nope."

Xander laughed as well, then started to get up.

"And the other reason?" Genblade perked, throwing his enemy a grin.

"Wanted to let you know something. Something important," Xander admitted, grabbing his coat off the back of his chair.

"What's that?"

He leaned in close to the glass, a wry smile on his lips. "It's not over."

Xander hung up the phone and turned to leave without another word, not even bothering to see Genblade's reaction.

Genblade smirked as he watched Xander leave the building, the large metal doors lock shut behind him. "Round two to you, Womb," he chuckled to himself, placing the phone gently back onto its receiver.

On the roof of the police station, Xander looked out upon his city.

Megan says I have to think positive. That I shouldn't have regrets.

He took in a deep breath, then let out a sigh.

"If you're innocent, you're hurt, or you're scared... I'll be there."

Xander smiled. For the first time in months, he didn't regret saying those words. He felt good about them. *Thank you, Megan.*

"I love you, Sara," he said, bringing out his knife and slicing his hand to trigger the transformation. "The fights just beginning, and I'm not giving up."

"Black Womb lives."

ABOUT THE AUTHOR

Matthew LeDrew holds an Honours Degree in English from the Memorial University of Newfoundland with a minor in Anthropology, and studied Journalism at College of the North Atlantic in Stephenville, Newfoundland. He was honoured to be a jury member of both the 2018 NLBA awards and the 2020 Arts and Letters Awards.

He has written twenty-four novels for Engen Books: the ten book Coral Beach Casefiles series, *The Long Road, Cinders, Sinister Intent, Faith, Family Values, Fate's Shadow, First Aid, Jacobi Street, Touch Your Nose, Infinity, The Tourniquet Reprisal, Exodus of Angels, Garden of the Eighth Circle, and The Rats of Refraction* the latter five of which with his co-author and wife Ellen Curtis.

He lives in Chapel Arm, Newfoundland.